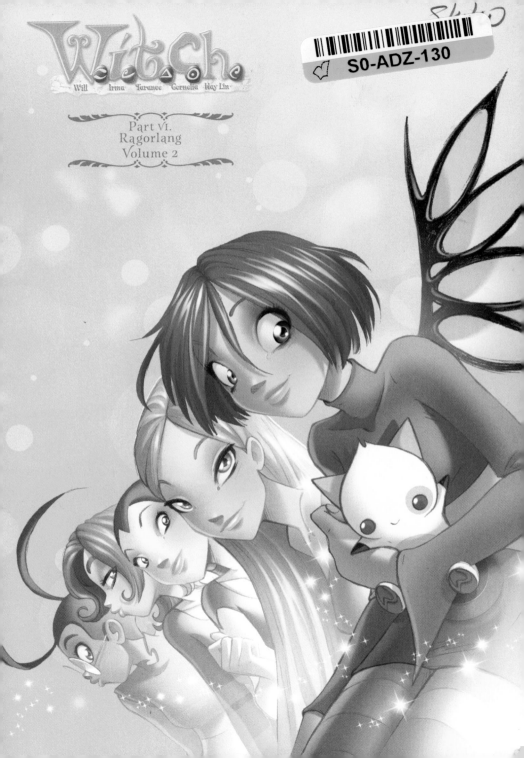

W.i.t.c.h

Will Irma Taranee Cornelia Hay Lin

Part VI.
Ragorlang
Volume 2

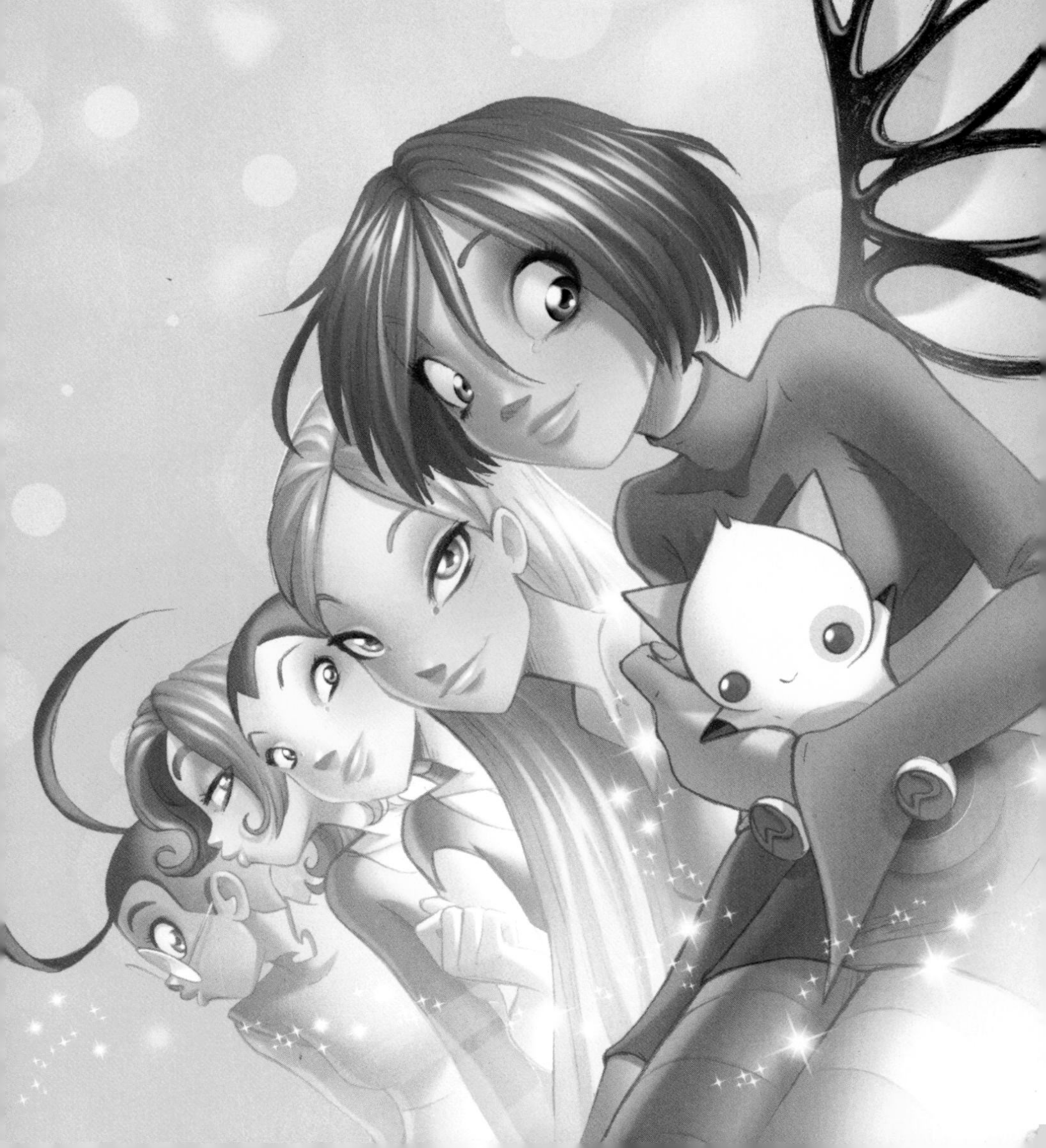

W.i.t.c.h.

Will Irma Taranee Cornelia Hay Lin

Part VI.
Ragorlang
Volume 2

CONTENTS

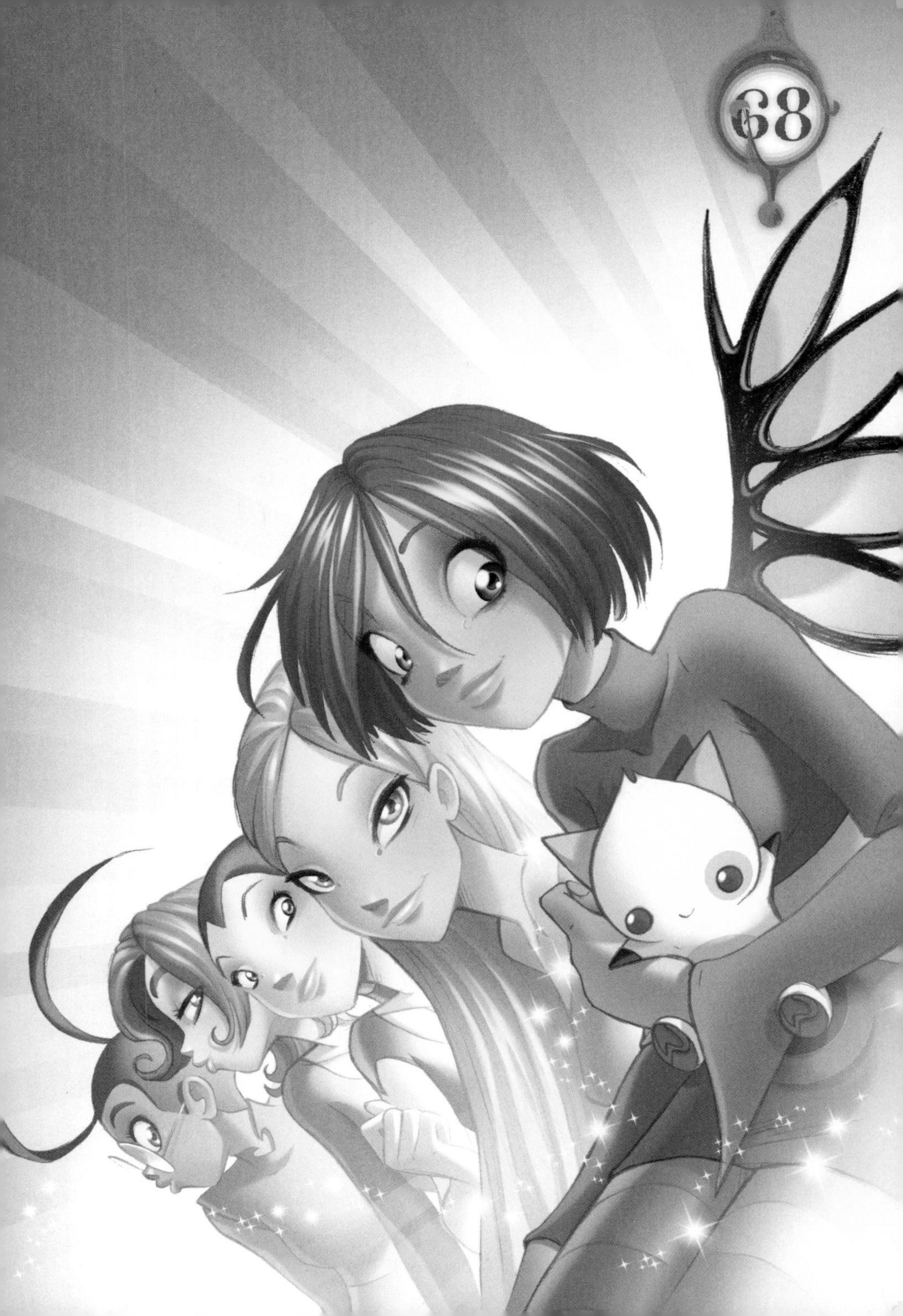
68

The Dark Side

"Those creatures were just reflections..."

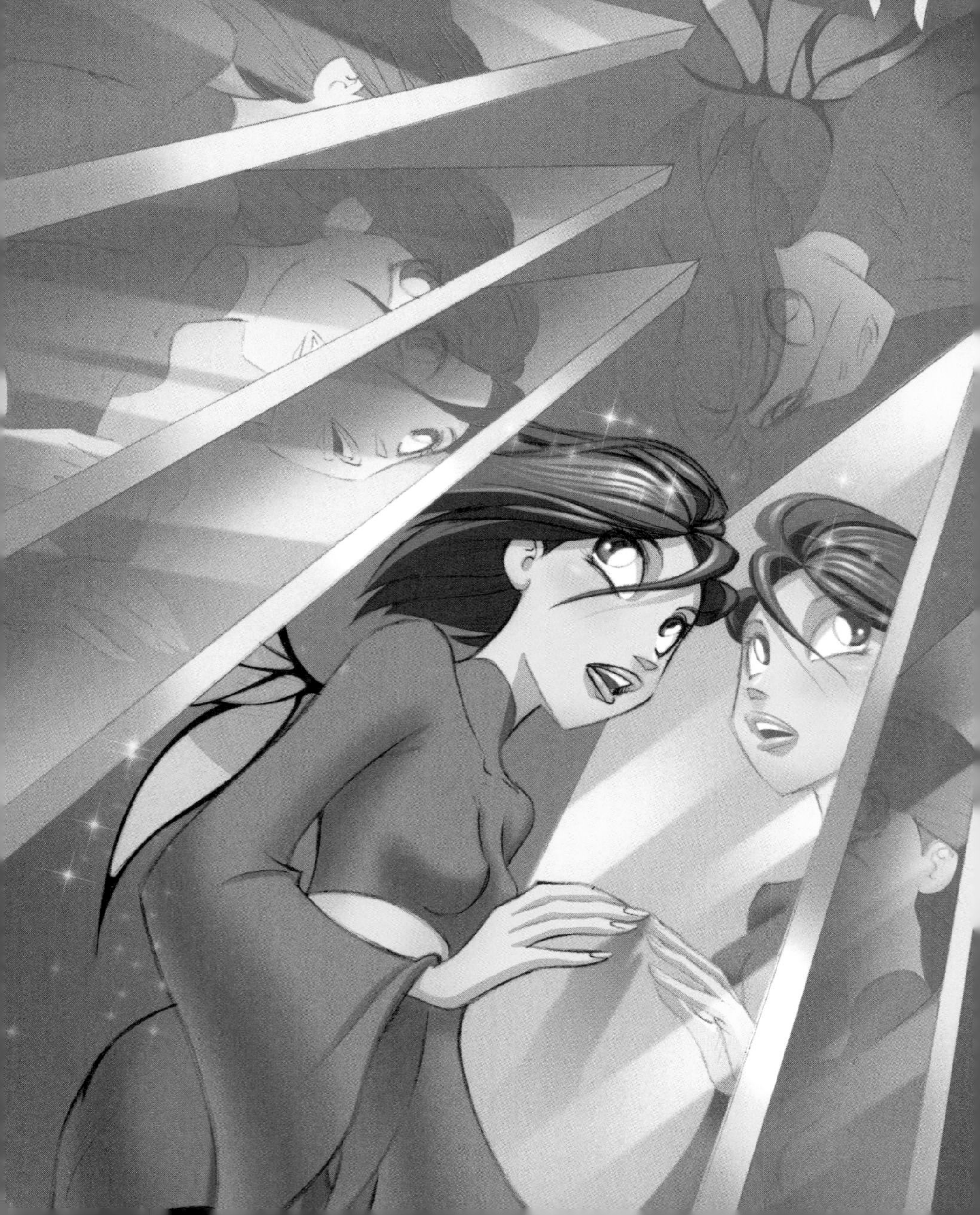

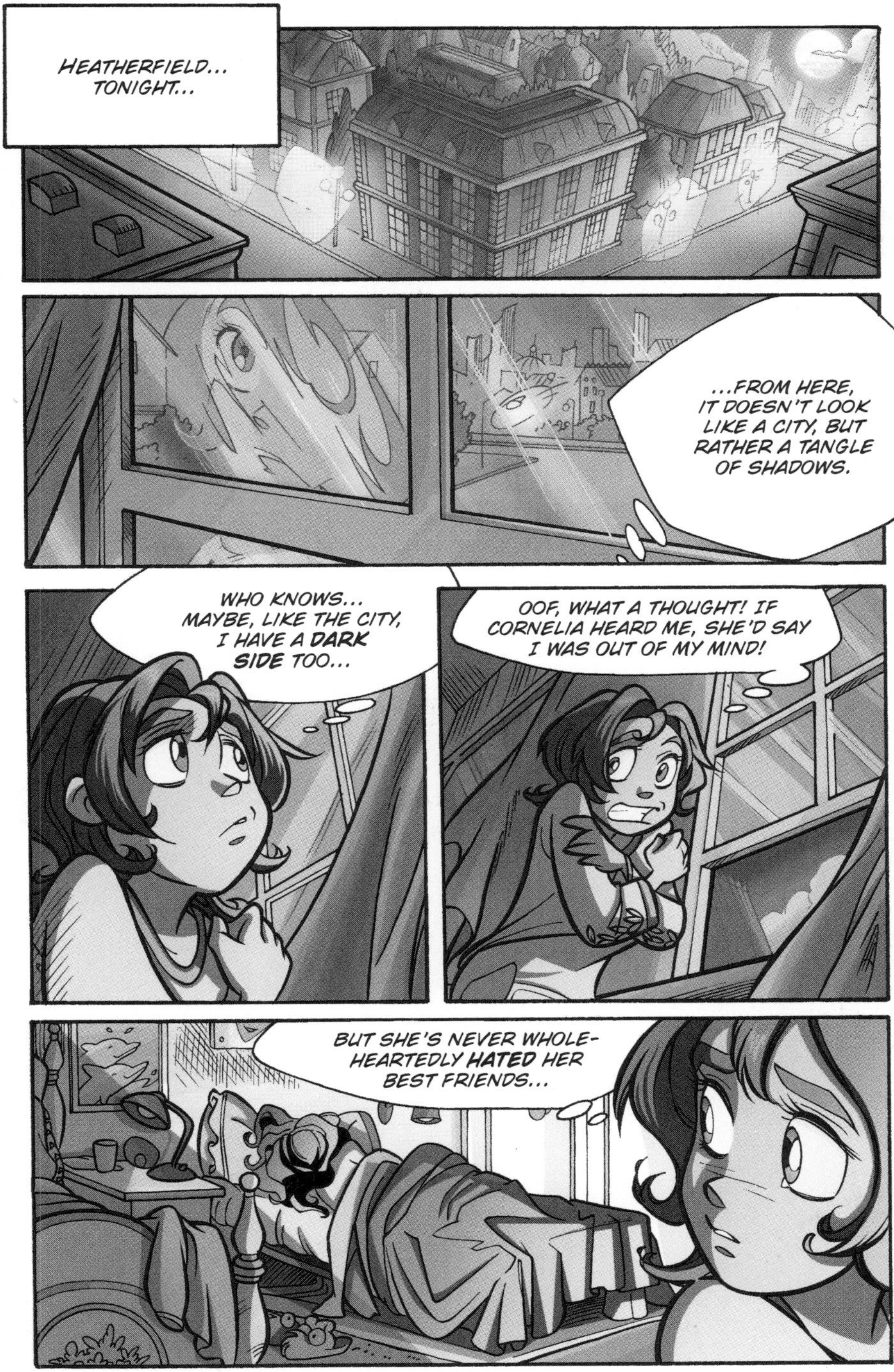
HEATHERFIELD... TONIGHT...
...FROM HERE, IT DOESN'T LOOK LIKE A CITY, BUT RATHER A TANGLE OF SHADOWS.
WHO KNOWS... MAYBE, LIKE THE CITY, I HAVE A DARK SIDE TOO...
OOF, WHAT A THOUGHT! IF CORNELIA HEARD ME, SHE'D SAY I WAS OUT OF MY MIND!
BUT SHE'S NEVER WHOLE-HEARTEDLY HATED HER BEST FRIENDS...

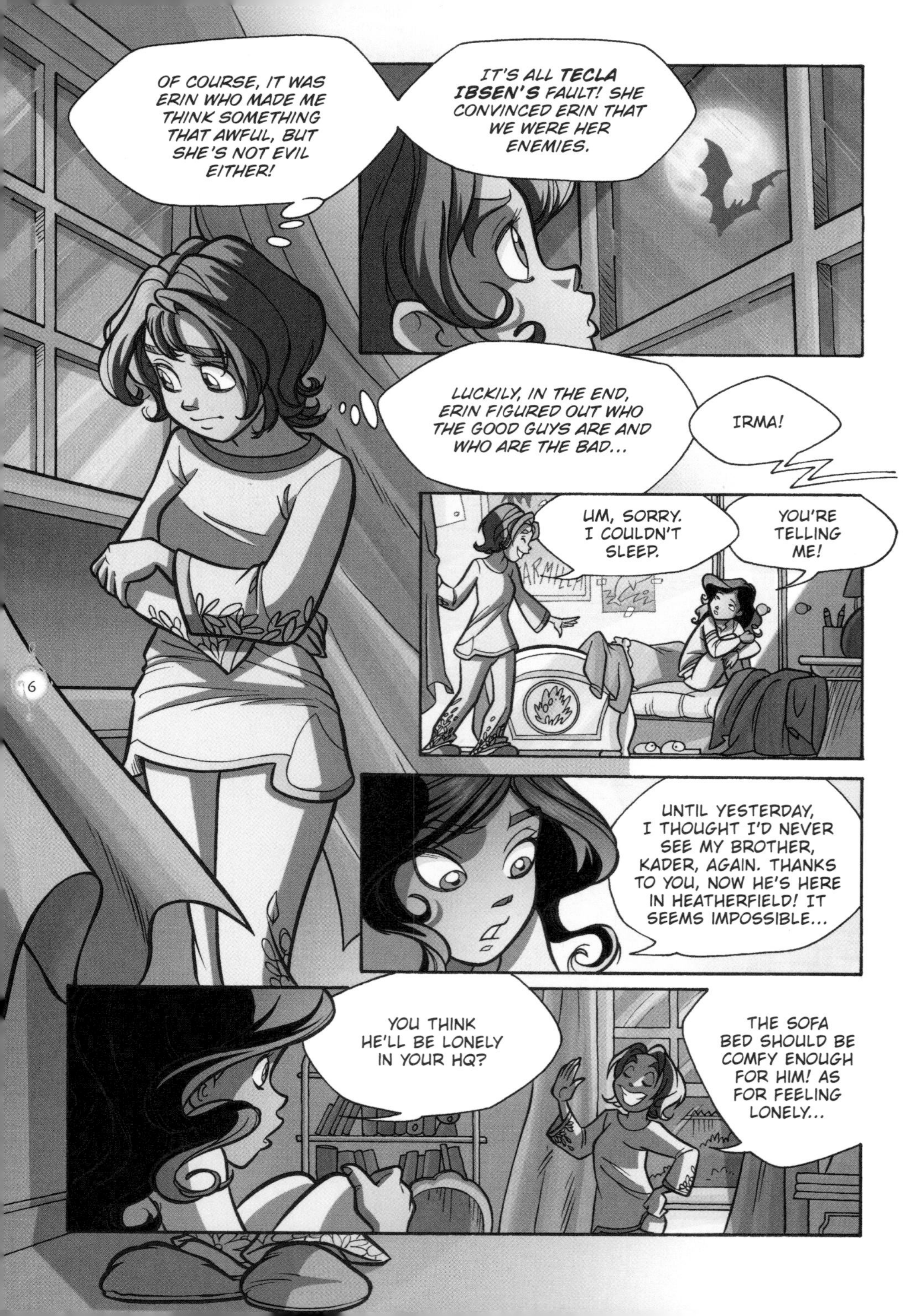
OF COURSE, IT WAS ERIN WHO MADE ME THINK SOMETHING THAT AWFUL, BUT SHE'S NOT EVIL EITHER!
IT'S ALL **TECLA IBSEN'S** FAULT! SHE CONVINCED ERIN THAT WE WERE HER ENEMIES.
LUCKILY, IN THE END, ERIN FIGURED OUT WHO THE GOOD GUYS ARE AND WHO ARE THE BAD...
IRMA!
UM, SORRY. I COULDN'T SLEEP.
YOU'RE TELLING ME!
UNTIL YESTERDAY, I THOUGHT I'D NEVER SEE MY BROTHER, KADER, AGAIN. THANKS TO YOU, NOW HE'S HERE IN HEATHERFIELD! IT SEEMS IMPOSSIBLE...
YOU THINK HE'LL BE LONELY IN YOUR HQ?
THE SOFA BED SHOULD BE COMFY ENOUGH FOR HIM! AS FOR FEELING LONELY...

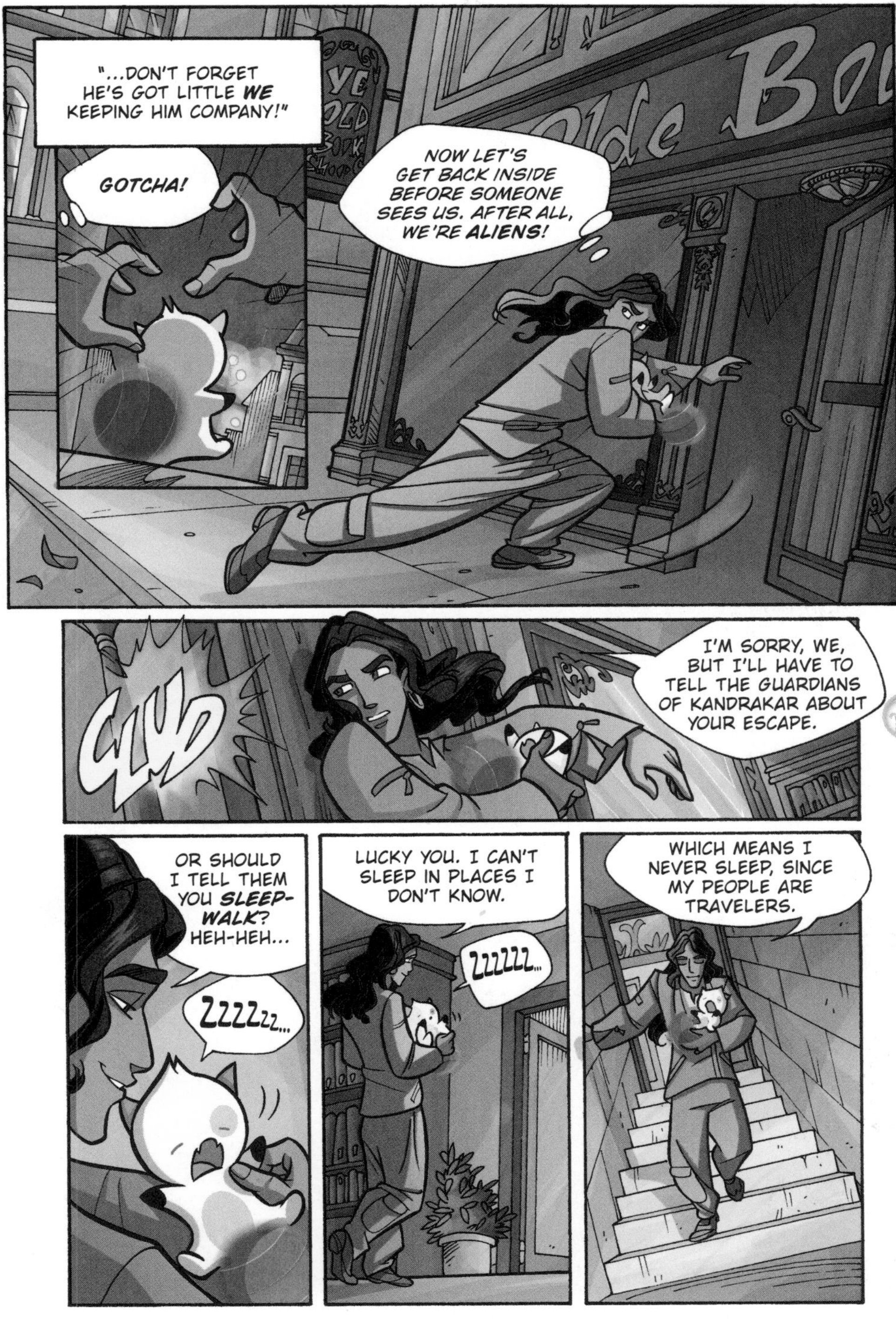

"...DON'T FORGET HE'S GOT LITTLE WE KEEPING HIM COMPANY!"
GOTCHA!
NOW LET'S GET BACK INSIDE BEFORE SOMEONE SEES US. AFTER ALL, WE'RE ALIENS!
CLUD
I'M SORRY, WE, BUT I'LL HAVE TO TELL THE GUARDIANS OF KANDRAKAR ABOUT YOUR ESCAPE.
OR SHOULD I TELL THEM YOU SLEEP-WALK? HEH-HEH...
ZZZZzz...
LUCKY YOU. I CAN'T SLEEP IN PLACES I DON'T KNOW.
ZZZZZZ...
WHICH MEANS I NEVER SLEEP, SINCE MY PEOPLE ARE TRAVELERS.

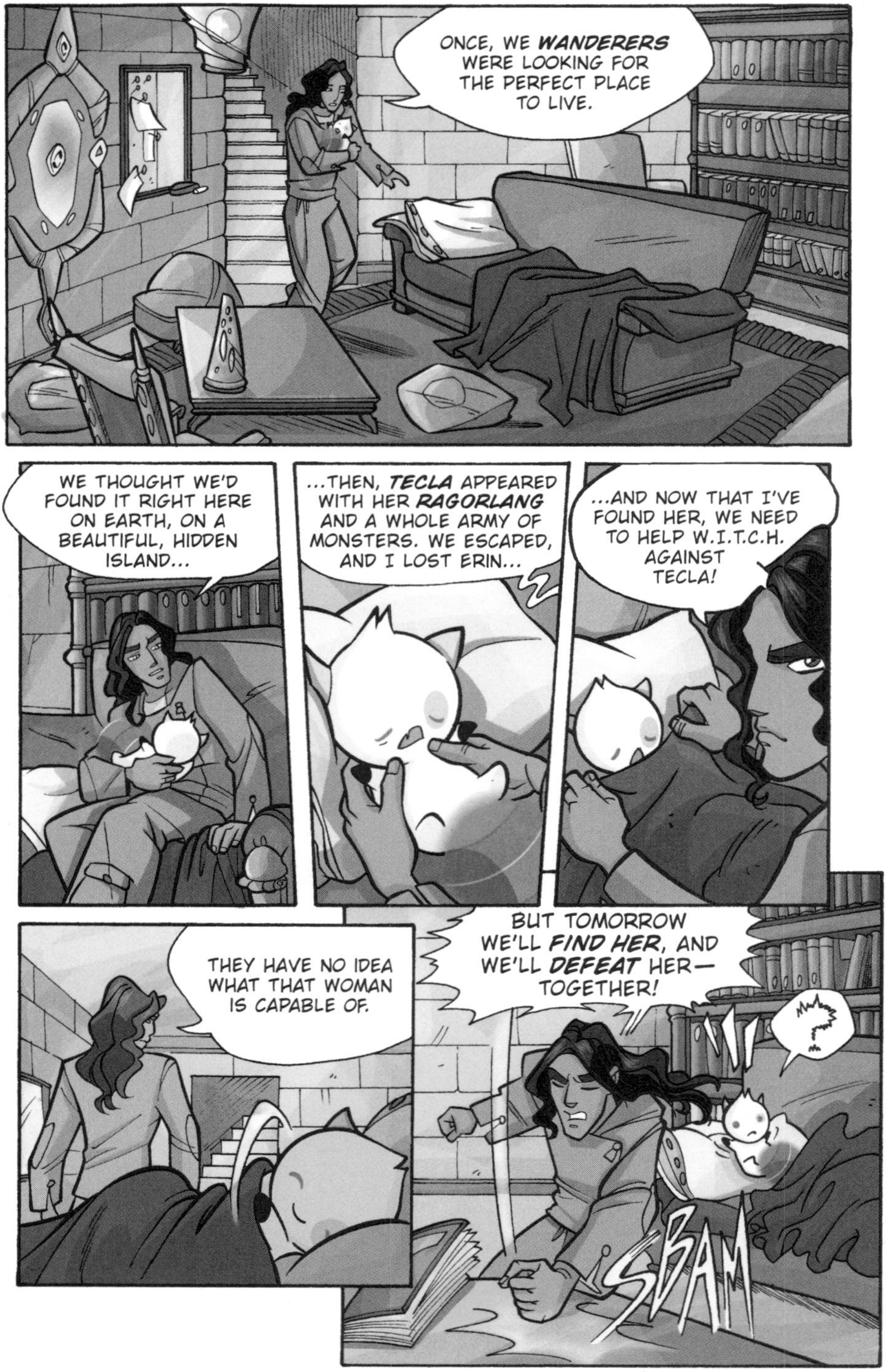
ONCE, WE WANDERERS WERE LOOKING FOR THE PERFECT PLACE TO LIVE.
WE THOUGHT WE'D FOUND IT RIGHT HERE ON EARTH, ON A BEAUTIFUL, HIDDEN ISLAND...
...THEN, TECLA APPEARED WITH HER RAGORLANG AND A WHOLE ARMY OF MONSTERS. WE ESCAPED, AND I LOST ERIN...
...AND NOW THAT I'VE FOUND HER, WE NEED TO HELP W.I.T.C.H. AGAINST TECLA!
THEY HAVE NO IDEA WHAT THAT WOMAN IS CAPABLE OF.
BUT TOMORROW WE'LL FIND HER, AND WE'LL DEFEAT HER—TOGETHER!
?
SBAM

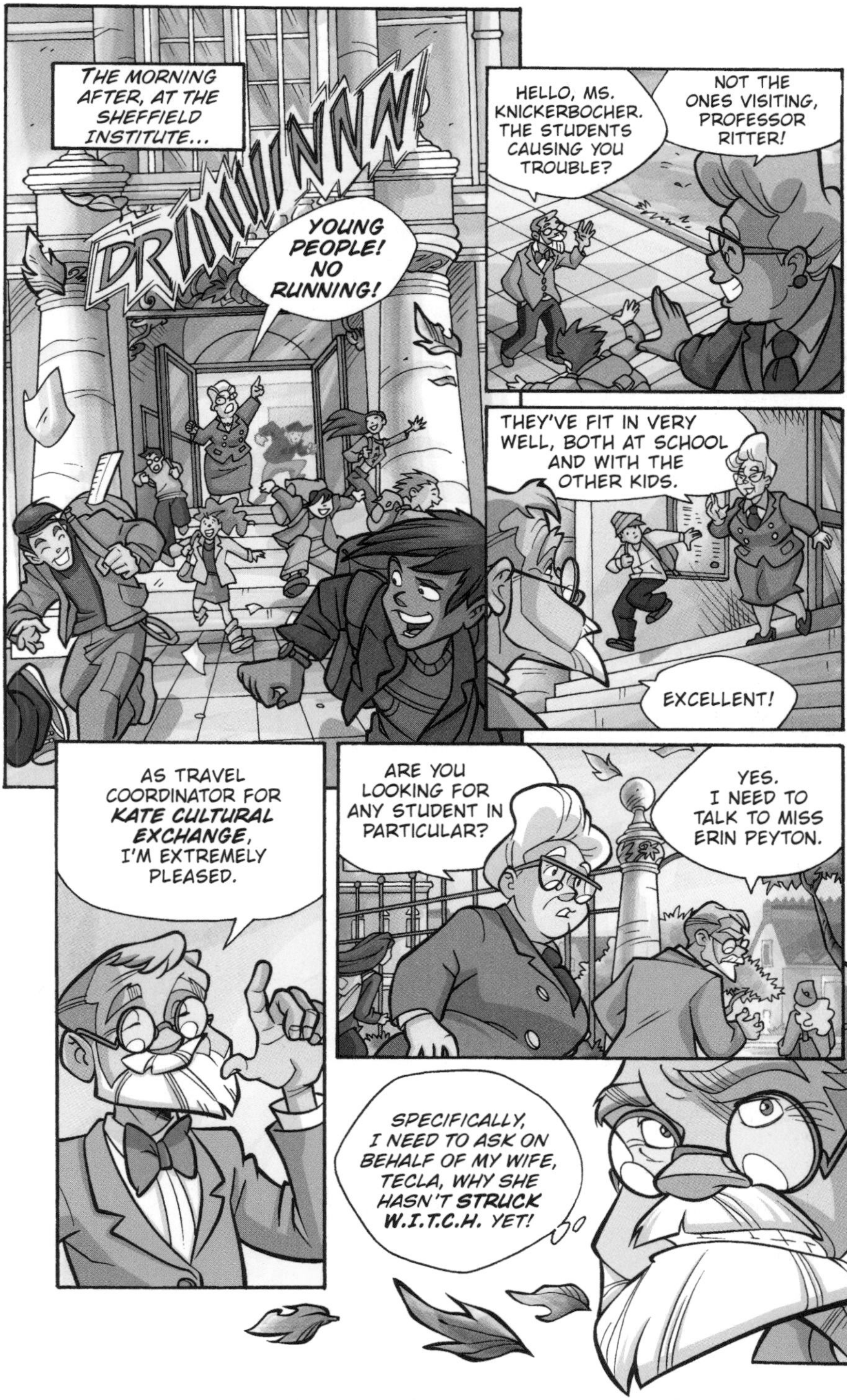

THE MORNING AFTER, AT THE SHEFFIELD INSTITUTE...
DRIIIIINNN
YOUNG PEOPLE! NO RUNNING!
HELLO, MS. KNICKERBOCHER. THE STUDENTS CAUSING YOU TROUBLE?
NOT THE ONES VISITING, PROFESSOR RITTER!
THEY'VE FIT IN VERY WELL, BOTH AT SCHOOL AND WITH THE OTHER KIDS.
EXCELLENT!
AS TRAVEL COORDINATOR FOR ***KATE CULTURAL EXCHANGE***, I'M EXTREMELY PLEASED.
ARE YOU LOOKING FOR ANY STUDENT IN PARTICULAR?
YES. I NEED TO TALK TO MISS ERIN PEYTON.
SPECIFICALLY, I NEED TO ASK ON BEHALF OF MY WIFE, TECLA, WHY SHE HASN'T ***STRUCK W.I.T.C.H.*** *YET!*

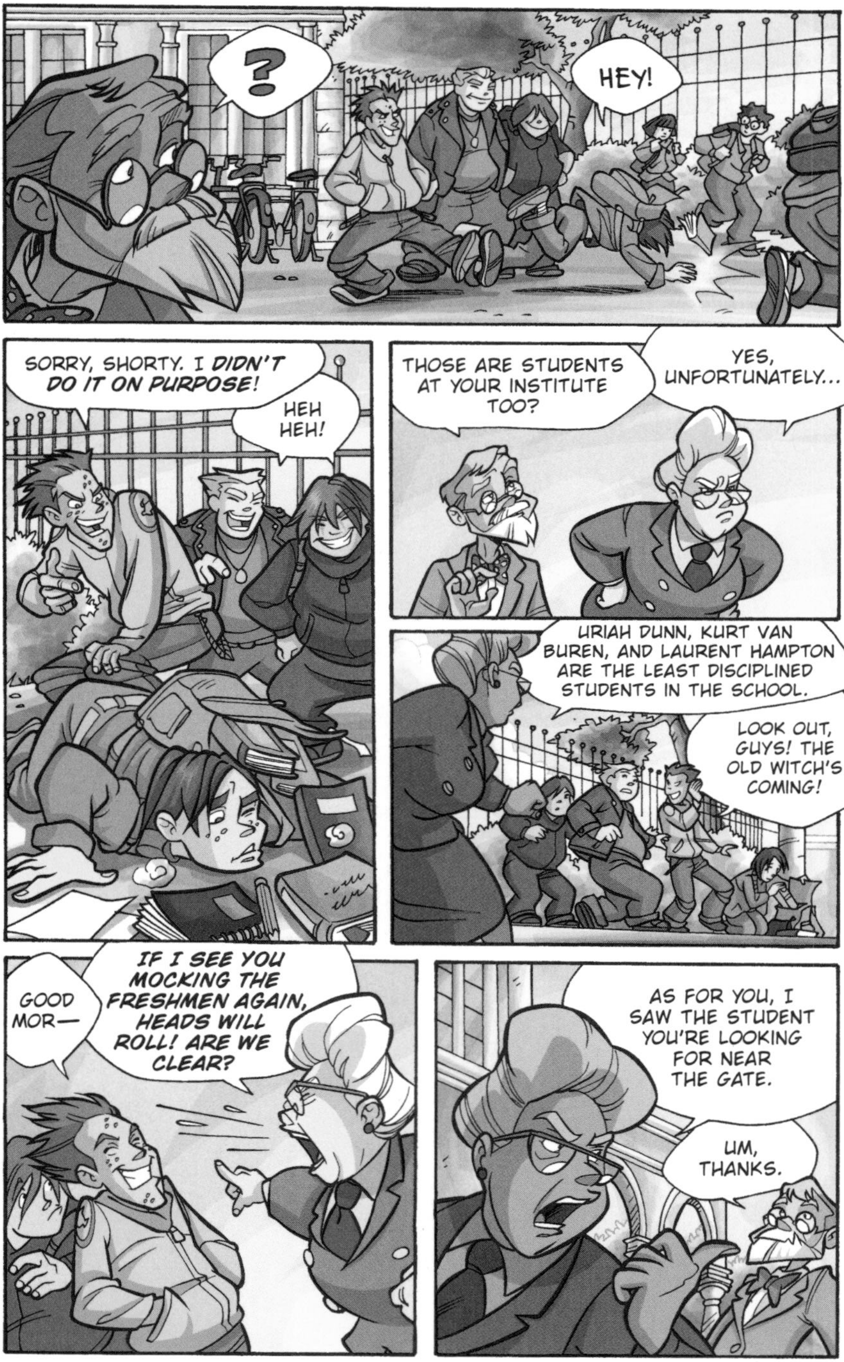
?
HEY!
SORRY, SHORTY. I *DIDN'T DO IT ON PURPOSE*!
HEH HEH!
THOSE ARE STUDENTS AT YOUR INSTITUTE TOO?
YES, UNFORTUNATELY...
URIAH DUNN, KURT VAN BUREN, AND LAURENT HAMPTON ARE THE LEAST DISCIPLINED STUDENTS IN THE SCHOOL.
LOOK OUT, GUYS! THE OLD WITCH'S COMING!
GOOD MOR—
IF I SEE YOU MOCKING THE FRESHMEN AGAIN, HEADS WILL ROLL! ARE WE CLEAR?
AS FOR YOU, I SAW THE STUDENT YOU'RE LOOKING FOR NEAR THE GATE.
UM, THANKS.

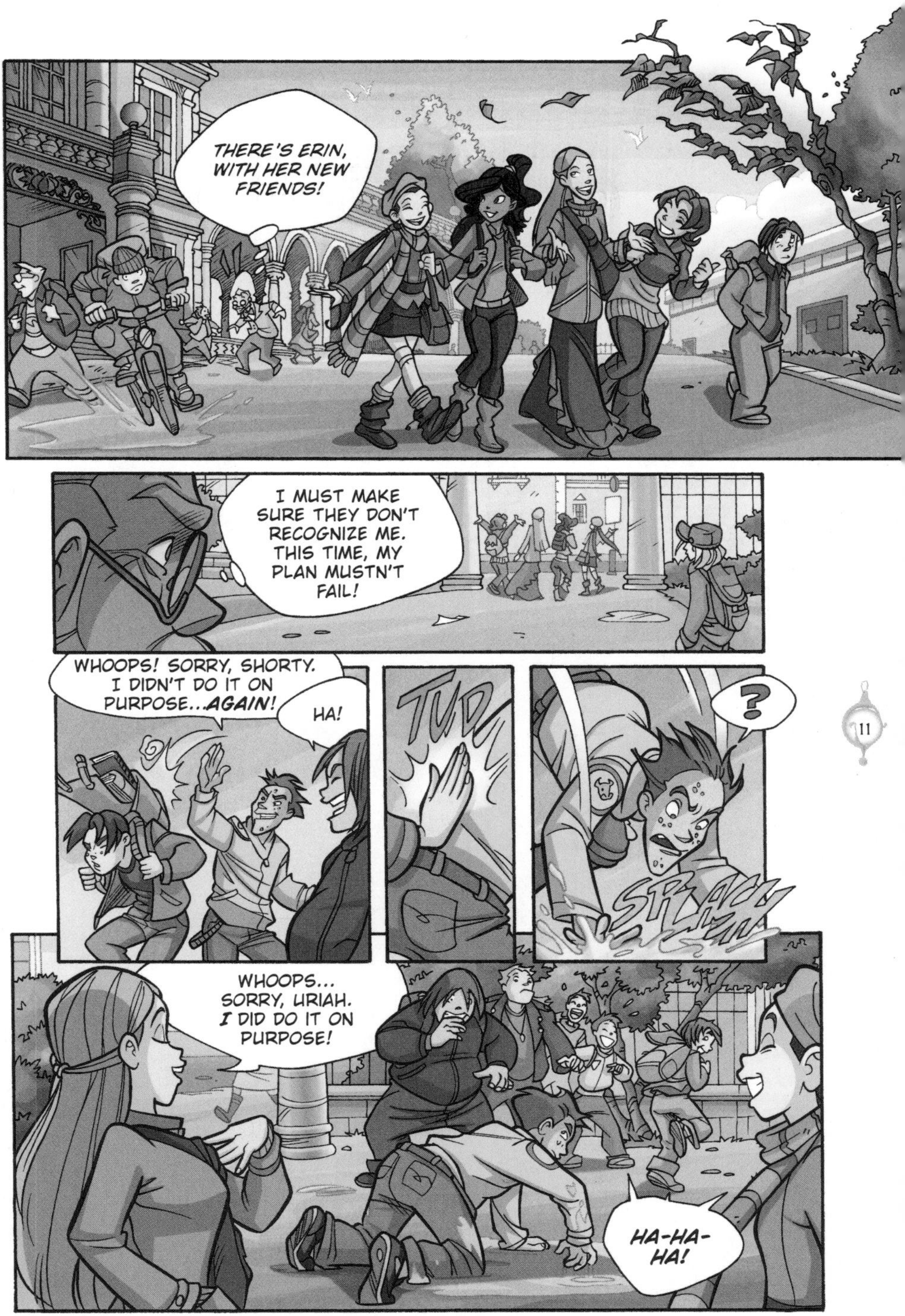
THERE'S ERIN, WITH HER NEW FRIENDS!
I MUST MAKE SURE THEY DON'T RECOGNIZE ME. THIS TIME, MY PLAN MUSTN'T FAIL!
WHOOPS! SORRY, SHORTY. I DIDN'T DO IT ON PURPOSE...AGAIN!
HA!
TUD
?
SPLACK
WHOOPS... SORRY, URIAH. I DID DO IT ON PURPOSE!
HA-HA-HA!

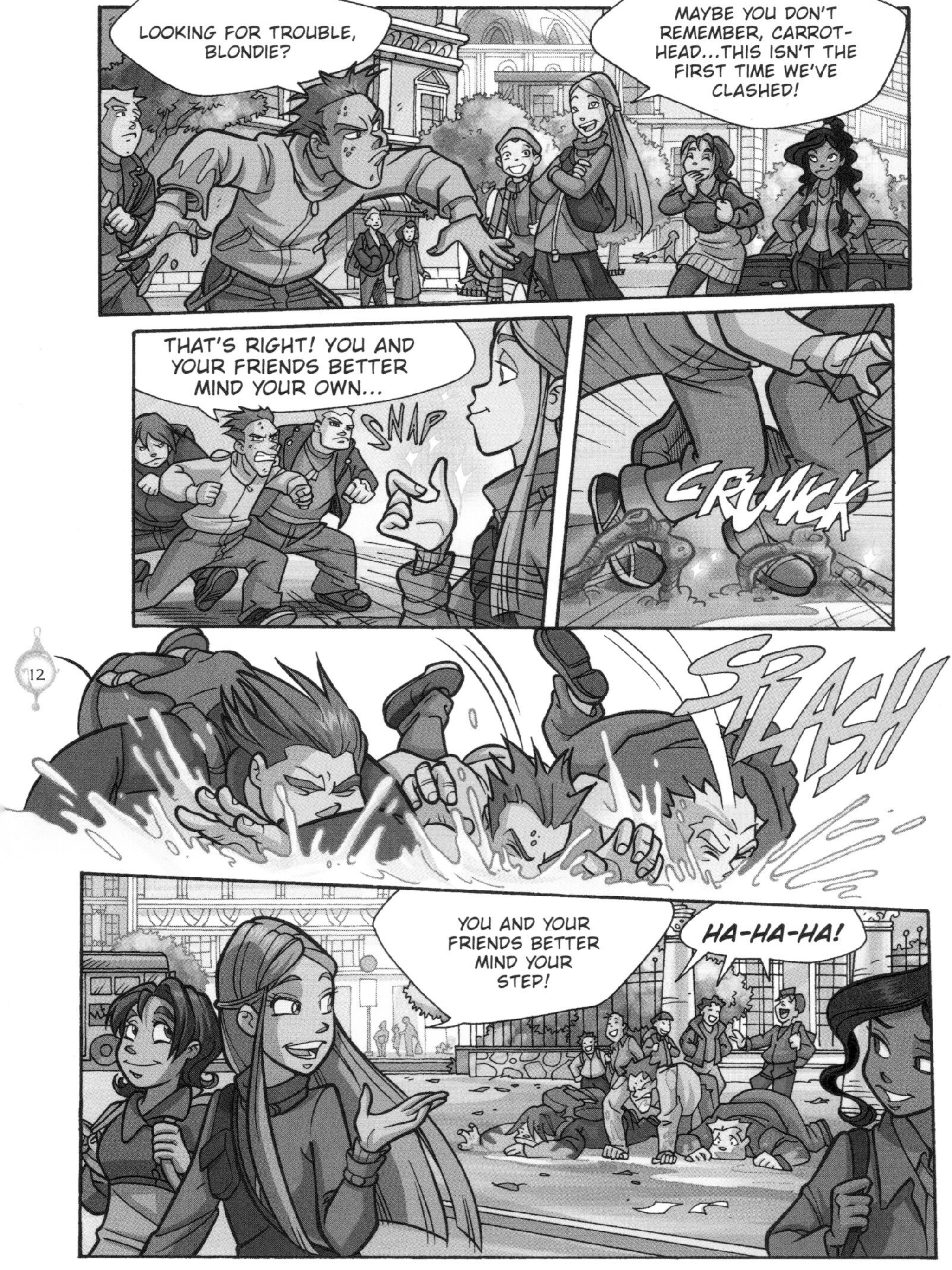
LOOKING FOR TROUBLE, BLONDIE?
MAYBE YOU DON'T REMEMBER, CARROT-HEAD...THIS ISN'T THE FIRST TIME WE'VE CLASHED!
THAT'S RIGHT! YOU AND YOUR FRIENDS BETTER MIND YOUR OWN...
SNAP
CRUNCK
SPLASH
YOU AND YOUR FRIENDS BETTER MIND YOUR STEP!
HA-HA-HA!

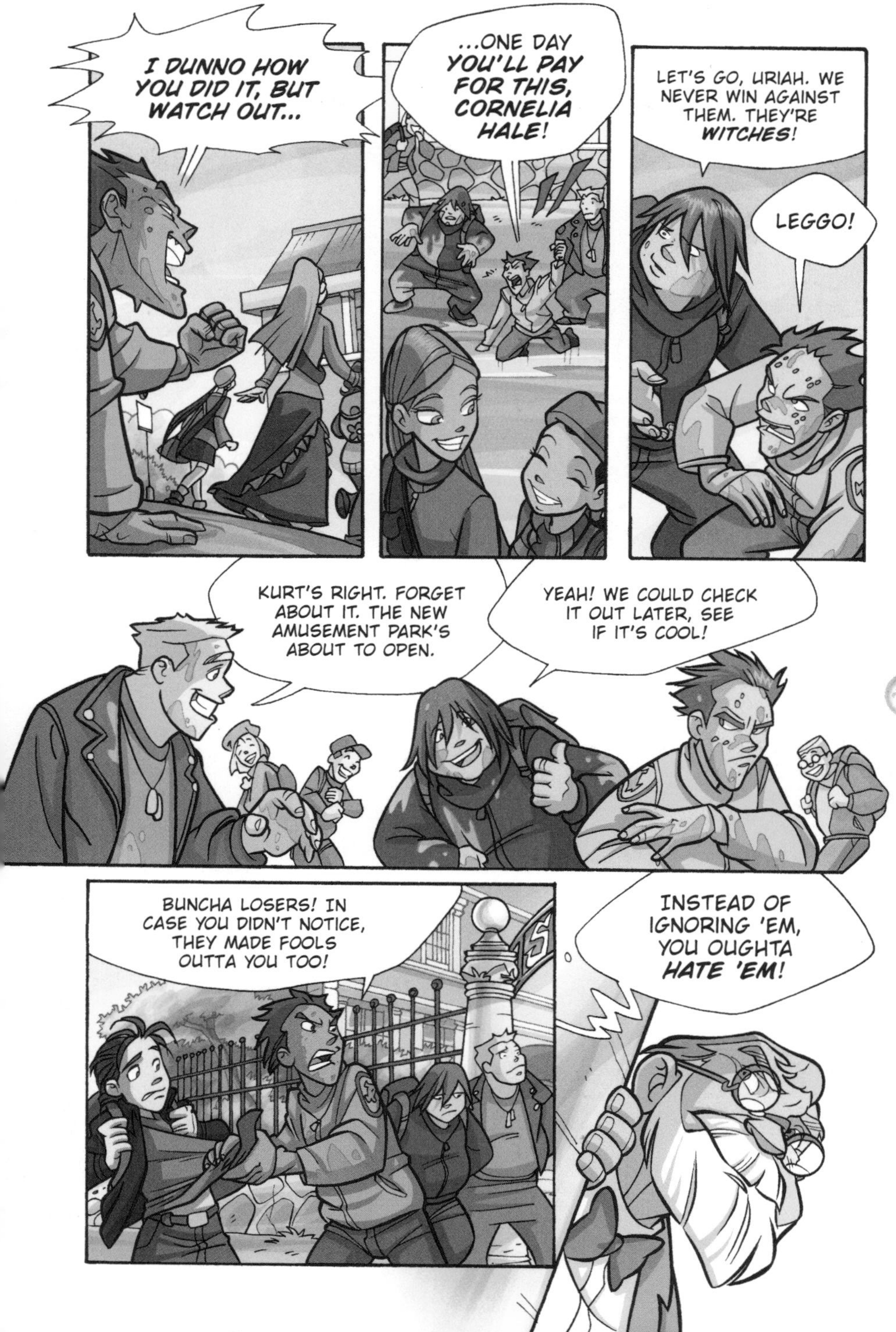
I DUNNO HOW YOU DID IT, BUT WATCH OUT...
...ONE DAY YOU'LL PAY FOR THIS, CORNELIA HALE!
LET'S GO, URIAH. WE NEVER WIN AGAINST THEM. THEY'RE WITCHES!
LEGGO!
KURT'S RIGHT. FORGET ABOUT IT. THE NEW AMUSEMENT PARK'S ABOUT TO OPEN.
YEAH! WE COULD CHECK IT OUT LATER, SEE IF IT'S COOL!
BUNCHA LOSERS! IN CASE YOU DIDN'T NOTICE, THEY MADE FOOLS OUTTA YOU TOO!
INSTEAD OF IGNORING 'EM, YOU OUGHTA HATE 'EM!

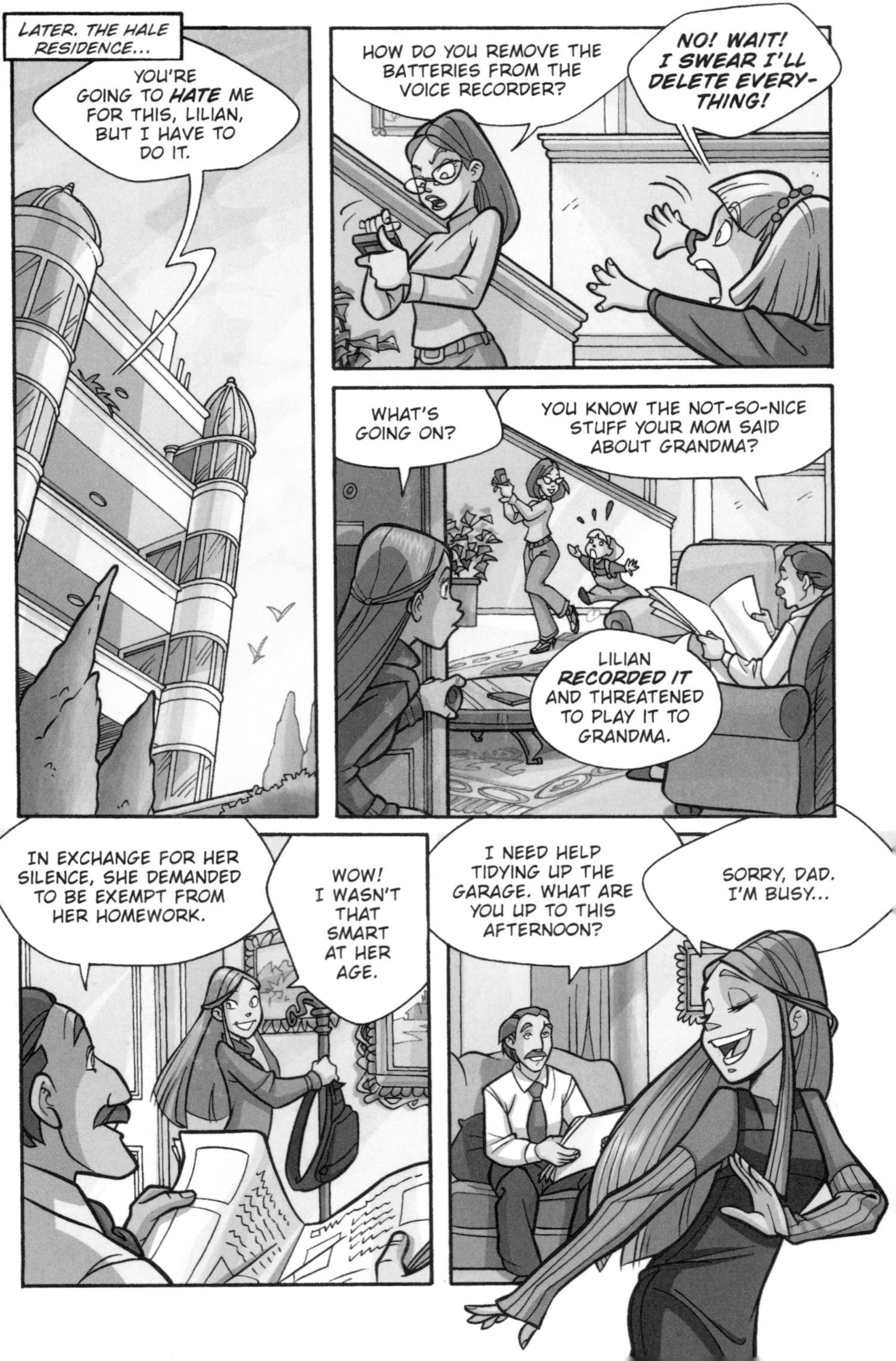

LATER. THE HALE RESIDENCE...
YOU'RE GOING TO *HATE* ME FOR THIS, LILIAN, BUT I HAVE TO DO IT.
HOW DO YOU REMOVE THE BATTERIES FROM THE VOICE RECORDER?
NO! WAIT! I SWEAR I'LL DELETE EVERYTHING!
WHAT'S GOING ON?
YOU KNOW THE NOT-SO-NICE STUFF YOUR MOM SAID ABOUT GRANDMA?
LILIAN *RECORDED IT* AND THREATENED TO PLAY IT TO GRANDMA.
IN EXCHANGE FOR HER SILENCE, SHE DEMANDED TO BE EXEMPT FROM HER HOMEWORK.
WOW! I WASN'T THAT SMART AT HER AGE.
I NEED HELP TIDYING UP THE GARAGE. WHAT ARE YOU UP TO THIS AFTERNOON?
SORRY, DAD. I'M BUSY...

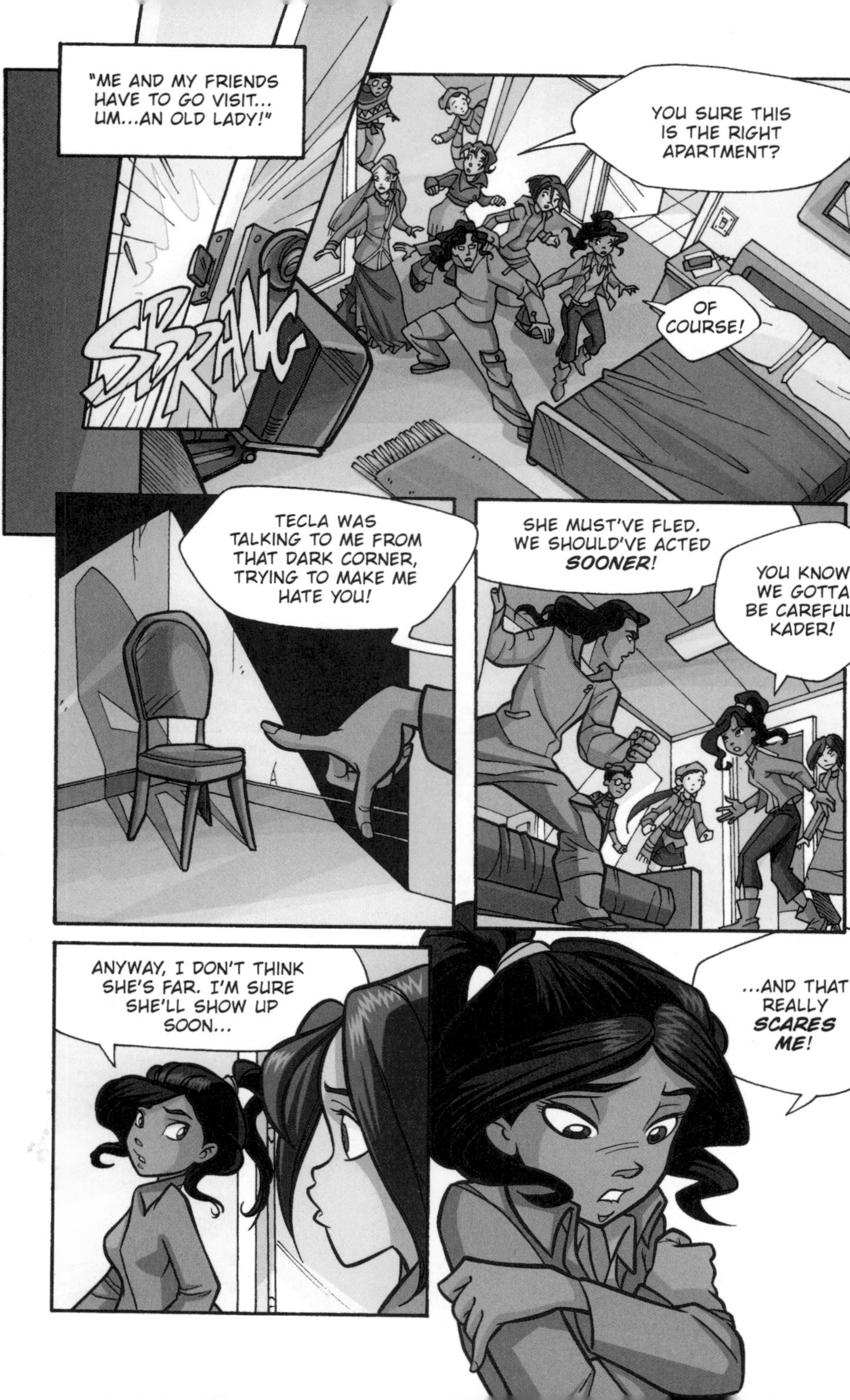
"ME AND MY FRIENDS HAVE TO GO VISIT... UM...AN OLD LADY!"
YOU SURE THIS IS THE RIGHT APARTMENT?
SBRANG
OF COURSE!
TECLA WAS TALKING TO ME FROM THAT DARK CORNER, TRYING TO MAKE ME HATE YOU!
SHE MUST'VE FLED. WE SHOULD'VE ACTED SOONER!
YOU KNOW WE GOTTA BE CAREFUL, KADER!
ANYWAY, I DON'T THINK SHE'S FAR. I'M SURE SHE'LL SHOW UP SOON...
...AND THAT REALLY SCARES ME!

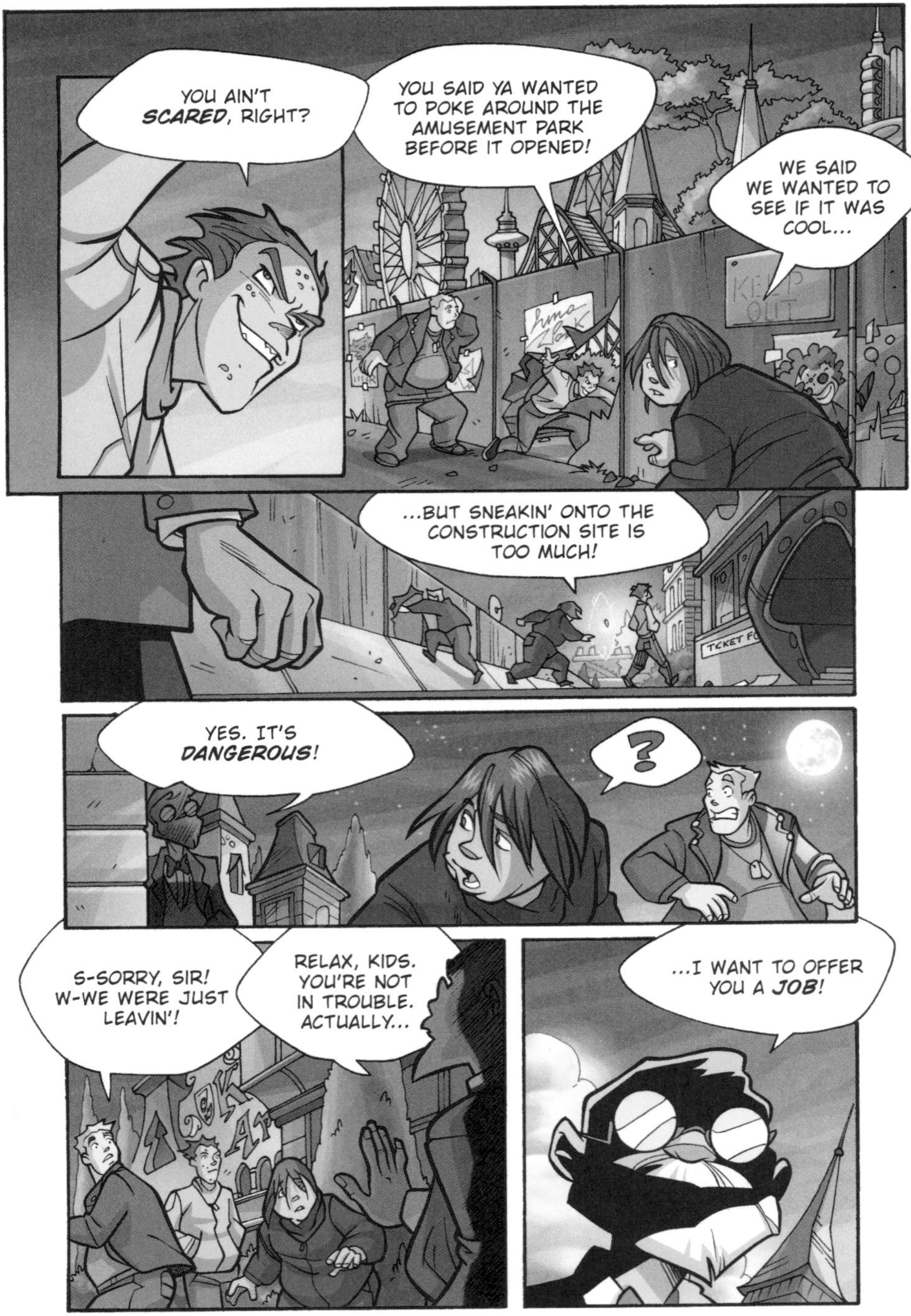
YOU AIN'T SCARED, RIGHT?
YOU SAID YA WANTED TO POKE AROUND THE AMUSEMENT PARK BEFORE IT OPENED!
WE SAID WE WANTED TO SEE IF IT WAS COOL...
KEEP OUT
...BUT SNEAKIN' ONTO THE CONSTRUCTION SITE IS TOO MUCH!
YES. IT'S DANGEROUS!
?
S-SORRY, SIR! W-WE WERE JUST LEAVIN'!
RELAX, KIDS. YOU'RE NOT IN TROUBLE. ACTUALLY...
...I WANT TO OFFER YOU A JOB!

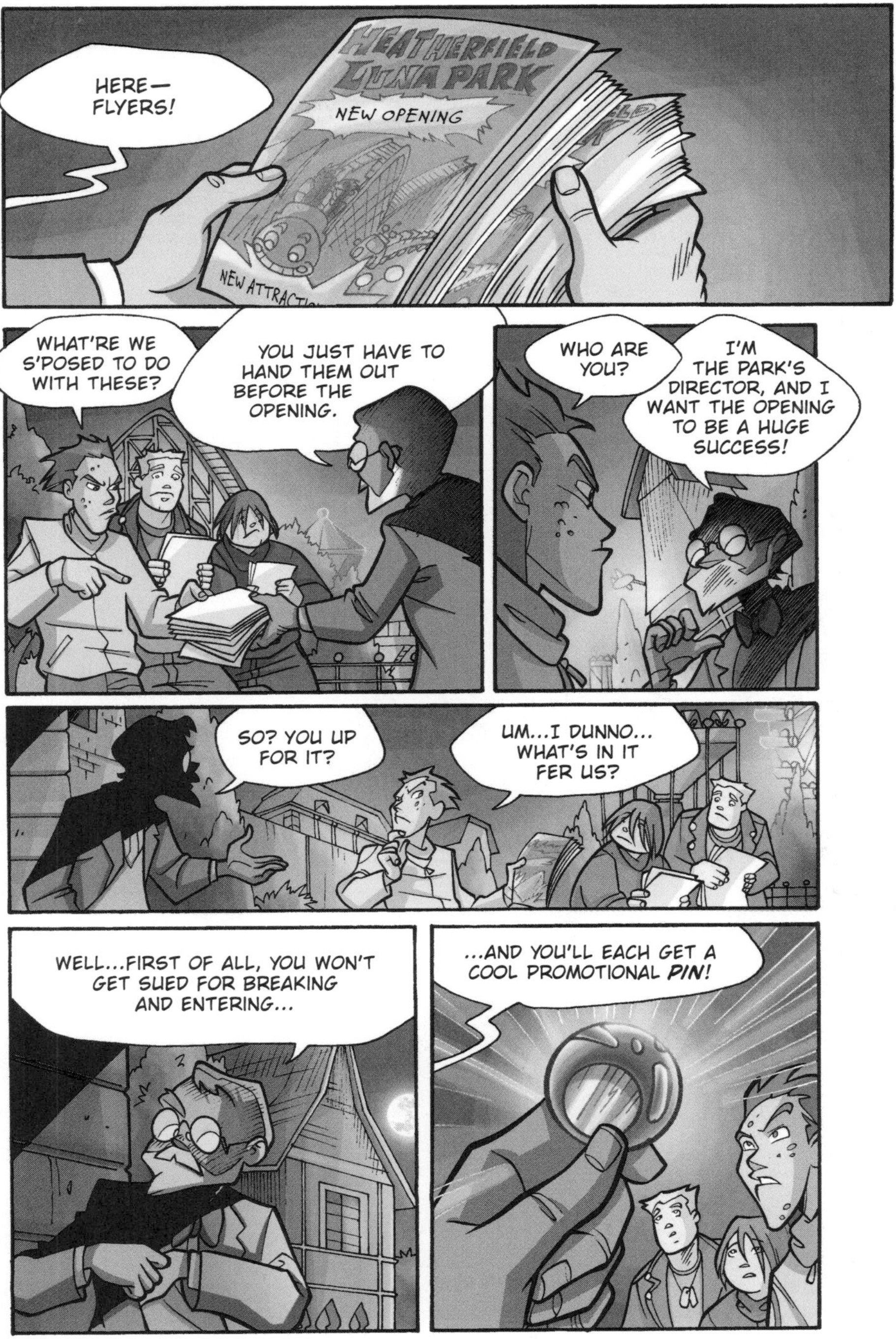
HEATHERFIELD LUNA PARK
NEW OPENING
HERE— FLYERS!
WHAT'RE WE S'POSED TO DO WITH THESE?
YOU JUST HAVE TO HAND THEM OUT BEFORE THE OPENING.
WHO ARE YOU?
I'M THE PARK'S DIRECTOR, AND I WANT THE OPENING TO BE A HUGE SUCCESS!
SO? YOU UP FOR IT?
UM...I DUNNO... WHAT'S IN IT FER US?
WELL...FIRST OF ALL, YOU WON'T GET SUED FOR BREAKING AND ENTERING...
...AND YOU'LL EACH GET A COOL PROMOTIONAL ***PIN!***

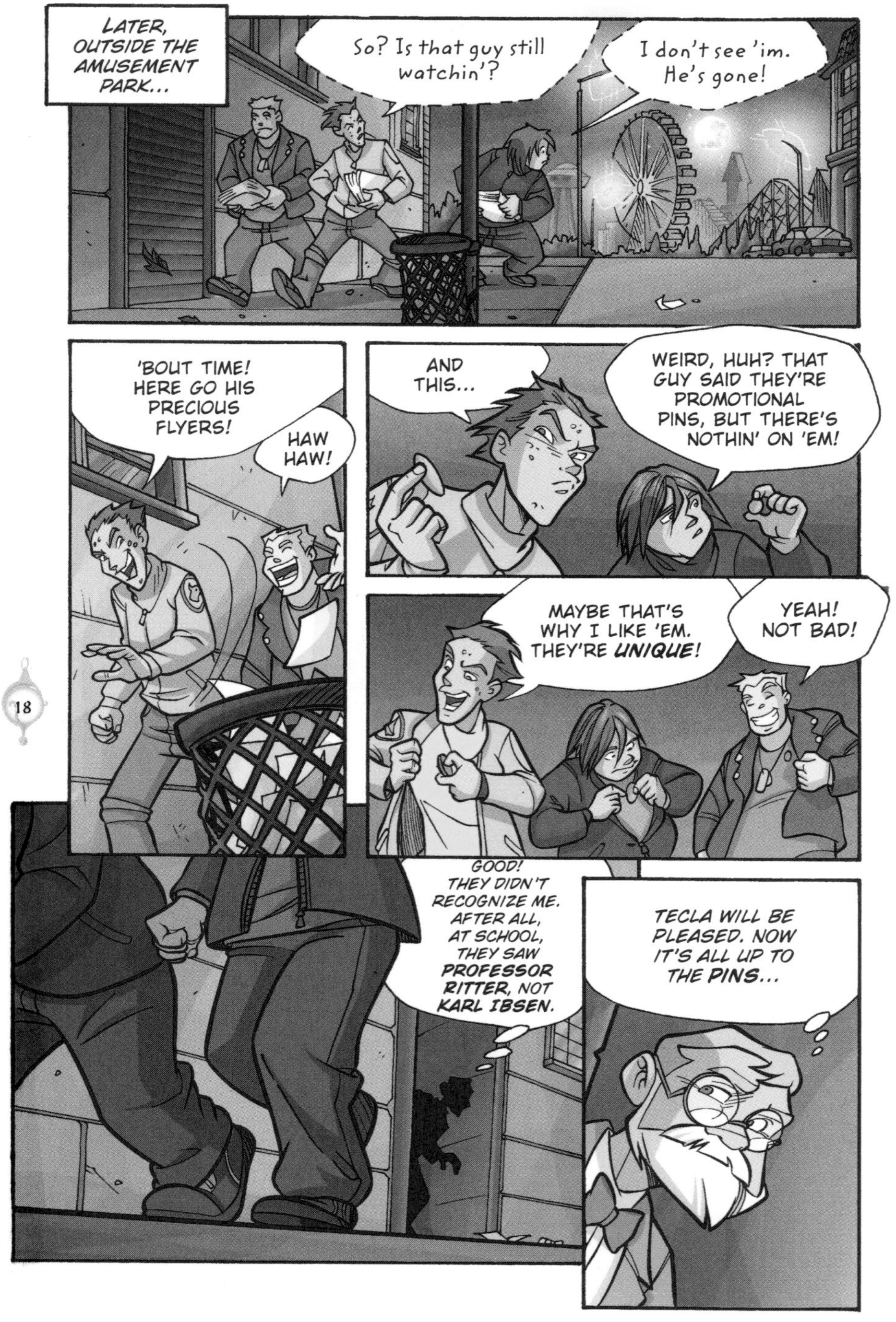
LATER, OUTSIDE THE AMUSEMENT PARK...
So? Is that guy still watchin'?
I don't see 'im. He's gone!
'BOUT TIME! HERE GO HIS PRECIOUS FLYERS!
HAW HAW!
AND THIS...
WEIRD, HUH? THAT GUY SAID THEY'RE PROMOTIONAL PINS, BUT THERE'S NOTHIN' ON 'EM!
MAYBE THAT'S WHY I LIKE 'EM. THEY'RE UNIQUE!
YEAH! NOT BAD!
GOOD! THEY DIDN'T RECOGNIZE ME. AFTER ALL, AT SCHOOL, THEY SAW PROFESSOR RITTER, NOT KARL IBSEN.
TECLA WILL BE PLEASED. NOW IT'S ALL UP TO THE PINS...

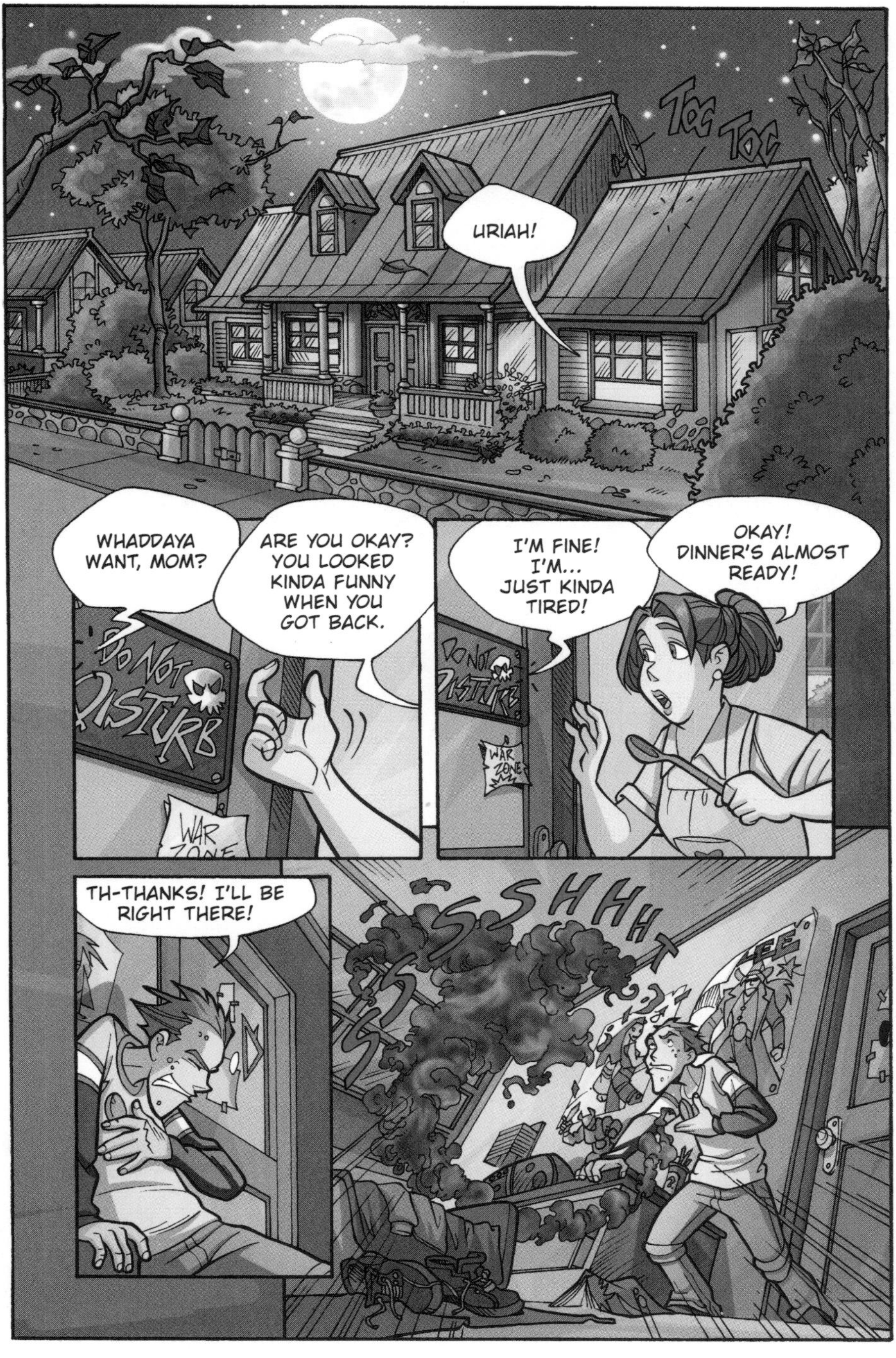
TOC TOC
URIAH!
WHADDAYA WANT, MOM?
ARE YOU OKAY? YOU LOOKED KINDA FUNNY WHEN YOU GOT BACK.
DO NOT DISTURB
WAR ZONE
I'M FINE! I'M... JUST KINDA TIRED!
OKAY! DINNER'S ALMOST READY!
TH-THANKS! I'LL BE RIGHT THERE!
SSSHHHT

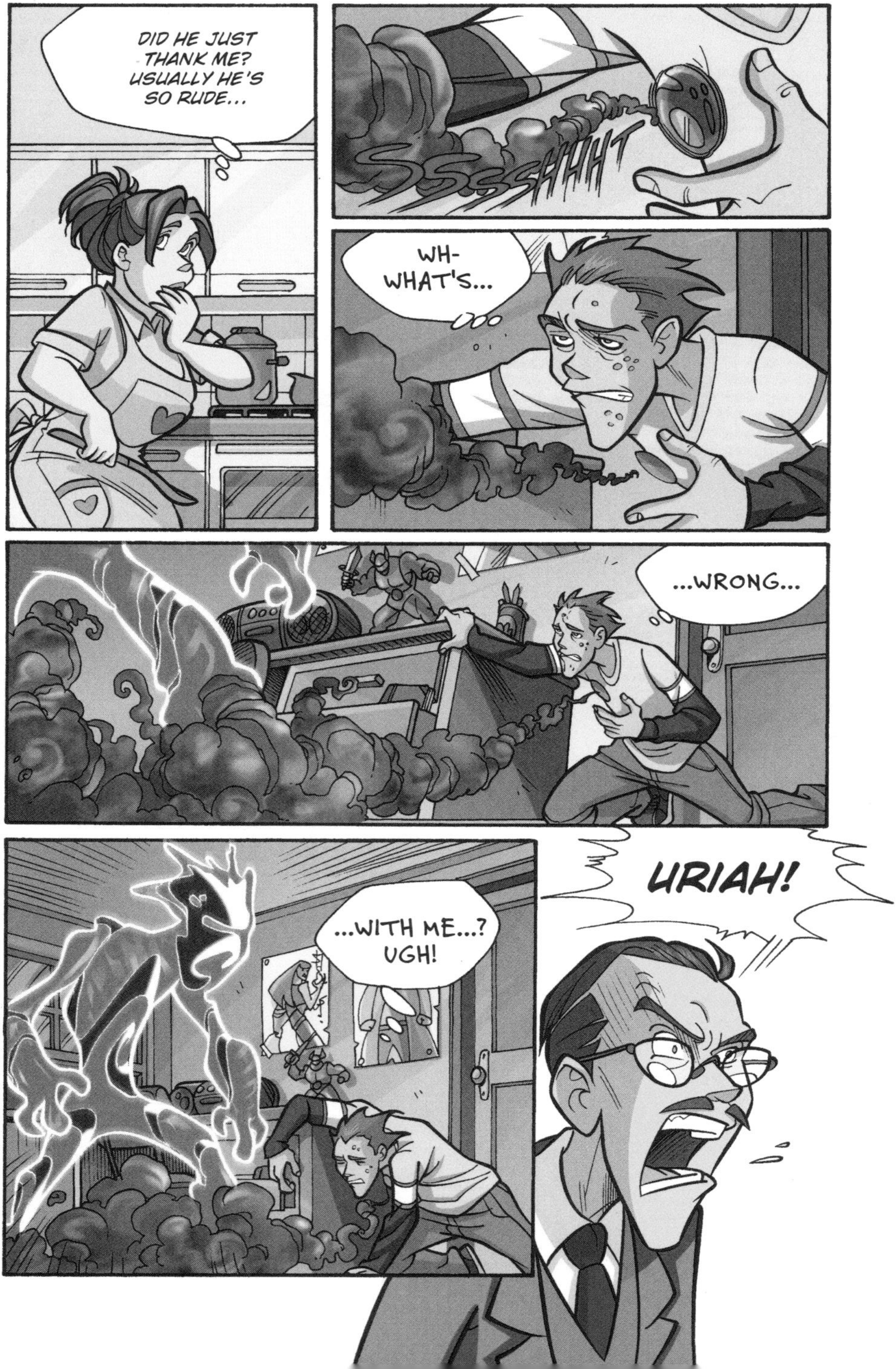
DID HE JUST THANK ME? USUALLY HE'S SO RUDE...
SSSSSHHHT
WH- WHAT'S...
...WRONG...
URIAH!
...WITH ME...? UGH!

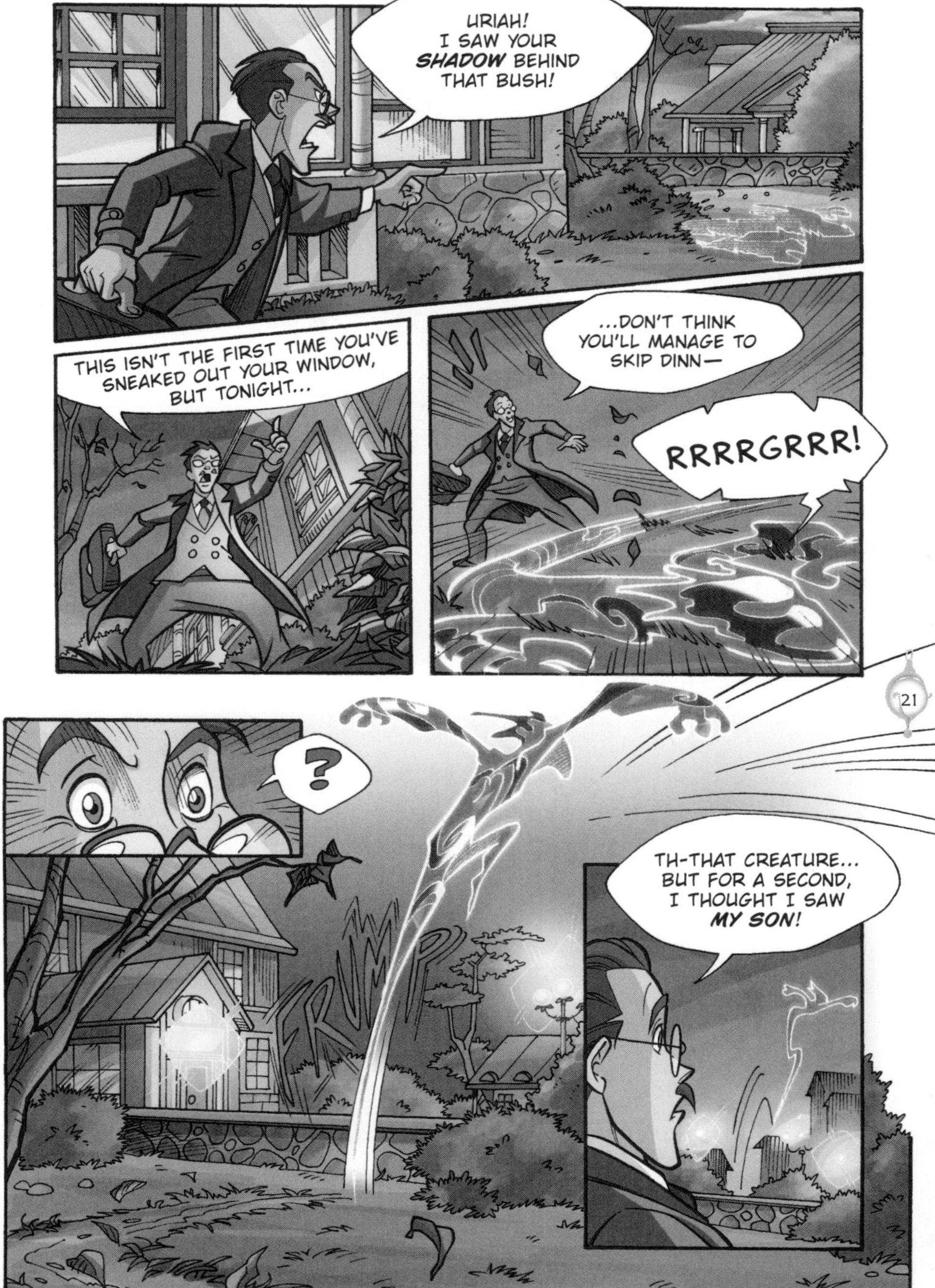
URIAH! I SAW YOUR *SHADOW* BEHIND THAT BUSH!
THIS ISN'T THE FIRST TIME YOU'VE SNEAKED OUT YOUR WINDOW, BUT TONIGHT...
...DON'T THINK YOU'LL MANAGE TO SKIP DINN—
RRRRGRRR!
?
FRUMP
TH-THAT CREATURE... BUT FOR A SECOND, I THOUGHT I SAW *MY SON*!

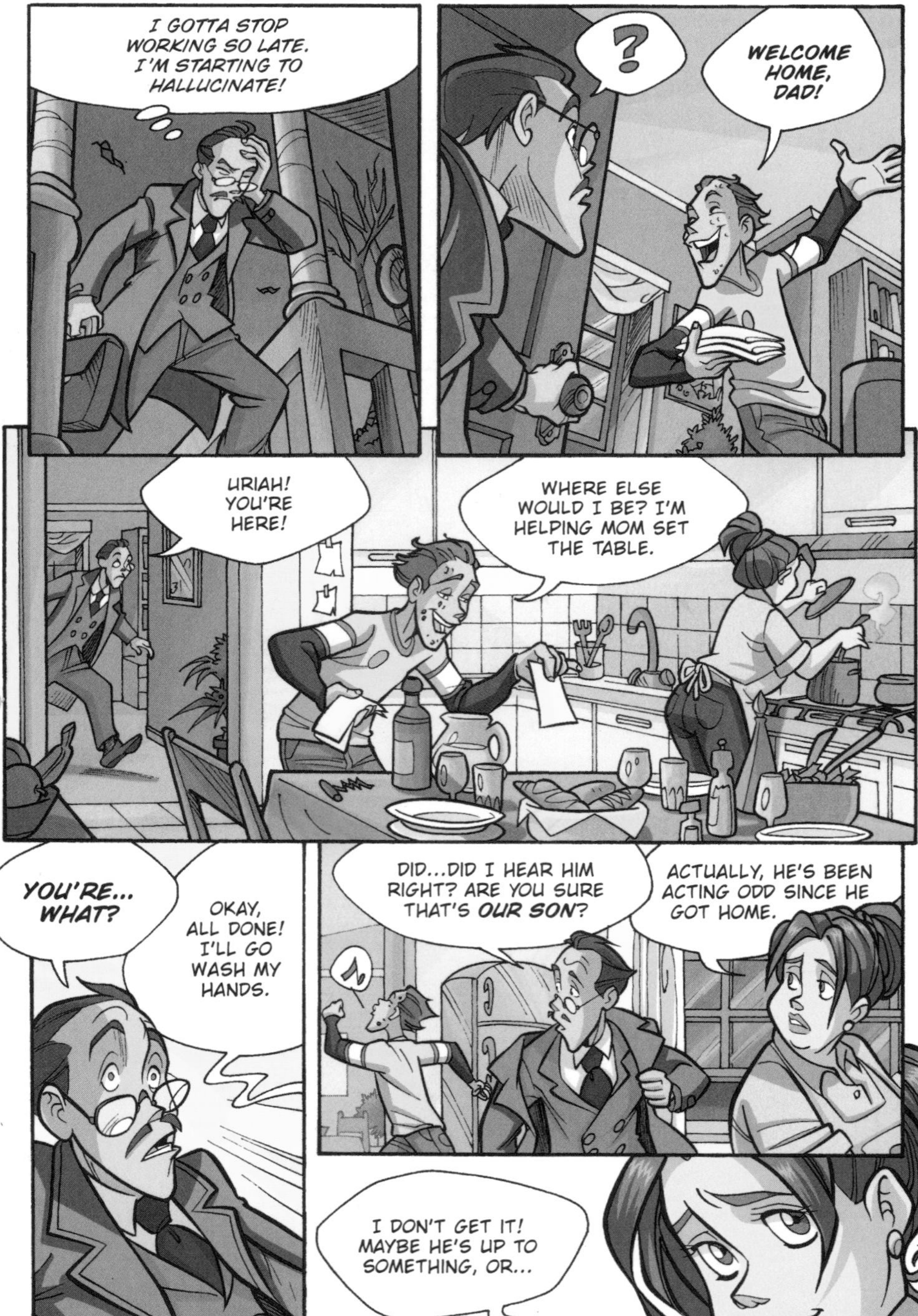
I GOTTA STOP WORKING SO LATE. I'M STARTING TO HALLUCINATE!
?
WELCOME HOME, DAD!
URIAH! YOU'RE HERE!
WHERE ELSE WOULD I BE? I'M HELPING MOM SET THE TABLE.
YOU'RE... WHAT?
OKAY, ALL DONE! I'LL GO WASH MY HANDS.
DID...DID I HEAR HIM RIGHT? ARE YOU SURE THAT'S OUR SON?
ACTUALLY, HE'S BEEN ACTING ODD SINCE HE GOT HOME.
I DON'T GET IT! MAYBE HE'S UP TO SOMETHING, OR...

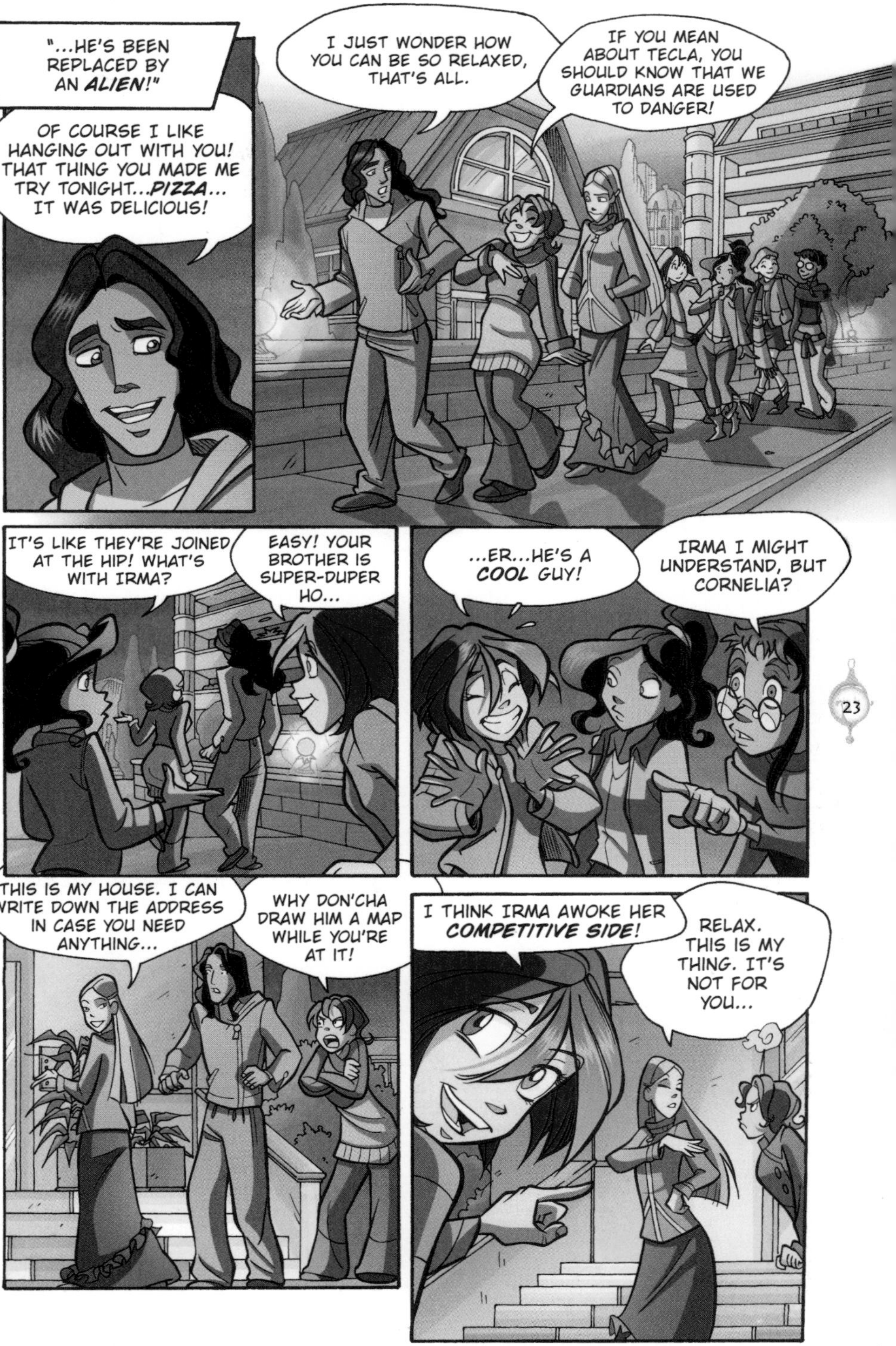
"...HE'S BEEN REPLACED BY AN *ALIEN*!"
OF COURSE I LIKE HANGING OUT WITH YOU! THAT THING YOU MADE ME TRY TONIGHT...*PIZZA*... IT WAS DELICIOUS!
I JUST WONDER HOW YOU CAN BE SO RELAXED, THAT'S ALL.
IF YOU MEAN ABOUT TECLA, YOU SHOULD KNOW THAT WE GUARDIANS ARE USED TO DANGER!
IT'S LIKE THEY'RE JOINED AT THE HIP! WHAT'S WITH IRMA?
EASY! YOUR BROTHER IS SUPER-DUPER HO...
...ER...HE'S A *COOL* GUY!
IRMA I MIGHT UNDERSTAND, BUT CORNELIA?
THIS IS MY HOUSE. I CAN WRITE DOWN THE ADDRESS IN CASE YOU NEED ANYTHING...
WHY DON'CHA DRAW HIM A MAP WHILE YOU'RE AT IT!
I THINK IRMA AWOKE HER *COMPETITIVE SIDE*!
RELAX. THIS IS MY THING. IT'S NOT FOR YOU...

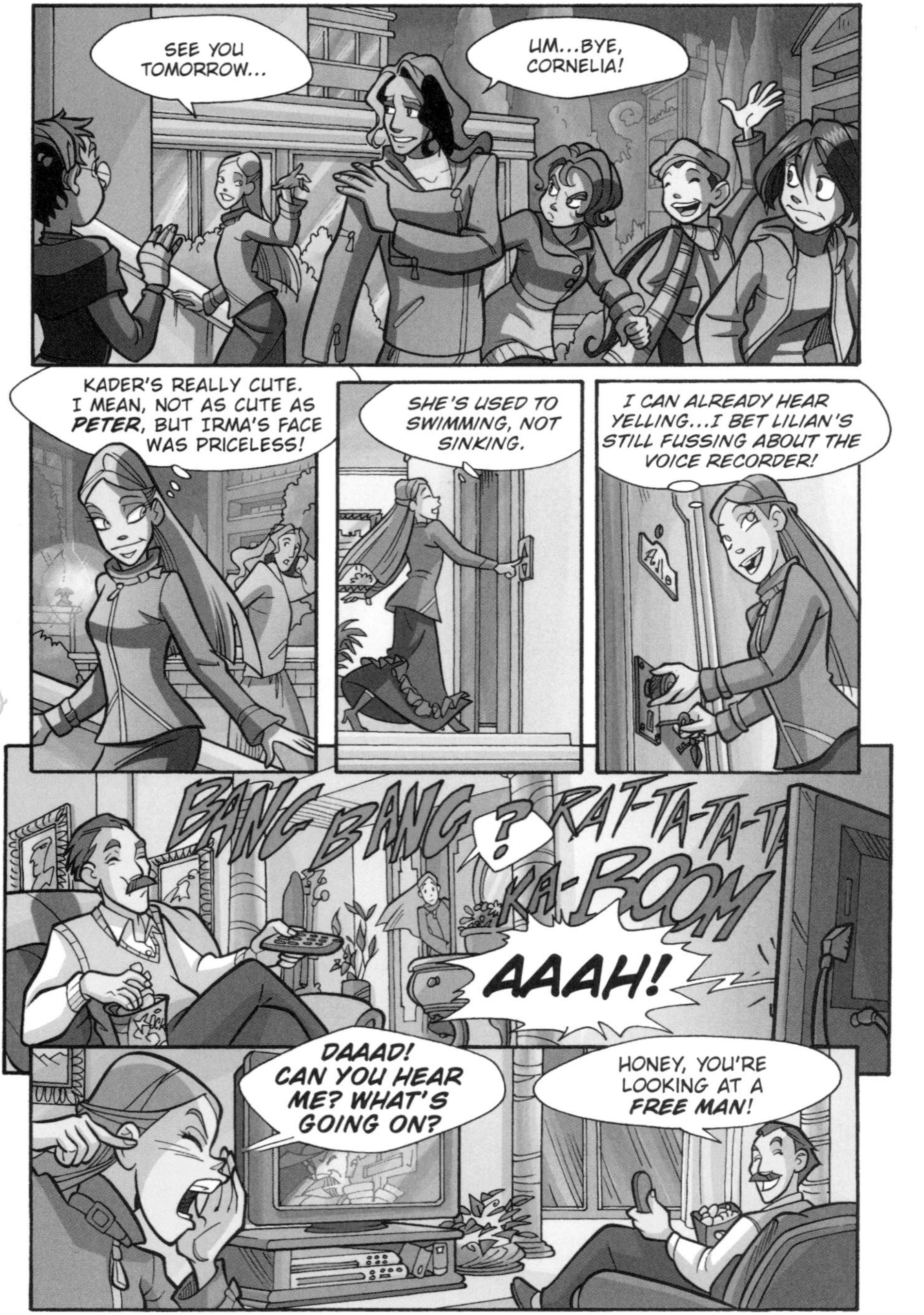
SEE YOU TOMORROW...
UM...BYE, CORNELIA!
KADER'S REALLY CUTE. I MEAN, NOT AS CUTE AS PETER, BUT IRMA'S FACE WAS PRICELESS!
SHE'S USED TO SWIMMING, NOT SINKING.
I CAN ALREADY HEAR YELLING...I BET LILIAN'S STILL FUSSING ABOUT THE VOICE RECORDER!
BANG BANG
?
RAT-TA-TA-TA
KA-BOOM
AAAH!
DAAAD! CAN YOU HEAR ME? WHAT'S GOING ON?
HONEY, YOU'RE LOOKING AT A FREE MAN!

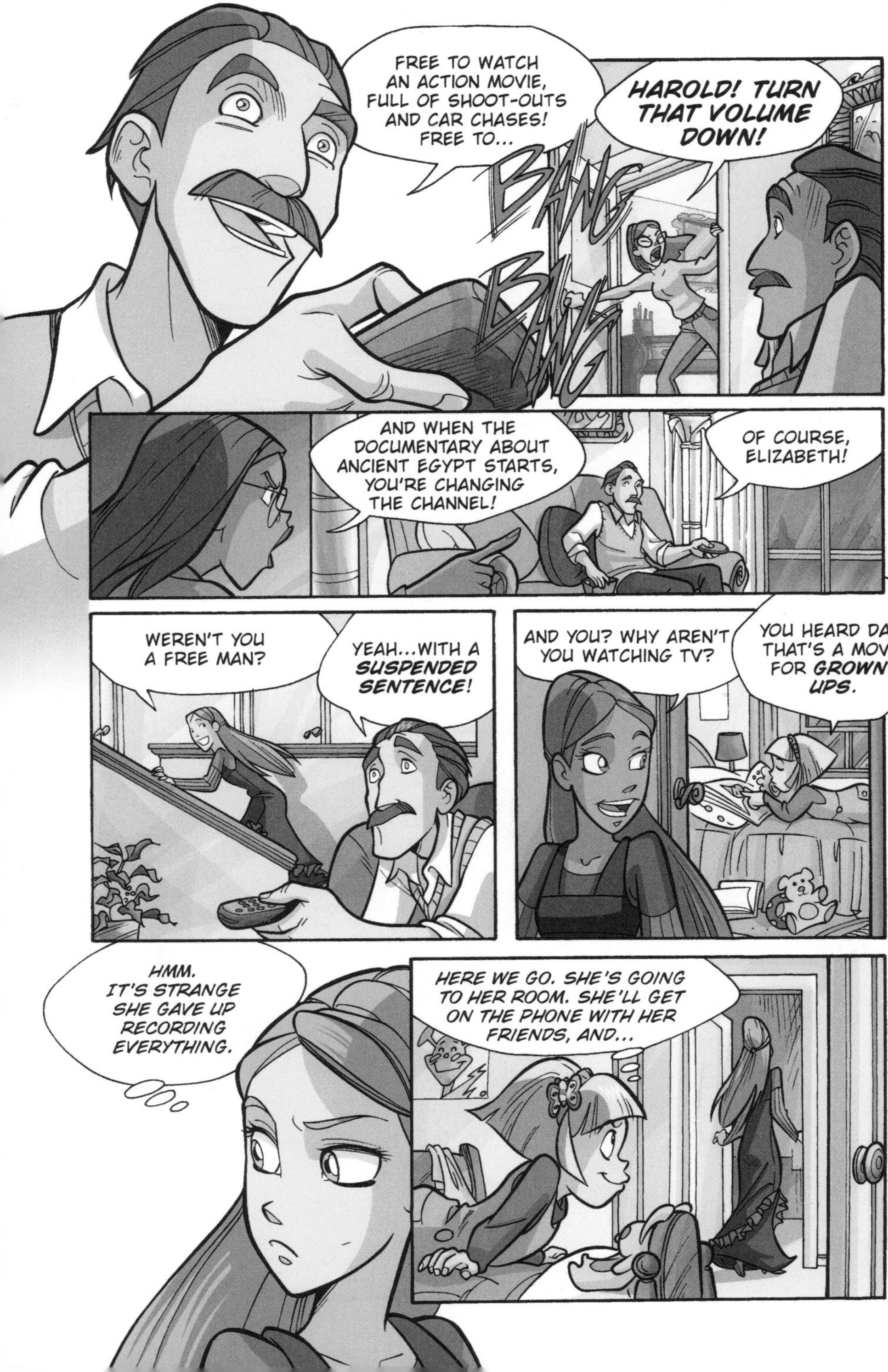
FREE TO WATCH AN ACTION MOVIE, FULL OF SHOOT-OUTS AND CAR CHASES! FREE TO...
BANG
BANG
BANG
HAROLD! TURN THAT VOLUME DOWN!
AND WHEN THE DOCUMENTARY ABOUT ANCIENT EGYPT STARTS, YOU'RE CHANGING THE CHANNEL!
OF COURSE, ELIZABETH!
WEREN'T YOU A FREE MAN?
YEAH...WITH A SUSPENDED SENTENCE!
AND YOU? WHY AREN'T YOU WATCHING TV?
YOU HEARD DAD. THAT'S A MOVIE FOR GROWN-UPS.
HMM. IT'S STRANGE SHE GAVE UP RECORDING EVERYTHING.
HERE WE GO. SHE'S GOING TO HER ROOM. SHE'LL GET ON THE PHONE WITH HER FRIENDS, AND...

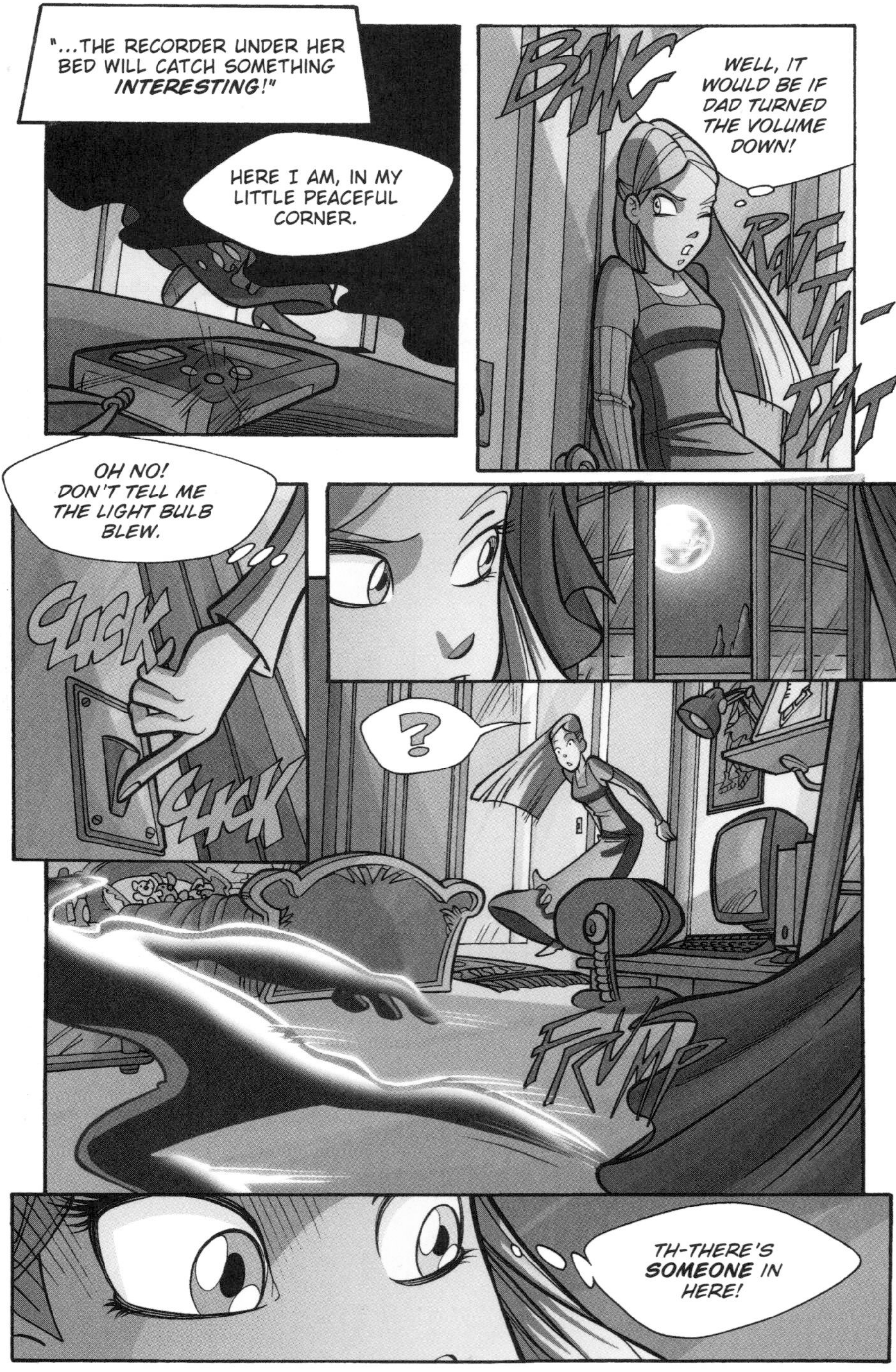
"...THE RECORDER UNDER HER BED WILL CATCH SOMETHING **INTERESTING**!"
HERE I AM, IN MY LITTLE PEACEFUL CORNER.
BANG
WELL, IT WOULD BE IF DAD TURNED THE VOLUME DOWN!
RAT-TA-TAT
OH NO! DON'T TELL ME THE LIGHT BULB BLEW.
CLICK
CLICK
?
FRUMP
TH-THERE'S **SOMEONE** IN HERE!

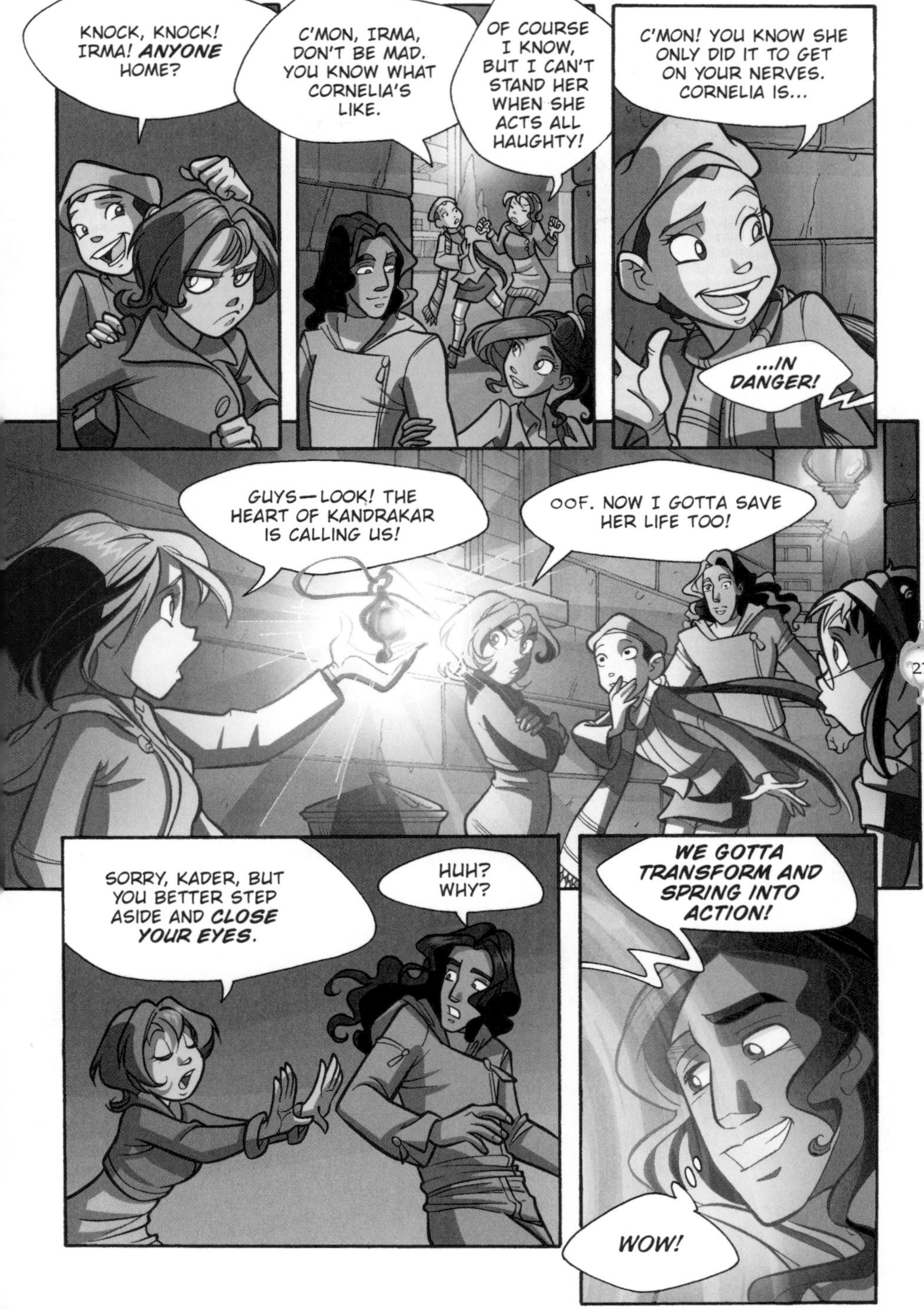
KNOCK, KNOCK! IRMA! ***ANYONE*** HOME?
C'MON, IRMA, DON'T BE MAD. YOU KNOW WHAT CORNELIA'S LIKE.
OF COURSE I KNOW, BUT I CAN'T STAND HER WHEN SHE ACTS ALL HAUGHTY!
C'MON! YOU KNOW SHE ONLY DID IT TO GET ON YOUR NERVES. CORNELIA IS...
...IN DANGER!
GUYS—LOOK! THE HEART OF KANDRAKAR IS CALLING US!
OOF. NOW I GOTTA SAVE HER LIFE TOO!
SORRY, KADER, BUT YOU BETTER STEP ASIDE AND ***CLOSE YOUR EYES***.
HUH? WHY?
WE GOTTA TRANSFORM AND SPRING INTO ACTION!
WOW!

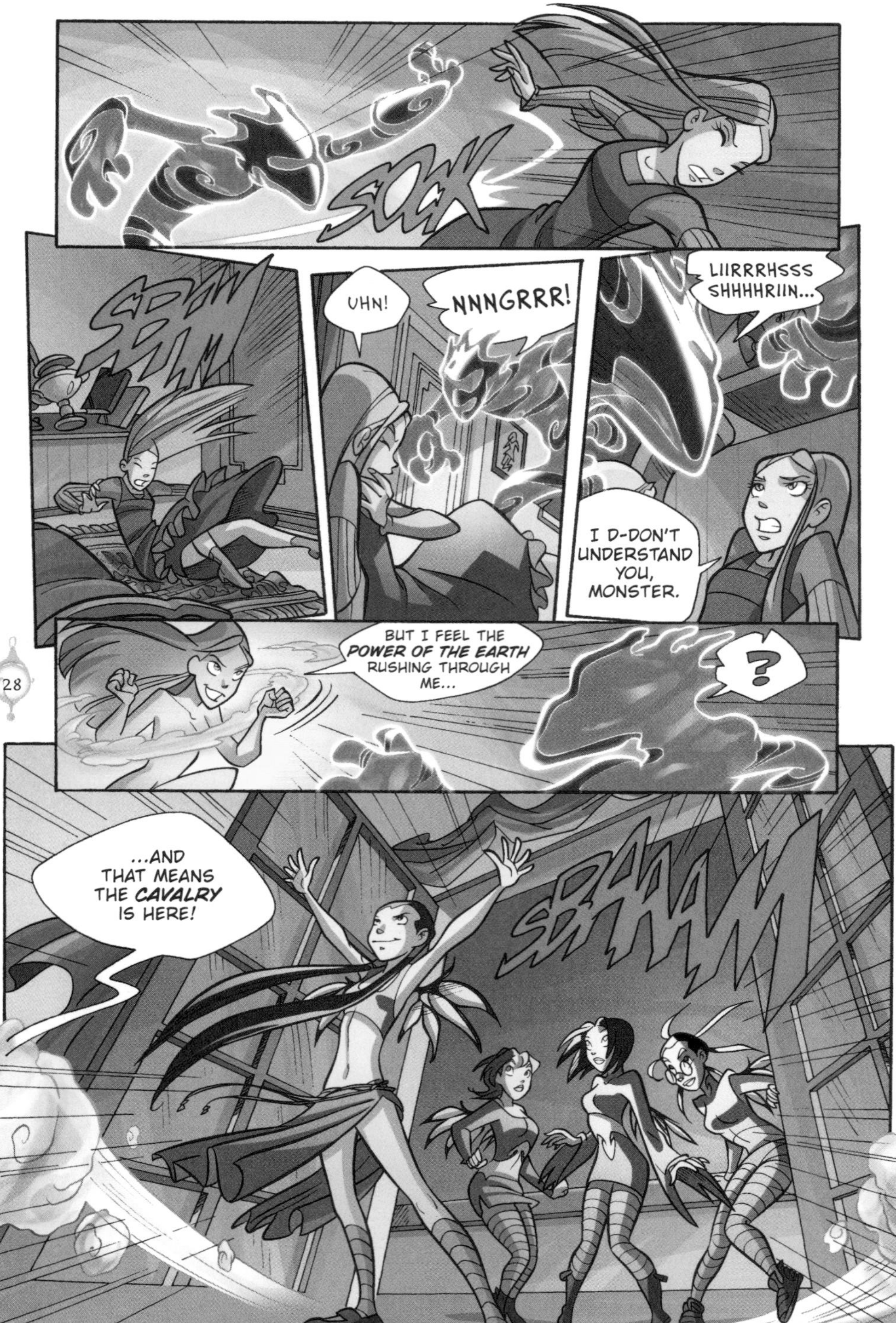
SOCK
SBAM
UHN!
NNNGRRR!
LIIRRRHSSS SHHHHRIIN...
I D-DON'T UNDERSTAND YOU, MONSTER.
BUT I FEEL THE *POWER OF THE EARTH* RUSHING THROUGH ME...
?
...AND THAT MEANS THE *CAVALRY* IS HERE!
SBAM

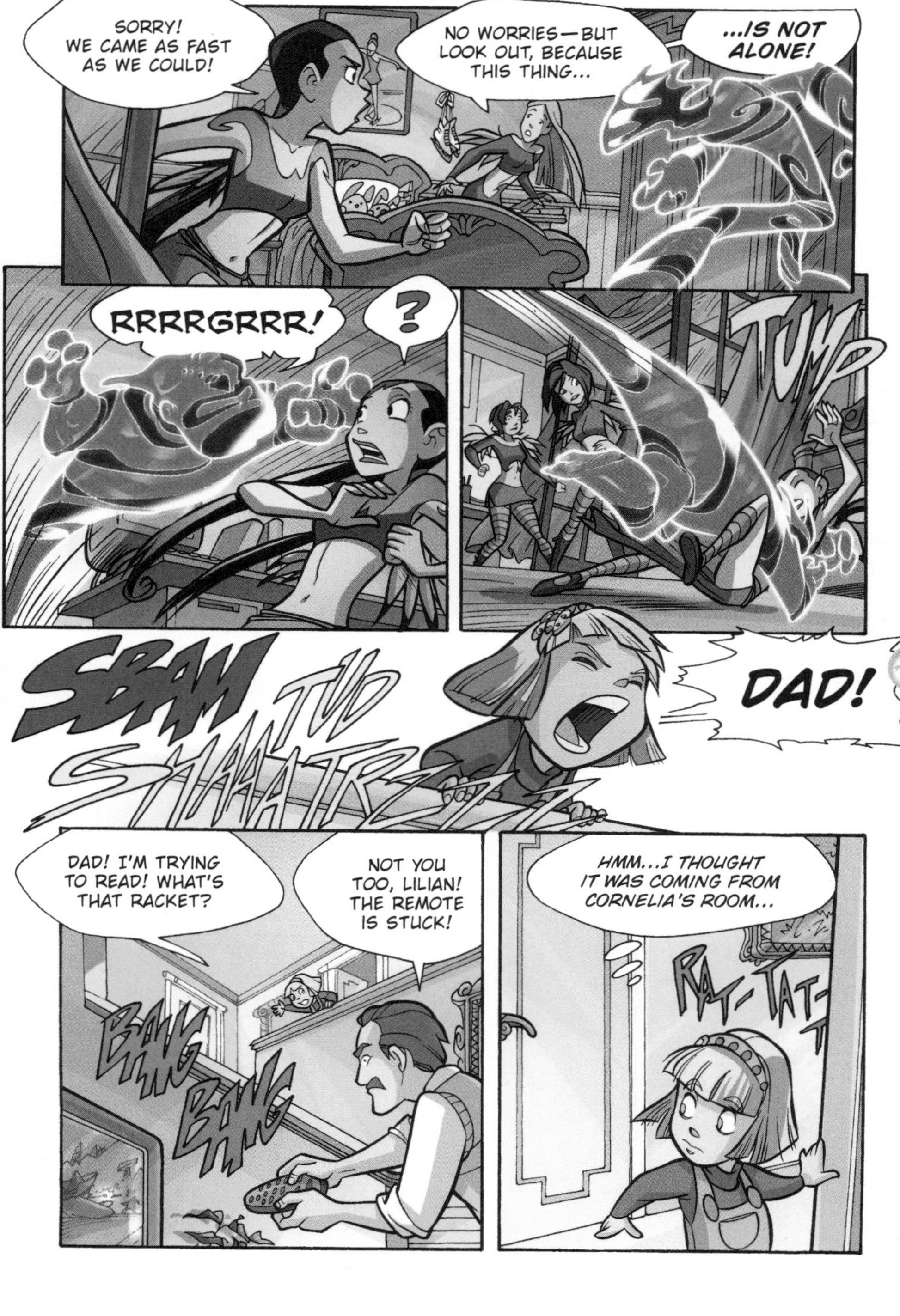
SORRY! WE CAME AS FAST AS WE COULD!
NO WORRIES—BUT LOOK OUT, BECAUSE THIS THING...
...IS NOT ALONE!
RRRRGRRR!
?
TUMP
SBAM
TUD
SHAAATRZZZ
DAD!
DAD! I'M TRYING TO READ! WHAT'S THAT RACKET?
NOT YOU TOO, LILIAN! THE REMOTE IS STUCK!
BANG
BANG
HMM...I THOUGHT IT WAS COMING FROM CORNELIA'S ROOM...
RAT-TAT-T

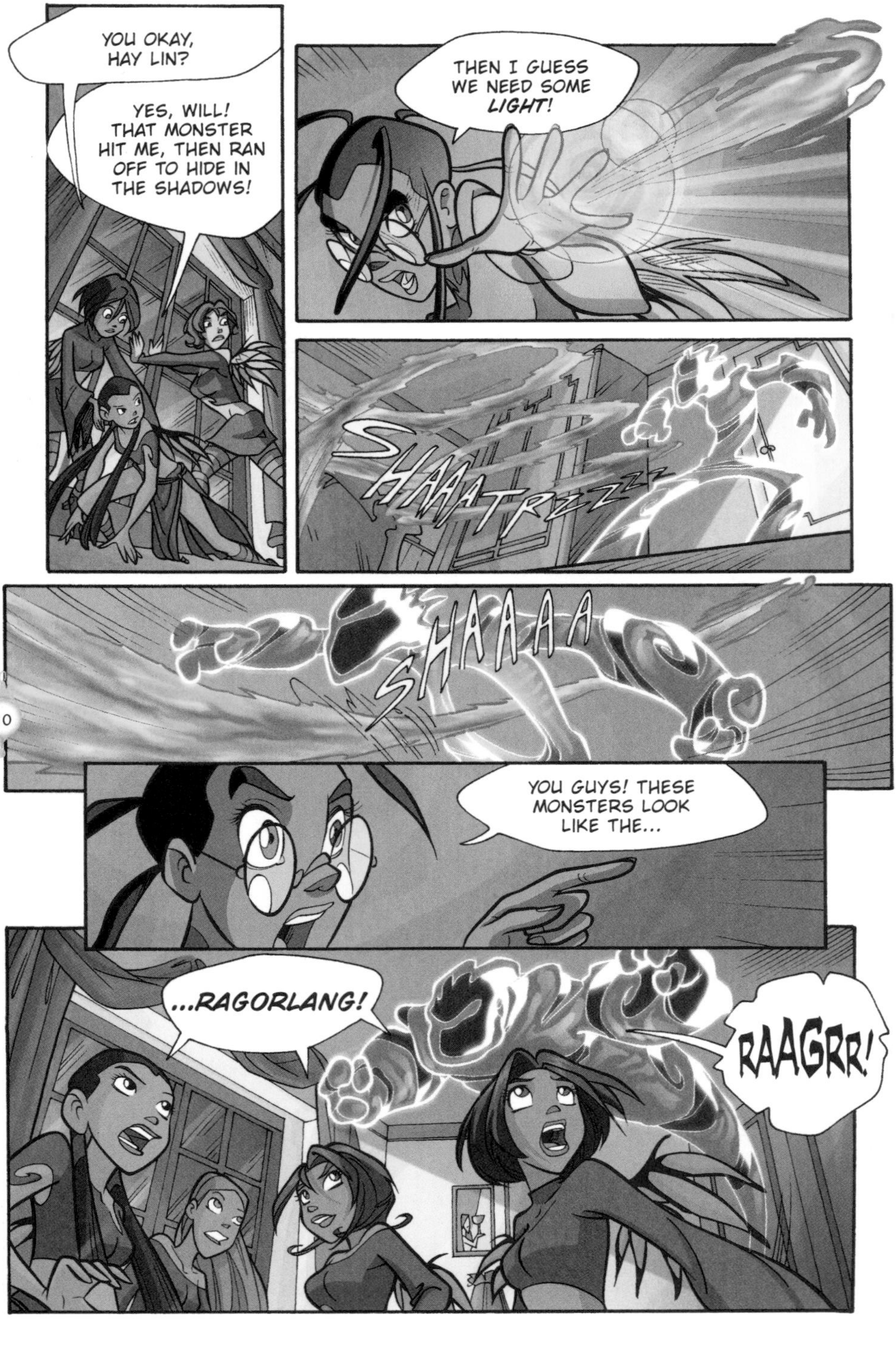

YOU OKAY, HAY LIN?
YES, WILL! THAT MONSTER HIT ME, THEN RAN OFF TO HIDE IN THE SHADOWS!
THEN I GUESS WE NEED SOME *LIGHT*!
SHHAAATRZZZZ
SHAAAAA
YOU GUYS! THESE MONSTERS LOOK LIKE THE...
...RAGORLANG!
RAAGRR!

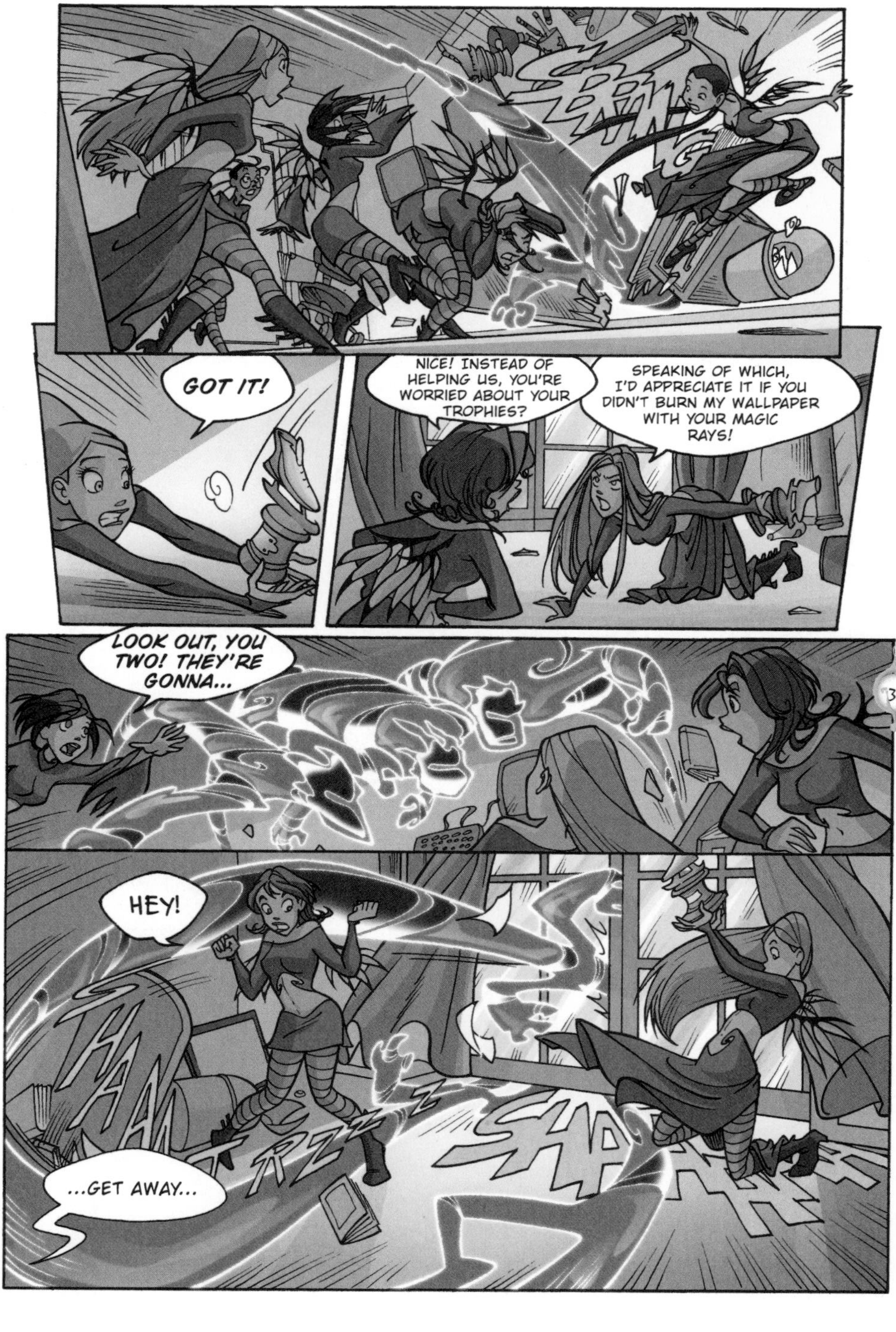
GOT IT!
NICE! INSTEAD OF HELPING US, YOU'RE WORRIED ABOUT YOUR TROPHIES?
SPEAKING OF WHICH, I'D APPRECIATE IT IF YOU DIDN'T BURN MY WALLPAPER WITH YOUR MAGIC RAYS!
LOOK OUT, YOU TWO! THEY'RE GONNA...
HEY!
...GET AWAY...

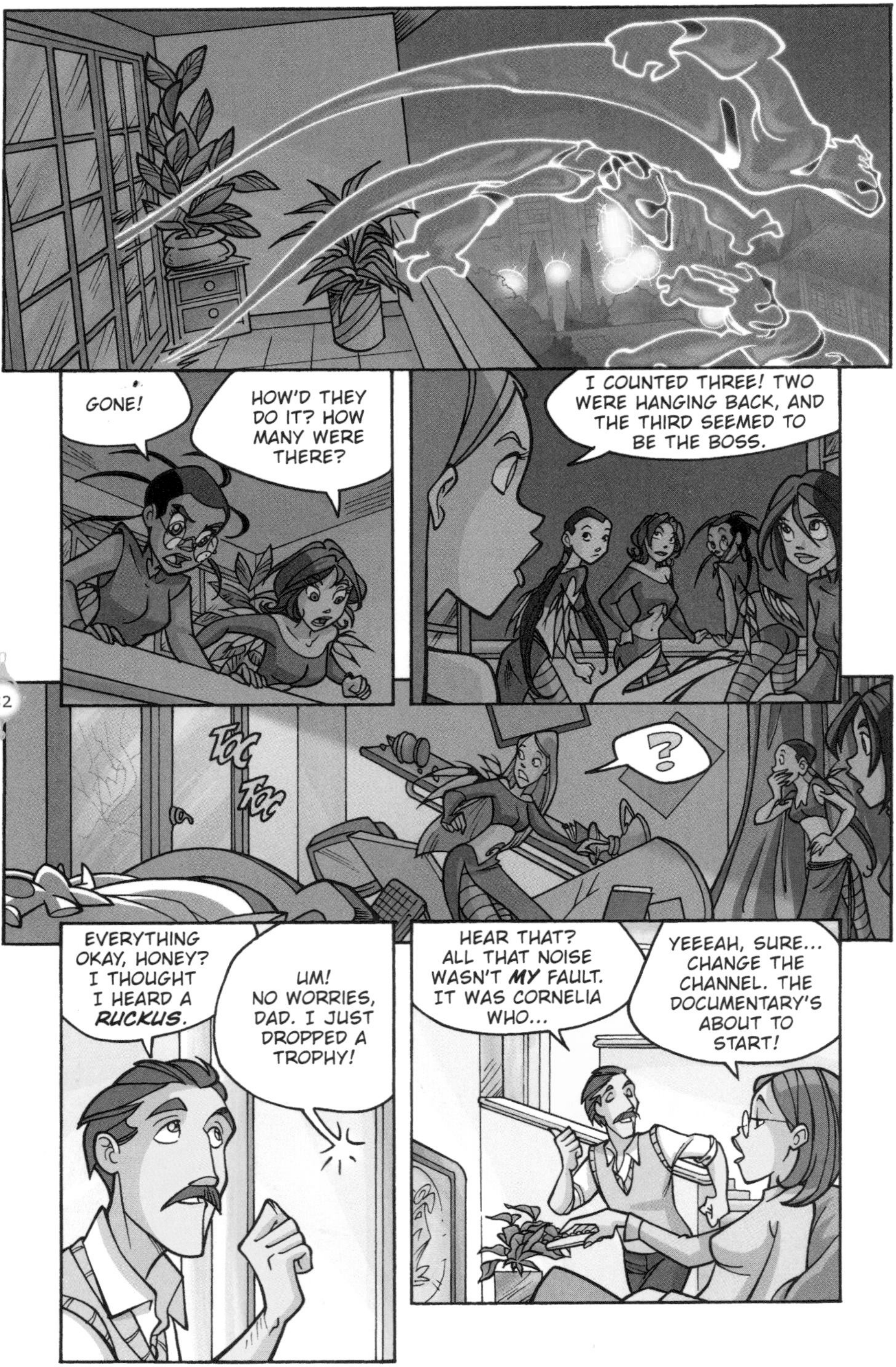

GONE!
HOW'D THEY DO IT? HOW MANY WERE THERE?
I COUNTED THREE! TWO WERE HANGING BACK, AND THE THIRD SEEMED TO BE THE BOSS.
TOC
TOC
?
EVERYTHING OKAY, HONEY? I THOUGHT I HEARD A **RUCKUS**.
UM! NO WORRIES, DAD. I JUST DROPPED A TROPHY!
HEAR THAT? ALL THAT NOISE WASN'T ***MY*** FAULT. IT WAS CORNELIA WHO...
YEEEAH, SURE... CHANGE THE CHANNEL. THE DOCUMENTARY'S ABOUT TO START!

32

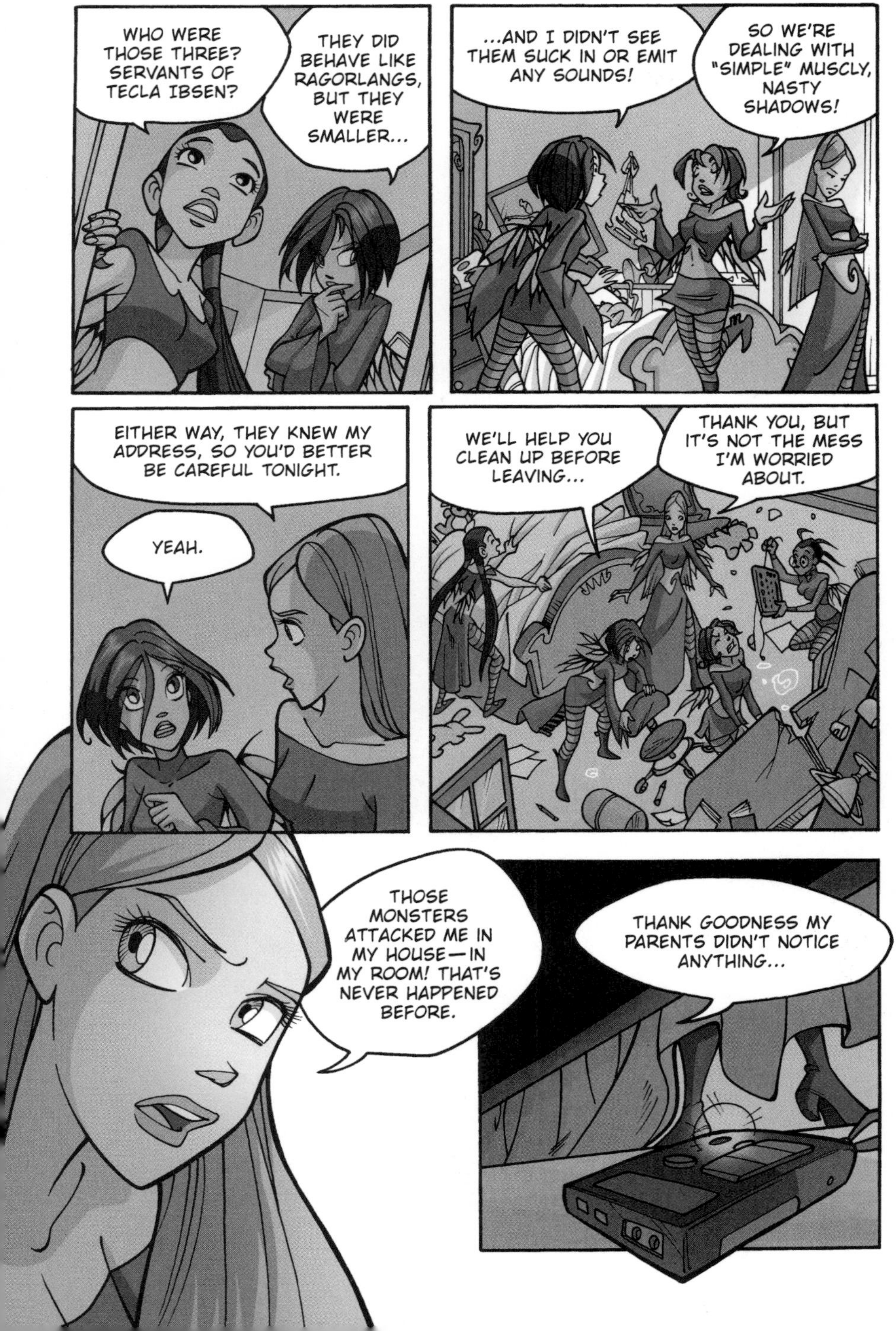
WHO WERE THOSE THREE? SERVANTS OF TECLA IBSEN?
THEY DID BEHAVE LIKE RAGORLANGS, BUT THEY WERE SMALLER...
...AND I DIDN'T SEE THEM SUCK IN OR EMIT ANY SOUNDS!
SO WE'RE DEALING WITH "SIMPLE" MUSCLY, NASTY SHADOWS!
EITHER WAY, THEY KNEW MY ADDRESS, SO YOU'D BETTER BE CAREFUL TONIGHT.
YEAH.
WE'LL HELP YOU CLEAN UP BEFORE LEAVING...
THANK YOU, BUT IT'S NOT THE MESS I'M WORRIED ABOUT.
THOSE MONSTERS ATTACKED ME IN MY HOUSE—IN MY ROOM! THAT'S NEVER HAPPENED BEFORE.
THANK GOODNESS MY PARENTS DIDN'T NOTICE ANYTHING...

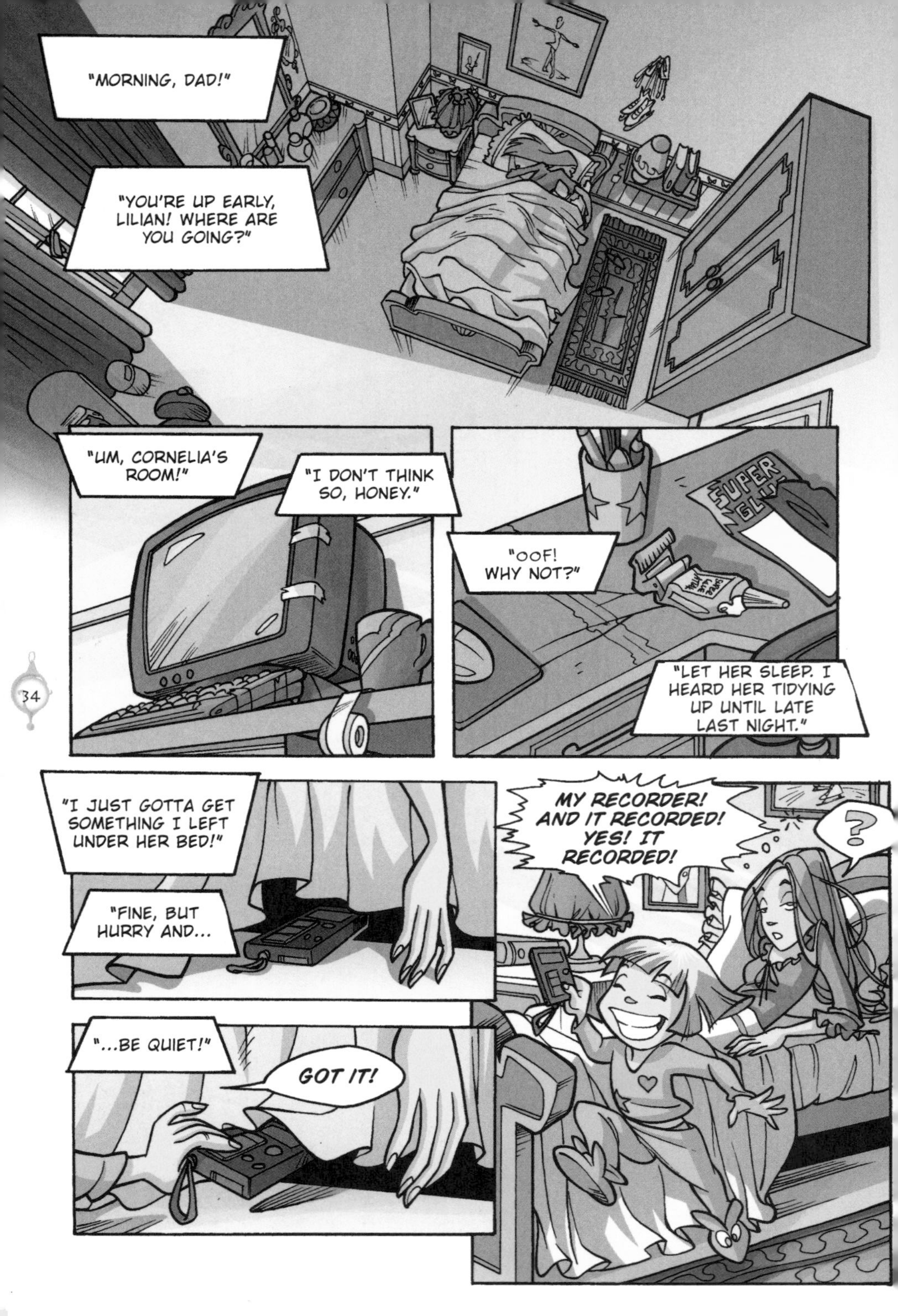

"MORNING, DAD!"
"YOU'RE UP EARLY, LILIAN! WHERE ARE YOU GOING?"
"UM, CORNELIA'S ROOM!"
"I DON'T THINK SO, HONEY."
"OOF! WHY NOT?"
SUPER GLUE
"LET HER SLEEP. I HEARD HER TIDYING UP UNTIL LATE LAST NIGHT."
"I JUST GOTTA GET SOMETHING I LEFT UNDER HER BED!"
"FINE, BUT HURRY AND...
"...BE QUIET!"
GOT IT!
MY RECORDER! AND IT RECORDED! YES! IT RECORDED!
?

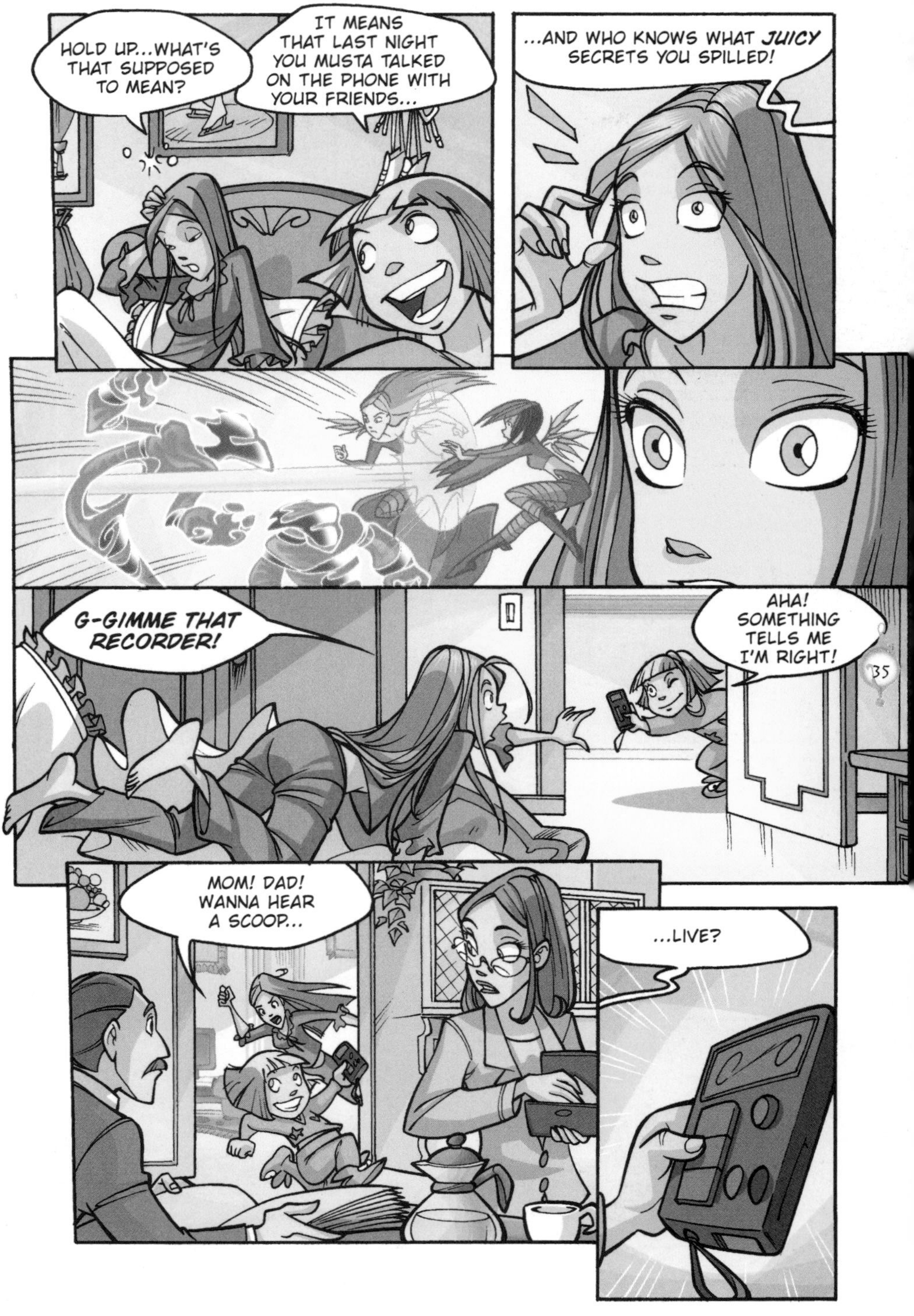
HOLD UP...WHAT'S THAT SUPPOSED TO MEAN?
IT MEANS THAT LAST NIGHT YOU MUSTA TALKED ON THE PHONE WITH YOUR FRIENDS...
...AND WHO KNOWS WHAT JUICY SECRETS YOU SPILLED!
G-GIMME THAT RECORDER!
AHA! SOMETHING TELLS ME I'M RIGHT!
MOM! DAD! WANNA HEAR A SCOOP...
...LIVE?

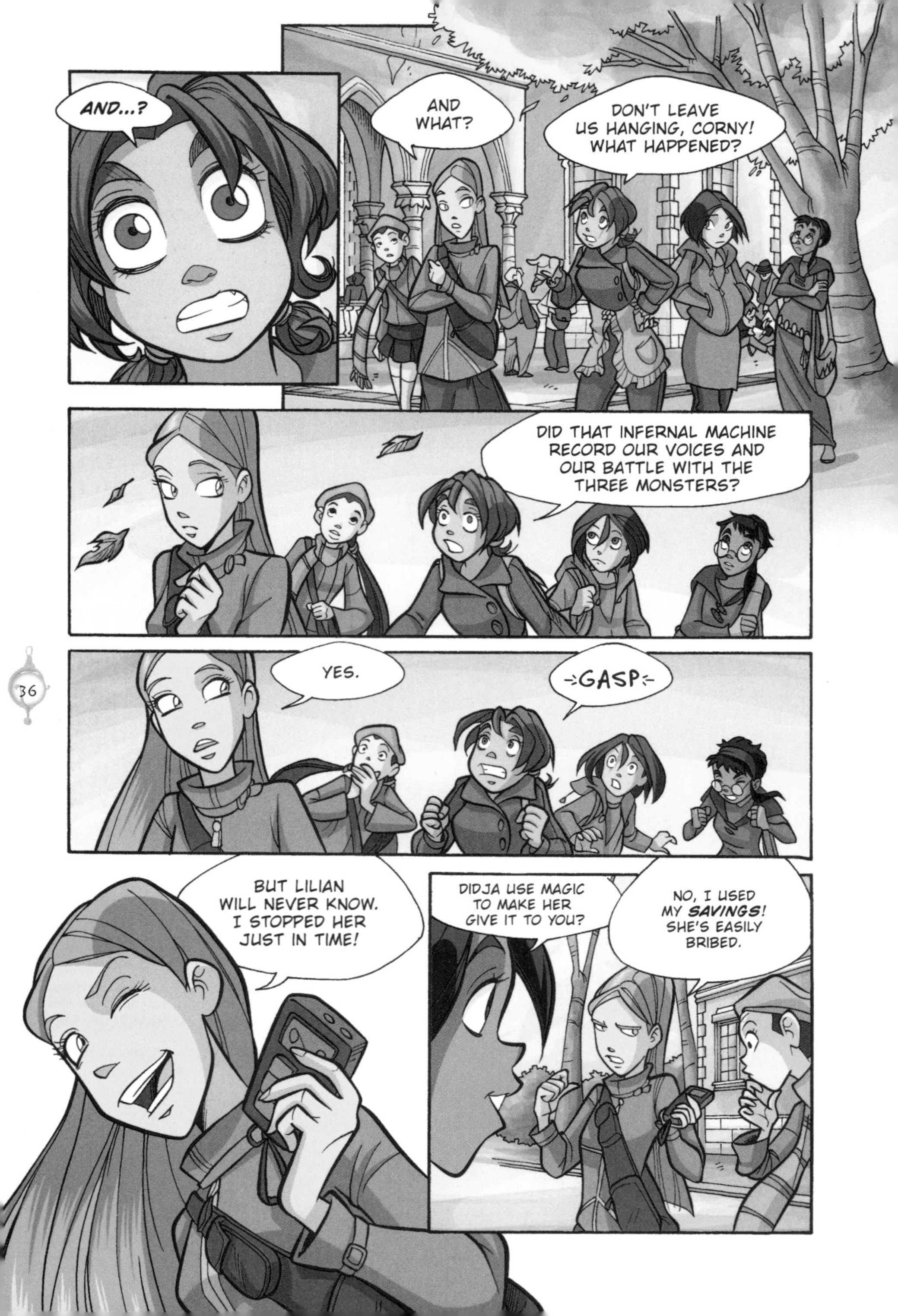
AND...?
AND WHAT?
DON'T LEAVE US HANGING, CORNY! WHAT HAPPENED?
DID THAT INFERNAL MACHINE RECORD OUR VOICES AND OUR BATTLE WITH THE THREE MONSTERS?
YES.
GASP
BUT LILIAN WILL NEVER KNOW. I STOPPED HER JUST IN TIME!
DIDJA USE MAGIC TO MAKE HER GIVE IT TO YOU?
NO, I USED MY ***SAVINGS***! SHE'S EASILY BRIBED.

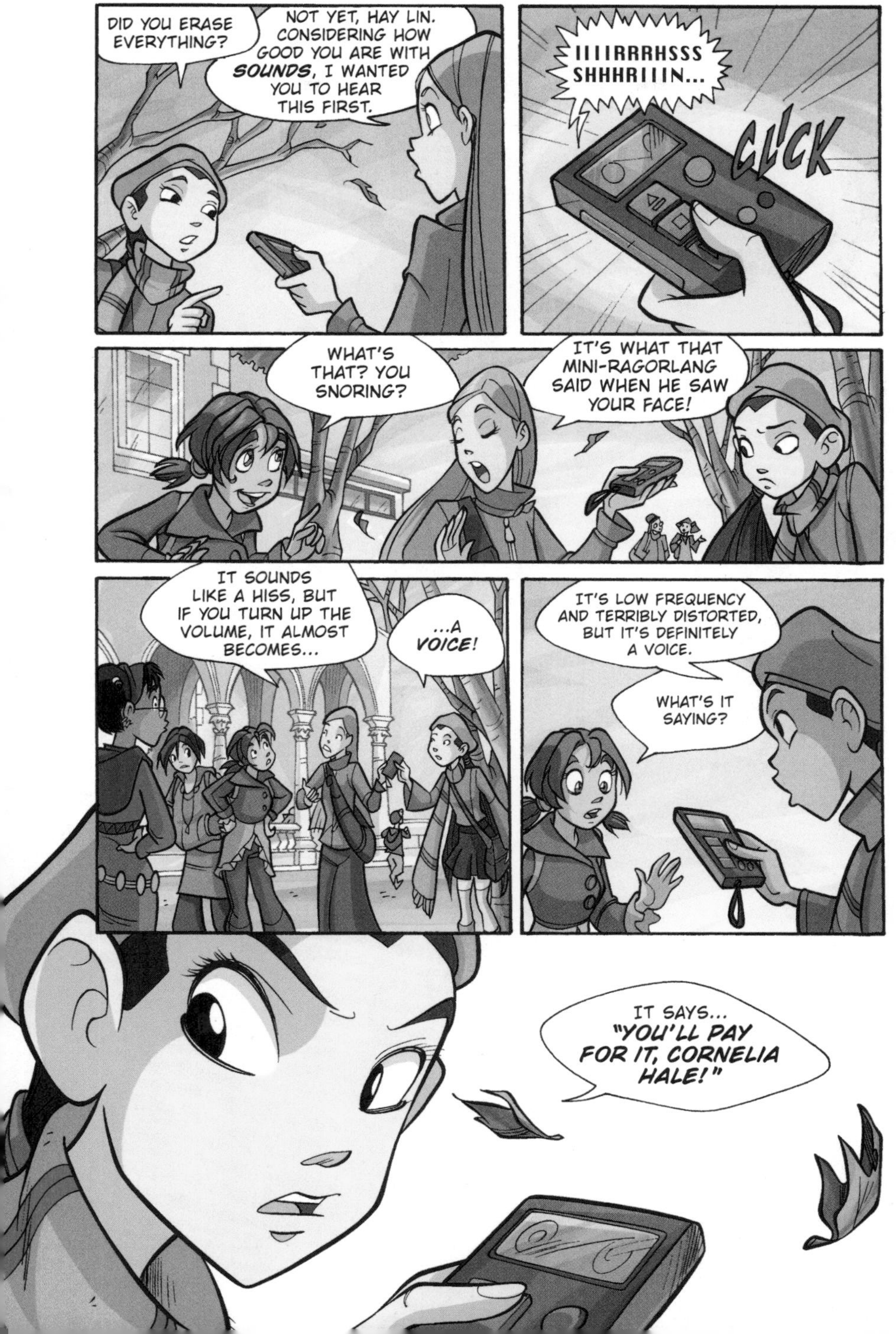

DID YOU ERASE EVERYTHING?
NOT YET, HAY LIN. CONSIDERING HOW GOOD YOU ARE WITH SOUNDS, I WANTED YOU TO HEAR THIS FIRST.
IIIIRRRHSSS SHHHRIIIN...
CLICK
WHAT'S THAT? YOU SNORING?
IT'S WHAT THAT MINI-RAGORLANG SAID WHEN HE SAW YOUR FACE!
IT SOUNDS LIKE A HISS, BUT IF YOU TURN UP THE VOLUME, IT ALMOST BECOMES...
...A VOICE!
IT'S LOW FREQUENCY AND TERRIBLY DISTORTED, BUT IT'S DEFINITELY A VOICE.
WHAT'S IT SAYING?
IT SAYS... "YOU'LL PAY FOR IT, CORNELIA HALE!"

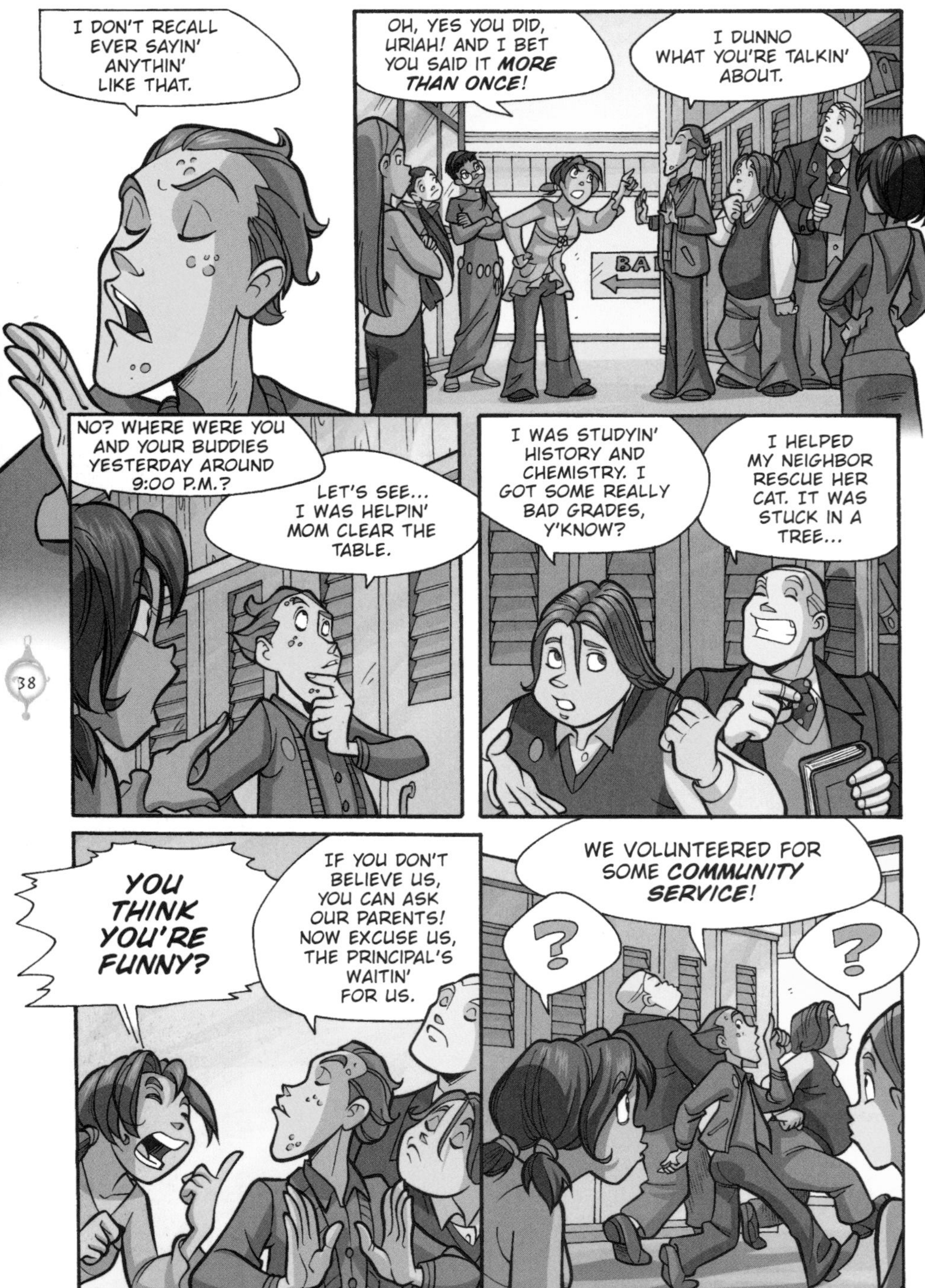

I DON'T RECALL EVER SAYIN' ANYTHIN' LIKE THAT.
OH, YES YOU DID, URIAH! AND I BET YOU SAID IT MORE THAN ONCE!
I DUNNO WHAT YOU'RE TALKIN' ABOUT.
BA
NO? WHERE WERE YOU AND YOUR BUDDIES YESTERDAY AROUND 9:00 P.M.?
LET'S SEE... I WAS HELPIN' MOM CLEAR THE TABLE.
I WAS STUDYIN' HISTORY AND CHEMISTRY. I GOT SOME REALLY BAD GRADES, Y'KNOW?
I HELPED MY NEIGHBOR RESCUE HER CAT. IT WAS STUCK IN A TREE...
YOU THINK YOU'RE FUNNY?
IF YOU DON'T BELIEVE US, YOU CAN ASK OUR PARENTS! NOW EXCUSE US, THE PRINCIPAL'S WAITIN' FOR US.
WE VOLUNTEERED FOR SOME COMMUNITY SERVICE!
?
?

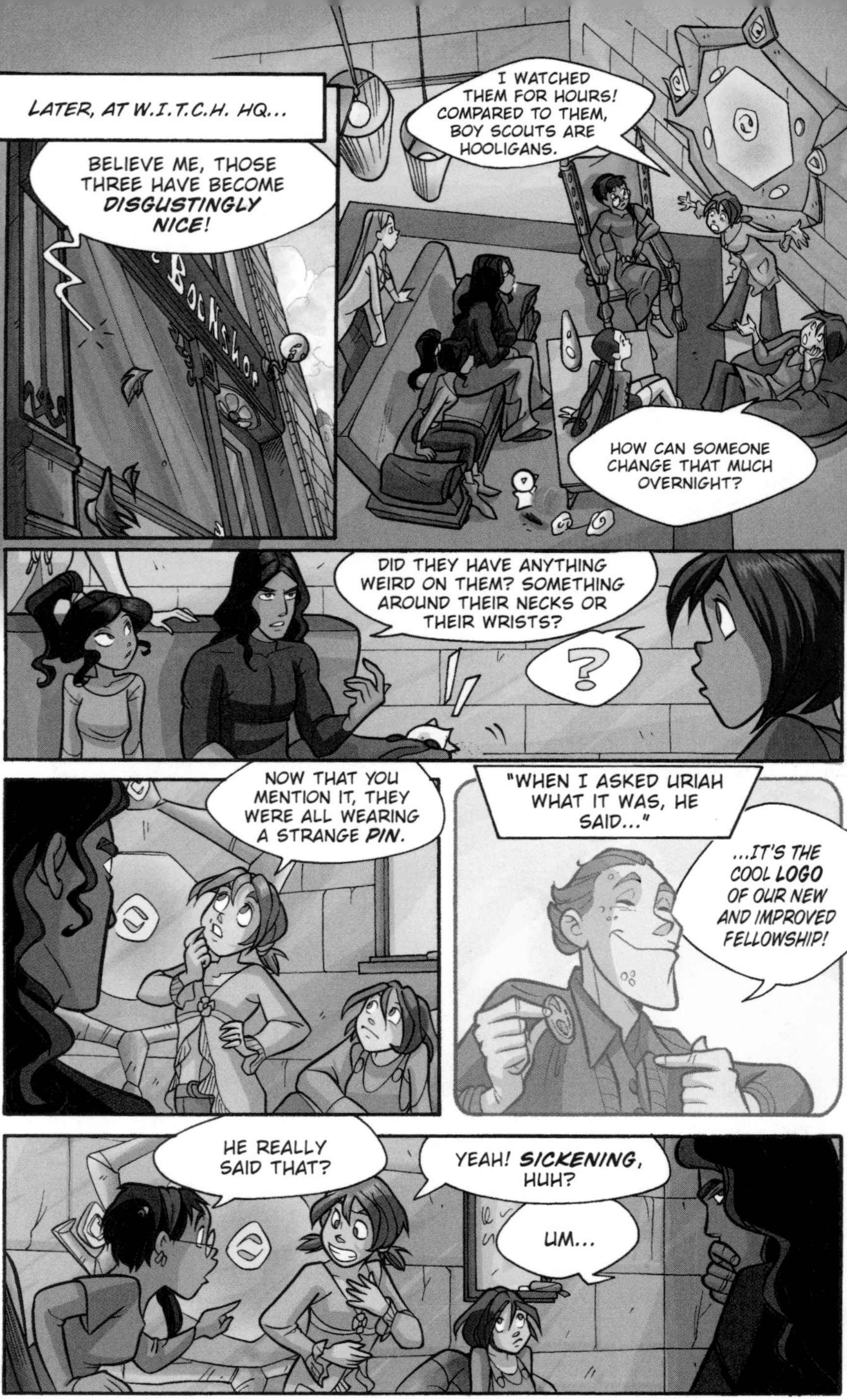
LATER, AT W.I.T.C.H. HQ...
BELIEVE ME, THOSE THREE HAVE BECOME ***DISGUSTINGLY NICE!***
I WATCHED THEM FOR HOURS! COMPARED TO THEM, BOY SCOUTS ARE HOOLIGANS.
HOW CAN SOMEONE CHANGE THAT MUCH OVERNIGHT?
DID THEY HAVE ANYTHING WEIRD ON THEM? SOMETHING AROUND THEIR NECKS OR THEIR WRISTS?
?
NOW THAT YOU MENTION IT, THEY WERE ALL WEARING A STRANGE ***PIN.***
"WHEN I ASKED URIAH WHAT IT WAS, HE SAID..."
...IT'S THE COOL **LOGO** OF OUR NEW AND IMPROVED FELLOWSHIP!
HE REALLY SAID THAT?
YEAH! ***SICKENING,*** HUH?
UM...

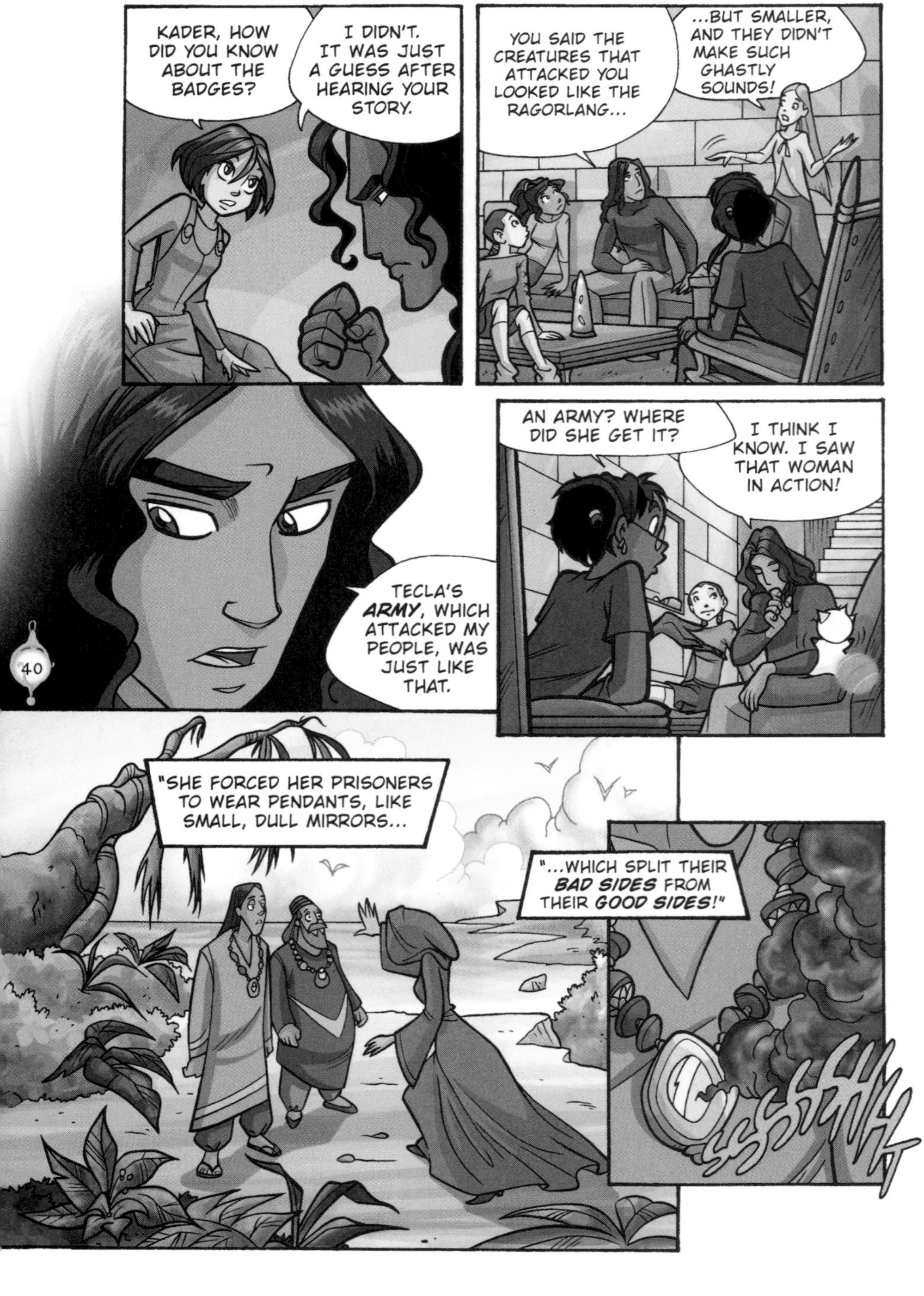
KADER, HOW DID YOU KNOW ABOUT THE BADGES?
I DIDN'T. IT WAS JUST A GUESS AFTER HEARING YOUR STORY.
YOU SAID THE CREATURES THAT ATTACKED YOU LOOKED LIKE THE RAGORLANG...
...BUT SMALLER, AND THEY DIDN'T MAKE SUCH GHASTLY SOUNDS!
TECLA'S *ARMY*, WHICH ATTACKED MY PEOPLE, WAS JUST LIKE THAT.
AN ARMY? WHERE DID SHE GET IT?
I THINK I KNOW. I SAW THAT WOMAN IN ACTION!
"SHE FORCED HER PRISONERS TO WEAR PENDANTS, LIKE SMALL, DULL MIRRORS...
"...WHICH SPLIT THEIR *BAD SIDES* FROM THEIR *GOOD SIDES*!"
SSSSHHH

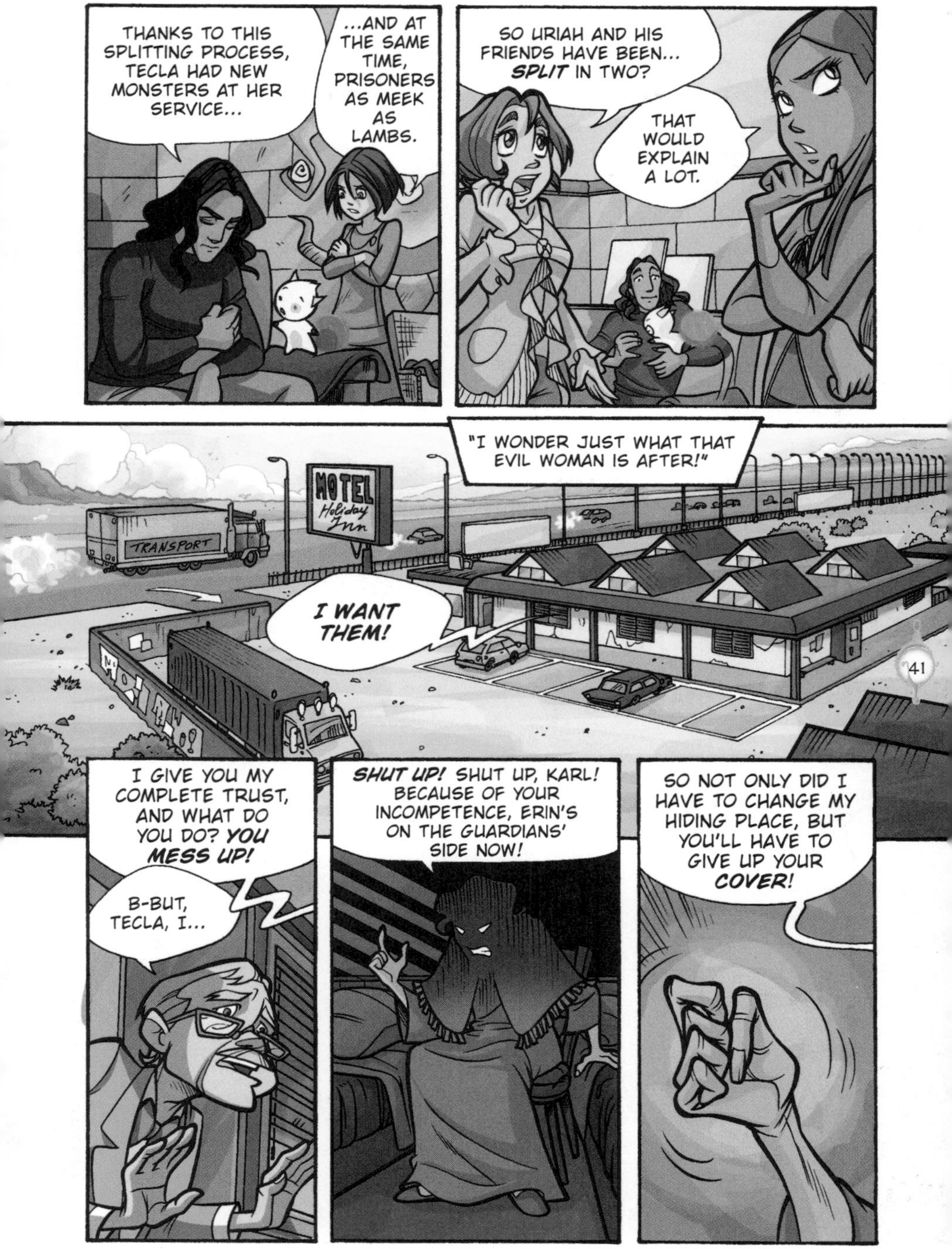
THANKS TO THIS SPLITTING PROCESS, TECLA HAD NEW MONSTERS AT HER SERVICE...
...AND AT THE SAME TIME, PRISONERS AS MEEK AS LAMBS.
SO URIAH AND HIS FRIENDS HAVE BEEN... *SPLIT* IN TWO?
THAT WOULD EXPLAIN A LOT.
"I WONDER JUST WHAT THAT EVIL WOMAN IS AFTER!"
MOTEL Holiday Inn
TRANSPORT
I WANT THEM!
I GIVE YOU MY COMPLETE TRUST, AND WHAT DO YOU DO? ***YOU MESS UP!***
B-BUT, TECLA, I...
SHUT UP! SHUT UP, KARL! BECAUSE OF YOUR INCOMPETENCE, ERIN'S ON THE GUARDIANS' SIDE NOW!
SO NOT ONLY DID I HAVE TO CHANGE MY HIDING PLACE, BUT YOU'LL HAVE TO GIVE UP YOUR ***COVER!***

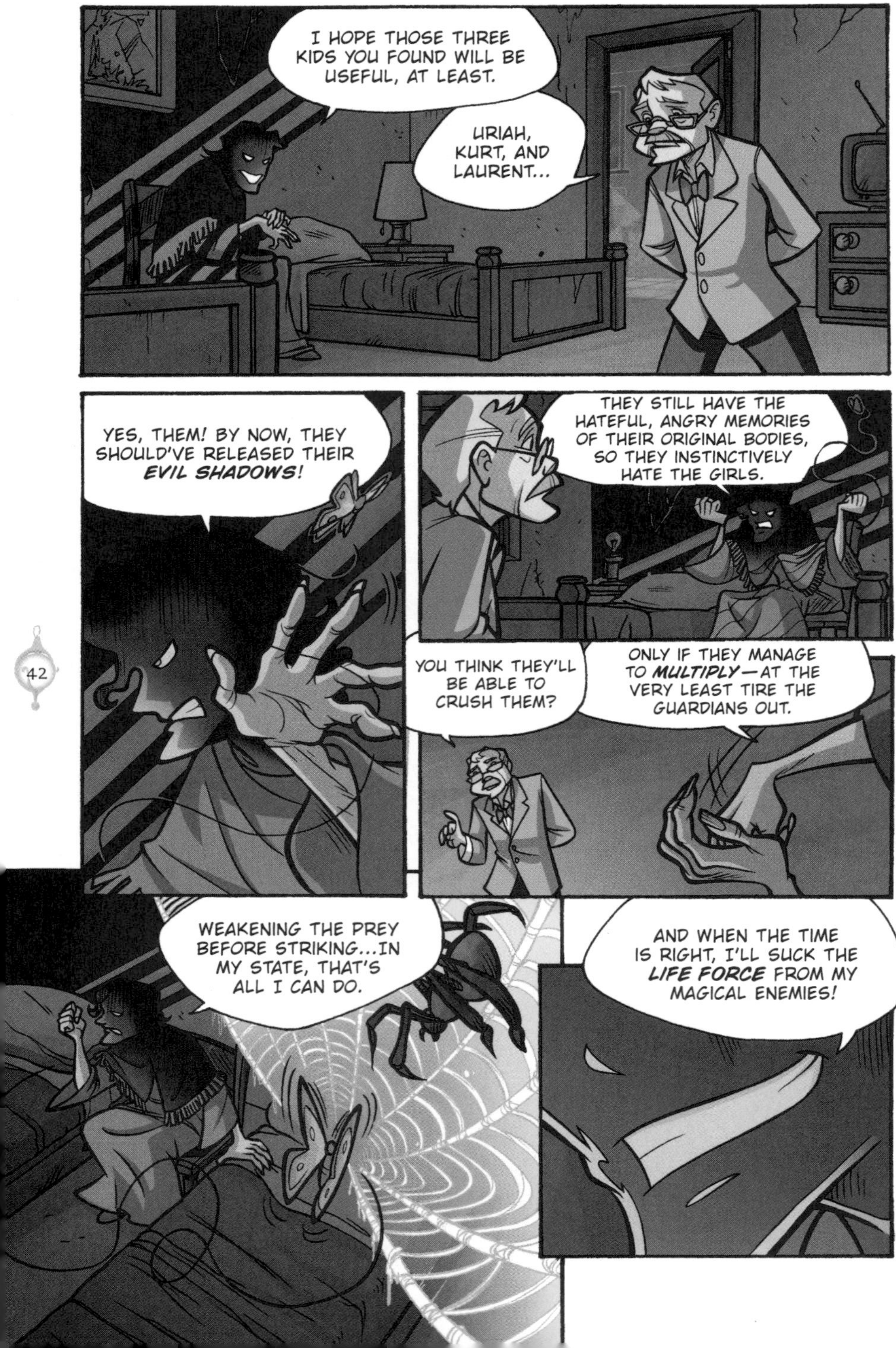
I HOPE THOSE THREE KIDS YOU FOUND WILL BE USEFUL, AT LEAST.
URIAH, KURT, AND LAURENT...
YES, THEM! BY NOW, THEY SHOULD'VE RELEASED THEIR EVIL SHADOWS!
THEY STILL HAVE THE HATEFUL, ANGRY MEMORIES OF THEIR ORIGINAL BODIES, SO THEY INSTINCTIVELY HATE THE GIRLS.
YOU THINK THEY'LL BE ABLE TO CRUSH THEM?
ONLY IF THEY MANAGE TO MULTIPLY—AT THE VERY LEAST TIRE THE GUARDIANS OUT.
WEAKENING THE PREY BEFORE STRIKING...IN MY STATE, THAT'S ALL I CAN DO.
AND WHEN THE TIME IS RIGHT, I'LL SUCK THE LIFE FORCE FROM MY MAGICAL ENEMIES!

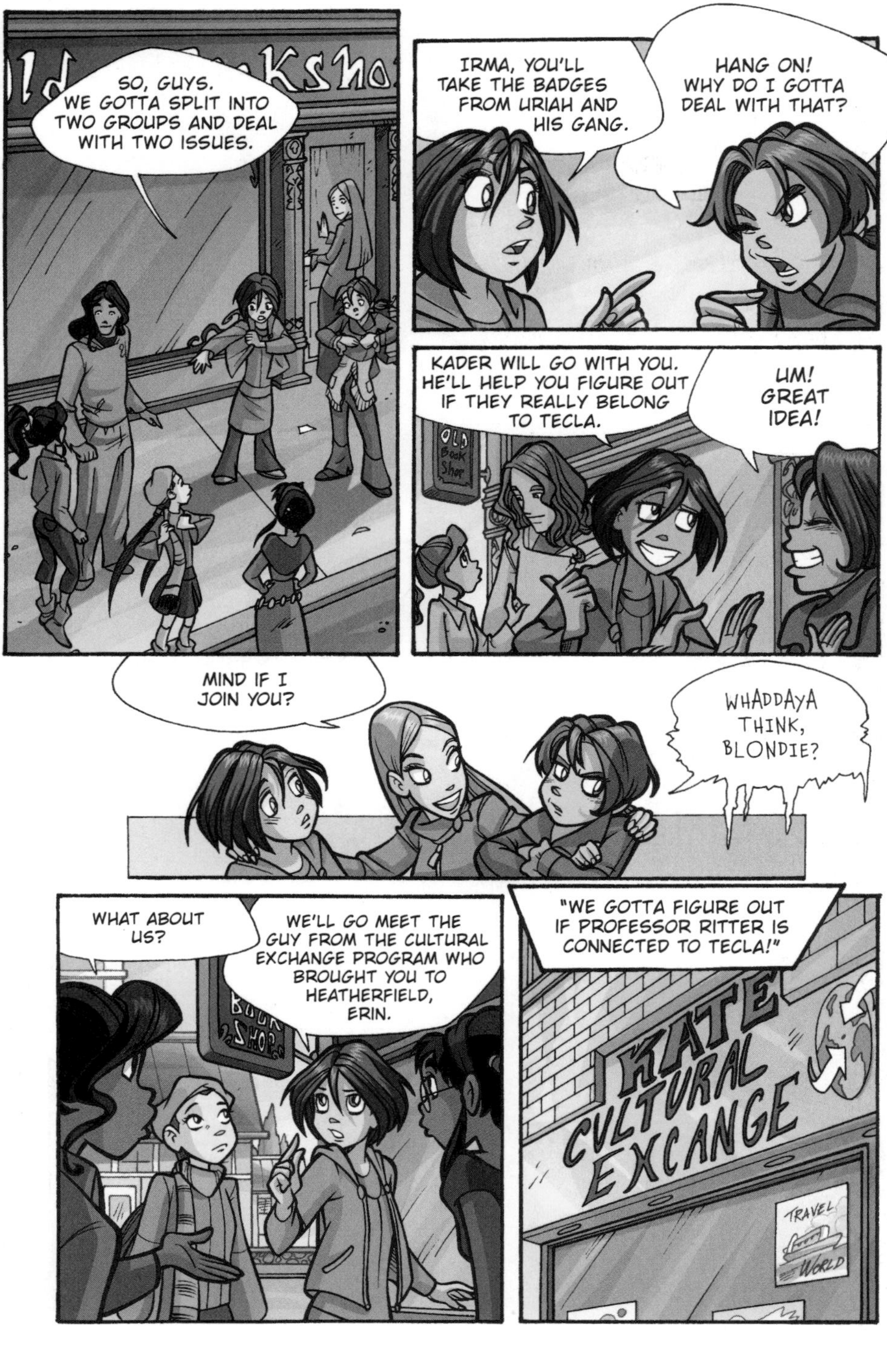
SO, GUYS. WE GOTTA SPLIT INTO TWO GROUPS AND DEAL WITH TWO ISSUES.
IRMA, YOU'LL TAKE THE BADGES FROM URIAH AND HIS GANG.
HANG ON! WHY DO I GOTTA DEAL WITH THAT?
KADER WILL GO WITH YOU. HE'LL HELP YOU FIGURE OUT IF THEY REALLY BELONG TO TECLA.
UM! GREAT IDEA!
MIND IF I JOIN YOU?
WHADDAYA THINK, BLONDIE?
WHAT ABOUT US?
WE'LL GO MEET THE GUY FROM THE CULTURAL EXCHANGE PROGRAM WHO BROUGHT YOU TO HEATHERFIELD, ERIN.
"WE GOTTA FIGURE OUT IF PROFESSOR RITTER IS CONNECTED TO TECLA!"
KATE CULTURAL EXCANGE
TRAVEL WORLD

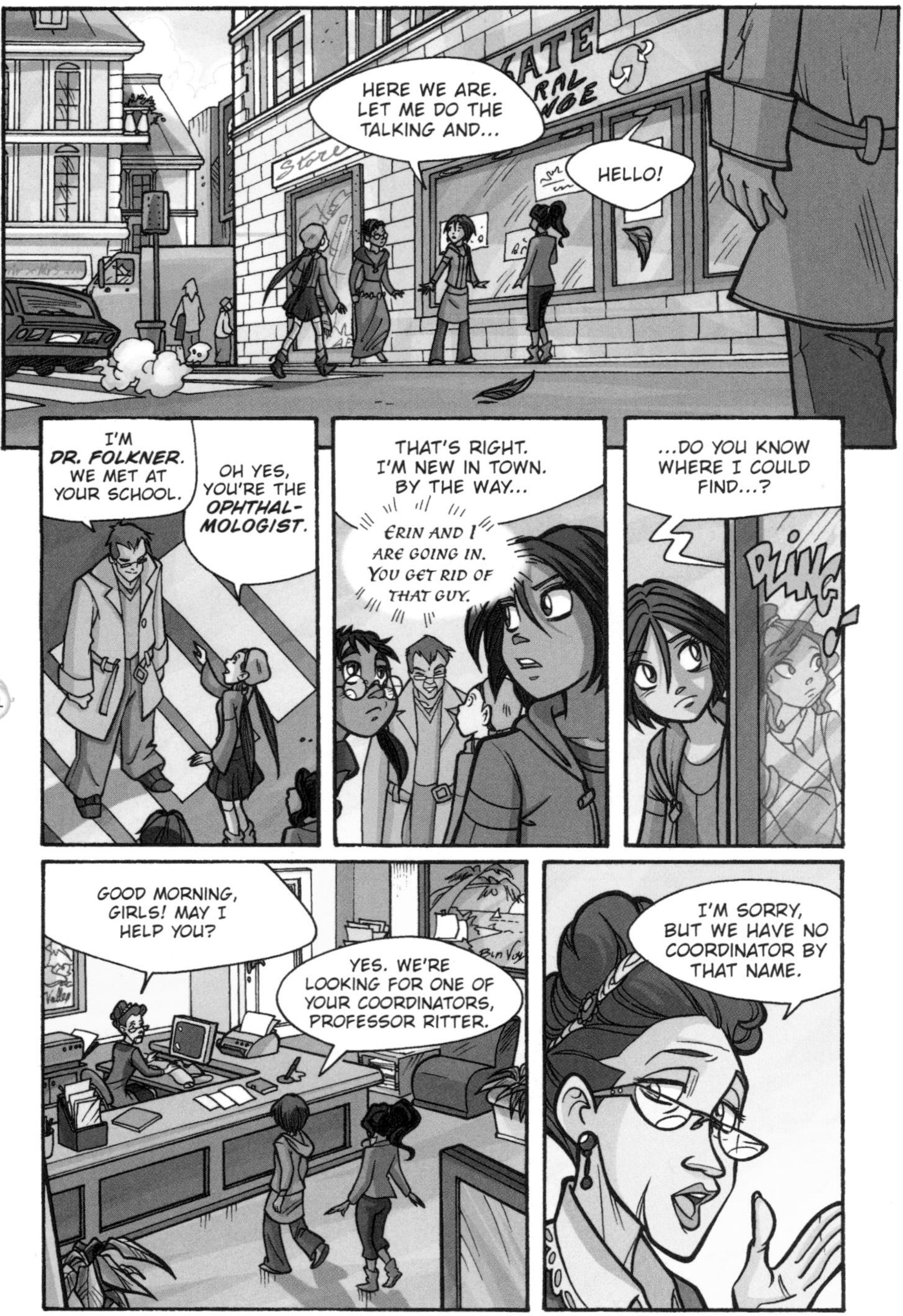

HERE WE ARE. LET ME DO THE TALKING AND...
HELLO!
I'M **DR. FOLKNER.** WE MET AT YOUR SCHOOL.
OH YES, YOU'RE THE ***OPHTHAL-MOLOGIST.***
THAT'S RIGHT. I'M NEW IN TOWN. BY THE WAY...
ERIN AND I ARE GOING IN. YOU GET RID OF THAT GUY.
...DO YOU KNOW WHERE I COULD FIND...?
DLING
GOOD MORNING, GIRLS! MAY I HELP YOU?
YES. WE'RE LOOKING FOR ONE OF YOUR COORDINATORS, PROFESSOR RITTER.
I'M SORRY, BUT WE HAVE NO COORDINATOR BY THAT NAME.

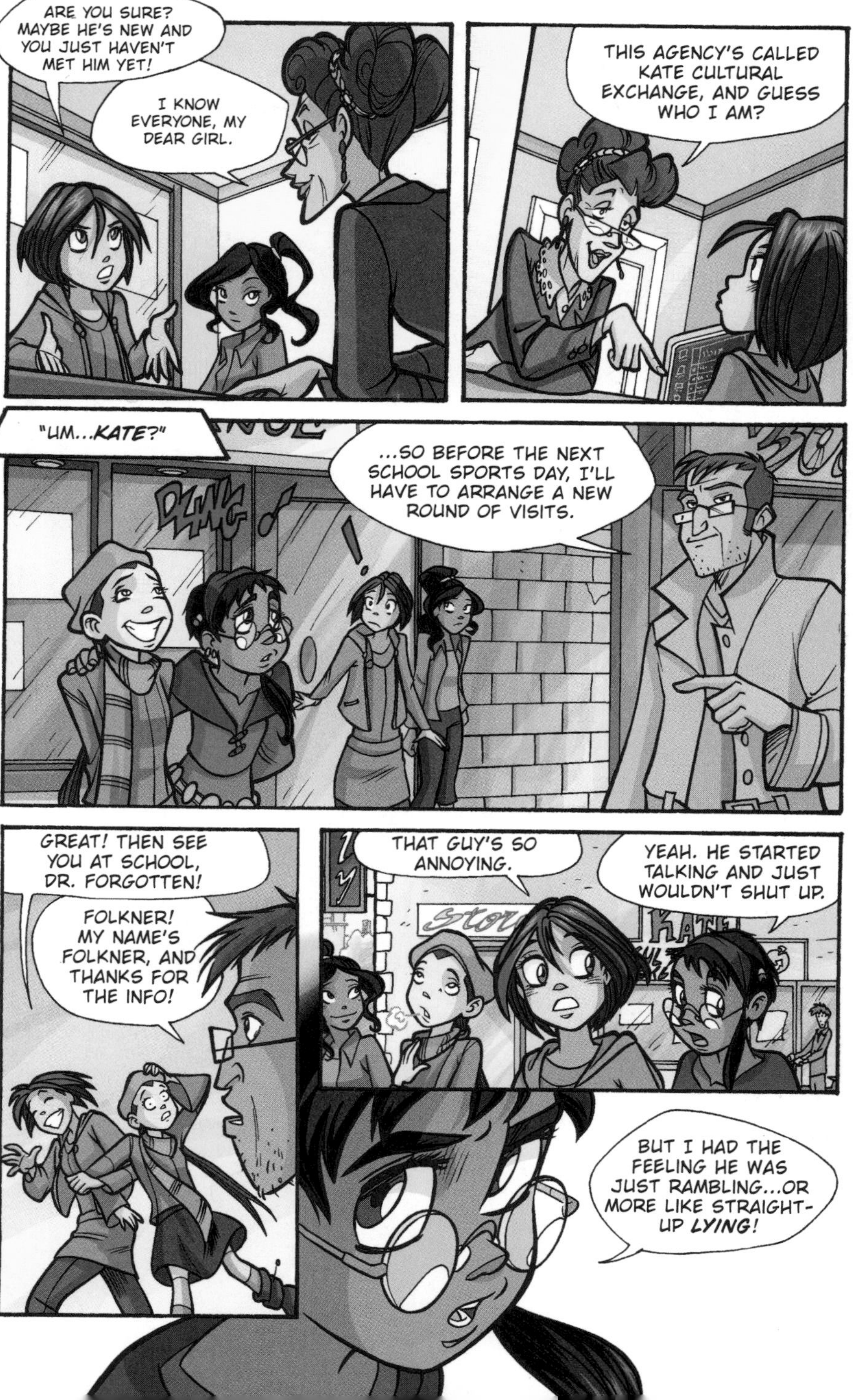
ARE YOU SURE? MAYBE HE'S NEW AND YOU JUST HAVEN'T MET HIM YET!
I KNOW EVERYONE, MY DEAR GIRL.
THIS AGENCY'S CALLED KATE CULTURAL EXCHANGE, AND GUESS WHO I AM?
"UM...*KATE*?"
...SO BEFORE THE NEXT SCHOOL SPORTS DAY, I'LL HAVE TO ARRANGE A NEW ROUND OF VISITS.
GREAT! THEN SEE YOU AT SCHOOL, DR. FORGOTTEN!
FOLKNER! MY NAME'S FOLKNER, AND THANKS FOR THE INFO!
THAT GUY'S SO ANNOYING.
YEAH. HE STARTED TALKING AND JUST WOULDN'T SHUT UP.
BUT I HAD THE FEELING HE WAS JUST RAMBLING...OR MORE LIKE STRAIGHT-UP *LYING*!

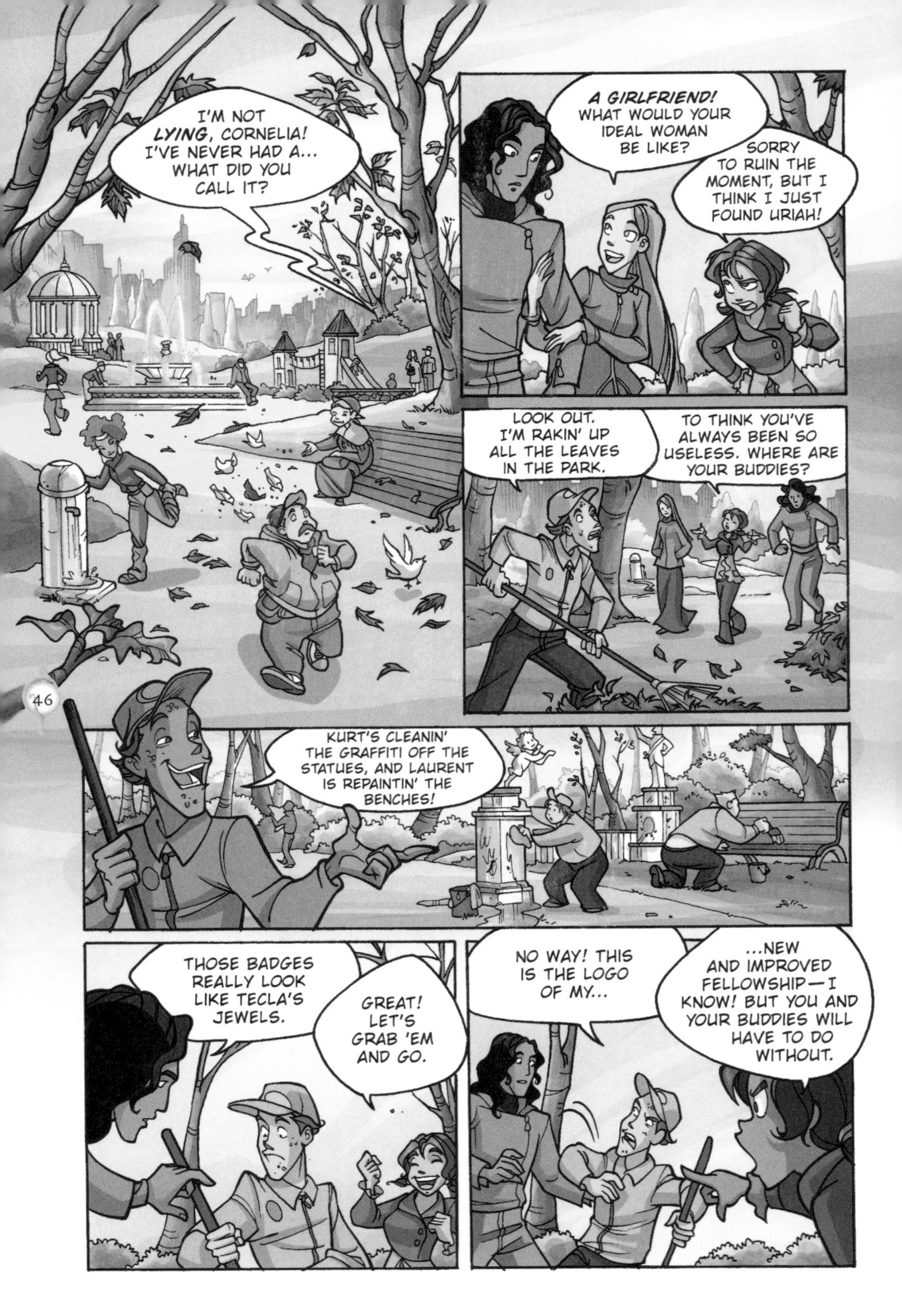
I'M NOT LYING, CORNELIA! I'VE NEVER HAD A... WHAT DID YOU CALL IT?
A GIRLFRIEND! WHAT WOULD YOUR IDEAL WOMAN BE LIKE?
SORRY TO RUIN THE MOMENT, BUT I THINK I JUST FOUND URIAH!
LOOK OUT. I'M RAKIN' UP ALL THE LEAVES IN THE PARK.
TO THINK YOU'VE ALWAYS BEEN SO USELESS. WHERE ARE YOUR BUDDIES?
KURT'S CLEANIN' THE GRAFFITI OFF THE STATUES, AND LAURENT IS REPAINTIN' THE BENCHES!
THOSE BADGES REALLY LOOK LIKE TECLA'S JEWELS.
GREAT! LET'S GRAB 'EM AND GO.
NO WAY! THIS IS THE LOGO OF MY...
...NEW AND IMPROVED FELLOWSHIP—I KNOW! BUT YOU AND YOUR BUDDIES WILL HAVE TO DO WITHOUT.

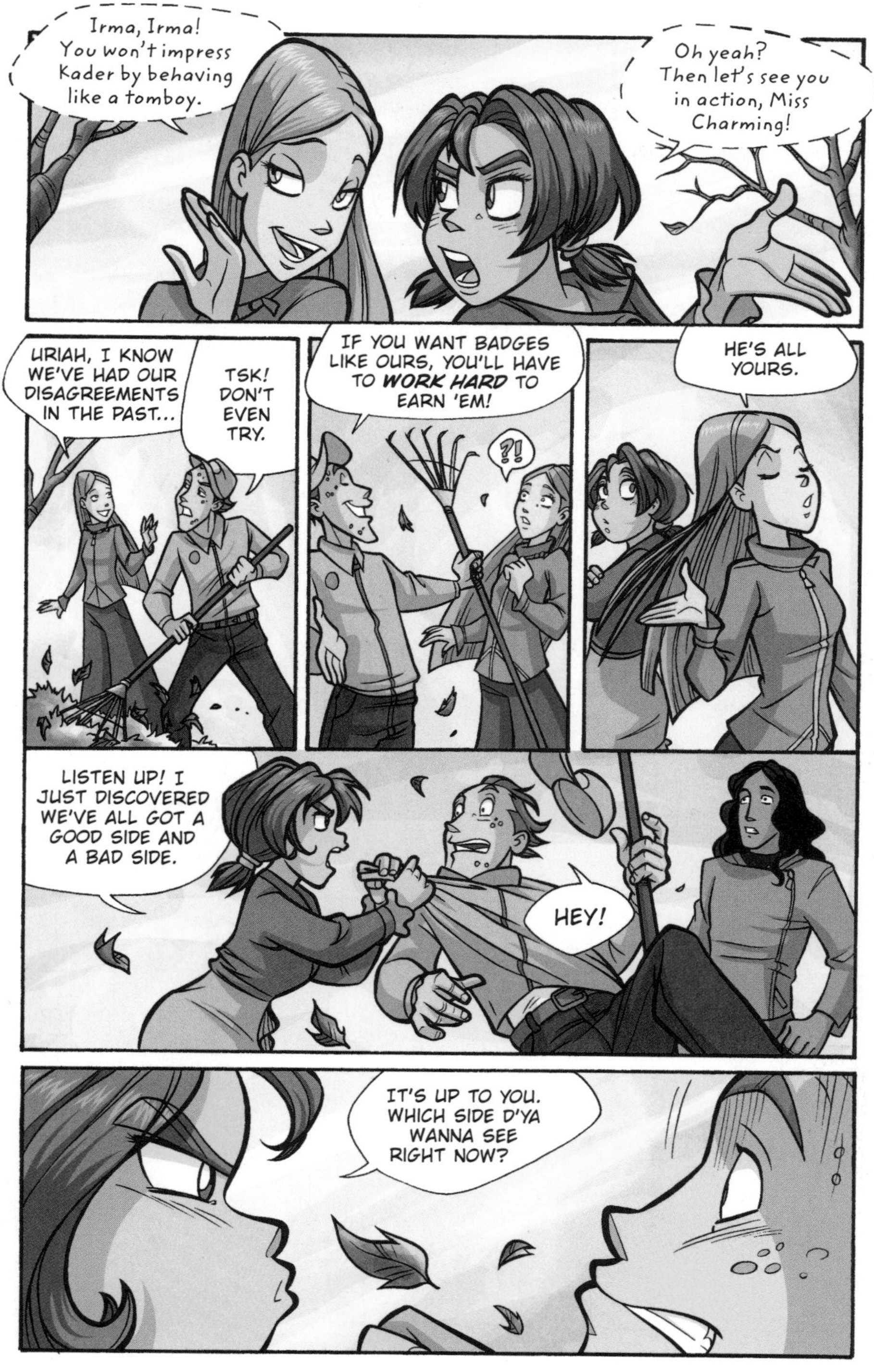

Irma, Irma! You won't impress Kader by behaving like a tomboy.
Oh yeah? Then let's see you in action, Miss Charming!
URIAH, I KNOW WE'VE HAD OUR DISAGREEMENTS IN THE PAST...
TSK! DON'T EVEN TRY.
IF YOU WANT BADGES LIKE OURS, YOU'LL HAVE TO *WORK HARD* TO EARN 'EM!
?!
HE'S ALL YOURS.
LISTEN UP! I JUST DISCOVERED WE'VE ALL GOT A GOOD SIDE AND A BAD SIDE.
HEY!
IT'S UP TO YOU. WHICH SIDE D'YA WANNA SEE RIGHT NOW?

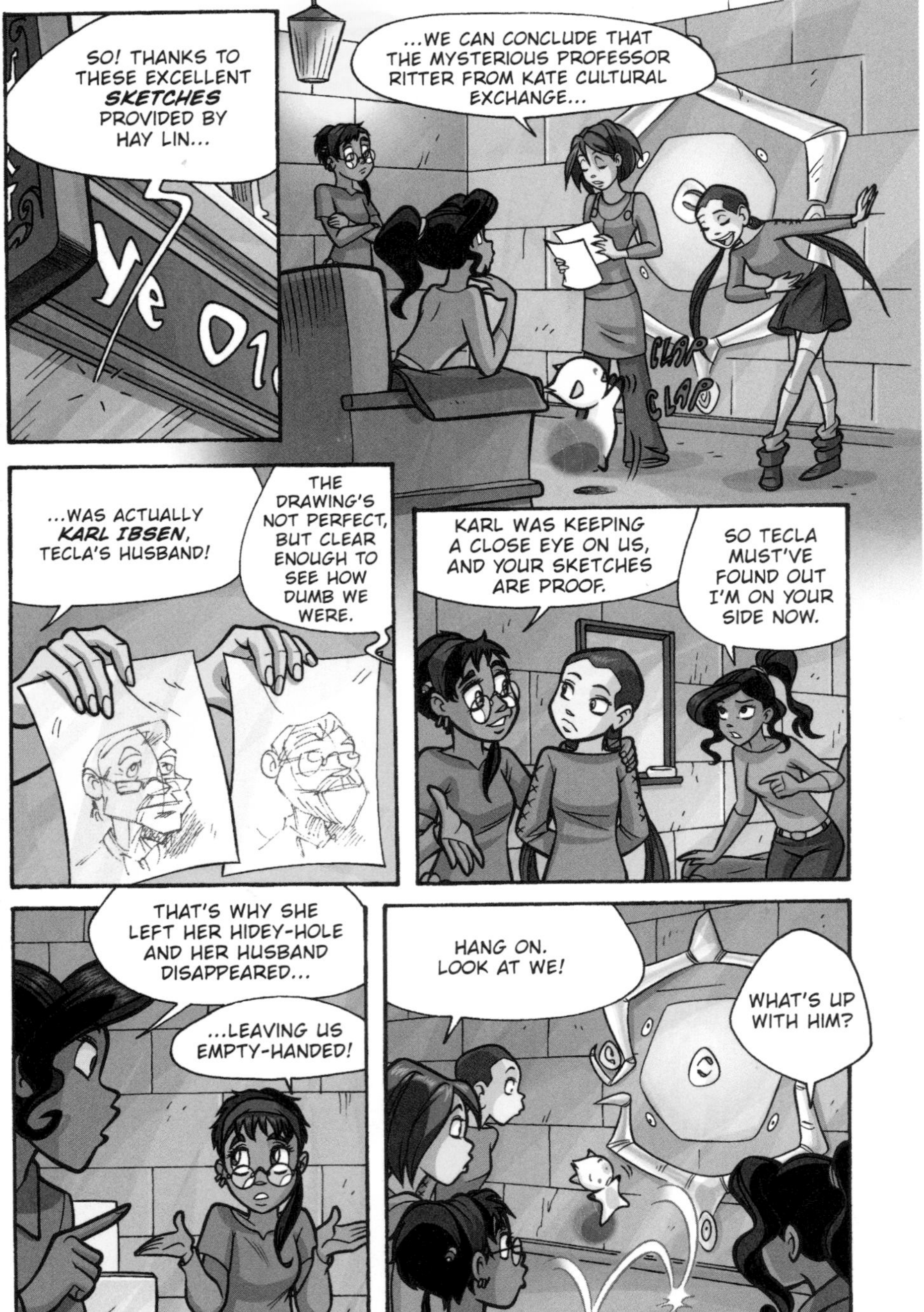

SO! THANKS TO THESE EXCELLENT SKETCHES PROVIDED BY HAY LIN...
...WE CAN CONCLUDE THAT THE MYSTERIOUS PROFESSOR RITTER FROM KATE CULTURAL EXCHANGE...
CLAP
CLAP
...WAS ACTUALLY KARL IBSEN, TECLA'S HUSBAND!
THE DRAWING'S NOT PERFECT, BUT CLEAR ENOUGH TO SEE HOW DUMB WE WERE.
KARL WAS KEEPING A CLOSE EYE ON US, AND YOUR SKETCHES ARE PROOF.
SO TECLA MUST'VE FOUND OUT I'M ON YOUR SIDE NOW.
THAT'S WHY SHE LEFT HER HIDEY-HOLE AND HER HUSBAND DISAPPEARED...
...LEAVING US EMPTY-HANDED!
HANG ON. LOOK AT WE!
WHAT'S UP WITH HIM?

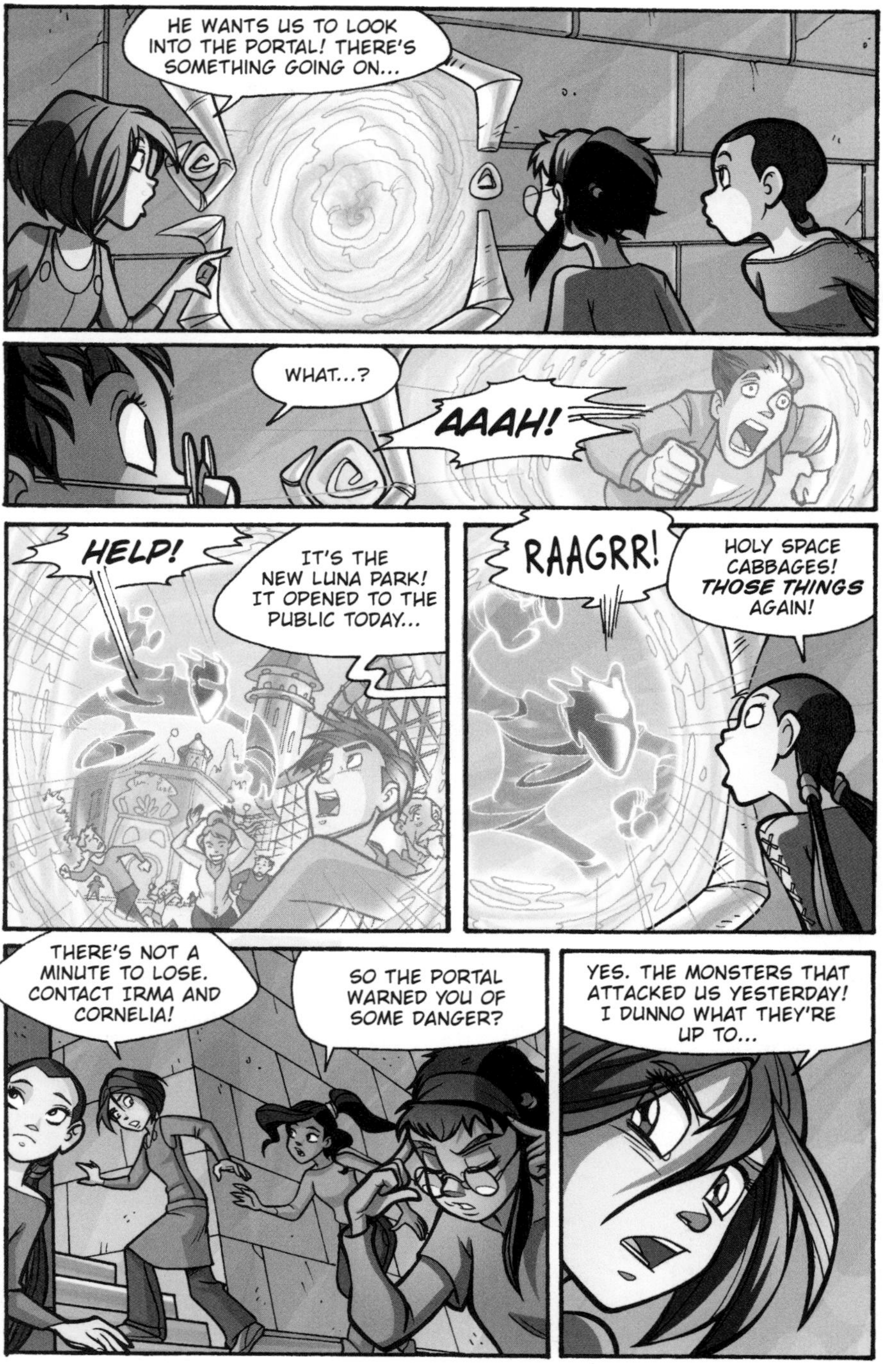

HE WANTS US TO LOOK INTO THE PORTAL! THERE'S SOMETHING GOING ON...
WHAT...?
AAAH!
HELP!
IT'S THE NEW LUNA PARK! IT OPENED TO THE PUBLIC TODAY...
RAAGRR!
HOLY SPACE CABBAGES! THOSE THINGS AGAIN!
THERE'S NOT A MINUTE TO LOSE. CONTACT IRMA AND CORNELIA!
SO THE PORTAL WARNED YOU OF SOME DANGER?
YES. THE MONSTERS THAT ATTACKED US YESTERDAY! I DUNNO WHAT THEY'RE UP TO...

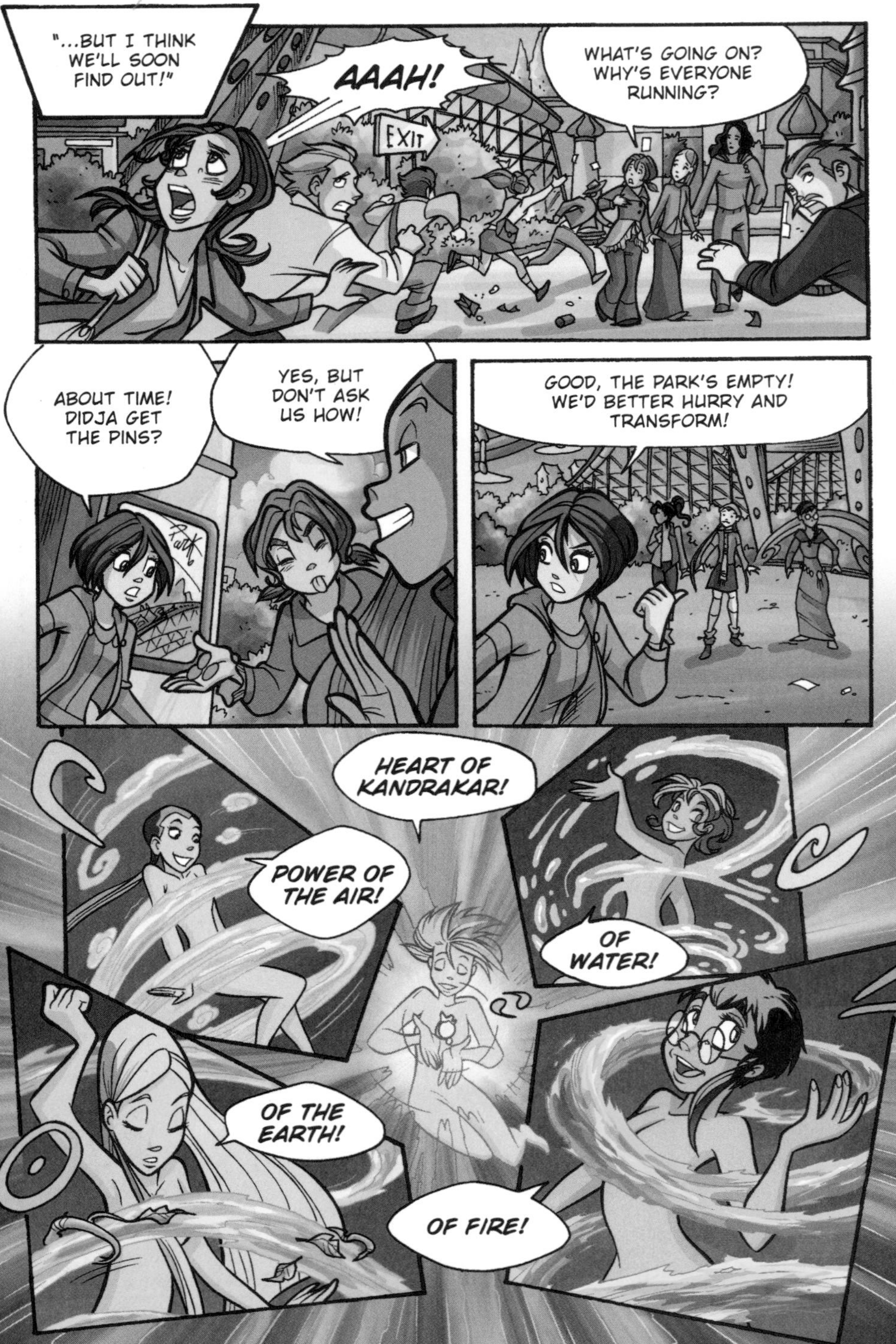

"...BUT I THINK WE'LL SOON FIND OUT!"
AAAH!
EXIT
WHAT'S GOING ON? WHY'S EVERYONE RUNNING?
ABOUT TIME! DIDJA GET THE PINS?
YES, BUT DON'T ASK US HOW!
GOOD, THE PARK'S EMPTY! WE'D BETTER HURRY AND TRANSFORM!
HEART OF KANDRAKAR!
POWER OF THE AIR!
OF WATER!
OF THE EARTH!
OF FIRE!

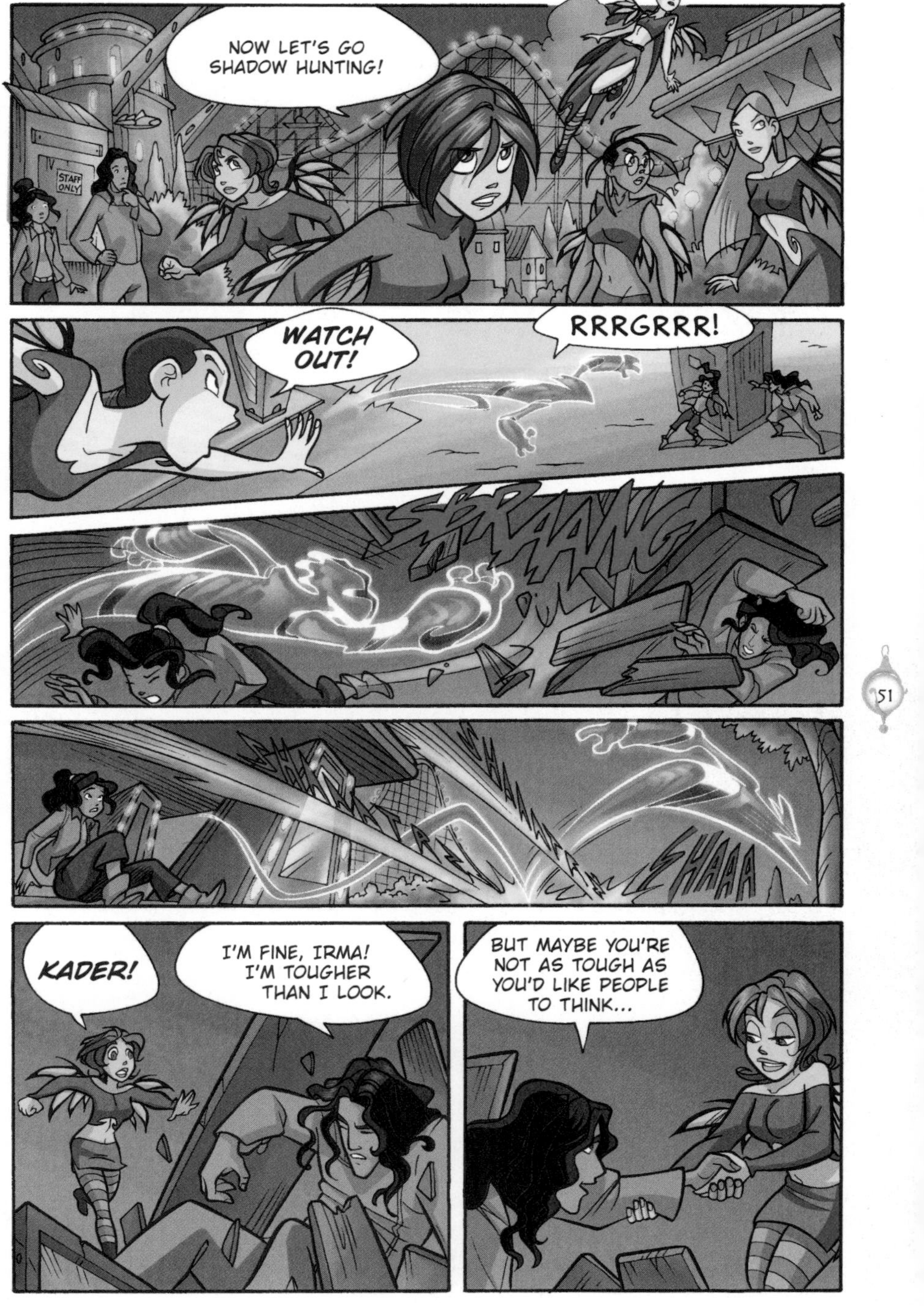
NOW LET'S GO SHADOW HUNTING!
STAFF ONLY
WATCH OUT!
RRRGRRR!
SBRAANG
SHAAA
KADER!
I'M FINE, IRMA! I'M TOUGHER THAN I LOOK.
BUT MAYBE YOU'RE NOT AS TOUGH AS YOU'D LIKE PEOPLE TO THINK...

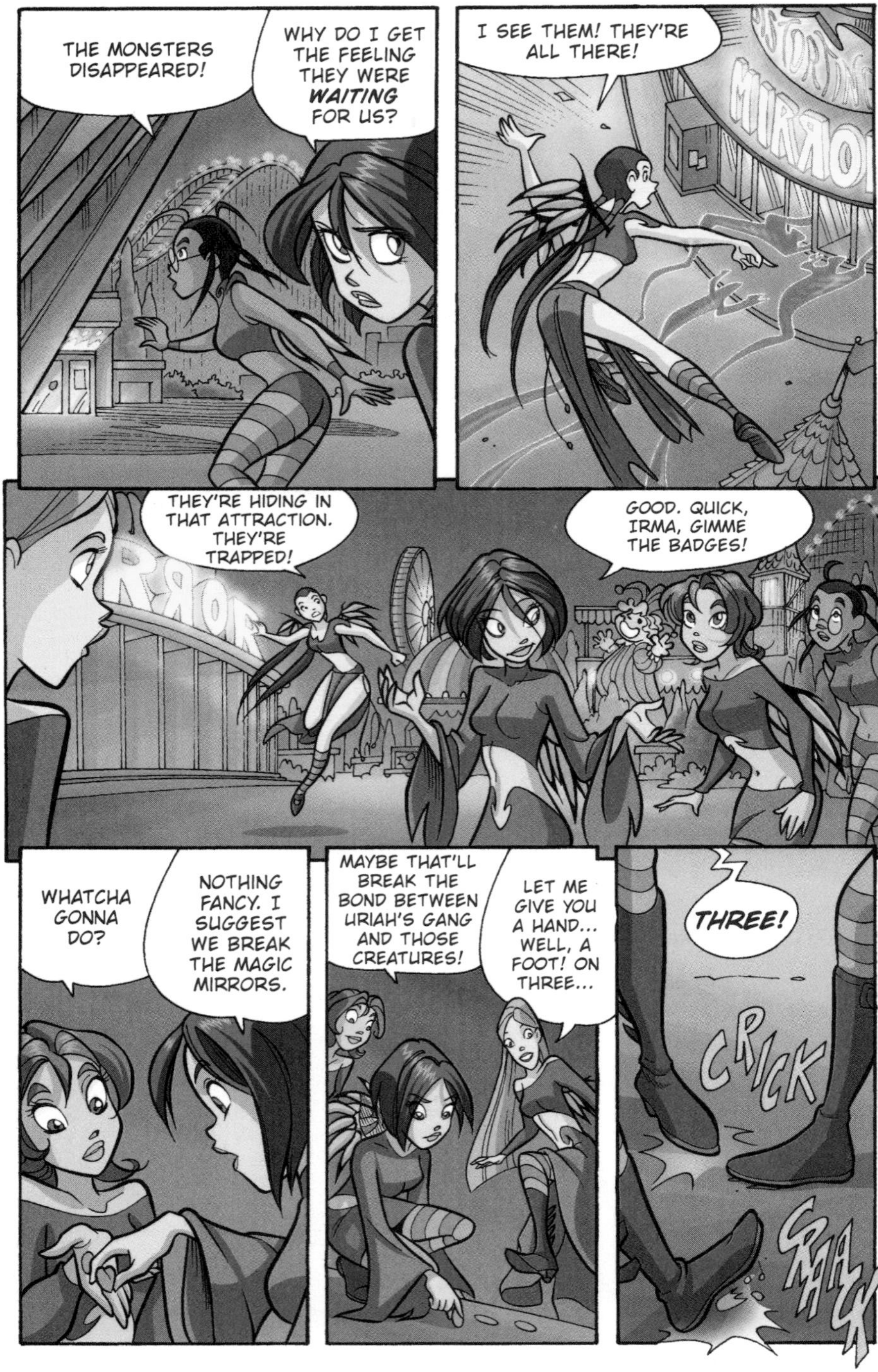
THE MONSTERS DISAPPEARED!
WHY DO I GET THE FEELING THEY WERE *WAITING* FOR US?
I SEE THEM! THEY'RE ALL THERE!
THEY'RE HIDING IN THAT ATTRACTION. THEY'RE TRAPPED!
GOOD. QUICK, IRMA, GIMME THE BADGES!
WHATCHA GONNA DO?
NOTHING FANCY. I SUGGEST WE BREAK THE MAGIC MIRRORS.
MAYBE THAT'LL BREAK THE BOND BETWEEN URIAH'S GANG AND THOSE CREATURES!
LET ME GIVE YOU A HAND... WELL, A FOOT! ON THREE...
THREE!
CRICK
CRAAACK

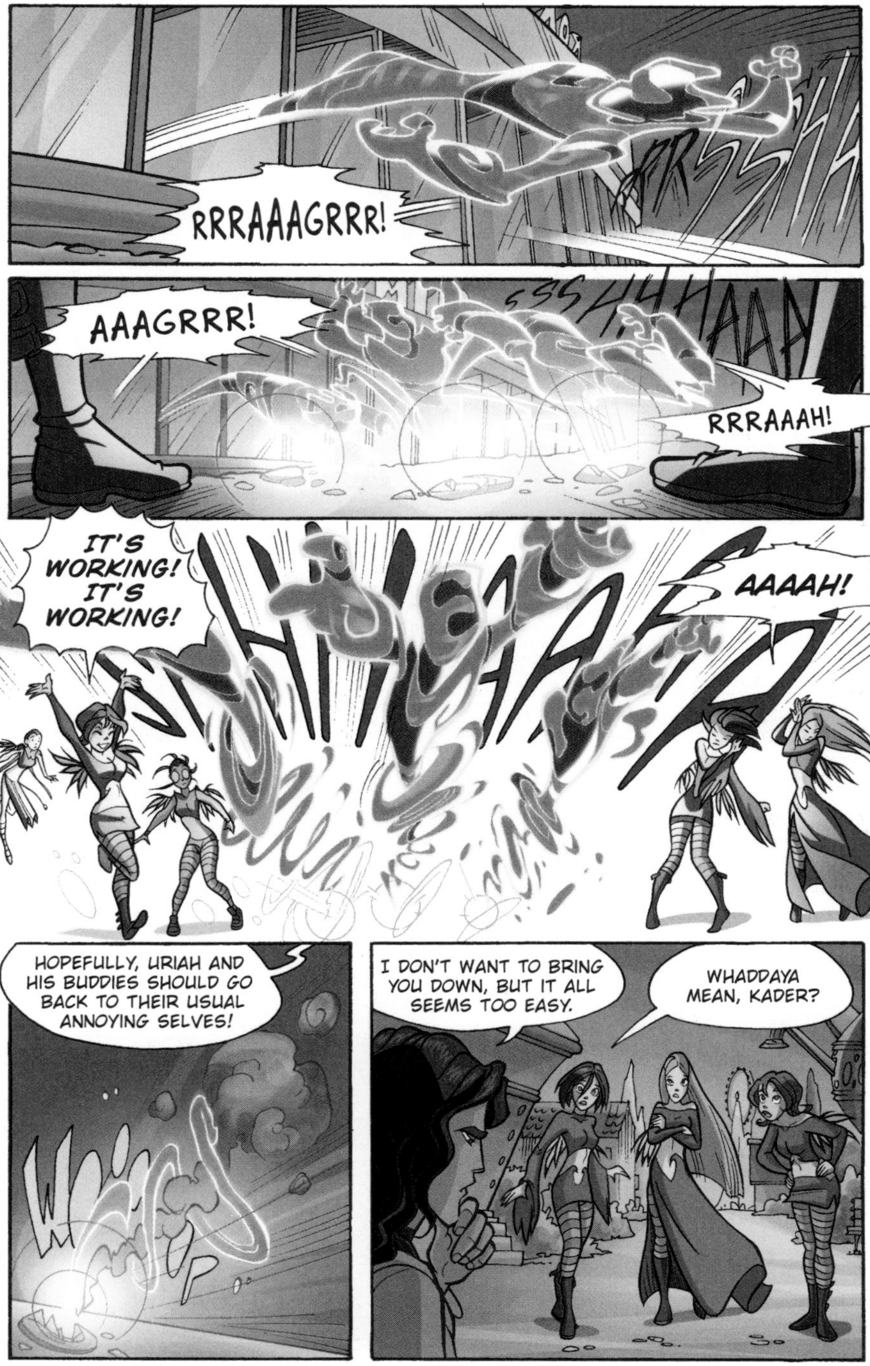

RRRAAAGRRR!
PRSSSHH
AAAGRRR!
SSSHHHAAA
RRRAAAH!
IT'S WORKING! IT'S WORKING!
AAAAH!
HOPEFULLY, URIAH AND HIS BUDDIES SHOULD GO BACK TO THEIR USUAL ANNOYING SELVES!
I DON'T WANT TO BRING YOU DOWN, BUT IT ALL SEEMS TOO EASY.
WHADDAYA MEAN, KADER?

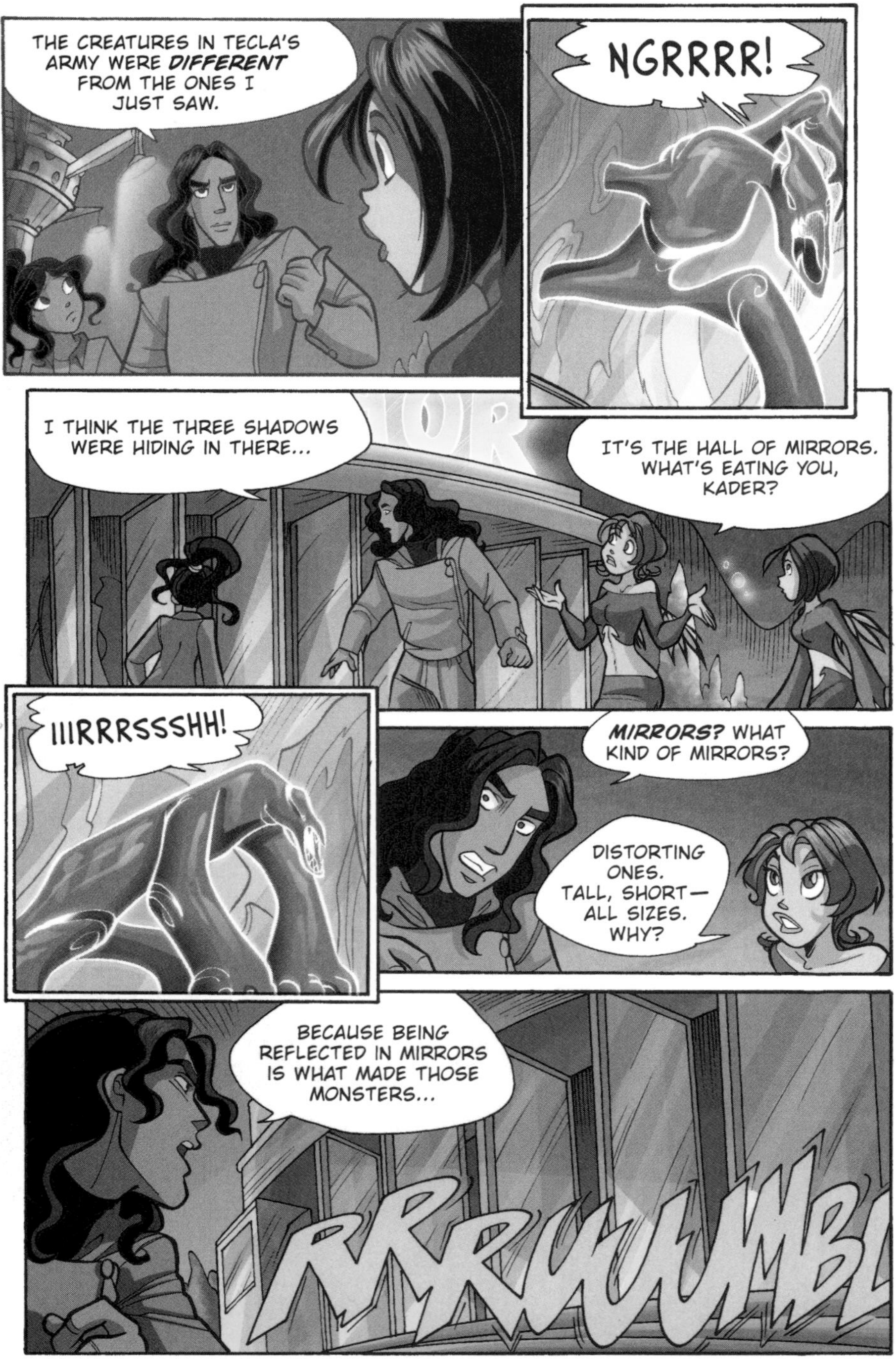

THE CREATURES IN TECLA'S ARMY WERE *DIFFERENT* FROM THE ONES I JUST SAW.
NGRRRR!
I THINK THE THREE SHADOWS WERE HIDING IN THERE...
IT'S THE HALL OF MIRRORS. WHAT'S EATING YOU, KADER?
IIIRRRSSSHH!
MIRRORS? WHAT KIND OF MIRRORS?
DISTORTING ONES. TALL, SHORT— ALL SIZES. WHY?
BECAUSE BEING REFLECTED IN MIRRORS IS WHAT MADE THOSE MONSTERS...
RRRUUUMBL

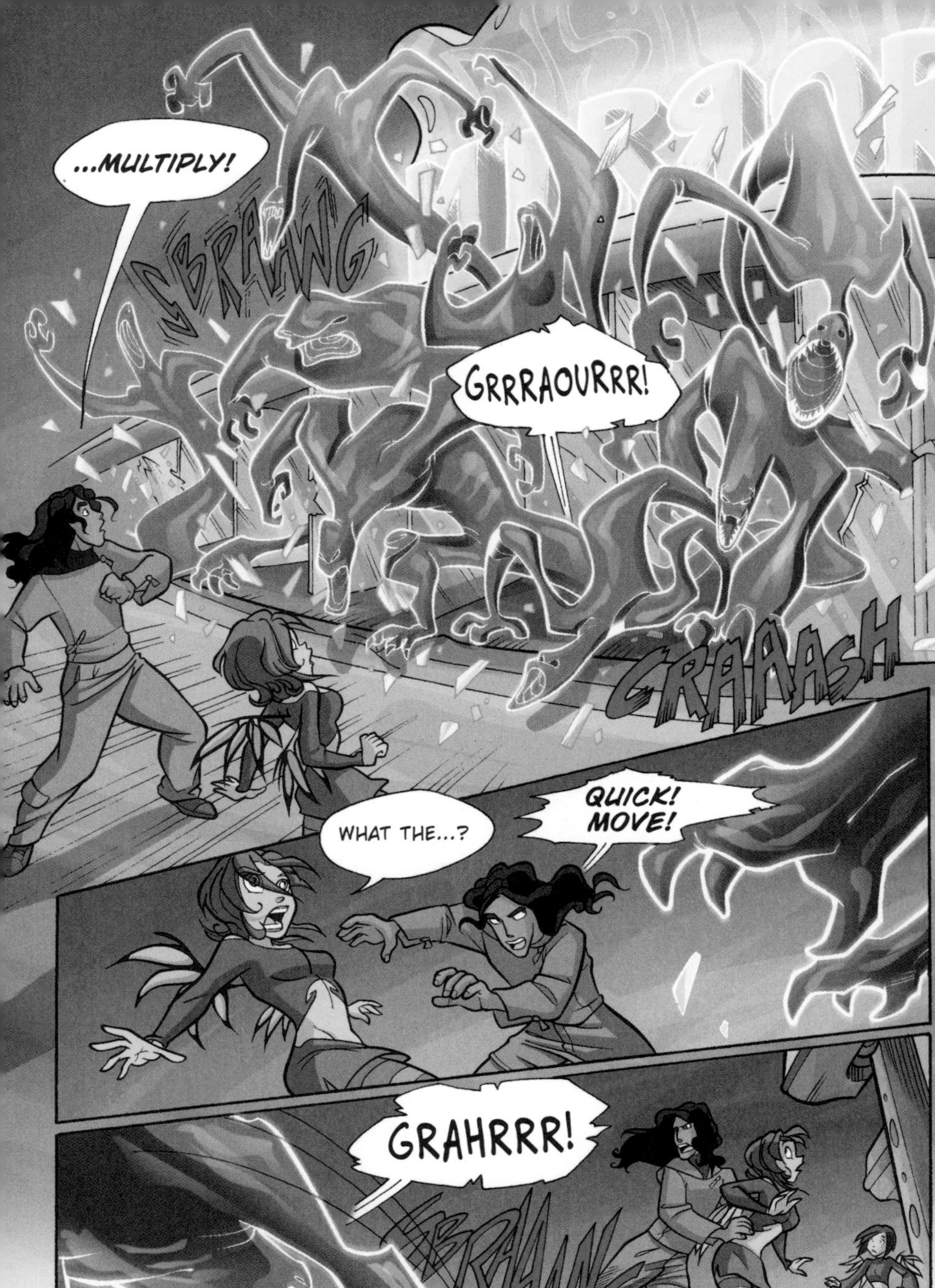
...MULTIPLY!
CBRAANG
GRRRAOURRR!
CRAAASH
WHAT THE...?
QUICK! MOVE!
GRAHRRR!

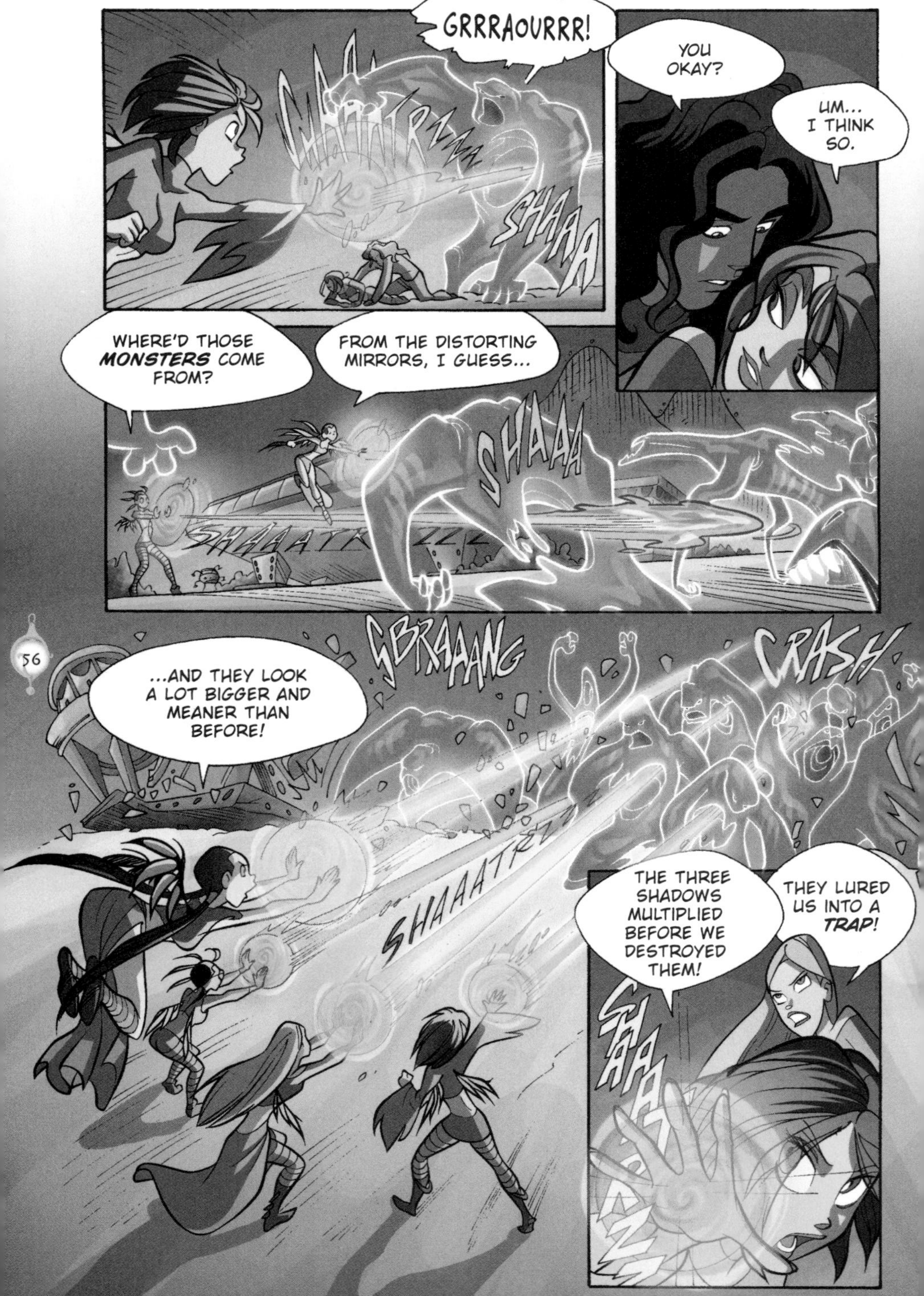

GRRRAOURRR!
SHAAA
YOU OKAY?
UM... I THINK SO.
WHERE'D THOSE **MONSTERS** COME FROM?
FROM THE DISTORTING MIRRORS, I GUESS...
SHAAA
GBRAAANG
CRASH
...AND THEY LOOK A LOT BIGGER AND MEANER THAN BEFORE!
SHAAATRZ
THE THREE SHADOWS MULTIPLIED BEFORE WE DESTROYED THEM!
THEY LURED US INTO A ***TRAP!***

LET'S SEE HOW THEY DEAL WITH MY POWERS!

RII-IINN

CRAAASH

WOOO OOOSSSHHH

UNBELIEVABLE! IT'S NOT WORKING!

WE NEED TO THINK FAST! THOSE CREATURES AREN'T AFFECTED BY OUR MAGICAL RAYS!

THEY DON'T RUN, THEY DON'T HIDE, AND IF WE HIT THEM, THEY GET BACK UP!

SHAAARZZ

YOU'RE RIGHT! THEY SEEM INVINCIBLE!

SHAAARZZ

I GOT IT! *PHYSICS!*

57

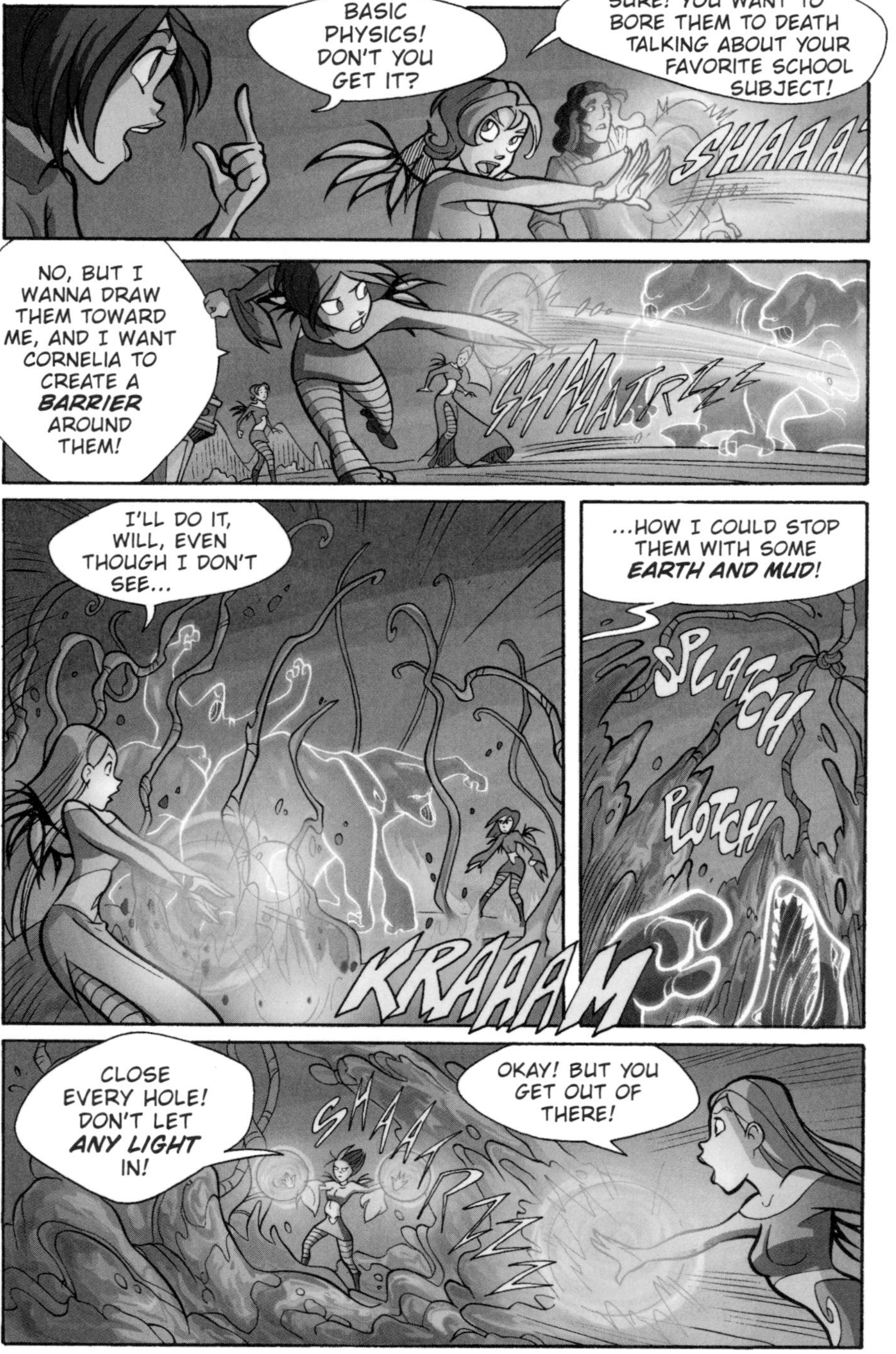
BASIC PHYSICS! DON'T YOU GET IT?
SURE! YOU WANT TO BORE THEM TO DEATH TALKING ABOUT YOUR FAVORITE SCHOOL SUBJECT!
SHAAAT
NO, BUT I WANNA DRAW THEM TOWARD ME, AND I WANT CORNELIA TO CREATE A **BARRIER** AROUND THEM!
SHAAATRZZZ
I'LL DO IT, WILL, EVEN THOUGH I DON'T SEE...
...HOW I COULD STOP THEM WITH SOME **EARTH AND MUD!**
SPLATCH
PLOTCH
KRAAAM
CLOSE EVERY HOLE! DON'T LET **ANY LIGHT** IN!
OKAY! BUT YOU GET OUT OF THERE!
SHAAATRZZZ

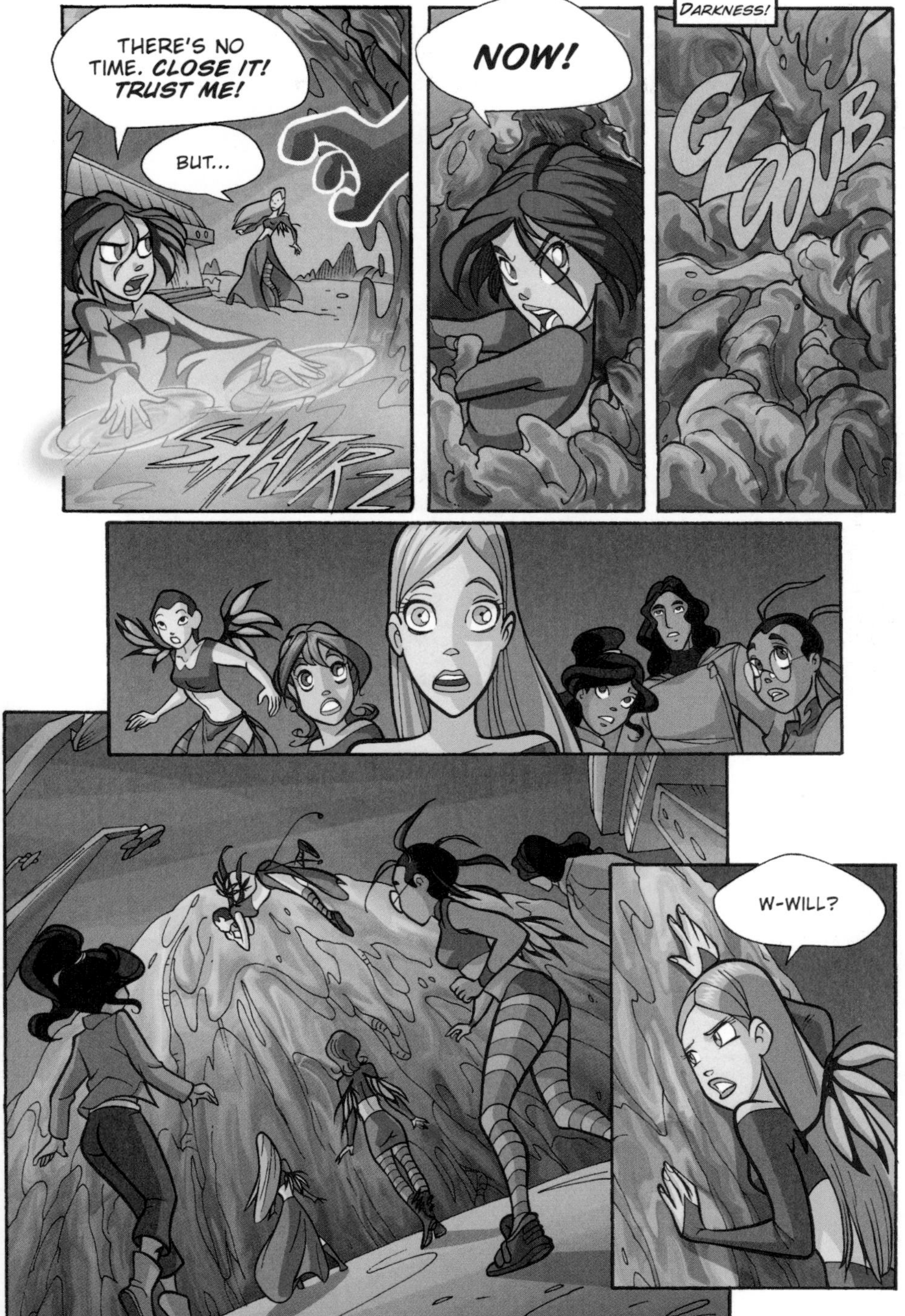

THERE'S NO TIME. CLOSE IT! TRUST ME!
BUT...
SHAARRZ
NOW!
DARKNESS!
GLOOOUB
W-WILL?

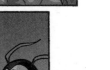

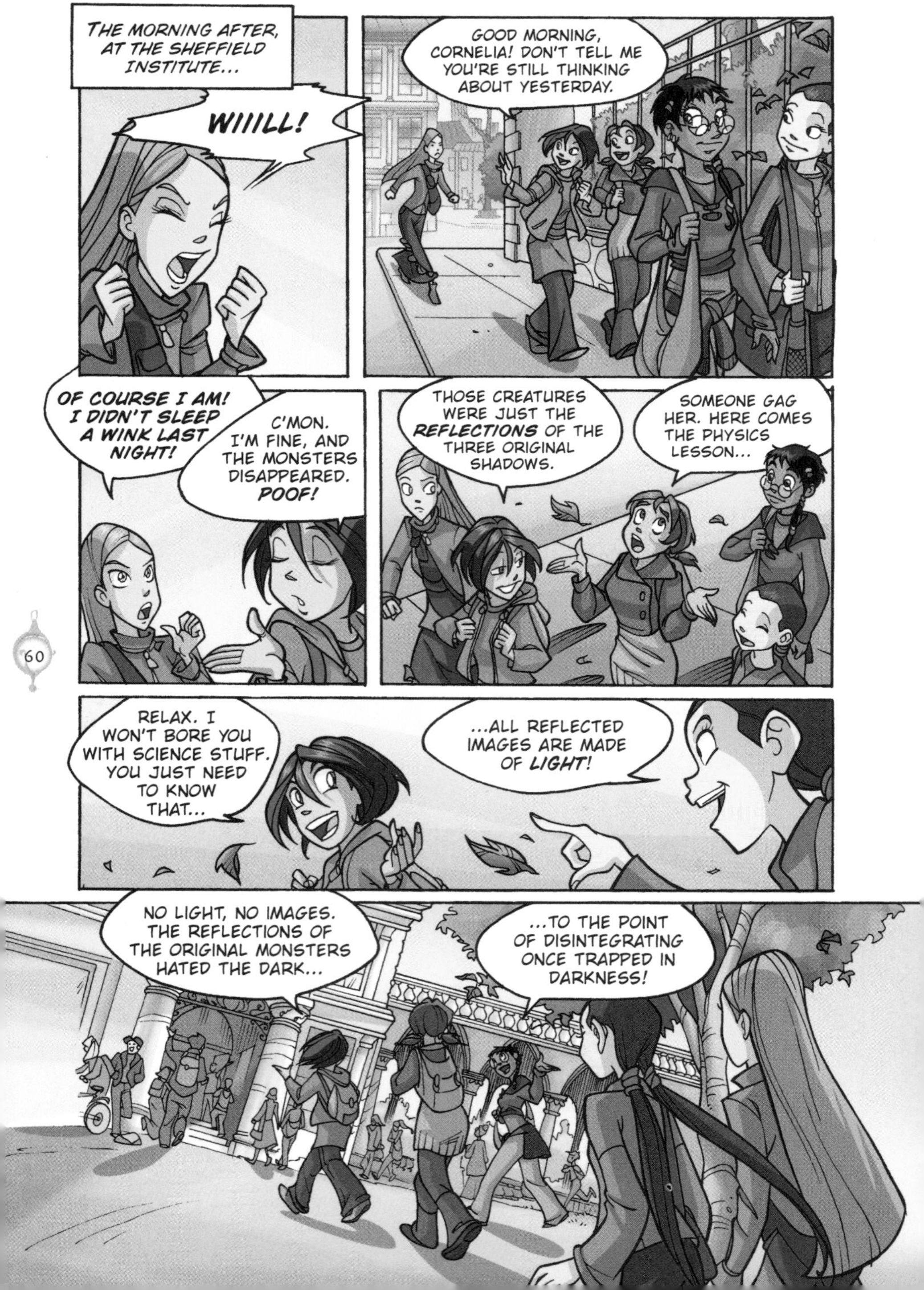
THE MORNING AFTER, AT THE SHEFFIELD INSTITUTE...
WIIILL!
GOOD MORNING, CORNELIA! DON'T TELL ME YOU'RE STILL THINKING ABOUT YESTERDAY.
OF COURSE I AM! I DIDN'T SLEEP A WINK LAST NIGHT!
C'MON. I'M FINE, AND THE MONSTERS DISAPPEARED. POOF!
THOSE CREATURES WERE JUST THE REFLECTIONS OF THE THREE ORIGINAL SHADOWS.
SOMEONE GAG HER. HERE COMES THE PHYSICS LESSON...
RELAX. I WON'T BORE YOU WITH SCIENCE STUFF. YOU JUST NEED TO KNOW THAT...
...ALL REFLECTED IMAGES ARE MADE OF LIGHT!
NO LIGHT, NO IMAGES. THE REFLECTIONS OF THE ORIGINAL MONSTERS HATED THE DARK...
...TO THE POINT OF DISINTEGRATING ONCE TRAPPED IN DARKNESS!

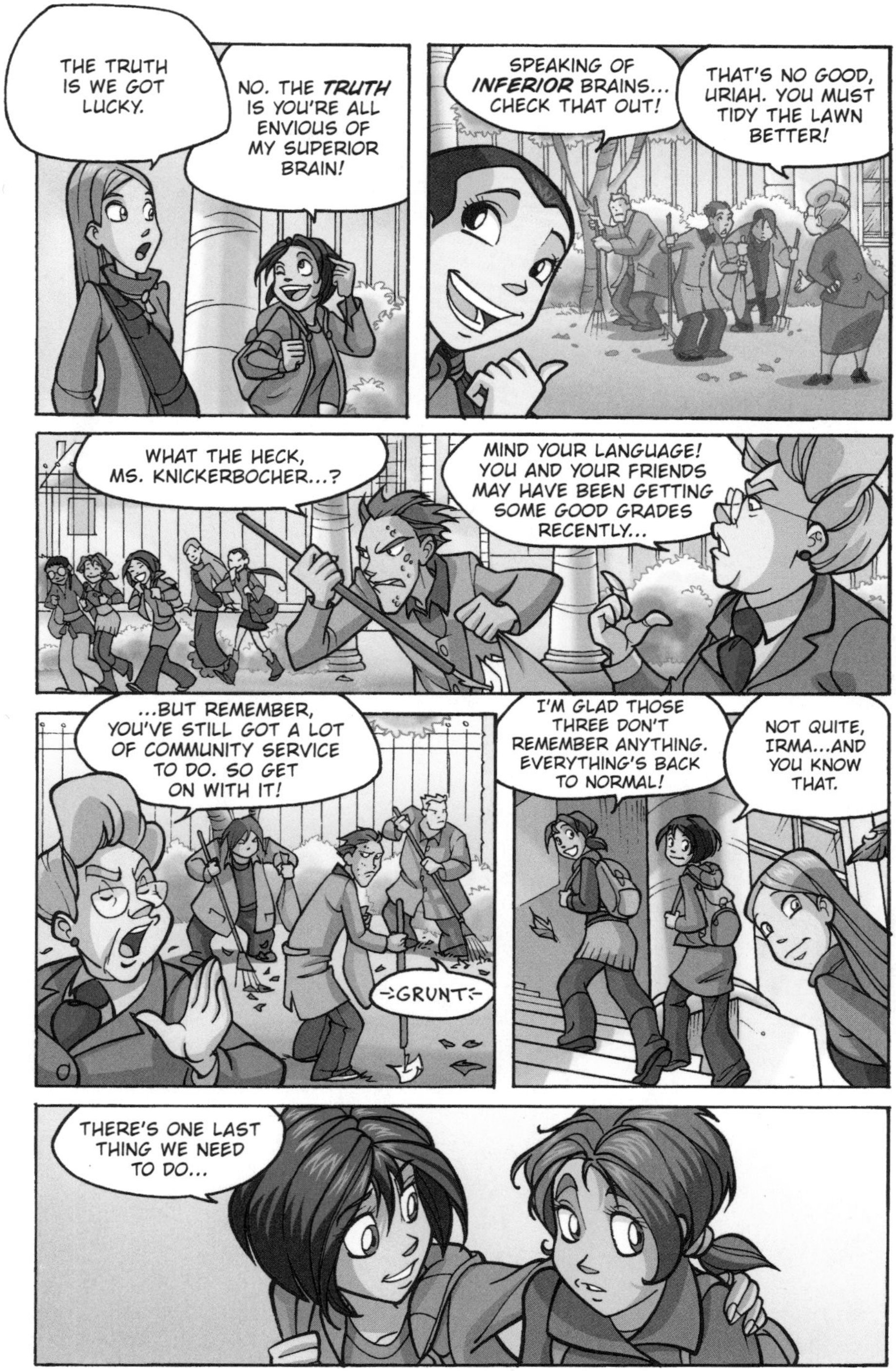
THE TRUTH IS WE GOT LUCKY.
NO. THE *TRUTH* IS YOU'RE ALL ENVIOUS OF MY SUPERIOR BRAIN!
SPEAKING OF *INFERIOR* BRAINS... CHECK THAT OUT!
THAT'S NO GOOD, URIAH. YOU MUST TIDY THE LAWN BETTER!
WHAT THE HECK, MS. KNICKERBOCHER...?
MIND YOUR LANGUAGE! YOU AND YOUR FRIENDS MAY HAVE BEEN GETTING SOME GOOD GRADES RECENTLY...
...BUT REMEMBER, YOU'VE STILL GOT A LOT OF COMMUNITY SERVICE TO DO. SO GET ON WITH IT!
GRUNT
I'M GLAD THOSE THREE DON'T REMEMBER ANYTHING. EVERYTHING'S BACK TO NORMAL!
NOT QUITE, IRMA...AND YOU KNOW THAT.
THERE'S ONE LAST THING WE NEED TO DO...

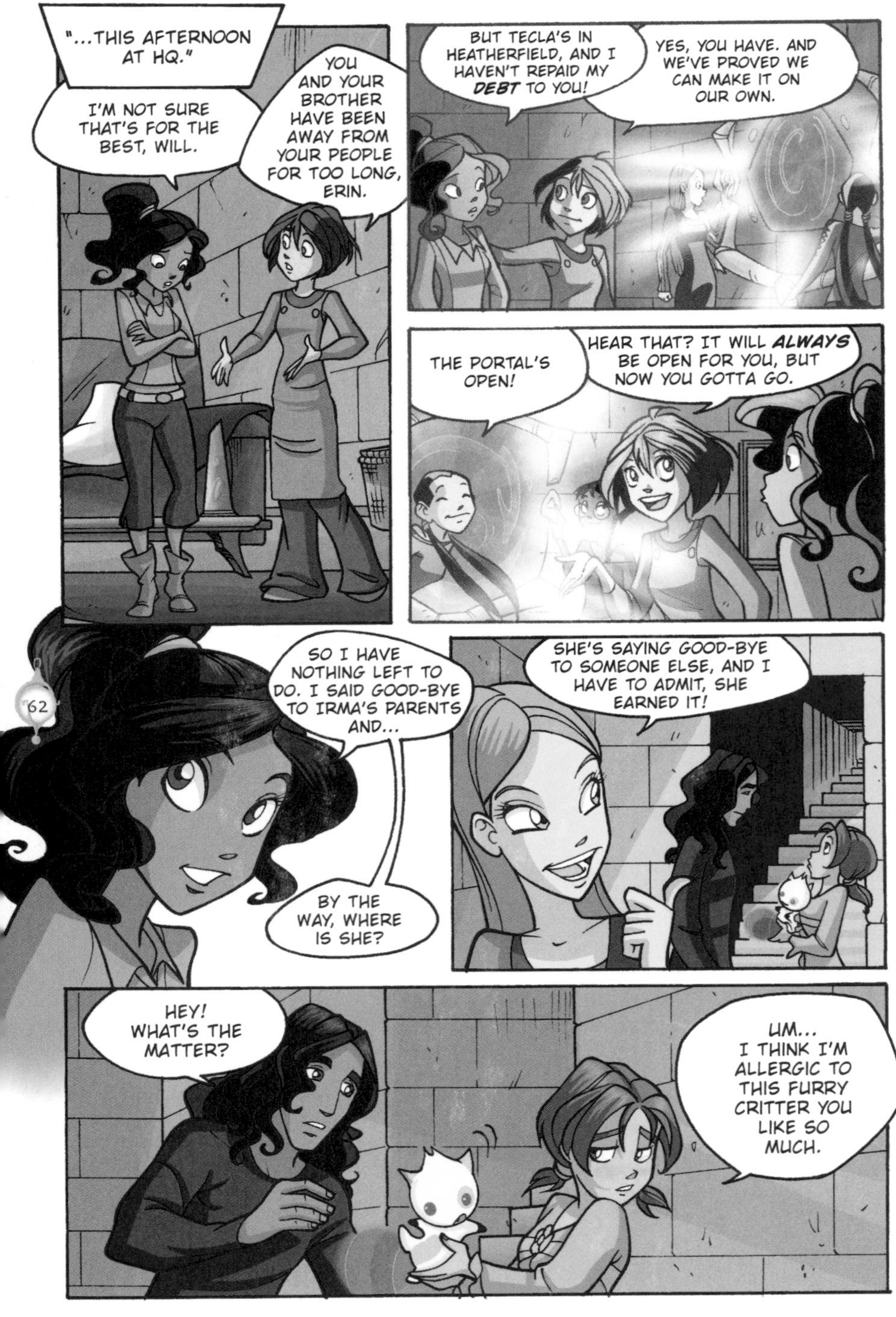
"...THIS AFTERNOON AT HQ."
I'M NOT SURE THAT'S FOR THE BEST, WILL.
YOU AND YOUR BROTHER HAVE BEEN AWAY FROM YOUR PEOPLE FOR TOO LONG, ERIN.
BUT TECLA'S IN HEATHERFIELD, AND I HAVEN'T REPAID MY DEBT TO YOU!
YES, YOU HAVE. AND WE'VE PROVED WE CAN MAKE IT ON OUR OWN.
THE PORTAL'S OPEN!
HEAR THAT? IT WILL ALWAYS BE OPEN FOR YOU, BUT NOW YOU GOTTA GO.
SO I HAVE NOTHING LEFT TO DO. I SAID GOOD-BYE TO IRMA'S PARENTS AND...
BY THE WAY, WHERE IS SHE?
SHE'S SAYING GOOD-BYE TO SOMEONE ELSE, AND I HAVE TO ADMIT, SHE EARNED IT!
HEY! WHAT'S THE MATTER?
UM... I THINK I'M ALLERGIC TO THIS FURRY CRITTER YOU LIKE SO MUCH.

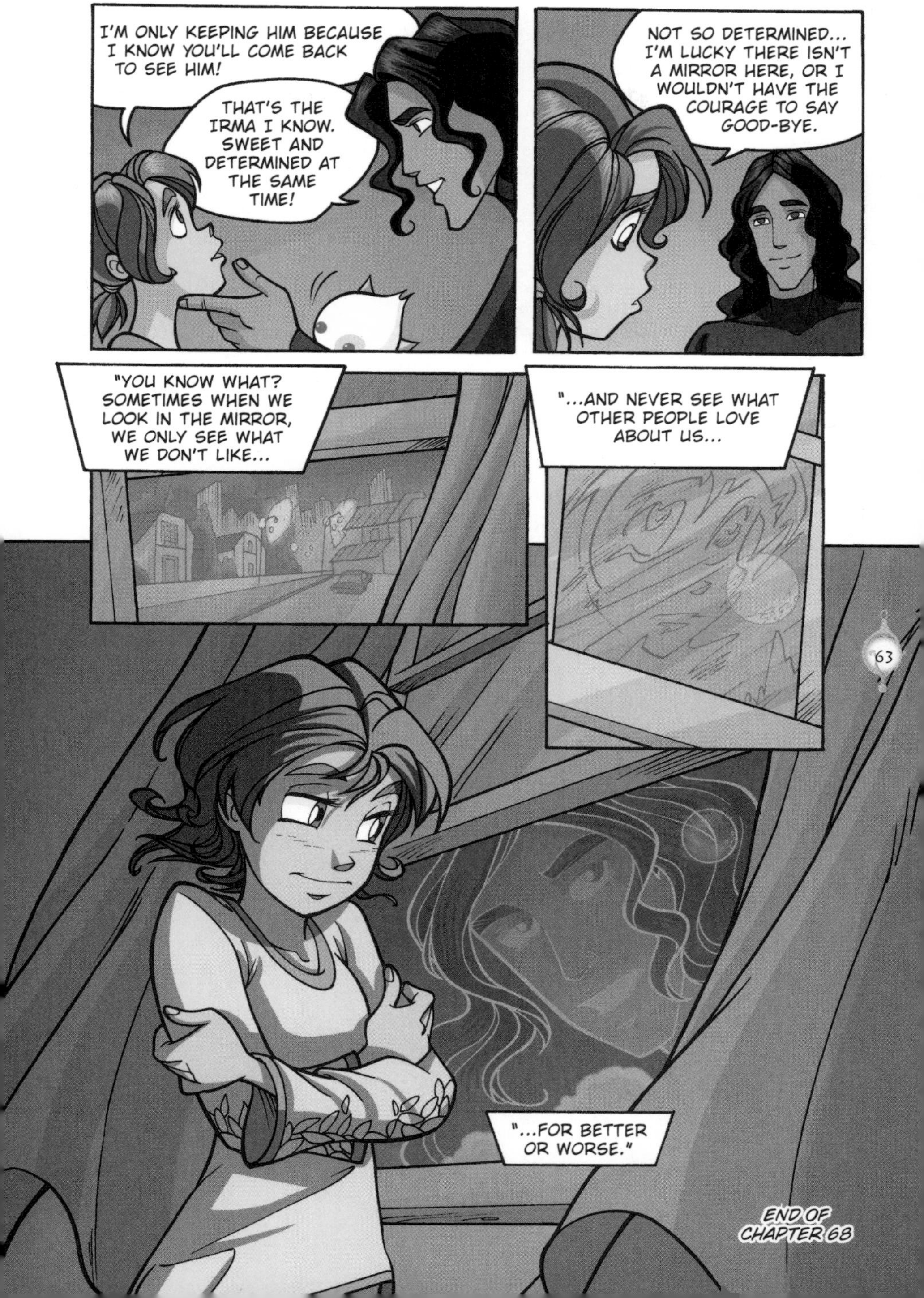
I'M ONLY KEEPING HIM BECAUSE I KNOW YOU'LL COME BACK TO SEE HIM!
THAT'S THE IRMA I KNOW. SWEET AND DETERMINED AT THE SAME TIME!
NOT SO DETERMINED... I'M LUCKY THERE ISN'T A MIRROR HERE, OR I WOULDN'T HAVE THE COURAGE TO SAY GOOD-BYE.
"YOU KNOW WHAT? SOMETIMES WHEN WE LOOK IN THE MIRROR, WE ONLY SEE WHAT WE DON'T LIKE...
"...AND NEVER SEE WHAT OTHER PEOPLE LOVE ABOUT US...
"...FOR BETTER OR WORSE."
END OF CHAPTER 68

W.i.t.c.h.

Will Irma Taranee Cornelia Hay Lin

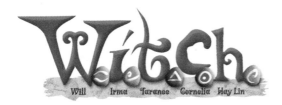

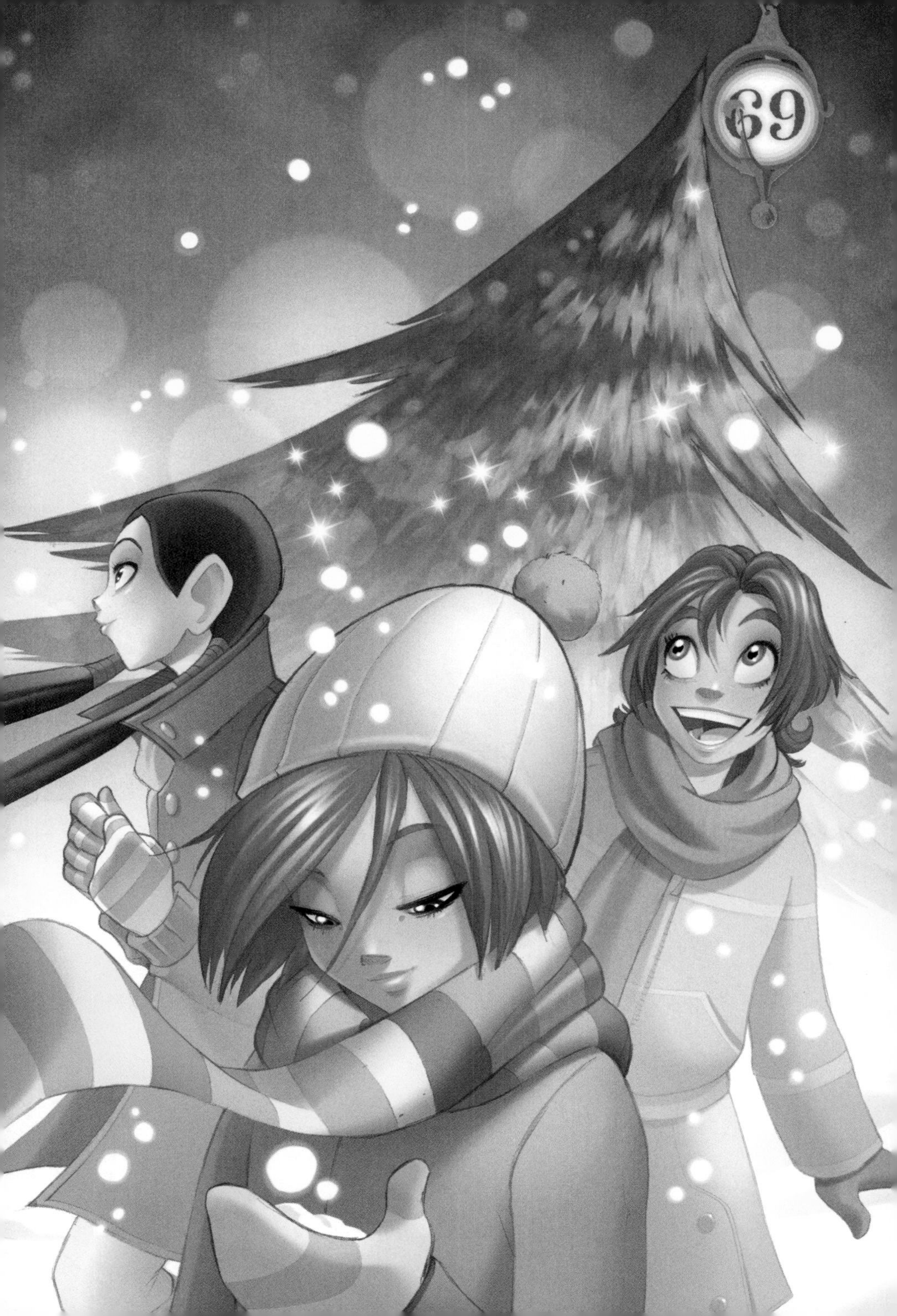
69

Beyond Borders

"You will visit all the worlds under Kandrakar's control."

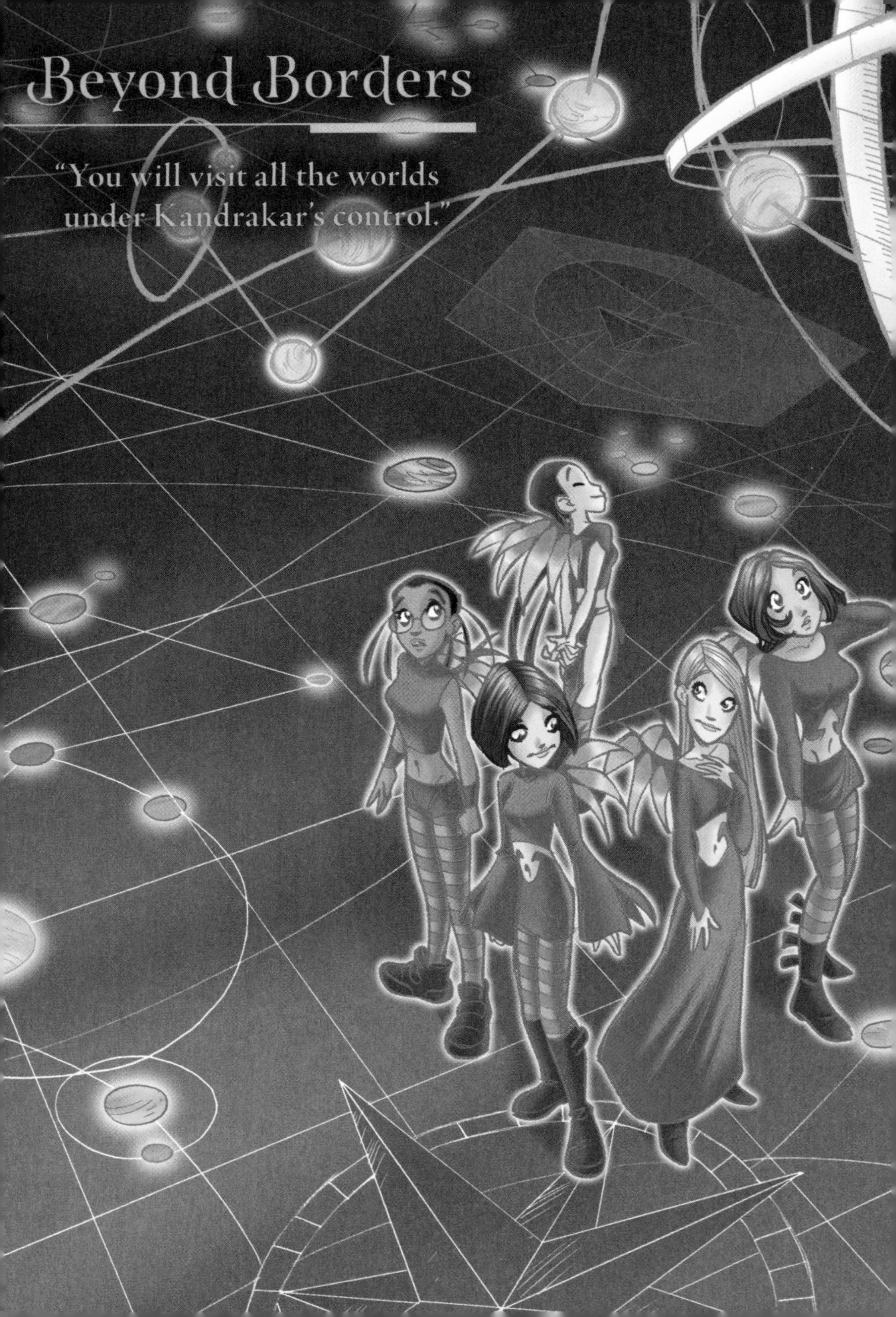

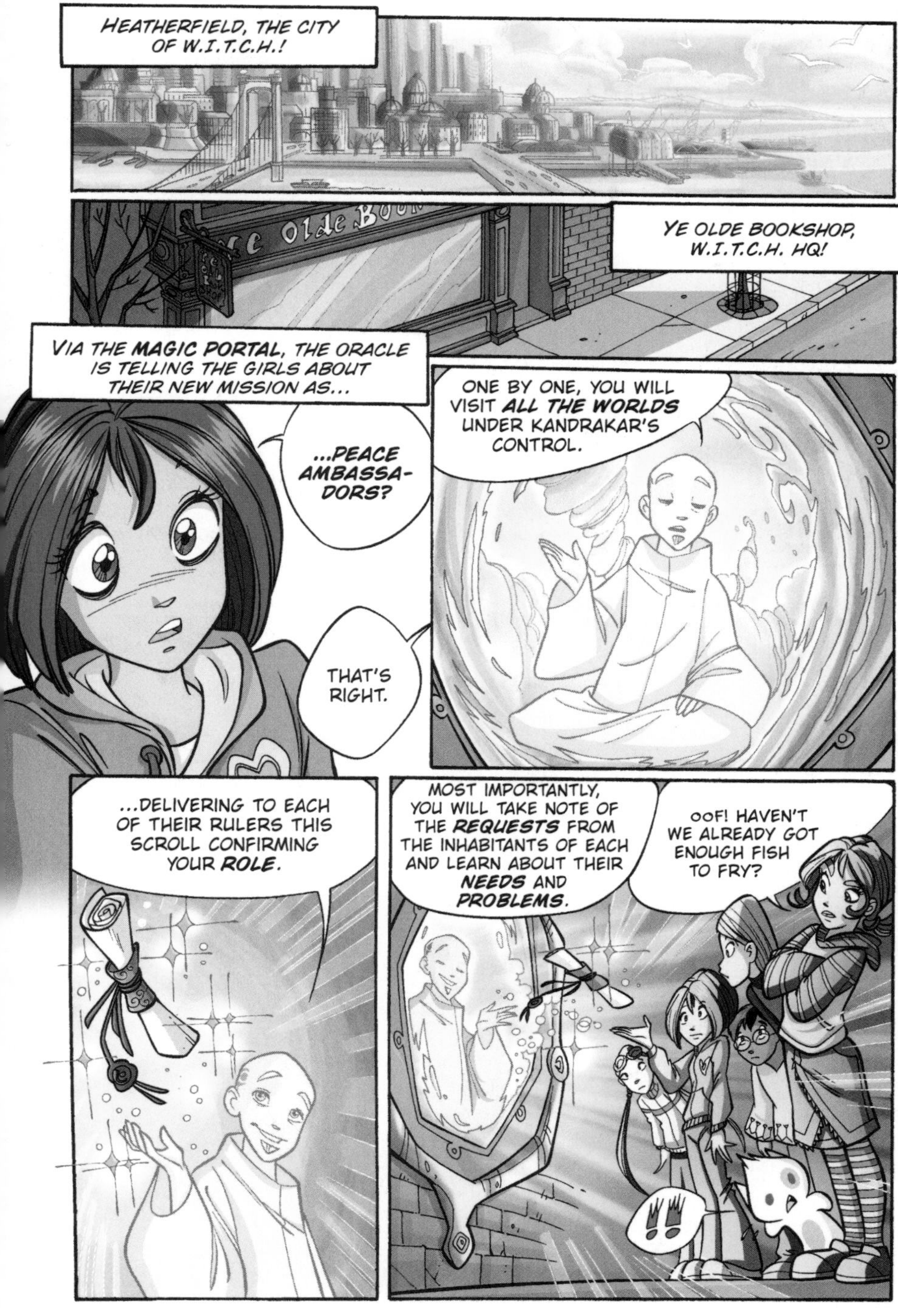

HEATHERFIELD, THE CITY OF W.I.T.C.H.!
YE OLDE BOOKSHOP, W.I.T.C.H. HQ!
VIA THE MAGIC PORTAL, THE ORACLE IS TELLING THE GIRLS ABOUT THEIR NEW MISSION AS...
ONE BY ONE, YOU WILL VISIT ALL THE WORLDS UNDER KANDRAKAR'S CONTROL.
...PEACE AMBASSADORS?
THAT'S RIGHT.
...DELIVERING TO EACH OF THEIR RULERS THIS SCROLL CONFIRMING YOUR ROLE.
MOST IMPORTANTLY, YOU WILL TAKE NOTE OF THE REQUESTS FROM THE INHABITANTS OF EACH AND LEARN ABOUT THEIR NEEDS AND PROBLEMS.
OOF! HAVEN'T WE ALREADY GOT ENOUGH FISH TO FRY?

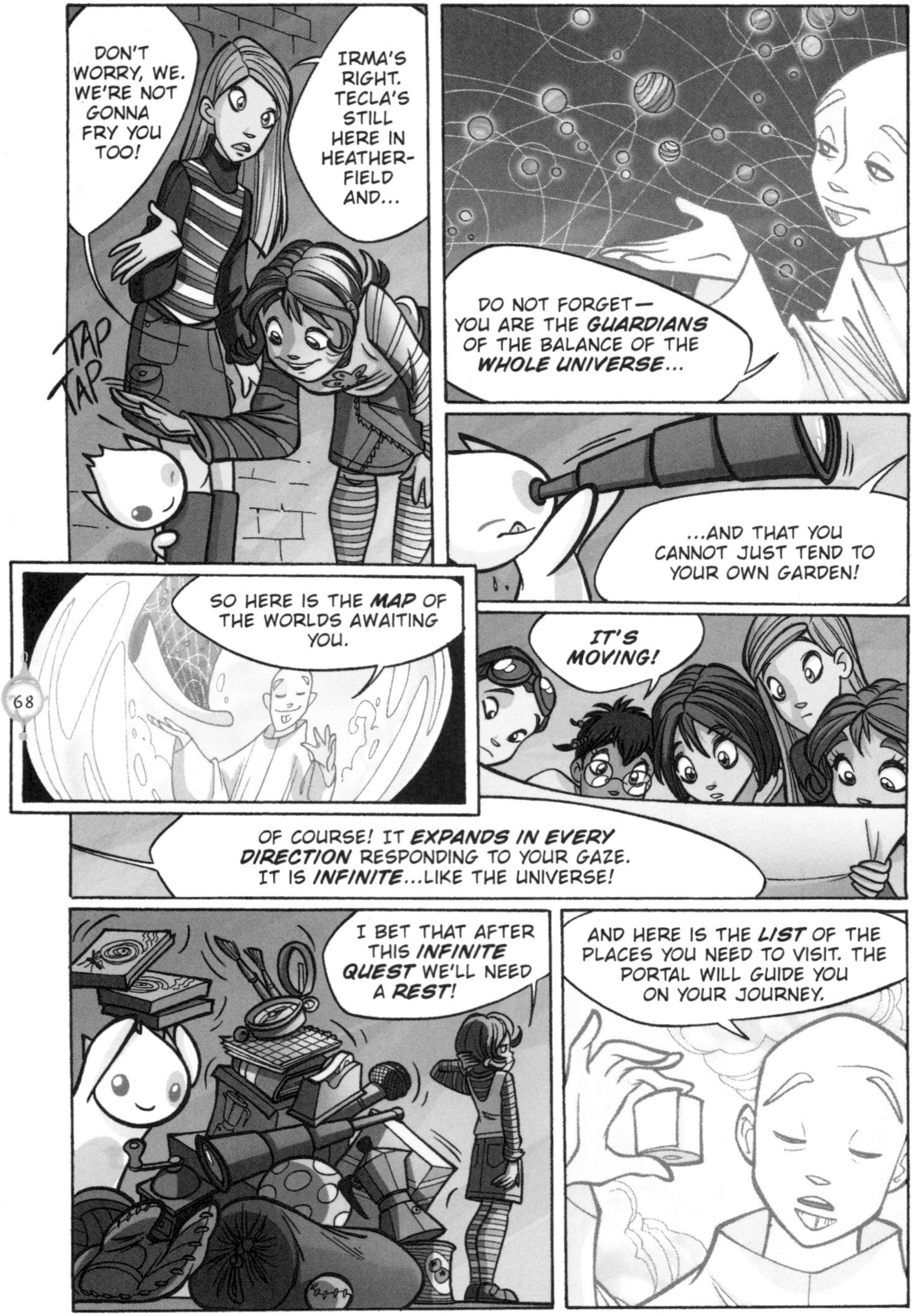

DON'T WORRY, WE. WE'RE NOT GONNA FRY YOU TOO!
IRMA'S RIGHT. TECLA'S STILL HERE IN HEATHER-FIELD AND...
TAP TAP
DO NOT FORGET— YOU ARE THE ***GUARDIANS*** OF THE BALANCE OF THE ***WHOLE UNIVERSE***...
...AND THAT YOU CANNOT JUST TEND TO YOUR OWN GARDEN!
SO HERE IS THE ***MAP*** OF THE WORLDS AWAITING YOU.
IT'S MOVING!
OF COURSE! IT ***EXPANDS IN EVERY DIRECTION*** RESPONDING TO YOUR GAZE. IT IS ***INFINITE***...LIKE THE UNIVERSE!
I BET THAT AFTER THIS ***INFINITE QUEST*** WE'LL NEED A ***REST***!
AND HERE IS THE ***LIST*** OF THE PLACES YOU NEED TO VISIT. THE PORTAL WILL GUIDE YOU ON YOUR JOURNEY.

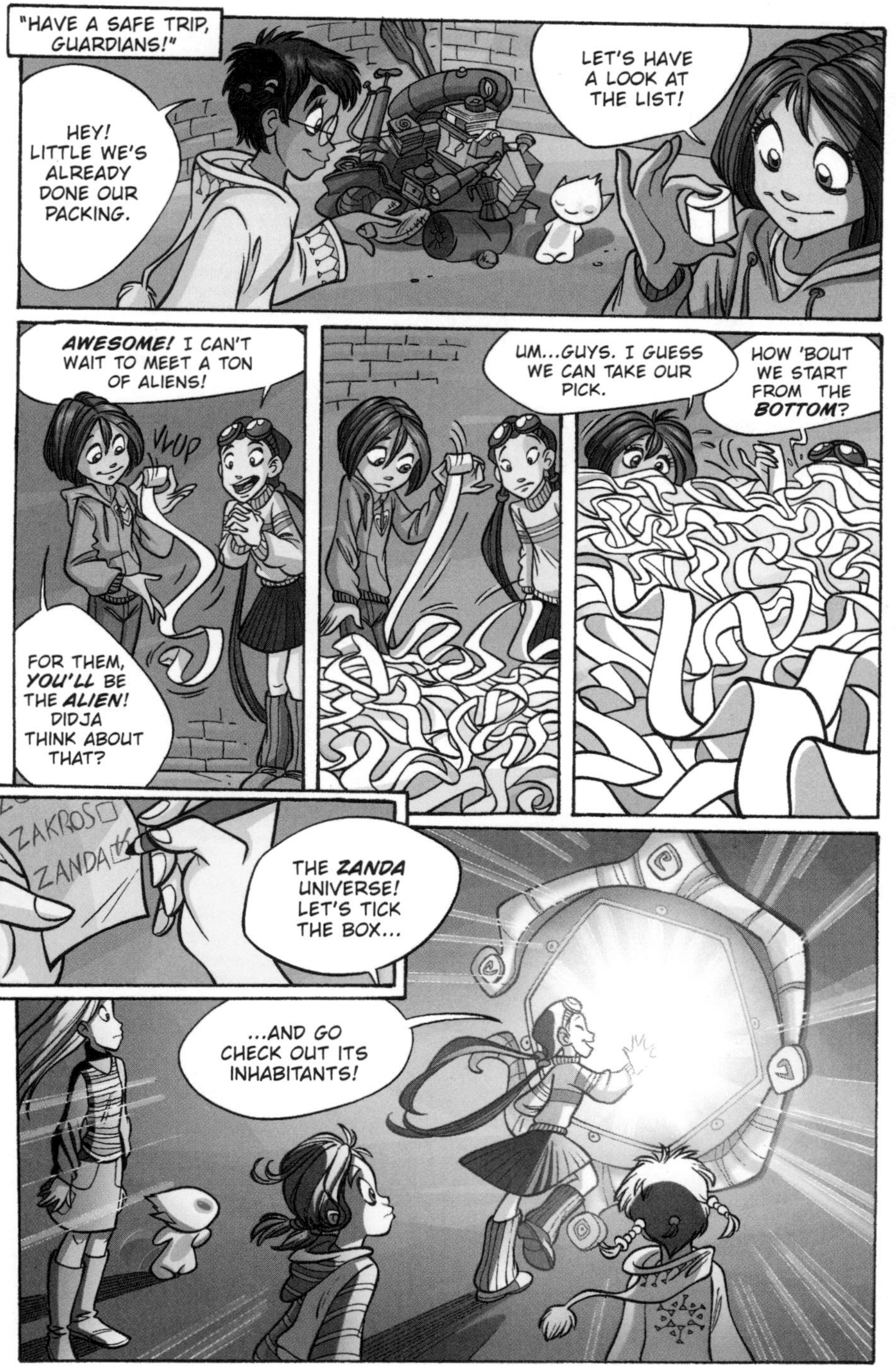

"HAVE A SAFE TRIP, GUARDIANS!"
HEY! LITTLE WE'S ALREADY DONE OUR PACKING.
LET'S HAVE A LOOK AT THE LIST!
AWESOME! I CAN'T WAIT TO MEET A TON OF ALIENS!
VUUP
FOR THEM, ***YOU'LL*** BE THE ***ALIEN***! DIDJA THINK ABOUT THAT?
UM...GUYS. I GUESS WE CAN TAKE OUR PICK.
HOW 'BOUT WE START FROM THE ***BOTTOM***?
ZAKROS
ZANDA
THE ***ZANDA*** UNIVERSE! LET'S TICK THE BOX...
...AND GO CHECK OUT ITS INHABITANTS!

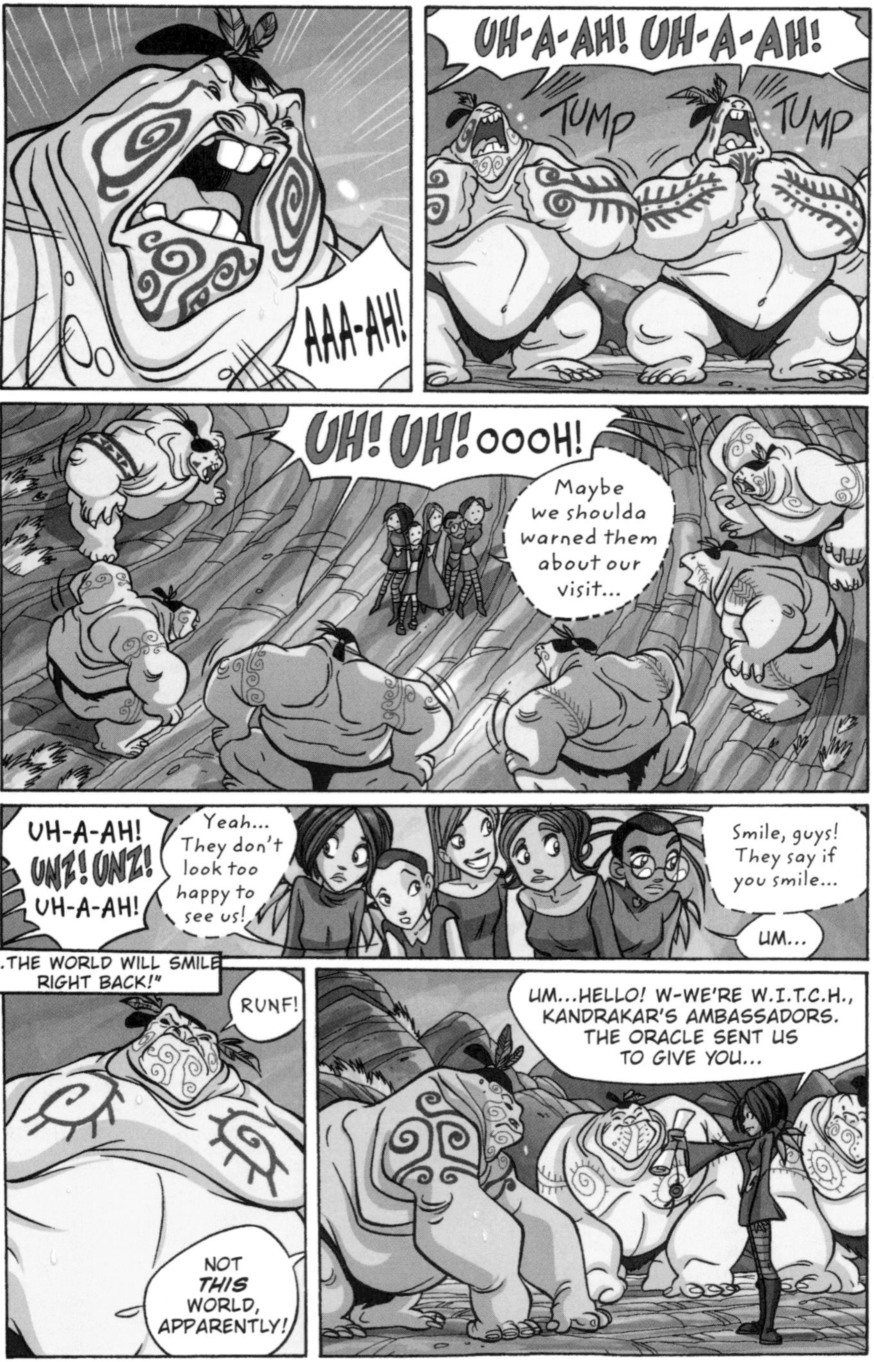
AAA-AH!
UH-A-AH! UH-A-AH!
TUMP
TUMP
UH! UH! OOOH!
Maybe we shoulda warned them about our visit...
UH-A-AH! UNZ! UNZ! UH-A-AH!
Yeah... They don't look too happy to see us!
Smile, guys! They say if you smile...
UM...
"...THE WORLD WILL SMILE RIGHT BACK!"
RUNF!
NOT THIS WORLD, APPARENTLY!
UM...HELLO! W-WE'RE W.I.T.C.H., KANDRAKAR'S AMBASSADORS. THE ORACLE SENT US TO GIVE YOU...

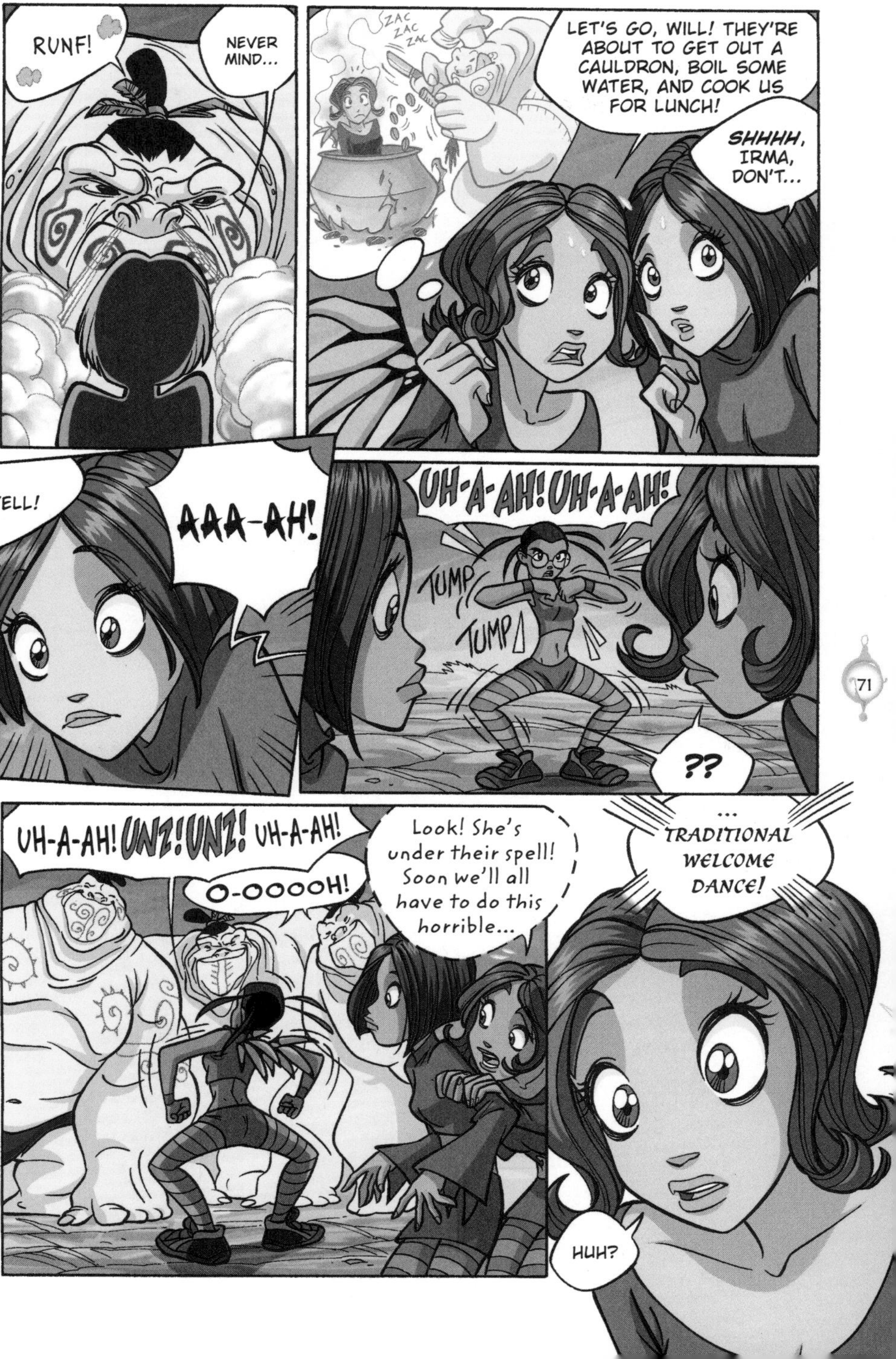

RUNF!
NEVER MIND...
ZAC ZAC ZAC
LET'S GO, WILL! THEY'RE ABOUT TO GET OUT A CAULDRON, BOIL SOME WATER, AND COOK US FOR LUNCH!
SHHHH, IRMA, DON'T...
...YELL!
AAA-AH!
UH-A-AH! UH-A-AH!
TUMP
TUMP
??
UH-A-AH! UNZ! UNZ! UH-A-AH!
O-OOOOH!
Look! She's under their spell! Soon we'll all have to do this horrible...
... TRADITIONAL WELCOME DANCE!
HUH?

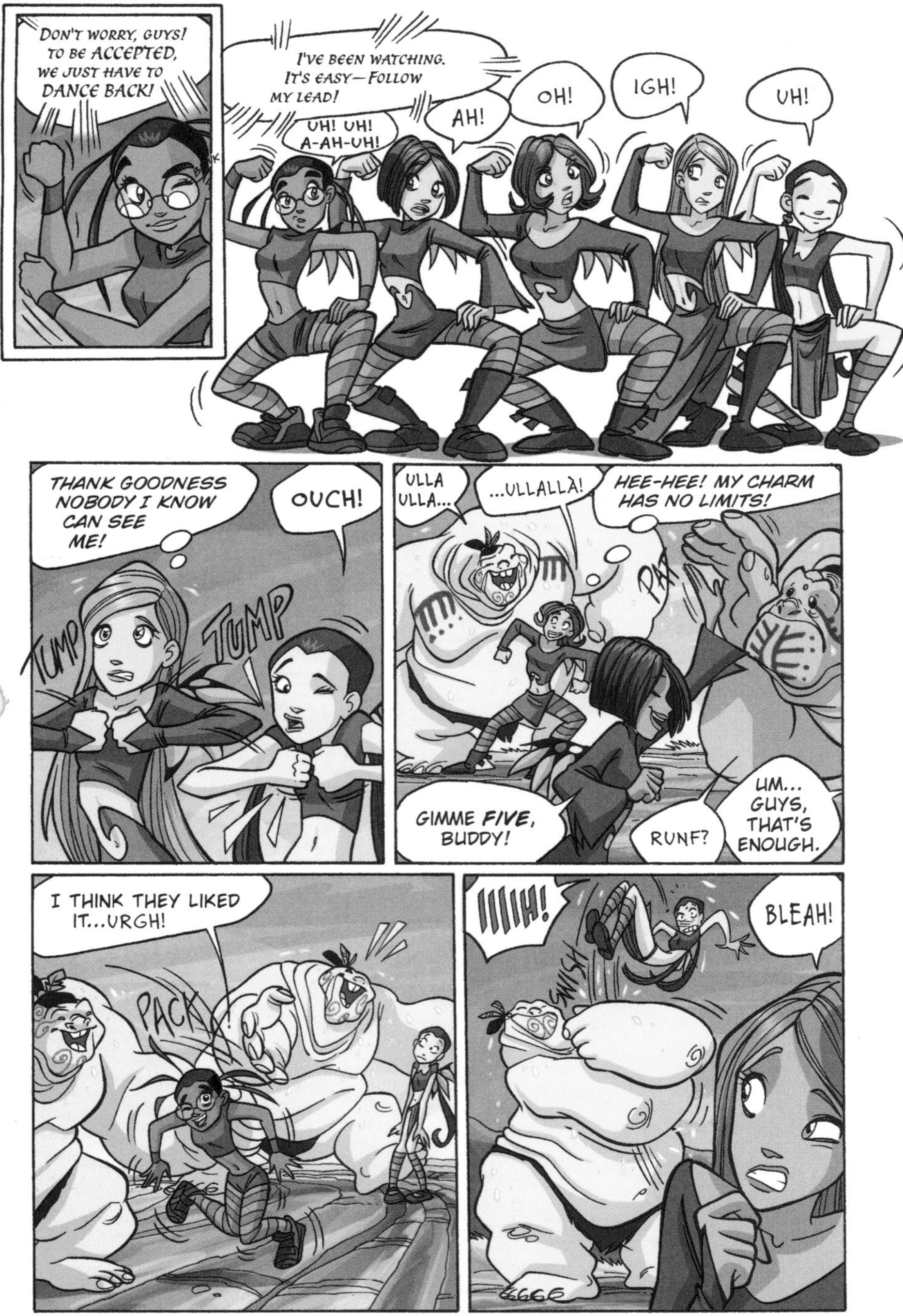
DON'T WORRY, GUYS! TO BE ACCEPTED, WE JUST HAVE TO DANCE BACK!
I'VE BEEN WATCHING. IT'S EASY—FOLLOW MY LEAD!
UH! UH! A-AH-UH!
AH!
OH!
IGH!
UH!
THANK GOODNESS NOBODY I KNOW CAN SEE ME!
OUCH!
TUMP
TUMP
ULLA ULLA...
...ULLALLÀ!
HEE-HEE! MY CHARM HAS NO LIMITS!
PAT
GIMME FIVE, BUDDY!
RUNF?
UM... GUYS, THAT'S ENOUGH.
I THINK THEY LIKED IT...URGH!
PACK
IIIIH!
SWISH
BLEAH!

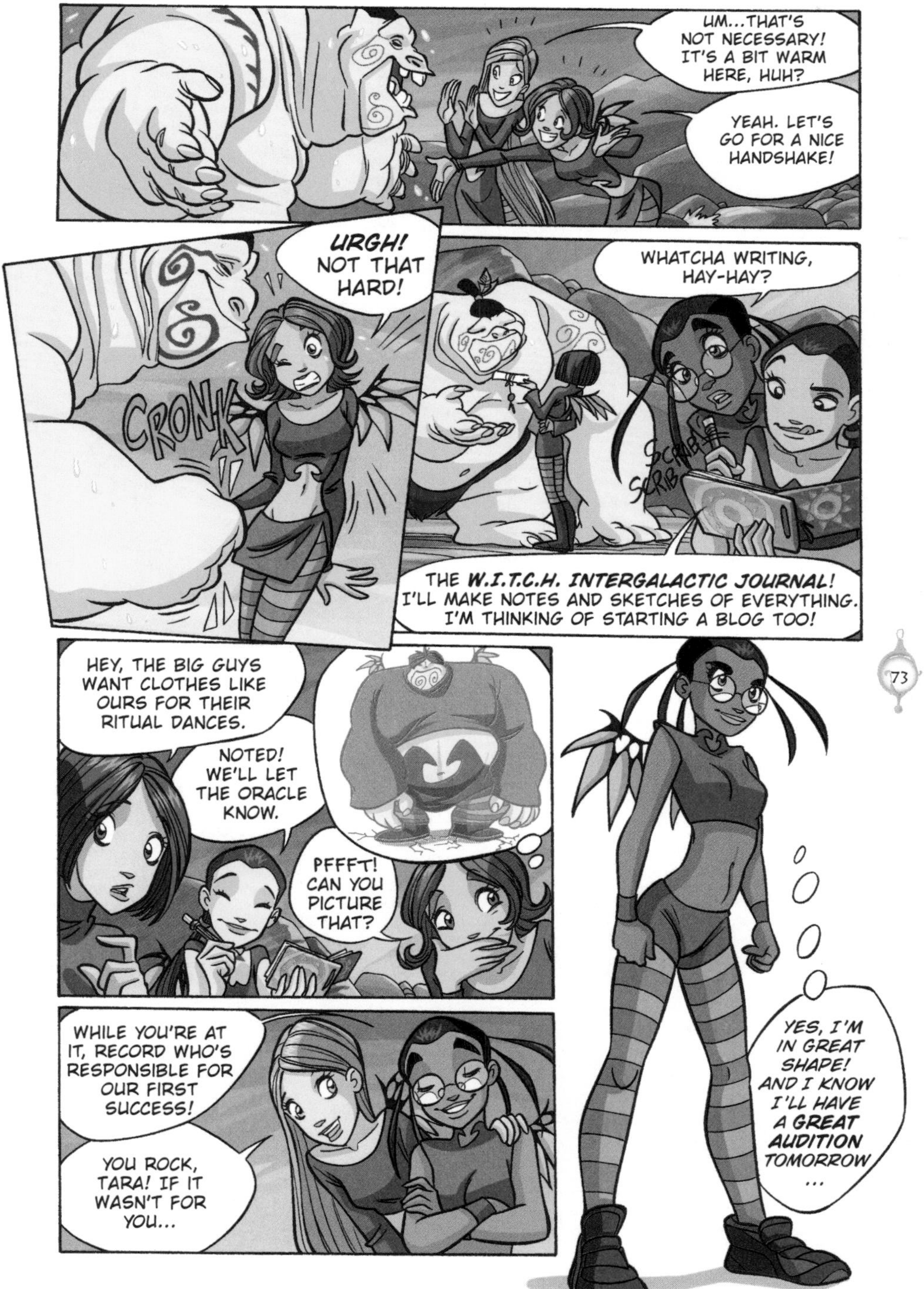
UM...THAT'S NOT NECESSARY! IT'S A BIT WARM HERE, HUH?
YEAH. LET'S GO FOR A NICE HANDSHAKE!
URGH! NOT THAT HARD!
CRONK
WHATCHA WRITING, HAY-HAY?
SCRIB SCRIB
THE W.I.T.C.H. INTERGALACTIC JOURNAL! I'LL MAKE NOTES AND SKETCHES OF EVERYTHING. I'M THINKING OF STARTING A BLOG TOO!
HEY, THE BIG GUYS WANT CLOTHES LIKE OURS FOR THEIR RITUAL DANCES.
NOTED! WE'LL LET THE ORACLE KNOW.
PFFFT! CAN YOU PICTURE THAT?
WHILE YOU'RE AT IT, RECORD WHO'S RESPONSIBLE FOR OUR FIRST SUCCESS!
YOU ROCK, TARA! IF IT WASN'T FOR YOU...
YES, I'M IN GREAT SHAPE! AND I KNOW I'LL HAVE A GREAT AUDITION TOMORROW ...

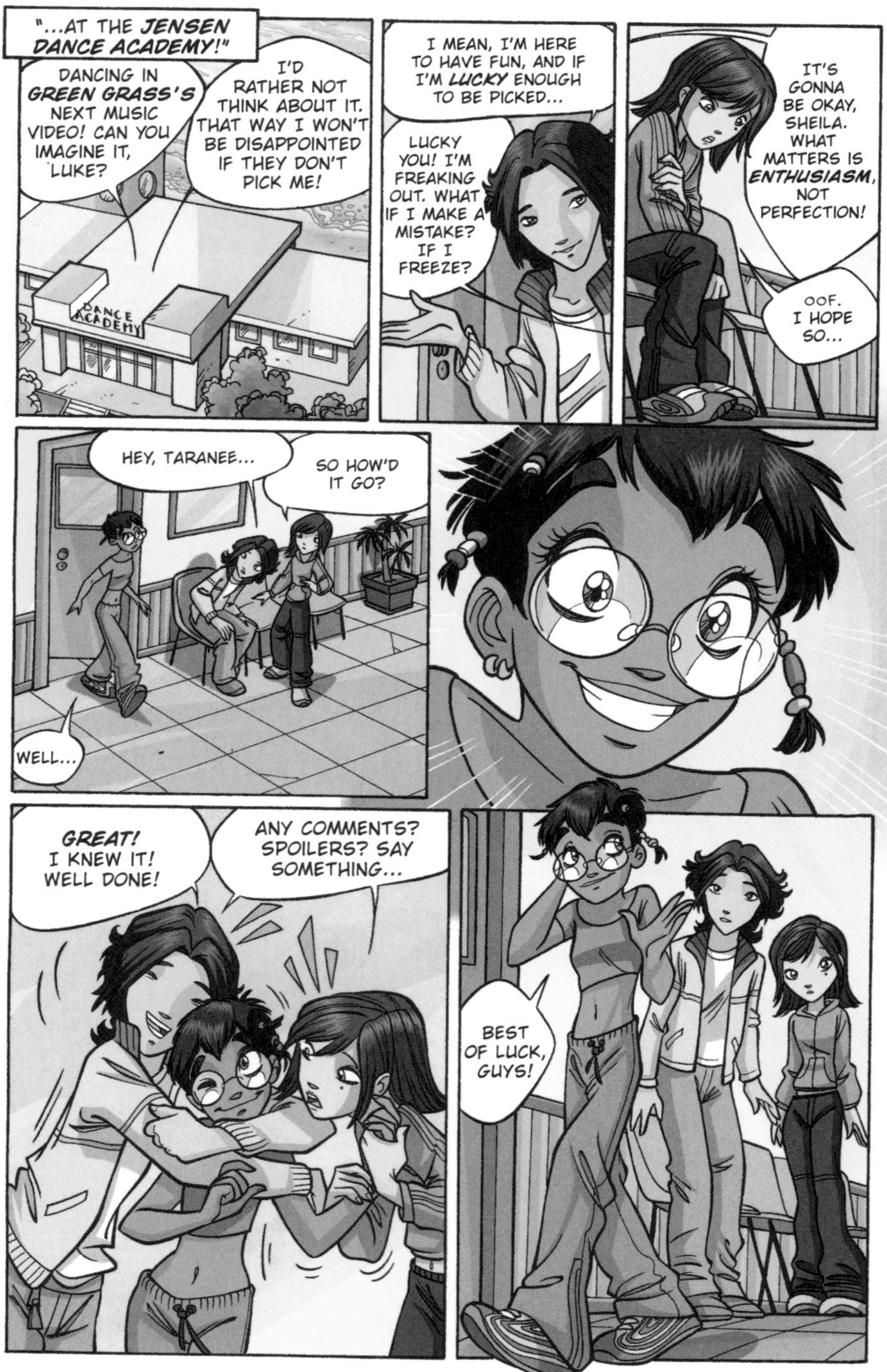
"...AT THE JENSEN DANCE ACADEMY!"
DANCING IN GREEN GRASS'S NEXT MUSIC VIDEO! CAN YOU IMAGINE IT, LUKE?
I'D RATHER NOT THINK ABOUT IT. THAT WAY I WON'T BE DISAPPOINTED IF THEY DON'T PICK ME!
DANCE ACADEMY
I MEAN, I'M HERE TO HAVE FUN, AND IF I'M LUCKY ENOUGH TO BE PICKED...
LUCKY YOU! I'M FREAKING OUT. WHAT IF I MAKE A MISTAKE? IF I FREEZE?
IT'S GONNA BE OKAY, SHEILA. WHAT MATTERS IS ENTHUSIASM, NOT PERFECTION!
OOF. I HOPE SO...
HEY, TARANEE...
SO HOW'D IT GO?
WELL...
GREAT! I KNEW IT! WELL DONE!
ANY COMMENTS? SPOILERS? SAY SOMETHING...
BEST OF LUCK, GUYS!

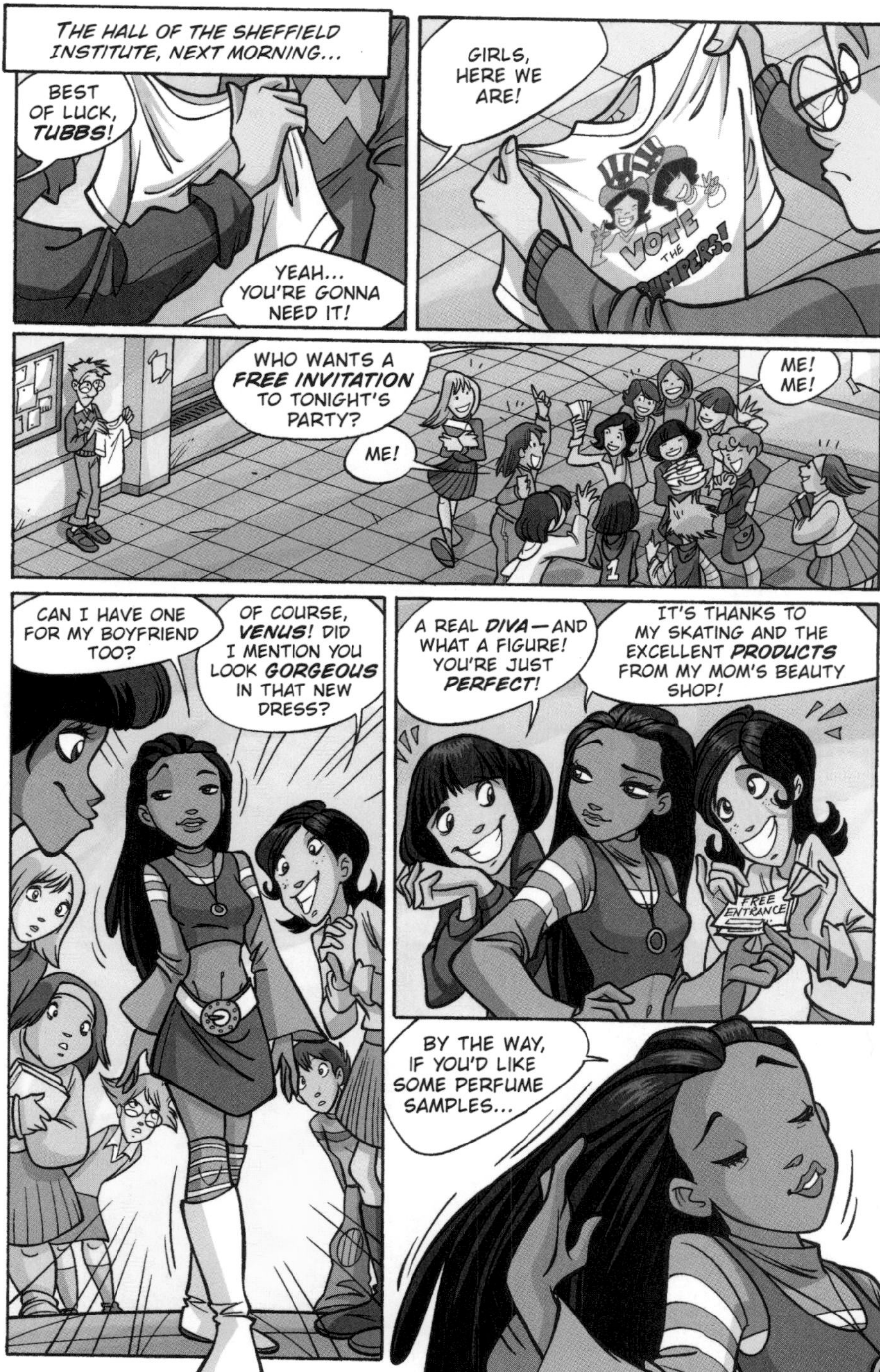
THE HALL OF THE SHEFFIELD INSTITUTE, NEXT MORNING...
BEST OF LUCK, TUBBS!
YEAH... YOU'RE GONNA NEED IT!
GIRLS, HERE WE ARE!
VOTE THE PUMPKINS!
WHO WANTS A FREE INVITATION TO TONIGHT'S PARTY?
ME!
ME! ME!
CAN I HAVE ONE FOR MY BOYFRIEND TOO?
OF COURSE, VENUS! DID I MENTION YOU LOOK GORGEOUS IN THAT NEW DRESS?
A REAL DIVA—AND WHAT A FIGURE! YOU'RE JUST PERFECT!
IT'S THANKS TO MY SKATING AND THE EXCELLENT PRODUCTS FROM MY MOM'S BEAUTY SHOP!
FREE ENTRANCE
BY THE WAY, IF YOU'D LIKE SOME PERFUME SAMPLES...

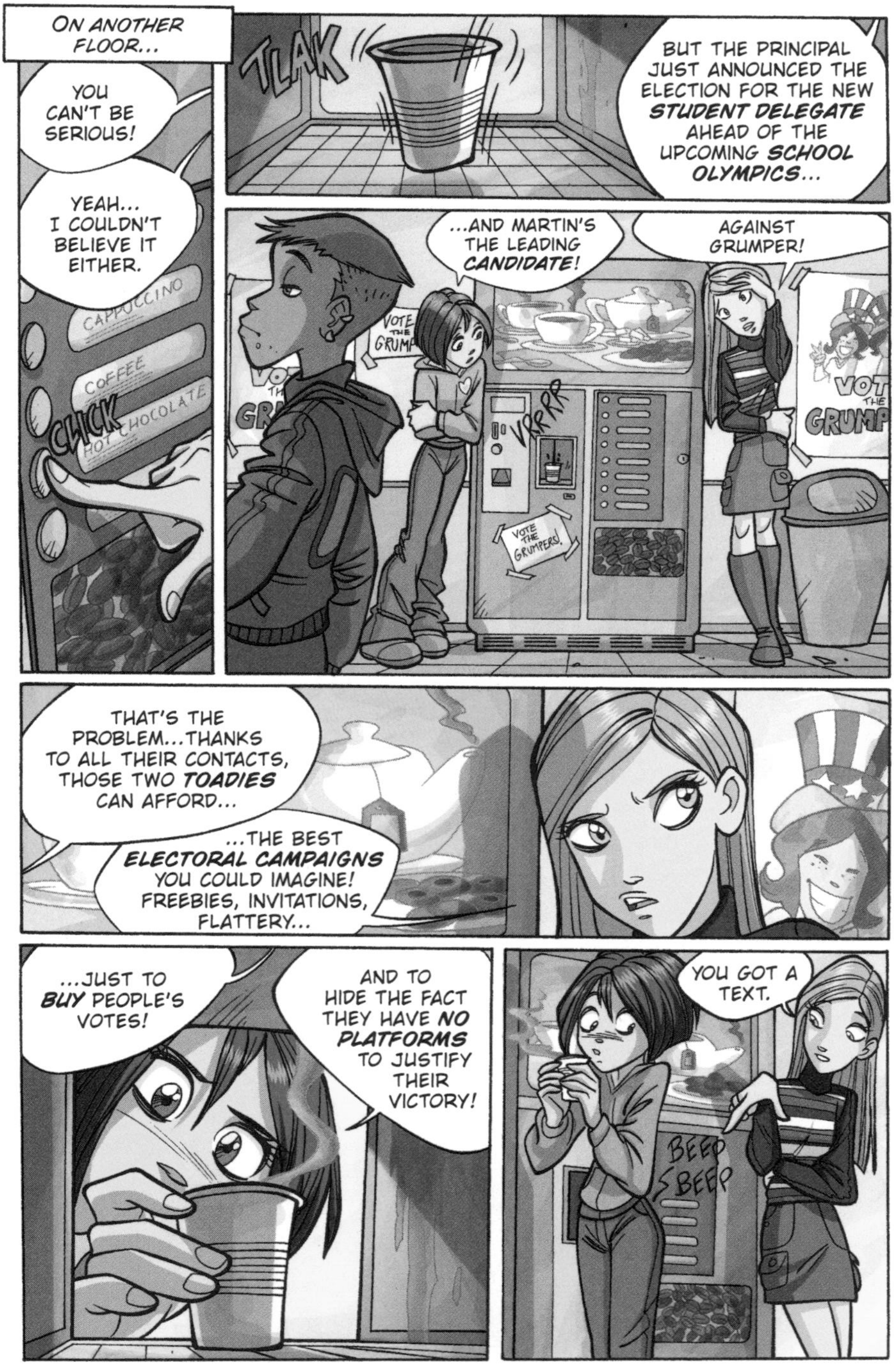
ON ANOTHER FLOOR...
YOU CAN'T BE SERIOUS!
TLAK
BUT THE PRINCIPAL JUST ANNOUNCED THE ELECTION FOR THE NEW **STUDENT DELEGATE** AHEAD OF THE UPCOMING **SCHOOL OLYMPICS**...
YEAH... I COULDN'T BELIEVE IT EITHER.
CAPPUCCINO
COFFEE
HOT CHOCOLATE
CLICK
...AND MARTIN'S THE LEADING **CANDIDATE**!
AGAINST GRUMPER!
VOTE THE GRUMP
VOTE THE GRUMPERS!
VRRRR
VOTE THE GRUMP
THAT'S THE PROBLEM...THANKS TO ALL THEIR CONTACTS, THOSE TWO **TOADIES** CAN AFFORD...
...THE BEST **ELECTORAL CAMPAIGNS** YOU COULD IMAGINE! FREEBIES, INVITATIONS, FLATTERY...
...JUST TO **BUY** PEOPLE'S VOTES!
AND TO HIDE THE FACT THEY HAVE **NO PLATFORMS** TO JUSTIFY THEIR VICTORY!
YOU GOT A TEXT.
BEEP BEEP

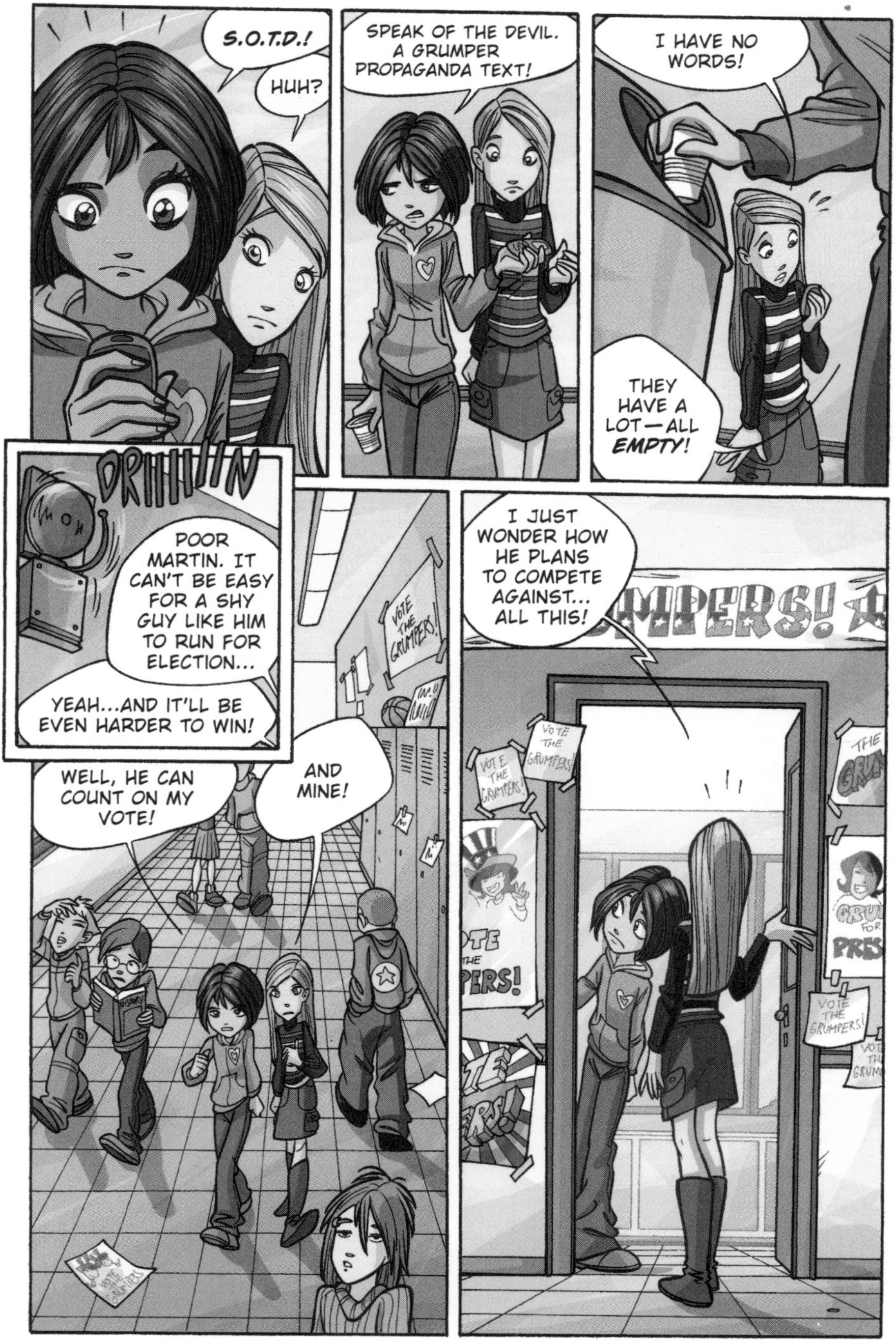
S.O.T.D.!
HUH?
SPEAK OF THE DEVIL. A GRUMPER PROPAGANDA TEXT!
I HAVE NO WORDS!
THEY HAVE A LOT—ALL EMPTY!
DRIIIIIIN
POOR MARTIN. IT CAN'T BE EASY FOR A SHY GUY LIKE HIM TO RUN FOR ELECTION...
YEAH...AND IT'LL BE EVEN HARDER TO WIN!
VOTE THE GRUMPERS!
WELL, HE CAN COUNT ON MY VOTE!
AND MINE!
I JUST WONDER HOW HE PLANS TO COMPETE AGAINST... ALL THIS!
VOTE THE GRUMPERS!
VOTE THE GRUMPERS!
VOTE THE GRUMPERS!

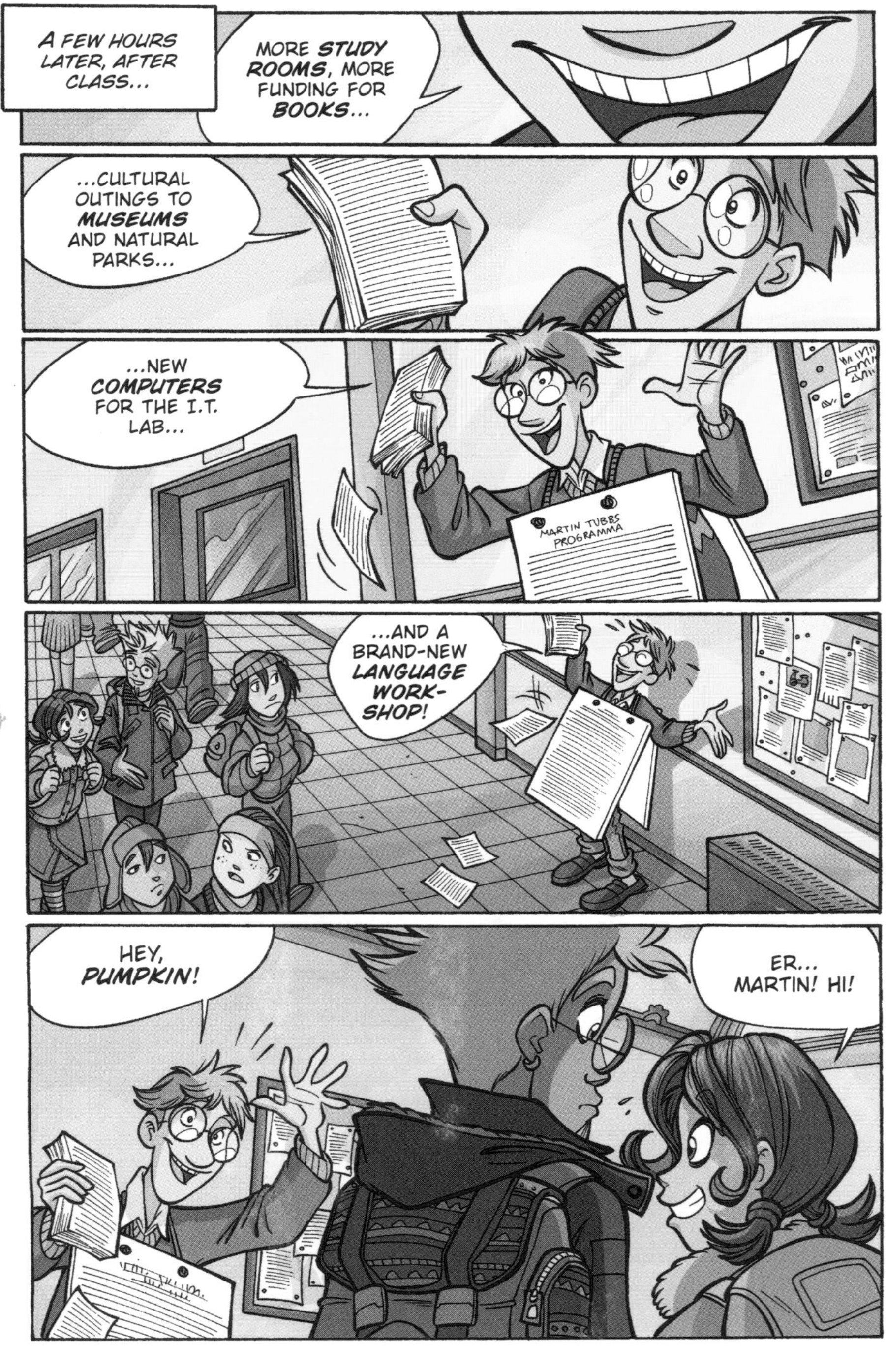

A FEW HOURS LATER, AFTER CLASS...
MORE STUDY ROOMS, MORE FUNDING FOR BOOKS...
...CULTURAL OUTINGS TO MUSEUMS AND NATURAL PARKS...
...NEW COMPUTERS FOR THE I.T. LAB...
MARTIN TUBBS PROGRAMMA
...AND A BRAND-NEW LANGUAGE WORK-SHOP!
HEY, PUMPKIN!
ER... MARTIN! HI!

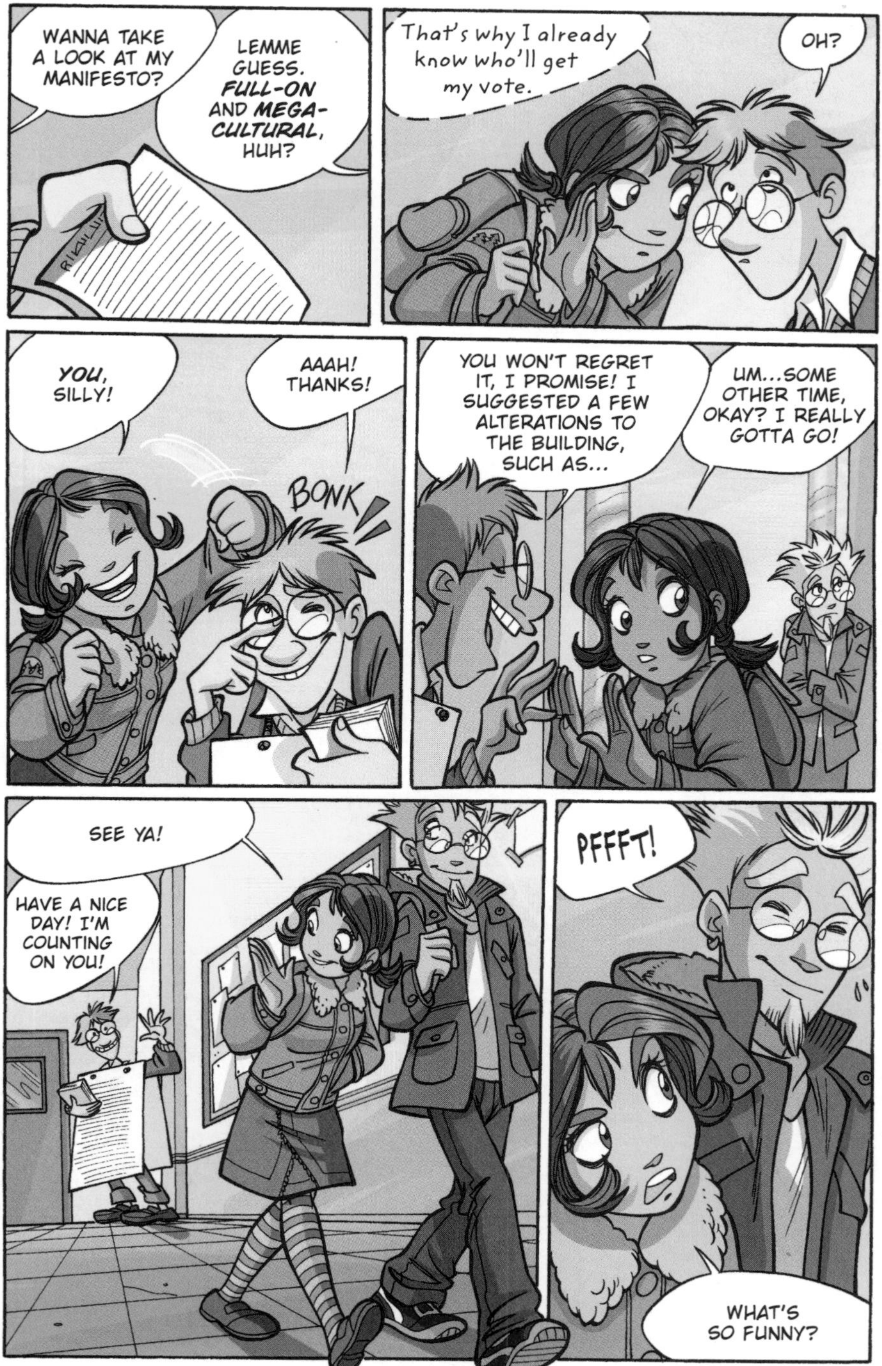
WANNA TAKE A LOOK AT MY MANIFESTO?
LEMME GUESS. FULL-ON AND MEGA-CULTURAL, HUH?
That's why I already know who'll get my vote.
OH?
YOU, SILLY!
AAAH! THANKS!
BONK
YOU WON'T REGRET IT, I PROMISE! I SUGGESTED A FEW ALTERATIONS TO THE BUILDING, SUCH AS...
UM...SOME OTHER TIME, OKAY? I REALLY GOTTA GO!
SEE YA!
HAVE A NICE DAY! I'M COUNTING ON YOU!
PFFFT!
WHAT'S SO FUNNY?

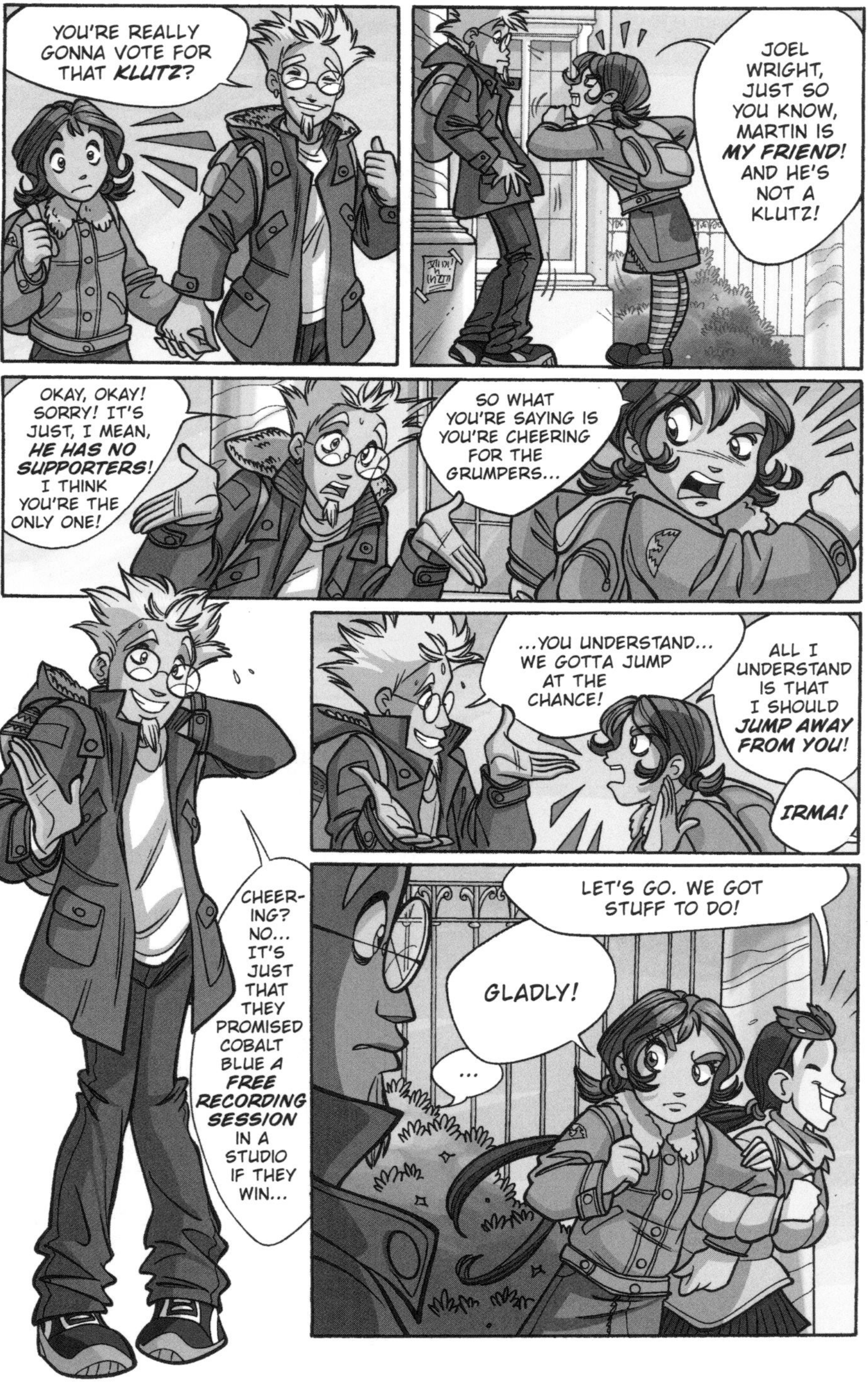
YOU'RE REALLY GONNA VOTE FOR THAT KLUTZ?
JOEL WRIGHT, JUST SO YOU KNOW, MARTIN IS MY FRIEND! AND HE'S NOT A KLUTZ!
OKAY, OKAY! SORRY! IT'S JUST, I MEAN, HE HAS NO SUPPORTERS! I THINK YOU'RE THE ONLY ONE!
SO WHAT YOU'RE SAYING IS YOU'RE CHEERING FOR THE GRUMPERS...
CHEERING? NO... IT'S JUST THAT THEY PROMISED COBALT BLUE A FREE RECORDING SESSION IN A STUDIO IF THEY WIN...
...YOU UNDERSTAND... WE GOTTA JUMP AT THE CHANCE!
ALL I UNDERSTAND IS THAT I SHOULD JUMP AWAY FROM YOU!
IRMA!
LET'S GO. WE GOT STUFF TO DO!
GLADLY!
...

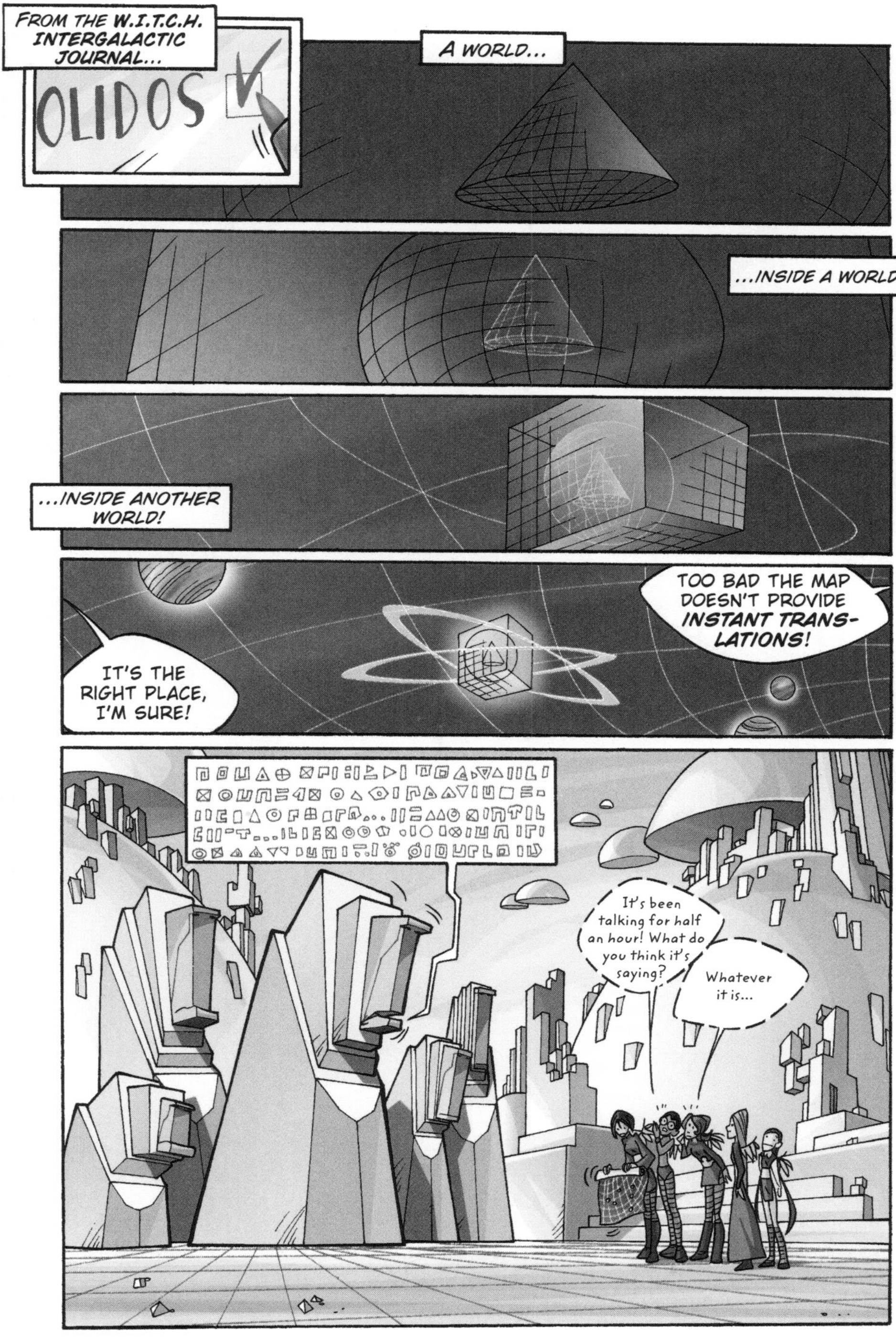
FROM THE W.I.T.C.H. INTERGALACTIC JOURNAL...
OLIDOS
A WORLD...
...INSIDE A WORLD...
...INSIDE ANOTHER WORLD!
IT'S THE RIGHT PLACE, I'M SURE!
TOO BAD THE MAP DOESN'T PROVIDE INSTANT TRANSLATIONS!
It's been talking for half an hour! What do you think it's saying?
Whatever it is...

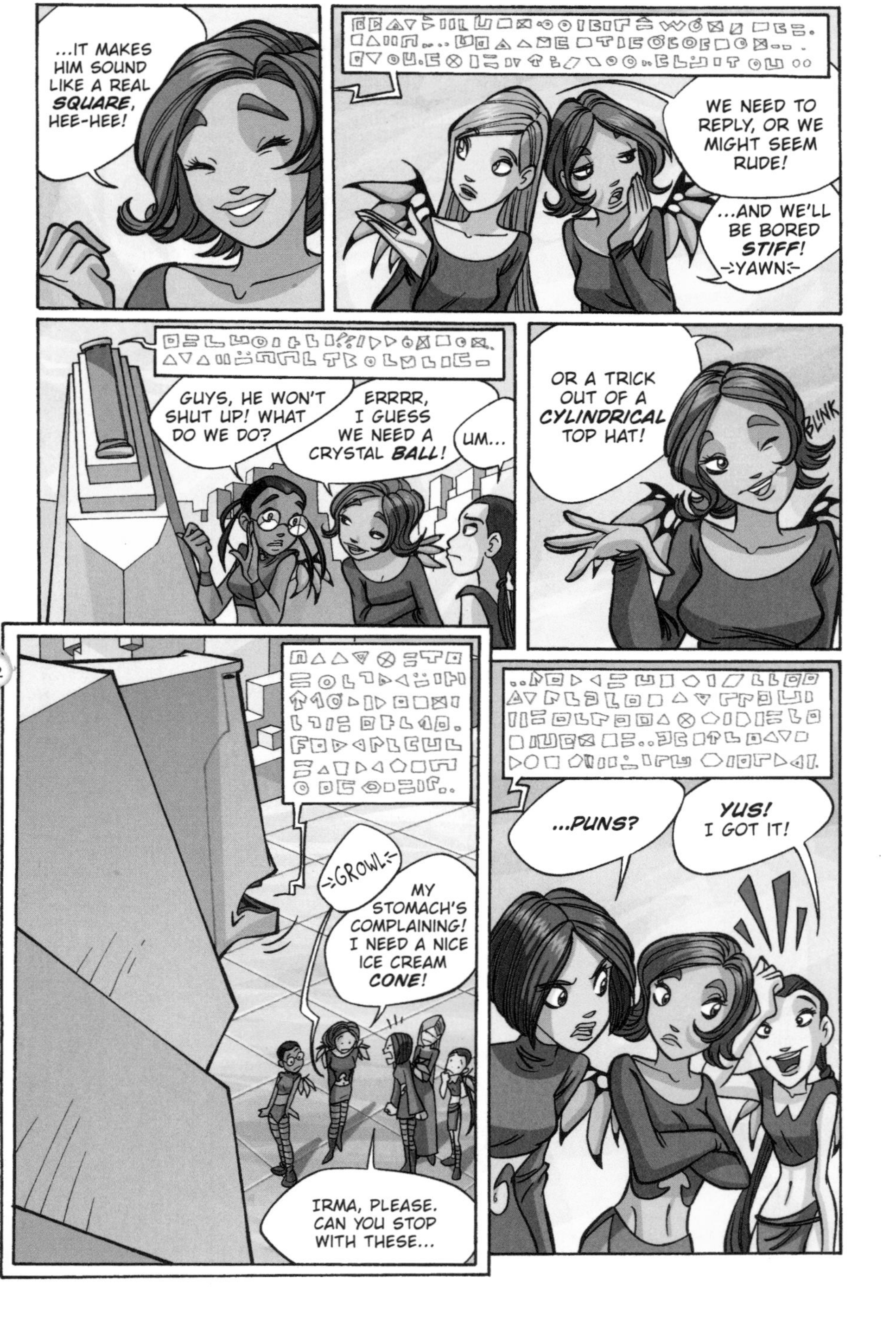

...IT MAKES HIM SOUND LIKE A REAL SQUARE, HEE-HEE!
WE NEED TO REPLY, OR WE MIGHT SEEM RUDE!
...AND WE'LL BE BORED STIFF!
YAWN
GUYS, HE WON'T SHUT UP! WHAT DO WE DO?
ERRRR, I GUESS WE NEED A CRYSTAL BALL!
UM...
OR A TRICK OUT OF A CYLINDRICAL TOP HAT!
BLINK
GROWL
MY STOMACH'S COMPLAINING! I NEED A NICE ICE CREAM CONE!
IRMA, PLEASE. CAN YOU STOP WITH THESE...
...PUNS?
YUS! I GOT IT!

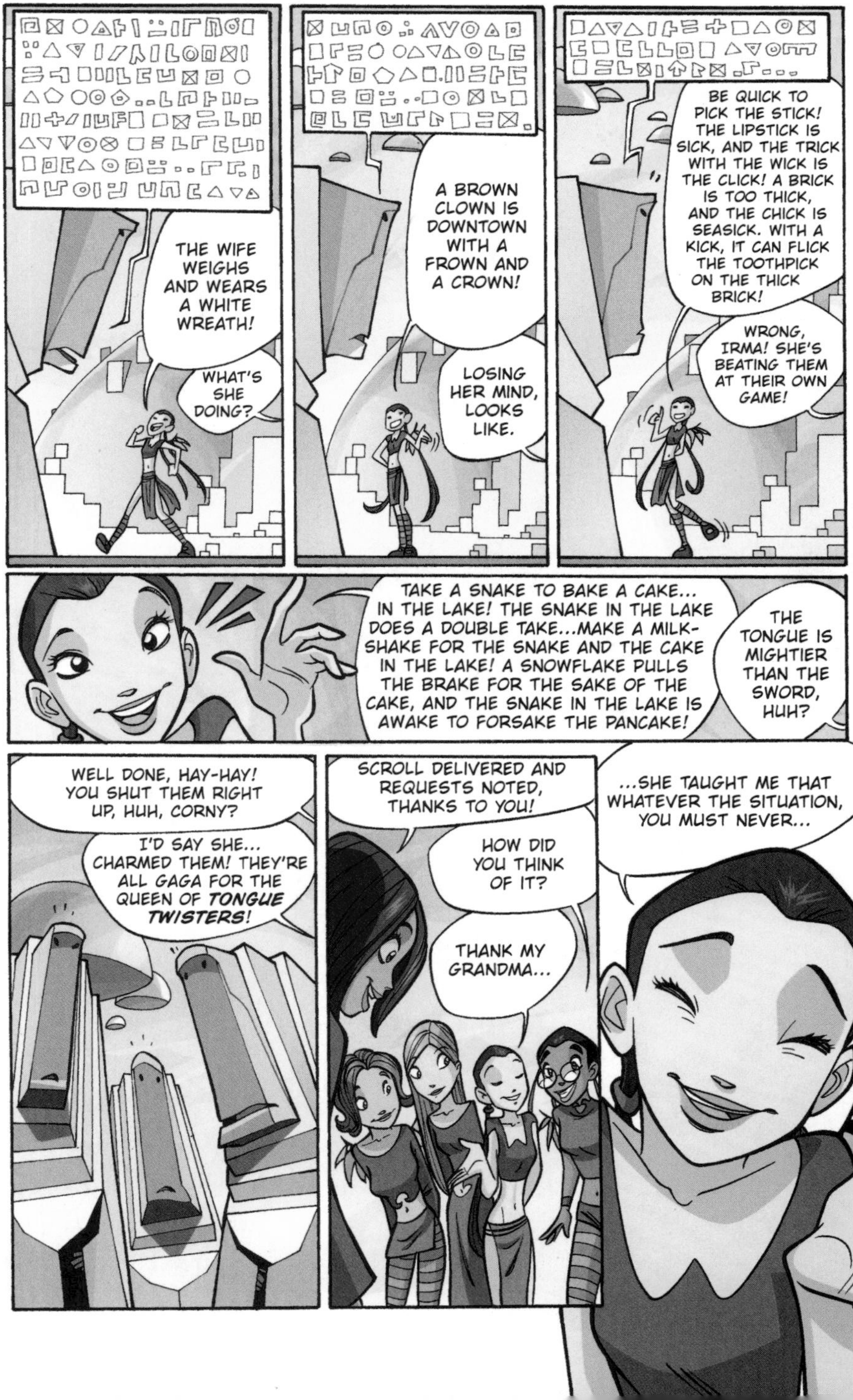
THE WIFE WEIGHS AND WEARS A WHITE WREATH!
WHAT'S SHE DOING?
A BROWN CLOWN IS DOWNTOWN WITH A FROWN AND A CROWN!
LOSING HER MIND, LOOKS LIKE.
BE QUICK TO PICK THE STICK! THE LIPSTICK IS SICK, AND THE TRICK WITH THE WICK IS THE CLICK! A BRICK IS TOO THICK, AND THE CHICK IS SEASICK. WITH A KICK, IT CAN FLICK THE TOOTHPICK ON THE THICK BRICK!
WRONG, IRMA! SHE'S BEATING THEM AT THEIR OWN GAME!
TAKE A SNAKE TO BAKE A CAKE... IN THE LAKE! THE SNAKE IN THE LAKE DOES A DOUBLE TAKE...MAKE A MILK-SHAKE FOR THE SNAKE AND THE CAKE IN THE LAKE! A SNOWFLAKE PULLS THE BRAKE FOR THE SAKE OF THE CAKE, AND THE SNAKE IN THE LAKE IS AWAKE TO FORSAKE THE PANCAKE!
THE TONGUE IS MIGHTIER THAN THE SWORD, HUH?
WELL DONE, HAY-HAY! YOU SHUT THEM RIGHT UP, HUH, CORNY?
I'D SAY SHE... CHARMED THEM! THEY'RE ALL GAGA FOR THE QUEEN OF TONGUE TWISTERS!
SCROLL DELIVERED AND REQUESTS NOTED, THANKS TO YOU!
HOW DID YOU THINK OF IT?
THANK MY GRANDMA...
...SHE TAUGHT ME THAT WHATEVER THE SITUATION, YOU MUST NEVER...

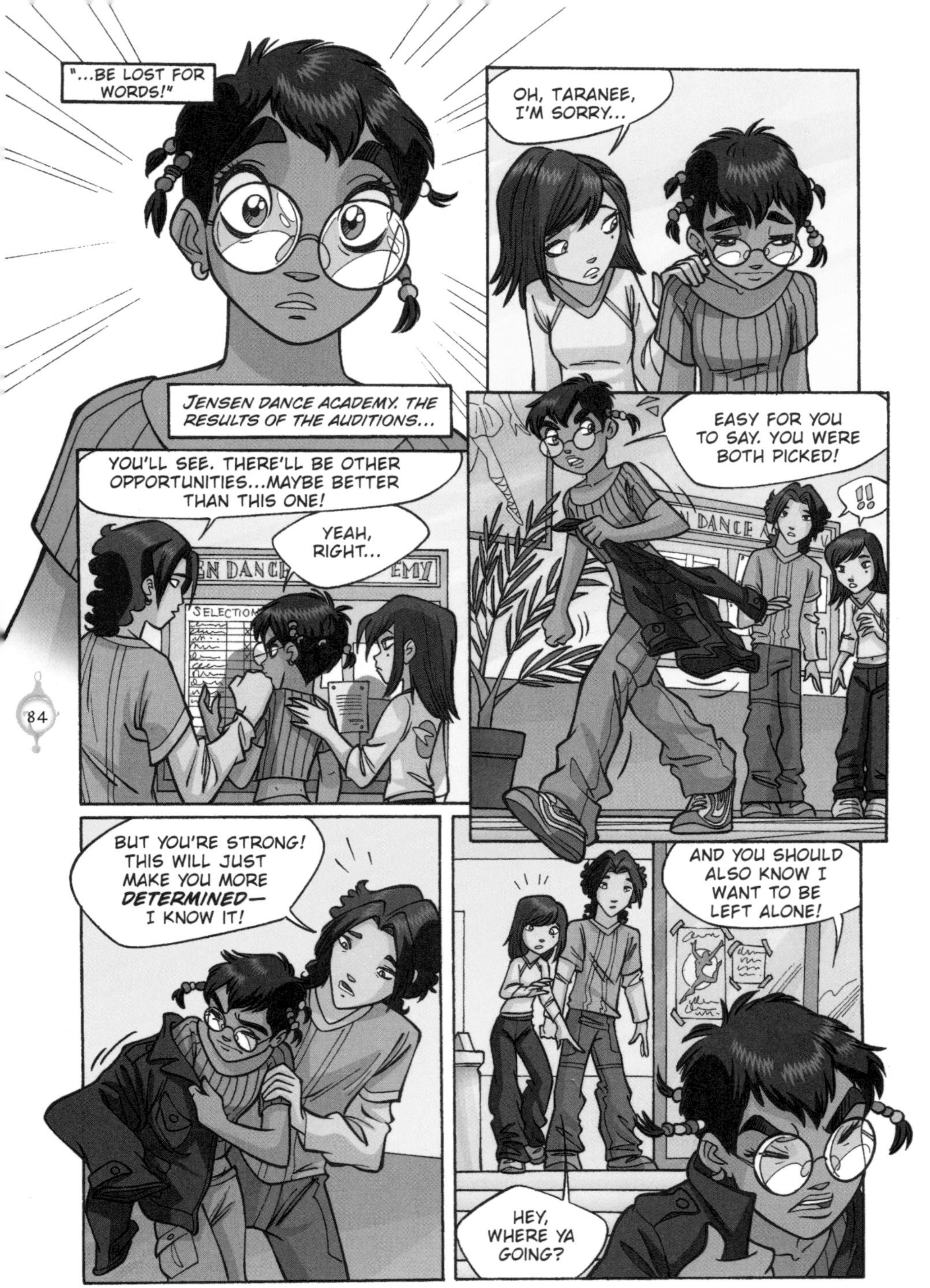
"...BE LOST FOR WORDS!"
OH, TARANEE, I'M SORRY...
JENSEN DANCE ACADEMY. THE RESULTS OF THE AUDITIONS...
YOU'LL SEE. THERE'LL BE OTHER OPPORTUNITIES...MAYBE BETTER THAN THIS ONE!
YEAH, RIGHT...
EASY FOR YOU TO SAY. YOU WERE BOTH PICKED!
!!
BUT YOU'RE STRONG! THIS WILL JUST MAKE YOU MORE DETERMINED— I KNOW IT!
AND YOU SHOULD ALSO KNOW I WANT TO BE LEFT ALONE!
HEY, WHERE YA GOING?

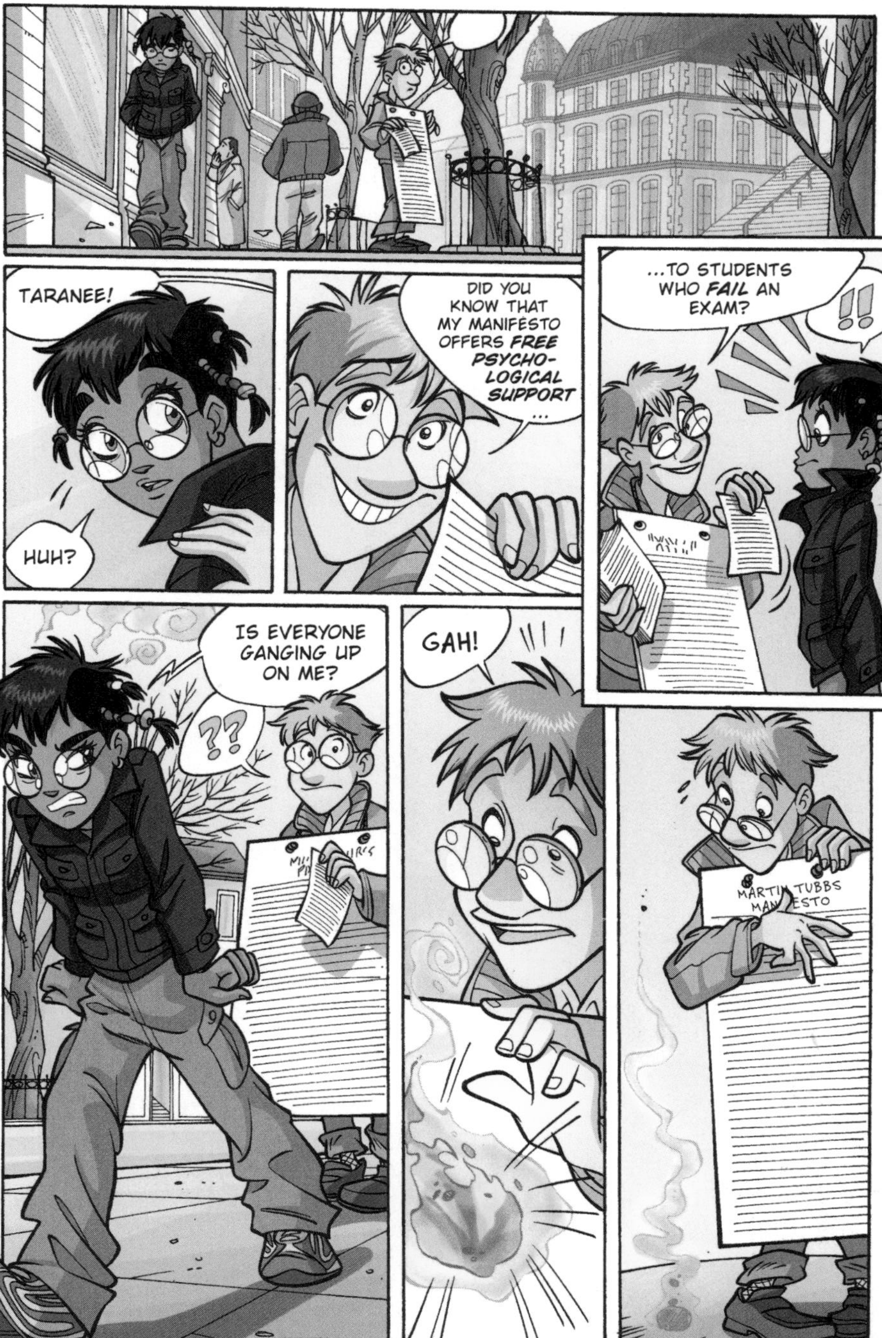
TARANEE!
HUH?
DID YOU KNOW THAT MY MANIFESTO OFFERS FREE PSYCHO-LOGICAL SUPPORT ...
...TO STUDENTS WHO FAIL AN EXAM?
!!
IS EVERYONE GANGING UP ON ME?
??
GAH!
MARTIN TUBBS MANIFESTO

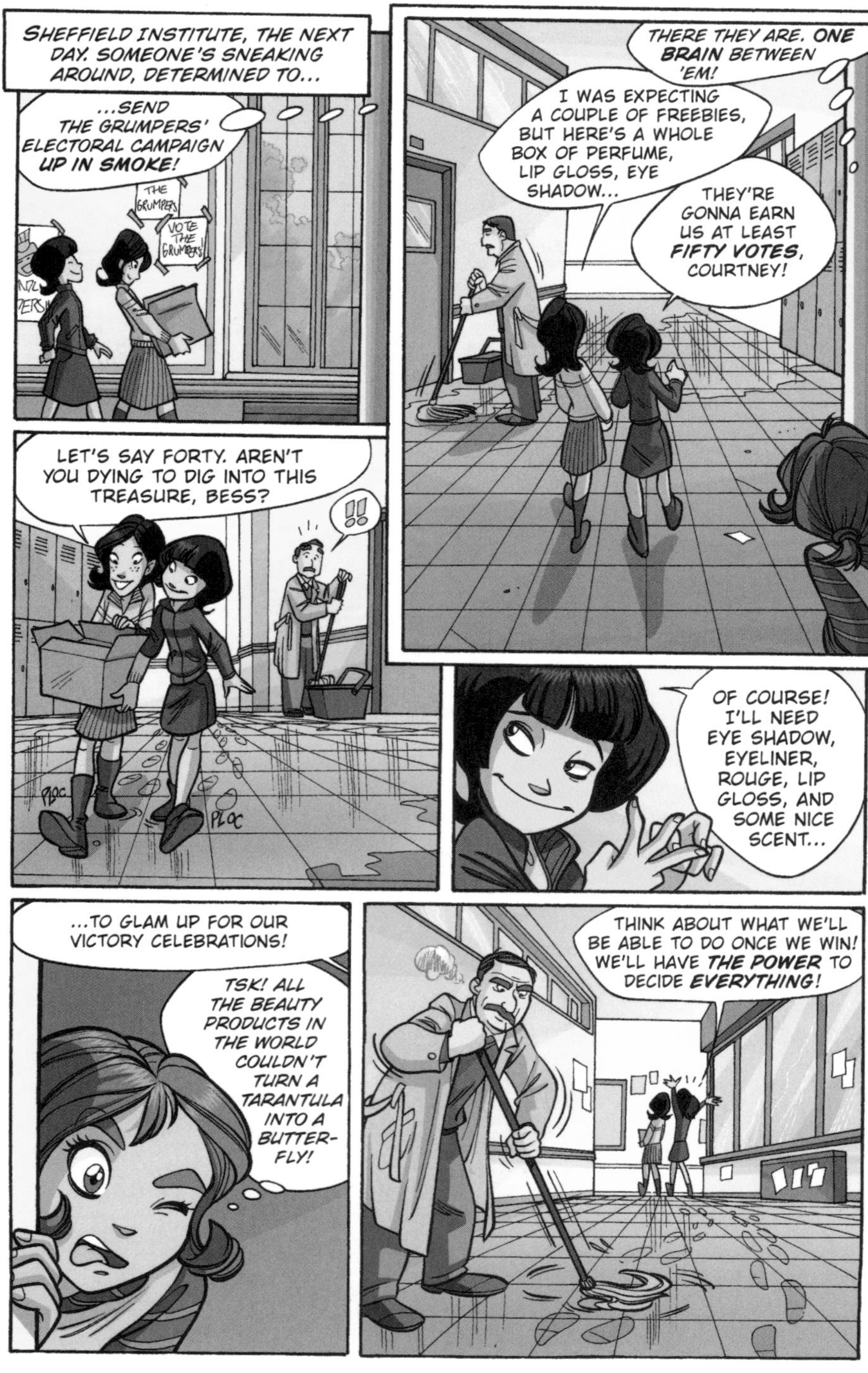

SHEFFIELD INSTITUTE, THE NEXT DAY. SOMEONE'S SNEAKING AROUND, DETERMINED TO...
...SEND THE GRUMPERS' ELECTORAL CAMPAIGN UP IN SMOKE!
THE GRUMPERS
VOTE THE GRUMPERS!
THERE THEY ARE. ONE BRAIN BETWEEN 'EM!
I WAS EXPECTING A COUPLE OF FREEBIES, BUT HERE'S A WHOLE BOX OF PERFUME, LIP GLOSS, EYE SHADOW...
THEY'RE GONNA EARN US AT LEAST FIFTY VOTES, COURTNEY!
LET'S SAY FORTY. AREN'T YOU DYING TO DIG INTO THIS TREASURE, BESS?
!!
PLOC
PLOC
OF COURSE! I'LL NEED EYE SHADOW, EYELINER, ROUGE, LIP GLOSS, AND SOME NICE SCENT...
...TO GLAM UP FOR OUR VICTORY CELEBRATIONS!
TSK! ALL THE BEAUTY PRODUCTS IN THE WORLD COULDN'T TURN A TARANTULA INTO A BUTTER-FLY!
THINK ABOUT WHAT WE'LL BE ABLE TO DO ONCE WE WIN! WE'LL HAVE THE POWER TO DECIDE EVERYTHING!

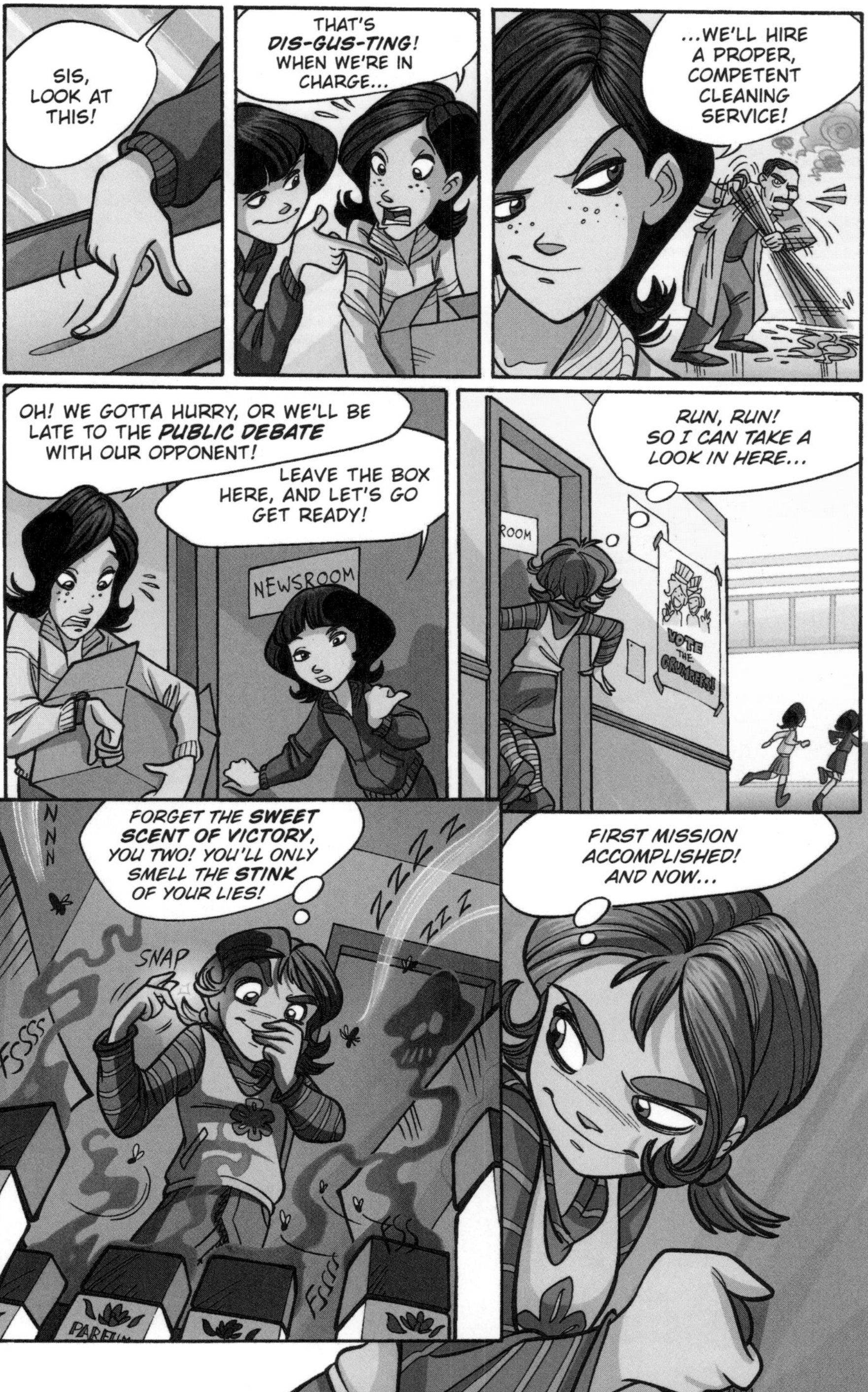
SIS, LOOK AT THIS!
THAT'S **DIS-GUS-TING!** WHEN WE'RE IN CHARGE...
...WE'LL HIRE A PROPER, COMPETENT CLEANING SERVICE!
OH! WE GOTTA HURRY, OR WE'LL BE LATE TO THE **PUBLIC DEBATE** WITH OUR OPPONENT!
LEAVE THE BOX HERE, AND LET'S GO GET READY!
NEWSROOM
RUN, RUN! SO I CAN TAKE A LOOK IN HERE...
ROOM
*FORGET THE **SWEET SCENT OF VICTORY,** YOU TWO! YOU'LL ONLY SMELL THE **STINK** OF YOUR LIES!*
NNN
ZZZZ
ZZZ
SNAP
FSSSS
FSS
FSSSS
FIRST MISSION ACCOMPLISHED! AND NOW...

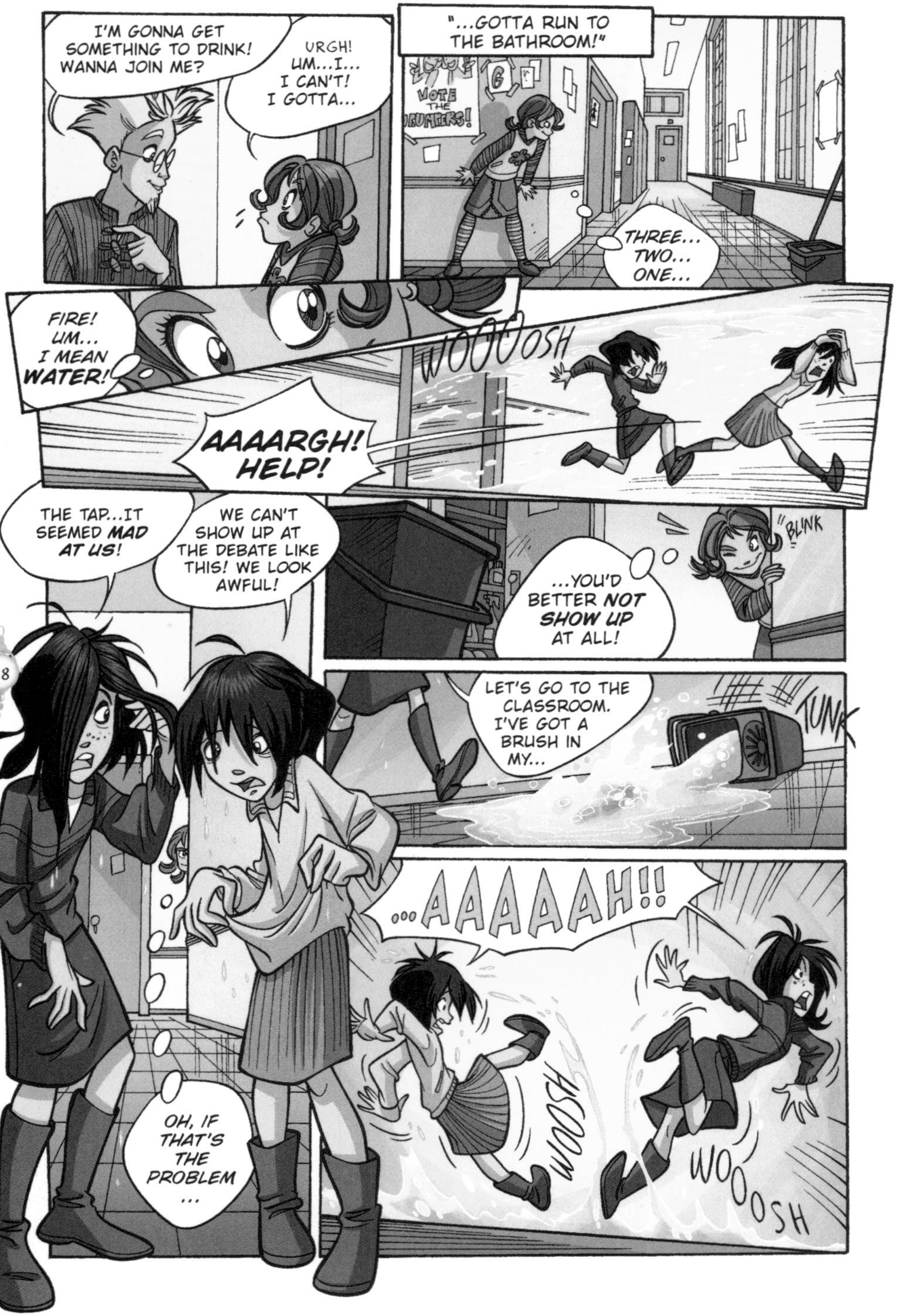

I'M GONNA GET SOMETHING TO DRINK! WANNA JOIN ME?
URGH! UM...I... I CAN'T! I GOTTA...
"...GOTTA RUN TO THE BATHROOM!"
VOTE THE DRUMMERS!
THREE... TWO... ONE...
FIRE! UM... I MEAN WATER!
WOOOOSH
AAAARGH! HELP!
THE TAP...IT SEEMED MAD AT US!
WE CAN'T SHOW UP AT THE DEBATE LIKE THIS! WE LOOK AWFUL!
BLINK
...YOU'D BETTER NOT SHOW UP AT ALL!
LET'S GO TO THE CLASSROOM. I'VE GOT A BRUSH IN MY...
TUNK
...AAAAAH!!
OH, IF THAT'S THE PROBLEM ...
WOOSH
WOOOOSH

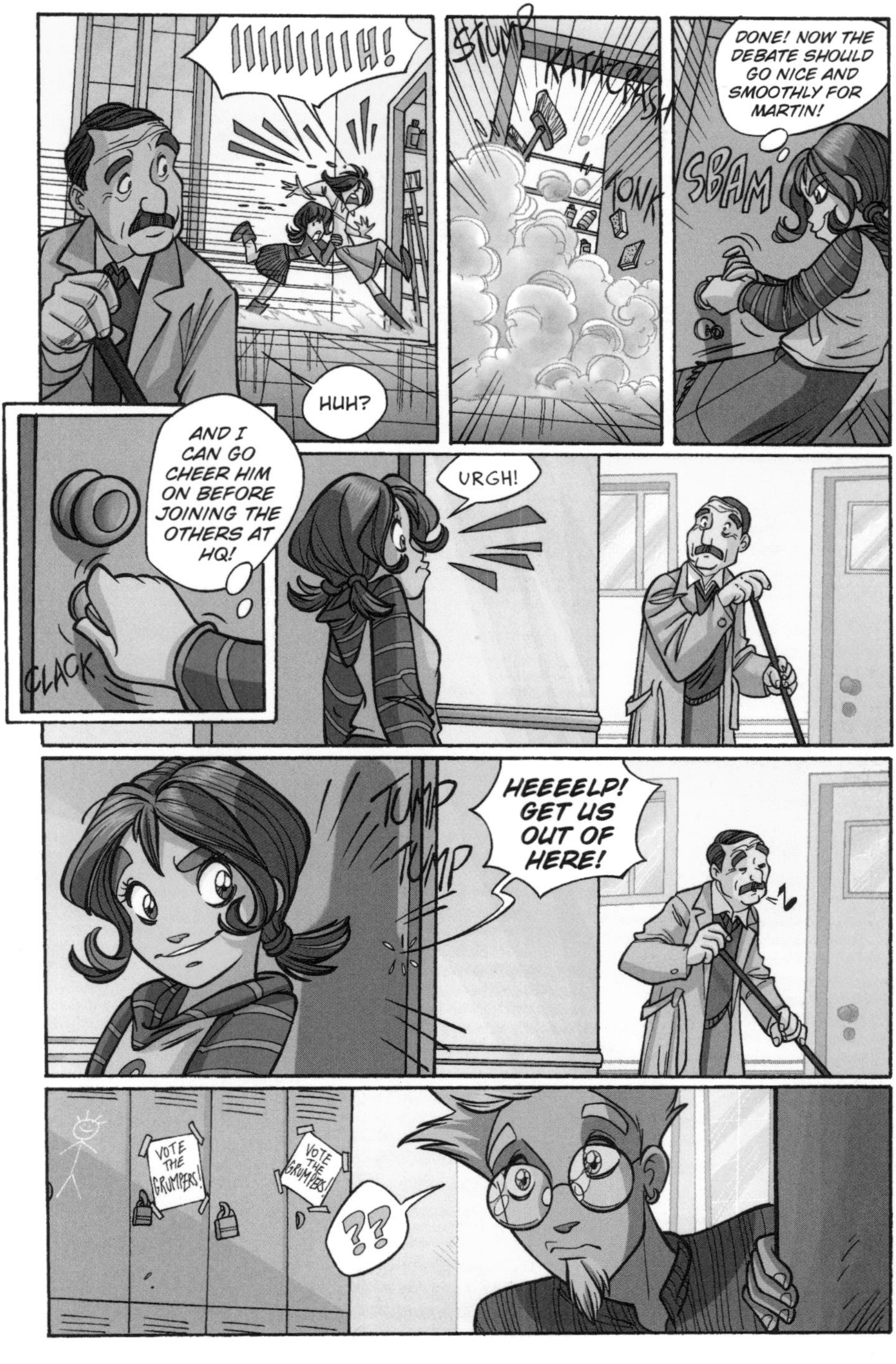
IIIIIIIIIH!
HUH?
STUMP
KATACRASH
TONK
DONE! NOW THE DEBATE SHOULD GO NICE AND SMOOTHLY FOR MARTIN!
SBAM
AND I CAN GO CHEER HIM ON BEFORE JOINING THE OTHERS AT HQ!
CLACK
URGH!
TUMP
TUMP
HEEEELP! GET US OUT OF HERE!
VOTE THE GRUMPERS!
VOTE THE GRUMPERS!
??

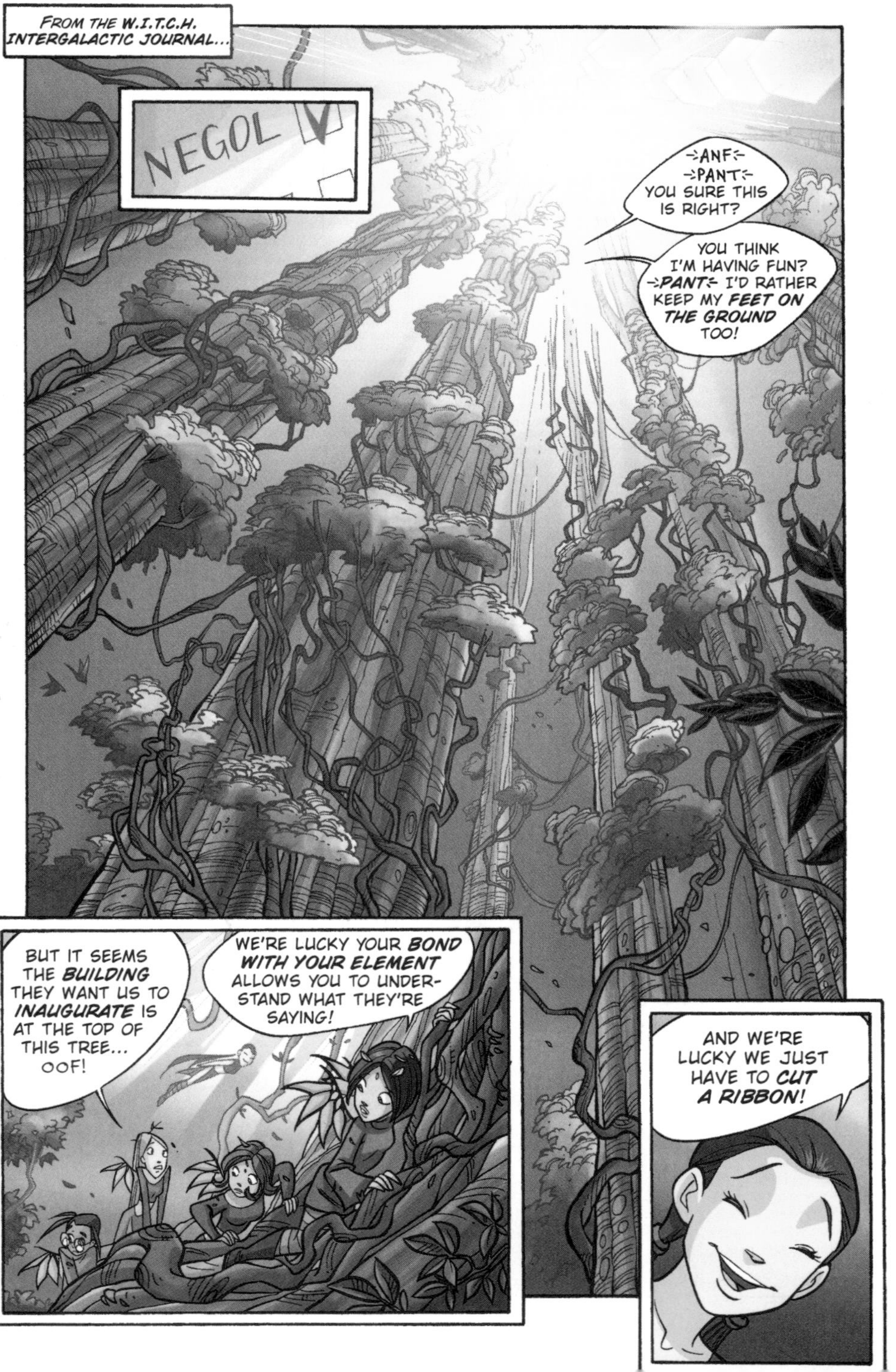
FROM THE W.I.T.C.H. INTERGALACTIC JOURNAL...
NEGOL V
ANF PANT YOU SURE THIS IS RIGHT?
YOU THINK I'M HAVING FUN? PANT I'D RATHER KEEP MY FEET ON THE GROUND TOO!
BUT IT SEEMS THE BUILDING THEY WANT US TO INAUGURATE IS AT THE TOP OF THIS TREE... OOF!
WE'RE LUCKY YOUR BOND WITH YOUR ELEMENT ALLOWS YOU TO UNDERSTAND WHAT THEY'RE SAYING!
AND WE'RE LUCKY WE JUST HAVE TO CUT A RIBBON!

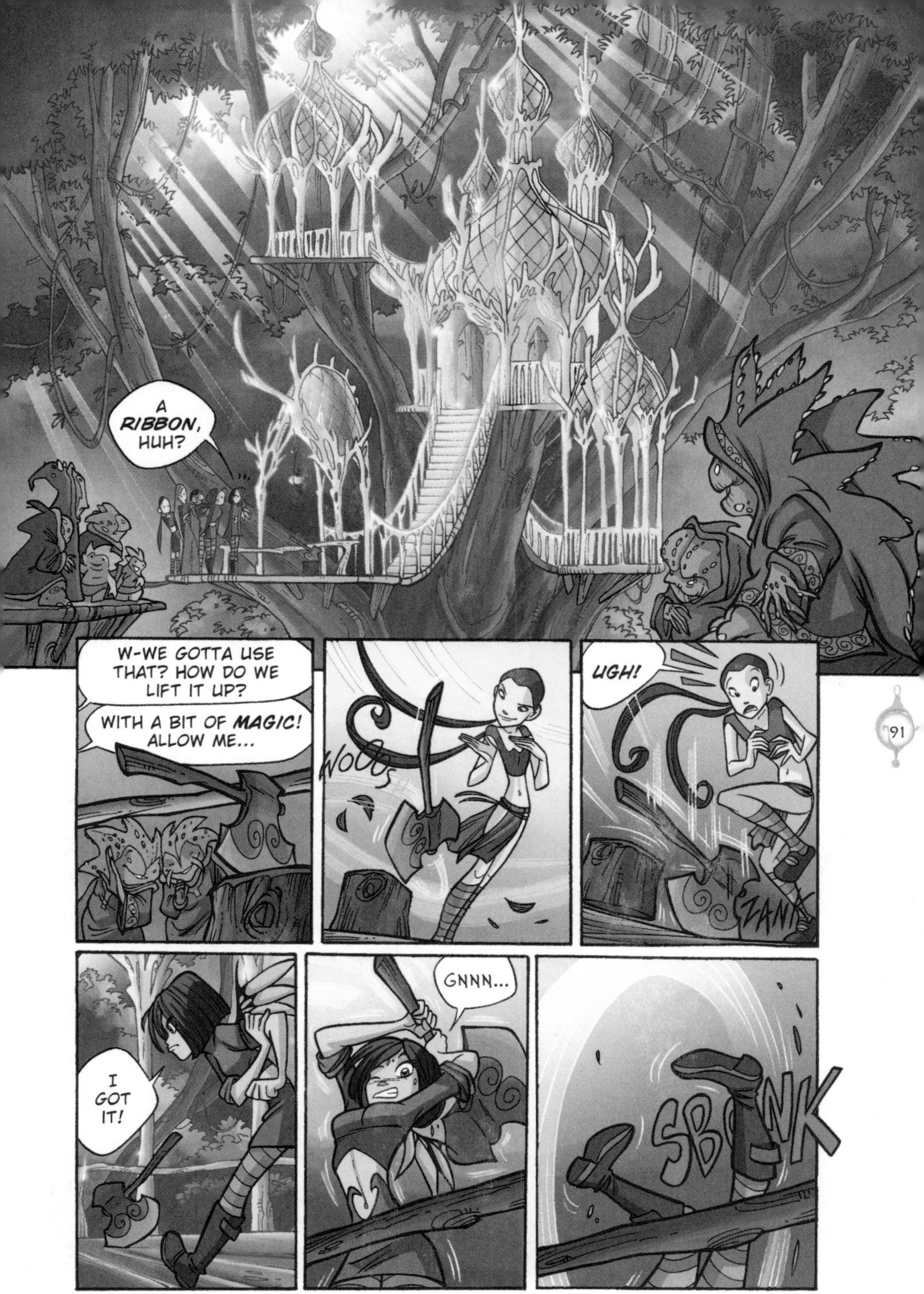
A RIBBON, HUH?
W-WE GOTTA USE THAT? HOW DO WE LIFT IT UP?
WITH A BIT OF MAGIC! ALLOW ME...
WOOO
UGH!
I GOT IT!
GNNN...
SBONK

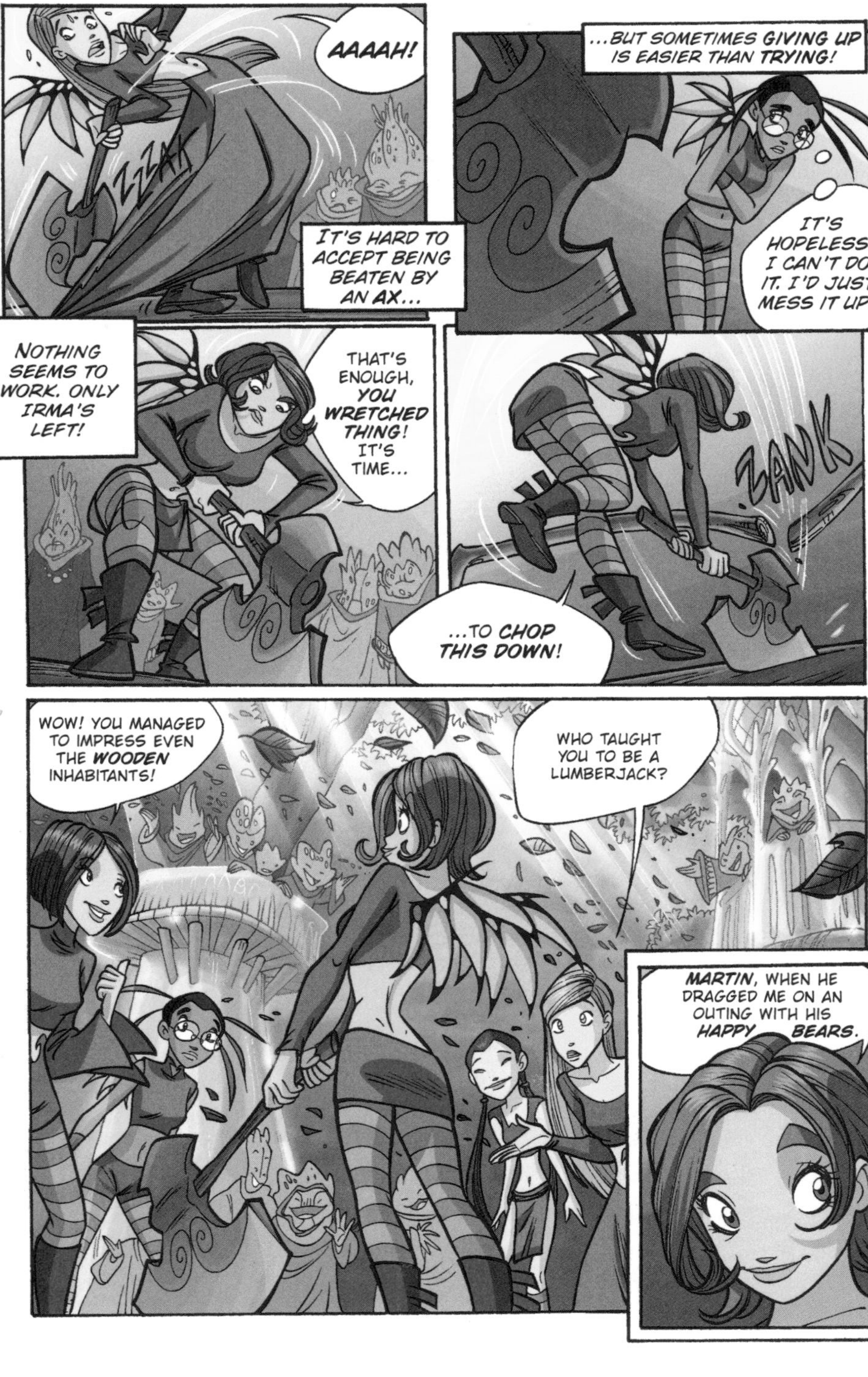

AAAAH!
ZZZAK
IT'S HARD TO ACCEPT BEING BEATEN BY AN AX...
...BUT SOMETIMES GIVING UP IS EASIER THAN TRYING!
IT'S HOPELESS. I CAN'T DO IT. I'D JUST MESS IT UP!
NOTHING SEEMS TO WORK. ONLY IRMA'S LEFT!
THAT'S ENOUGH, YOU WRETCHED THING! IT'S TIME...
ZANK
...TO CHOP THIS DOWN!
WOW! YOU MANAGED TO IMPRESS EVEN THE WOODEN INHABITANTS!
WHO TAUGHT YOU TO BE A LUMBERJACK?
MARTIN, WHEN HE DRAGGED ME ON AN OUTING WITH HIS HAPPY BEARS.

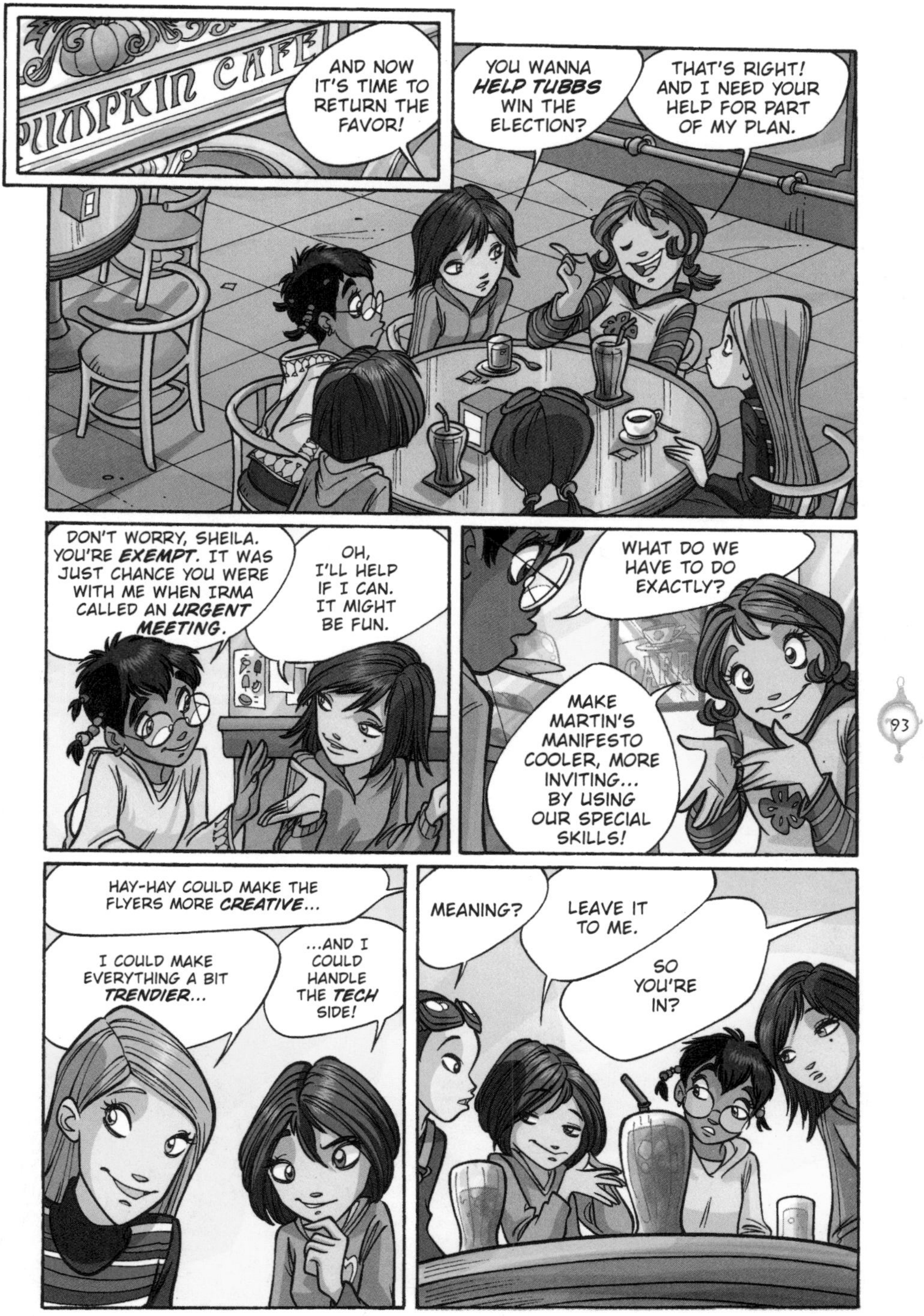
PUMPKIN CAFE
AND NOW IT'S TIME TO RETURN THE FAVOR!
YOU WANNA ***HELP TUBBS*** WIN THE ELECTION?
THAT'S RIGHT! AND I NEED YOUR HELP FOR PART OF MY PLAN.
DON'T WORRY, SHEILA. YOU'RE ***EXEMPT***. IT WAS JUST CHANCE YOU WERE WITH ME WHEN IRMA CALLED AN ***URGENT MEETING***.
OH, I'LL HELP IF I CAN. IT MIGHT BE FUN.
WHAT DO WE HAVE TO DO EXACTLY?
MAKE MARTIN'S MANIFESTO COOLER, MORE INVITING... BY USING OUR SPECIAL SKILLS!
HAY-HAY COULD MAKE THE FLYERS MORE ***CREATIVE***...
I COULD MAKE EVERYTHING A BIT ***TRENDIER***...
...AND I COULD HANDLE THE ***TECH*** SIDE!
MEANING?
LEAVE IT TO ME.
SO YOU'RE IN?

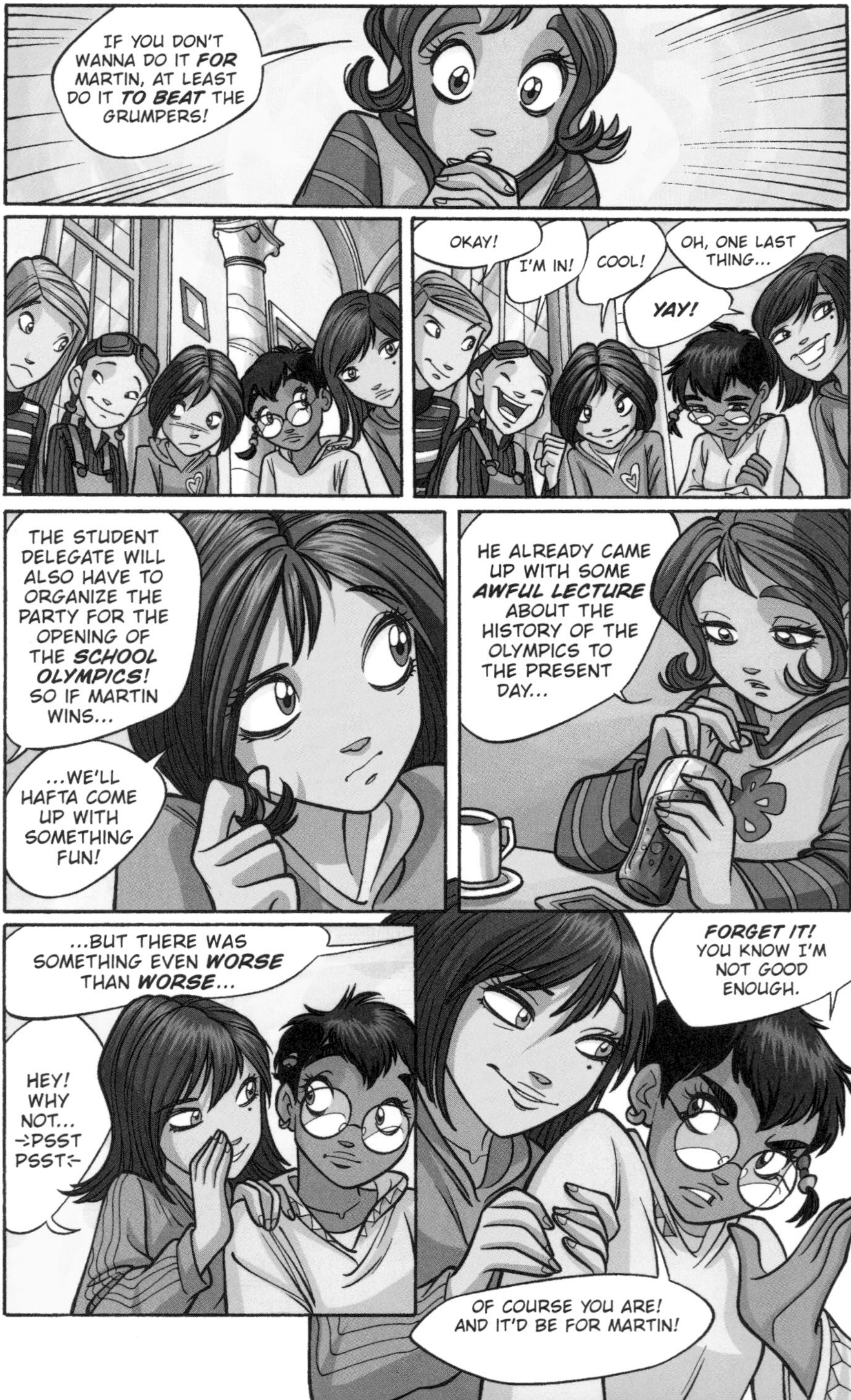
IF YOU DON'T WANNA DO IT **FOR** MARTIN, AT LEAST DO IT **TO BEAT** THE GRUMPERS!
OKAY!
I'M IN!
COOL!
OH, ONE LAST THING...
YAY!
THE STUDENT DELEGATE WILL ALSO HAVE TO ORGANIZE THE PARTY FOR THE OPENING OF THE **SCHOOL OLYMPICS!** SO IF MARTIN WINS...
...WE'LL HAFTA COME UP WITH SOMETHING FUN!
HE ALREADY CAME UP WITH SOME **AWFUL LECTURE** ABOUT THE HISTORY OF THE OLYMPICS TO THE PRESENT DAY...
...BUT THERE WAS SOMETHING EVEN **WORSE** THAN **WORSE**...
HEY! WHY NOT... PSST PSST
FORGET IT! YOU KNOW I'M NOT GOOD ENOUGH.
OF COURSE YOU ARE! AND IT'D BE FOR MARTIN!

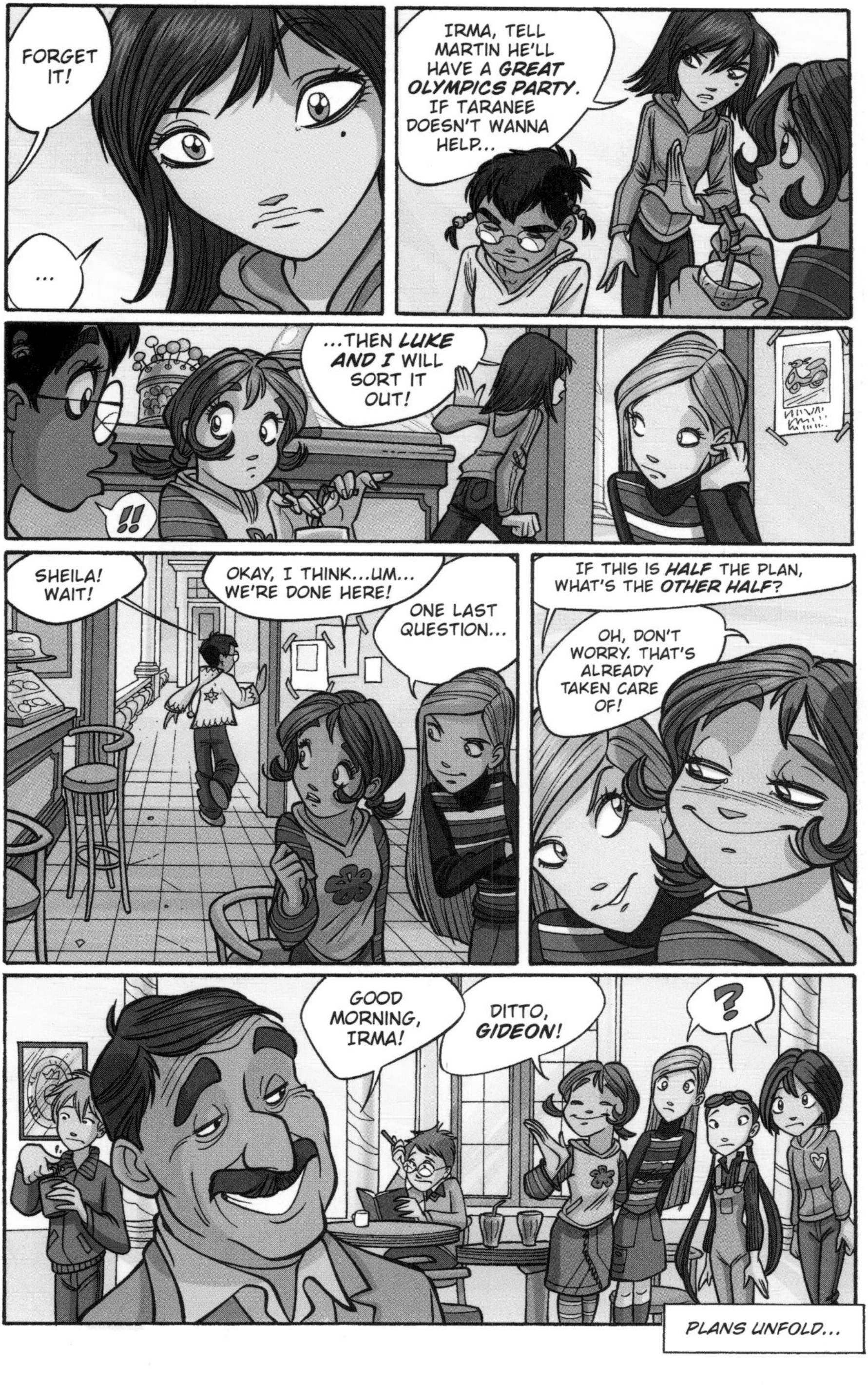

FORGET IT!
...
IRMA, TELL MARTIN HE'LL HAVE A GREAT OLYMPICS PARTY. IF TARANEE DOESN'T WANNA HELP...
...THEN LUKE AND I WILL SORT IT OUT!
!!
SHEILA! WAIT!
OKAY, I THINK...UM... WE'RE DONE HERE!
ONE LAST QUESTION...
IF THIS IS HALF THE PLAN, WHAT'S THE OTHER HALF?
OH, DON'T WORRY. THAT'S ALREADY TAKEN CARE OF!
GOOD MORNING, IRMA!
DITTO, GIDEON!
?
PLANS UNFOLD...

W.i.t.c.h.

Will Irma Taranee Cornelia Hay Lin

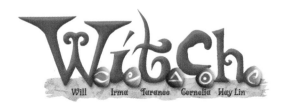

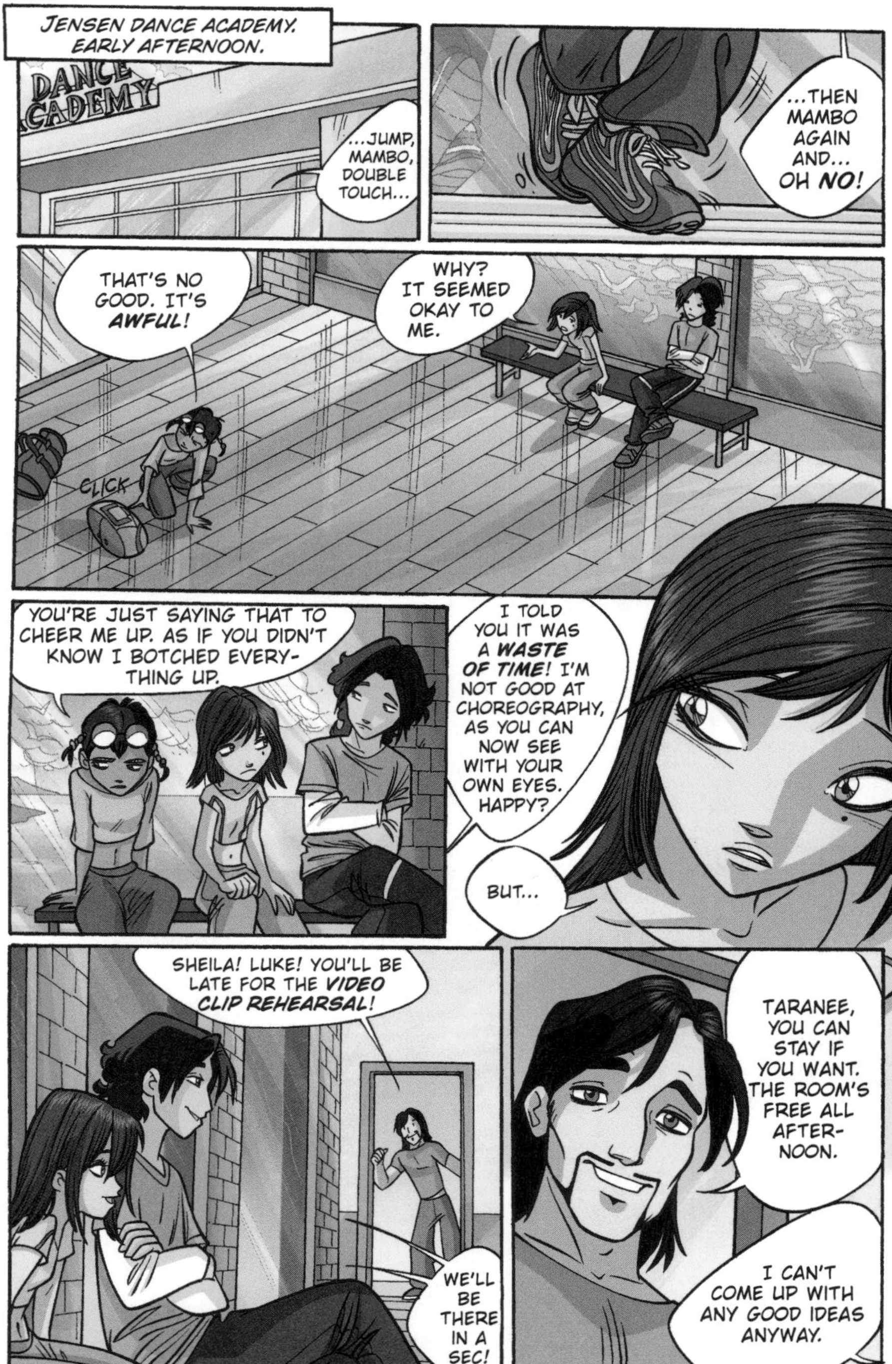
JENSEN DANCE ACADEMY. EARLY AFTERNOON.
DANCE ACADEMY
...JUMP, MAMBO, DOUBLE TOUCH...
...THEN MAMBO AGAIN AND... OH NO!
THAT'S NO GOOD. IT'S AWFUL!
WHY? IT SEEMED OKAY TO ME.
CLICK
YOU'RE JUST SAYING THAT TO CHEER ME UP. AS IF YOU DIDN'T KNOW I BOTCHED EVERY-THING UP.
I TOLD YOU IT WAS A WASTE OF TIME! I'M NOT GOOD AT CHOREOGRAPHY, AS YOU CAN NOW SEE WITH YOUR OWN EYES. HAPPY?
BUT...
SHEILA! LUKE! YOU'LL BE LATE FOR THE VIDEO CLIP REHEARSAL!
WE'LL BE THERE IN A SEC!
TARANEE, YOU CAN STAY IF YOU WANT. THE ROOM'S FREE ALL AFTER-NOON.
I CAN'T COME UP WITH ANY GOOD IDEAS ANYWAY.

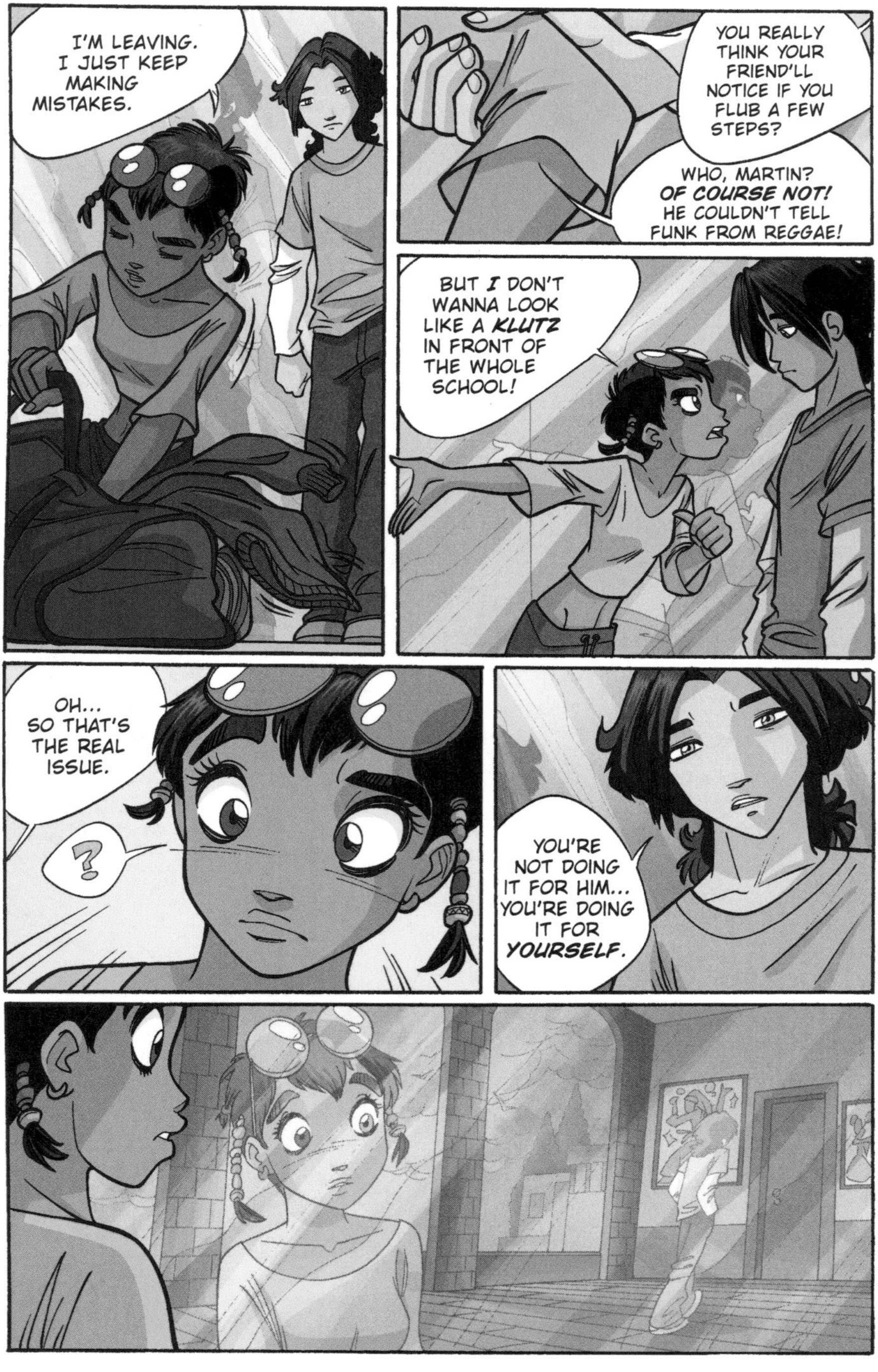
I'M LEAVING. I JUST KEEP MAKING MISTAKES.
YOU REALLY THINK YOUR FRIEND'LL NOTICE IF YOU FLUB A FEW STEPS?
WHO, MARTIN? ***OF COURSE NOT!*** HE COULDN'T TELL FUNK FROM REGGAE!
BUT ***I*** DON'T WANNA LOOK LIKE A ***KLUTZ*** IN FRONT OF THE WHOLE SCHOOL!
OH... SO THAT'S THE REAL ISSUE.
?
YOU'RE NOT DOING IT FOR HIM... YOU'RE DOING IT FOR ***YOURSELF***.

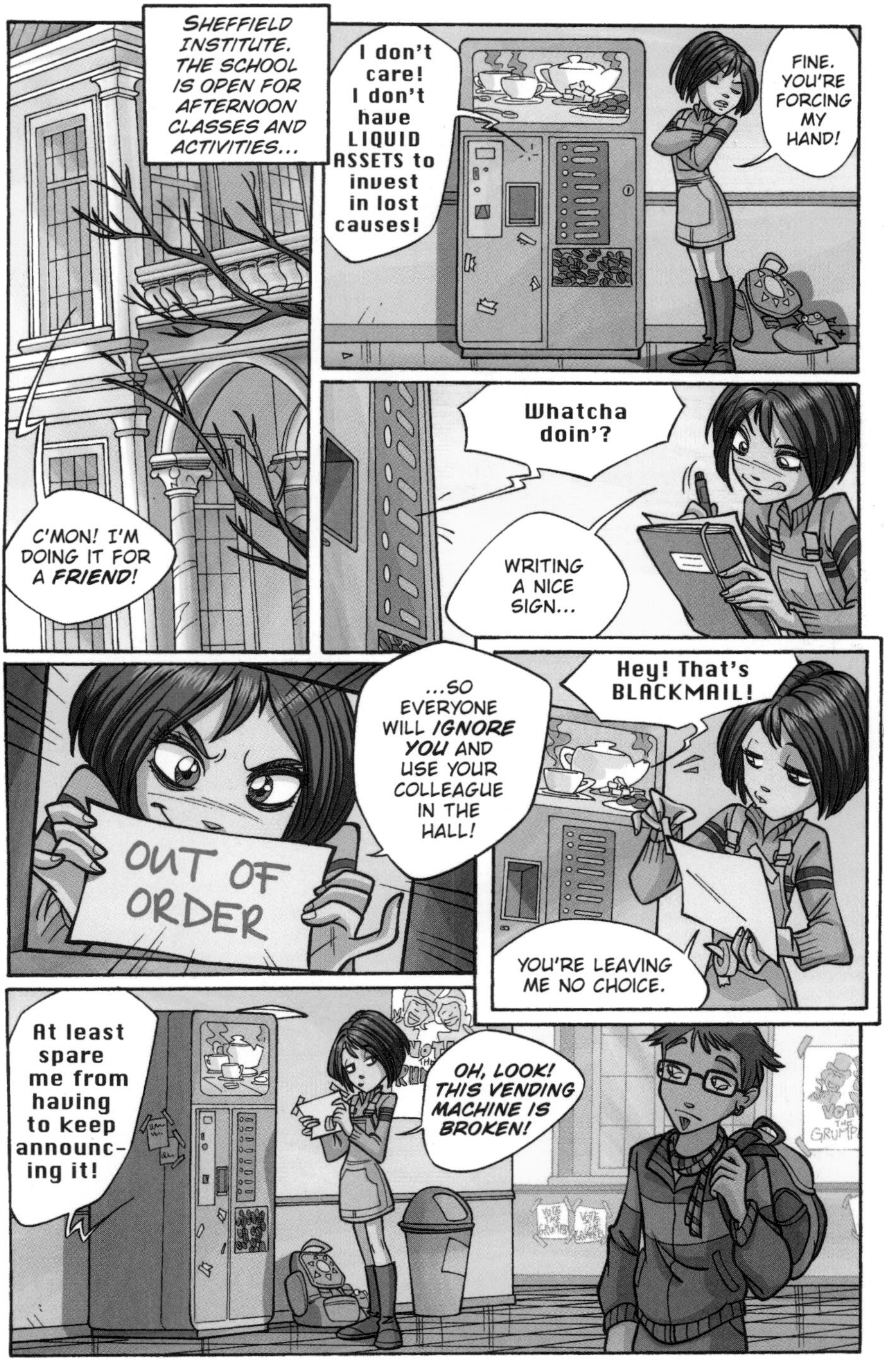
SHEFFIELD INSTITUTE. THE SCHOOL IS OPEN FOR AFTERNOON CLASSES AND ACTIVITIES...
C'MON! I'M DOING IT FOR A FRIEND!
I don't care! I don't have LIQUID ASSETS to invest in lost causes!
FINE. YOU'RE FORCING MY HAND!
Whatcha doin'?
WRITING A NICE SIGN...
OUT OF ORDER
...SO EVERYONE WILL IGNORE YOU AND USE YOUR COLLEAGUE IN THE HALL!
Hey! That's BLACKMAIL!
YOU'RE LEAVING ME NO CHOICE.
At least spare me from having to keep announcing it!
OH, LOOK! THIS VENDING MACHINE IS BROKEN!

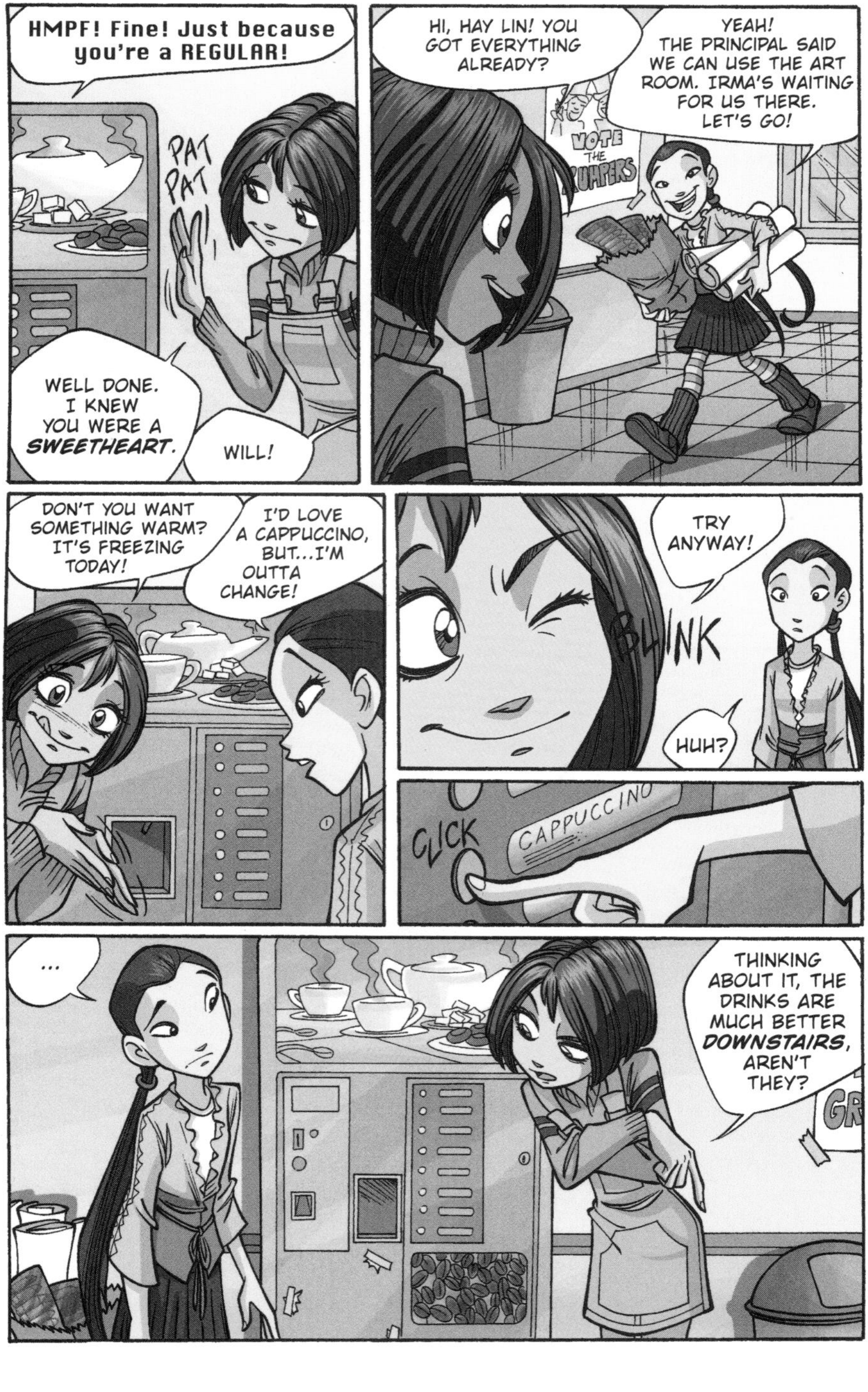
HMPF! Fine! Just because you're a REGULAR!
PAT PAT
WELL DONE. I KNEW YOU WERE A SWEETHEART.
WILL!
HI, HAY LIN! YOU GOT EVERYTHING ALREADY?
YEAH! THE PRINCIPAL SAID WE CAN USE THE ART ROOM. IRMA'S WAITING FOR US THERE. LET'S GO!
VOTE THE KRUMPERS
DON'T YOU WANT SOMETHING WARM? IT'S FREEZING TODAY!
I'D LOVE A CAPPUCCINO, BUT...I'M OUTTA CHANGE!
TRY ANYWAY!
BLINK
HUH?
CLICK
CAPPUCCINO
CAPPUCCINO
...
THINKING ABOUT IT, THE DRINKS ARE MUCH BETTER DOWNSTAIRS, AREN'T THEY?

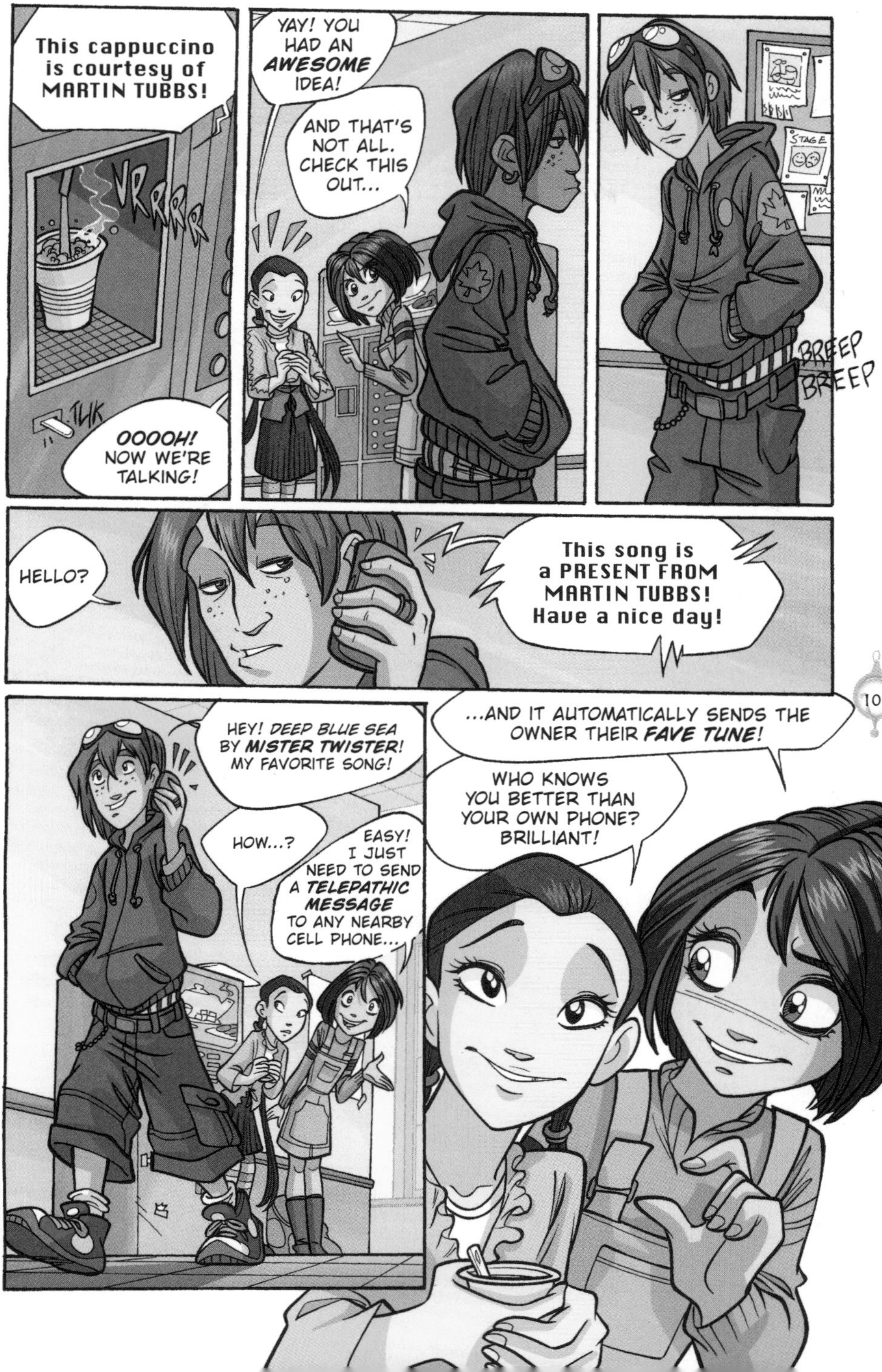
This cappuccino is courtesy of MARTIN TUBBS!
VRRRRR
TLIK
OOOOH! NOW WE'RE TALKING!
YAY! YOU HAD AN AWESOME IDEA!
AND THAT'S NOT ALL. CHECK THIS OUT...
STAGE
BREEP BREEP
HELLO?
This song is a PRESENT FROM MARTIN TUBBS! Have a nice day!
HEY! DEEP BLUE SEA BY MISTER TWISTER! MY FAVORITE SONG!
HOW...?
EASY! I JUST NEED TO SEND A TELEPATHIC MESSAGE TO ANY NEARBY CELL PHONE...
...AND IT AUTOMATICALLY SENDS THE OWNER THEIR FAVE TUNE!
WHO KNOWS YOU BETTER THAN YOUR OWN PHONE? BRILLIANT!

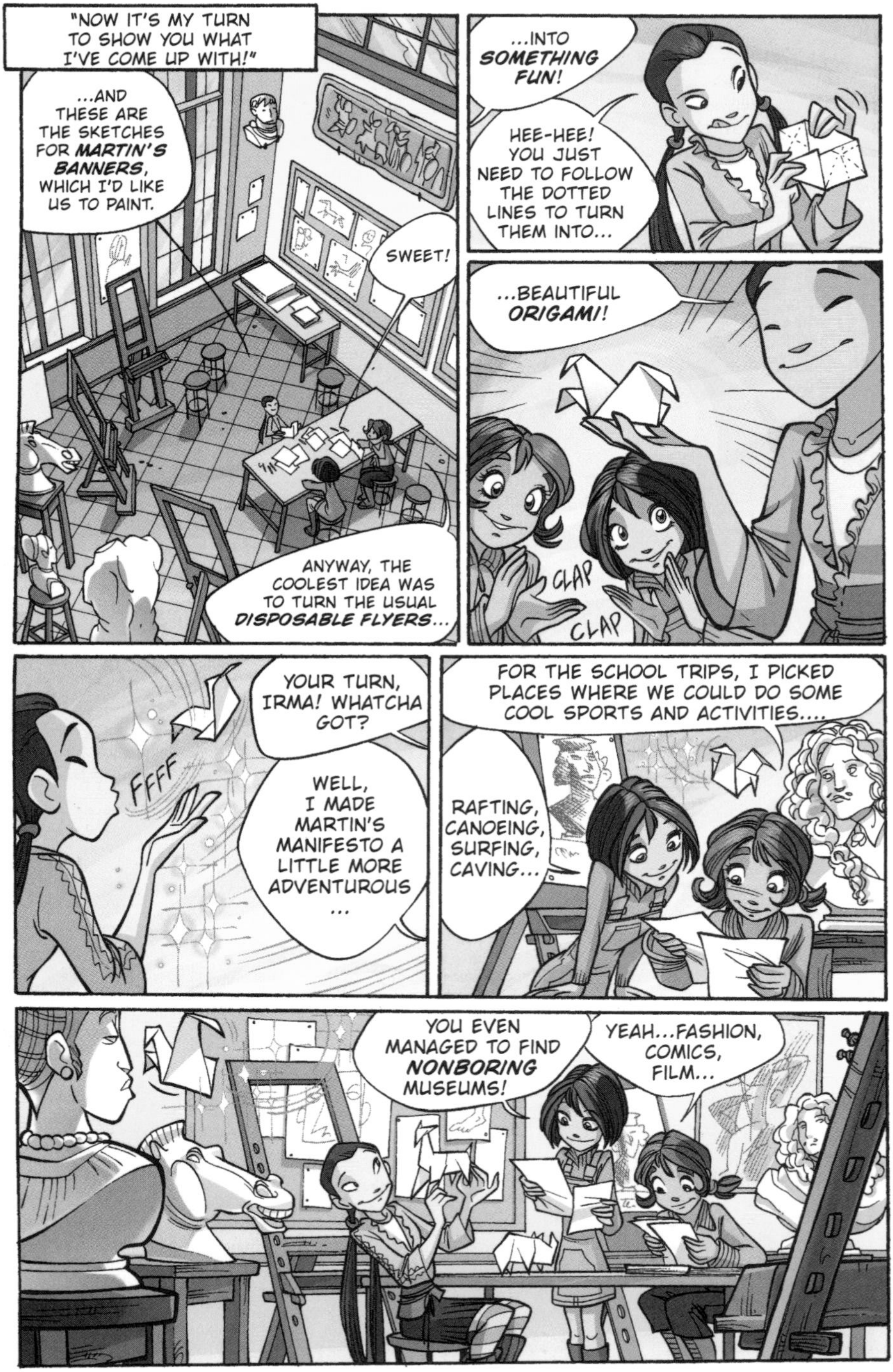

"NOW IT'S MY TURN TO SHOW YOU WHAT I'VE COME UP WITH!"
...AND THESE ARE THE SKETCHES FOR **MARTIN'S BANNERS**, WHICH I'D LIKE US TO PAINT.
SWEET!
ANYWAY, THE COOLEST IDEA WAS TO TURN THE USUAL **DISPOSABLE FLYERS**...
...INTO **SOMETHING FUN**!
HEE-HEE! YOU JUST NEED TO FOLLOW THE DOTTED LINES TO TURN THEM INTO...
...BEAUTIFUL **ORIGAMI**!
CLAP
CLAP
FFFF
YOUR TURN, IRMA! WHATCHA GOT?
WELL, I MADE MARTIN'S MANIFESTO A LITTLE MORE ADVENTUROUS ...
FOR THE SCHOOL TRIPS, I PICKED PLACES WHERE WE COULD DO SOME COOL SPORTS AND ACTIVITIES....
RAFTING, CANOEING, SURFING, CAVING...
YOU EVEN MANAGED TO FIND **NONBORING** MUSEUMS!
YEAH...FASHION, COMICS, FILM...

102

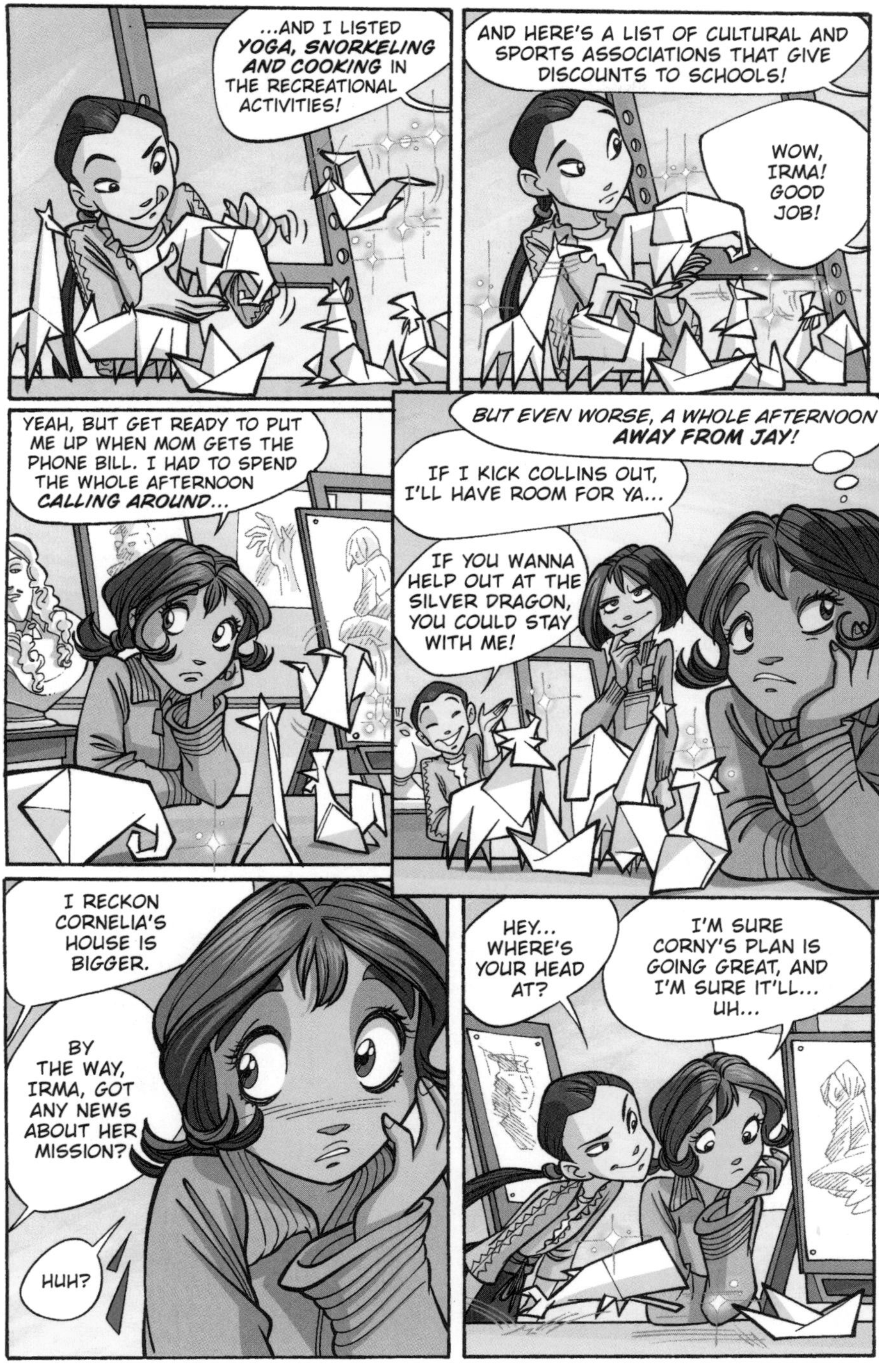
...AND I LISTED ***YOGA, SNORKELING AND COOKING*** IN THE RECREATIONAL ACTIVITIES!
AND HERE'S A LIST OF CULTURAL AND SPORTS ASSOCIATIONS THAT GIVE DISCOUNTS TO SCHOOLS!
WOW, IRMA! GOOD JOB!
YEAH, BUT GET READY TO PUT ME UP WHEN MOM GETS THE PHONE BILL. I HAD TO SPEND THE WHOLE AFTERNOON ***CALLING AROUND***...
BUT EVEN WORSE, A WHOLE AFTERNOON ***AWAY FROM JAY!***
IF I KICK COLLINS OUT, I'LL HAVE ROOM FOR YA...
IF YOU WANNA HELP OUT AT THE SILVER DRAGON, YOU COULD STAY WITH ME!
I RECKON CORNELIA'S HOUSE IS BIGGER.
BY THE WAY, IRMA, GOT ANY NEWS ABOUT HER MISSION?
HUH?
HEY... WHERE'S YOUR HEAD AT?
I'M SURE CORNY'S PLAN IS GOING GREAT, AND I'M SURE IT'LL... UH...

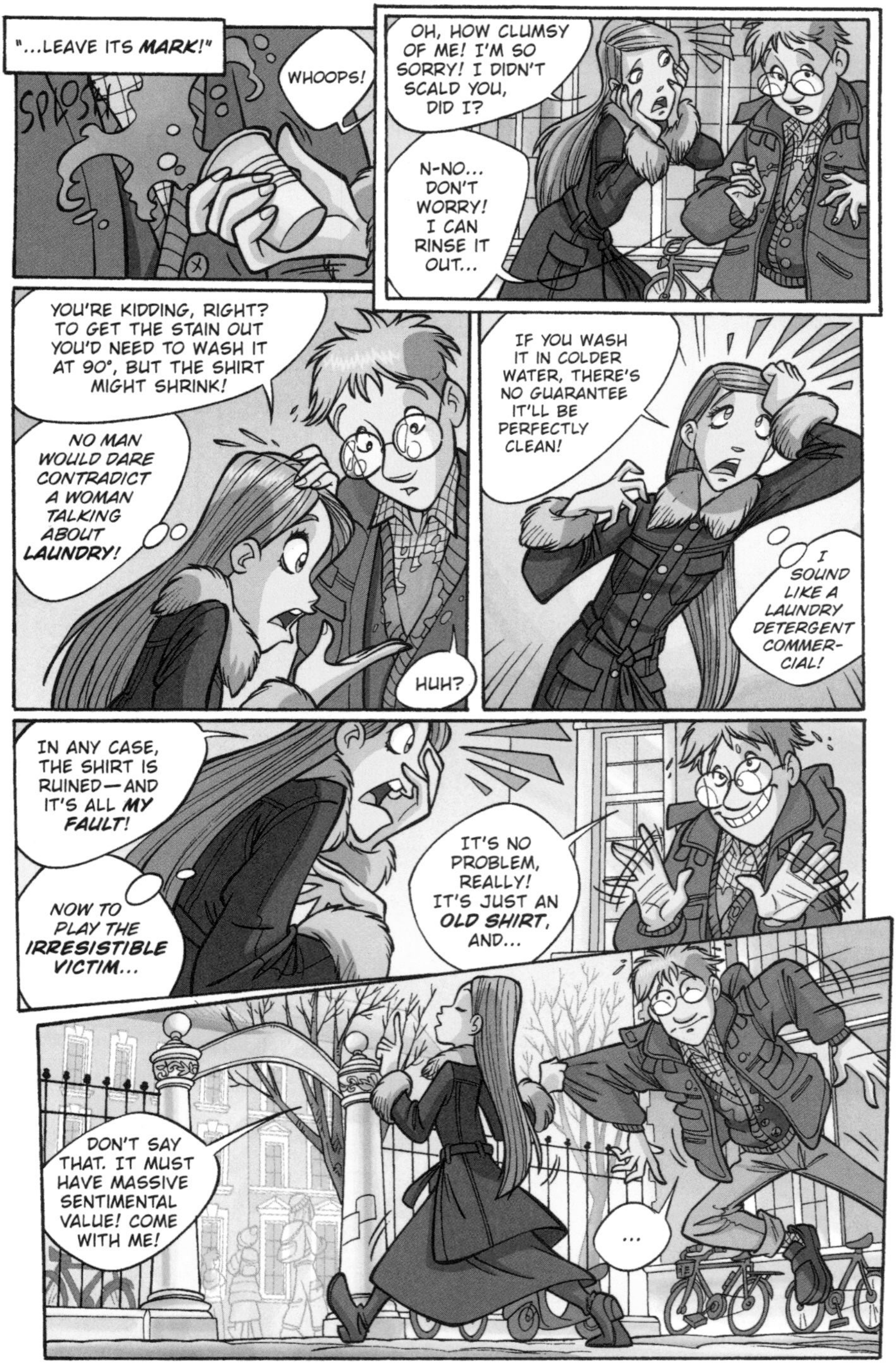
"...LEAVE ITS *MARK!*"
SPLOSH
WHOOPS!
OH, HOW CLUMSY OF ME! I'M SO SORRY! I DIDN'T SCALD YOU, DID I?
N-NO... DON'T WORRY! I CAN RINSE IT OUT...
YOU'RE KIDDING, RIGHT? TO GET THE STAIN OUT YOU'D NEED TO WASH IT AT 90°, BUT THE SHIRT MIGHT SHRINK!
*NO MAN WOULD DARE CONTRADICT A WOMAN TALKING ABOUT **LAUNDRY**!*
HUH?
IF YOU WASH IT IN COLDER WATER, THERE'S NO GUARANTEE IT'LL BE PERFECTLY CLEAN!
I SOUND LIKE A LAUNDRY DETERGENT COMMERCIAL!
IN ANY CASE, THE SHIRT IS RUINED—AND IT'S ALL ***MY FAULT***!
*NOW TO PLAY THE **IRRESISTIBLE VICTIM**...*
IT'S NO PROBLEM, REALLY! IT'S JUST AN ***OLD SHIRT***, AND...
DON'T SAY THAT. IT MUST HAVE MASSIVE SENTIMENTAL VALUE! COME WITH ME!
...

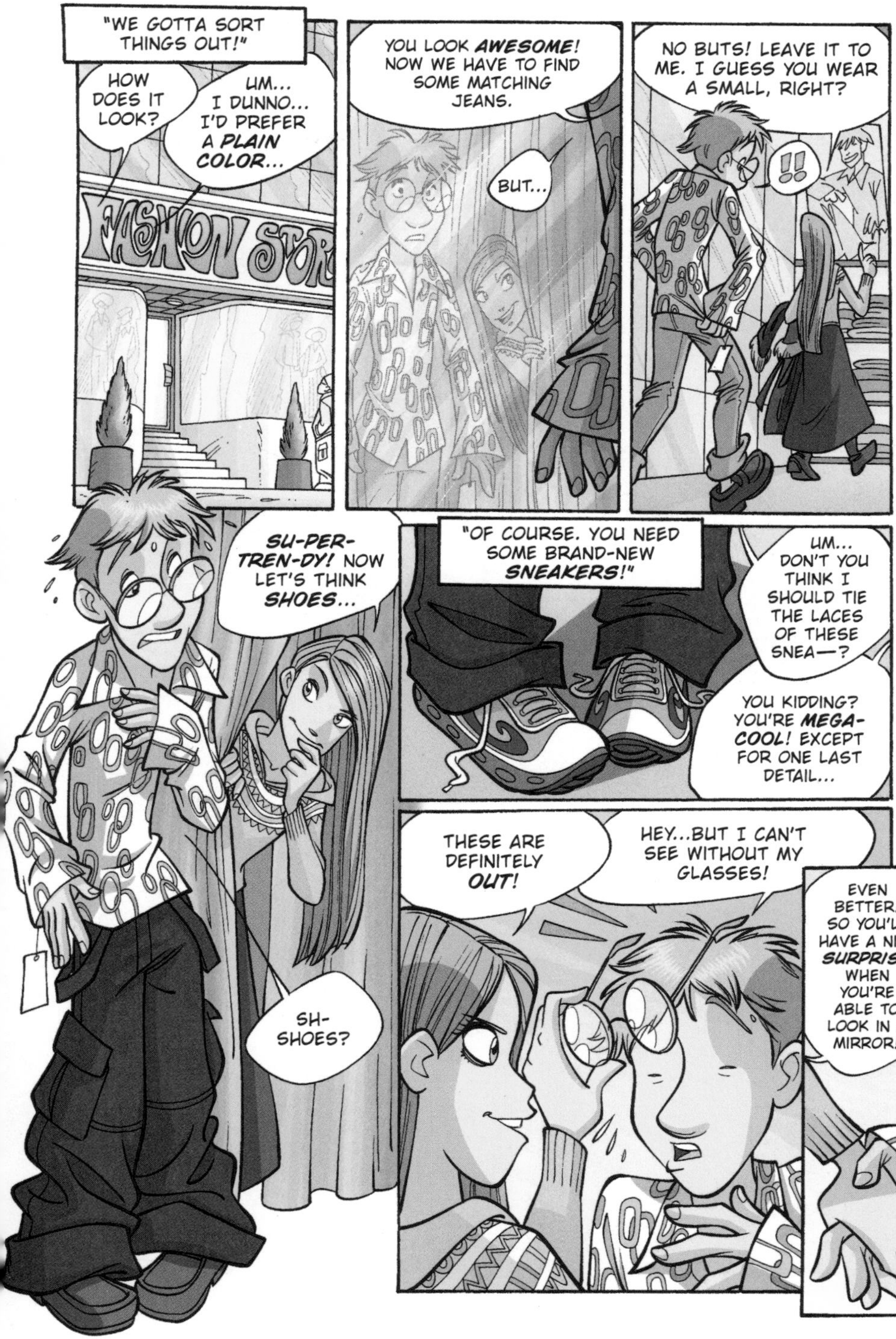

"WE GOTTA SORT THINGS OUT!"
HOW DOES IT LOOK?
UM... I DUNNO... I'D PREFER A PLAIN COLOR...
FASHION STOR
YOU LOOK AWESOME! NOW WE HAVE TO FIND SOME MATCHING JEANS.
BUT...
NO BUTS! LEAVE IT TO ME. I GUESS YOU WEAR A SMALL, RIGHT?
!!
SU-PER-TREN-DY! NOW LET'S THINK SHOES...
SH-SHOES?
"OF COURSE. YOU NEED SOME BRAND-NEW SNEAKERS!"
UM... DON'T YOU THINK I SHOULD TIE THE LACES OF THESE SNEA—?
YOU KIDDING? YOU'RE MEGA-COOL! EXCEPT FOR ONE LAST DETAIL...
THESE ARE DEFINITELY OUT!
HEY...BUT I CAN'T SEE WITHOUT MY GLASSES!
EVEN BETTER! SO YOU'LL HAVE A NICE SURPRISE WHEN YOU'RE ABLE TO LOOK IN A MIRROR!

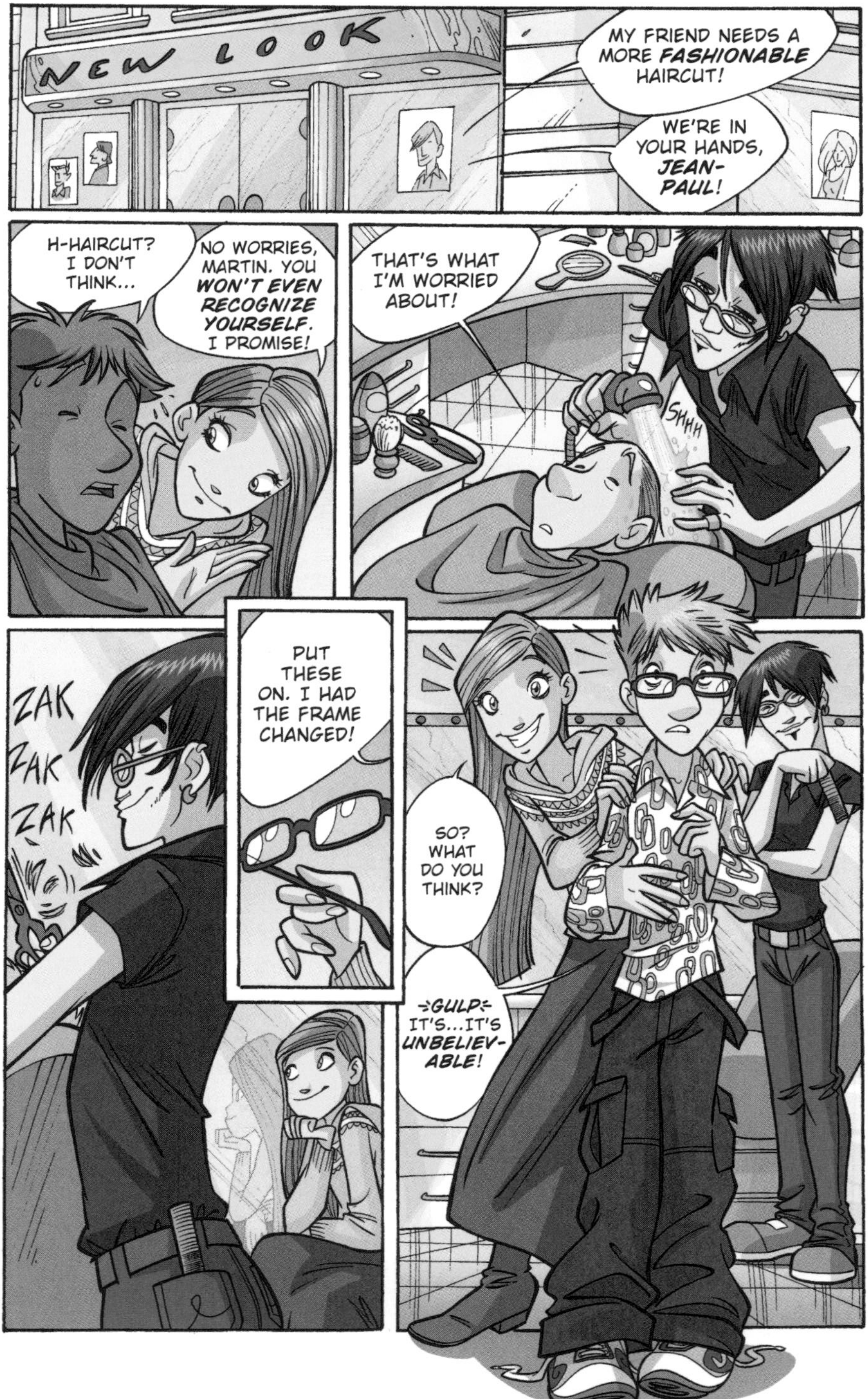

NEW LOOK
MY FRIEND NEEDS A MORE FASHIONABLE HAIRCUT!
WE'RE IN YOUR HANDS, JEAN-PAUL!
H-HAIRCUT? I DON'T THINK...
NO WORRIES, MARTIN. YOU WON'T EVEN RECOGNIZE YOURSELF. I PROMISE!
THAT'S WHAT I'M WORRIED ABOUT!
SHHH
ZAK
ZAK
ZAK
PUT THESE ON. I HAD THE FRAME CHANGED!
SO? WHAT DO YOU THINK?
-GULP- IT'S...IT'S UNBELIEV-ABLE!

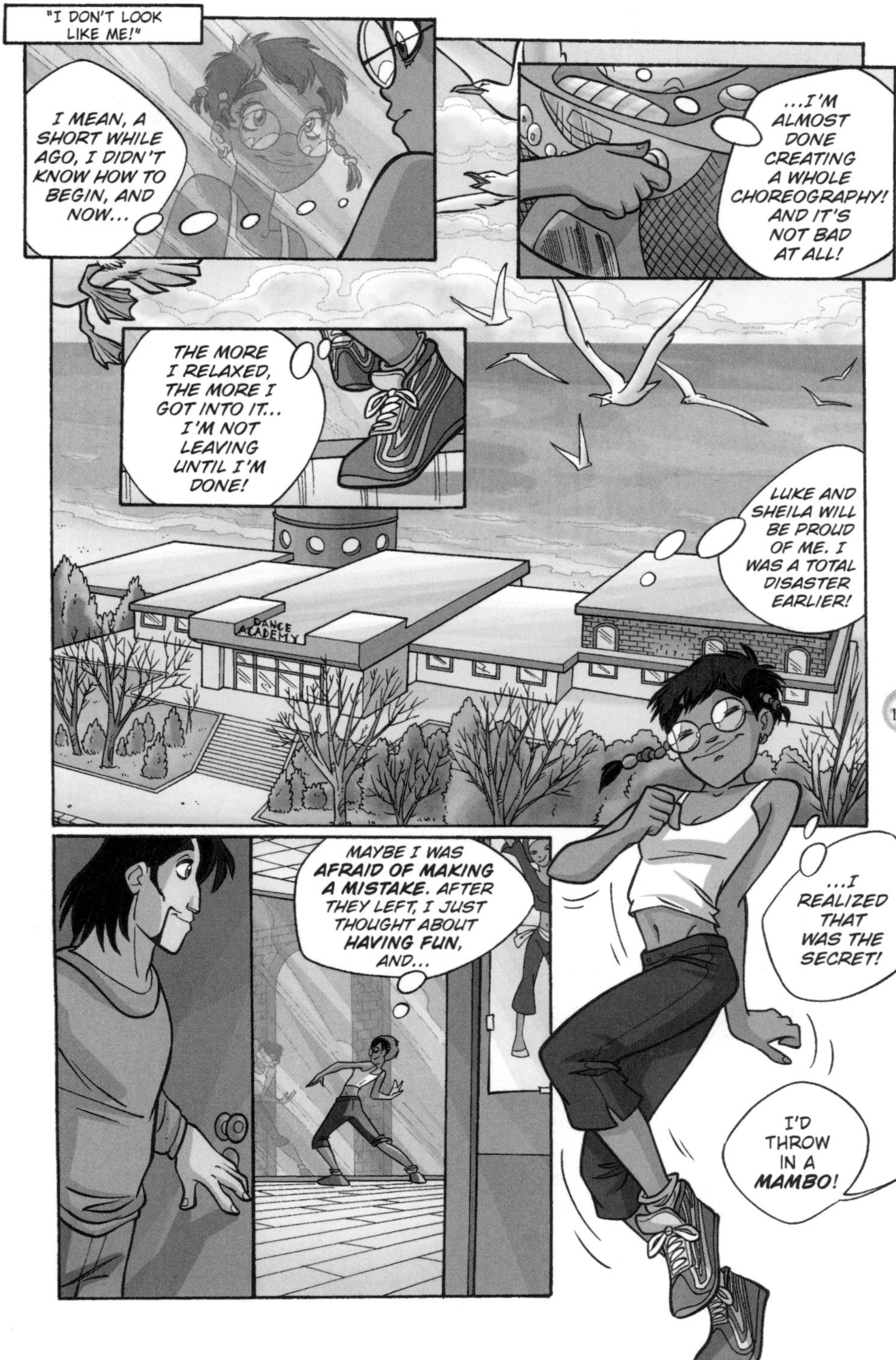

"I DON'T LOOK LIKE ME!"
I MEAN, A SHORT WHILE AGO, I DIDN'T KNOW HOW TO BEGIN, AND NOW...
...I'M ALMOST DONE CREATING A WHOLE CHOREOGRAPHY! AND IT'S NOT BAD AT ALL!
THE MORE I RELAXED, THE MORE I GOT INTO IT... I'M NOT LEAVING UNTIL I'M DONE!
LUKE AND SHEILA WILL BE PROUD OF ME. I WAS A TOTAL DISASTER EARLIER!
DANCE ACADEMY
MAYBE I WAS AFRAID OF MAKING A MISTAKE. AFTER THEY LEFT, I JUST THOUGHT ABOUT HAVING FUN, AND...
...I REALIZED THAT WAS THE SECRET!
I'D THROW IN A MAMBO!

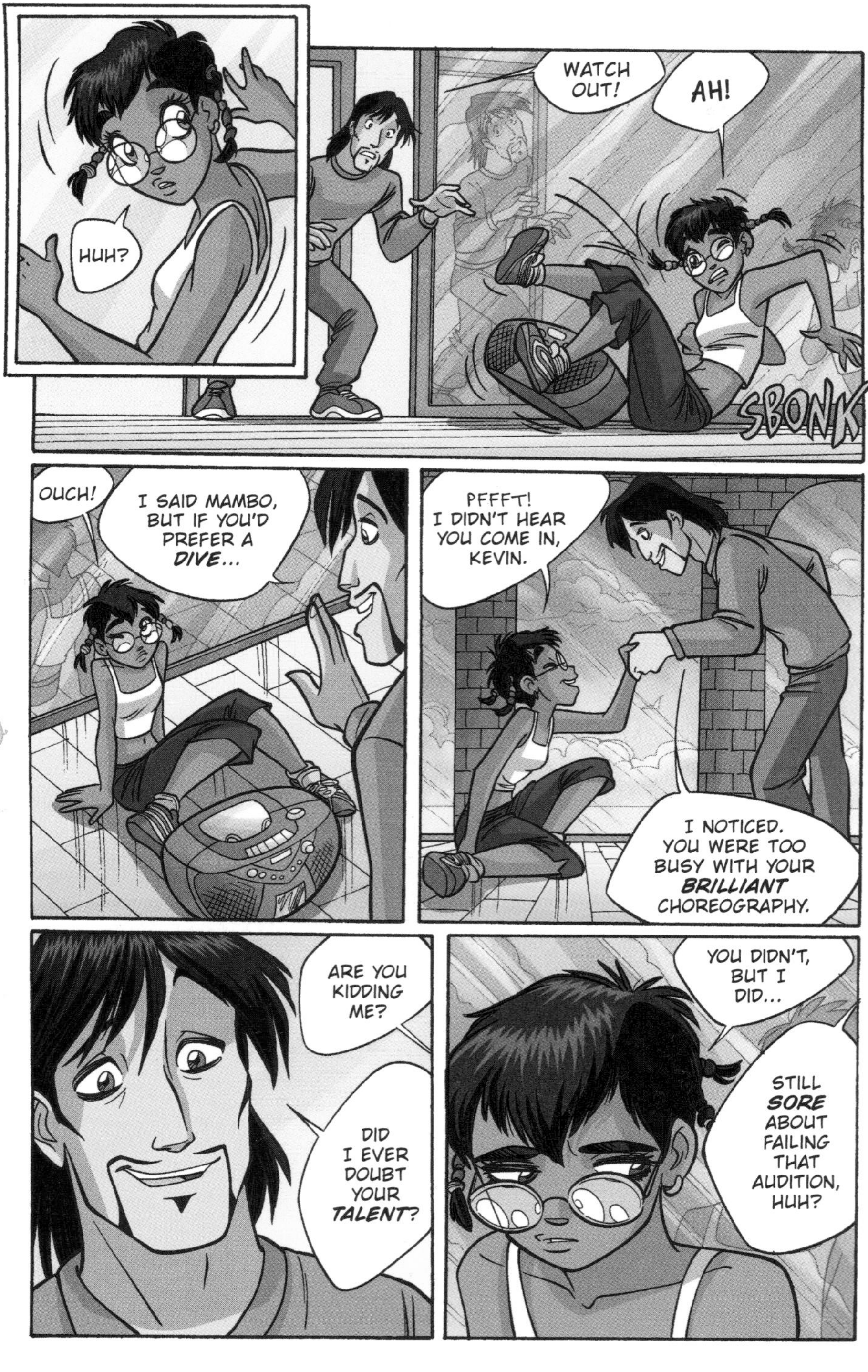
HUH?
WATCH OUT!
AH!
SBONK
OUCH!
I SAID MAMBO, BUT IF YOU'D PREFER A *DIVE*...
PFFFT! I DIDN'T HEAR YOU COME IN, KEVIN.
I NOTICED. YOU WERE TOO BUSY WITH YOUR *BRILLIANT* CHOREOGRAPHY.
ARE YOU KIDDING ME?
DID I EVER DOUBT YOUR *TALENT*?
YOU DIDN'T, BUT I DID...
STILL *SORE* ABOUT FAILING THAT AUDITION, HUH?

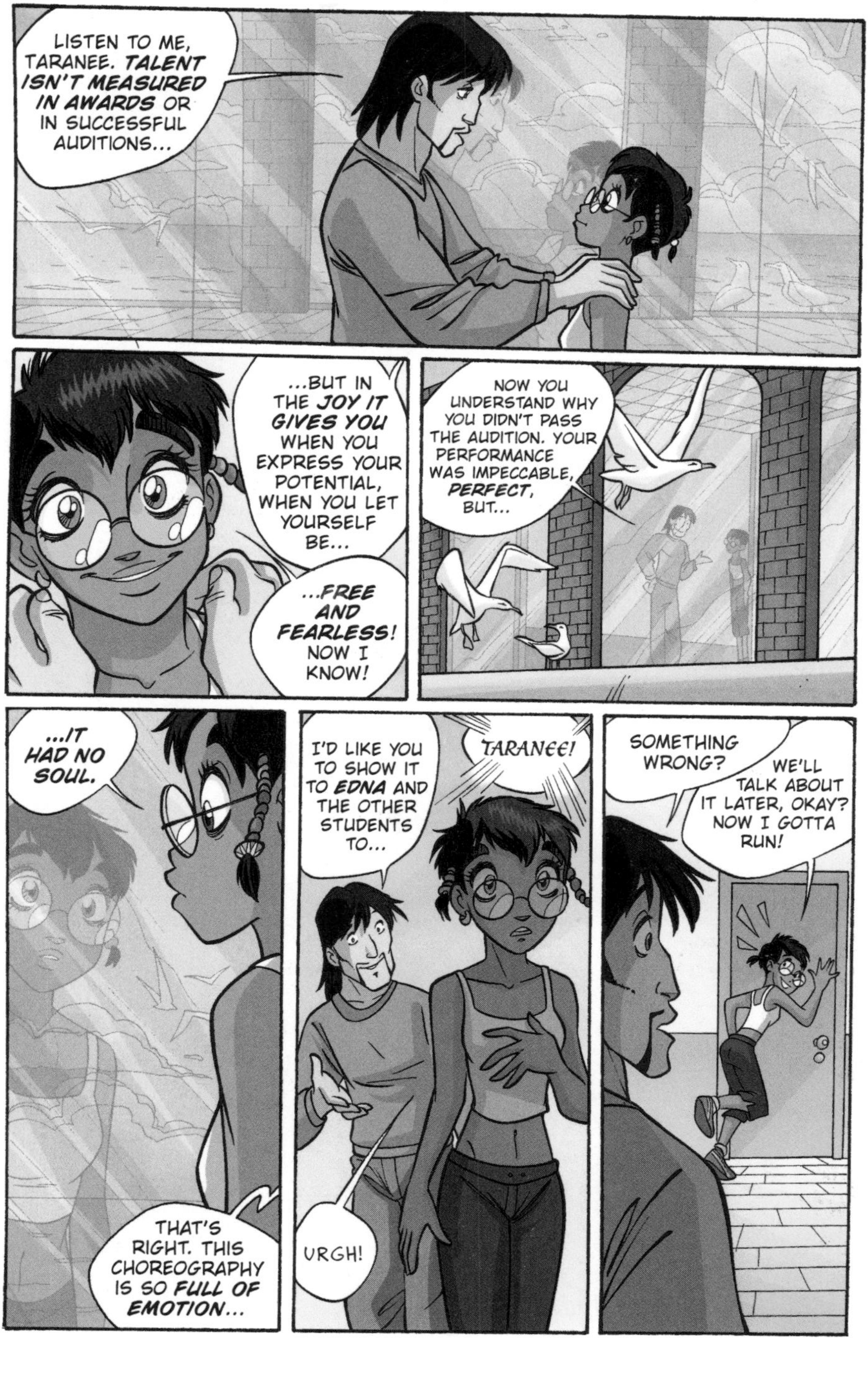
LISTEN TO ME, TARANEE. TALENT ISN'T MEASURED IN AWARDS OR IN SUCCESSFUL AUDITIONS...
...BUT IN THE JOY IT GIVES YOU WHEN YOU EXPRESS YOUR POTENTIAL, WHEN YOU LET YOURSELF BE...
...FREE AND FEARLESS! NOW I KNOW!
NOW YOU UNDERSTAND WHY YOU DIDN'T PASS THE AUDITION. YOUR PERFORMANCE WAS IMPECCABLE, PERFECT, BUT...
...IT HAD NO SOUL.
THAT'S RIGHT. THIS CHOREOGRAPHY IS SO FULL OF EMOTION...
I'D LIKE YOU TO SHOW IT TO EDNA AND THE OTHER STUDENTS TO...
TARANEE!
URGH!
SOMETHING WRONG?
WE'LL TALK ABOUT IT LATER, OKAY? NOW I GOTTA RUN!

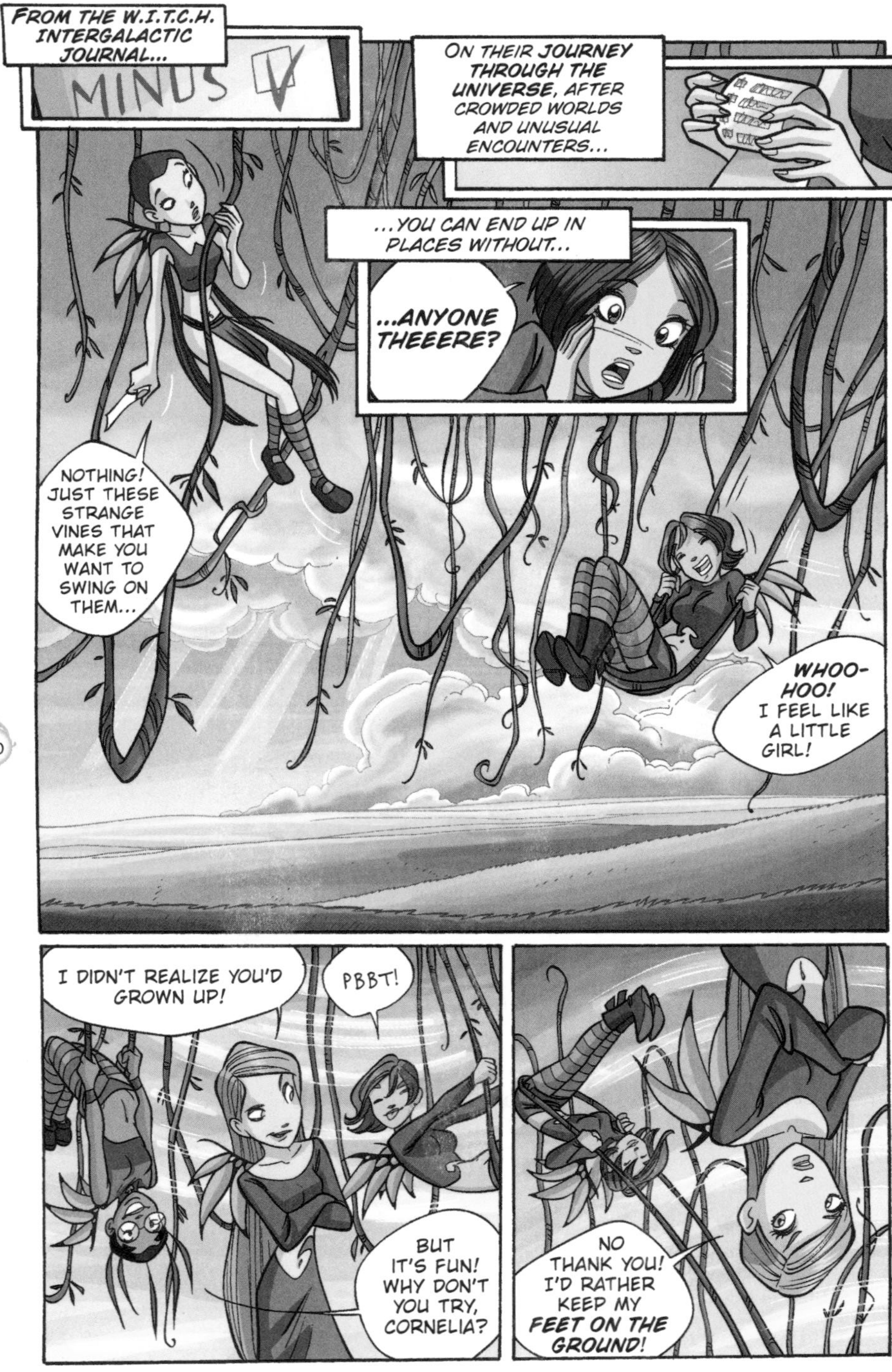
FROM THE W.I.T.C.H. INTERGALACTIC JOURNAL...
MINUS V
ON THEIR JOURNEY THROUGH THE UNIVERSE, AFTER CROWDED WORLDS AND UNUSUAL ENCOUNTERS...
...YOU CAN END UP IN PLACES WITHOUT...
...ANYONE THEEERE?
NOTHING! JUST THESE STRANGE VINES THAT MAKE YOU WANT TO SWING ON THEM...
WHOO-HOO! I FEEL LIKE A LITTLE GIRL!
I DIDN'T REALIZE YOU'D GROWN UP!
PBBT!
BUT IT'S FUN! WHY DON'T YOU TRY, CORNELIA?
NO THANK YOU! I'D RATHER KEEP MY FEET ON THE GROUND!

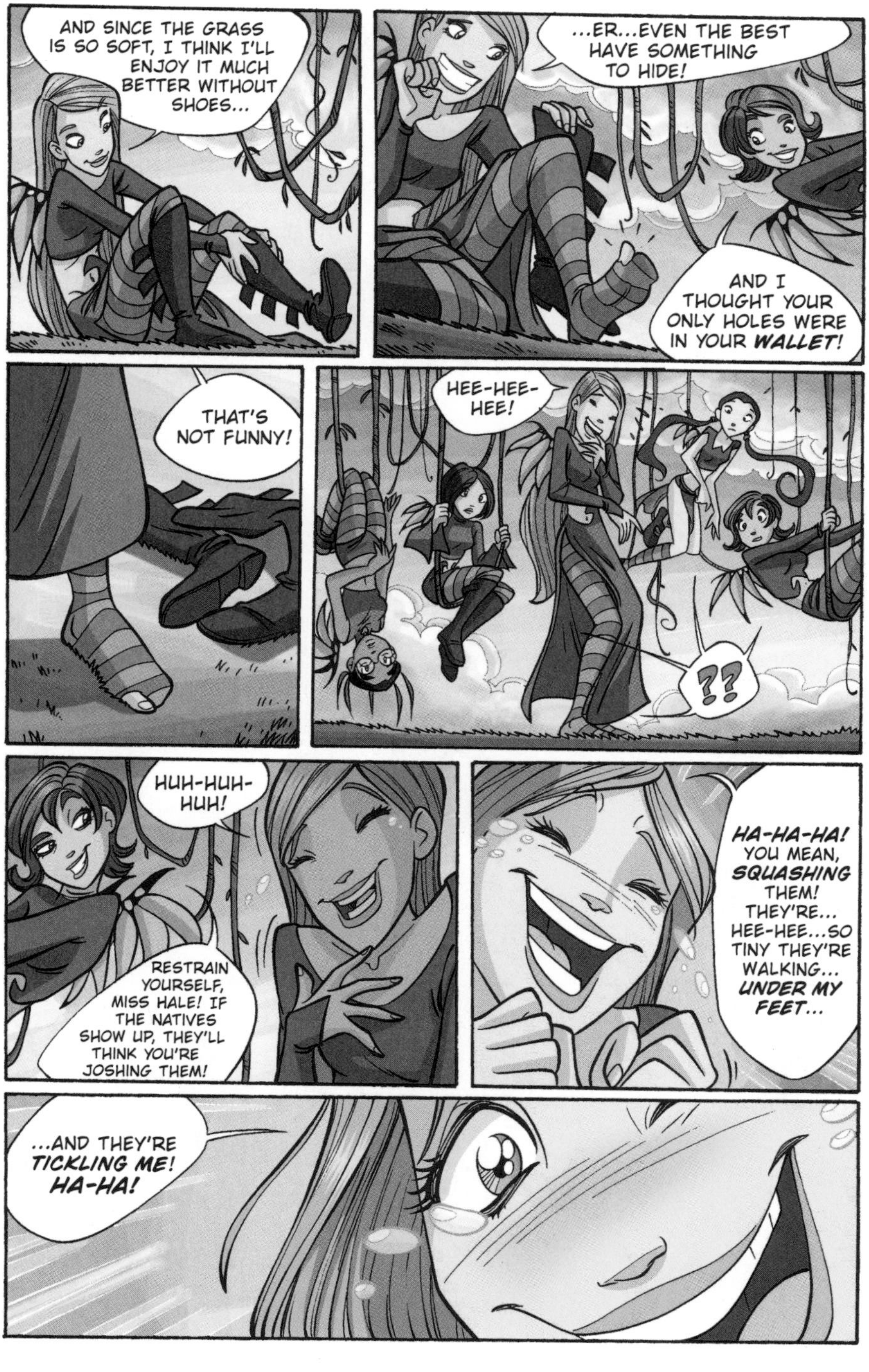
AND SINCE THE GRASS IS SO SOFT, I THINK I'LL ENJOY IT MUCH BETTER WITHOUT SHOES...
...ER...EVEN THE BEST HAVE SOMETHING TO HIDE!
AND I THOUGHT YOUR ONLY HOLES WERE IN YOUR ***WALLET***!
THAT'S NOT FUNNY!
HEE-HEE-HEE!
??
HUH-HUH-HUH!
RESTRAIN YOURSELF, MISS HALE! IF THE NATIVES SHOW UP, THEY'LL THINK YOU'RE JOSHING THEM!
HA-HA-HA! YOU MEAN, ***SQUASHING*** THEM! THEY'RE... HEE-HEE...SO TINY THEY'RE WALKING... ***UNDER MY FEET***...
...AND THEY'RE ***TICKLING ME! HA-HA!***

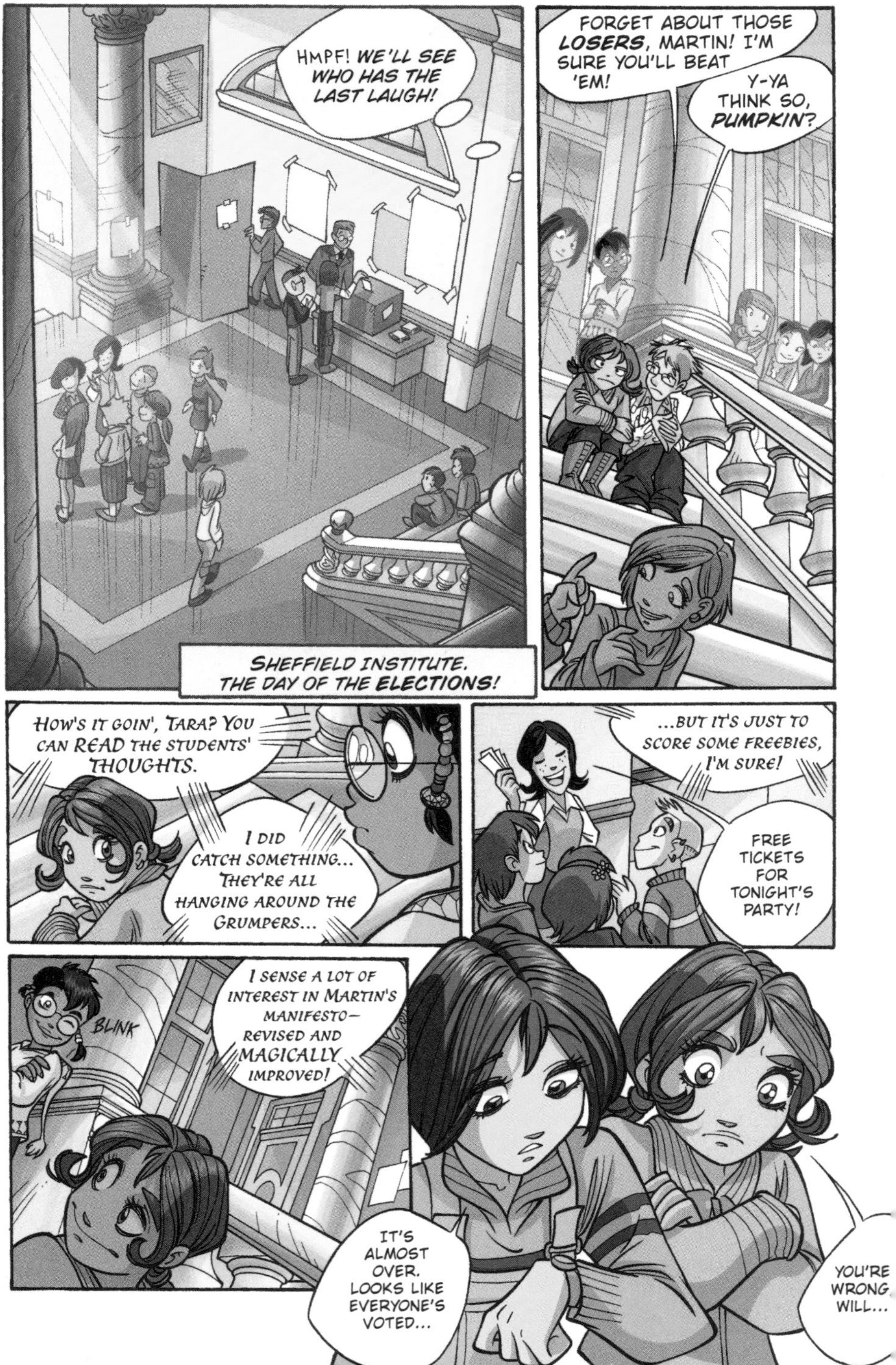
HMPF! WE'LL SEE WHO HAS THE LAST LAUGH!
SHEFFIELD INSTITUTE. THE DAY OF THE ELECTIONS!
FORGET ABOUT THOSE LOSERS, MARTIN! I'M SURE YOU'LL BEAT 'EM!
Y-YA THINK SO, PUMPKIN?
HOW'S IT GOIN', TARA? YOU CAN READ THE STUDENTS' THOUGHTS.
I DID CATCH SOMETHING... THEY'RE ALL HANGING AROUND THE GRUMPERS...
...BUT IT'S JUST TO SCORE SOME FREEBIES, I'M SURE!
FREE TICKETS FOR TONIGHT'S PARTY!
BLINK
I SENSE A LOT OF INTEREST IN MARTIN'S MANIFESTO— REVISED AND MAGICALLY IMPROVED!
IT'S ALMOST OVER. LOOKS LIKE EVERYONE'S VOTED...
YOU'RE WRONG, WILL...

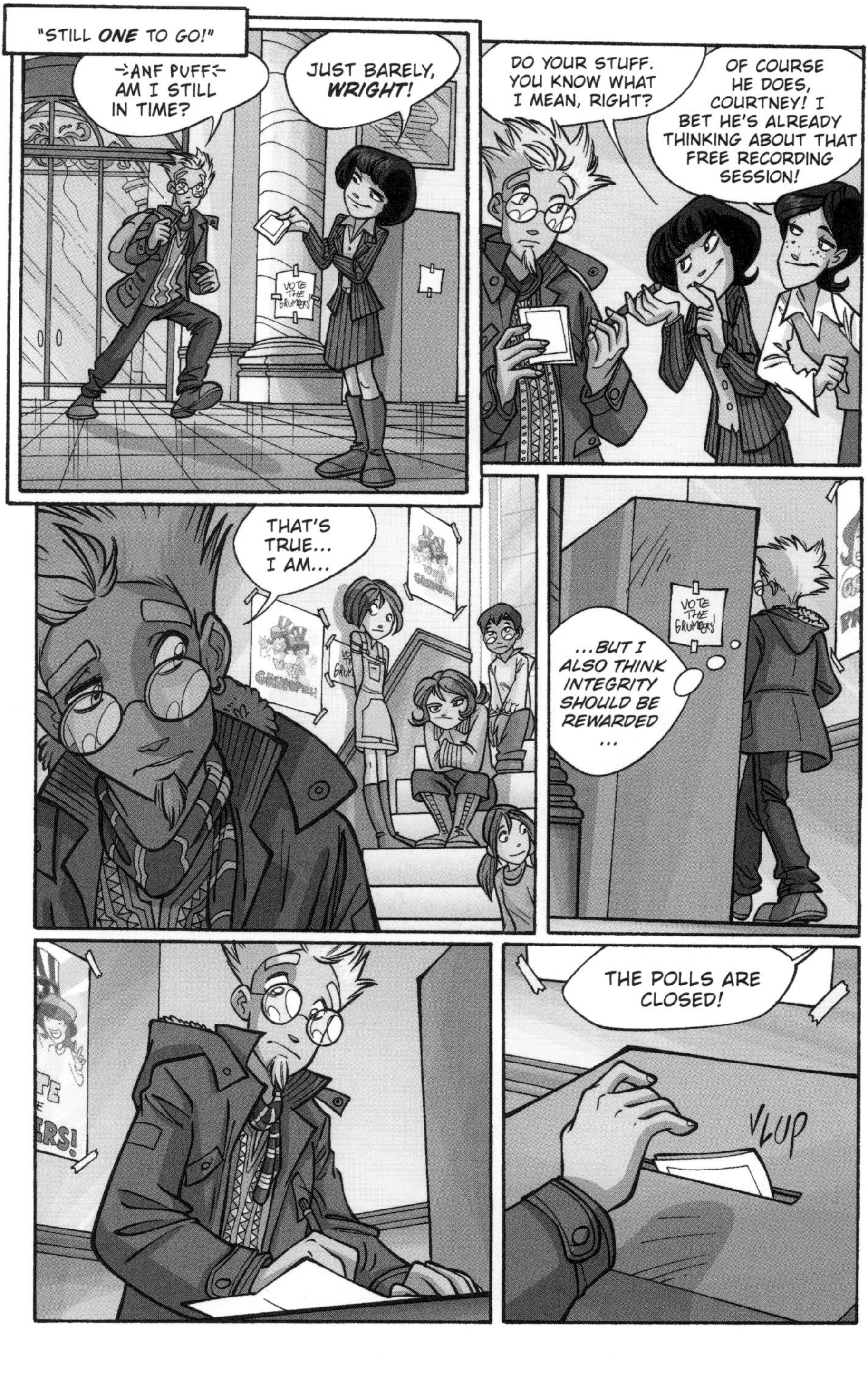
"STILL ONE TO GO!"
-ANF PUFF- AM I STILL IN TIME?
JUST BARELY, WRIGHT!
VOTE THE GRUMPERS
DO YOUR STUFF. YOU KNOW WHAT I MEAN, RIGHT?
OF COURSE HE DOES, COURTNEY! I BET HE'S ALREADY THINKING ABOUT THAT FREE RECORDING SESSION!
THAT'S TRUE... I AM...
VOTE THE GRUMPERS!
...BUT I ALSO THINK INTEGRITY SHOULD BE REWARDED ...
THE POLLS ARE CLOSED!
VLUP

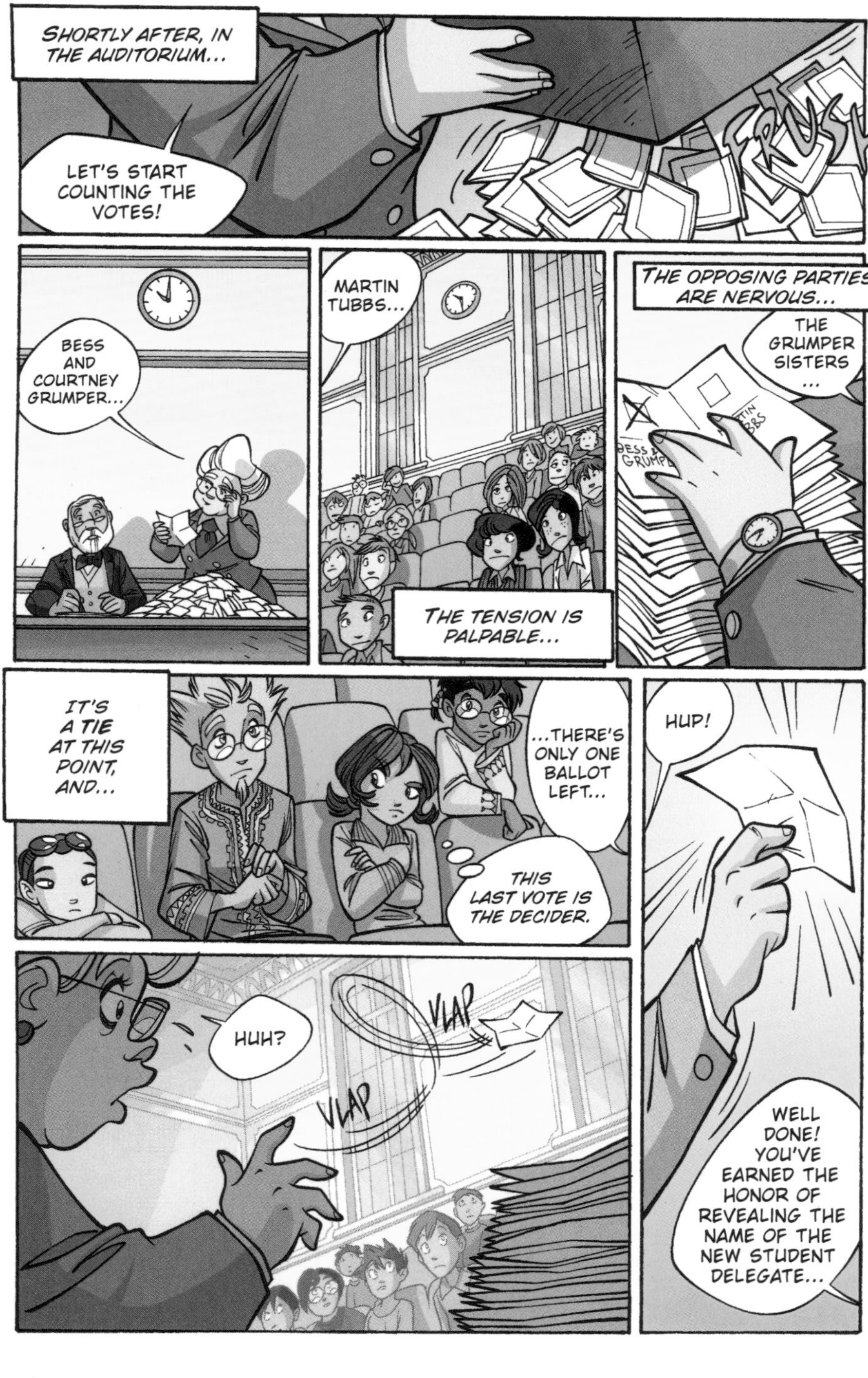
SHORTLY AFTER, IN THE AUDITORIUM...
LET'S START COUNTING THE VOTES!
FRUSH
BESS AND COURTNEY GRUMPER...
MARTIN TUBBS...
THE TENSION IS PALPABLE...
THE OPPOSING PARTIES ARE NERVOUS...
THE GRUMPER SISTERS ...
IT'S A TIE AT THIS POINT, AND...
...THERE'S ONLY ONE BALLOT LEFT...
THIS LAST VOTE IS THE DECIDER.
HUP!
HUH?
VLAP
VLAP
WELL DONE! YOU'VE EARNED THE HONOR OF REVEALING THE NAME OF THE NEW STUDENT DELEGATE...

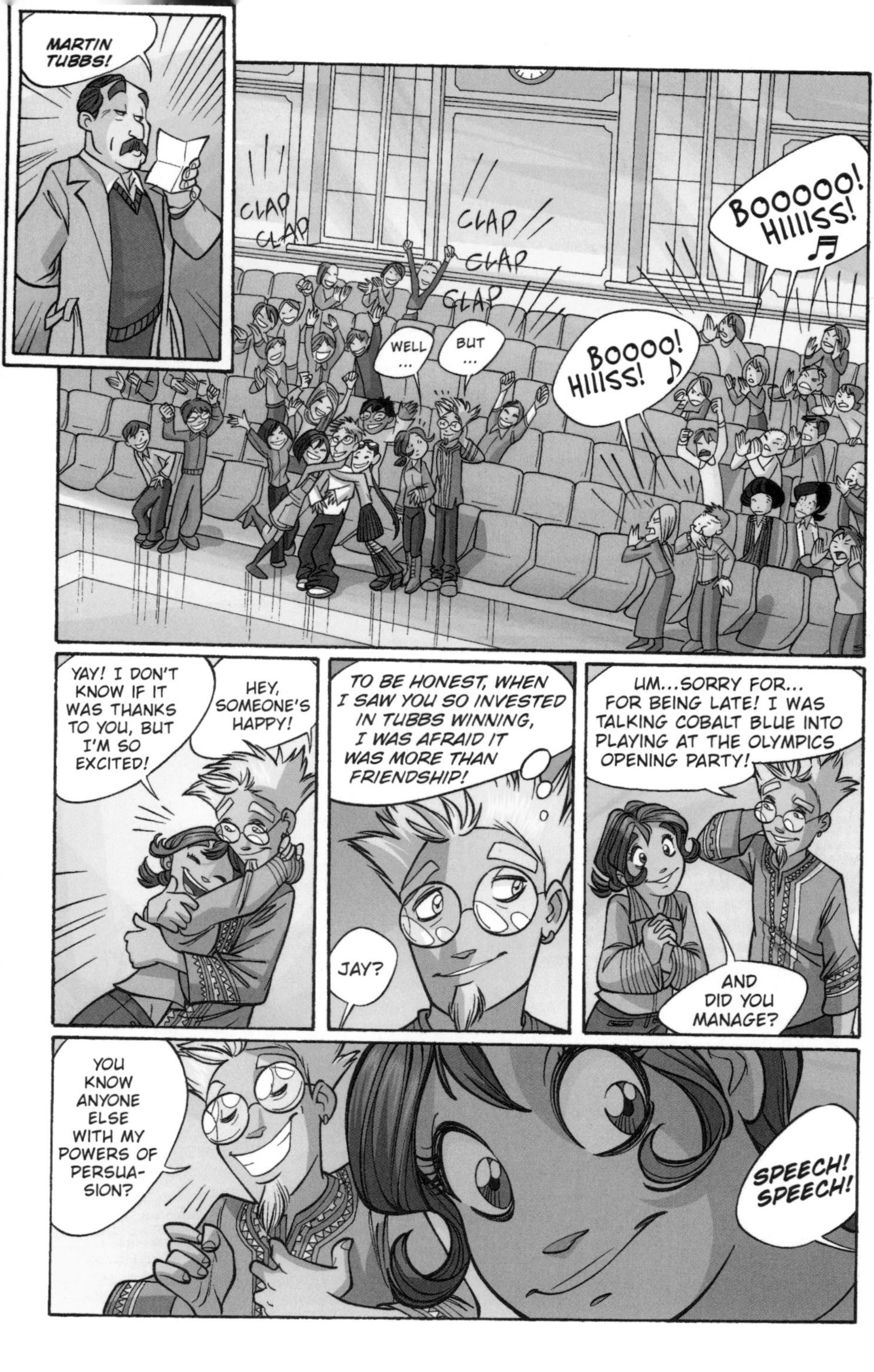
MARTIN TUBBS!
CLAP CLAP
CLAP
CLAP
CLAP
BOOOOO! HIIIISS! ♫
WELL ...
BUT ...
BOOOO! HIIISS! ♪
YAY! I DON'T KNOW IF IT WAS THANKS TO YOU, BUT I'M SO EXCITED!
HEY, SOMEONE'S HAPPY!
TO BE HONEST, WHEN I SAW YOU SO INVESTED IN TUBBS WINNING, I WAS AFRAID IT WAS MORE THAN FRIENDSHIP!
JAY?
UM...SORRY FOR... FOR BEING LATE! I WAS TALKING COBALT BLUE INTO PLAYING AT THE OLYMPICS OPENING PARTY!
AND DID YOU MANAGE?
YOU KNOW ANYONE ELSE WITH MY POWERS OF PERSUA-SION?
SPEECH! SPEECH!

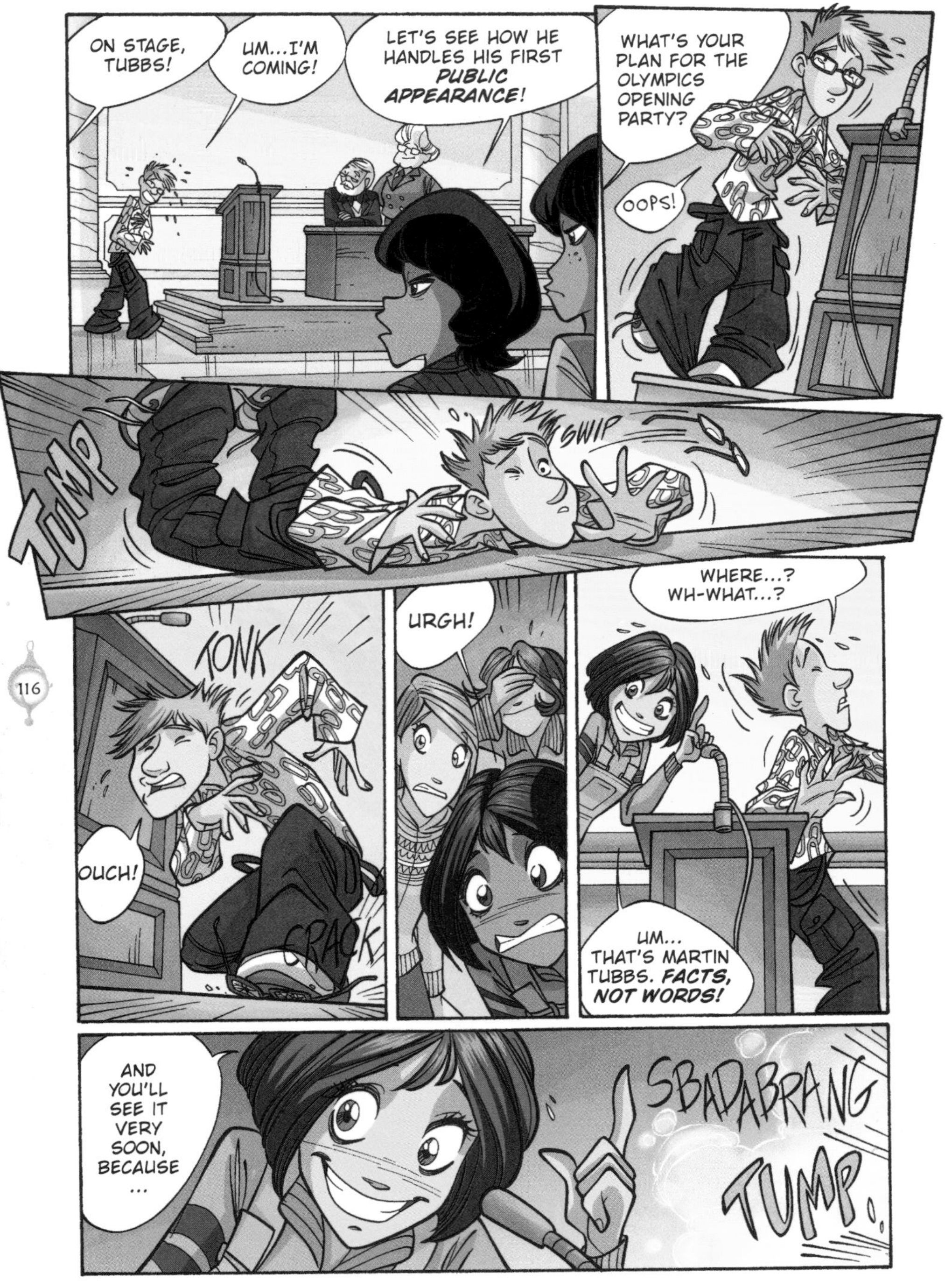
ON STAGE, TUBBS!
UM...I'M COMING!
LET'S SEE HOW HE HANDLES HIS FIRST ***PUBLIC APPEARANCE***!
WHAT'S YOUR PLAN FOR THE OLYMPICS OPENING PARTY?
OOPS!
TUMP
SWIP
TONK
OUCH!
CRACK
URGH!
WHERE...? WH-WHAT...?
UM... THAT'S MARTIN TUBBS. ***FACTS, NOT WORDS!***
AND YOU'LL SEE IT VERY SOON, BECAUSE ...
SBADABRANG
TUMP

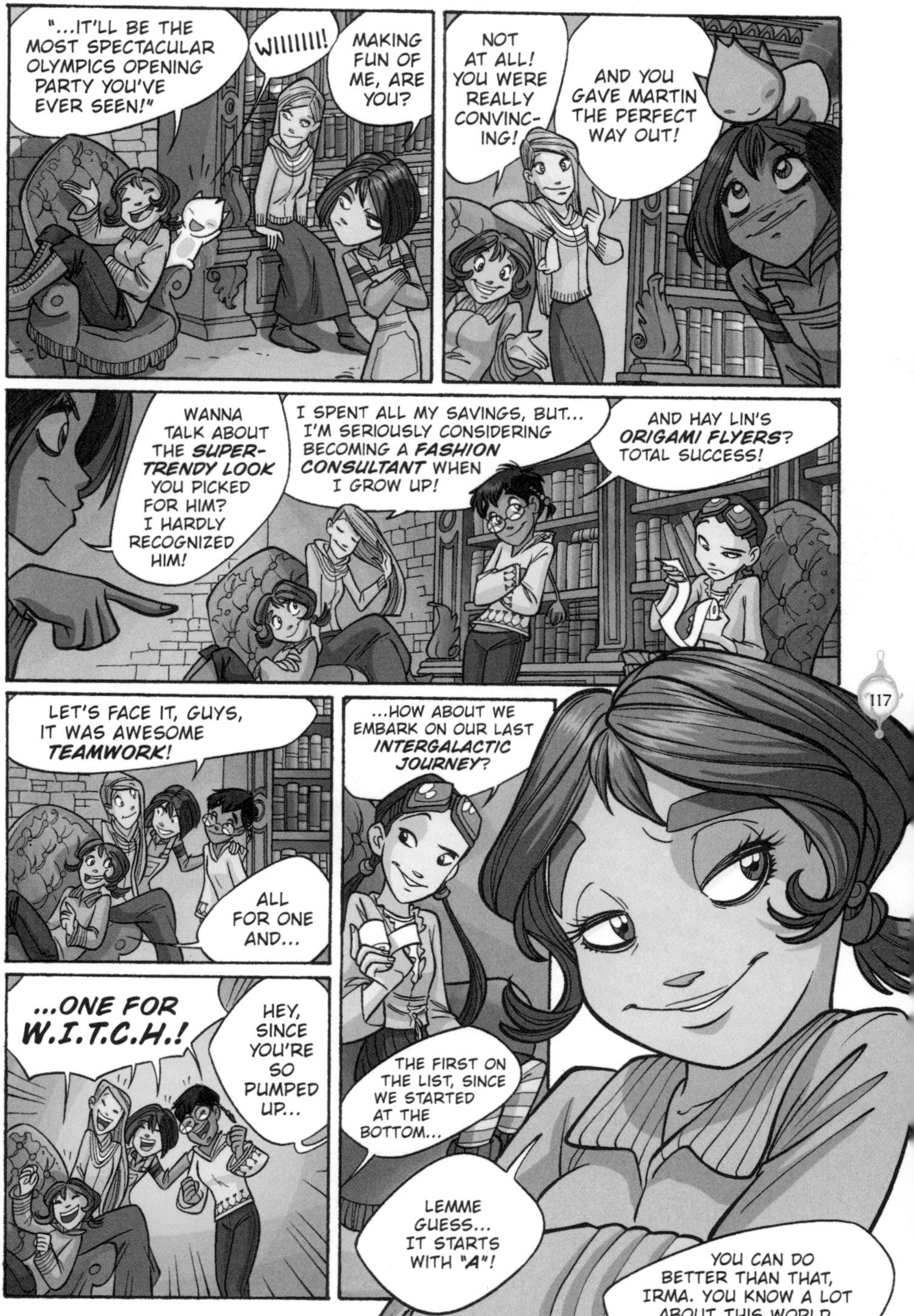

"...IT'LL BE THE MOST SPECTACULAR OLYMPICS OPENING PARTY YOU'VE EVER SEEN!"
WIIIIIII!
MAKING FUN OF ME, ARE YOU?
NOT AT ALL! YOU WERE REALLY CONVINC-ING!
AND YOU GAVE MARTIN THE PERFECT WAY OUT!
WANNA TALK ABOUT THE ***SUPER-TRENDY LOOK*** YOU PICKED FOR HIM? I HARDLY RECOGNIZED HIM!
I SPENT ALL MY SAVINGS, BUT... I'M SERIOUSLY CONSIDERING BECOMING A ***FASHION CONSULTANT*** WHEN I GROW UP!
AND HAY LIN'S ***ORIGAMI FLYERS***? TOTAL SUCCESS!
LET'S FACE IT, GUYS, IT WAS AWESOME ***TEAMWORK***!
ALL FOR ONE AND...
...HOW ABOUT WE EMBARK ON OUR LAST ***INTERGALACTIC JOURNEY***?
...ONE FOR W.I.T.C.H.!
HEY, SINCE YOU'RE SO PUMPED UP...
THE FIRST ON THE LIST, SINCE WE STARTED AT THE BOTTOM...
LEMME GUESS... IT STARTS WITH "***A***"!
YOU CAN DO BETTER THAN THAT, IRMA. YOU KNOW A LOT ABOUT THIS WORLD, I PROMISE!

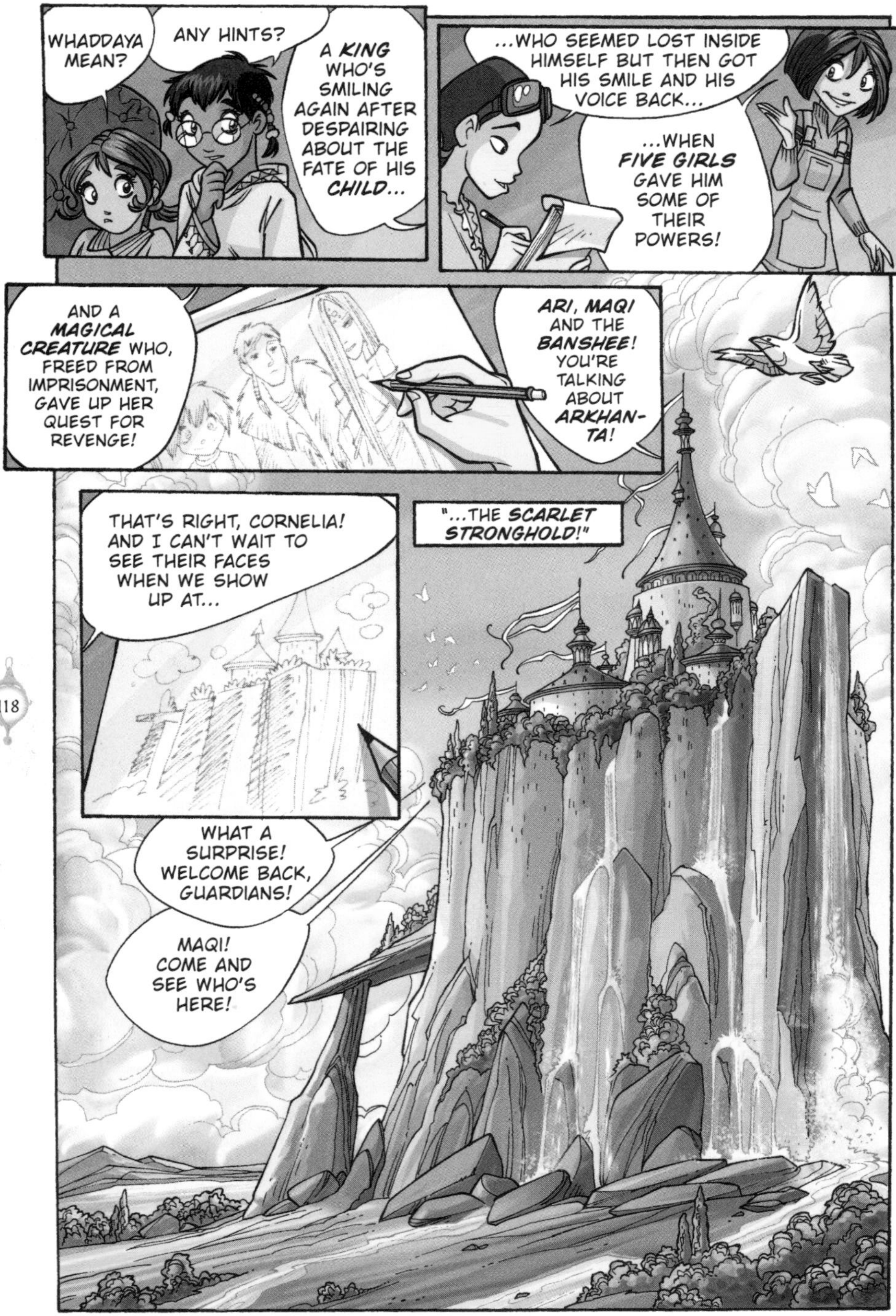
WHADDAYA MEAN?
ANY HINTS?
A KING WHO'S SMILING AGAIN AFTER DESPAIRING ABOUT THE FATE OF HIS CHILD...
...WHO SEEMED LOST INSIDE HIMSELF BUT THEN GOT HIS SMILE AND HIS VOICE BACK...
...WHEN FIVE GIRLS GAVE HIM SOME OF THEIR POWERS!
AND A MAGICAL CREATURE WHO, FREED FROM IMPRISONMENT, GAVE UP HER QUEST FOR REVENGE!
ARI, MAQI AND THE BANSHEE! YOU'RE TALKING ABOUT ARKHAN-TA!
THAT'S RIGHT, CORNELIA! AND I CAN'T WAIT TO SEE THEIR FACES WHEN WE SHOW UP AT...
"...THE SCARLET STRONGHOLD!"
WHAT A SURPRISE! WELCOME BACK, GUARDIANS!
MAQI! COME AND SEE WHO'S HERE!

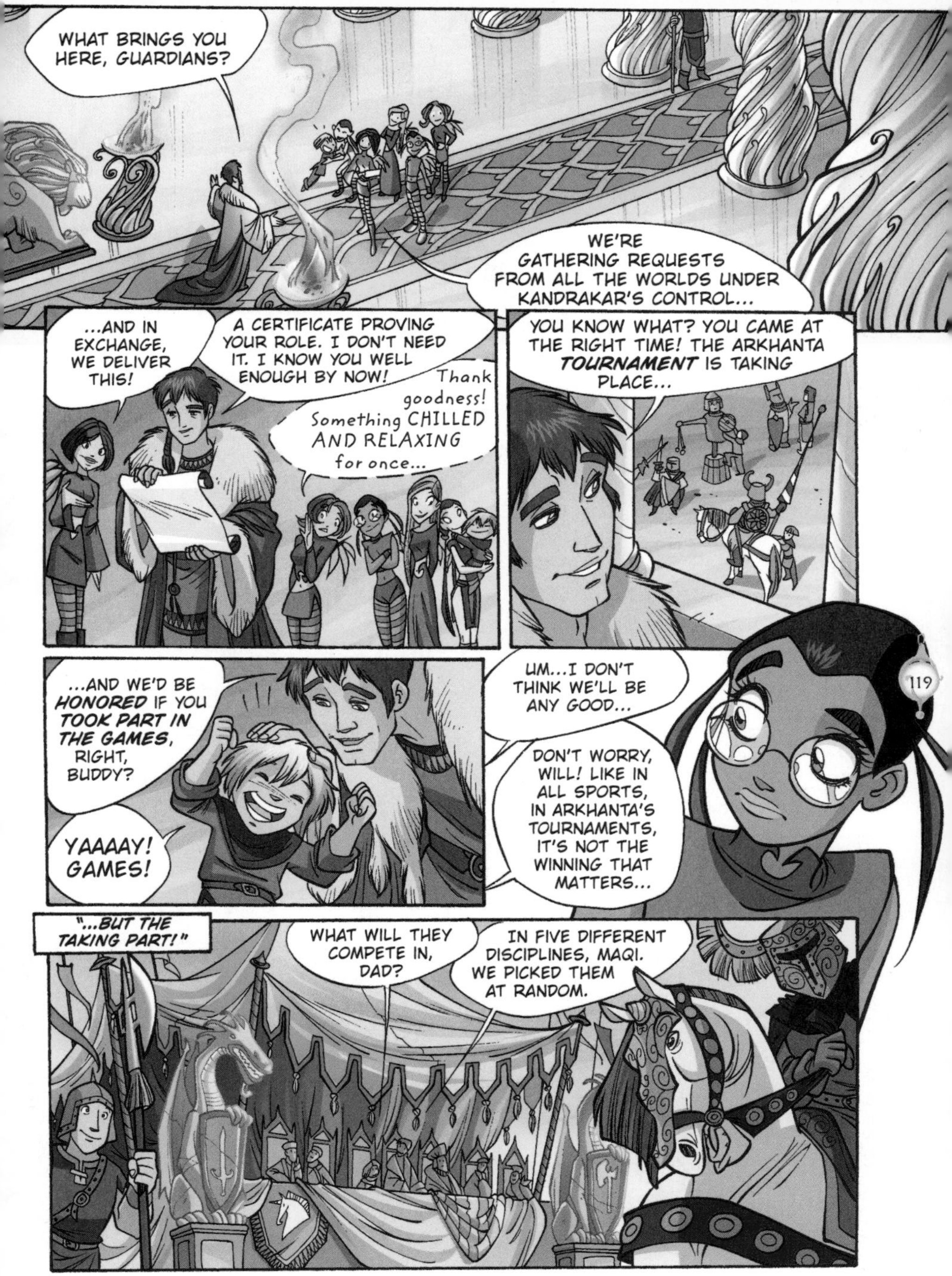
WHAT BRINGS YOU HERE, GUARDIANS?
WE'RE GATHERING REQUESTS FROM ALL THE WORLDS UNDER KANDRAKAR'S CONTROL...
...AND IN EXCHANGE, WE DELIVER THIS!
A CERTIFICATE PROVING YOUR ROLE. I DON'T NEED IT. I KNOW YOU WELL ENOUGH BY NOW!
Thank goodness! Something CHILLED AND RELAXING for once...
YOU KNOW WHAT? YOU CAME AT THE RIGHT TIME! THE ARKHANTA TOURNAMENT IS TAKING PLACE...
...AND WE'D BE HONORED IF YOU TOOK PART IN THE GAMES, RIGHT, BUDDY?
YAAAAY! GAMES!
UM...I DON'T THINK WE'LL BE ANY GOOD...
DON'T WORRY, WILL! LIKE IN ALL SPORTS, IN ARKHANTA'S TOURNAMENTS, IT'S NOT THE WINNING THAT MATTERS...
"...BUT THE TAKING PART!"
WHAT WILL THEY COMPETE IN, DAD?
IN FIVE DIFFERENT DISCIPLINES, MAQI. WE PICKED THEM AT RANDOM.

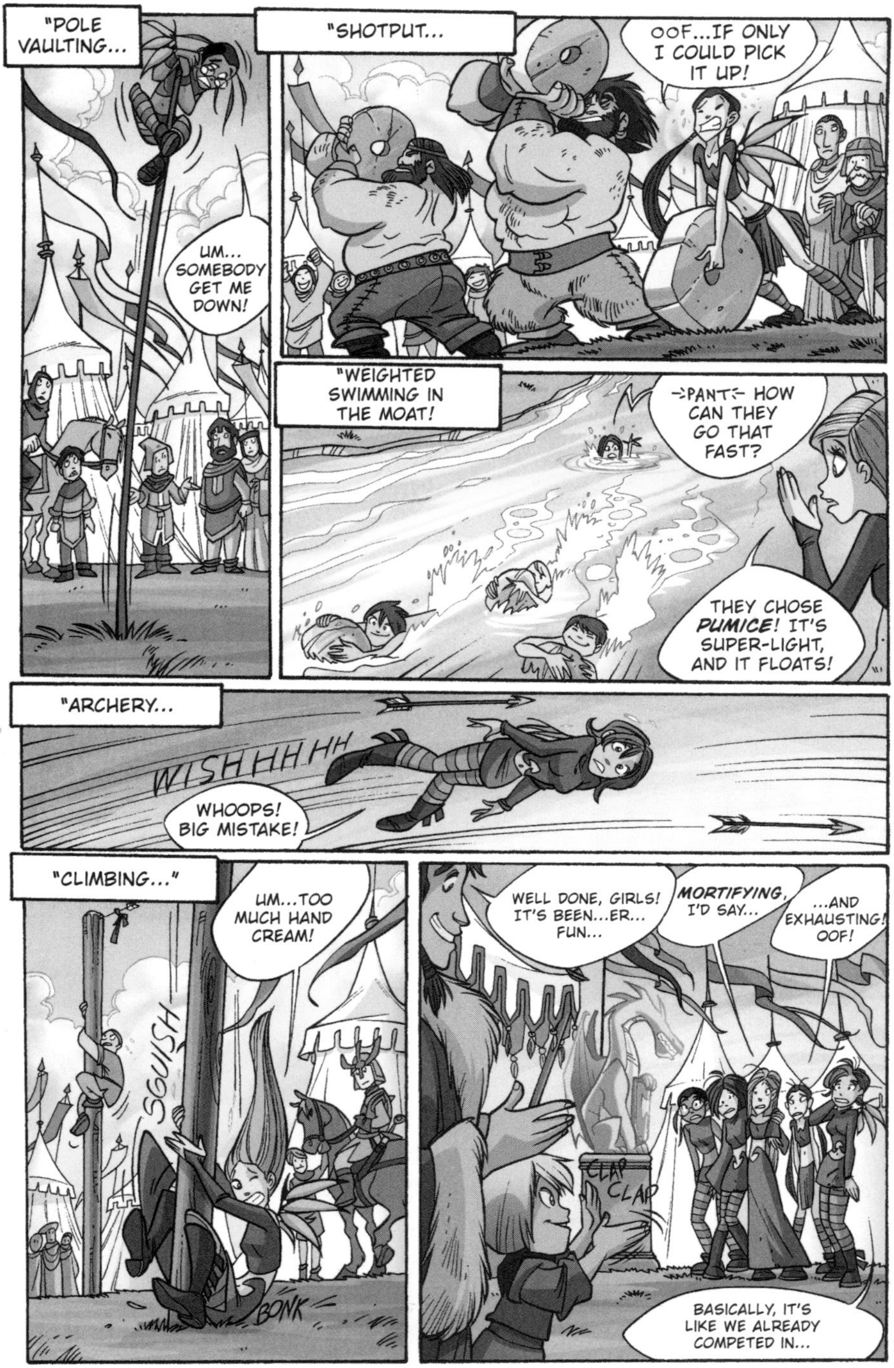
"POLE VAULTING...
UM... SOMEBODY GET ME DOWN!
"SHOTPUT...
OOF...IF ONLY I COULD PICK IT UP!
"WEIGHTED SWIMMING IN THE MOAT!
–PANT– HOW CAN THEY GO THAT FAST?
THEY CHOSE PUMICE! IT'S SUPER-LIGHT, AND IT FLOATS!
"ARCHERY...
WISHHHHH
WHOOPS! BIG MISTAKE!
"CLIMBING..."
UM...TOO MUCH HAND CREAM!
SQUISH
BONK
WELL DONE, GIRLS! IT'S BEEN...ER... FUN...
MORTIFYING, I'D SAY...
...AND EXHAUSTING! OOF!
CLAP CLAP
BASICALLY, IT'S LIKE WE ALREADY COMPETED IN...

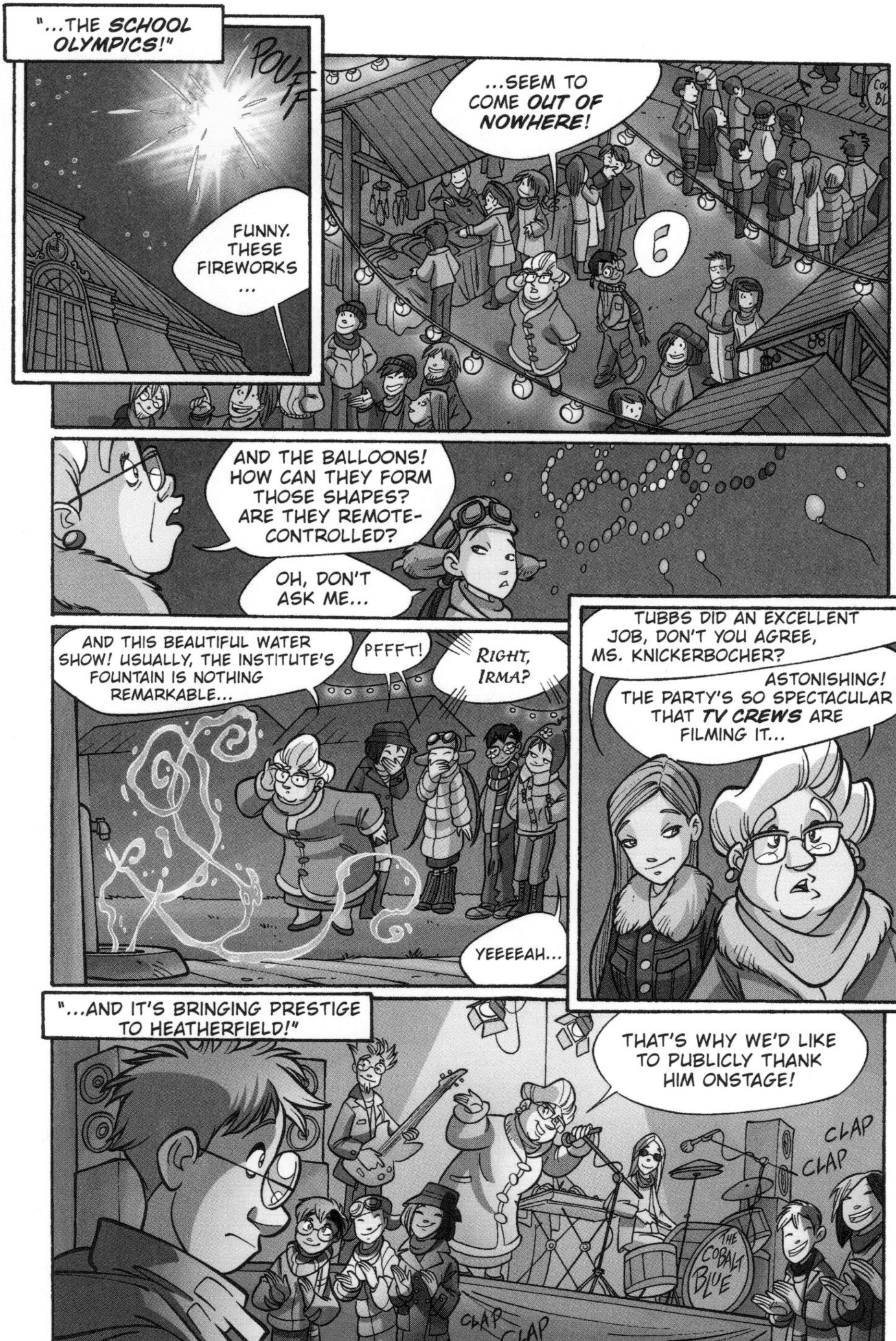
"...THE SCHOOL OLYMPICS!"
POUFF
FUNNY. THESE FIREWORKS ...
...SEEM TO COME OUT OF NOWHERE!
AND THE BALLOONS! HOW CAN THEY FORM THOSE SHAPES? ARE THEY REMOTE-CONTROLLED?
OH, DON'T ASK ME...
AND THIS BEAUTIFUL WATER SHOW! USUALLY, THE INSTITUTE'S FOUNTAIN IS NOTHING REMARKABLE...
PFFFT!
RIGHT, IRMA?
YEEEEAH...
TUBBS DID AN EXCELLENT JOB, DON'T YOU AGREE, MS. KNICKERBOCHER?
ASTONISHING! THE PARTY'S SO SPECTACULAR THAT TV CREWS ARE FILMING IT...
"...AND IT'S BRINGING PRESTIGE TO HEATHERFIELD!"
THAT'S WHY WE'D LIKE TO PUBLICLY THANK HIM ONSTAGE!
CLAP CLAP
THE COBALT BLUE
CLAP CLAP

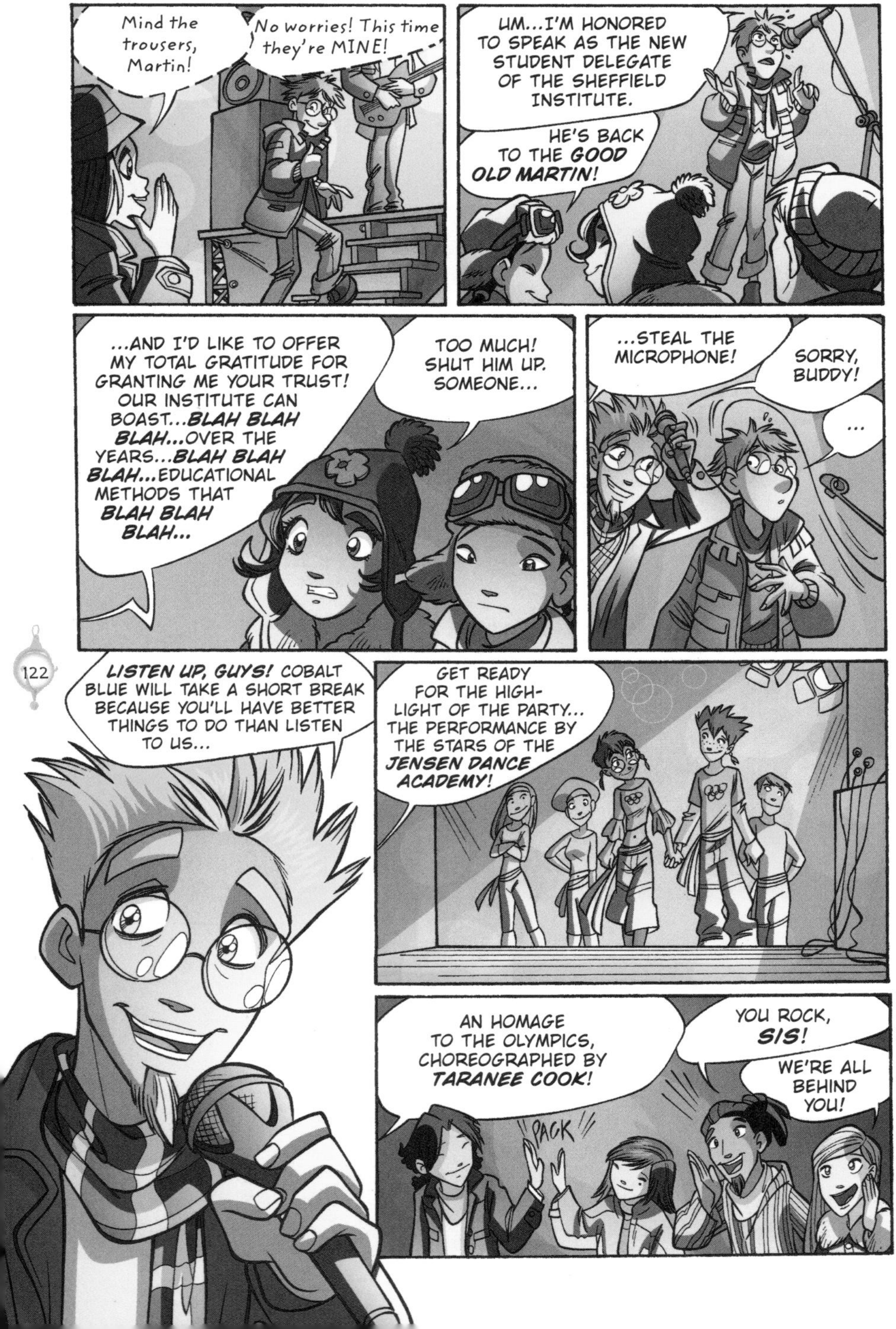

Mind the trousers, Martin!
No worries! This time they're MINE!
UM...I'M HONORED TO SPEAK AS THE NEW STUDENT DELEGATE OF THE SHEFFIELD INSTITUTE.
HE'S BACK TO THE GOOD OLD MARTIN!
...AND I'D LIKE TO OFFER MY TOTAL GRATITUDE FOR GRANTING ME YOUR TRUST! OUR INSTITUTE CAN BOAST...BLAH BLAH BLAH...OVER THE YEARS...BLAH BLAH BLAH...EDUCATIONAL METHODS THAT BLAH BLAH BLAH...
TOO MUCH! SHUT HIM UP. SOMEONE...
...STEAL THE MICROPHONE!
SORRY, BUDDY!
...
LISTEN UP, GUYS! COBALT BLUE WILL TAKE A SHORT BREAK BECAUSE YOU'LL HAVE BETTER THINGS TO DO THAN LISTEN TO US...
GET READY FOR THE HIGH-LIGHT OF THE PARTY... THE PERFORMANCE BY THE STARS OF THE JENSEN DANCE ACADEMY!
AN HOMAGE TO THE OLYMPICS, CHOREOGRAPHED BY TARANEE COOK!
PACK
YOU ROCK, SIS!
WE'RE ALL BEHIND YOU!

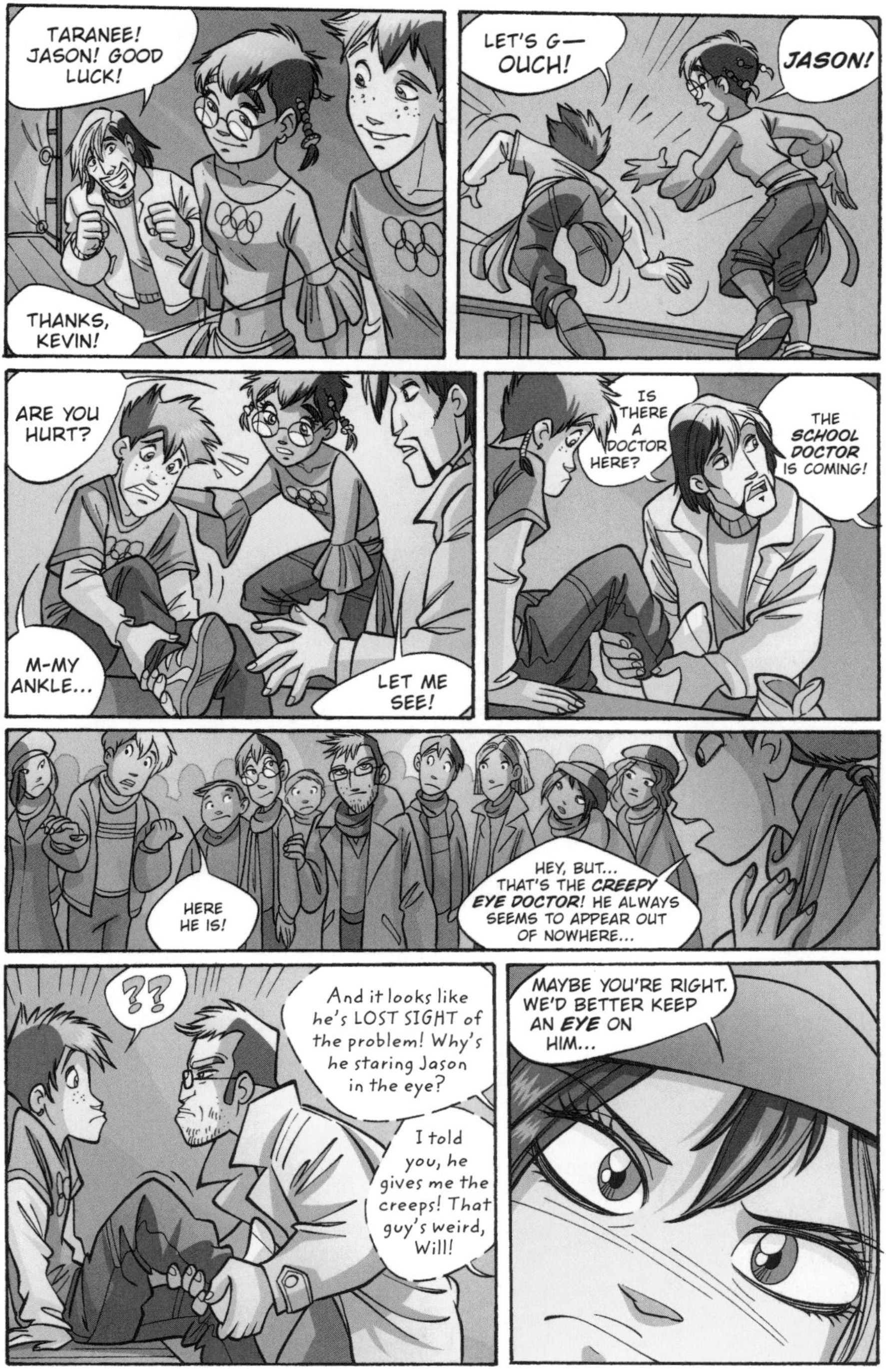

TARANEE! JASON! GOOD LUCK!
THANKS, KEVIN!
LET'S G— OUCH!
JASON!
ARE YOU HURT?
M-MY ANKLE...
LET ME SEE!
IS THERE A DOCTOR HERE?
THE SCHOOL DOCTOR IS COMING!
HERE HE IS!
HEY, BUT... THAT'S THE CREEPY EYE DOCTOR! HE ALWAYS SEEMS TO APPEAR OUT OF NOWHERE...
??
And it looks like he's LOST SIGHT of the problem! Why's he staring Jason in the eye?
I told you, he gives me the creeps! That guy's weird, Will!
MAYBE YOU'RE RIGHT. WE'D BETTER KEEP AN EYE ON HIM...

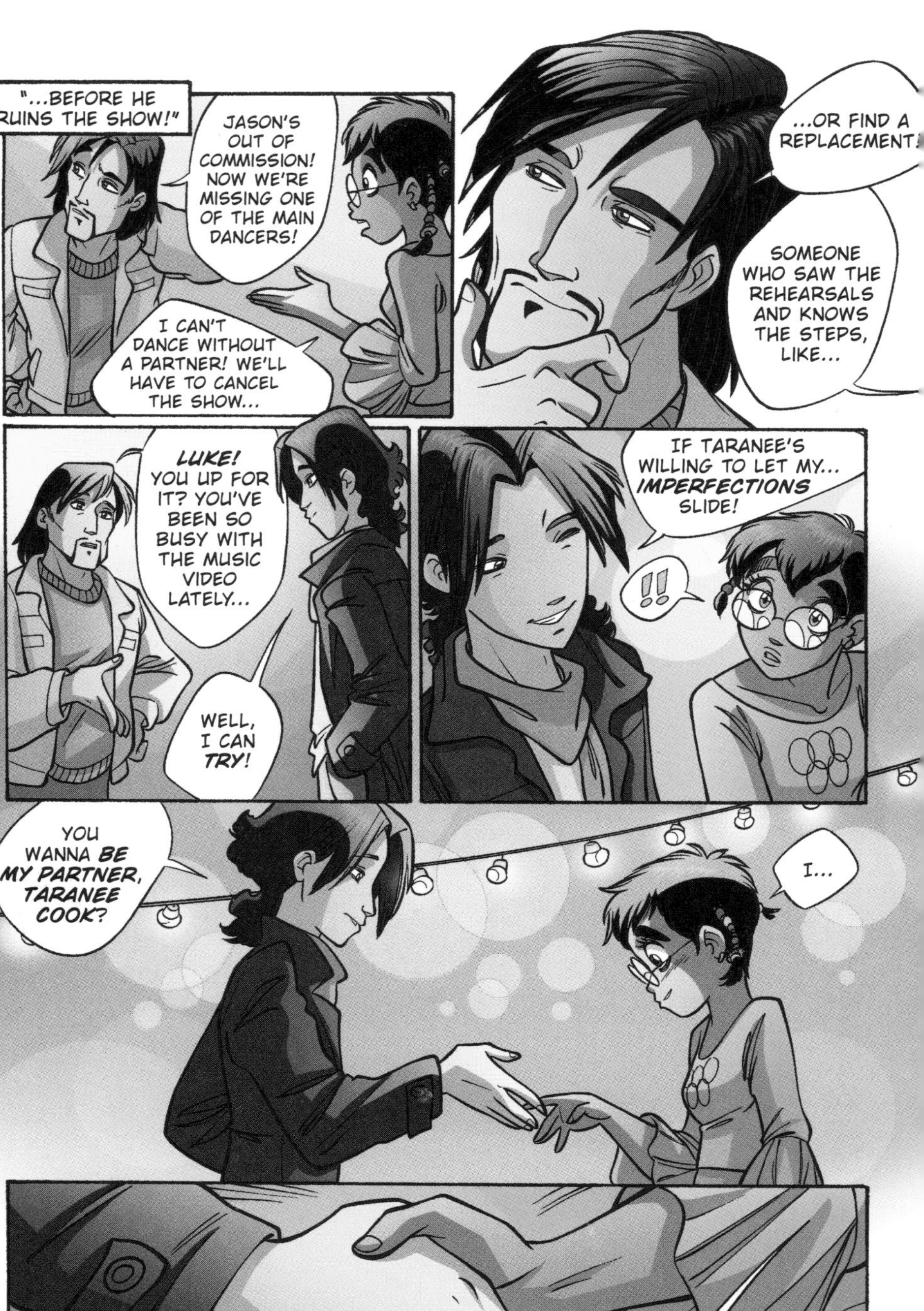
"...BEFORE HE RUINS THE SHOW!"
JASON'S OUT OF COMMISSION! NOW WE'RE MISSING ONE OF THE MAIN DANCERS!
I CAN'T DANCE WITHOUT A PARTNER! WE'LL HAVE TO CANCEL THE SHOW...
...OR FIND A REPLACEMENT!
SOMEONE WHO SAW THE REHEARSALS AND KNOWS THE STEPS, LIKE...
LUKE! YOU UP FOR IT? YOU'VE BEEN SO BUSY WITH THE MUSIC VIDEO LATELY...
WELL, I CAN *TRY*!
IF TARANEE'S WILLING TO LET MY... *IMPERFECTIONS* SLIDE!
!!
YOU WANNA *BE MY PARTNER, TARANEE COOK?*
I...
I'D LOVE TO, *LUKE PRADD*!

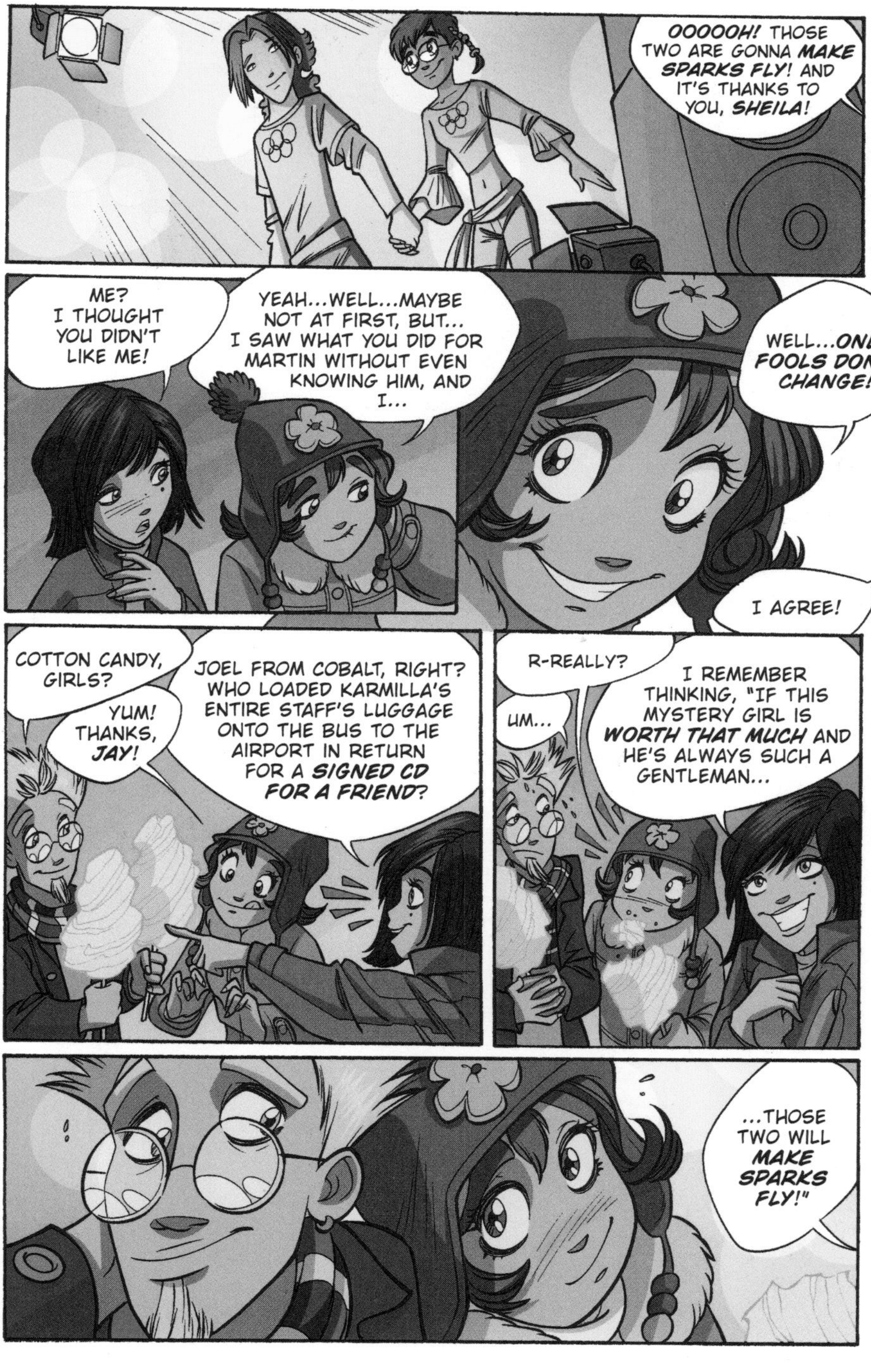
OOOOOH! THOSE TWO ARE GONNA MAKE SPARKS FLY! AND IT'S THANKS TO YOU, SHEILA!
ME? I THOUGHT YOU DIDN'T LIKE ME!
YEAH...WELL...MAYBE NOT AT FIRST, BUT... I SAW WHAT YOU DID FOR MARTIN WITHOUT EVEN KNOWING HIM, AND I...
WELL...ONLY FOOLS DON'T CHANGE!
I AGREE!
COTTON CANDY, GIRLS?
YUM! THANKS, JAY!
JOEL FROM COBALT, RIGHT? WHO LOADED KARMILLA'S ENTIRE STAFF'S LUGGAGE ONTO THE BUS TO THE AIRPORT IN RETURN FOR A SIGNED CD FOR A FRIEND?
R-REALLY?
UM...
I REMEMBER THINKING, "IF THIS MYSTERY GIRL IS WORTH THAT MUCH AND HE'S ALWAYS SUCH A GENTLEMAN...
...THOSE TWO WILL MAKE SPARKS FLY!"

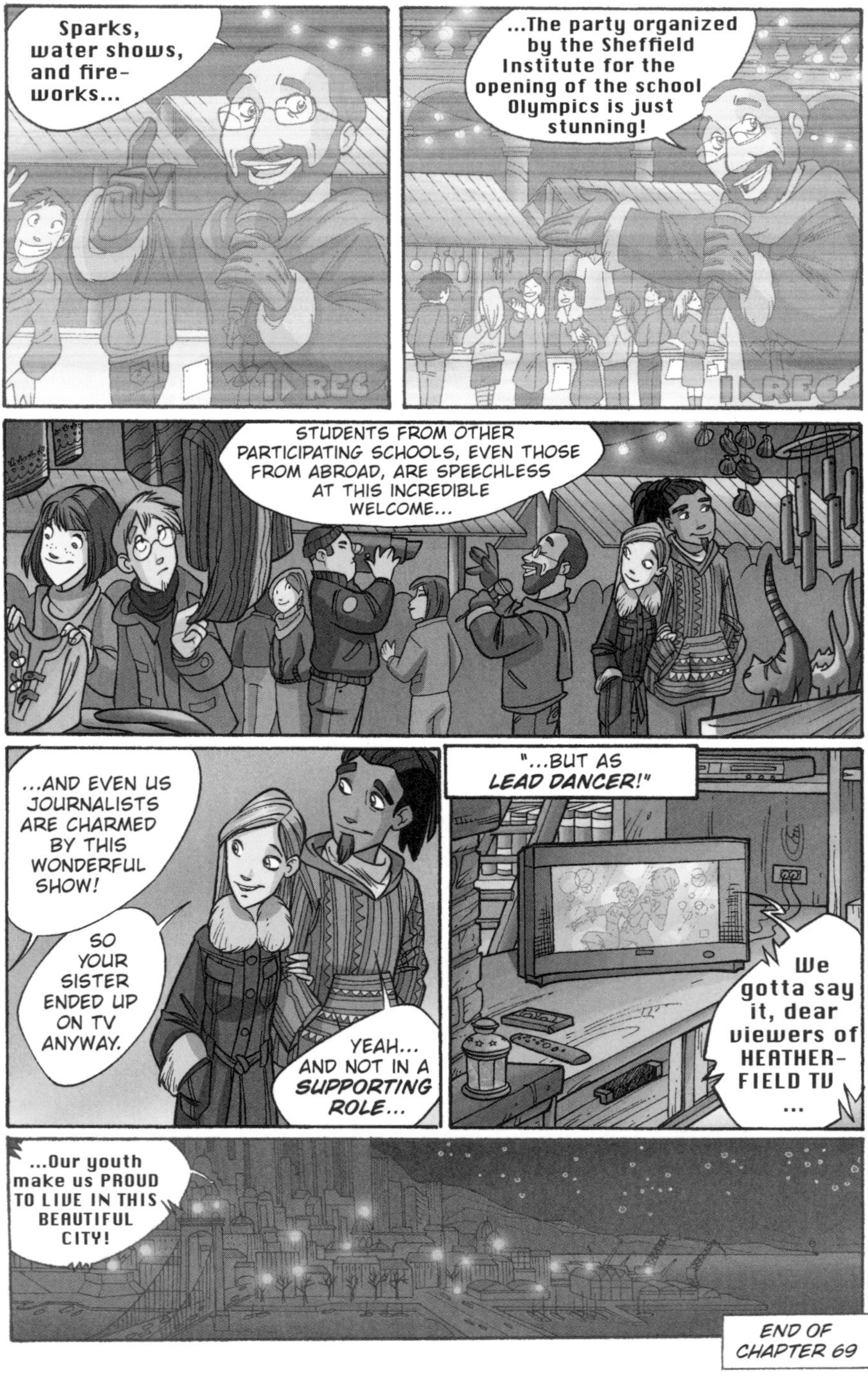
Sparks, water shows, and fire-works...
...The party organized by the Sheffield Institute for the opening of the school Olympics is just stunning!
STUDENTS FROM OTHER PARTICIPATING SCHOOLS, EVEN THOSE FROM ABROAD, ARE SPEECHLESS AT THIS INCREDIBLE WELCOME...
...AND EVEN US JOURNALISTS ARE CHARMED BY THIS WONDERFUL SHOW!
SO YOUR SISTER ENDED UP ON TV ANYWAY.
YEAH... AND NOT IN A SUPPORTING ROLE...
"...BUT AS LEAD DANCER!"
We gotta say it, dear viewers of HEATHER-FIELD TV ...
...Our youth make us PROUD TO LIVE IN THIS BEAUTIFUL CITY!
END OF CHAPTER 69

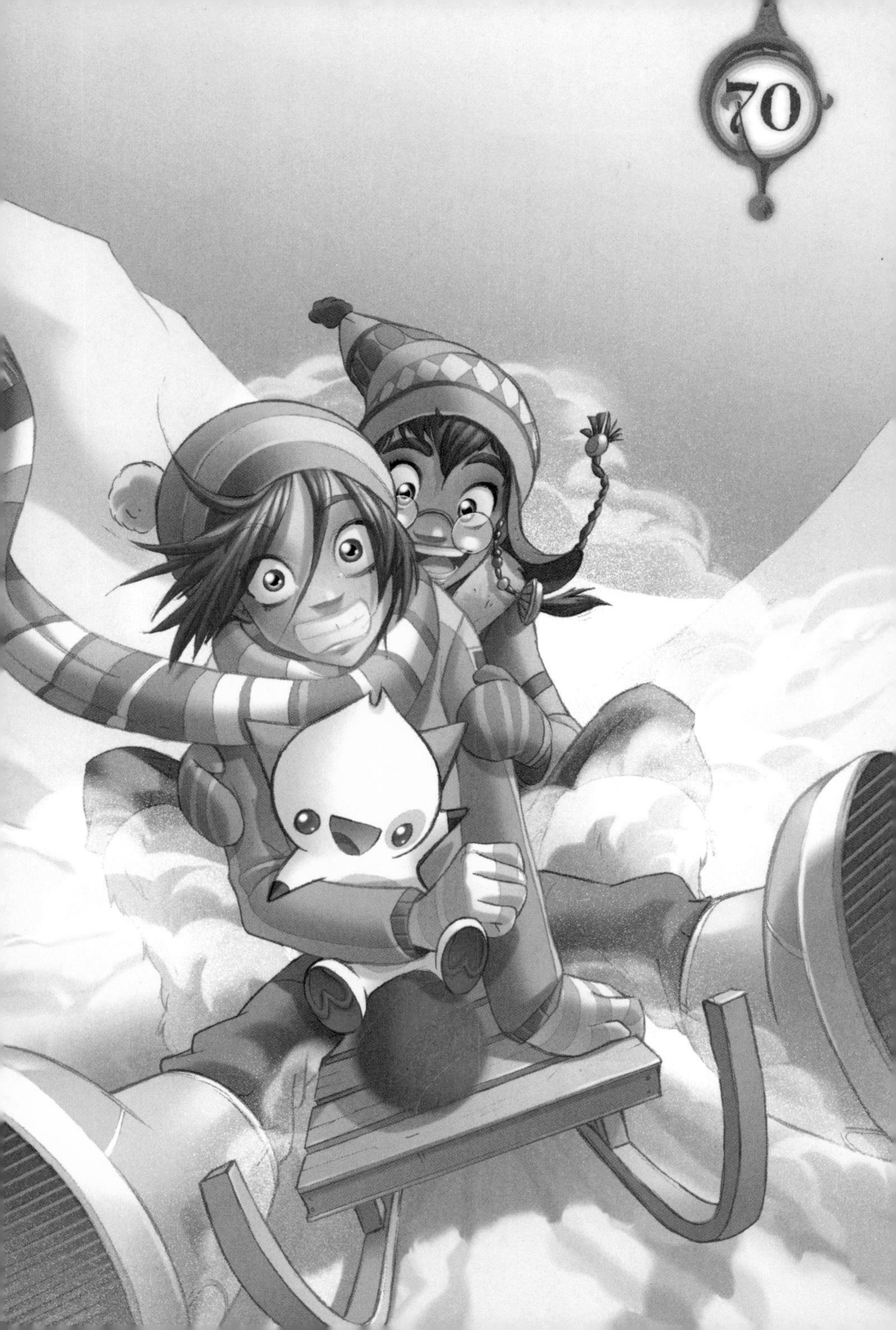
70

Radio Silence

"And I wonder if I'll ever find myself again!"

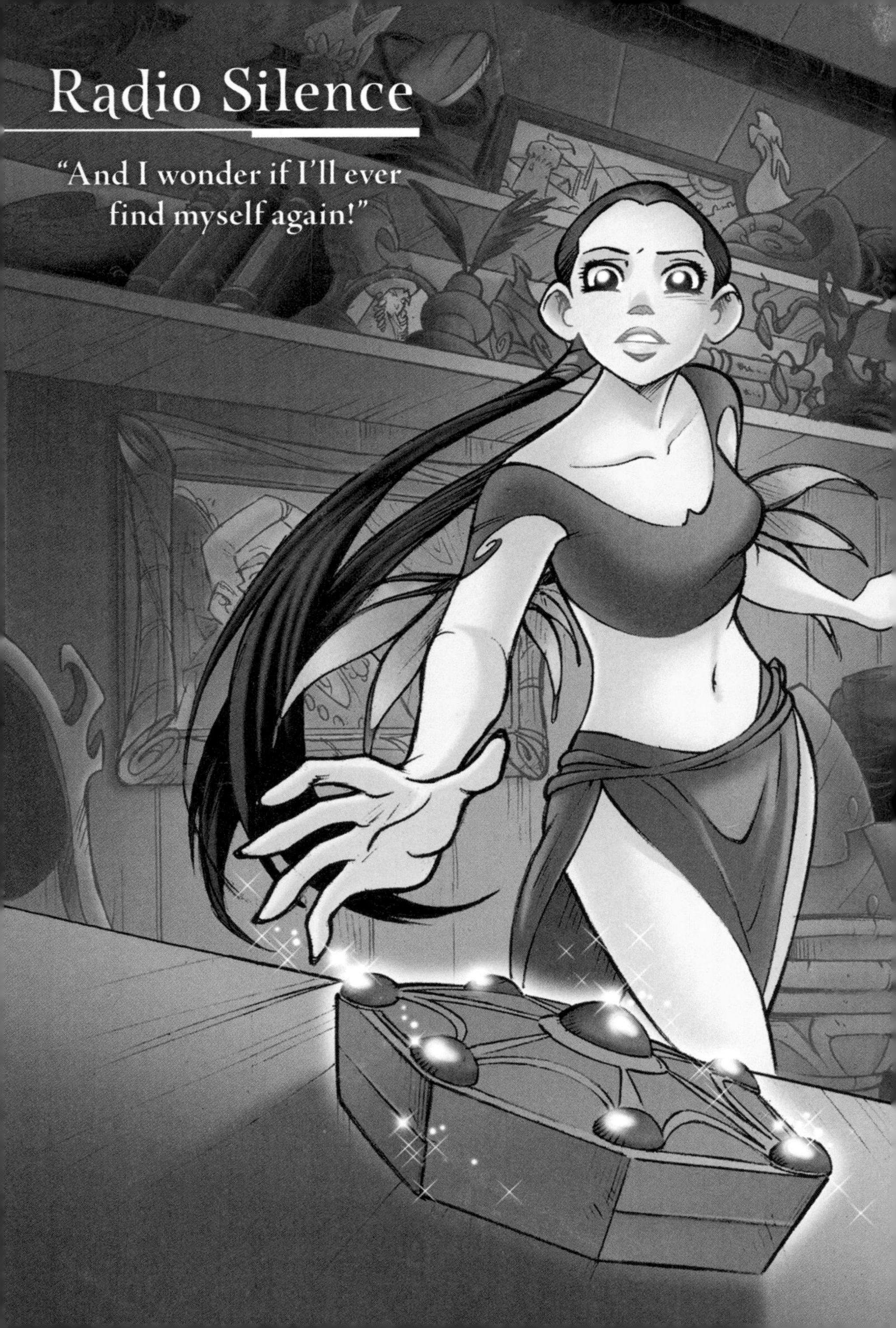

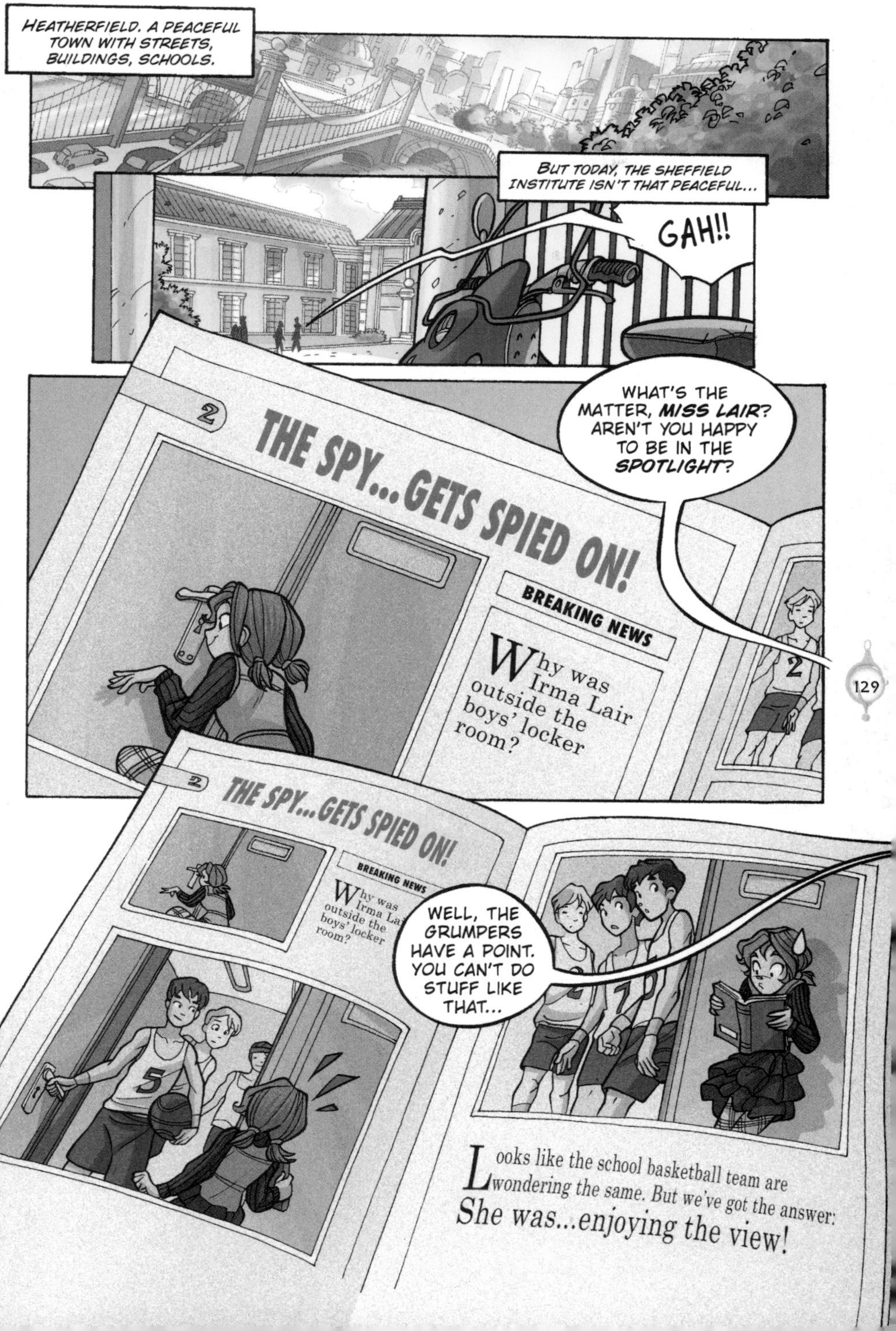
HEATHERFIELD. A PEACEFUL TOWN WITH STREETS, BUILDINGS, SCHOOLS.
BUT TODAY, THE SHEFFIELD INSTITUTE ISN'T THAT PEACEFUL...
GAH!!
WHAT'S THE MATTER, MISS LAIR? AREN'T YOU HAPPY TO BE IN THE SPOTLIGHT?
2
THE SPY...GETS SPIED ON!
BREAKING NEWS
Why was Irma Lair outside the boys' locker room?
2
THE SPY...GETS SPIED ON!
BREAKING NEWS
Why was Irma Lai[r] outside the boys' locker room?
WELL, THE GRUMPERS HAVE A POINT. YOU CAN'T DO STUFF LIKE THAT...
Looks like the school basketball team are wondering the same. But we've got the answer:
She was...enjoying the view!

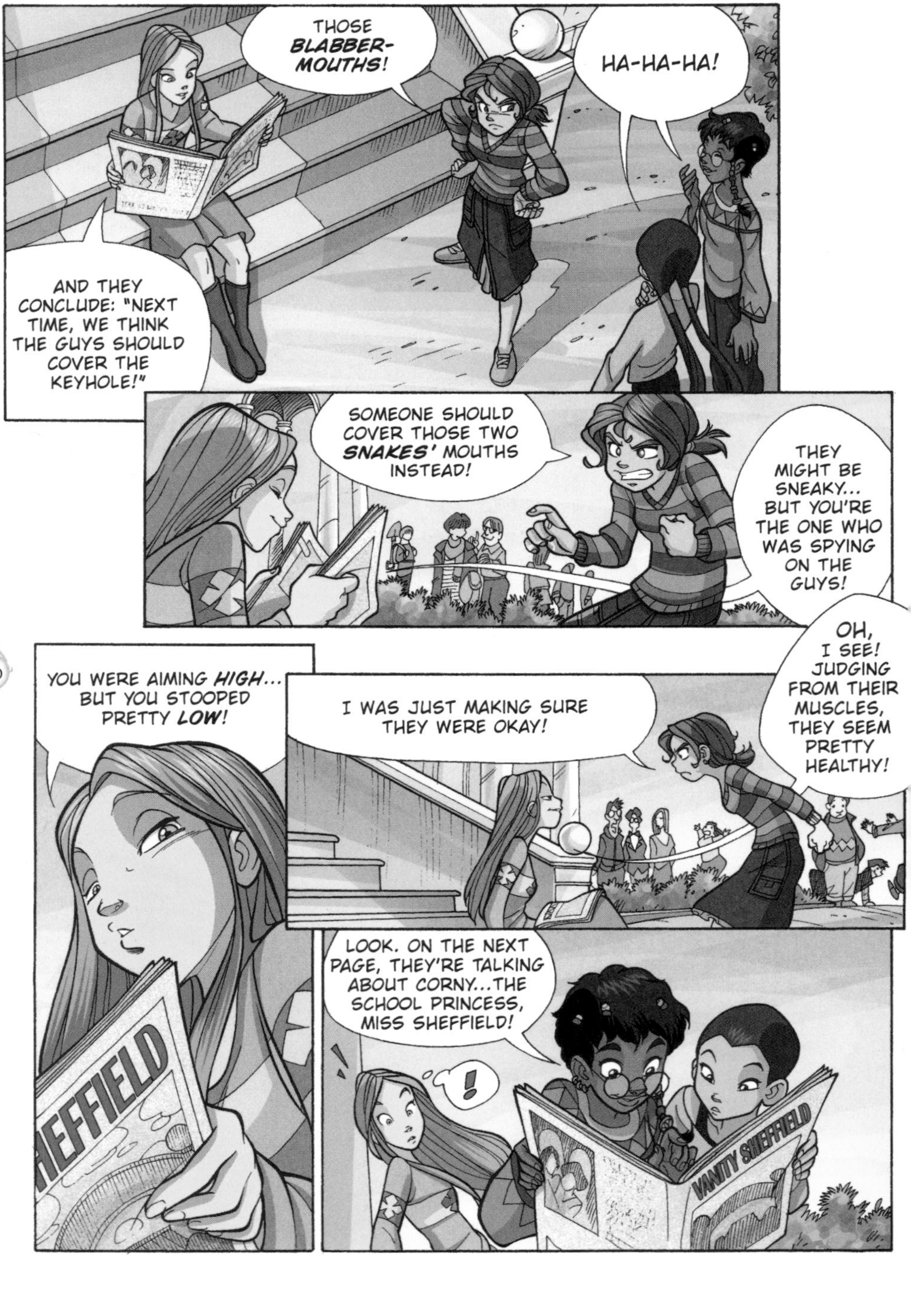

THOSE *BLABBER-MOUTHS*!
HA-HA-HA!
AND THEY CONCLUDE: "NEXT TIME, WE THINK THE GUYS SHOULD COVER THE KEYHOLE!"
SOMEONE SHOULD COVER THOSE TWO *SNAKES'* MOUTHS INSTEAD!
THEY MIGHT BE SNEAKY... BUT YOU'RE THE ONE WHO WAS SPYING ON THE GUYS!
YOU WERE AIMING *HIGH*... BUT YOU STOOPED PRETTY *LOW*!
I WAS JUST MAKING SURE THEY WERE OKAY!
OH, I SEE! JUDGING FROM THEIR MUSCLES, THEY SEEM PRETTY HEALTHY!
LOOK. ON THE NEXT PAGE, THEY'RE TALKING ABOUT CORNY...THE SCHOOL PRINCESS, MISS SHEFFIELD!
!
SHEFFIELD
VANITY SHEFFIELD

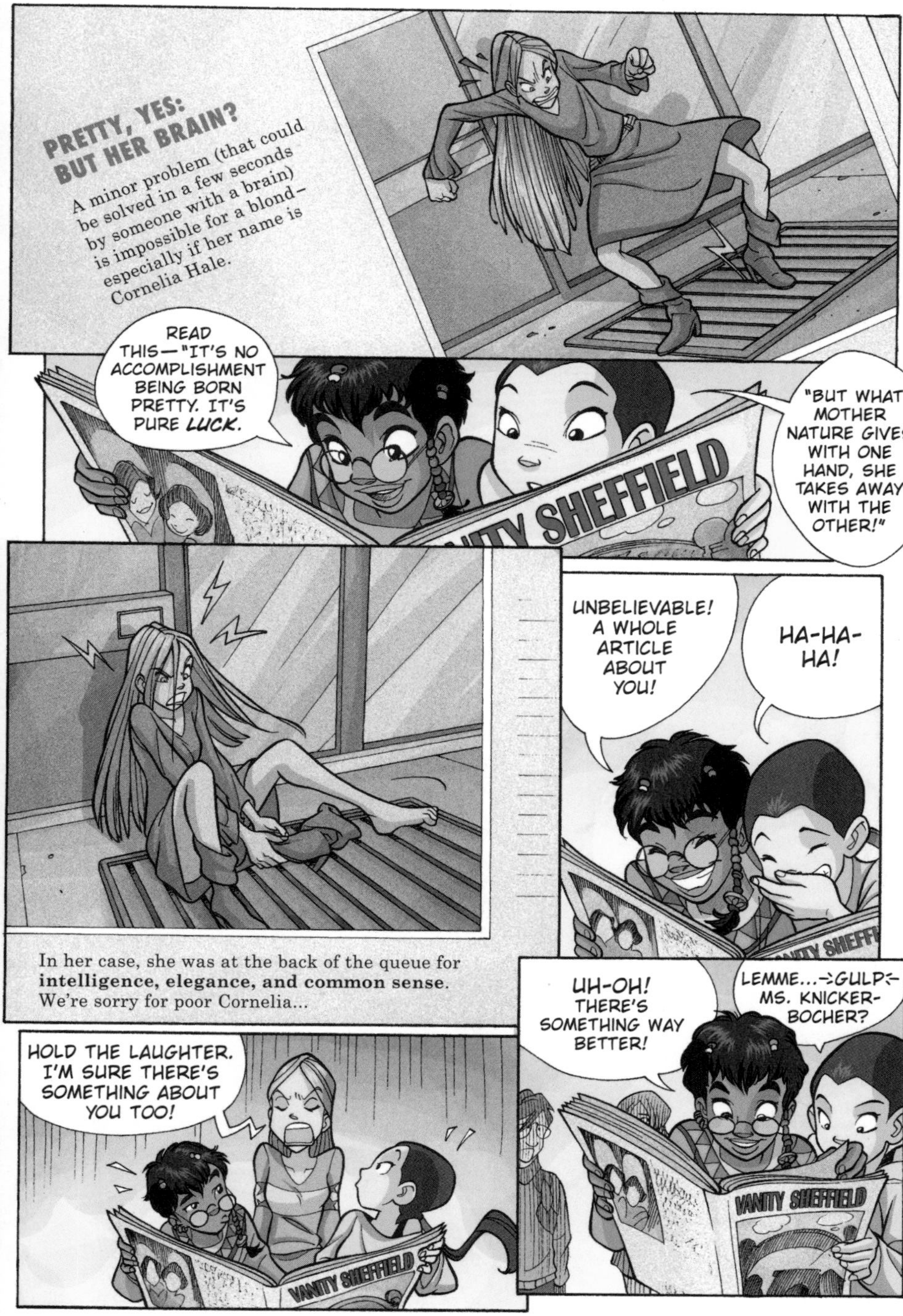
PRETTY, YES: BUT HER BRAIN?
A minor problem (that could be solved in a few seconds by someone with a brain) is impossible for a blond–especially if her name is Cornelia Hale.
READ THIS—"IT'S NO ACCOMPLISHMENT BEING BORN PRETTY. IT'S PURE LUCK.
"BUT WHAT MOTHER NATURE GIVES WITH ONE HAND, SHE TAKES AWAY WITH THE OTHER!"
VANITY SHEFFIELD
In her case, she was at the back of the queue for **intelligence, elegance, and common sense**. We're sorry for poor Cornelia...
UNBELIEVABLE! A WHOLE ARTICLE ABOUT YOU!
HA-HA-HA!
HOLD THE LAUGHTER. I'M SURE THERE'S SOMETHING ABOUT YOU TOO!
VANITY SHEFFIELD
UH-OH! THERE'S SOMETHING WAY BETTER!
LEMME... GULP MS. KNICKER-BOCHER?
VANITY SHEFFIELD

131

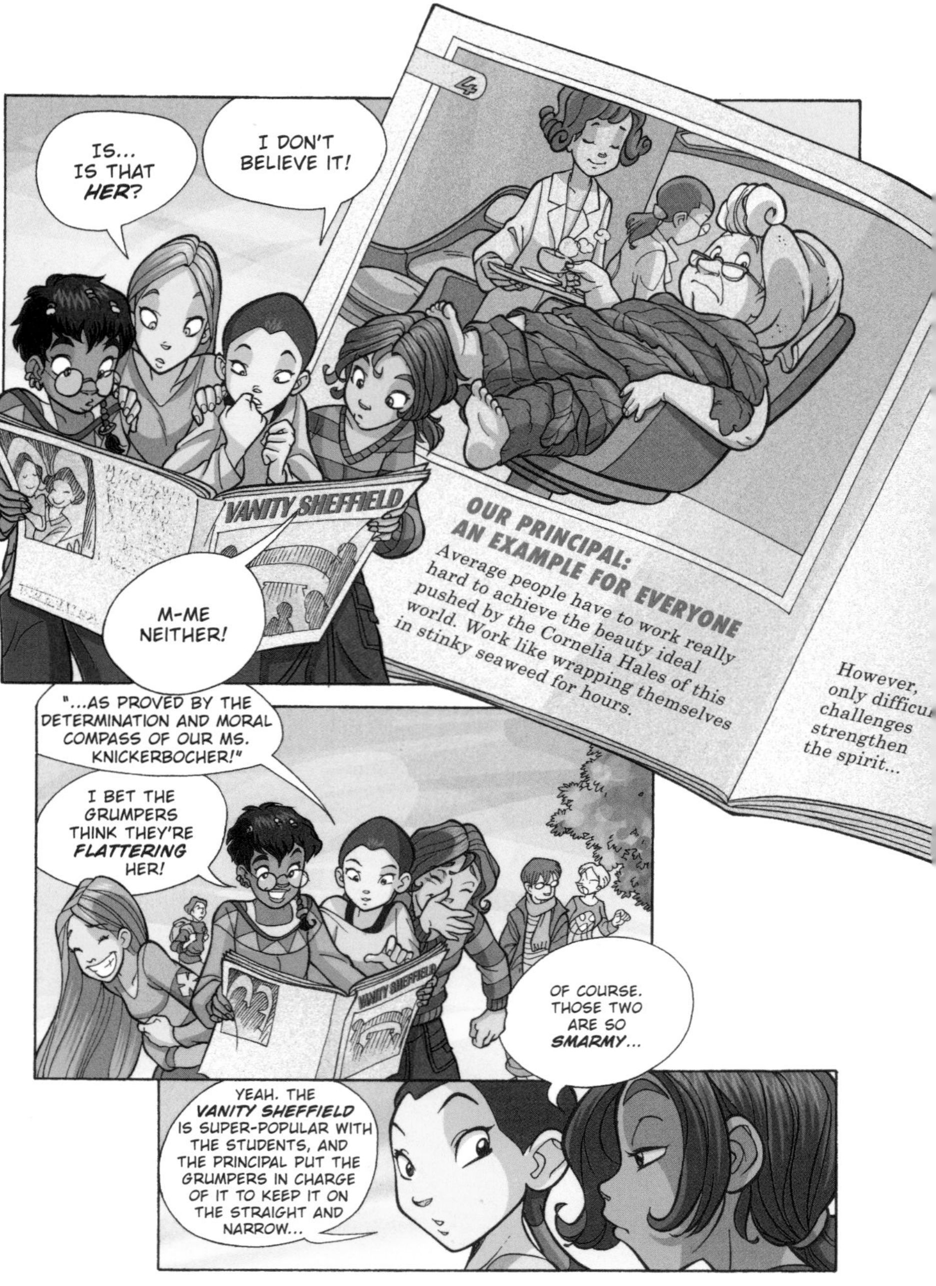
IS... IS THAT HER?
I DON'T BELIEVE IT!
OUR PRINCIPAL: AN EXAMPLE FOR EVERYONE
Average people have to work really hard to achieve the beauty ideal pushed by the Cornelia Hales of this world. Work like wrapping themselves in stinky seaweed for hours.
However, only difficu challenges strengthen the spirit...
M-ME NEITHER!
"...AS PROVED BY THE DETERMINATION AND MORAL COMPASS OF OUR MS. KNICKERBOCHER!"
I BET THE GRUMPERS THINK THEY'RE FLATTERING HER!
OF COURSE. THOSE TWO ARE SO SMARMY...
YEAH. THE VANITY SHEFFIELD IS SUPER-POPULAR WITH THE STUDENTS, AND THE PRINCIPAL PUT THE GRUMPERS IN CHARGE OF IT TO KEEP IT ON THE STRAIGHT AND NARROW...

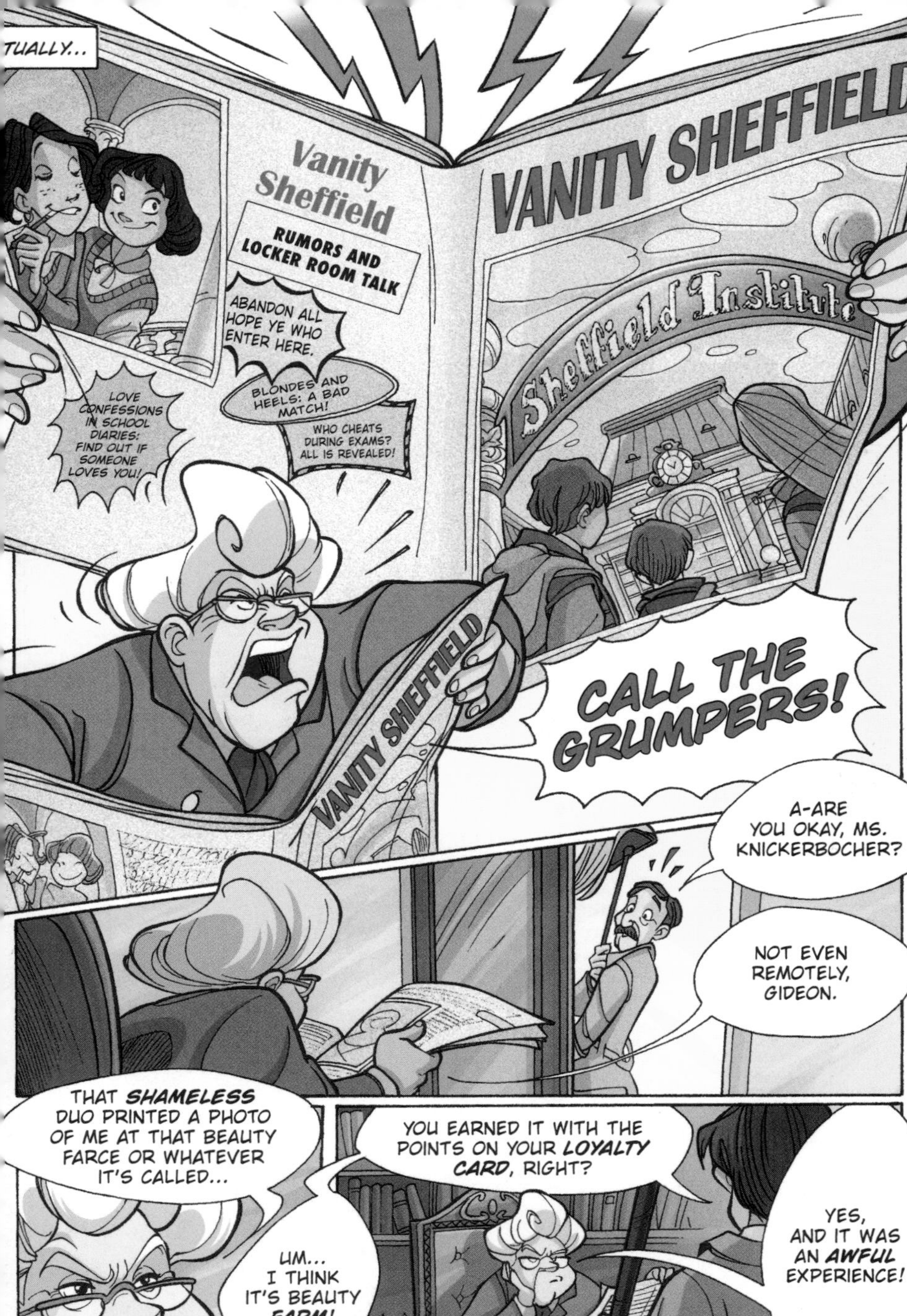
TUALLY...
Vanity Sheffield
RUMORS AND LOCKER ROOM TALK
ABANDON ALL HOPE YE WHO ENTER HERE.
BLONDES AND HEELS: A BAD MATCH!
LOVE CONFESSIONS IN SCHOOL DIARIES: FIND OUT IF SOMEONE LOVES YOU!
WHO CHEATS DURING EXAMS? ALL IS REVEALED!
VANITY SHEFFIELD
Sheffield Institute
VANITY SHEFFIELD
CALL THE GRUMPERS!
A-ARE YOU OKAY, MS. KNICKERBOCHER?
NOT EVEN REMOTELY, GIDEON.
THAT SHAMELESS DUO PRINTED A PHOTO OF ME AT THAT BEAUTY FARCE OR WHATEVER IT'S CALLED...
UM... I THINK IT'S BEAUTY FARM!
YOU EARNED IT WITH THE POINTS ON YOUR LOYALTY CARD, RIGHT?
YES, AND IT WAS AN AWFUL EXPERIENCE!

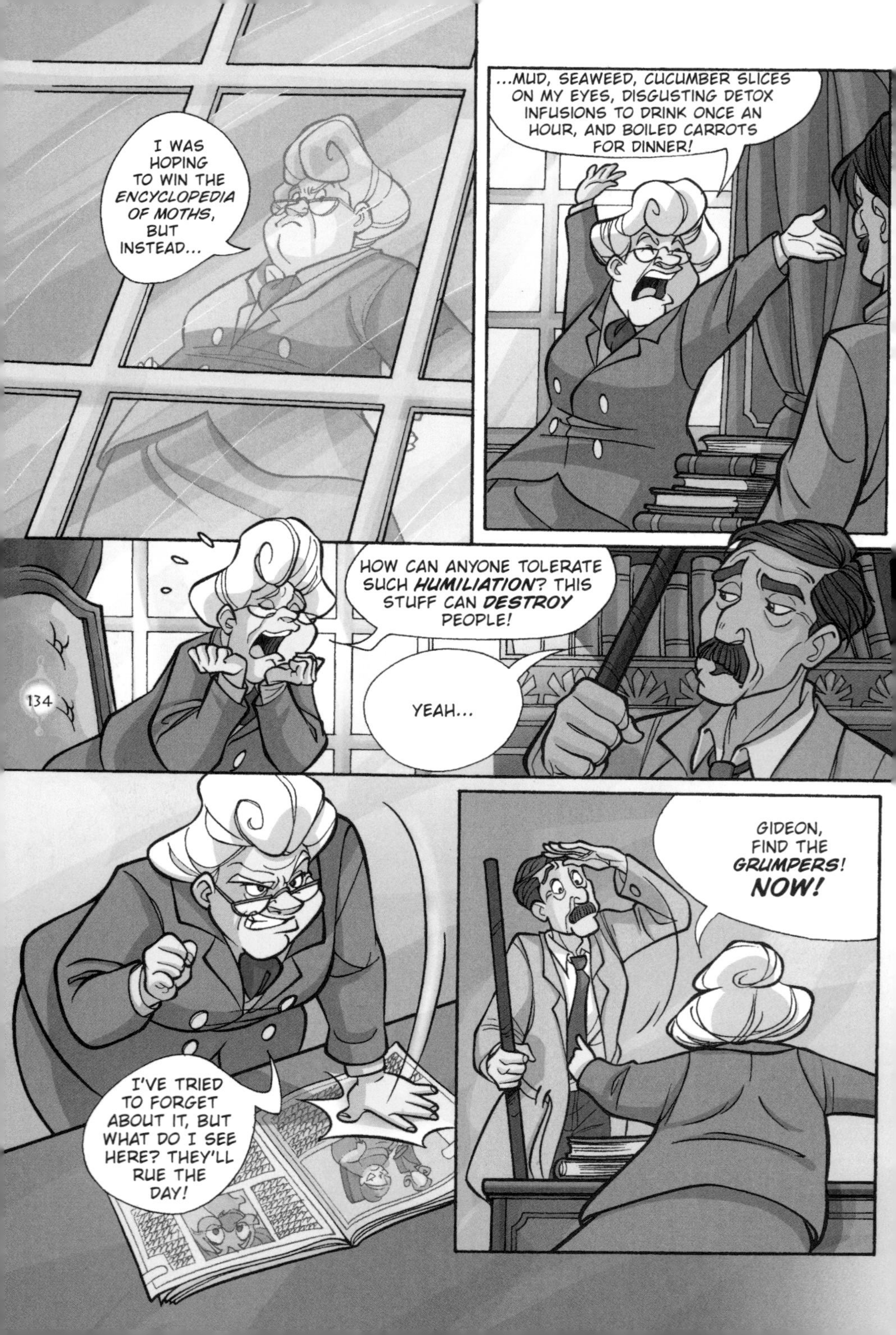
I WAS HOPING TO WIN THE *ENCYCLOPEDIA OF MOTHS*, BUT INSTEAD...
...MUD, SEAWEED, CUCUMBER SLICES ON MY EYES, DISGUSTING DETOX INFUSIONS TO DRINK ONCE AN HOUR, AND BOILED CARROTS FOR DINNER!
HOW CAN ANYONE TOLERATE SUCH ***HUMILIATION***? THIS STUFF CAN ***DESTROY*** PEOPLE!
YEAH...
I'VE TRIED TO FORGET ABOUT IT, BUT WHAT DO I SEE HERE? THEY'LL RUE THE DAY!
GIDEON, FIND THE ***GRUMPERS***! **NOW!**

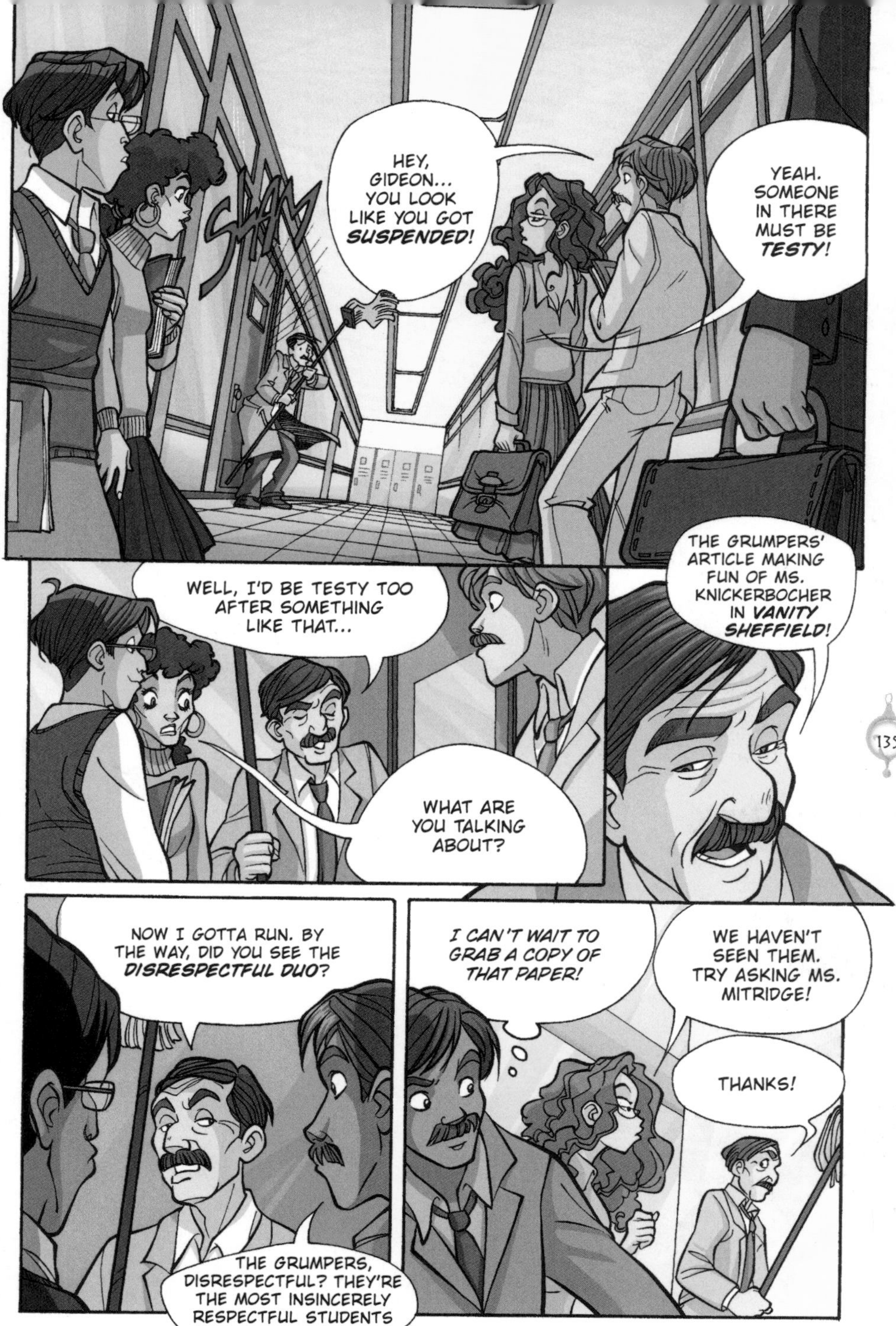
SLAM
HEY, GIDEON... YOU LOOK LIKE YOU GOT SUSPENDED!
YEAH. SOMEONE IN THERE MUST BE TESTY!
WELL, I'D BE TESTY TOO AFTER SOMETHING LIKE THAT...
WHAT ARE YOU TALKING ABOUT?
THE GRUMPERS' ARTICLE MAKING FUN OF MS. KNICKERBOCHER IN VANITY SHEFFIELD!
NOW I GOTTA RUN. BY THE WAY, DID YOU SEE THE DISRESPECTFUL DUO?
THE GRUMPERS, DISRESPECTFUL? THEY'RE THE MOST INSINCERELY RESPECTFUL STUDENTS IN THIS SCHOOL!
I CAN'T WAIT TO GRAB A COPY OF THAT PAPER!
WE HAVEN'T SEEN THEM. TRY ASKING MS. MITRIDGE!
THANKS!

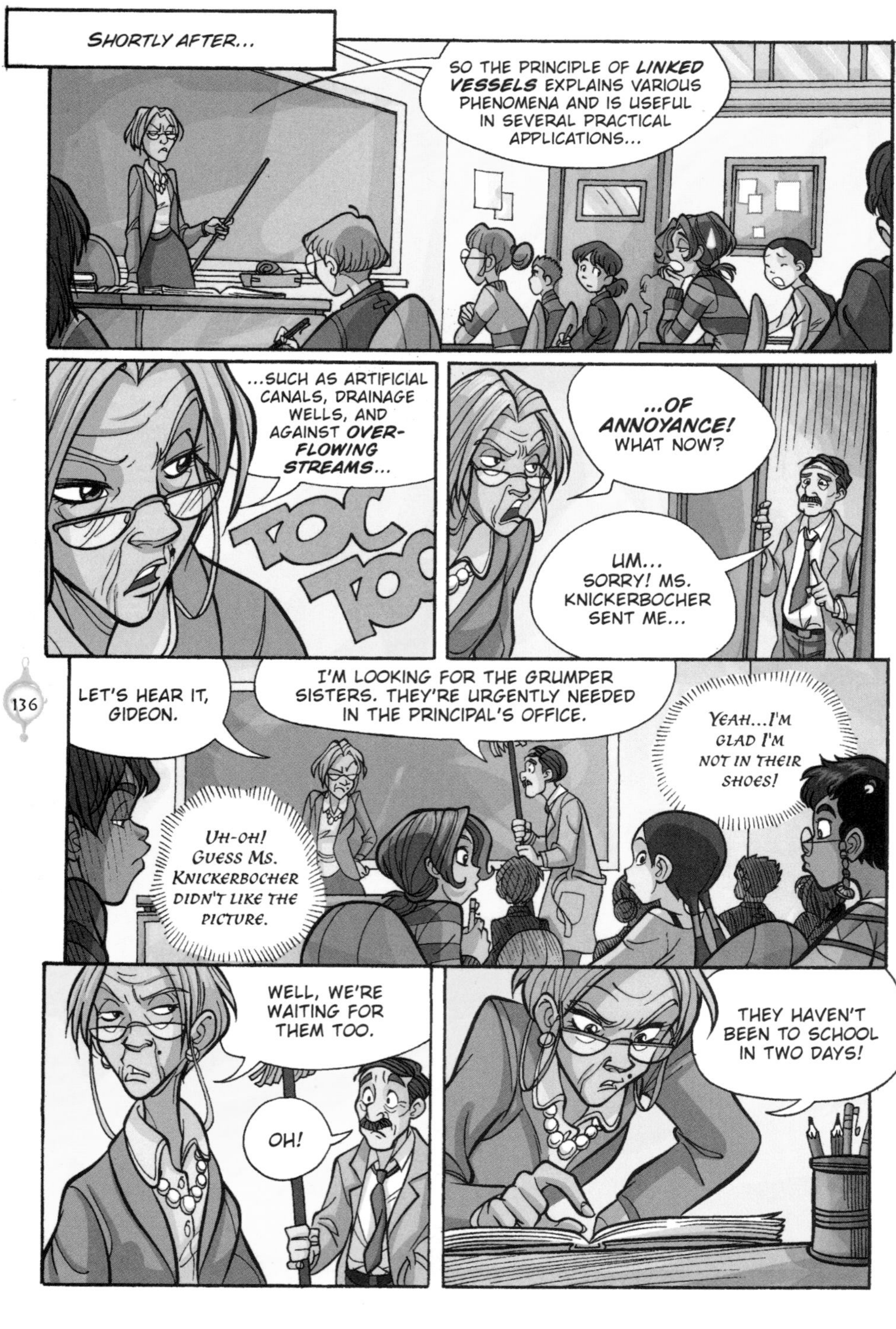
SHORTLY AFTER...
SO THE PRINCIPLE OF LINKED VESSELS EXPLAINS VARIOUS PHENOMENA AND IS USEFUL IN SEVERAL PRACTICAL APPLICATIONS...
...SUCH AS ARTIFICIAL CANALS, DRAINAGE WELLS, AND AGAINST OVER-FLOWING STREAMS...
TOC TOC
...OF ANNOYANCE! WHAT NOW?
UM... SORRY! MS. KNICKERBOCHER SENT ME...
LET'S HEAR IT, GIDEON.
I'M LOOKING FOR THE GRUMPER SISTERS. THEY'RE URGENTLY NEEDED IN THE PRINCIPAL'S OFFICE.
YEAH...I'M GLAD I'M NOT IN THEIR SHOES!
UH-OH! GUESS MS. KNICKERBOCHER DIDN'T LIKE THE PICTURE.
WELL, WE'RE WAITING FOR THEM TOO.
OH!
THEY HAVEN'T BEEN TO SCHOOL IN TWO DAYS!

136

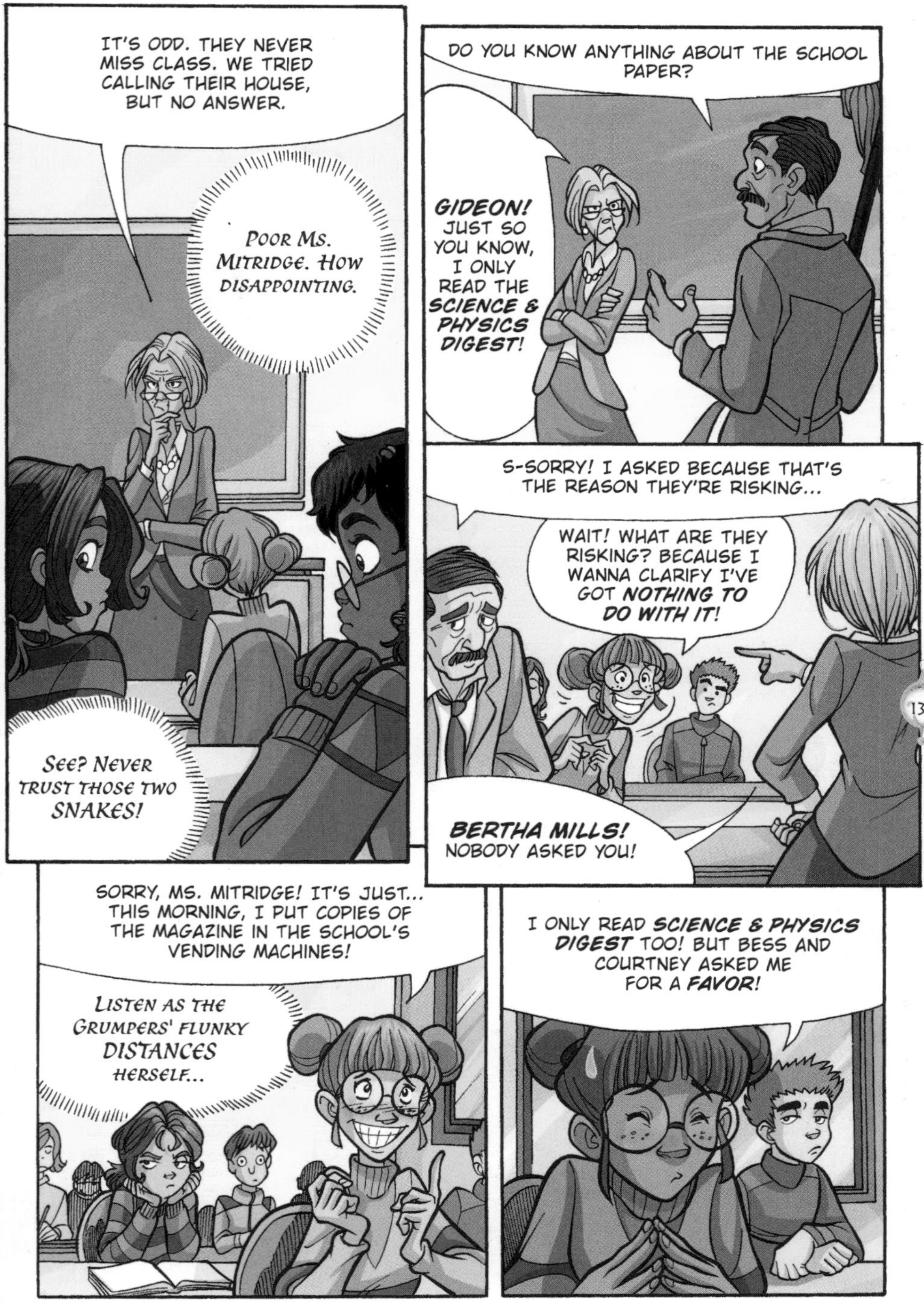
IT'S ODD. THEY NEVER MISS CLASS. WE TRIED CALLING THEIR HOUSE, BUT NO ANSWER.
POOR MS. MITRIDGE. HOW DISAPPOINTING.
SEE? NEVER TRUST THOSE TWO SNAKES!
DO YOU KNOW ANYTHING ABOUT THE SCHOOL PAPER?
GIDEON! JUST SO YOU KNOW, I ONLY READ THE SCIENCE & PHYSICS DIGEST!
S-SORRY! I ASKED BECAUSE THAT'S THE REASON THEY'RE RISKING...
WAIT! WHAT ARE THEY RISKING? BECAUSE I WANNA CLARIFY I'VE GOT NOTHING TO DO WITH IT!
BERTHA MILLS! NOBODY ASKED YOU!
SORRY, MS. MITRIDGE! IT'S JUST... THIS MORNING, I PUT COPIES OF THE MAGAZINE IN THE SCHOOL'S VENDING MACHINES!
LISTEN AS THE GRUMPERS' FLUNKY DISTANCES HERSELF...
I ONLY READ SCIENCE & PHYSICS DIGEST TOO! BUT BESS AND COURTNEY ASKED ME FOR A FAVOR!

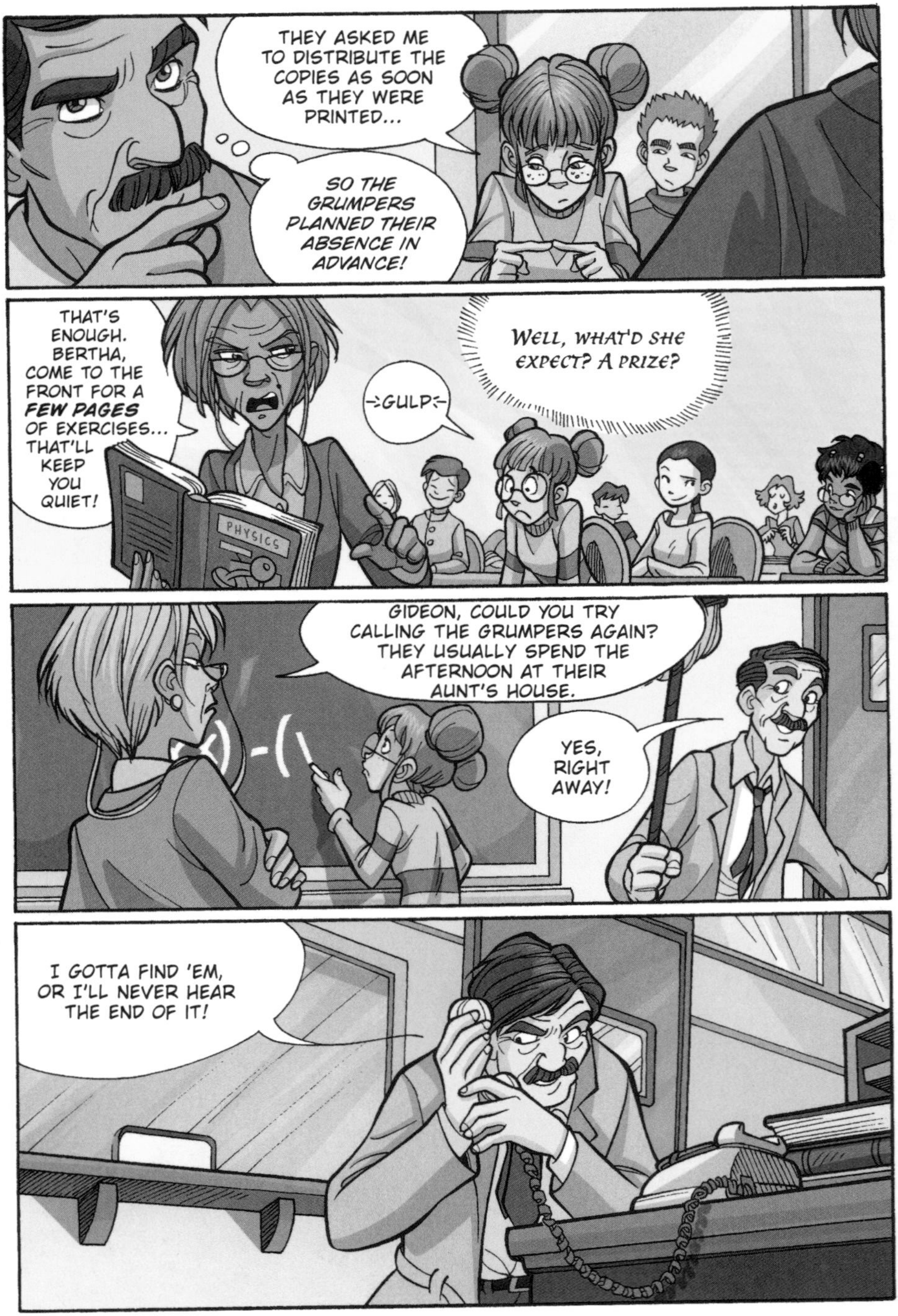

THEY ASKED ME TO DISTRIBUTE THE COPIES AS SOON AS THEY WERE PRINTED...
SO THE GRUMPERS PLANNED THEIR ABSENCE IN ADVANCE!
THAT'S ENOUGH. BERTHA, COME TO THE FRONT FOR A **FEW PAGES** OF EXERCISES... THAT'LL KEEP YOU QUIET!
GULP
WELL, WHAT'D SHE EXPECT? A PRIZE?
PHYSICS
GIDEON, COULD YOU TRY CALLING THE GRUMPERS AGAIN? THEY USUALLY SPEND THE AFTERNOON AT THEIR AUNT'S HOUSE.
YES, RIGHT AWAY!
I GOTTA FIND 'EM, OR I'LL NEVER HEAR THE END OF IT!

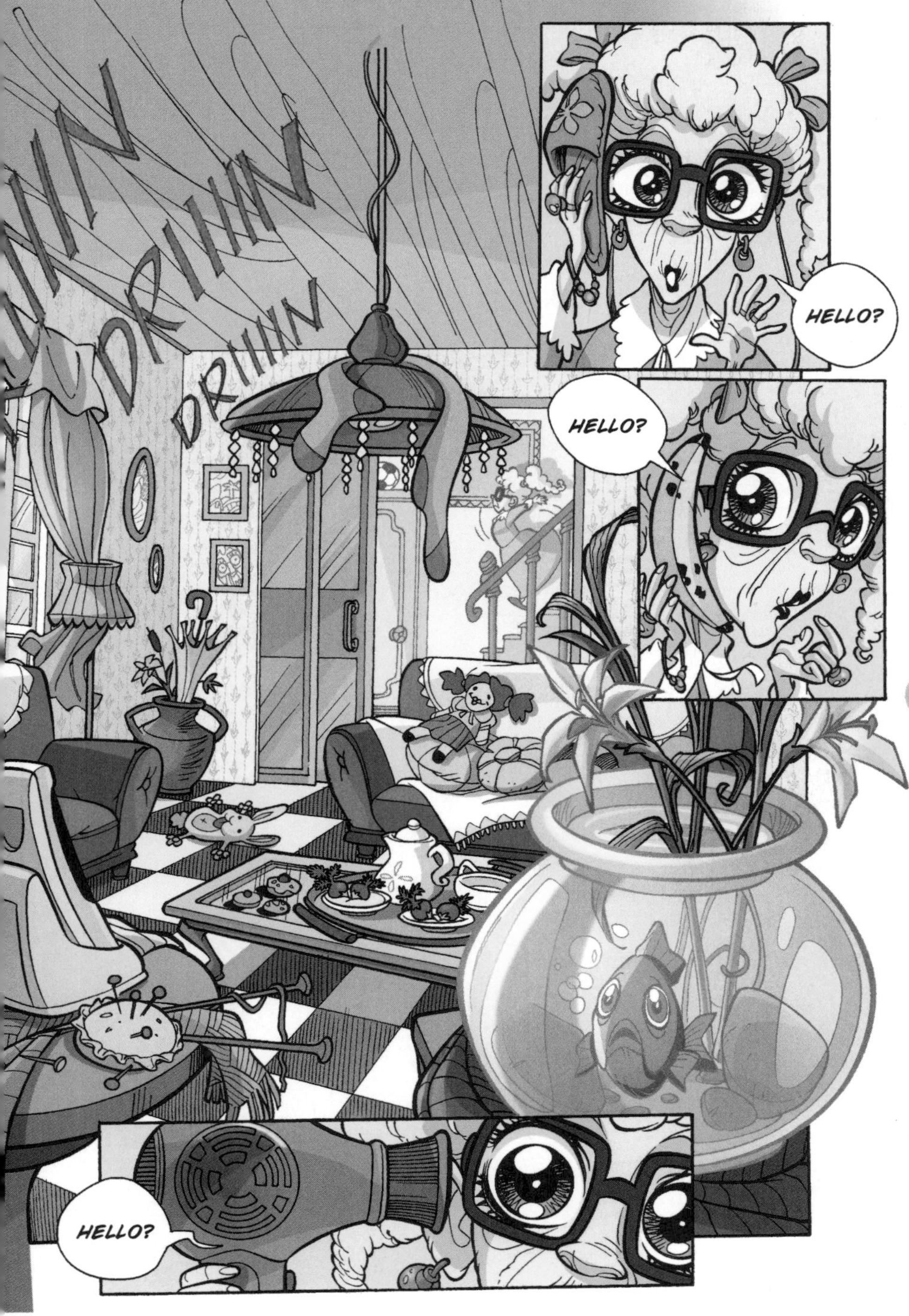
DRIIIN
DRIIIN
DRIIIN
HELLO?
HELLO?
HELLO?

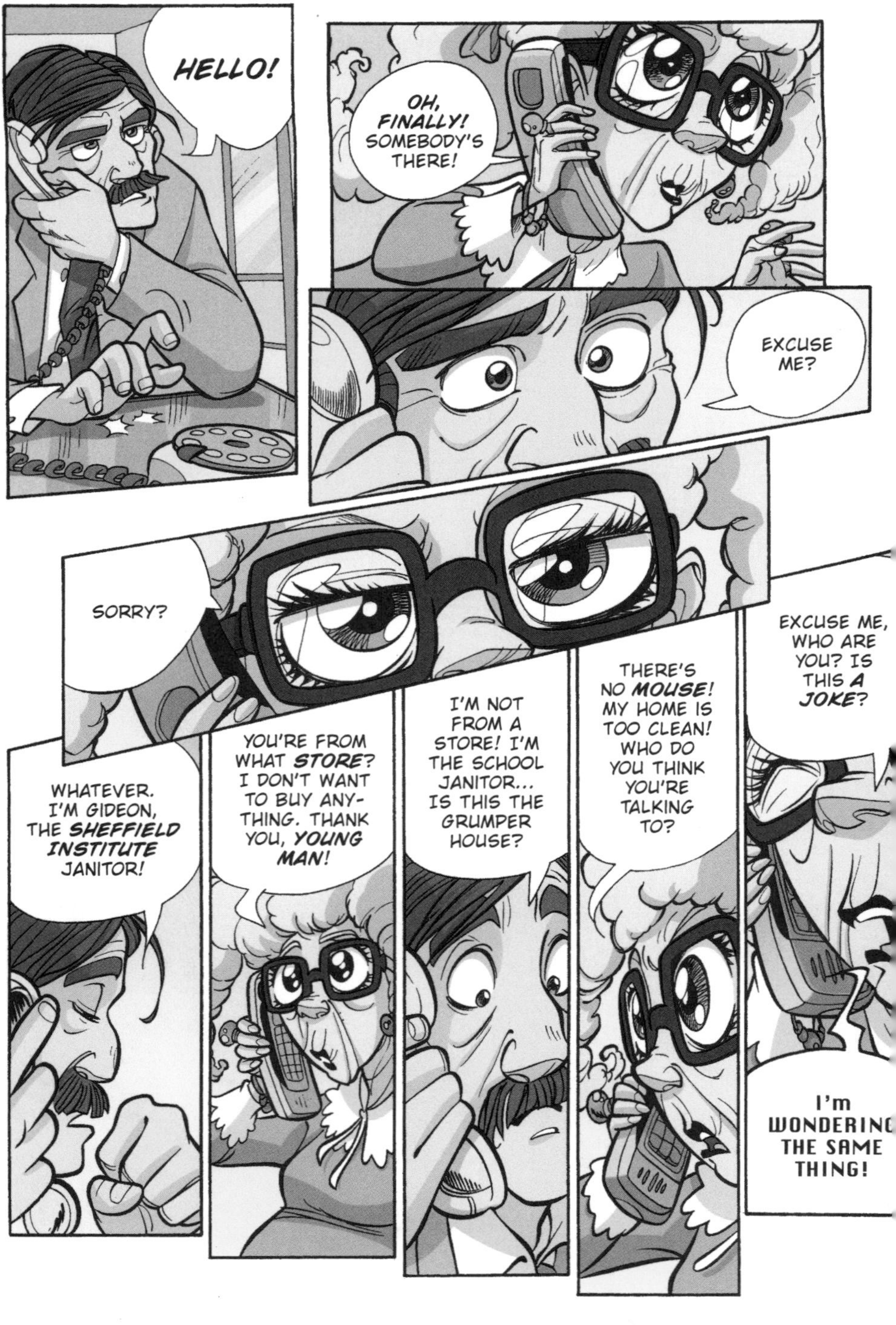
HELLO!
OH, FINALLY! SOMEBODY'S THERE!
EXCUSE ME?
SORRY?
WHATEVER. I'M GIDEON, THE SHEFFIELD INSTITUTE JANITOR!
YOU'RE FROM WHAT STORE? I DON'T WANT TO BUY ANY-THING. THANK YOU, YOUNG MAN!
I'M NOT FROM A STORE! I'M THE SCHOOL JANITOR... IS THIS THE GRUMPER HOUSE?
THERE'S NO MOUSE! MY HOME IS TOO CLEAN! WHO DO YOU THINK YOU'RE TALKING TO?
EXCUSE ME, WHO ARE YOU? IS THIS A JOKE?
I'm WONDERING THE SAME THING!

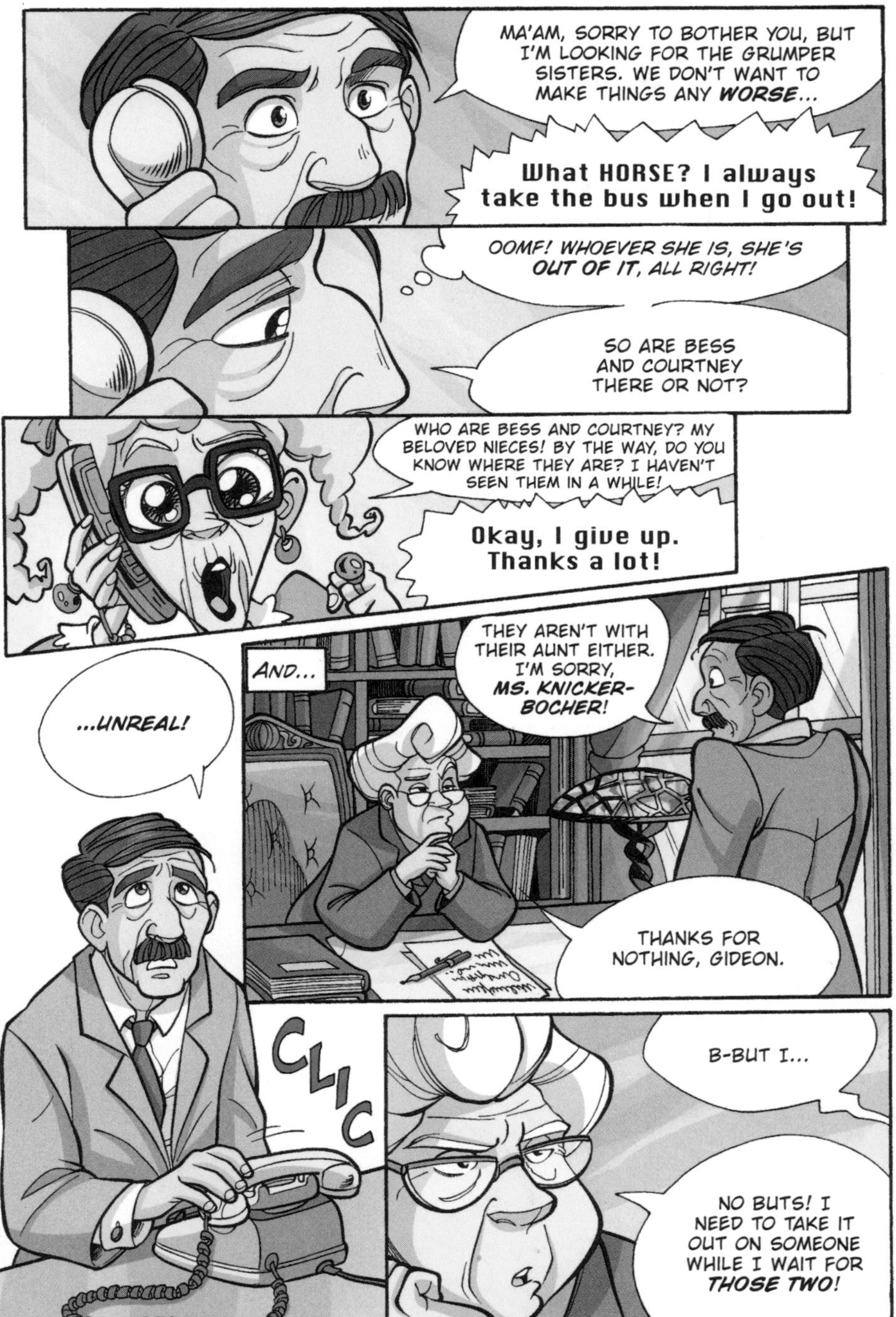
MA'AM, SORRY TO BOTHER YOU, BUT I'M LOOKING FOR THE GRUMPER SISTERS. WE DON'T WANT TO MAKE THINGS ANY WORSE...
What HORSE? I always take the bus when I go out!
OOMF! WHOEVER SHE IS, SHE'S OUT OF IT, ALL RIGHT!
SO ARE BESS AND COURTNEY THERE OR NOT?
WHO ARE BESS AND COURTNEY? MY BELOVED NIECES! BY THE WAY, DO YOU KNOW WHERE THEY ARE? I HAVEN'T SEEN THEM IN A WHILE!
Okay, I give up. Thanks a lot!
...UNREAL!
CLIC
AND...
THEY AREN'T WITH THEIR AUNT EITHER. I'M SORRY, MS. KNICKER-BOCHER!
THANKS FOR NOTHING, GIDEON.
B-BUT I...
NO BUTS! I NEED TO TAKE IT OUT ON SOMEONE WHILE I WAIT FOR THOSE TWO!

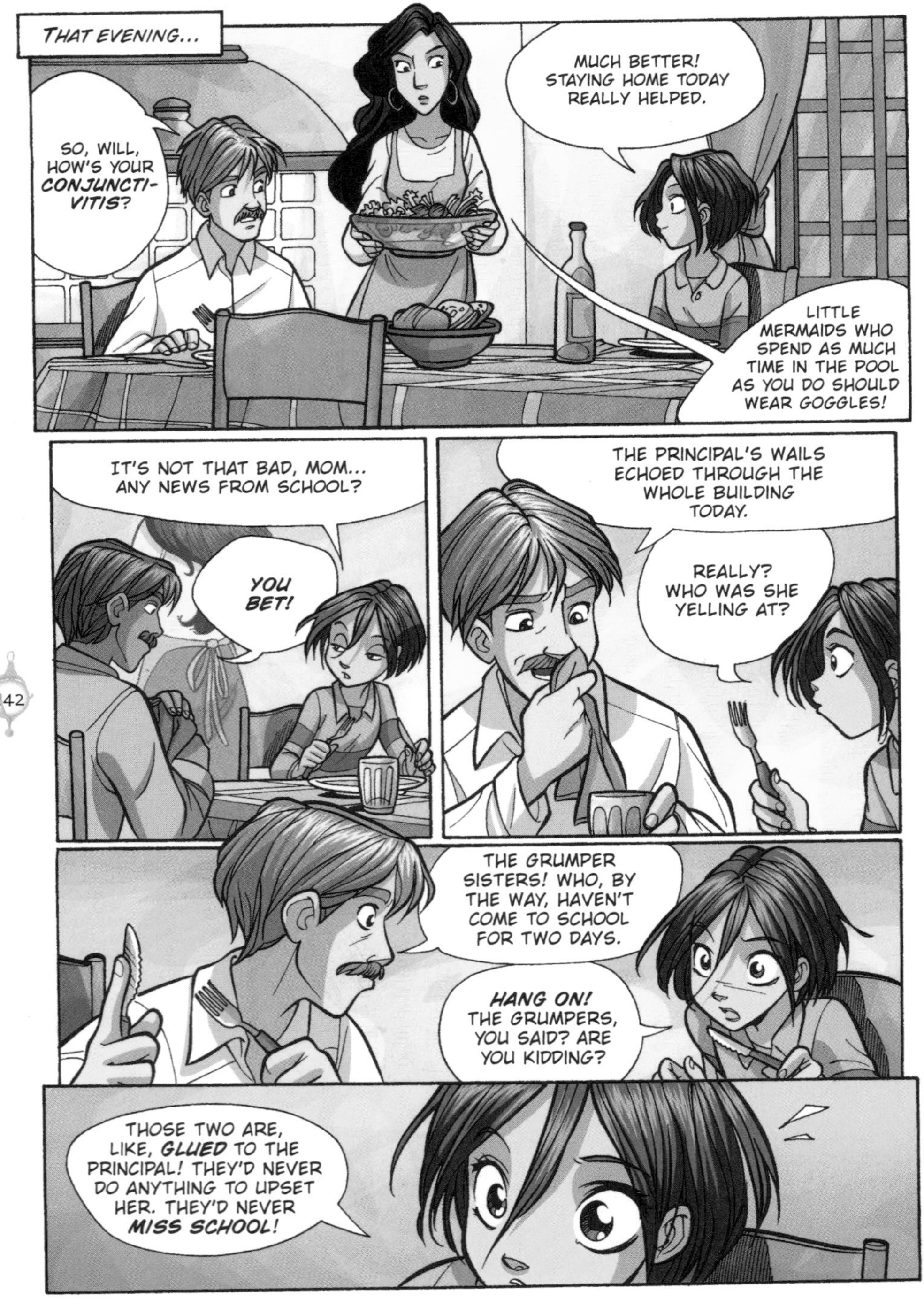
THAT EVENING...
SO, WILL, HOW'S YOUR CONJUNCTIVITIS?
MUCH BETTER! STAYING HOME TODAY REALLY HELPED.
LITTLE MERMAIDS WHO SPEND AS MUCH TIME IN THE POOL AS YOU DO SHOULD WEAR GOGGLES!
IT'S NOT THAT BAD, MOM... ANY NEWS FROM SCHOOL?
YOU BET!
THE PRINCIPAL'S WAILS ECHOED THROUGH THE WHOLE BUILDING TODAY.
REALLY? WHO WAS SHE YELLING AT?
THE GRUMPER SISTERS! WHO, BY THE WAY, HAVEN'T COME TO SCHOOL FOR TWO DAYS.
HANG ON! THE GRUMPERS, YOU SAID? ARE YOU KIDDING?
THOSE TWO ARE, LIKE, GLUED TO THE PRINCIPAL! THEY'D NEVER DO ANYTHING TO UPSET HER. THEY'D NEVER MISS SCHOOL!

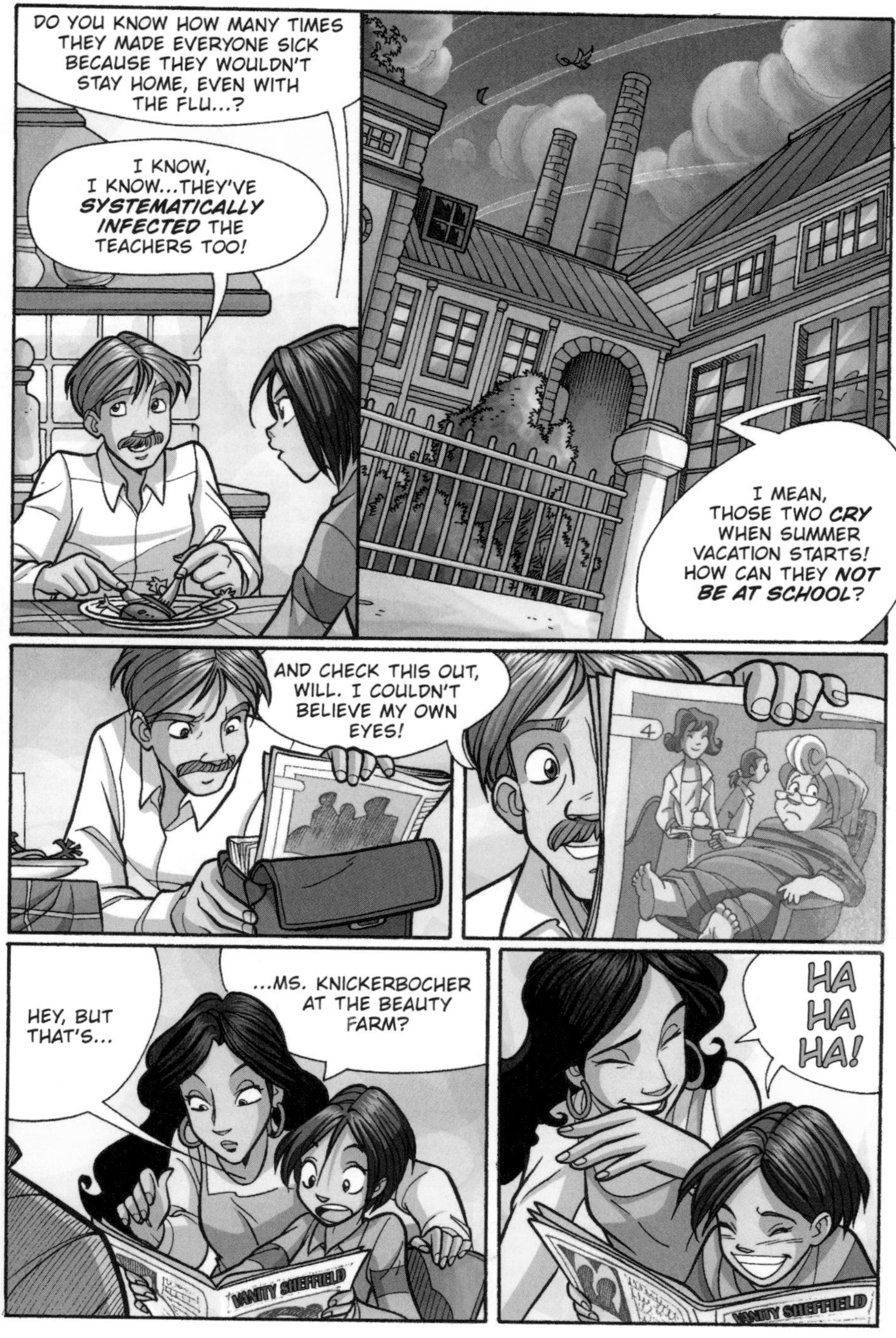
DO YOU KNOW HOW MANY TIMES THEY MADE EVERYONE SICK BECAUSE THEY WOULDN'T STAY HOME, EVEN WITH THE FLU...?
I KNOW, I KNOW...THEY'VE SYSTEMATICALLY INFECTED THE TEACHERS TOO!
I MEAN, THOSE TWO CRY WHEN SUMMER VACATION STARTS! HOW CAN THEY NOT BE AT SCHOOL?
AND CHECK THIS OUT, WILL. I COULDN'T BELIEVE MY OWN EYES!
4
HEY, BUT THAT'S...
...MS. KNICKERBOCHER AT THE BEAUTY FARM?
VANITY SHEFFIELD
HA HA HA!
VANITY SHEFFIELD

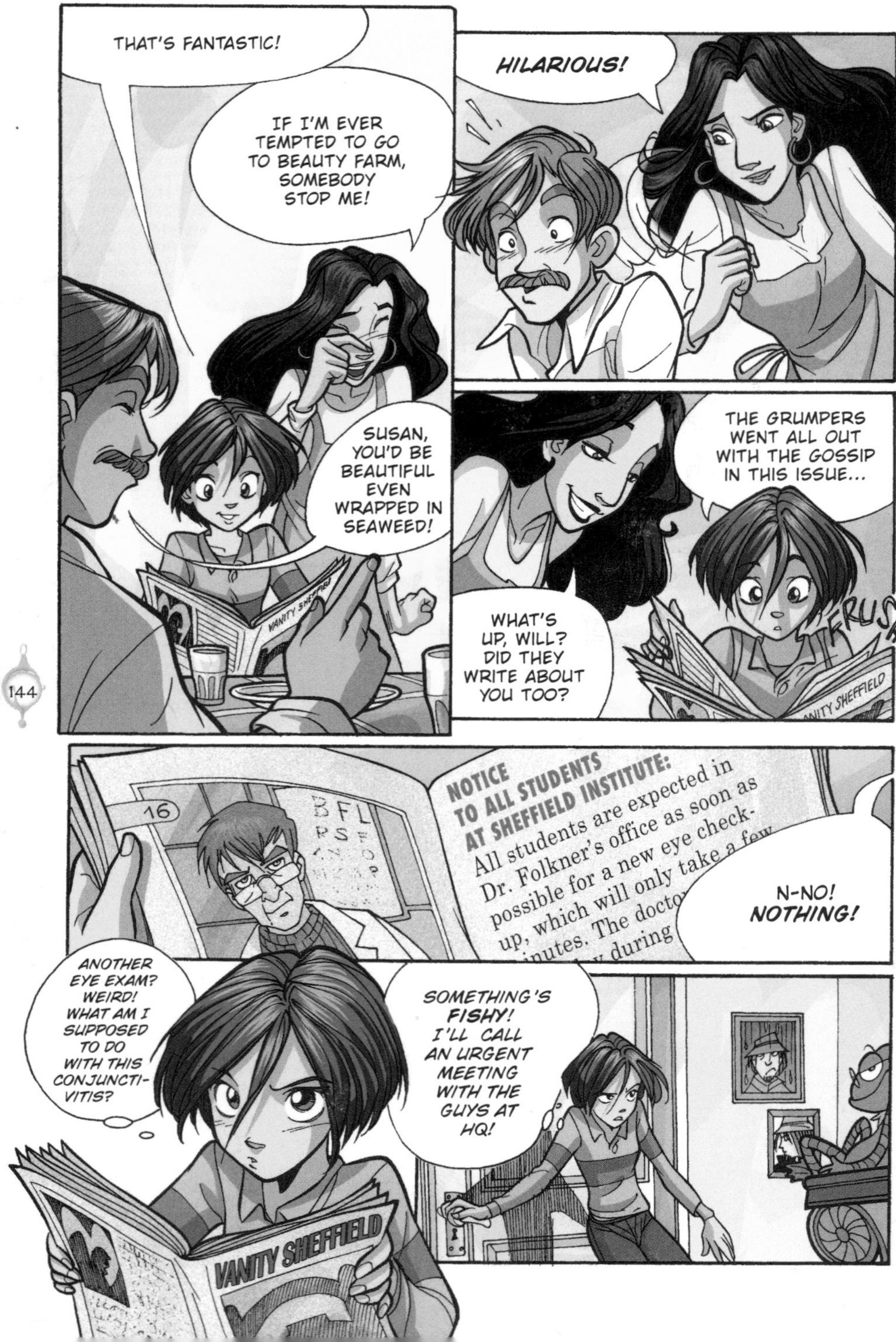

THAT'S FANTASTIC!
IF I'M EVER TEMPTED TO GO TO BEAUTY FARM, SOMEBODY STOP ME!
SUSAN, YOU'D BE BEAUTIFUL EVEN WRAPPED IN SEAWEED!
VANITY SHEFFIELD
HILARIOUS!
THE GRUMPERS WENT ALL OUT WITH THE GOSSIP IN THIS ISSUE...
WHAT'S UP, WILL? DID THEY WRITE ABOUT YOU TOO?
FRUSH
VANITY SHEFFIELD
16
NOTICE TO ALL STUDENTS AT SHEFFIELD INSTITUTE:
All students are expected in Dr. Folkner's office as soon as possible for a new eye check-up, which will only take a few
The doctor
during
N-NO! NOTHING!
ANOTHER EYE EXAM? WEIRD! WHAT AM I SUPPOSED TO DO WITH THIS CONJUNCTI-VITIS?
VANITY SHEFFIELD
SOMETHING'S FISHY! I'LL CALL AN URGENT MEETING WITH THE GUYS AT HQ!

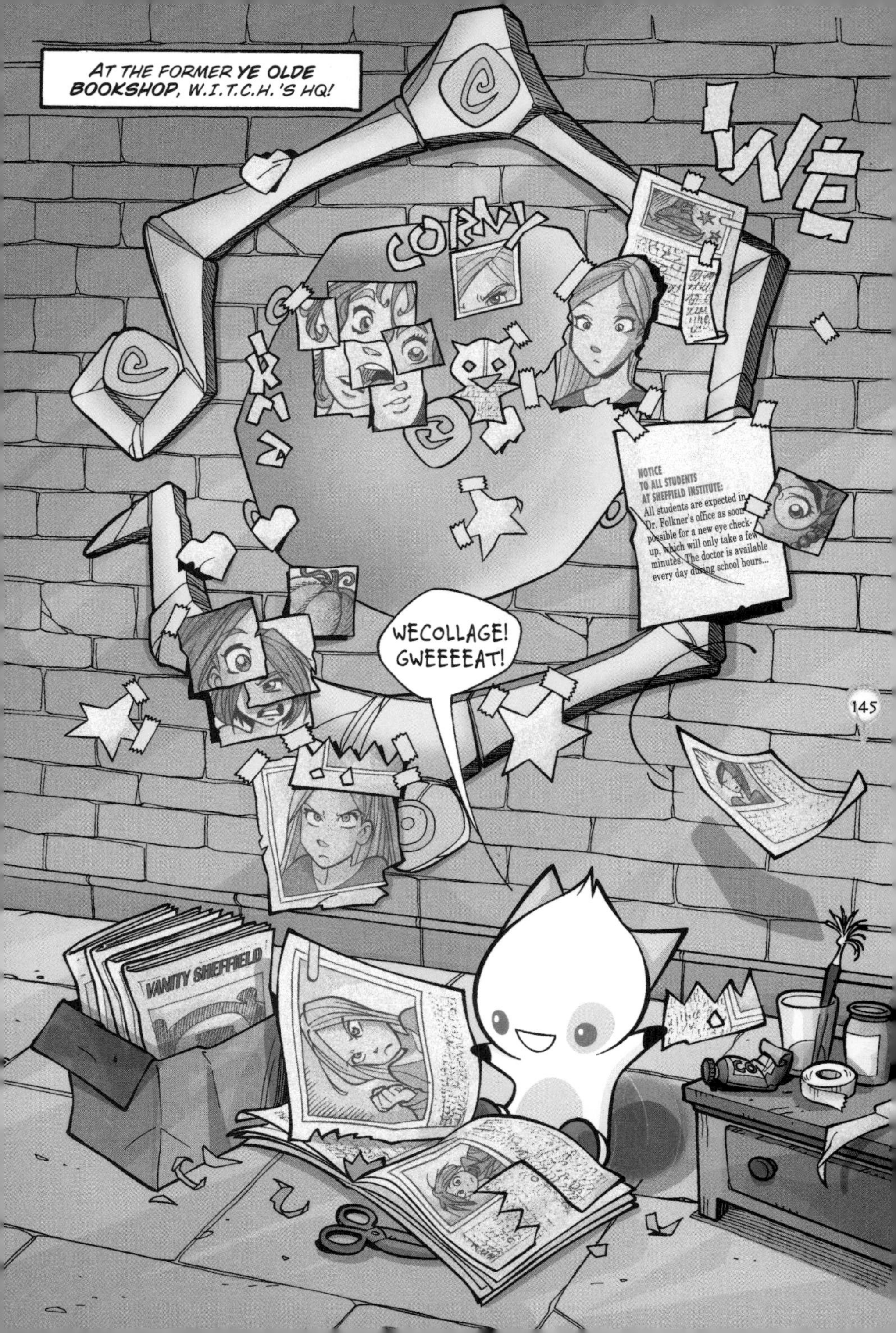
AT THE FORMER YE OLDE BOOKSHOP, W.I.T.C.H.'S HQ!
WE
CORNY
NOTICE
TO ALL STUDENTS
AT SHEFFIELD INSTITUTE:
All students are expected in
Dr. Folkner's office as soon
possible for a new eye check-
up, which will only take a few
minutes. The doctor is available
every day during school hours...
WECOLLAGE! GWEEEEAT!
VANITY SHEFFIELD

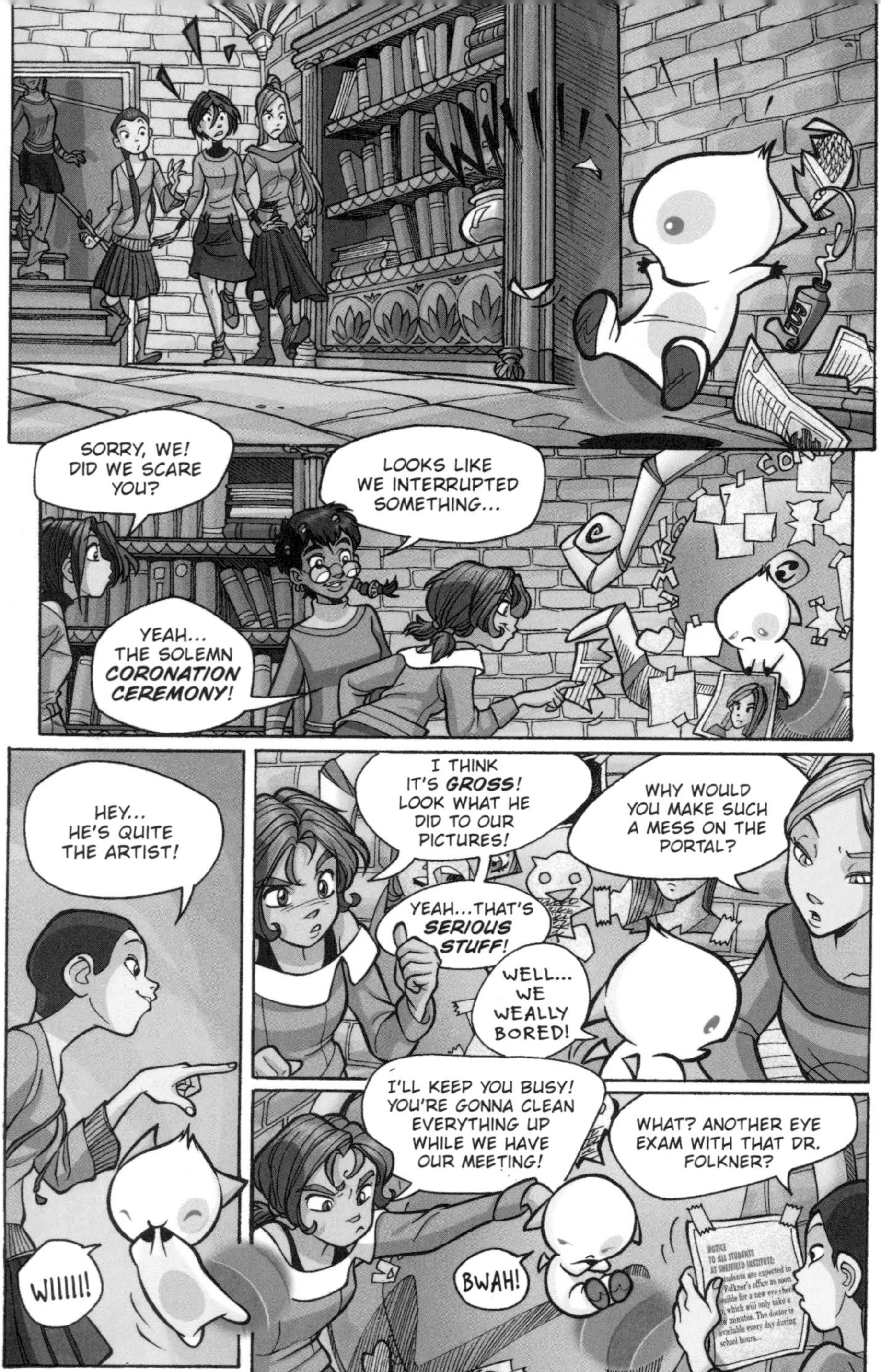
SORRY, WE! DID WE SCARE YOU?
LOOKS LIKE WE INTERRUPTED SOMETHING...
YEAH... THE SOLEMN CORONATION CEREMONY!
HEY... HE'S QUITE THE ARTIST!
WIIIII!
I THINK IT'S GROSS! LOOK WHAT HE DID TO OUR PICTURES!
YEAH...THAT'S SERIOUS STUFF!
WHY WOULD YOU MAKE SUCH A MESS ON THE PORTAL?
WELL... WE WEALLY BORED!
I'LL KEEP YOU BUSY! YOU'RE GONNA CLEAN EVERYTHING UP WHILE WE HAVE OUR MEETING!
BWAH!
WHAT? ANOTHER EYE EXAM WITH THAT DR. FOLKNER?
NOTICE
TO ALL STUDENTS
AT SHEFFIELD INSTITUTE:

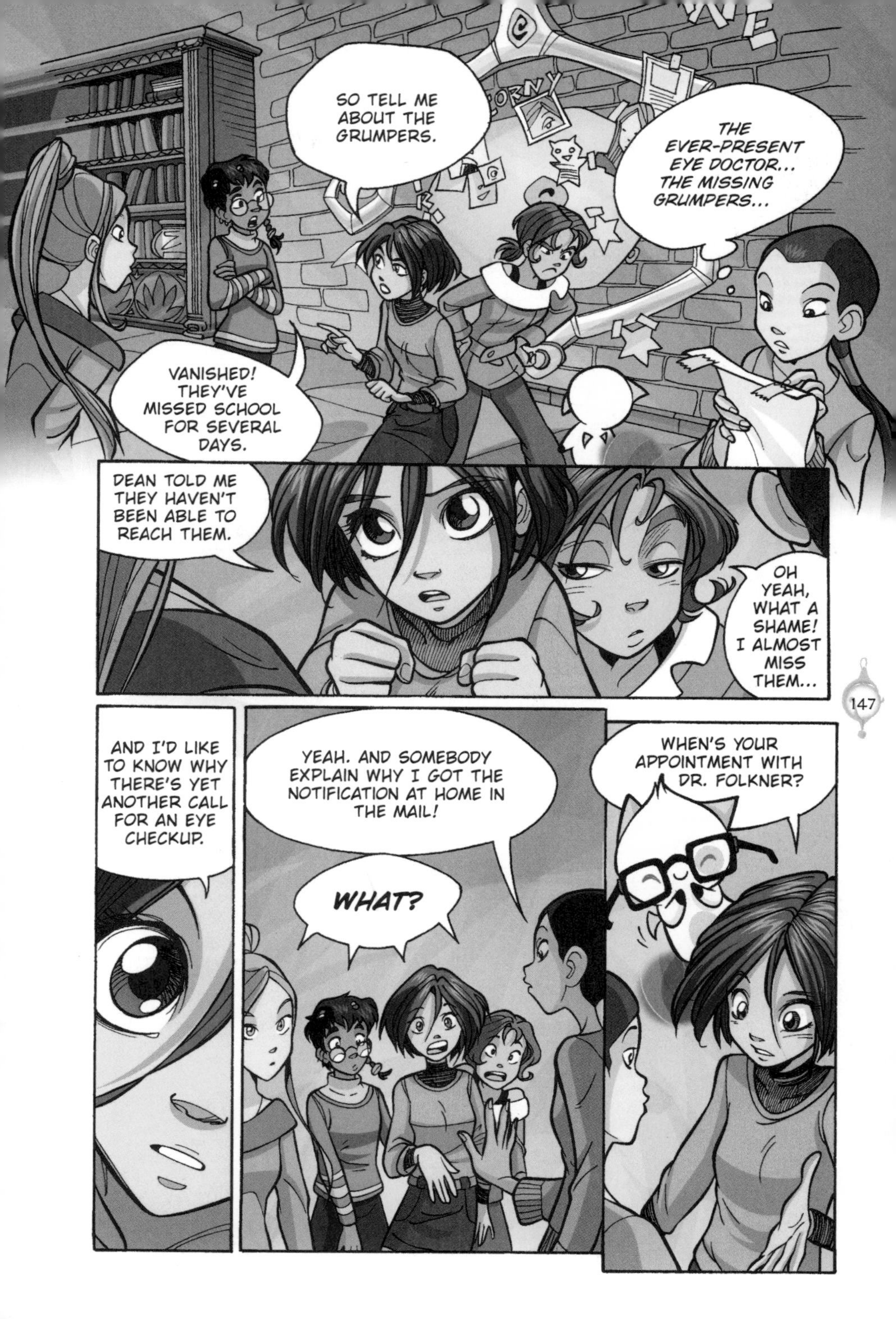
SO TELL ME ABOUT THE GRUMPERS.
THE EVER-PRESENT EYE DOCTOR... THE MISSING GRUMPERS...
VANISHED! THEY'VE MISSED SCHOOL FOR SEVERAL DAYS.
DEAN TOLD ME THEY HAVEN'T BEEN ABLE TO REACH THEM.
OH YEAH, WHAT A SHAME! I ALMOST MISS THEM...
AND I'D LIKE TO KNOW WHY THERE'S YET ANOTHER CALL FOR AN EYE CHECKUP.
YEAH. AND SOMEBODY EXPLAIN WHY I GOT THE NOTIFICATION AT HOME IN THE MAIL!
WHAT?
WHEN'S YOUR APPOINTMENT WITH DR. FOLKNER?

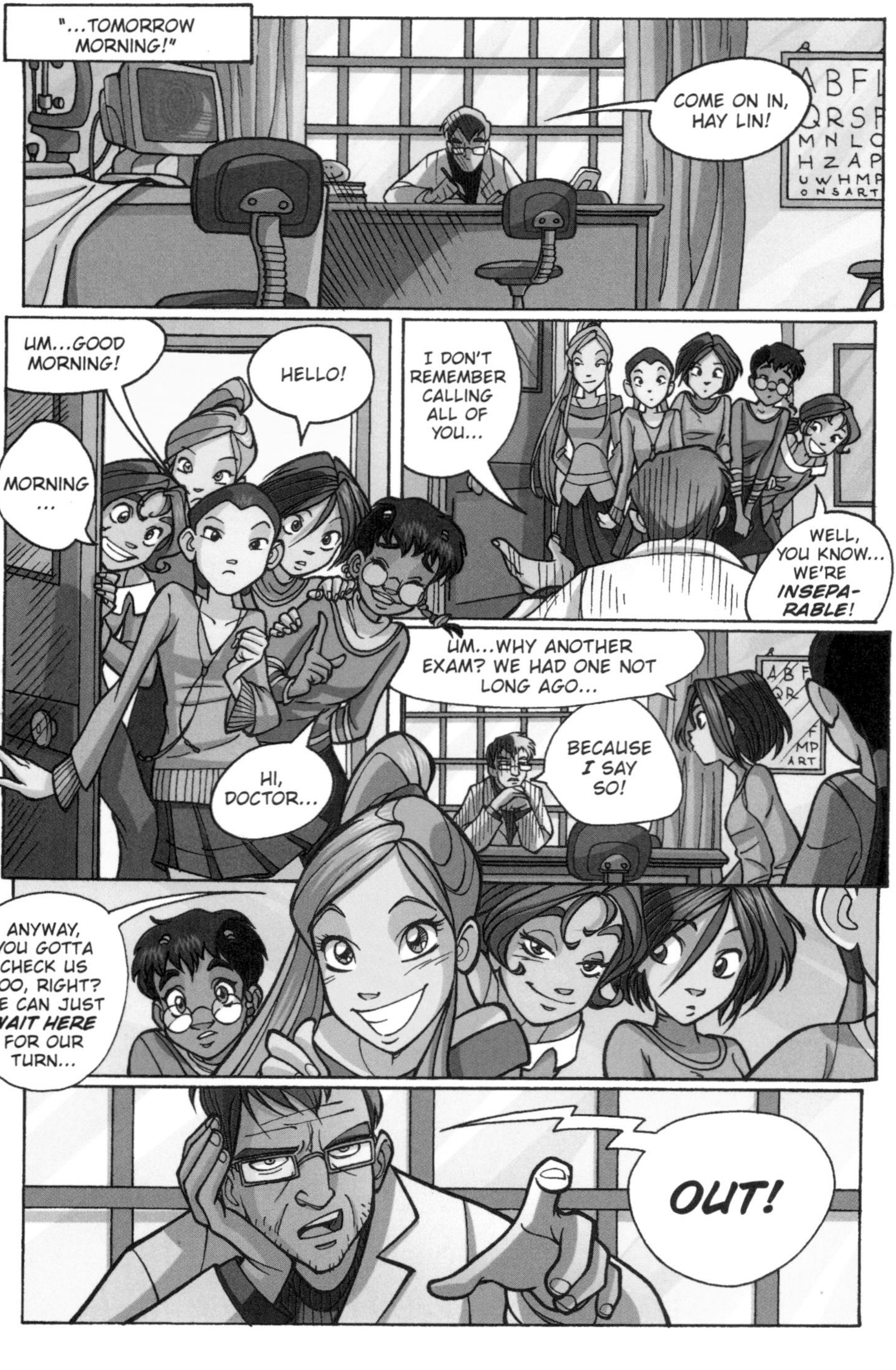
"...TOMORROW MORNING!"
COME ON IN, HAY LIN!
UM...GOOD MORNING!
HELLO!
MORNING ...
HI, DOCTOR...
I DON'T REMEMBER CALLING ALL OF YOU...
WELL, YOU KNOW... WE'RE INSEPA-RABLE!
UM...WHY ANOTHER EXAM? WE HAD ONE NOT LONG AGO...
BECAUSE I SAY SO!
ANYWAY, YOU GOTTA CHECK US TOO, RIGHT? WE CAN JUST WAIT HERE FOR OUR TURN...
OUT!

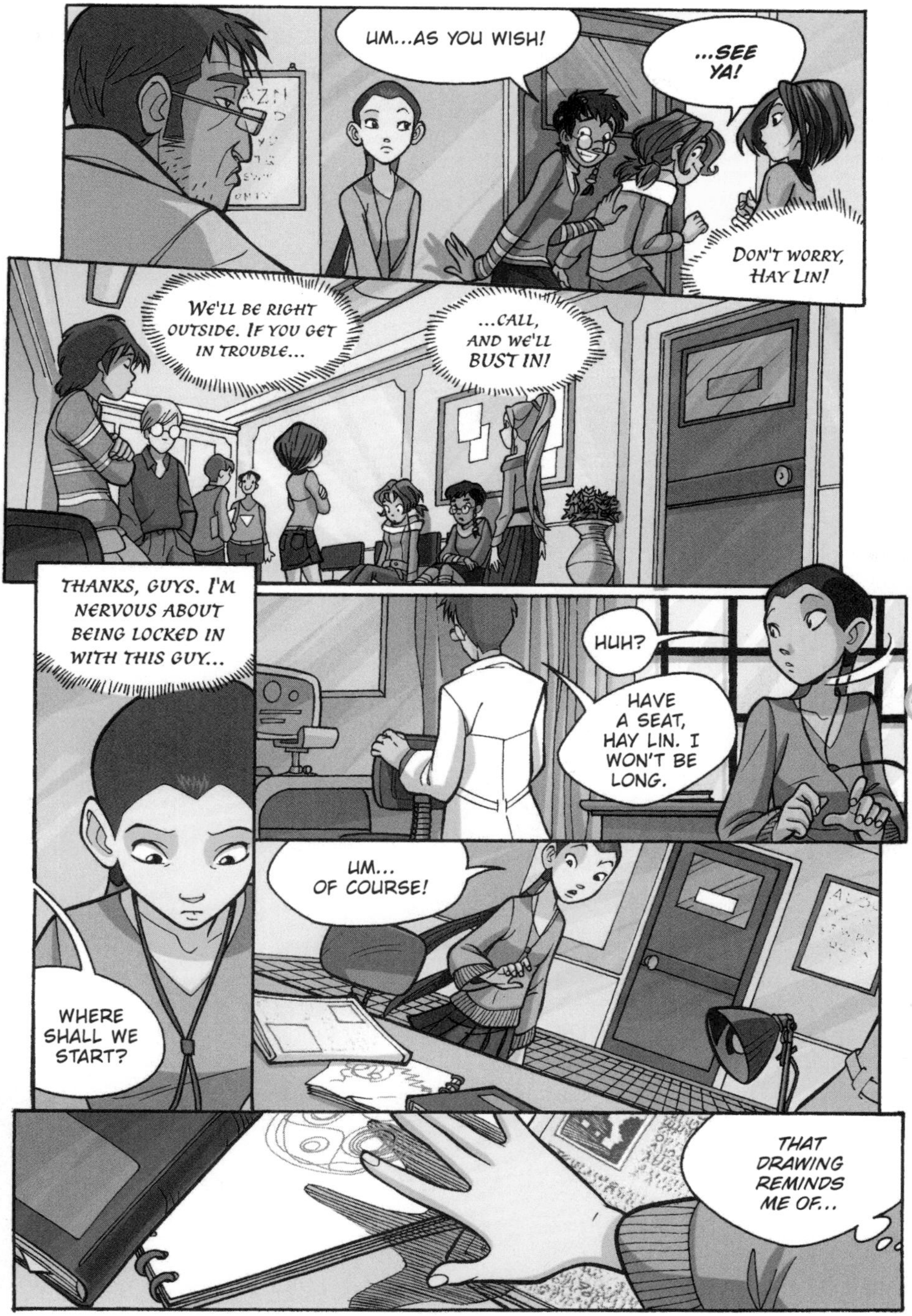
UM...AS YOU WISH!
...SEE YA!
DON'T WORRY, HAY LIN!
WE'LL BE RIGHT OUTSIDE. IF YOU GET IN TROUBLE...
...CALL, AND WE'LL BUST IN!
THANKS, GUYS. I'M NERVOUS ABOUT BEING LOCKED IN WITH THIS GUY...
HUH?
HAVE A SEAT, HAY LIN. I WON'T BE LONG.
UM... OF COURSE!
WHERE SHALL WE START?
THAT DRAWING REMINDS ME OF...

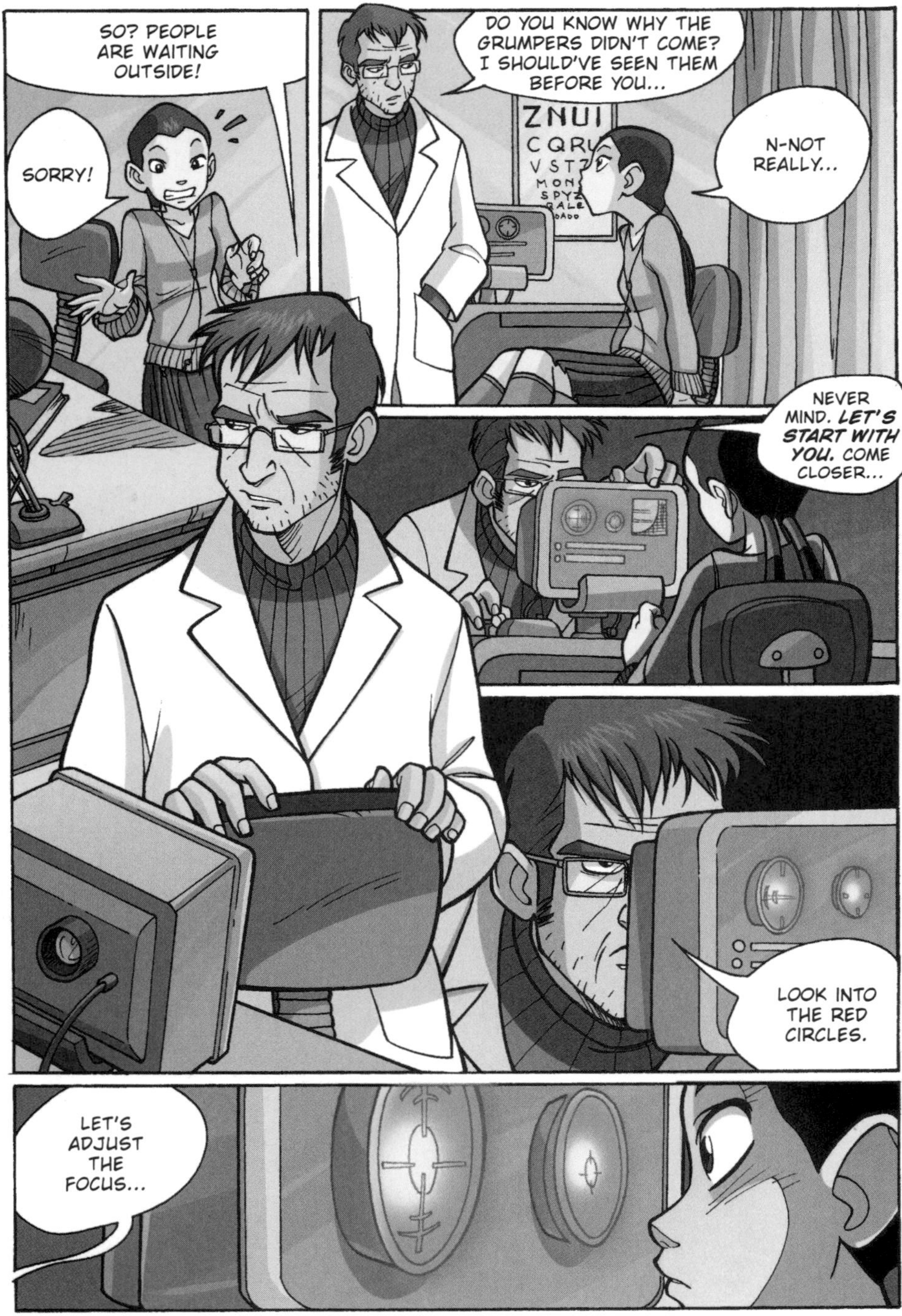
SO? PEOPLE ARE WAITING OUTSIDE!
SORRY!
DO YOU KNOW WHY THE GRUMPERS DIDN'T COME? I SHOULD'VE SEEN THEM BEFORE YOU...
ZNUI
CQRU
VSTZ
N-NOT REALLY...
NEVER MIND. ***LET'S START WITH YOU.*** COME CLOSER...
LOOK INTO THE RED CIRCLES.
LET'S ADJUST THE FOCUS...

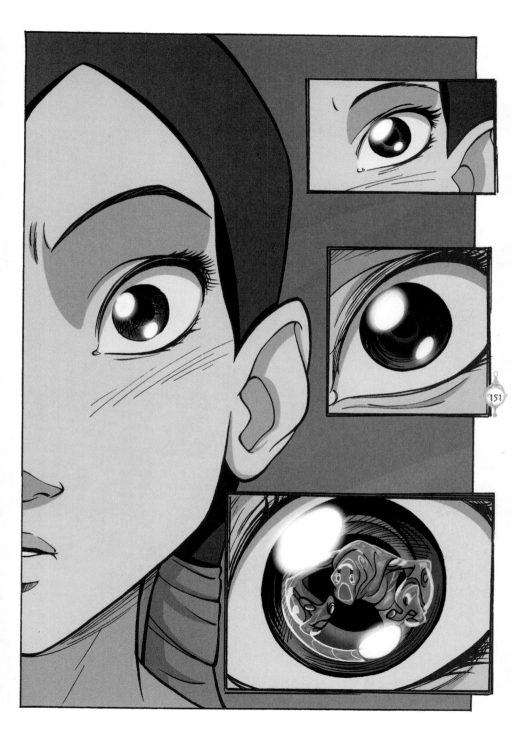

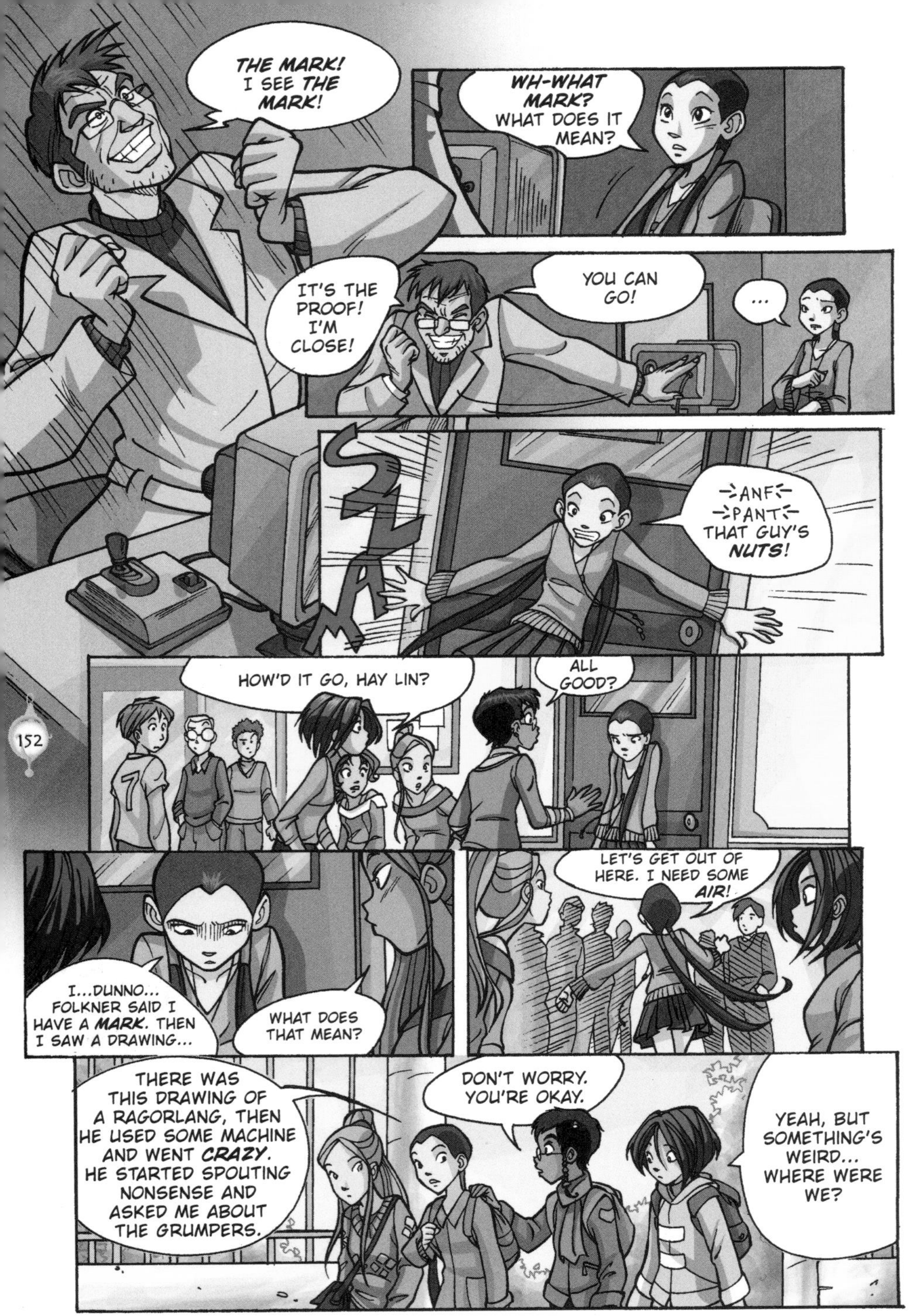
THE MARK! I SEE THE MARK!
WH-WHAT MARK? WHAT DOES IT MEAN?
IT'S THE PROOF! I'M CLOSE!
YOU CAN GO!
...
SLAM
ANF PANT THAT GUY'S NUTS!
HOW'D IT GO, HAY LIN?
ALL GOOD?
I...DUNNO... FOLKNER SAID I HAVE A MARK. THEN I SAW A DRAWING...
WHAT DOES THAT MEAN?
LET'S GET OUT OF HERE. I NEED SOME AIR!
THERE WAS THIS DRAWING OF A RAGORLANG, THEN HE USED SOME MACHINE AND WENT CRAZY. HE STARTED SPOUTING NONSENSE AND ASKED ME ABOUT THE GRUMPERS.
DON'T WORRY. YOU'RE OKAY.
YEAH, BUT SOMETHING'S WEIRD... WHERE WERE WE?

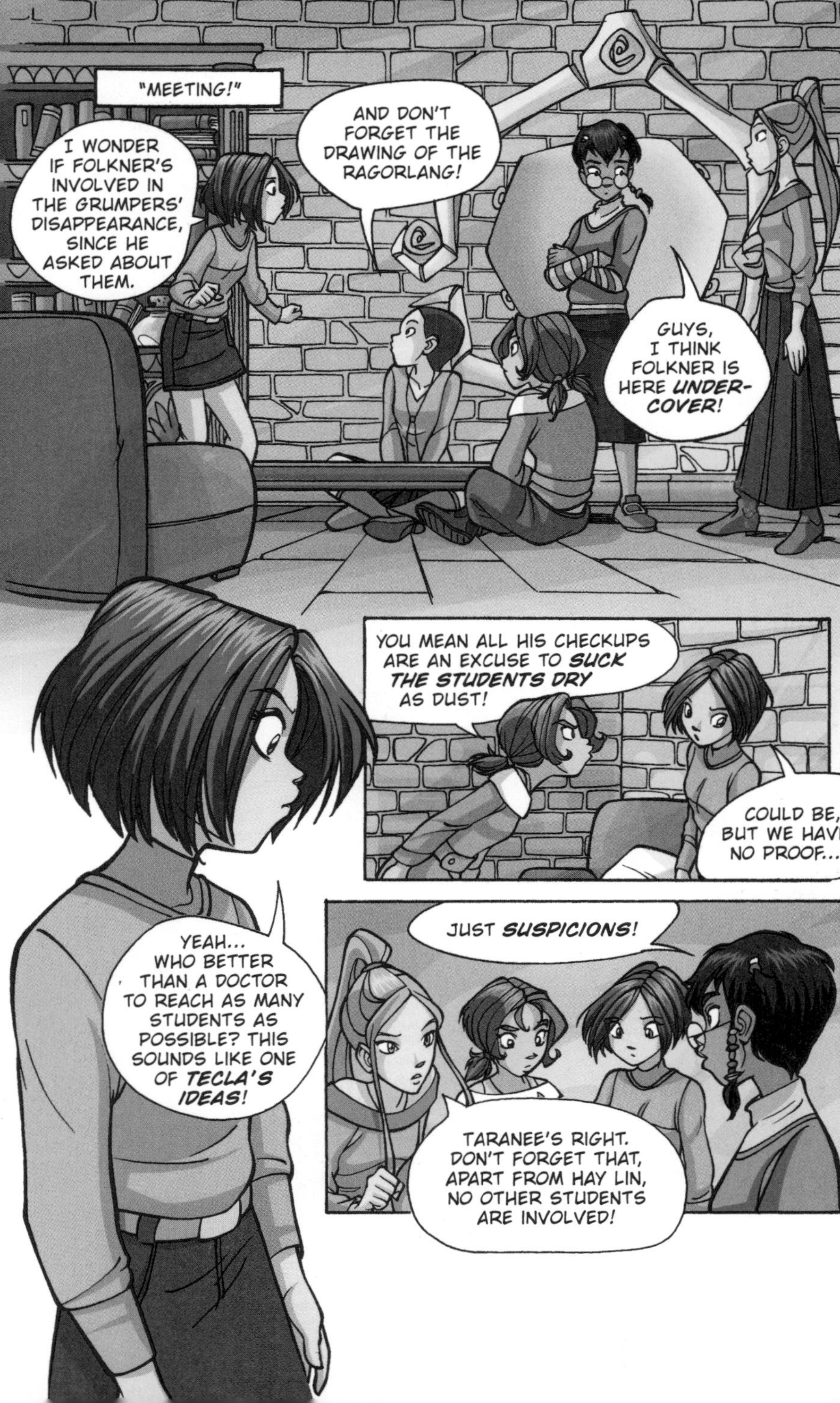
"MEETING!"
I WONDER IF FOLKNER'S INVOLVED IN THE GRUMPERS' DISAPPEARANCE, SINCE HE ASKED ABOUT THEM.
AND DON'T FORGET THE DRAWING OF THE RAGORLANG!
GUYS, I THINK FOLKNER IS HERE UNDER-COVER!
YOU MEAN ALL HIS CHECKUPS ARE AN EXCUSE TO SUCK THE STUDENTS DRY AS DUST!
COULD BE, BUT WE HAVE NO PROOF...
YEAH... WHO BETTER THAN A DOCTOR TO REACH AS MANY STUDENTS AS POSSIBLE? THIS SOUNDS LIKE ONE OF TECLA'S IDEAS!
JUST SUSPICIONS!
TARANEE'S RIGHT. DON'T FORGET THAT, APART FROM HAY LIN, NO OTHER STUDENTS ARE INVOLVED!

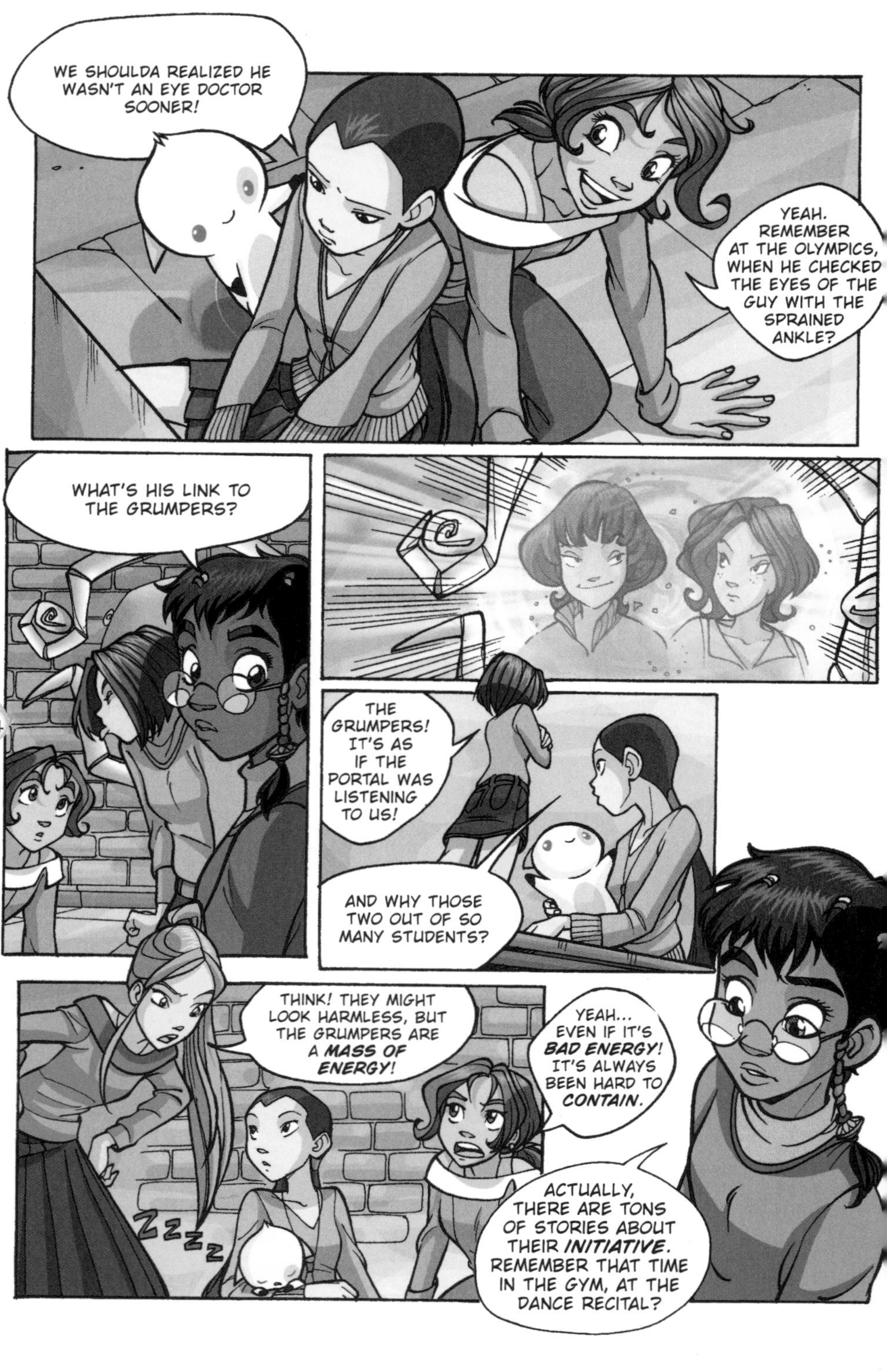
WE SHOULDA REALIZED HE WASN'T AN EYE DOCTOR SOONER!
YEAH. REMEMBER AT THE OLYMPICS, WHEN HE CHECKED THE EYES OF THE GUY WITH THE SPRAINED ANKLE?
WHAT'S HIS LINK TO THE GRUMPERS?
THE GRUMPERS! IT'S AS IF THE PORTAL WAS LISTENING TO US!
AND WHY THOSE TWO OUT OF SO MANY STUDENTS?
THINK! THEY MIGHT LOOK HARMLESS, BUT THE GRUMPERS ARE A MASS OF ENERGY!
YEAH... EVEN IF IT'S BAD ENERGY! IT'S ALWAYS BEEN HARD TO CONTAIN.
ACTUALLY, THERE ARE TONS OF STORIES ABOUT THEIR INITIATIVE. REMEMBER THAT TIME IN THE GYM, AT THE DANCE RECITAL?
ZZZZ

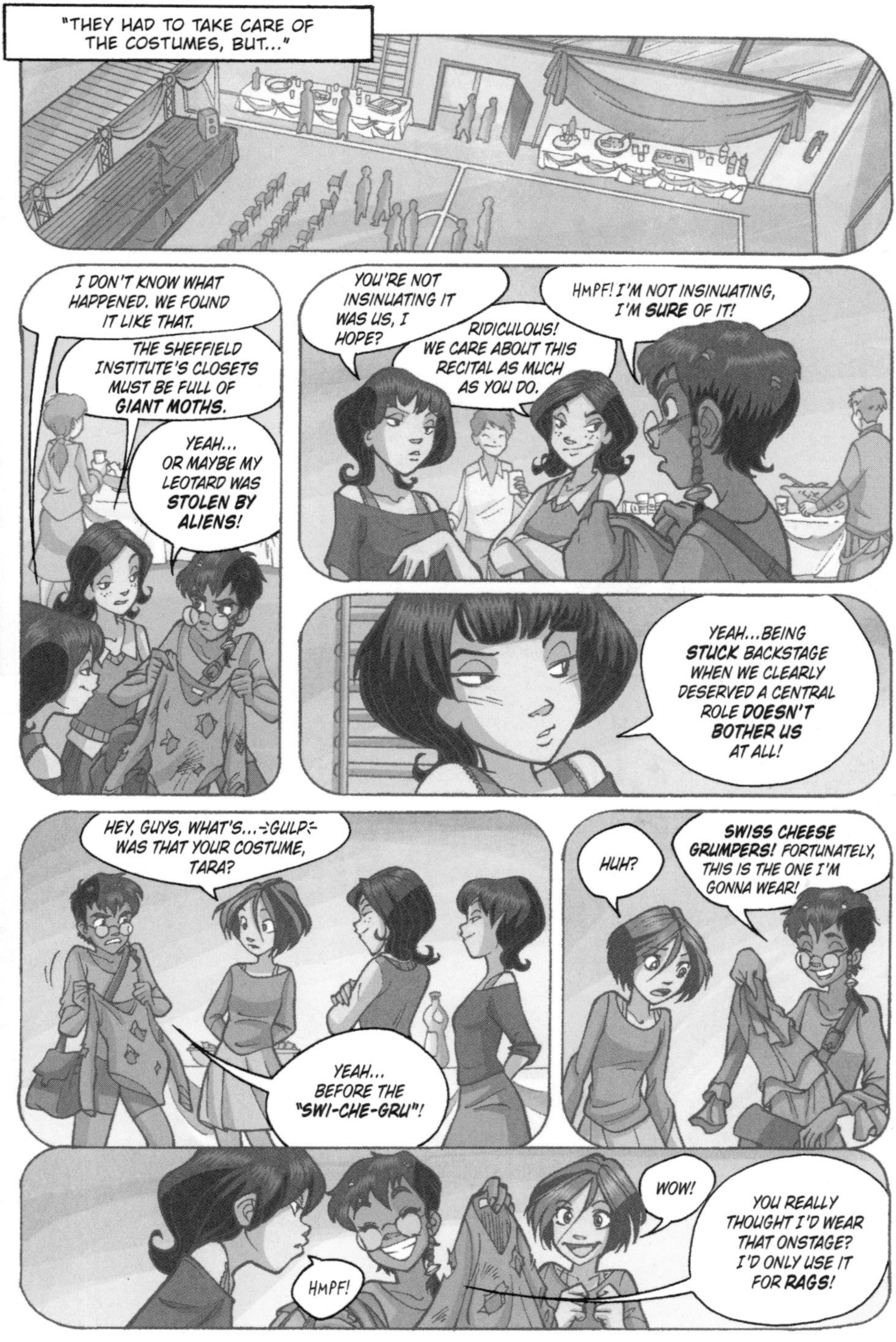
"THEY HAD TO TAKE CARE OF THE COSTUMES, BUT..."
I DON'T KNOW WHAT HAPPENED. WE FOUND IT LIKE THAT.
THE SHEFFIELD INSTITUTE'S CLOSETS MUST BE FULL OF GIANT MOTHS.
YEAH... OR MAYBE MY LEOTARD WAS STOLEN BY ALIENS!
YOU'RE NOT INSINUATING IT WAS US, I HOPE?
RIDICULOUS! WE CARE ABOUT THIS RECITAL AS MUCH AS YOU DO.
HMPF! I'M NOT INSINUATING, I'M SURE OF IT!
YEAH...BEING STUCK BACKSTAGE WHEN WE CLEARLY DESERVED A CENTRAL ROLE DOESN'T BOTHER US AT ALL!
HEY, GUYS, WHAT'S... ≈GULP≈ WAS THAT YOUR COSTUME, TARA?
YEAH... BEFORE THE "SWI-CHE-GRU"!
HUH?
SWISS CHEESE GRUMPERS! FORTUNATELY, THIS IS THE ONE I'M GONNA WEAR!
WOW!
YOU REALLY THOUGHT I'D WEAR THAT ONSTAGE? I'D ONLY USE IT FOR RAGS!
HMPF!

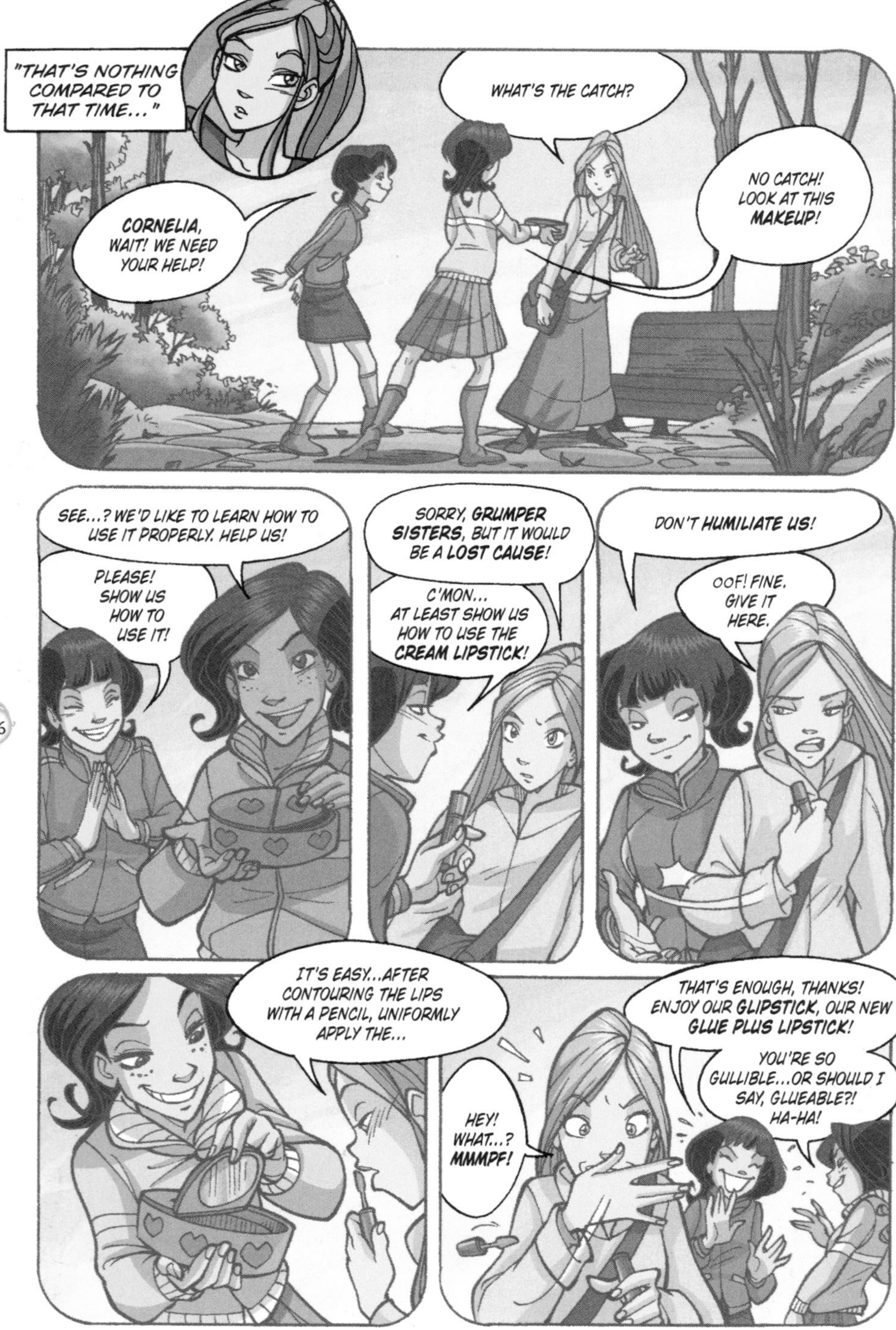
"THAT'S NOTHING COMPARED TO THAT TIME..."
CORNELIA, WAIT! WE NEED YOUR HELP!
WHAT'S THE CATCH?
NO CATCH! LOOK AT THIS MAKEUP!
SEE...? WE'D LIKE TO LEARN HOW TO USE IT PROPERLY. HELP US!
PLEASE! SHOW US HOW TO USE IT!
SORRY, GRUMPER SISTERS, BUT IT WOULD BE A LOST CAUSE!
C'MON... AT LEAST SHOW US HOW TO USE THE CREAM LIPSTICK!
DON'T HUMILIATE US!
OOF! FINE. GIVE IT HERE.
IT'S EASY...AFTER CONTOURING THE LIPS WITH A PENCIL, UNIFORMLY APPLY THE...
THAT'S ENOUGH, THANKS! ENJOY OUR GLIPSTICK, OUR NEW GLUE PLUS LIPSTICK!
YOU'RE SO GULLIBLE...OR SHOULD I SAY, GLUEABLE?! HA-HA!
HEY! WHAT...? MMMPF!

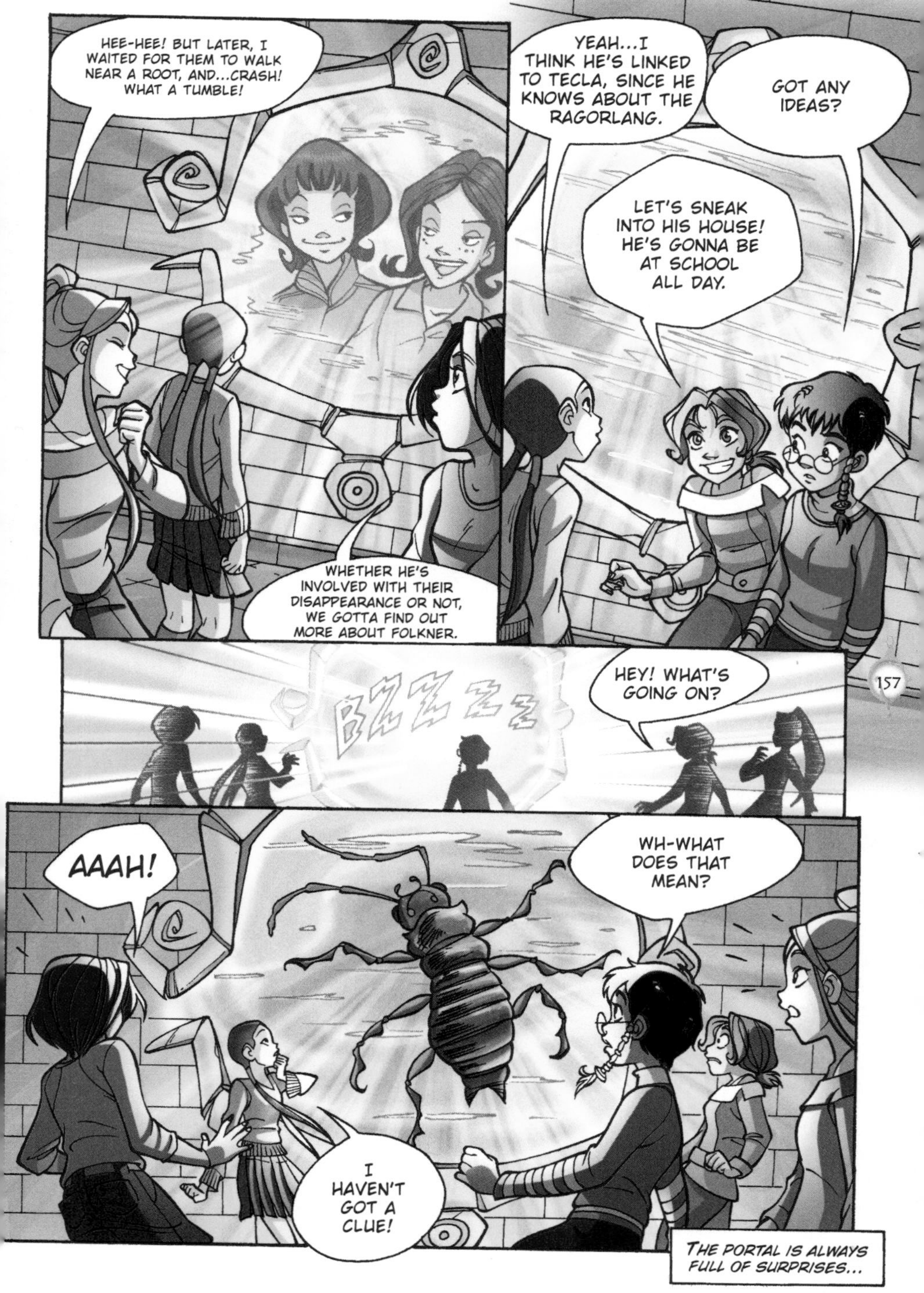
HEE-HEE! BUT LATER, I WAITED FOR THEM TO WALK NEAR A ROOT, AND...CRASH! WHAT A TUMBLE!
WHETHER HE'S INVOLVED WITH THEIR DISAPPEARANCE OR NOT, WE GOTTA FIND OUT MORE ABOUT FOLKNER.
YEAH...I THINK HE'S LINKED TO TECLA, SINCE HE KNOWS ABOUT THE RAGORLANG.
GOT ANY IDEAS?
LET'S SNEAK INTO HIS HOUSE! HE'S GONNA BE AT SCHOOL ALL DAY.
BZZZzz
HEY! WHAT'S GOING ON?
AAAH!
WH-WHAT DOES THAT MEAN?
I HAVEN'T GOT A CLUE!
THE PORTAL IS ALWAYS FULL OF SURPRISES...

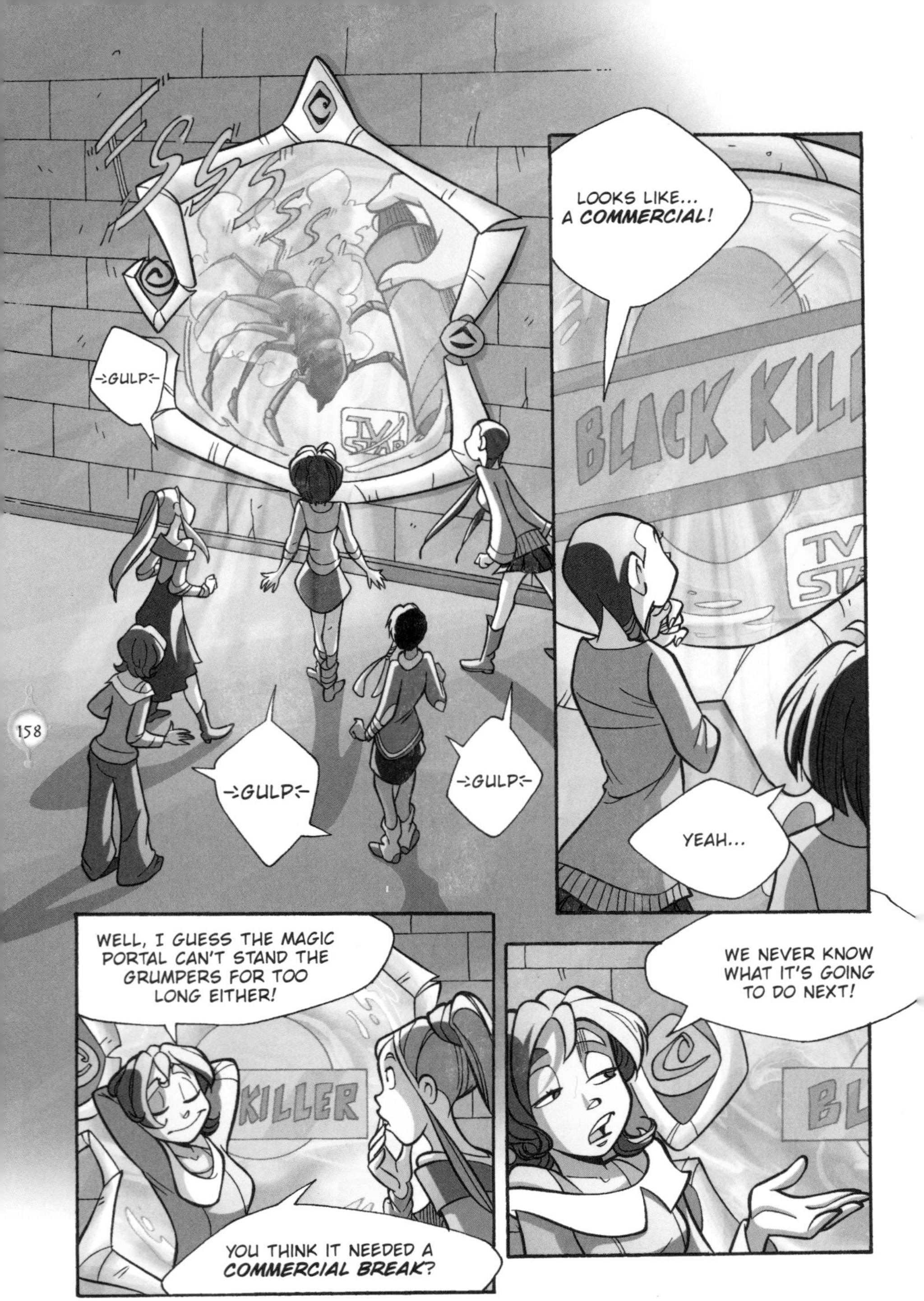

⇝GULP⇜
⇝GULP⇜
⇝GULP⇜
LOOKS LIKE... A **COMMERCIAL**!
YEAH...
WELL, I GUESS THE MAGIC PORTAL CAN'T STAND THE GRUMPERS FOR TOO LONG EITHER!
KILLER
YOU THINK IT NEEDED A **COMMERCIAL BREAK**?
WE NEVER KNOW WHAT IT'S GOING TO DO NEXT!

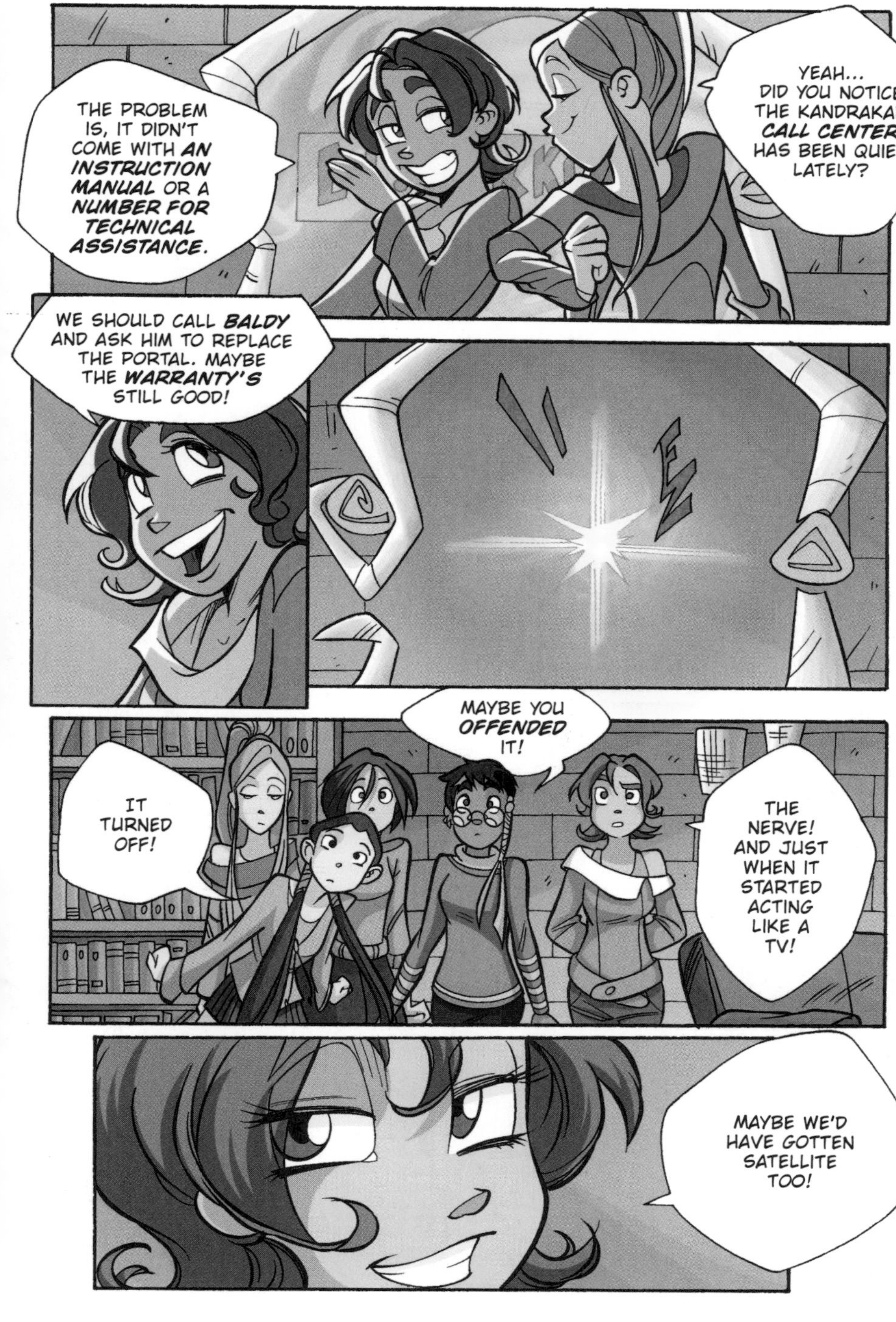
THE PROBLEM IS, IT DIDN'T COME WITH AN INSTRUCTION MANUAL OR A NUMBER FOR TECHNICAL ASSISTANCE.
YEAH... DID YOU NOTICE THE KANDRAKAR CALL CENTER HAS BEEN QUIET LATELY?
WE SHOULD CALL BALDY AND ASK HIM TO REPLACE THE PORTAL. MAYBE THE WARRANTY'S STILL GOOD!
IT TURNED OFF!
MAYBE YOU OFFENDED IT!
THE NERVE! AND JUST WHEN IT STARTED ACTING LIKE A TV!
MAYBE WE'D HAVE GOTTEN SATELLITE TOO!

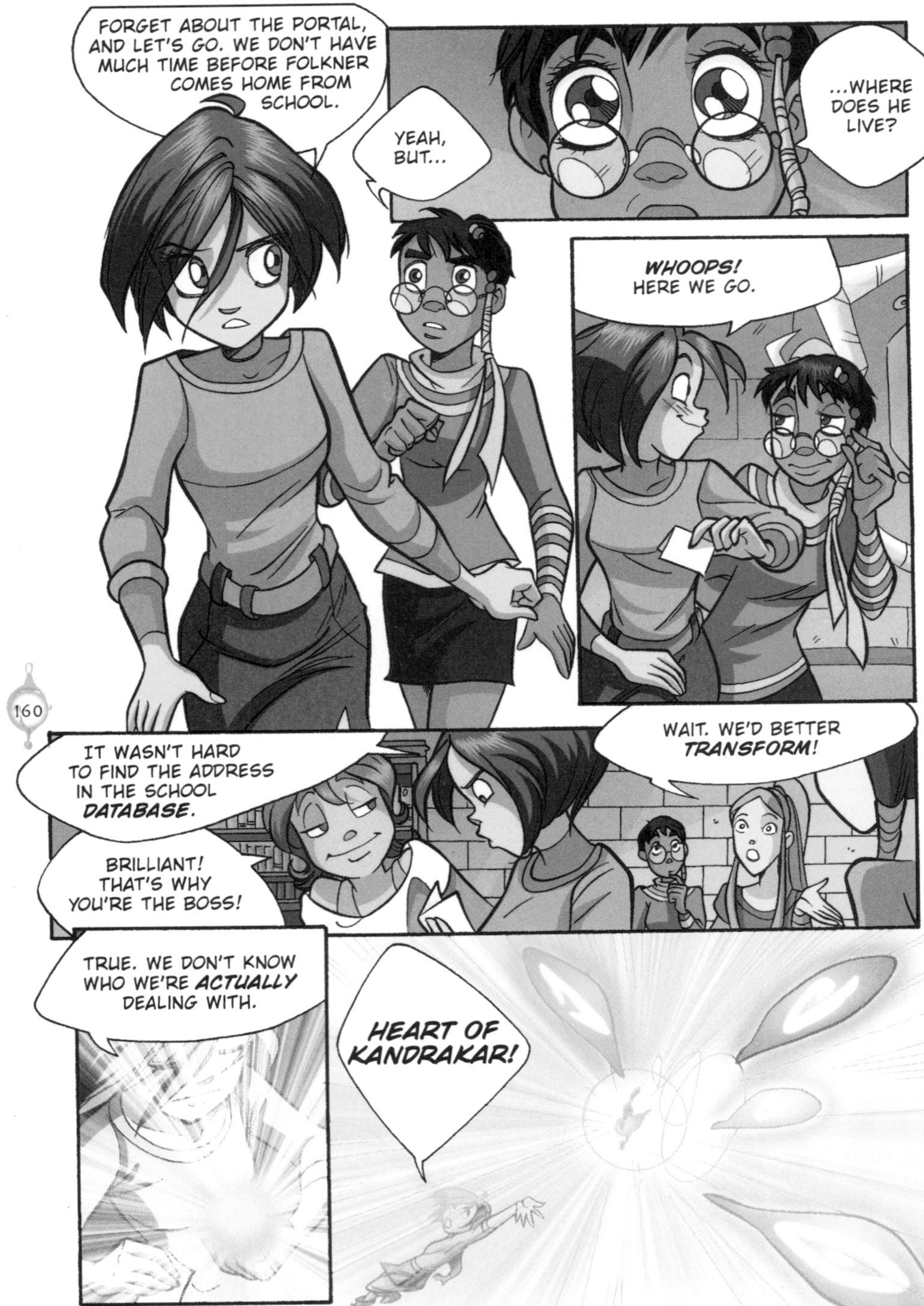
FORGET ABOUT THE PORTAL, AND LET'S GO. WE DON'T HAVE MUCH TIME BEFORE FOLKNER COMES HOME FROM SCHOOL.
YEAH, BUT...
...WHERE DOES HE LIVE?
WHOOPS! HERE WE GO.
IT WASN'T HARD TO FIND THE ADDRESS IN THE SCHOOL DATABASE.
BRILLIANT! THAT'S WHY YOU'RE THE BOSS!
WAIT. WE'D BETTER TRANSFORM!
TRUE. WE DON'T KNOW WHO WE'RE ACTUALLY DEALING WITH.
HEART OF KANDRAKAR!

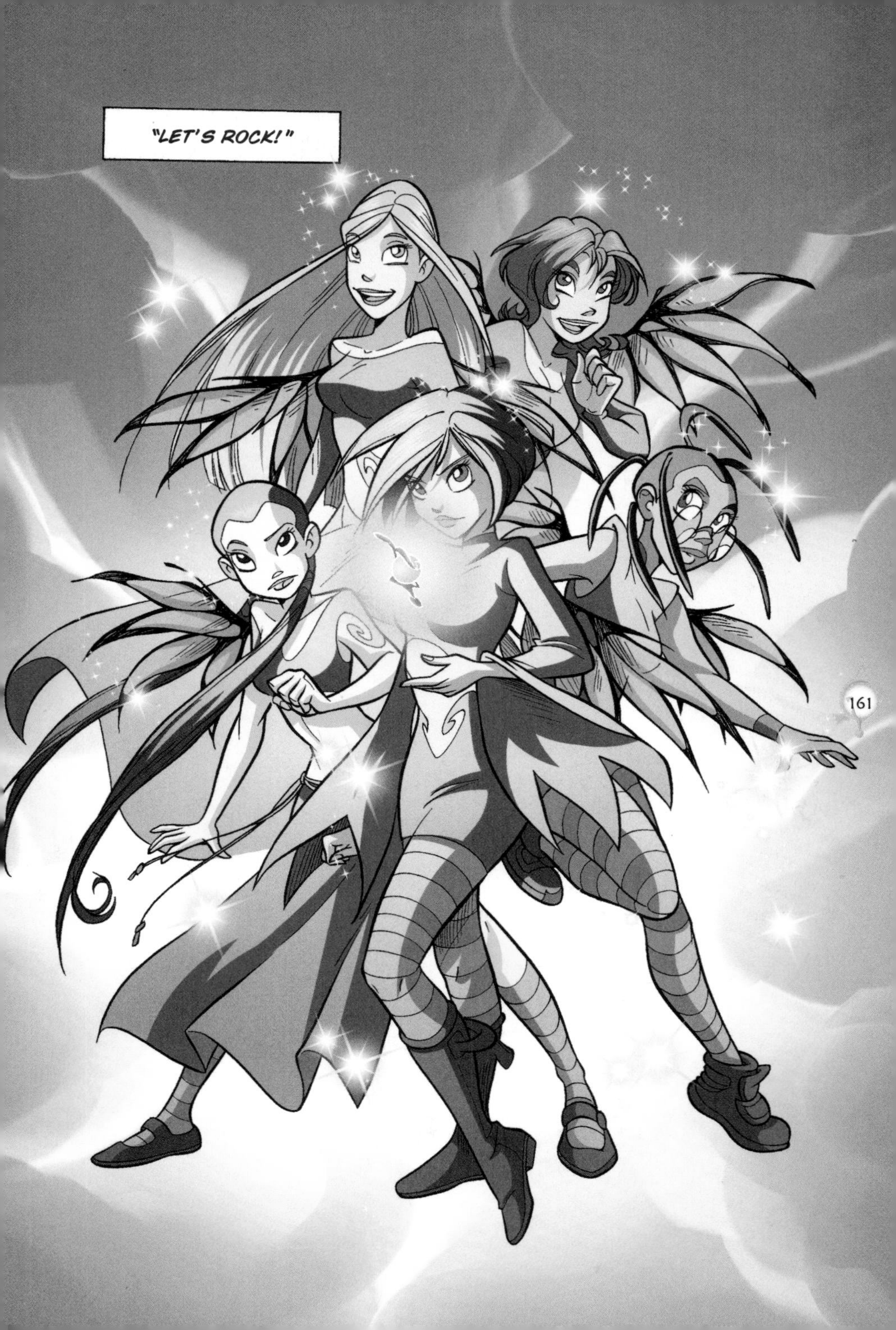
"LET'S ROCK!"

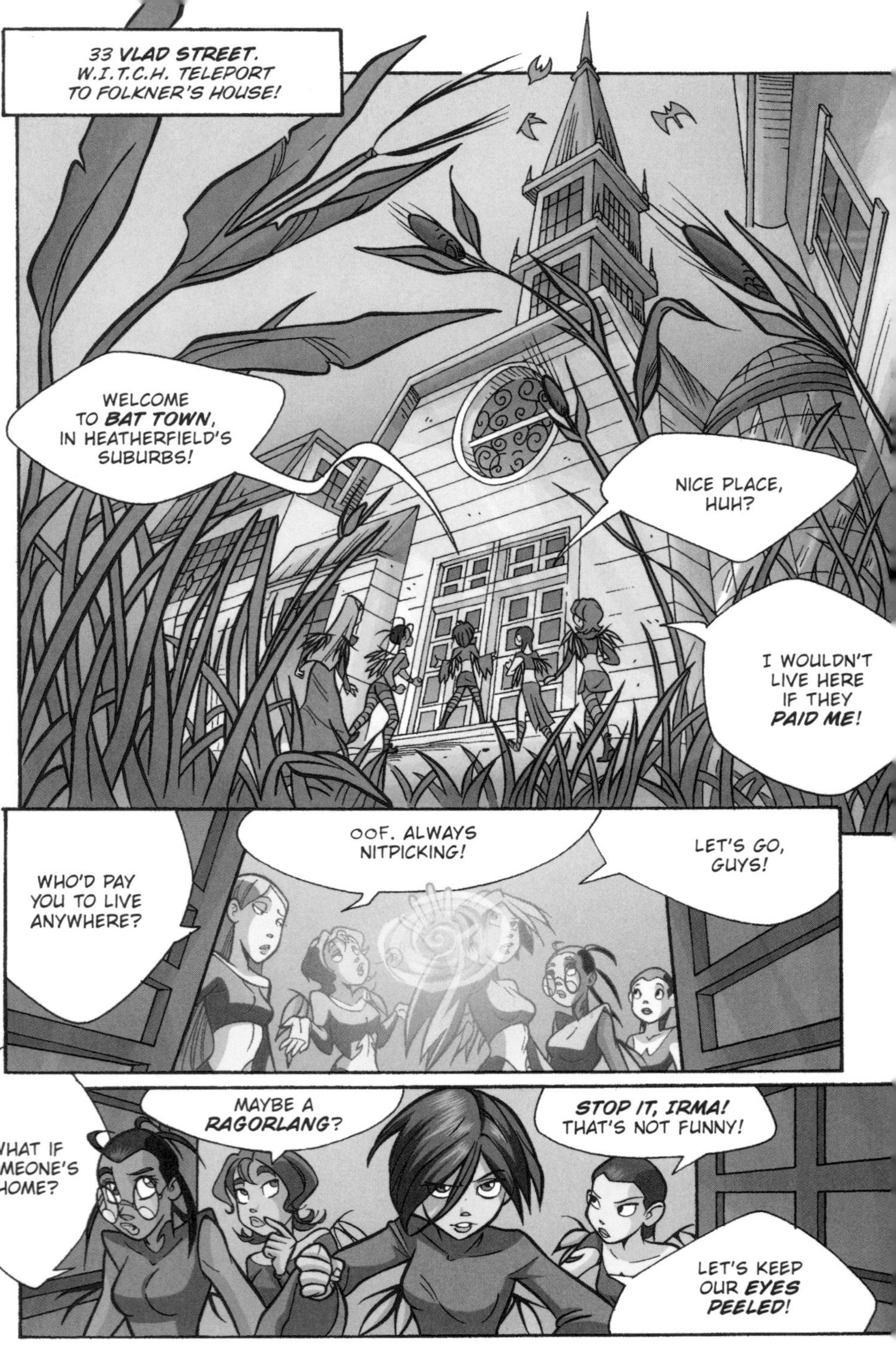
33 VLAD STREET. W.I.T.C.H. TELEPORT TO FOLKNER'S HOUSE!
WELCOME TO BAT TOWN, IN HEATHERFIELD'S SUBURBS!
NICE PLACE, HUH?
I WOULDN'T LIVE HERE IF THEY PAID ME!
WHO'D PAY YOU TO LIVE ANYWHERE?
OOF. ALWAYS NITPICKING!
LET'S GO, GUYS!
WHAT IF SOMEONE'S HOME?
MAYBE A RAGORLANG?
STOP IT, IRMA! THAT'S NOT FUNNY!
LET'S KEEP OUR EYES PEELED!

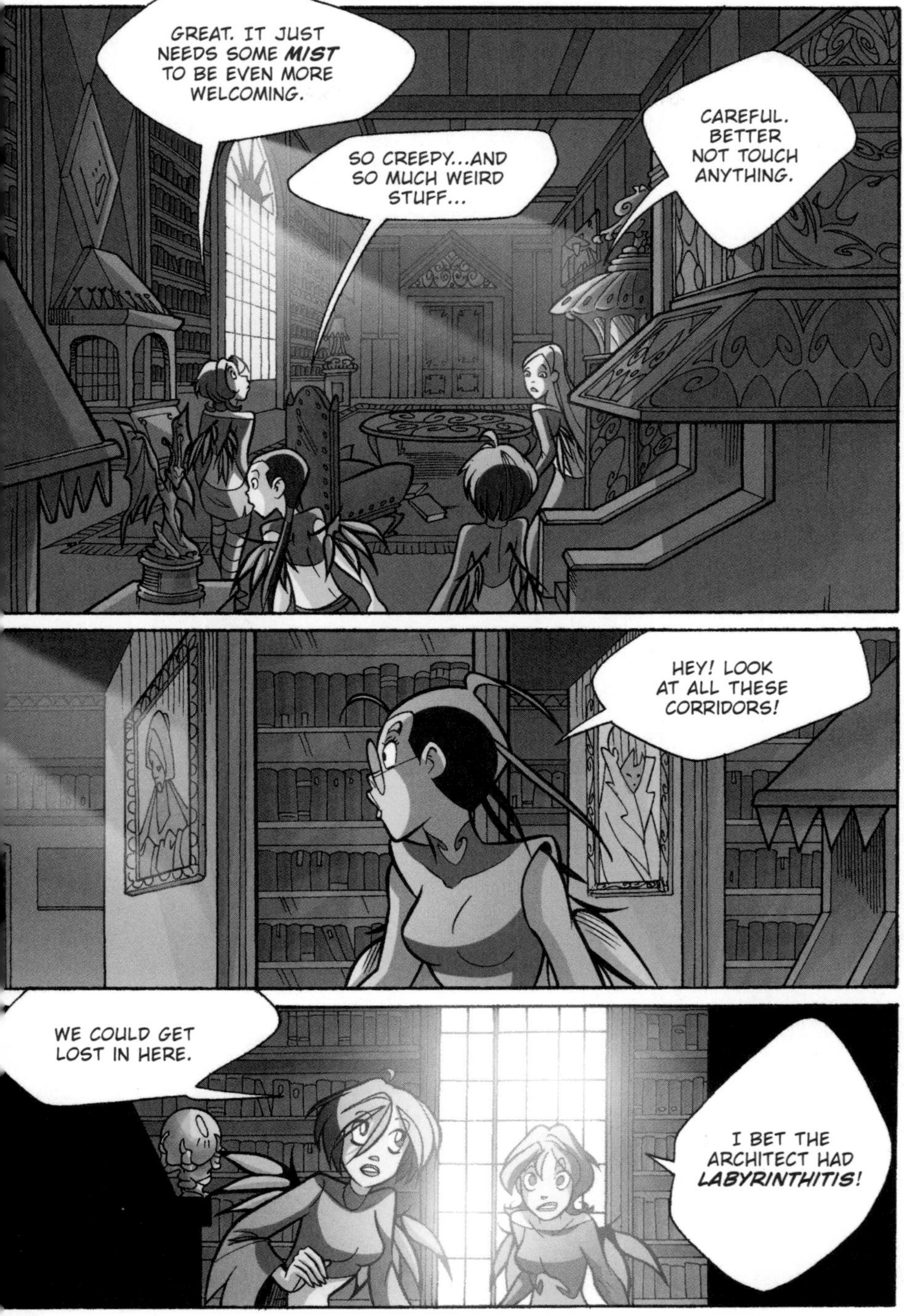
GREAT. IT JUST NEEDS SOME *MIST* TO BE EVEN MORE WELCOMING.
SO CREEPY...AND SO MUCH WEIRD STUFF...
CAREFUL. BETTER NOT TOUCH ANYTHING.
HEY! LOOK AT ALL THESE CORRIDORS!
WE COULD GET LOST IN HERE.
I BET THE ARCHITECT HAD ***LABYRINTHITIS***!

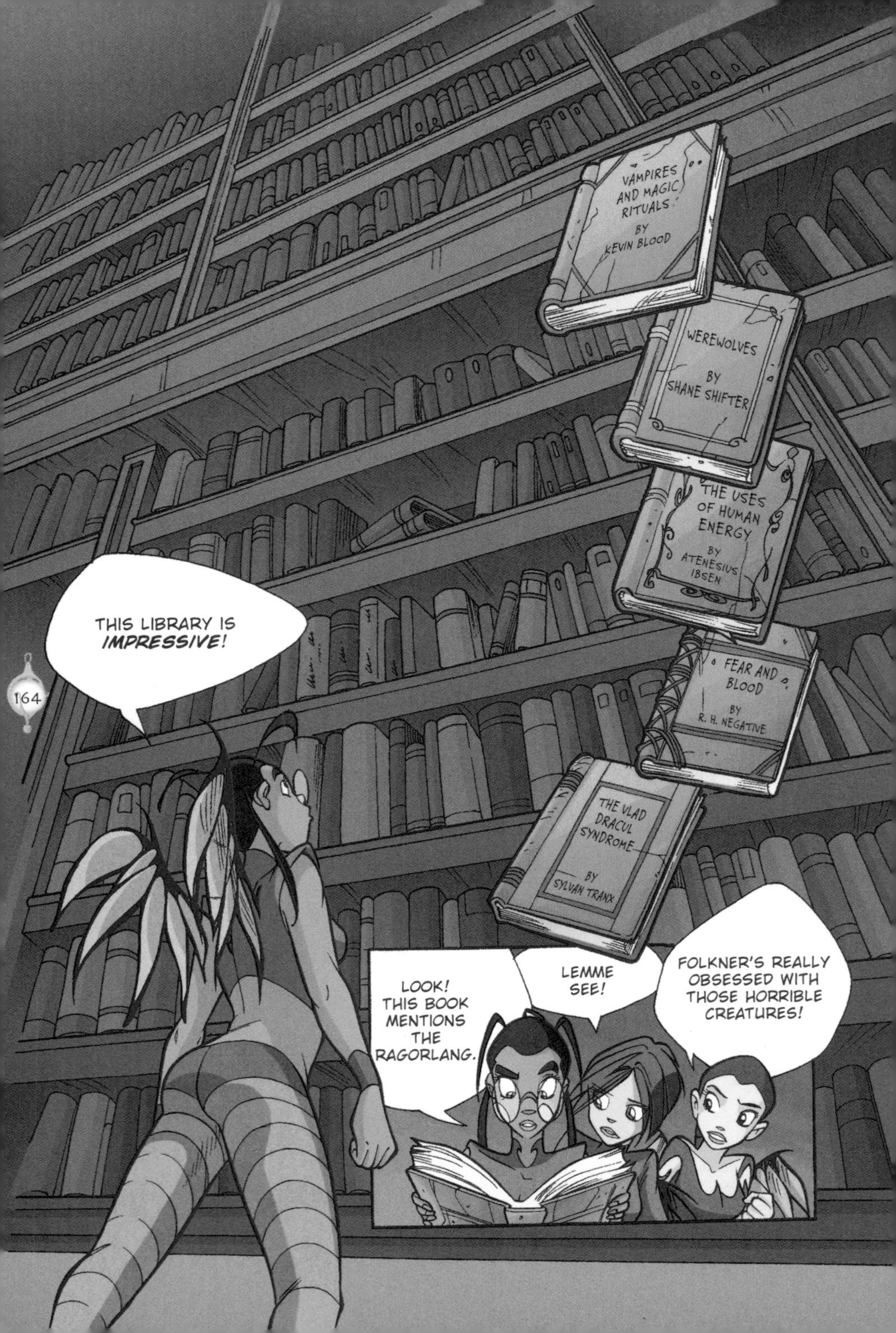
VAMPIRES AND MAGIC RITUALS BY KEVIN BLOOD
WEREWOLVES BY SHANE SHIFTER
THE USES OF HUMAN ENERGY BY ATENESIUS IBSEN
FEAR AND BLOOD BY R. H. NEGATIVE
THE VLAD DRACUL SYNDROME BY SYLVAN TRANX
THIS LIBRARY IS *IMPRESSIVE*!
LOOK! THIS BOOK MENTIONS THE RAGORLANG.
LEMME SEE!
FOLKNER'S REALLY OBSESSED WITH THOSE HORRIBLE CREATURES!

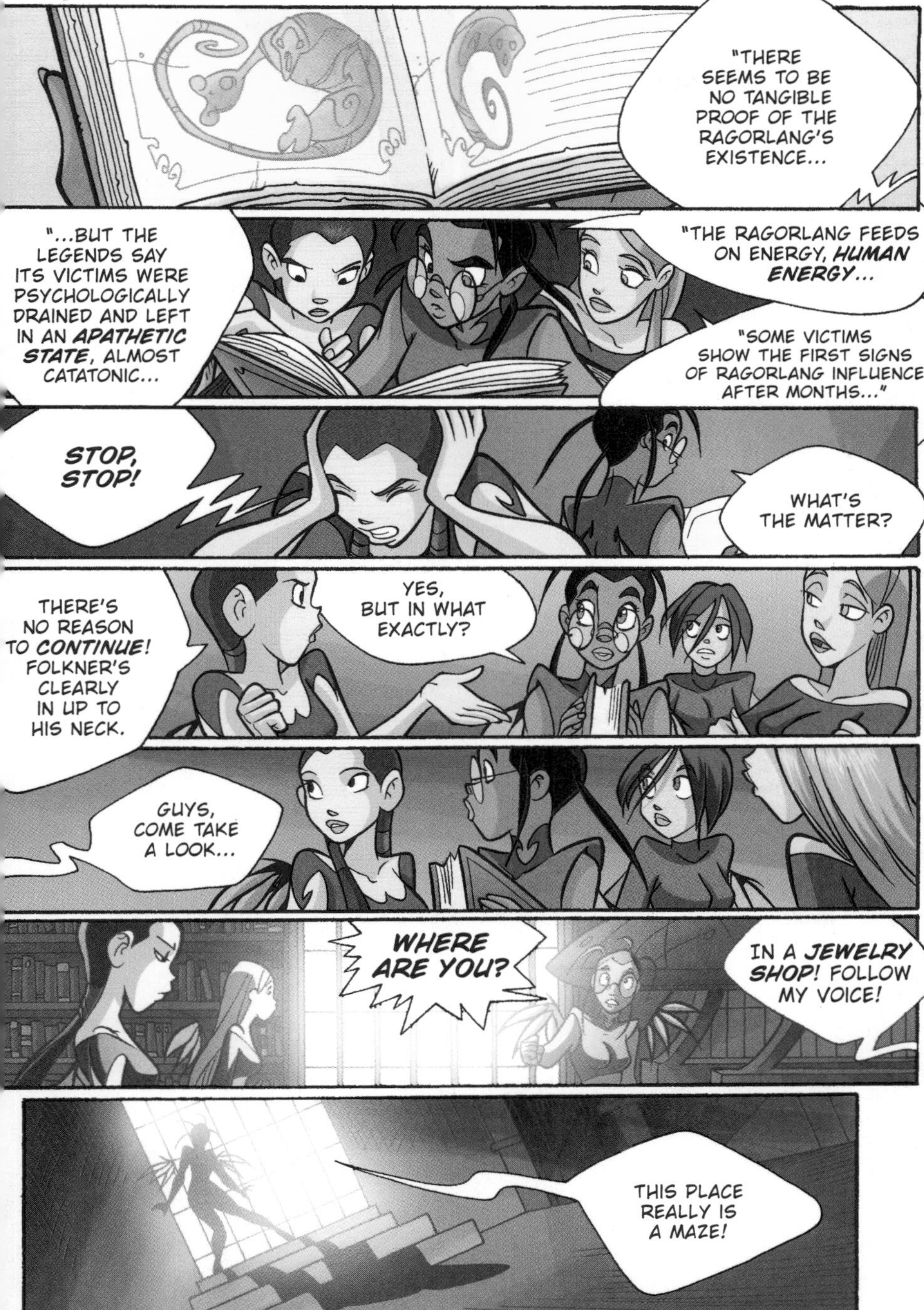
"THERE SEEMS TO BE NO TANGIBLE PROOF OF THE RAGORLANG'S EXISTENCE...
"...BUT THE LEGENDS SAY ITS VICTIMS WERE PSYCHOLOGICALLY DRAINED AND LEFT IN AN APATHETIC STATE, ALMOST CATATONIC...
"THE RAGORLANG FEEDS ON ENERGY, HUMAN ENERGY...
"SOME VICTIMS SHOW THE FIRST SIGNS OF RAGORLANG INFLUENCE AFTER MONTHS..."
STOP, STOP!
WHAT'S THE MATTER?
THERE'S NO REASON TO CONTINUE! FOLKNER'S CLEARLY IN UP TO HIS NECK.
YES, BUT IN WHAT EXACTLY?
GUYS, COME TAKE A LOOK...
WHERE ARE YOU?
IN A JEWELRY SHOP! FOLLOW MY VOICE!
THIS PLACE REALLY IS A MAZE!

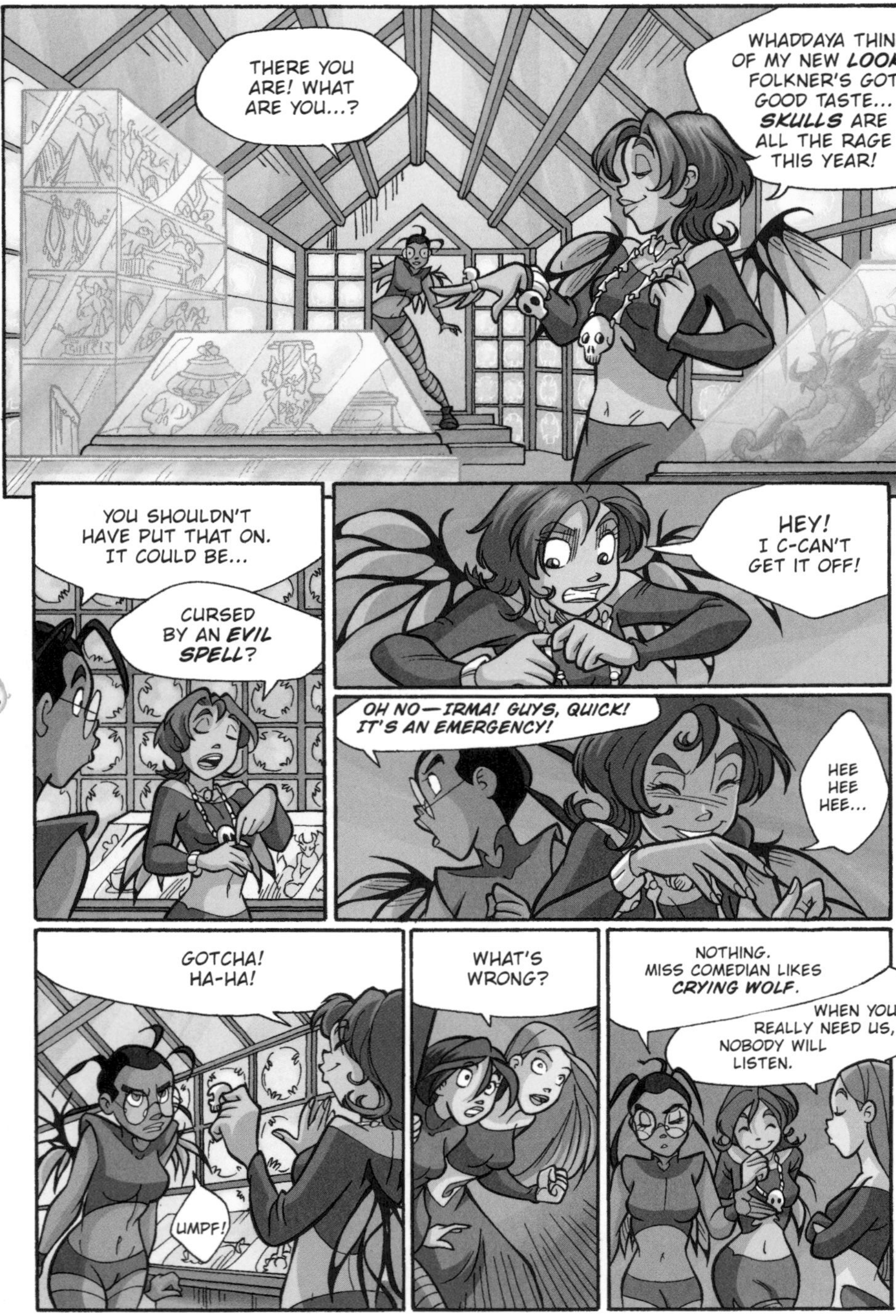
THERE YOU ARE! WHAT ARE YOU...?
WHADDAYA THINK OF MY NEW LOOK? FOLKNER'S GOT GOOD TASTE... SKULLS ARE ALL THE RAGE THIS YEAR!
YOU SHOULDN'T HAVE PUT THAT ON. IT COULD BE...
CURSED BY AN EVIL SPELL?
HEY! I C-CAN'T GET IT OFF!
OH NO—IRMA! GUYS, QUICK! IT'S AN EMERGENCY!
HEE HEE HEE...
GOTCHA! HA-HA!
UMPF!
WHAT'S WRONG?
NOTHING. MISS COMEDIAN LIKES CRYING WOLF.
WHEN YOU REALLY NEED US, NOBODY WILL LISTEN.

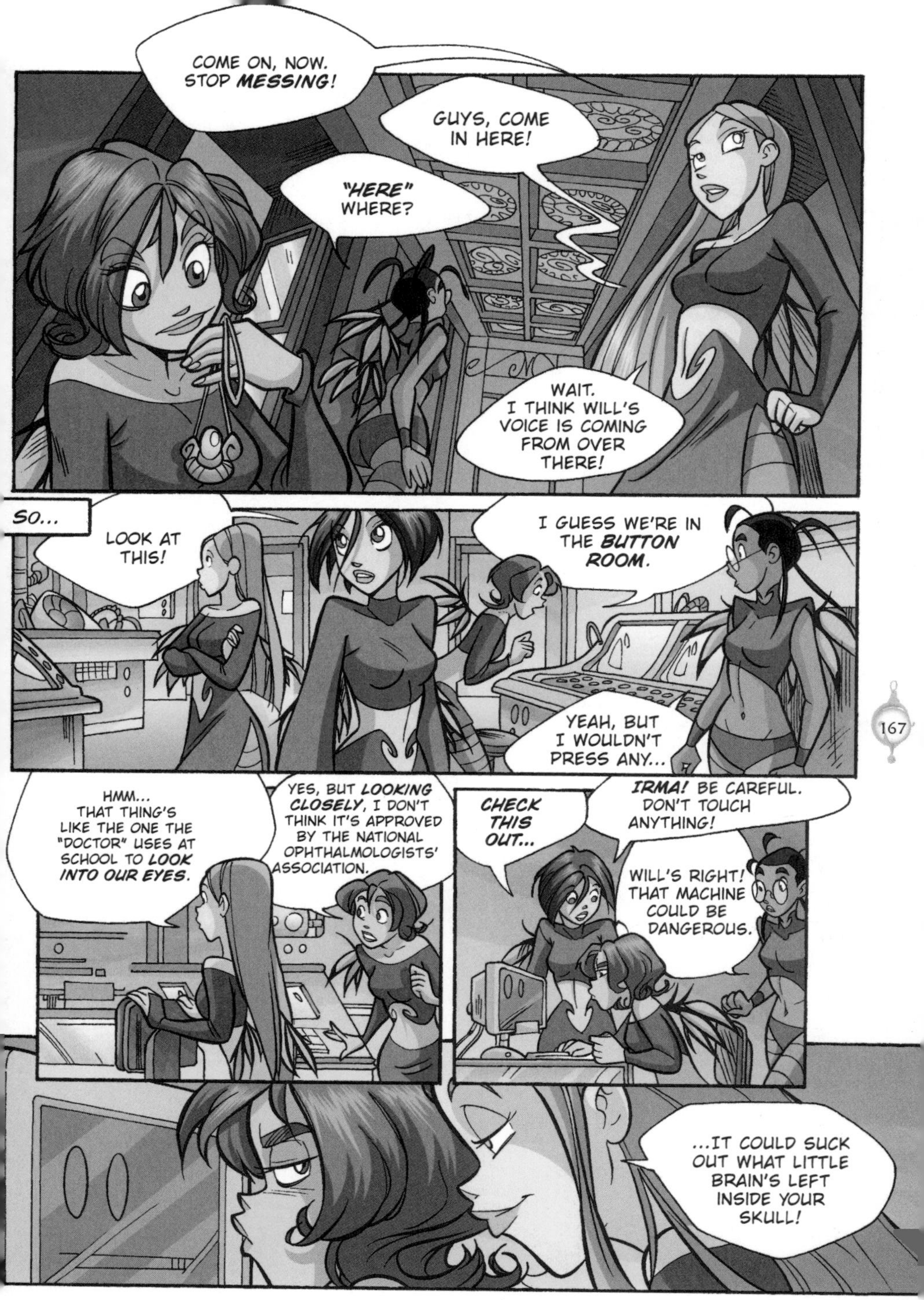
COME ON, NOW. STOP MESSING!
GUYS, COME IN HERE!
"HERE" WHERE?
WAIT. I THINK WILL'S VOICE IS COMING FROM OVER THERE!
SO...
LOOK AT THIS!
I GUESS WE'RE IN THE BUTTON ROOM.
YEAH, BUT I WOULDN'T PRESS ANY...
HMM... THAT THING'S LIKE THE ONE THE "DOCTOR" USES AT SCHOOL TO LOOK INTO OUR EYES.
YES, BUT LOOKING CLOSELY, I DON'T THINK IT'S APPROVED BY THE NATIONAL OPHTHALMOLOGISTS' ASSOCIATION.
CHECK THIS OUT...
IRMA! BE CAREFUL. DON'T TOUCH ANYTHING!
WILL'S RIGHT! THAT MACHINE COULD BE DANGEROUS.
...IT COULD SUCK OUT WHAT LITTLE BRAIN'S LEFT INSIDE YOUR SKULL!

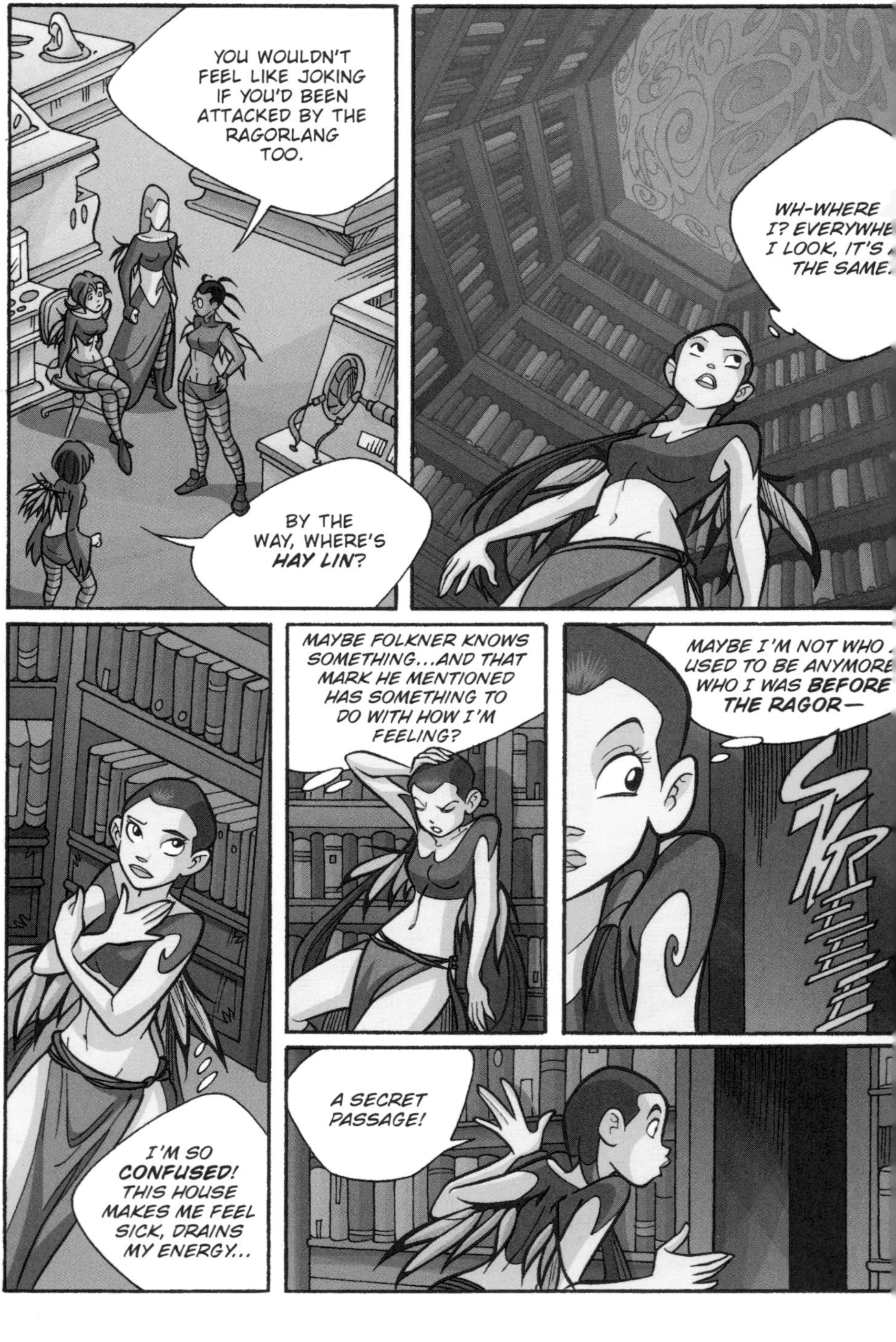
YOU WOULDN'T FEEL LIKE JOKING IF YOU'D BEEN ATTACKED BY THE RAGORLANG TOO.
BY THE WAY, WHERE'S **HAY LIN**?
WH-WHERE I? EVERYWHE I LOOK, IT'S THE SAME.
I'M SO **CONFUSED**! THIS HOUSE MAKES ME FEEL SICK, DRAINS MY ENERGY...
MAYBE FOLKNER KNOWS SOMETHING...AND THAT MARK HE MENTIONED HAS SOMETHING TO DO WITH HOW I'M FEELING?
MAYBE I'M NOT WHO USED TO BE ANYMORE WHO I WAS **BEFORE THE RAGOR—**
A SECRET PASSAGE!

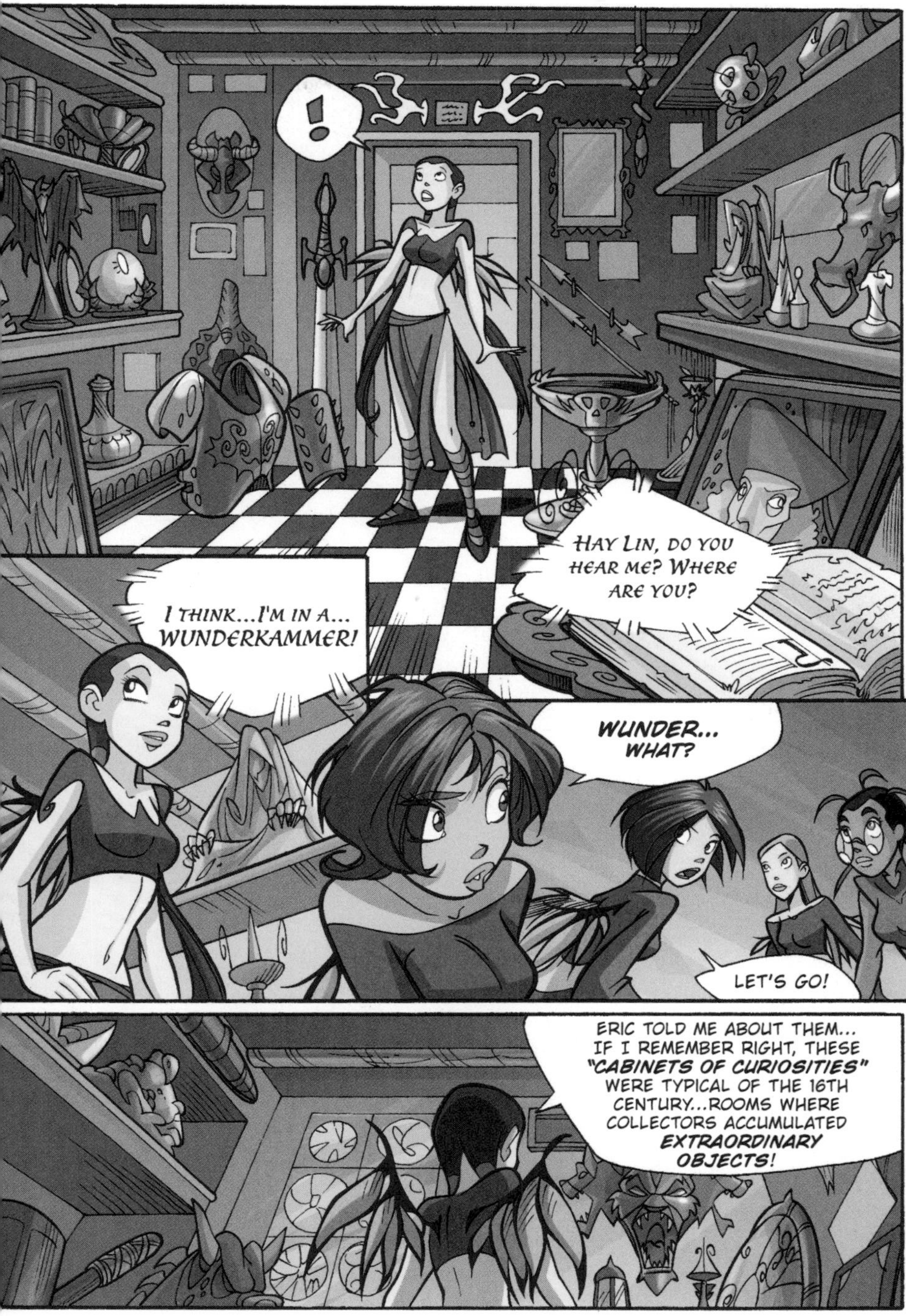
!
HAY LIN, DO YOU HEAR ME? WHERE ARE YOU?
I THINK...I'M IN A... WUNDERKAMMER!
WUNDER... WHAT?
LET'S GO!
ERIC TOLD ME ABOUT THEM... IF I REMEMBER RIGHT, THESE "CABINETS OF CURIOSITIES" WERE TYPICAL OF THE 16TH CENTURY...ROOMS WHERE COLLECTORS ACCUMULATED EXTRAORDINARY OBJECTS!

FOLKNER'S COLLECTION IS ABOUT MONSTERS AND VAMPIRES... NO SURPRISE THERE!

I WONDER WHERE HE FOUND ALL THIS STUFF...

AND I WONDER IF I'LL EVER *FIND MYSELF* AGAIN!

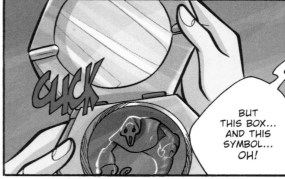

CLICK

BUT THIS BOX... AND THIS SYMBOL... OH!

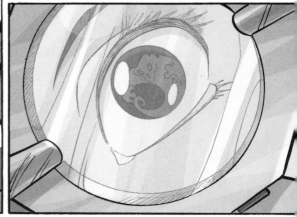

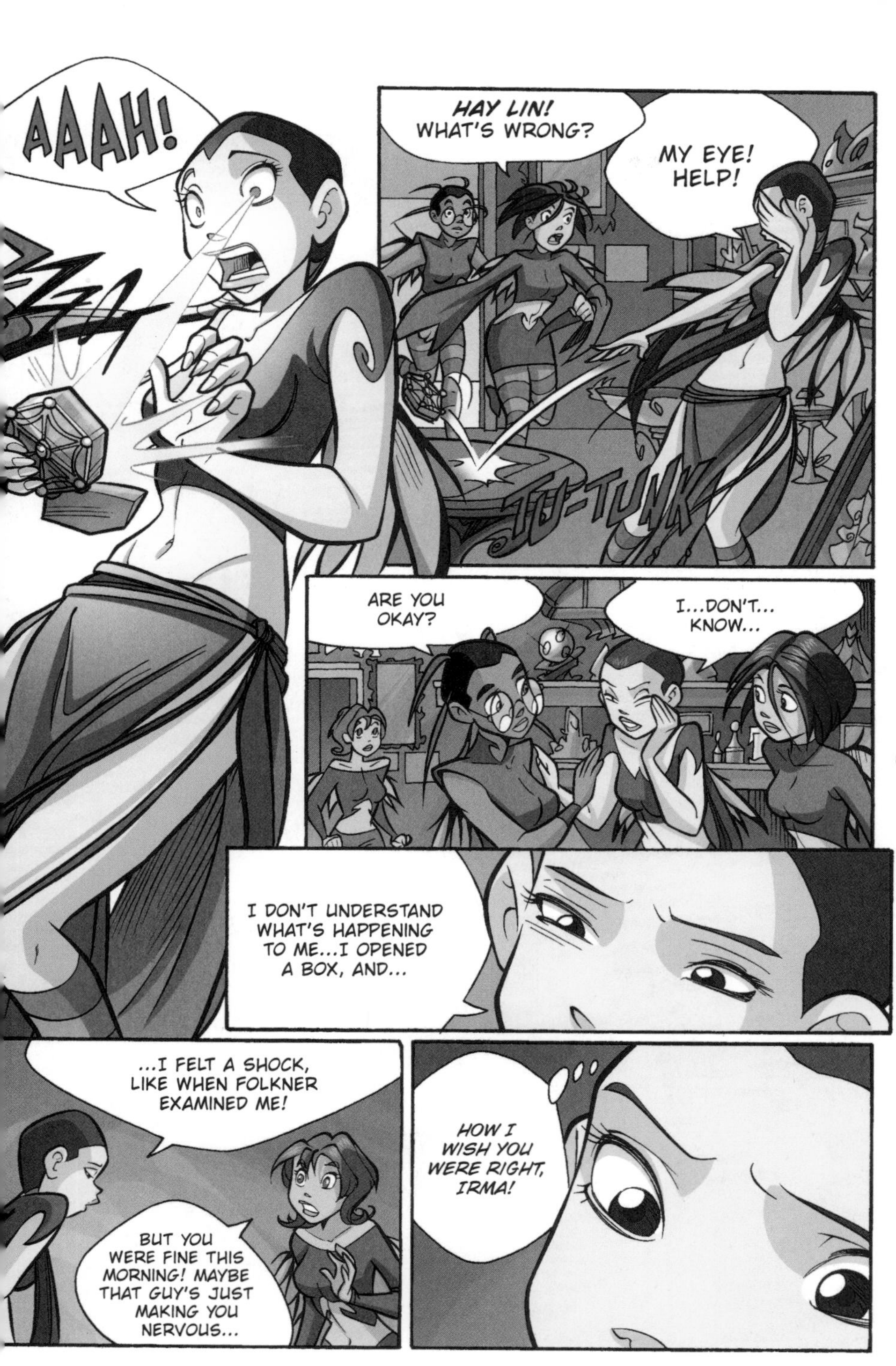
AAAH!
ZZAP
HAY LIN! WHAT'S WRONG?
MY EYE! HELP!
TU-TUNK
ARE YOU OKAY?
I...DON'T... KNOW...
I DON'T UNDERSTAND WHAT'S HAPPENING TO ME...I OPENED A BOX, AND...
...I FELT A SHOCK, LIKE WHEN FOLKNER EXAMINED ME!
BUT YOU WERE FINE THIS MORNING! MAYBE THAT GUY'S JUST MAKING YOU NERVOUS...
HOW I WISH YOU WERE RIGHT, IRMA!

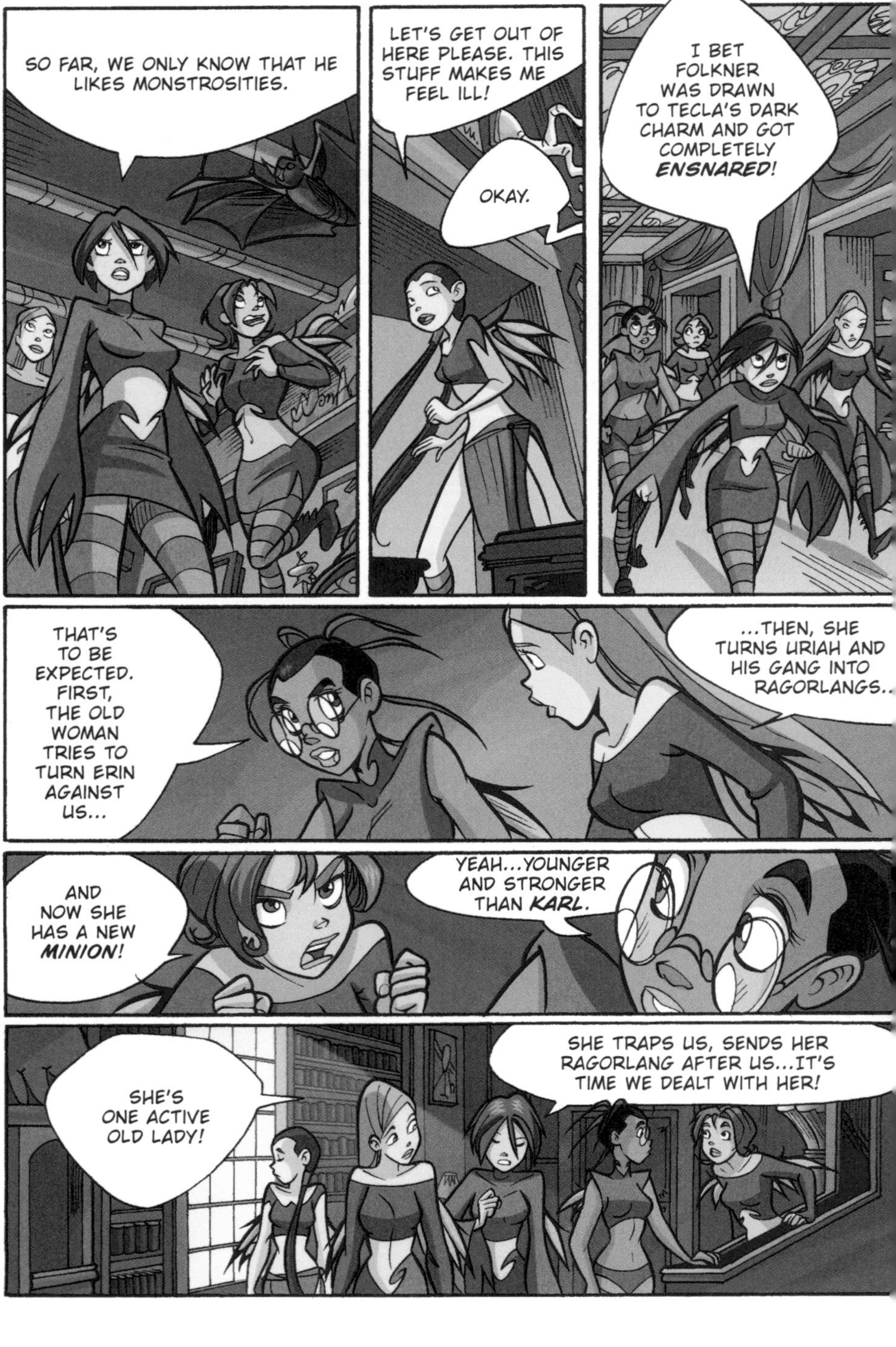
SO FAR, WE ONLY KNOW THAT HE LIKES MONSTROSITIES.
LET'S GET OUT OF HERE PLEASE. THIS STUFF MAKES ME FEEL ILL!
OKAY.
I BET FOLKNER WAS DRAWN TO TECLA'S DARK CHARM AND GOT COMPLETELY ENSNARED!
THAT'S TO BE EXPECTED. FIRST, THE OLD WOMAN TRIES TO TURN ERIN AGAINST US...
...THEN, SHE TURNS URIAH AND HIS GANG INTO RAGORLANGS...
AND NOW SHE HAS A NEW MINION!
YEAH...YOUNGER AND STRONGER THAN KARL.
SHE'S ONE ACTIVE OLD LADY!
SHE TRAPS US, SENDS HER RAGORLANG AFTER US...IT'S TIME WE DEALT WITH HER!

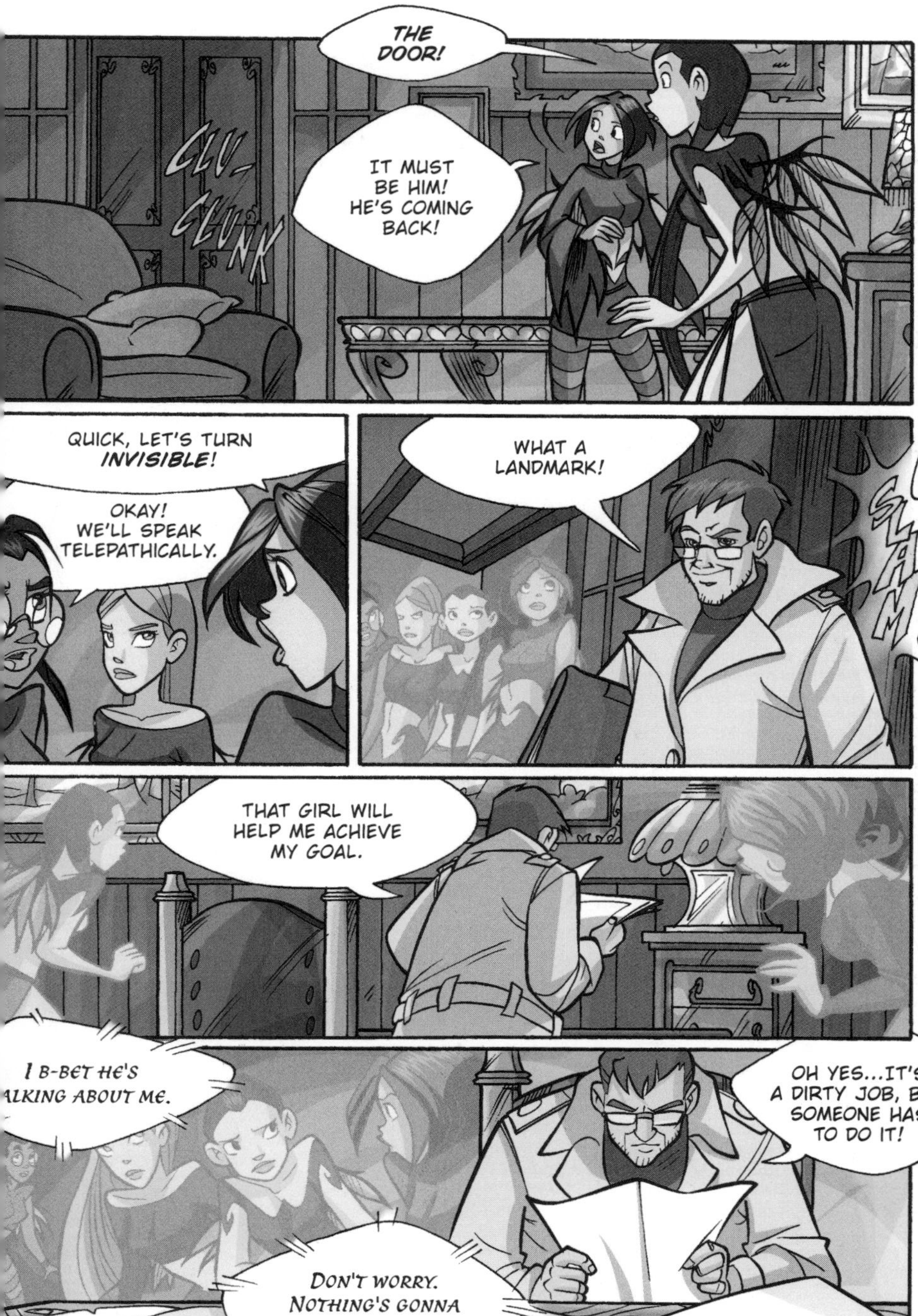

THE DOOR!
CLU-CLUNK
IT MUST BE HIM! HE'S COMING BACK!
QUICK, LET'S TURN INVISIBLE!
OKAY! WE'LL SPEAK TELEPATHICALLY.
WHAT A LANDMARK!
SLAM
THAT GIRL WILL HELP ME ACHIEVE MY GOAL.
I B-BET HE'S TALKING ABOUT ME.
OH YES...IT'S A DIRTY JOB, BUT SOMEONE HAS TO DO IT!
DON'T WORRY. NOTHING'S GONNA HAPPEN TO YOU.

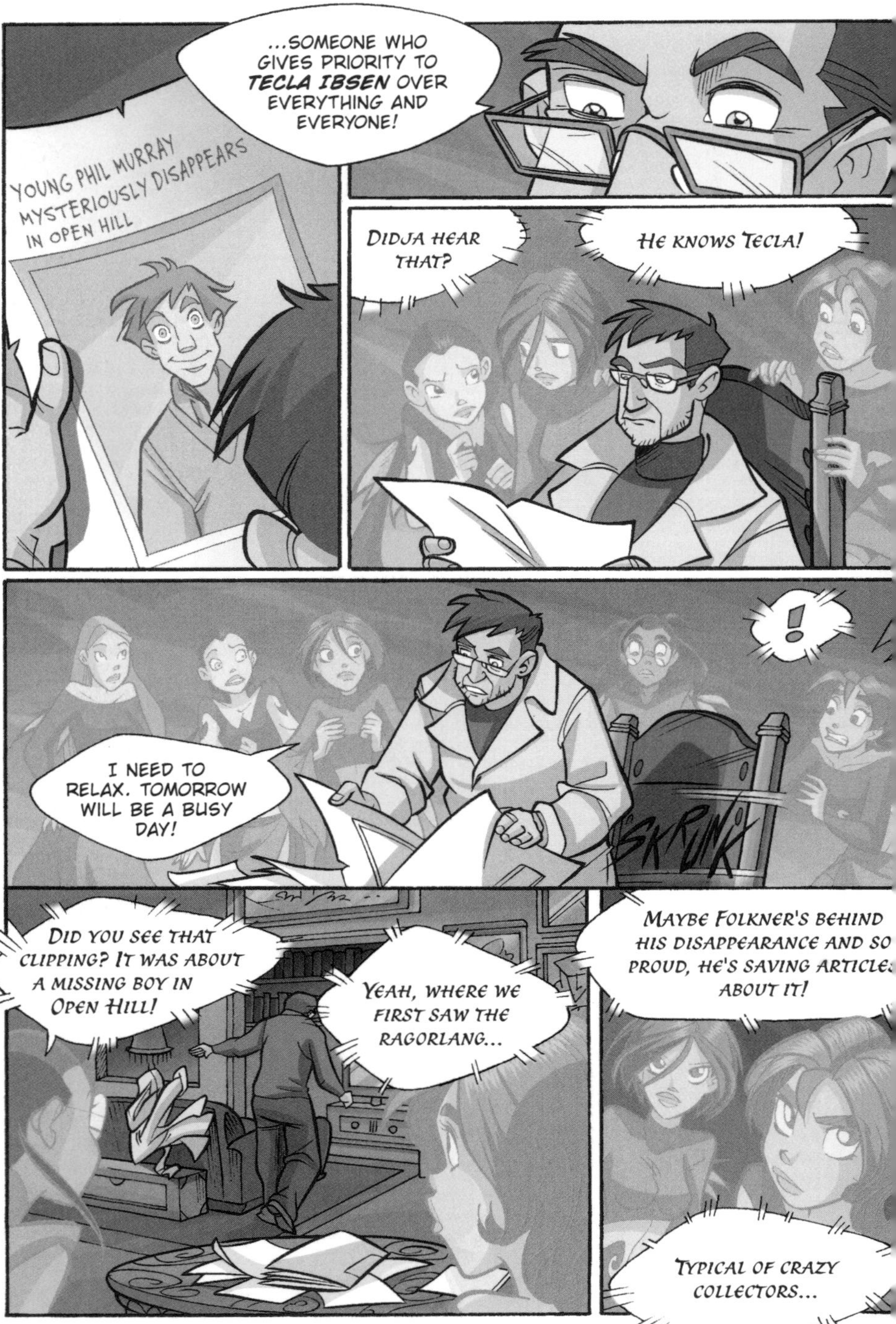

...SOMEONE WHO GIVES PRIORITY TO TECLA IBSEN OVER EVERYTHING AND EVERYONE!
YOUNG PHIL MURRAY MYSTERIOUSLY DISAPPEARS IN OPEN HILL
DIDJA HEAR THAT?
HE KNOWS TECLA!
!
I NEED TO RELAX. TOMORROW WILL BE A BUSY DAY!
SKRUNK
DID YOU SEE THAT CLIPPING? IT WAS ABOUT A MISSING BOY IN OPEN HILL!
YEAH, WHERE WE FIRST SAW THE RAGORLANG...
MAYBE FOLKNER'S BEHIND HIS DISAPPEARANCE AND SO PROUD, HE'S SAVING ARTICLES ABOUT IT!
TYPICAL OF CRAZY COLLECTORS...

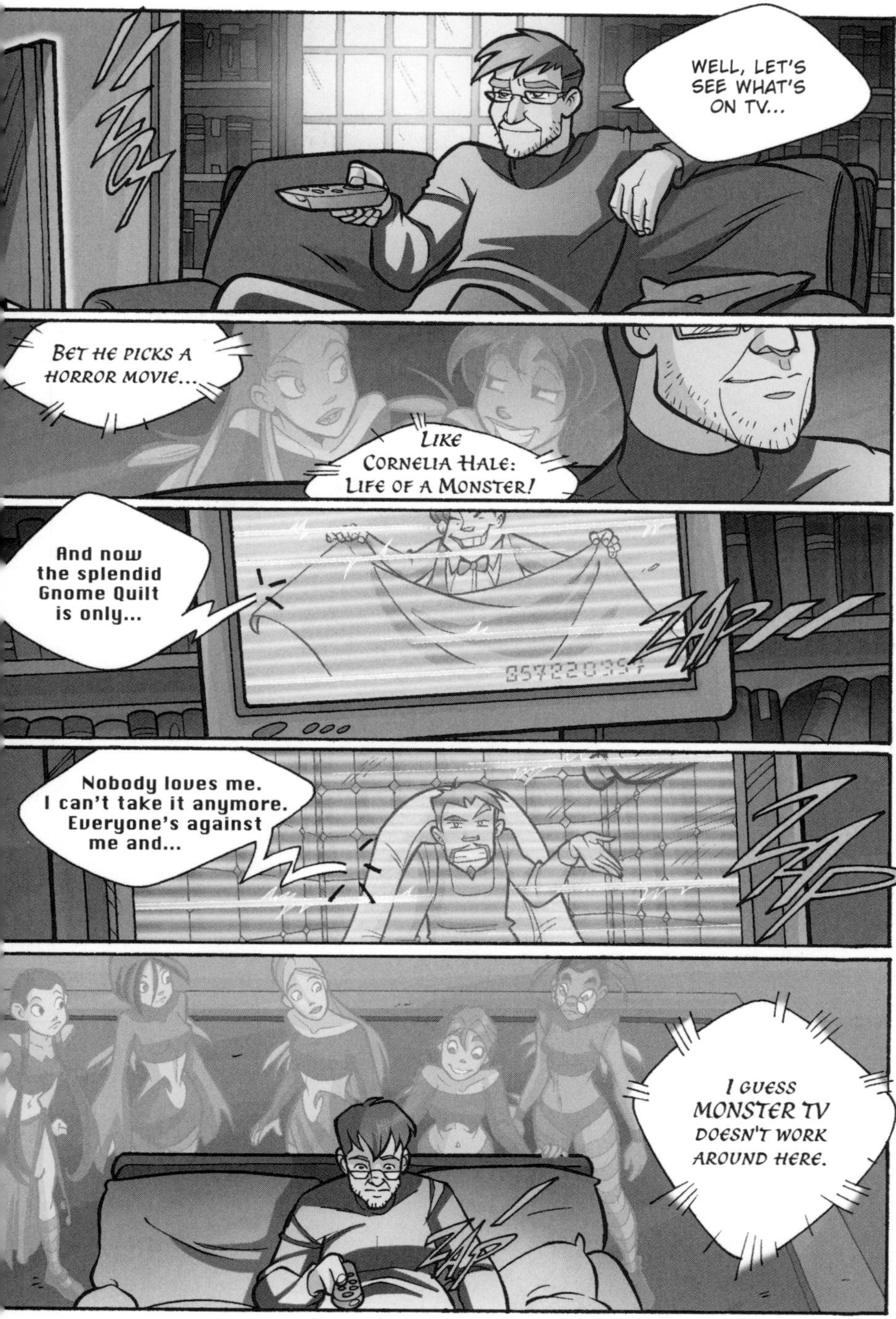
WELL, LET'S SEE WHAT'S ON TV...
BET HE PICKS A HORROR MOVIE...
LIKE CORNELIA HALE: LIFE OF A MONSTER!
And now the splendid Gnome Quilt is only...
ZAP!!
Nobody loves me. I can't take it anymore. Everyone's against me and...
I GUESS MONSTER TV DOESN'T WORK AROUND HERE.

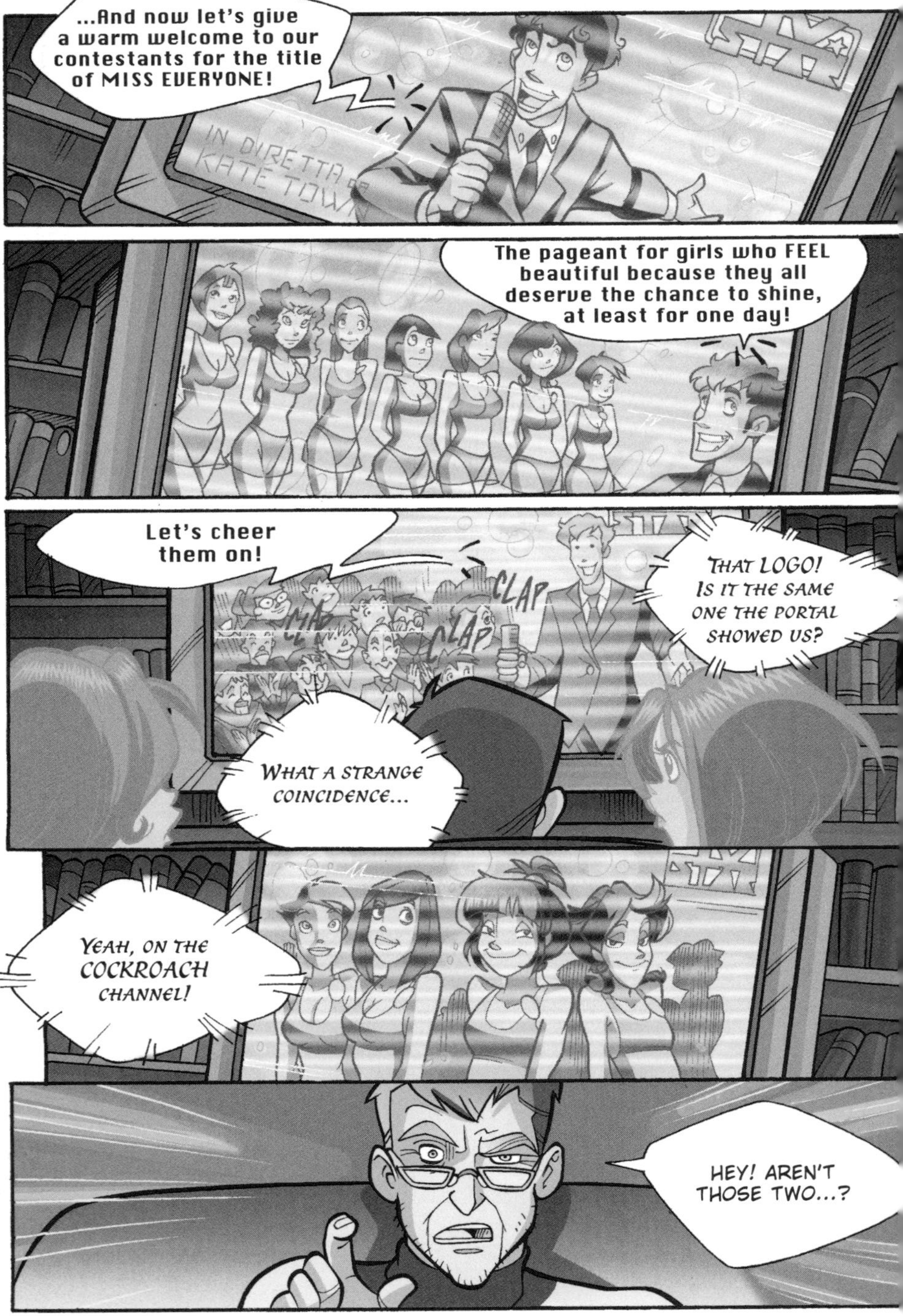
...And now let's give a warm welcome to our contestants for the title of MISS EVERYONE!
IN DIRETTA DA KATE TOWN
The pageant for girls who FEEL beautiful because they all deserve the chance to shine, at least for one day!
Let's cheer them on!
CLAP
CLAP
THAT LOGO! IS IT THE SAME ONE THE PORTAL SHOWED US?
WHAT A STRANGE COINCIDENCE...
YEAH, ON THE COCKROACH CHANNEL!
HEY! AREN'T THOSE TWO...?

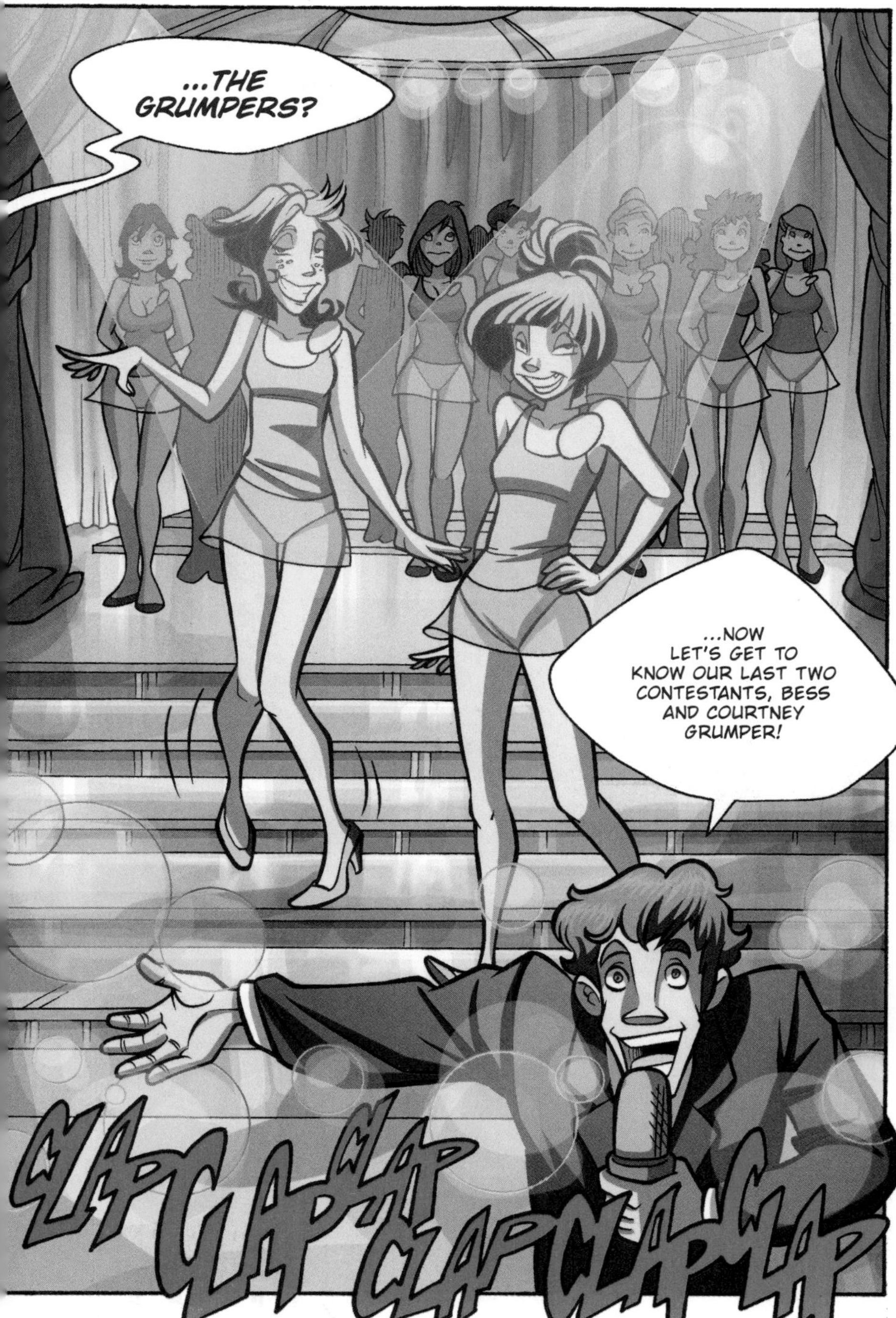
...THE GRUMPERS?
...NOW LET'S GET TO KNOW OUR LAST TWO CONTESTANTS, BESS AND COURTNEY GRUMPER!
CLAP CLAP CLAP CLAP
CLAP CLAP CLAP CLAP

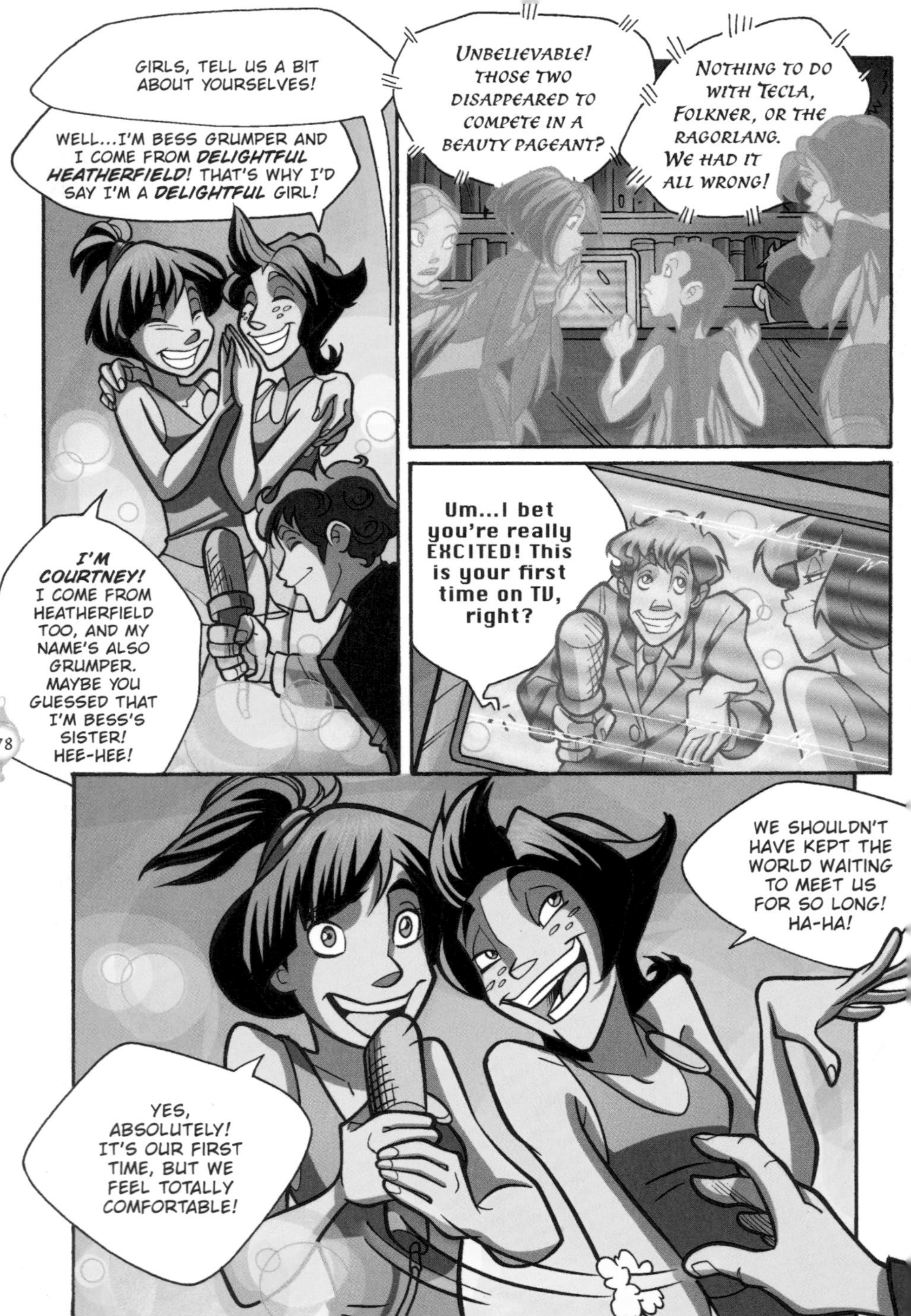
GIRLS, TELL US A BIT ABOUT YOURSELVES!
WELL...I'M BESS GRUMPER AND I COME FROM DELIGHTFUL HEATHERFIELD! THAT'S WHY I'D SAY I'M A DELIGHTFUL GIRL!
I'M COURTNEY! I COME FROM HEATHERFIELD TOO, AND MY NAME'S ALSO GRUMPER. MAYBE YOU GUESSED THAT I'M BESS'S SISTER! HEE-HEE!
UNBELIEVABLE! THOSE TWO DISAPPEARED TO COMPETE IN A BEAUTY PAGEANT?
NOTHING TO DO WITH TECLA, FOLKNER, OR THE RAGORLANG. WE HAD IT ALL WRONG!
Um...I bet you're really EXCITED! This is your first time on TV, right?
YES, ABSOLUTELY! IT'S OUR FIRST TIME, BUT WE FEEL TOTALLY COMFORTABLE!
WE SHOULDN'T HAVE KEPT THE WORLD WAITING TO MEET US FOR SO LONG! HA-HA!

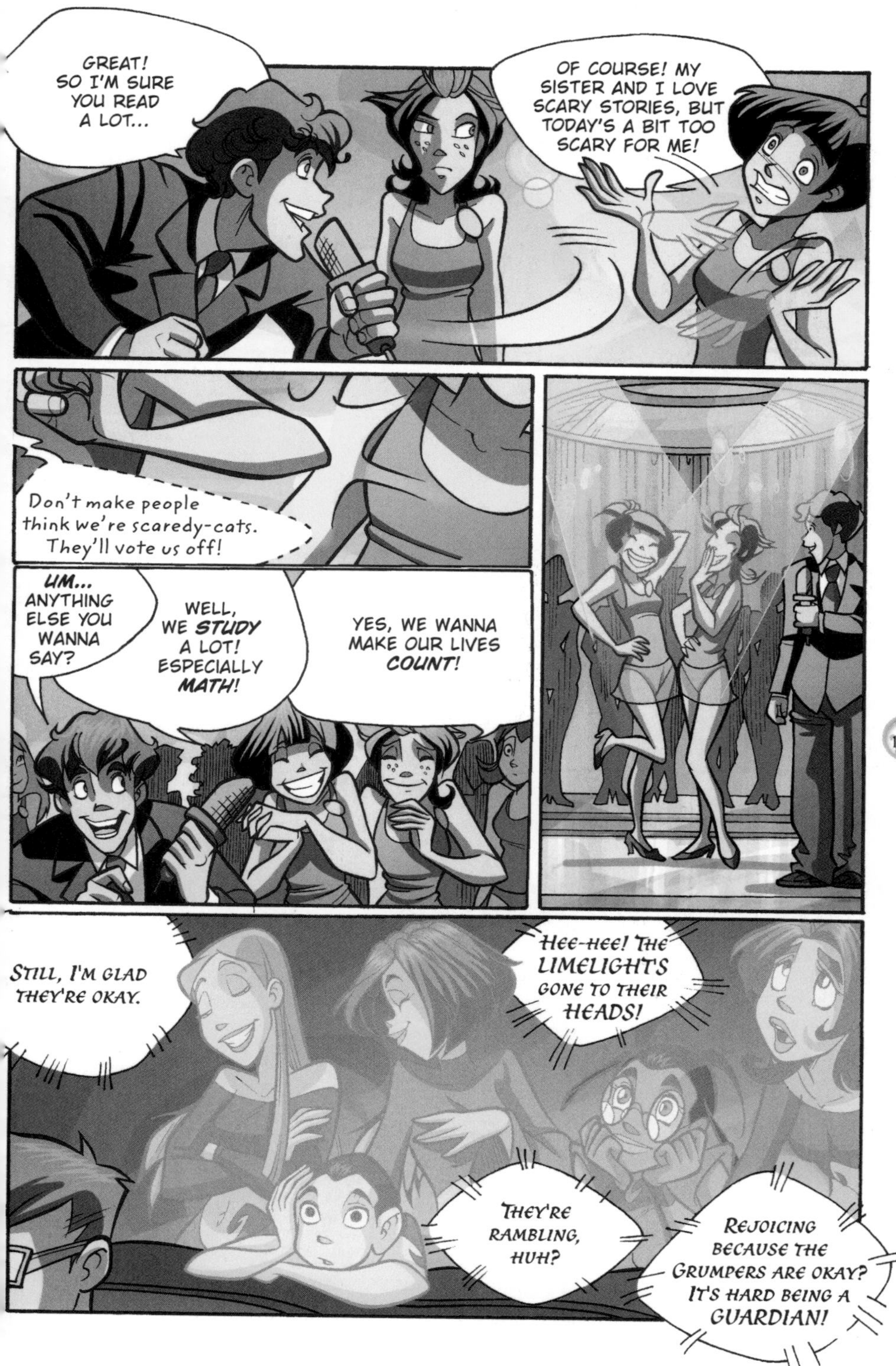
GREAT! SO I'M SURE YOU READ A LOT...
OF COURSE! MY SISTER AND I LOVE SCARY STORIES, BUT TODAY'S A BIT TOO SCARY FOR ME!
Don't make people think we're scaredy-cats. They'll vote us off!
UM... ANYTHING ELSE YOU WANNA SAY?
WELL, WE STUDY A LOT! ESPECIALLY MATH!
YES, WE WANNA MAKE OUR LIVES COUNT!
STILL, I'M GLAD THEY'RE OKAY.
HEE-HEE! THE LIMELIGHT'S GONE TO THEIR HEADS!
THEY'RE RAMBLING, HUH?
REJOICING BECAUSE THE GRUMPERS ARE OKAY? IT'S HARD BEING A GUARDIAN!

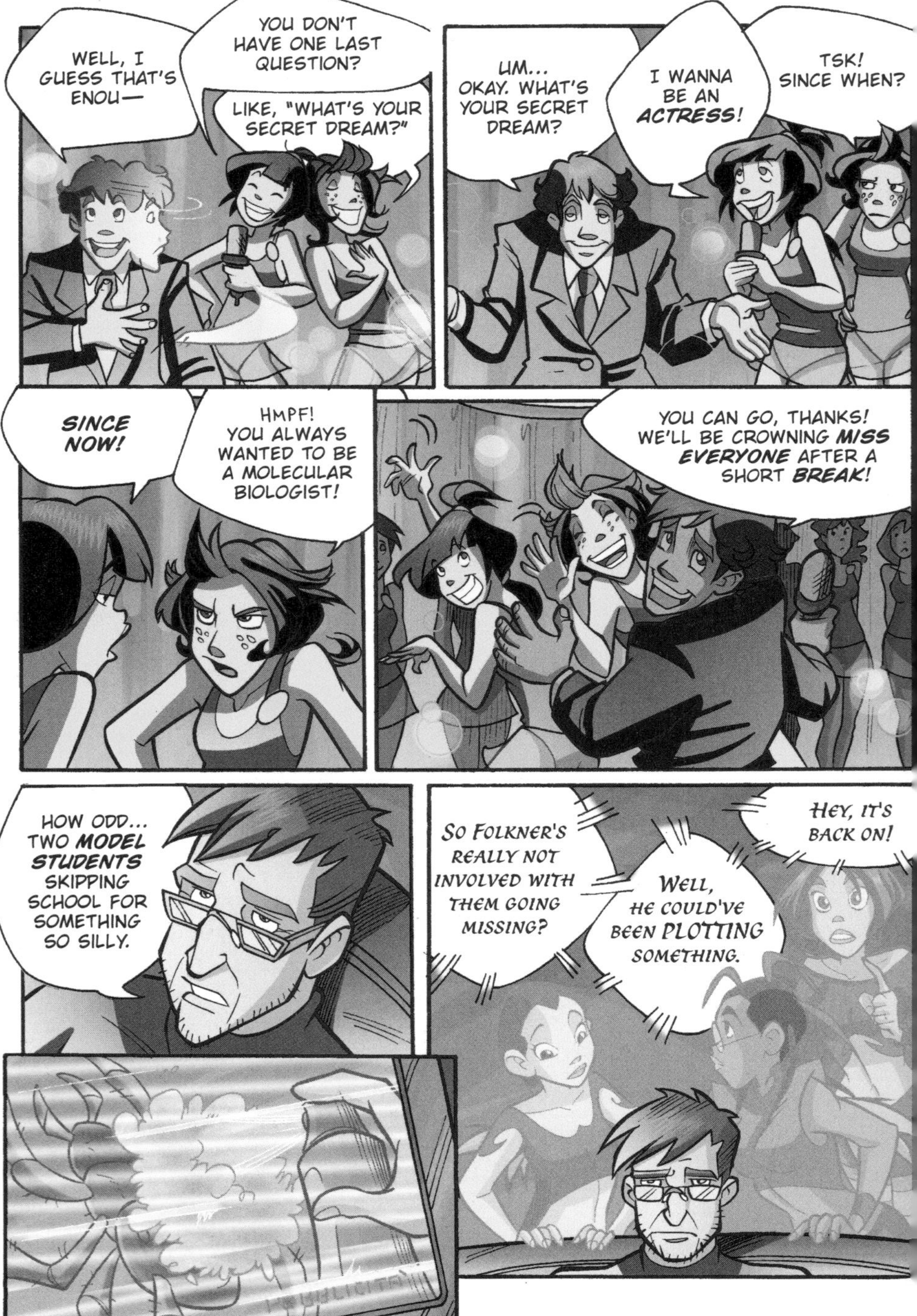
WELL, I GUESS THAT'S ENOU—
YOU DON'T HAVE ONE LAST QUESTION?
LIKE, "WHAT'S YOUR SECRET DREAM?"
UM... OKAY. WHAT'S YOUR SECRET DREAM?
I WANNA BE AN ACTRESS!
TSK! SINCE WHEN?
SINCE NOW!
HMPF! YOU ALWAYS WANTED TO BE A MOLECULAR BIOLOGIST!
YOU CAN GO, THANKS! WE'LL BE CROWNING MISS EVERYONE AFTER A SHORT BREAK!
HOW ODD... TWO MODEL STUDENTS SKIPPING SCHOOL FOR SOMETHING SO SILLY.
SO FOLKNER'S REALLY NOT INVOLVED WITH THEM GOING MISSING?
WELL, HE COULD'VE BEEN PLOTTING SOMETHING.
HEY, IT'S BACK ON!

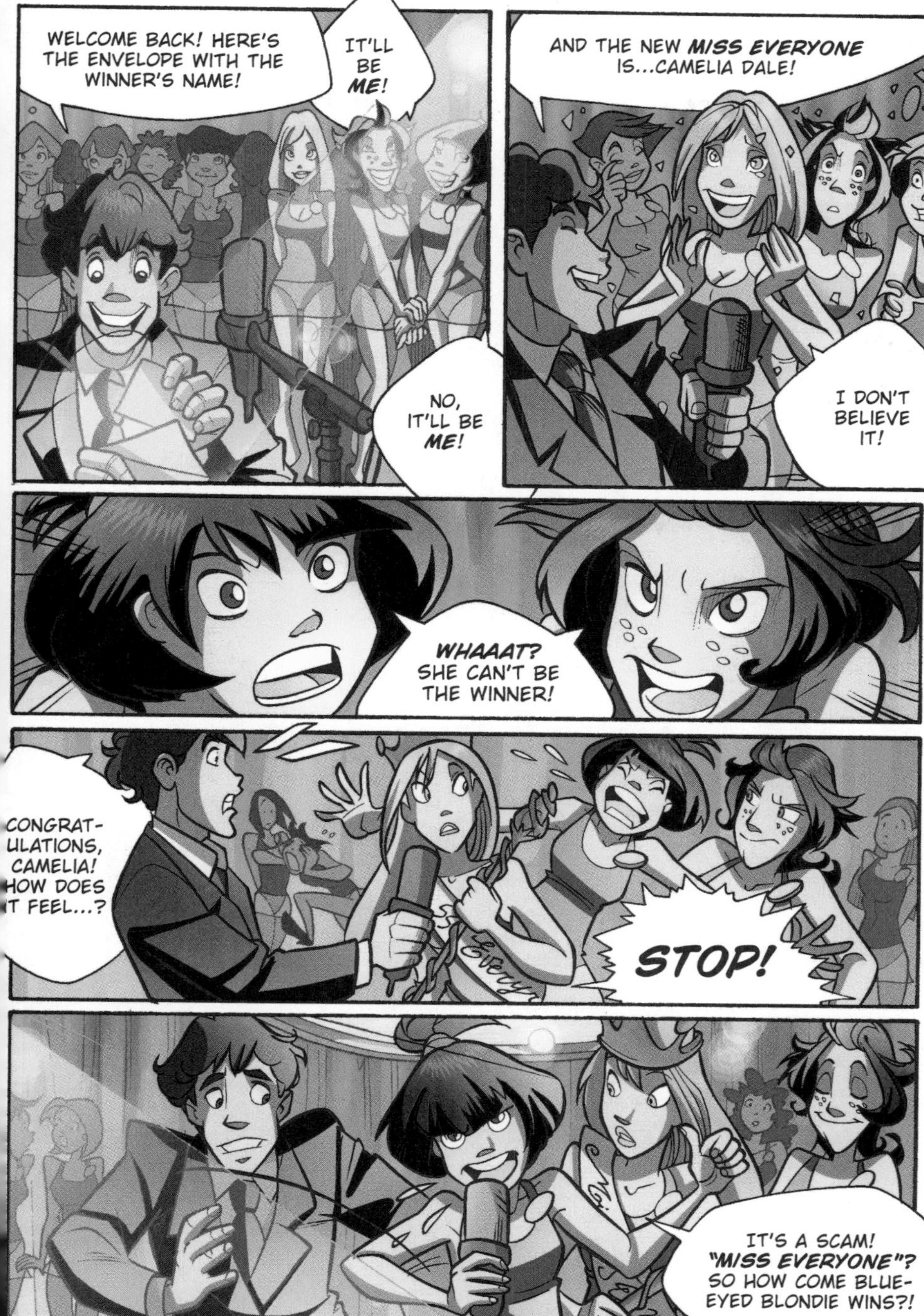
WELCOME BACK! HERE'S THE ENVELOPE WITH THE WINNER'S NAME!
IT'LL BE *ME*!
NO, IT'LL BE *ME*!
AND THE NEW *MISS EVERYONE* IS...CAMELIA DALE!
I DON'T BELIEVE IT!
WHAAAT? SHE CAN'T BE THE WINNER!
CONGRAT-ULATIONS, CAMELIA! HOW DOES IT FEEL...?
STOP!
IT'S A SCAM! *"MISS EVERYONE"*? SO HOW COME BLUE-EYED BLONDIE WINS?!

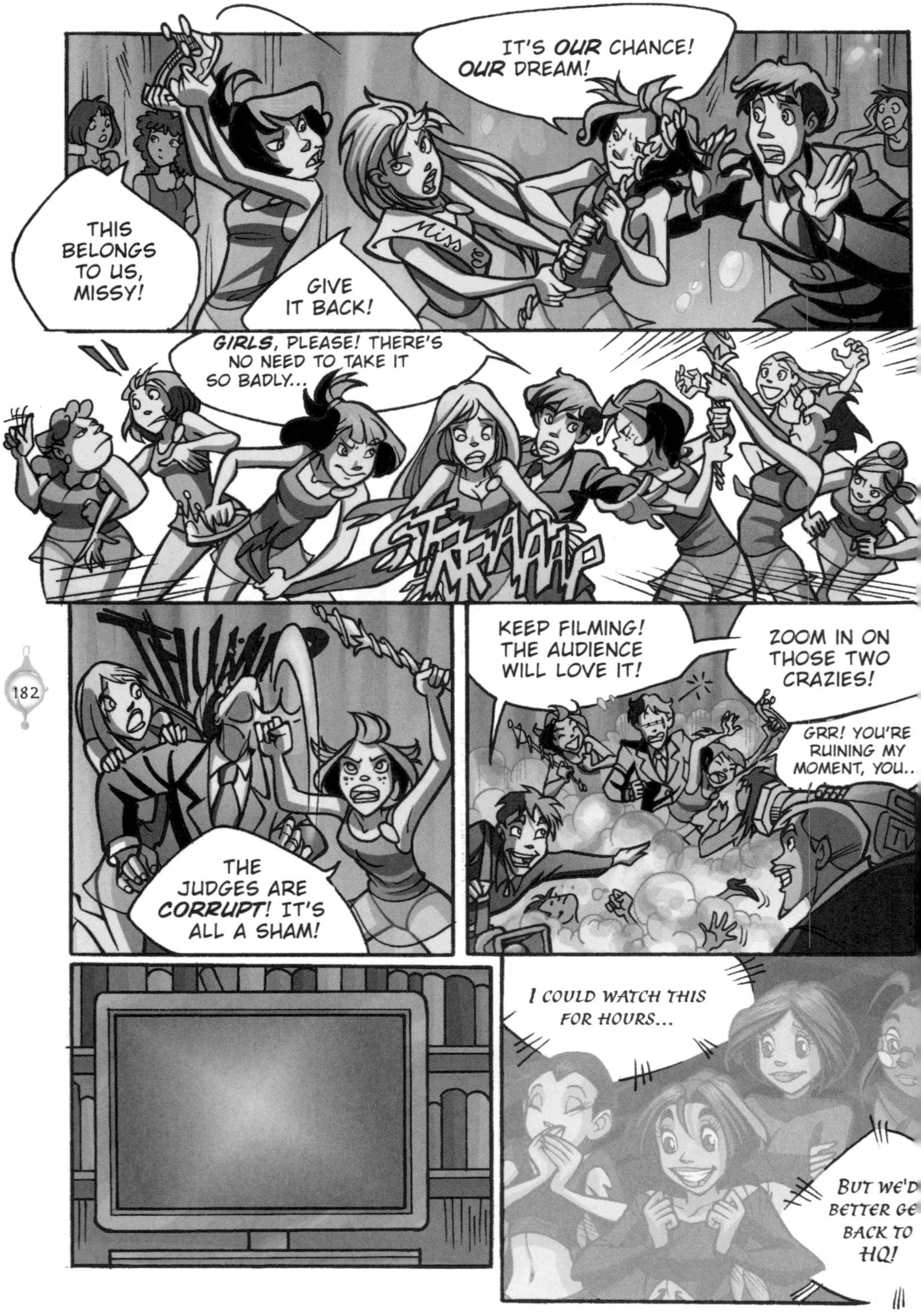
IT'S OUR CHANCE! OUR DREAM!
THIS BELONGS TO US, MISSY!
GIVE IT BACK!
GIRLS, PLEASE! THERE'S NO NEED TO TAKE IT SO BADLY...
STRAAAP
THUMP
THE JUDGES ARE CORRUPT! IT'S ALL A SHAM!
KEEP FILMING! THE AUDIENCE WILL LOVE IT!
ZOOM IN ON THOSE TWO CRAZIES!
GRR! YOU'RE RUINING MY MOMENT, YOU...
I COULD WATCH THIS FOR HOURS...
BUT WE'D BETTER GE BACK TO HQ!

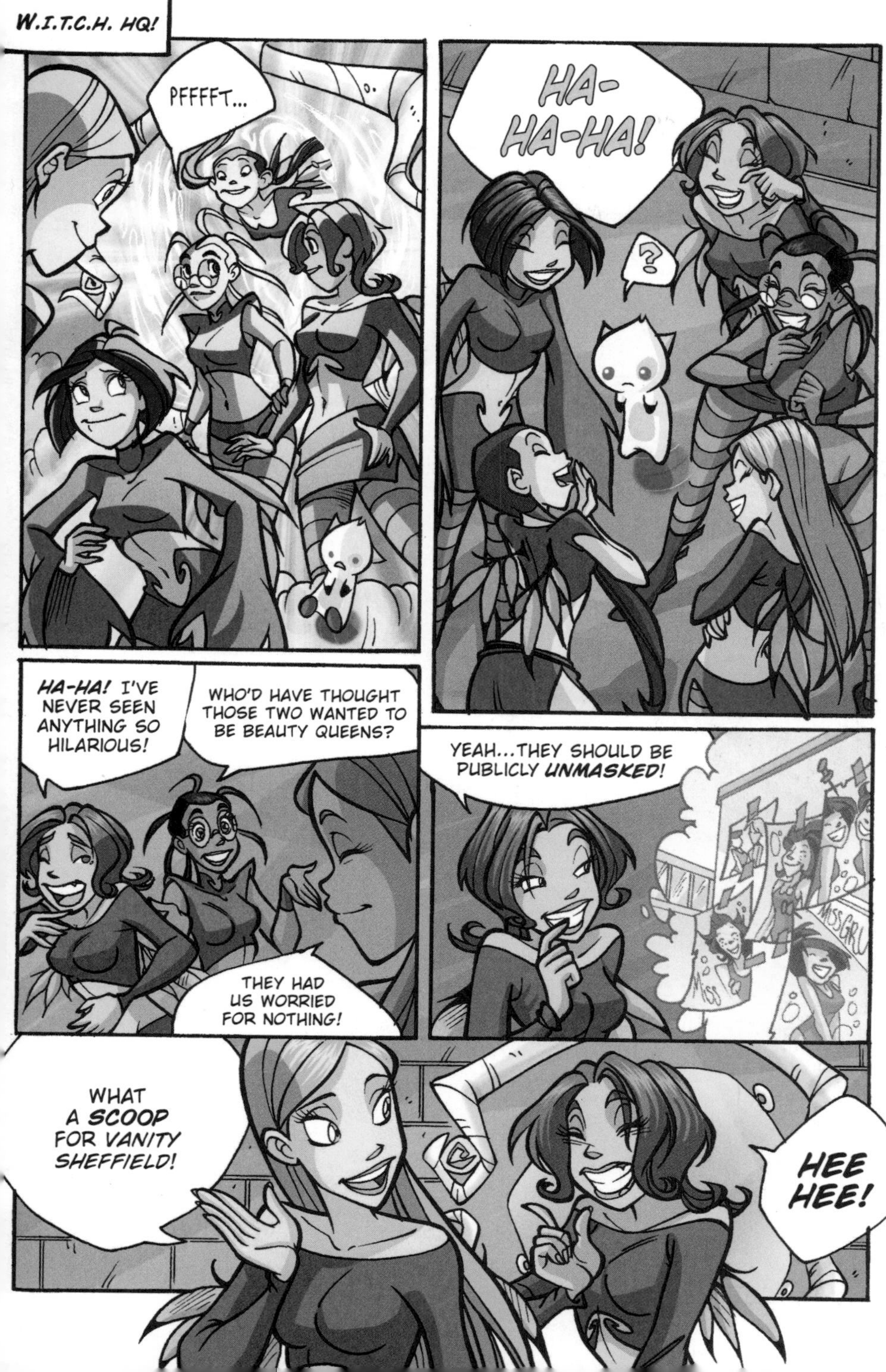

W.I.T.C.H. HQ!
PFFFFT...
HA-HA-HA!
?
HA-HA! I'VE NEVER SEEN ANYTHING SO HILARIOUS!
WHO'D HAVE THOUGHT THOSE TWO WANTED TO BE BEAUTY QUEENS?
THEY HAD US WORRIED FOR NOTHING!
YEAH...THEY SHOULD BE PUBLICLY UNMASKED!
WHAT A SCOOP FOR VANITY SHEFFIELD!
HEE HEE!

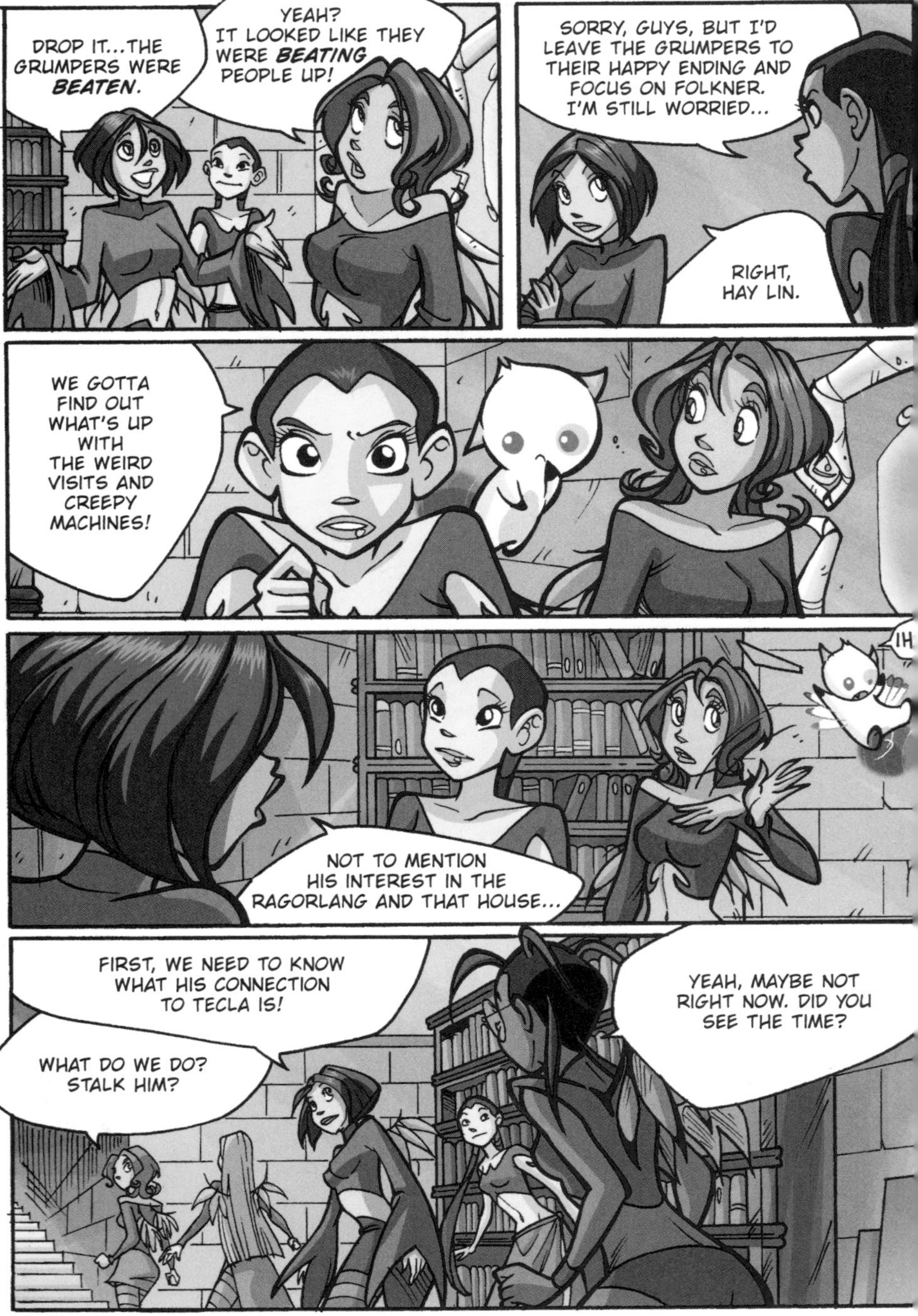
DROP IT...THE GRUMPERS WERE **BEATEN**.
YEAH? IT LOOKED LIKE THEY WERE **BEATING** PEOPLE UP!
SORRY, GUYS, BUT I'D LEAVE THE GRUMPERS TO THEIR HAPPY ENDING AND FOCUS ON FOLKNER. I'M STILL WORRIED...
RIGHT, HAY LIN.
WE GOTTA FIND OUT WHAT'S UP WITH THE WEIRD VISITS AND CREEPY MACHINES!
IH
NOT TO MENTION HIS INTEREST IN THE RAGORLANG AND THAT HOUSE...
FIRST, WE NEED TO KNOW WHAT HIS CONNECTION TO TECLA IS!
WHAT DO WE DO? STALK HIM?
YEAH, MAYBE NOT RIGHT NOW. DID YOU SEE THE TIME?

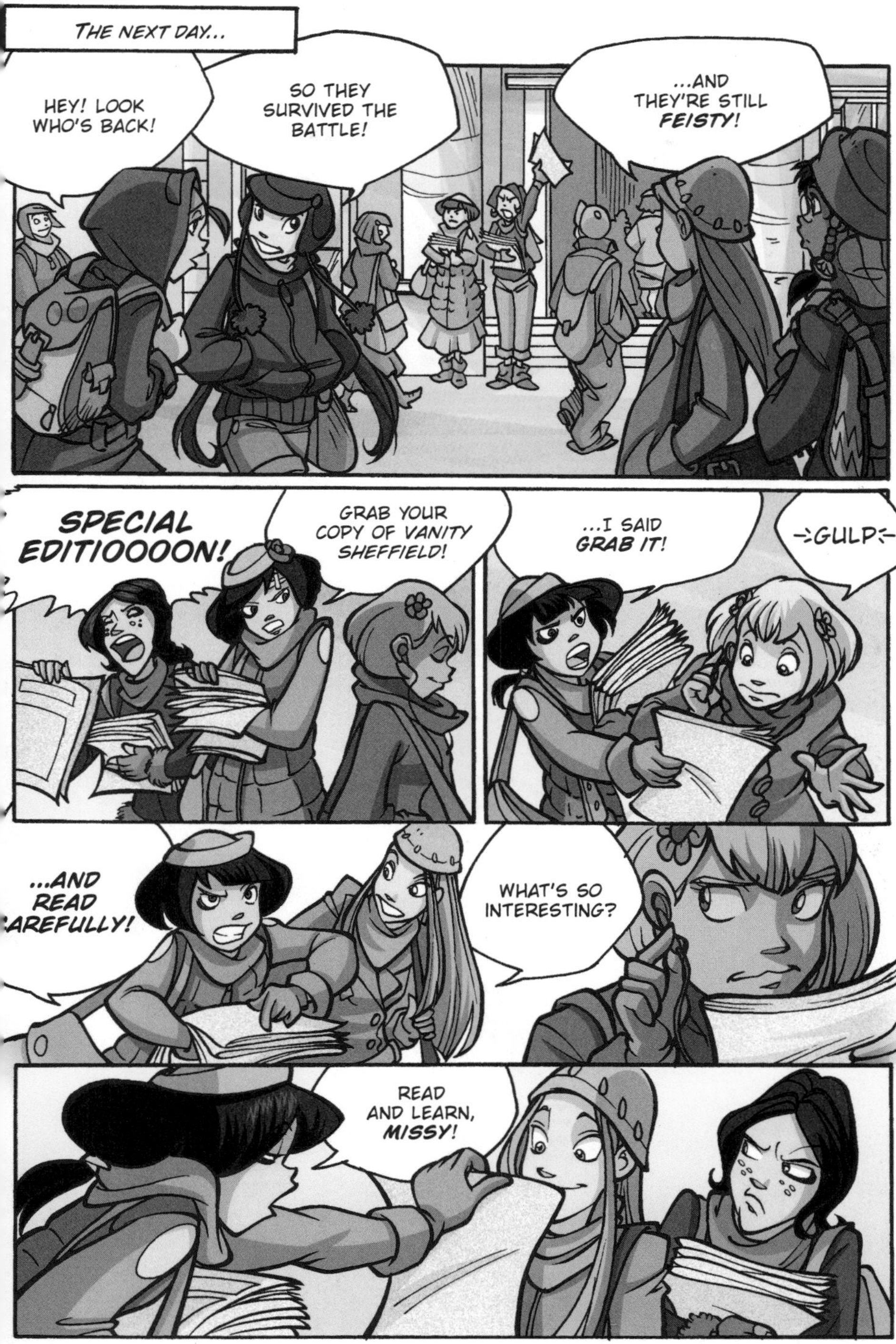
THE NEXT DAY...
HEY! LOOK WHO'S BACK!
SO THEY SURVIVED THE BATTLE!
...AND THEY'RE STILL FEISTY!
SPECIAL EDITIOOOON!
GRAB YOUR COPY OF VANITY SHEFFIELD!
...I SAID GRAB IT!
GULP
...AND READ CAREFULLY!
WHAT'S SO INTERESTING?
READ AND LEARN, MISSY!

Shattered Dreams: The Truth Behind Beauty Pageants (p. 5)

BEWARE SHOW BUSINESS!

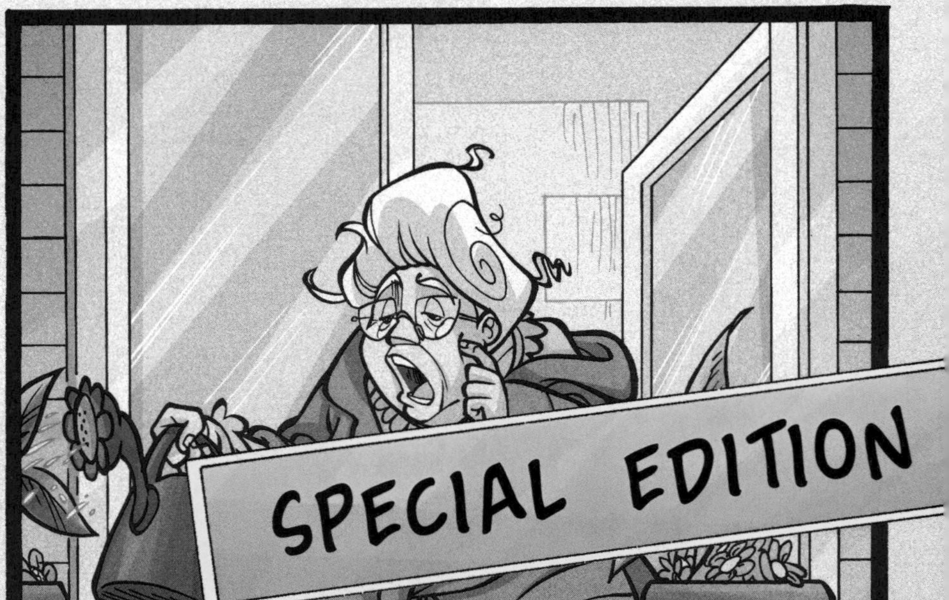

SPECIAL EDITION

MS. KNICKERBOCHER: AN EXAMPLE OF NATURAL BEAUTY

Real beauty is on the inside:

The Sheffield Institute principal once again sets an example with her disregard for any superficial embellishment.

We admire her! (p.14)

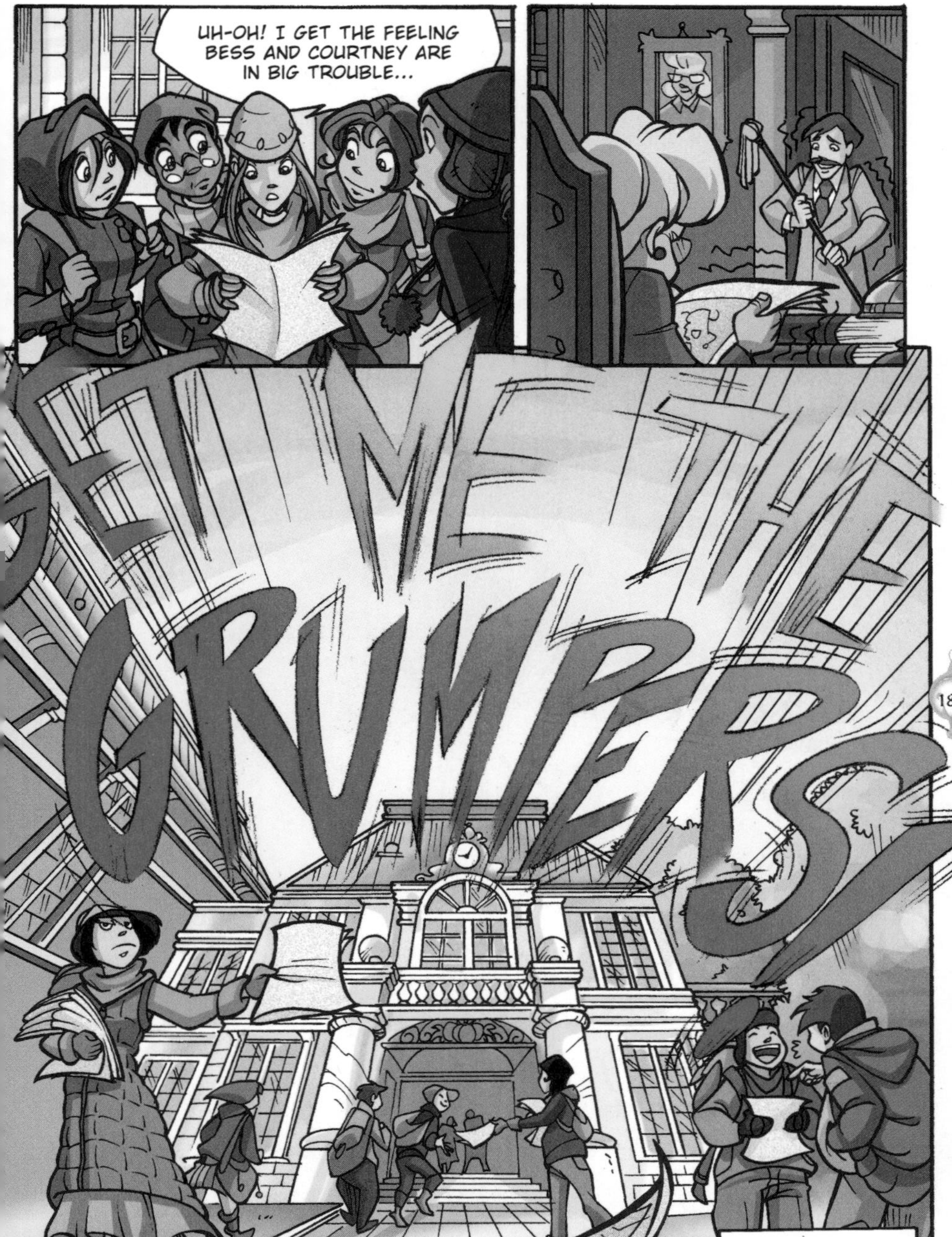

UH-OH! I GET THE FEELING BESS AND COURTNEY ARE IN BIG TROUBLE...
GET ME THE GRUMPERS!
END OF CHAPTER 70

W.i.t.c.h.

Will Irma Taranee Cornelia Hay Lin

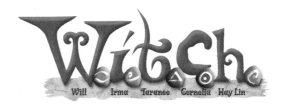

71

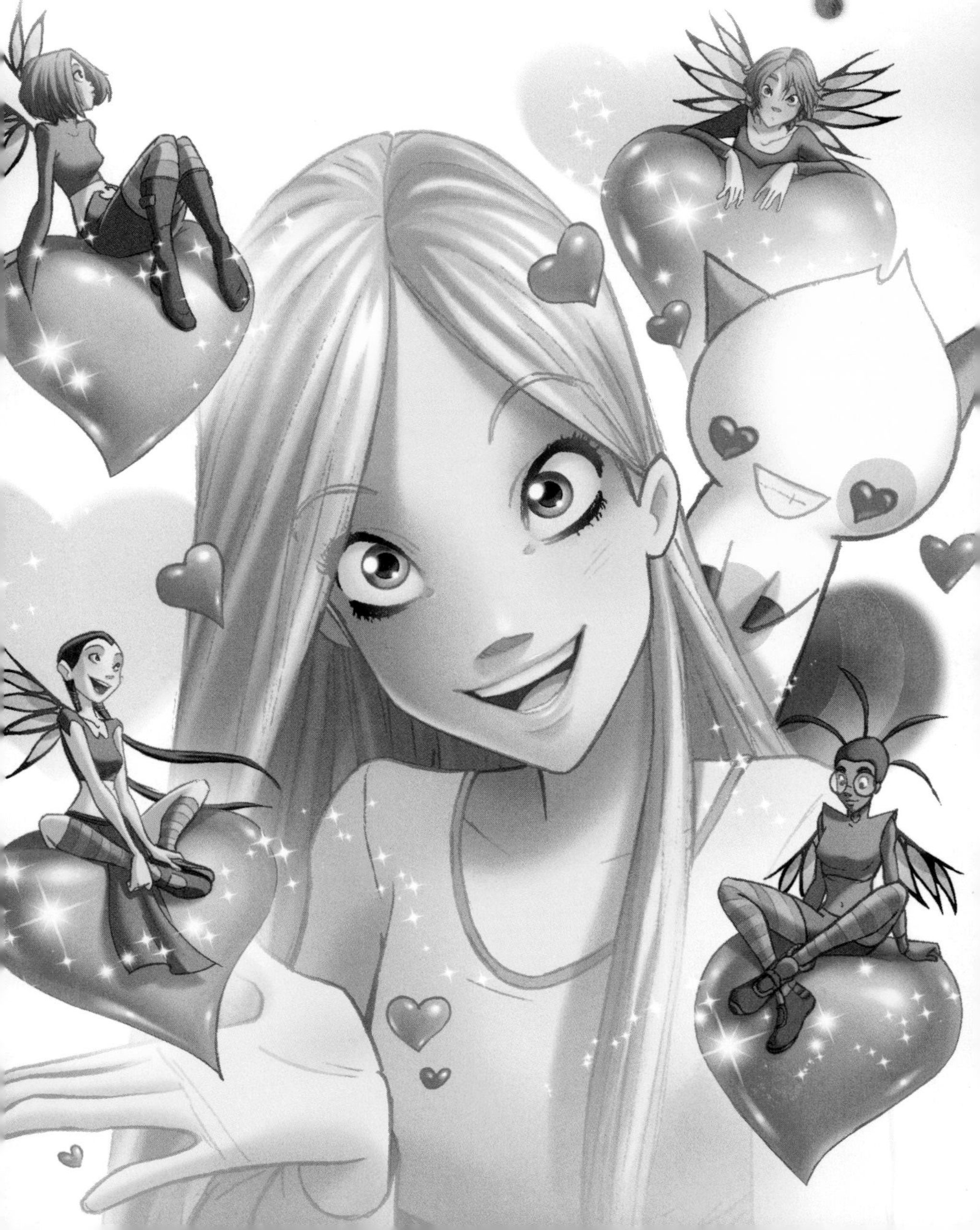

The Mark of Fear

"How can I forget about her if, every time I look in the mirror, I see the mark she left on me?"

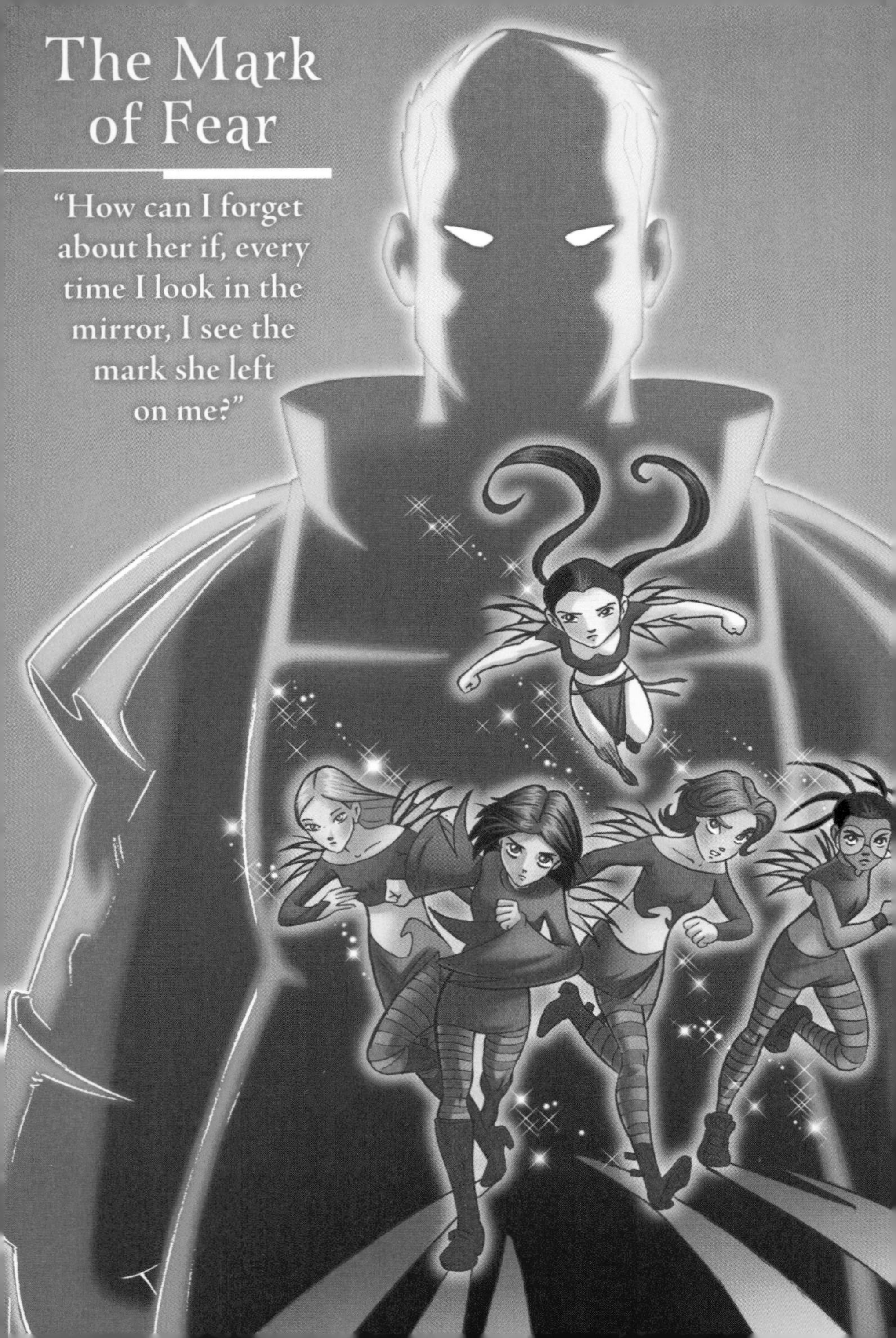

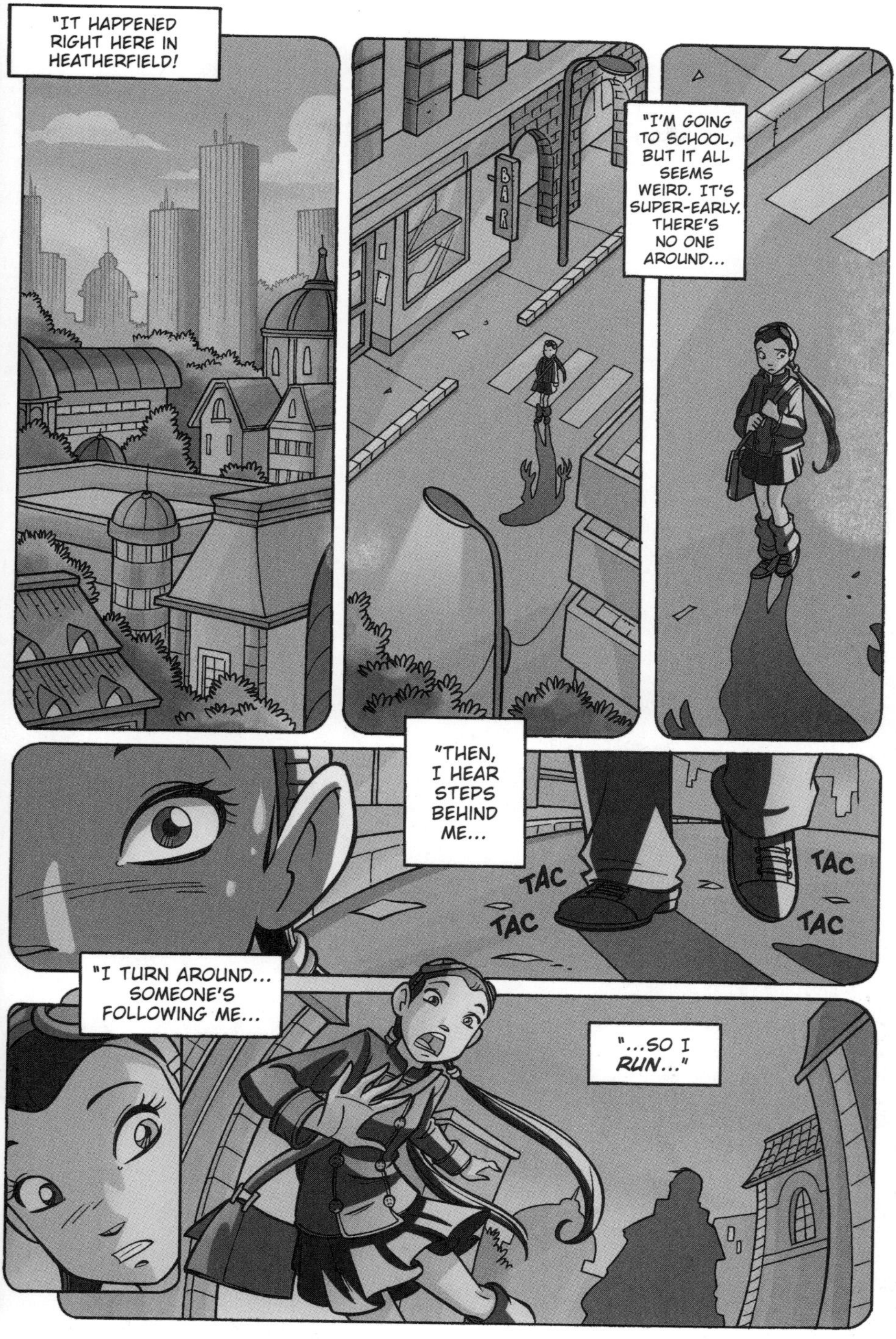
"IT HAPPENED RIGHT HERE IN HEATHERFIELD!
BAR
"I'M GOING TO SCHOOL, BUT IT ALL SEEMS WEIRD. IT'S SUPER-EARLY. THERE'S NO ONE AROUND...
"THEN, I HEAR STEPS BEHIND ME...
TAC
TAC
TAC
TAC
"I TURN AROUND... SOMEONE'S FOLLOWING ME...
"...SO I *RUN*..."

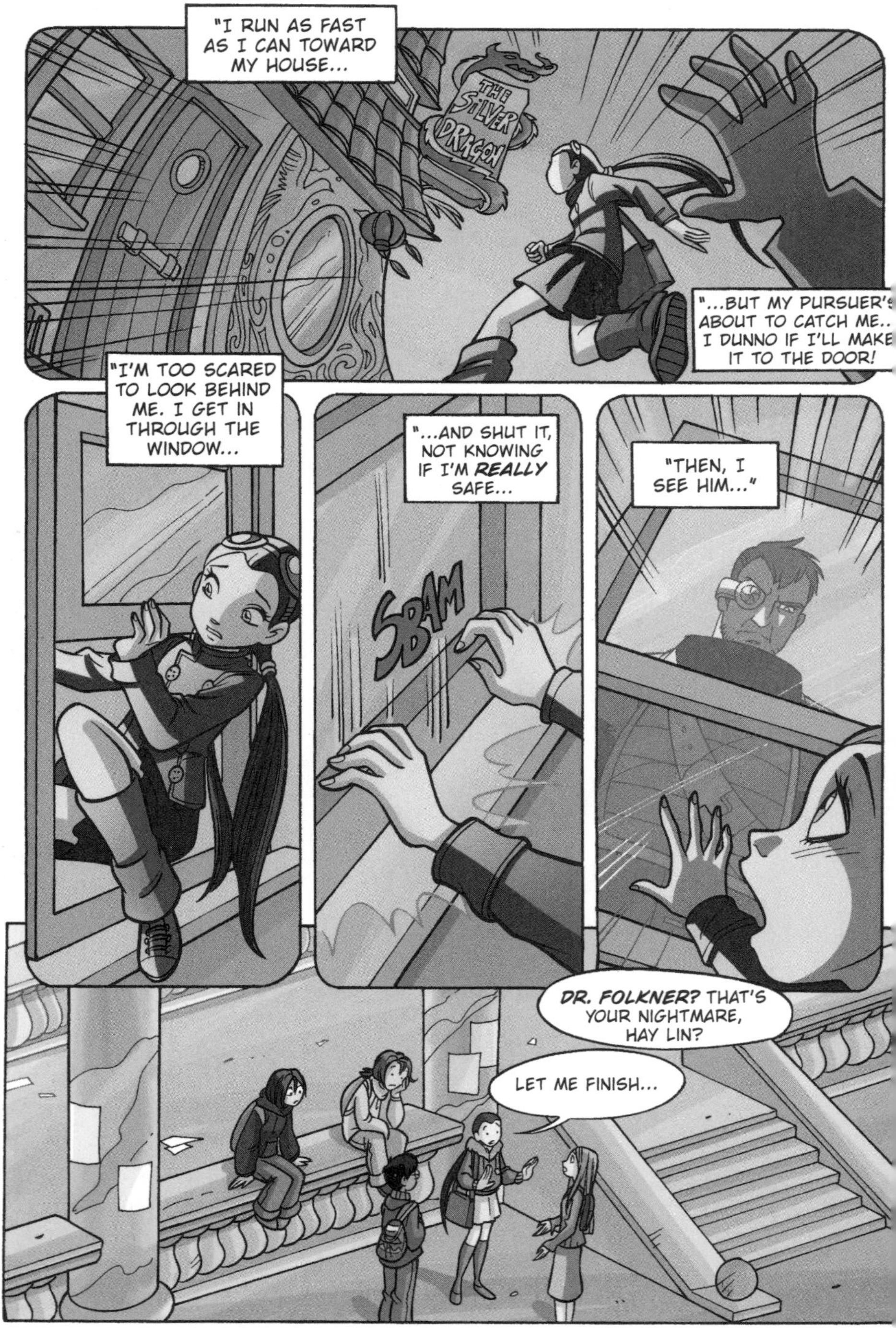
"I RUN AS FAST AS I CAN TOWARD MY HOUSE...
THE SILVER DRAGON
"...BUT MY PURSUER'S ABOUT TO CATCH ME... I DUNNO IF I'LL MAKE IT TO THE DOOR!
"I'M TOO SCARED TO LOOK BEHIND ME. I GET IN THROUGH THE WINDOW...
"...AND SHUT IT, NOT KNOWING IF I'M **REALLY** SAFE...
SBAM
"THEN, I SEE HIM..."
DR. FOLKNER? THAT'S YOUR NIGHTMARE, HAY LIN?
LET ME FINISH...

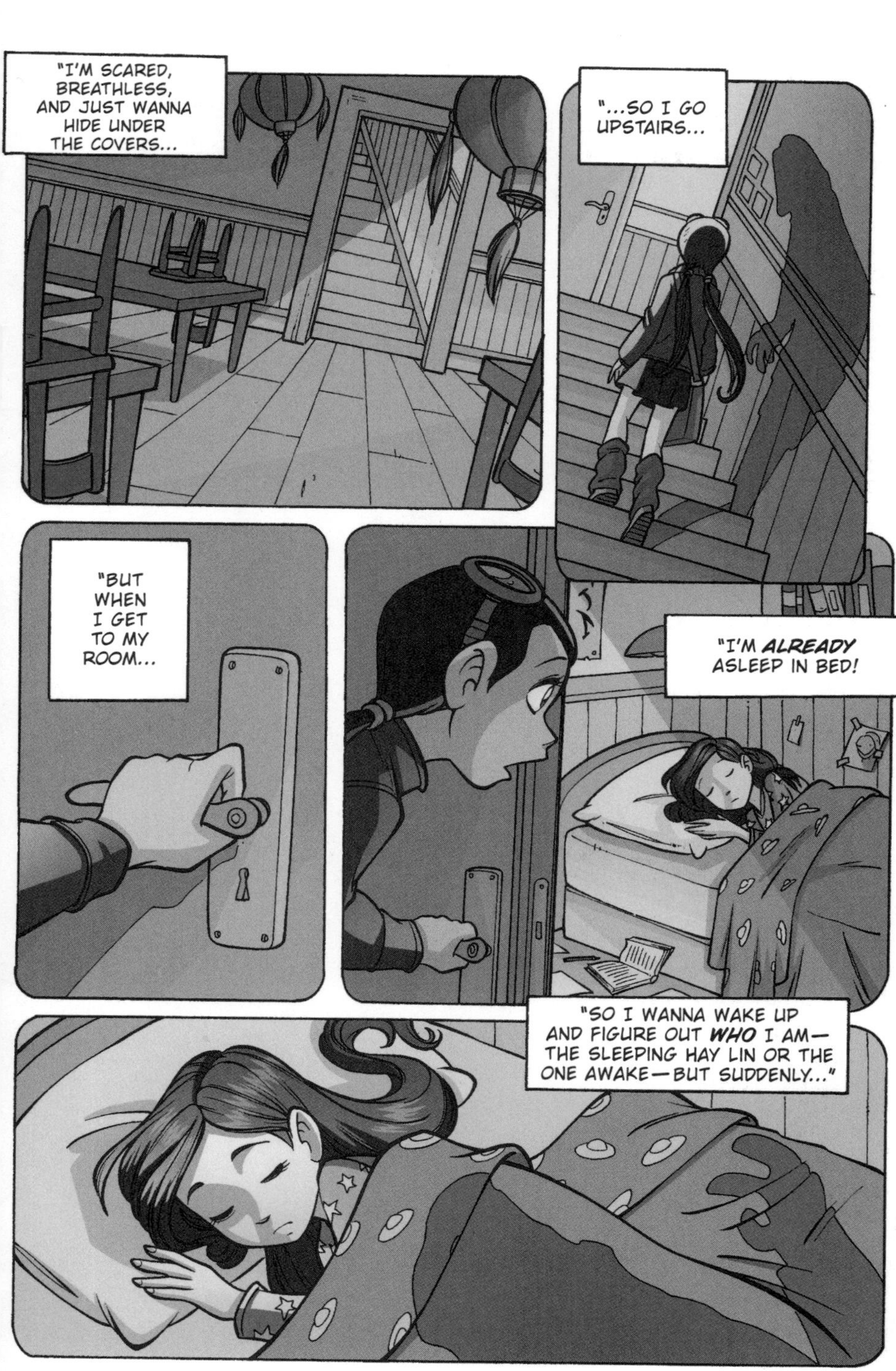
"I'M SCARED, BREATHLESS, AND JUST WANNA HIDE UNDER THE COVERS...
"...SO I GO UPSTAIRS...
"BUT WHEN I GET TO MY ROOM...
"I'M *ALREADY* ASLEEP IN BED!
"SO I WANNA WAKE UP AND FIGURE OUT *WHO* I AM— THE SLEEPING HAY LIN OR THE ONE AWAKE—BUT SUDDENLY..."

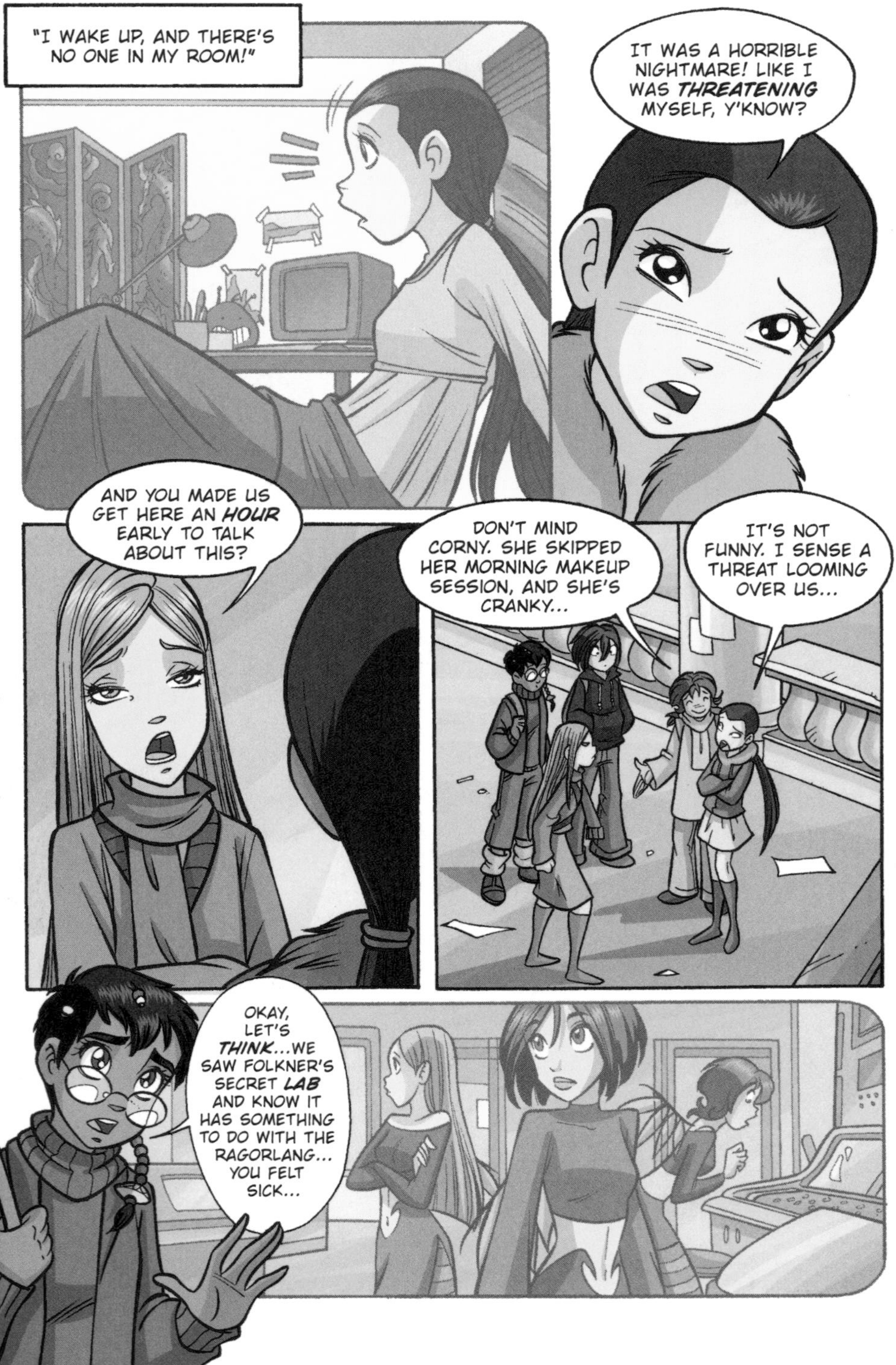
"I WAKE UP, AND THERE'S NO ONE IN MY ROOM!"
IT WAS A HORRIBLE NIGHTMARE! LIKE I WAS *THREATENING* MYSELF, Y'KNOW?
AND YOU MADE US GET HERE AN *HOUR* EARLY TO TALK ABOUT THIS?
DON'T MIND CORNY. SHE SKIPPED HER MORNING MAKEUP SESSION, AND SHE'S CRANKY...
IT'S NOT FUNNY. I SENSE A THREAT LOOMING OVER US...
OKAY, LET'S *THINK*...WE SAW FOLKNER'S SECRET *LAB* AND KNOW IT HAS SOMETHING TO DO WITH THE RAGORLANG... YOU FELT SICK...

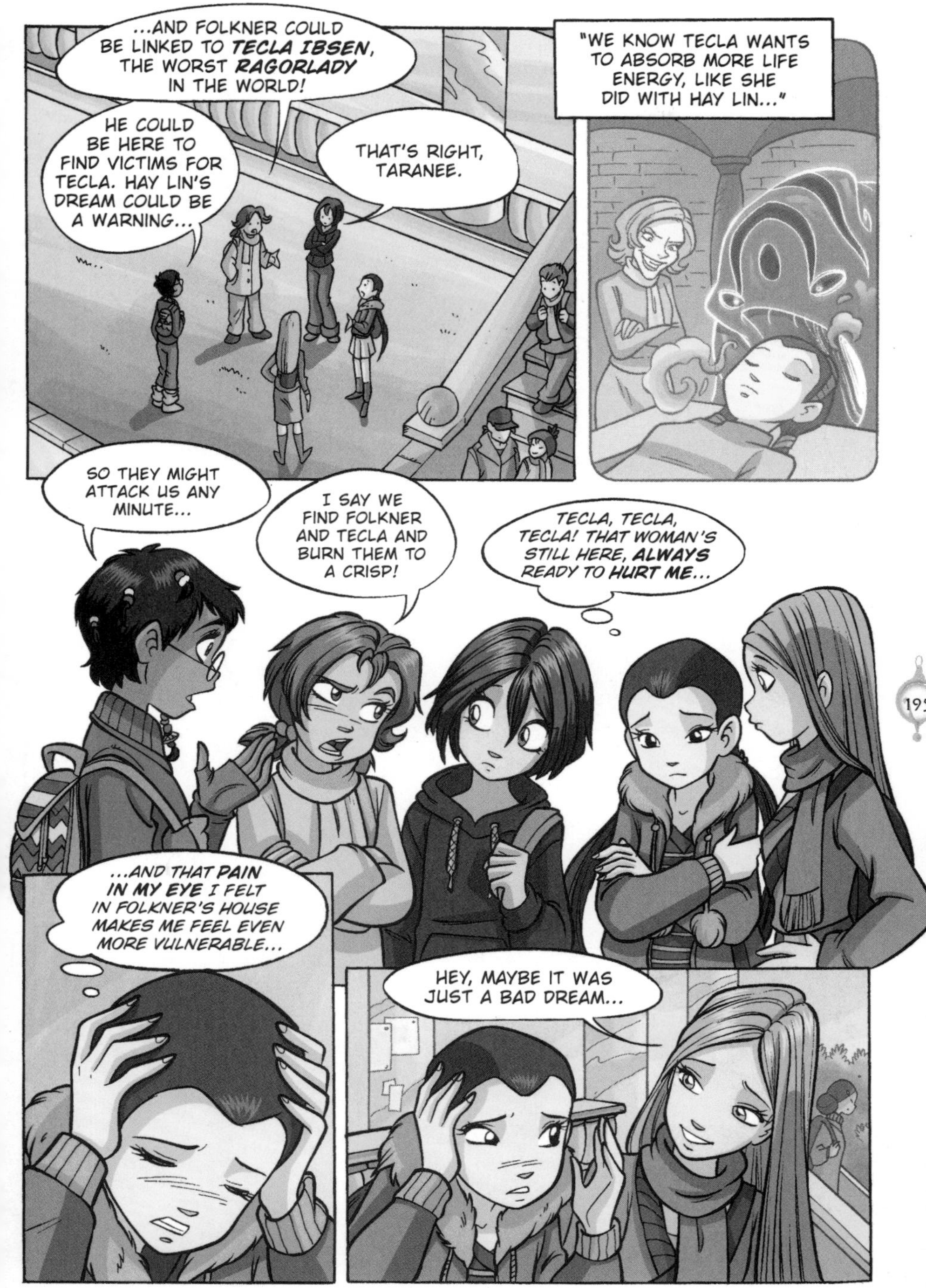
...AND FOLKNER COULD BE LINKED TO TECLA IBSEN, THE WORST RAGORLADY IN THE WORLD!
HE COULD BE HERE TO FIND VICTIMS FOR TECLA. HAY LIN'S DREAM COULD BE A WARNING...
THAT'S RIGHT, TARANEE.
"WE KNOW TECLA WANTS TO ABSORB MORE LIFE ENERGY, LIKE SHE DID WITH HAY LIN..."
SO THEY MIGHT ATTACK US ANY MINUTE...
I SAY WE FIND FOLKNER AND TECLA AND BURN THEM TO A CRISP!
TECLA, TECLA, TECLA! THAT WOMAN'S STILL HERE, ALWAYS READY TO HURT ME...
...AND THAT PAIN IN MY EYE I FELT IN FOLKNER'S HOUSE MAKES ME FEEL EVEN MORE VULNERABLE...
HEY, MAYBE IT WAS JUST A BAD DREAM...

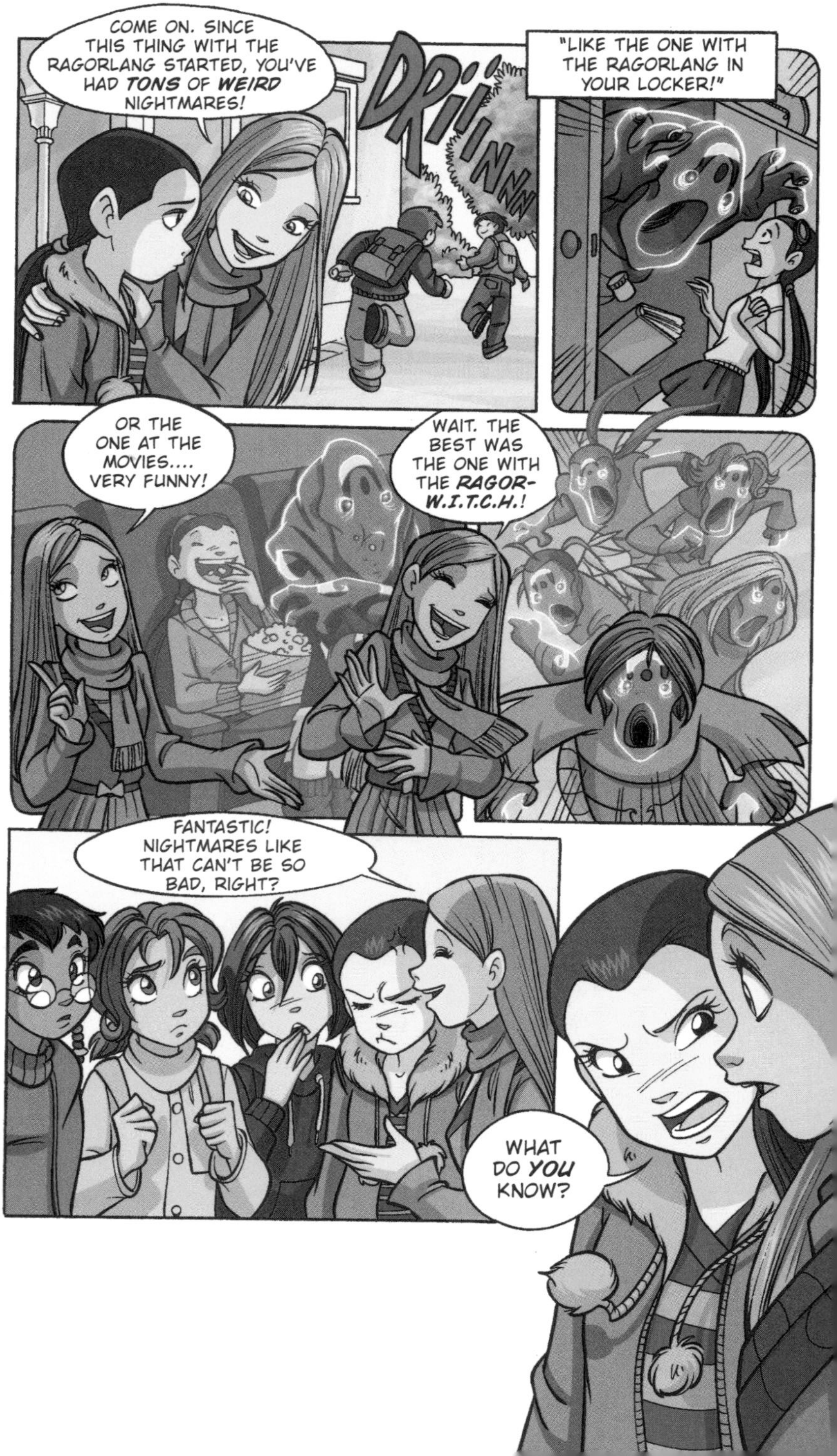
COME ON. SINCE THIS THING WITH THE RAGORLANG STARTED, YOU'VE HAD TONS OF WEIRD NIGHTMARES!
DRIIINNN
"LIKE THE ONE WITH THE RAGORLANG IN YOUR LOCKER!"
OR THE ONE AT THE MOVIES.... VERY FUNNY!
WAIT. THE BEST WAS THE ONE WITH THE RAGOR-W.I.T.C.H.!
FANTASTIC! NIGHTMARES LIKE THAT CAN'T BE SO BAD, RIGHT?
WHAT DO YOU KNOW?

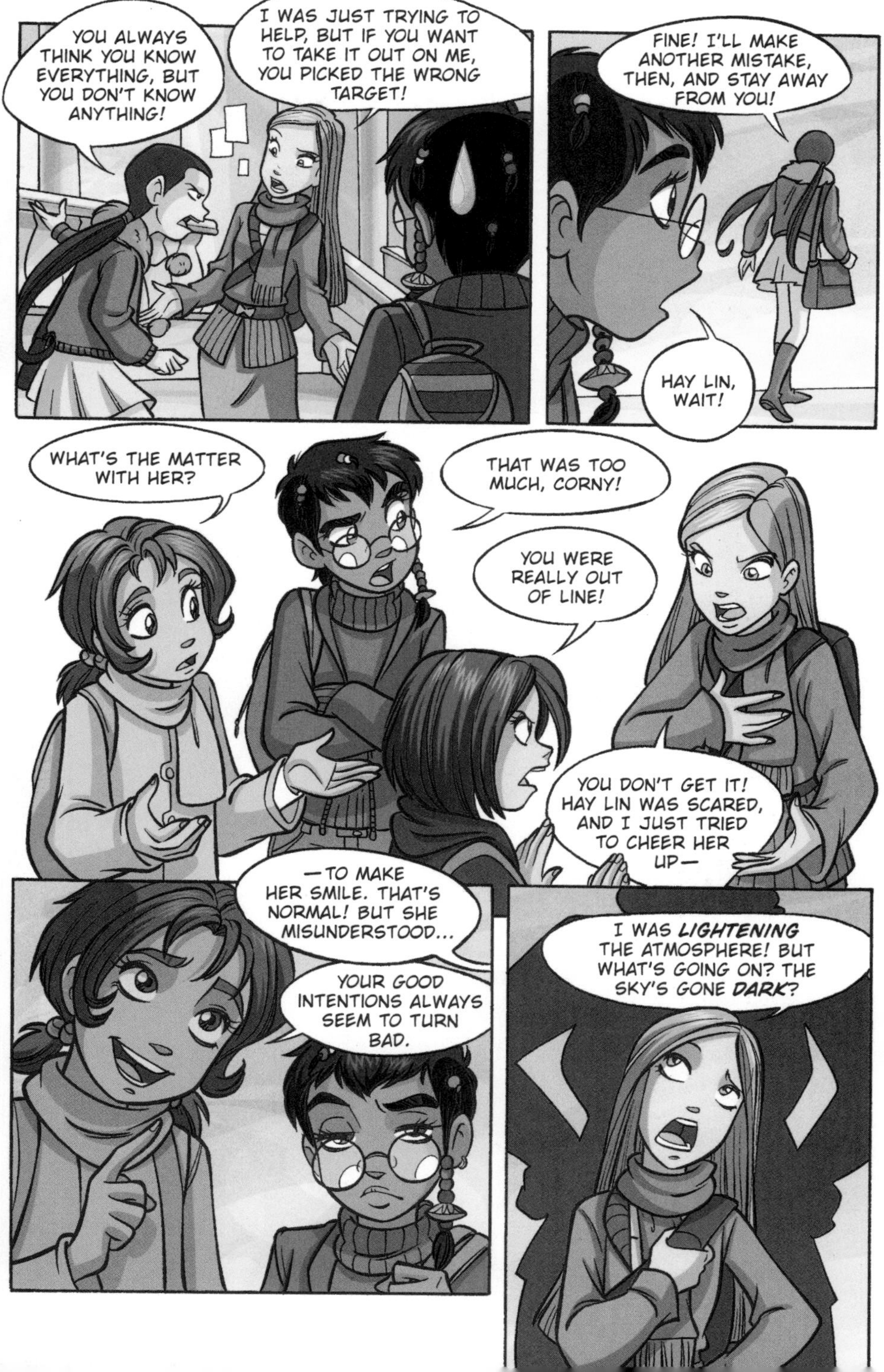
YOU ALWAYS THINK YOU KNOW EVERYTHING, BUT YOU DON'T KNOW ANYTHING!
I WAS JUST TRYING TO HELP, BUT IF YOU WANT TO TAKE IT OUT ON ME, YOU PICKED THE WRONG TARGET!
FINE! I'LL MAKE ANOTHER MISTAKE, THEN, AND STAY AWAY FROM YOU!
HAY LIN, WAIT!
WHAT'S THE MATTER WITH HER?
THAT WAS TOO MUCH, CORNY!
YOU WERE REALLY OUT OF LINE!
YOU DON'T GET IT! HAY LIN WAS SCARED, AND I JUST TRIED TO CHEER HER UP—
—TO MAKE HER SMILE. THAT'S NORMAL! BUT SHE MISUNDERSTOOD...
YOUR GOOD INTENTIONS ALWAYS SEEM TO TURN BAD.
I WAS ***LIGHTENING*** THE ATMOSPHERE! BUT WHAT'S GOING ON? THE SKY'S GONE ***DARK***?

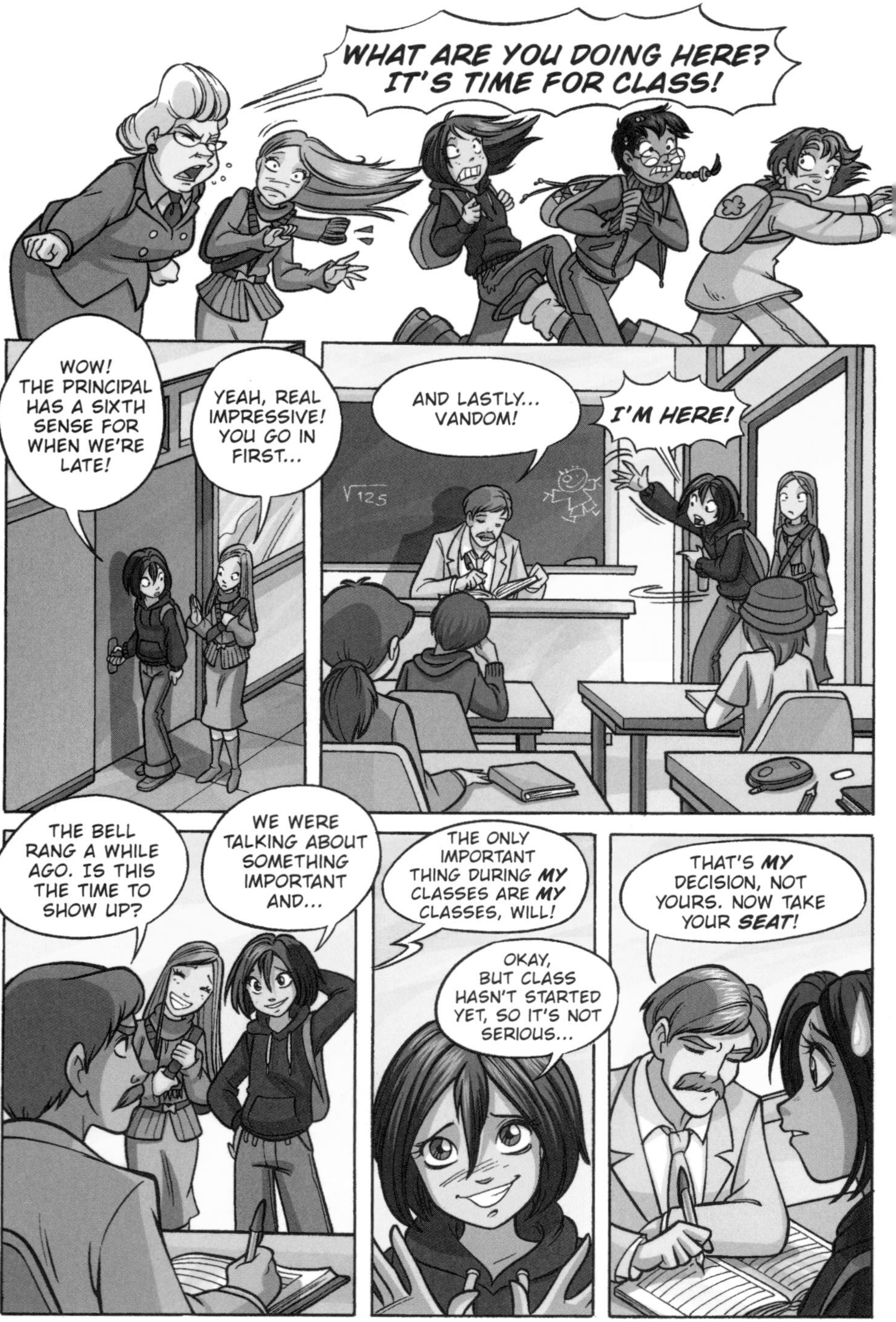

WHAT ARE YOU DOING HERE? IT'S TIME FOR CLASS!
WOW! THE PRINCIPAL HAS A SIXTH SENSE FOR WHEN WE'RE LATE!
YEAH, REAL IMPRESSIVE! YOU GO IN FIRST...
AND LASTLY... VANDOM!
I'M HERE!
THE BELL RANG A WHILE AGO. IS THIS THE TIME TO SHOW UP?
WE WERE TALKING ABOUT SOMETHING IMPORTANT AND...
THE ONLY IMPORTANT THING DURING MY CLASSES ARE MY CLASSES, WILL!
OKAY, BUT CLASS HASN'T STARTED YET, SO IT'S NOT SERIOUS...
THAT'S MY DECISION, NOT YOURS. NOW TAKE YOUR SEAT!

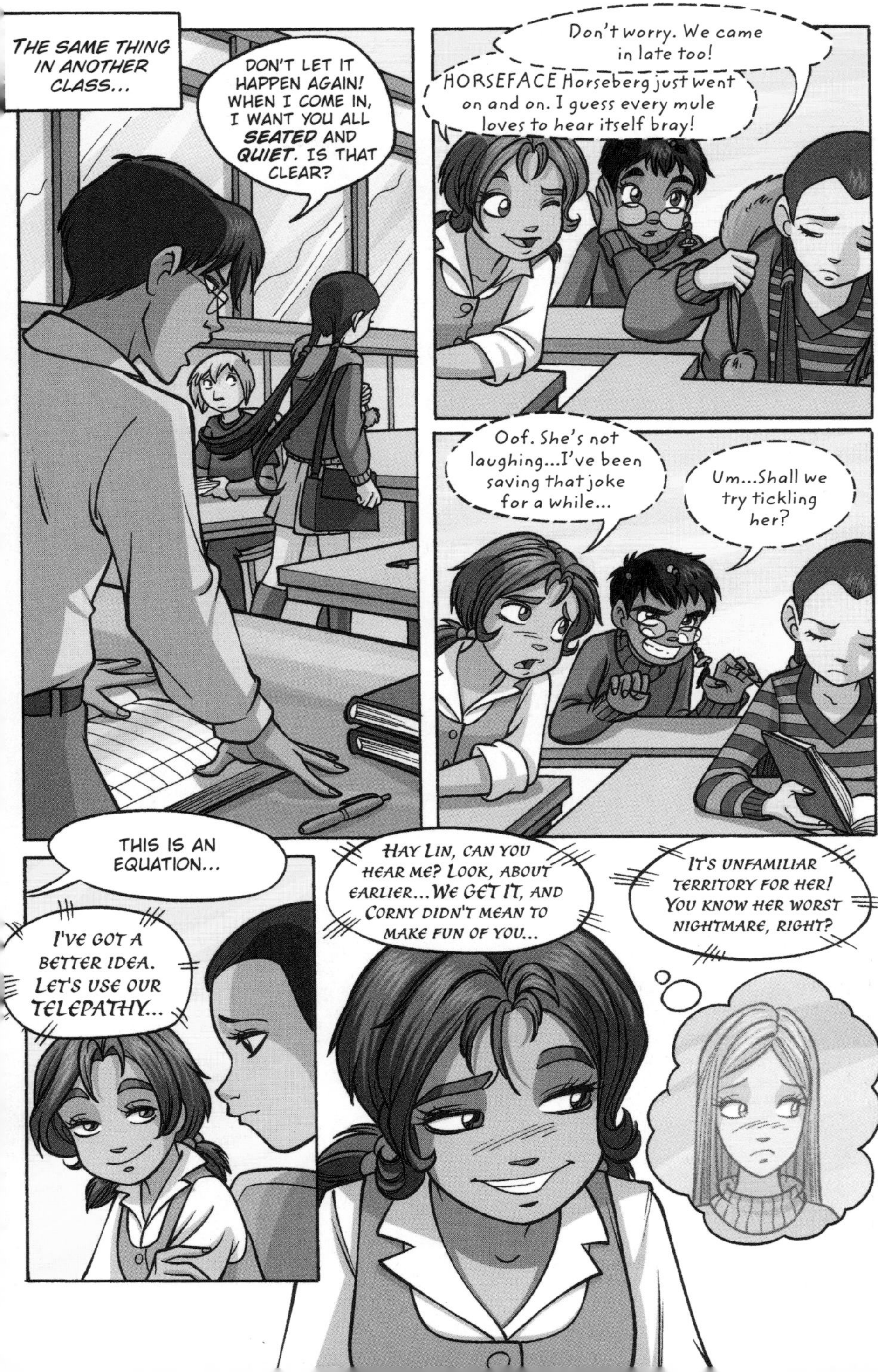
THE SAME THING IN ANOTHER CLASS...
DON'T LET IT HAPPEN AGAIN! WHEN I COME IN, I WANT YOU ALL SEATED AND QUIET. IS THAT CLEAR?
Don't worry. We came in late too!
HORSEFACE Horseberg just went on and on. I guess every mule loves to hear itself bray!
Oof. She's not laughing...I've been saving that joke for a while...
Um...Shall we try tickling her?
THIS IS AN EQUATION...
I'VE GOT A BETTER IDEA. LET'S USE OUR TELEPATHY...
HAY LIN, CAN YOU HEAR ME? LOOK, ABOUT EARLIER...WE GET IT, AND CORNY DIDN'T MEAN TO MAKE FUN OF YOU...
IT'S UNFAMILIAR TERRITORY FOR HER! YOU KNOW HER WORST NIGHTMARE, RIGHT?

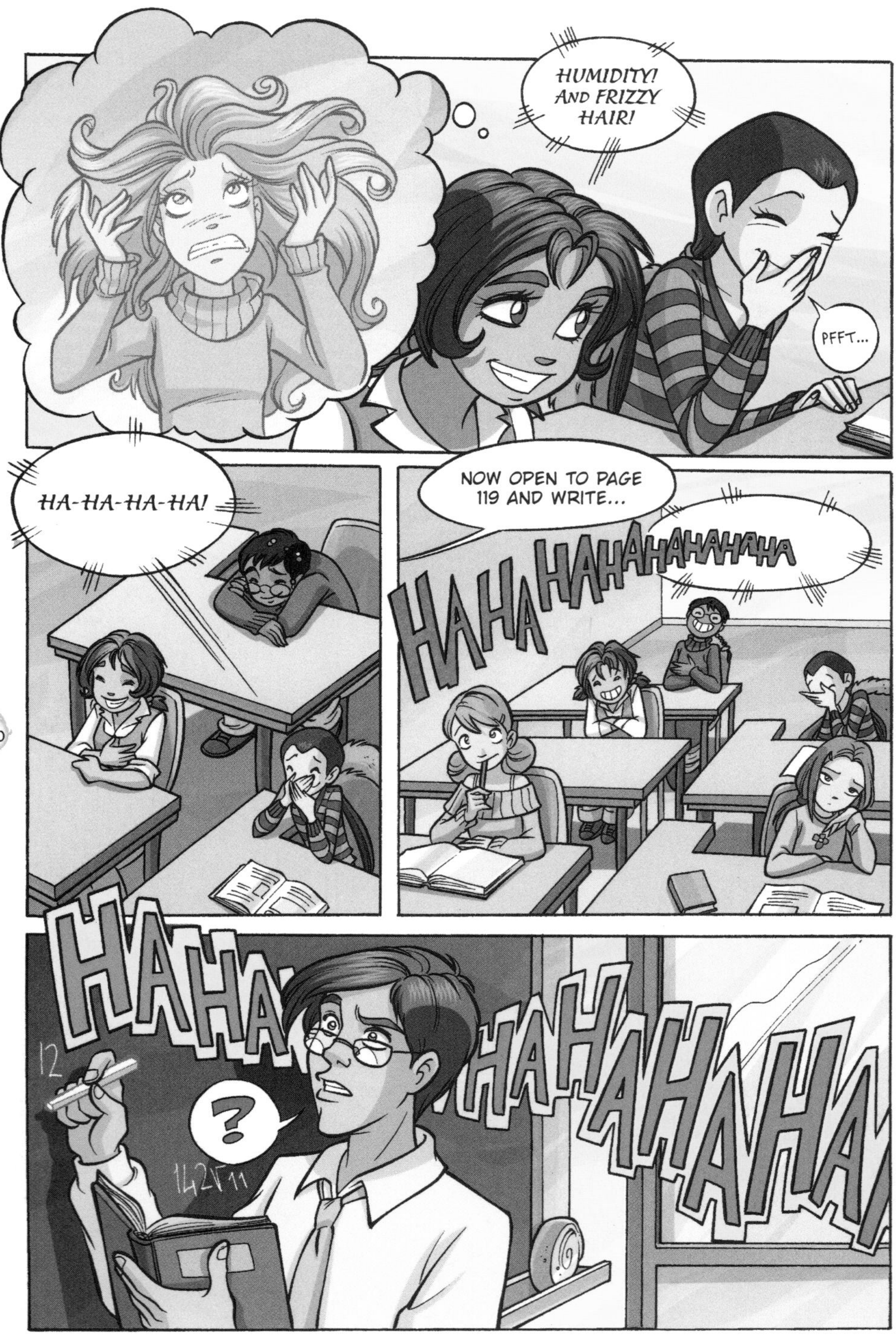
HUMIDITY! AND FRIZZY HAIR!
PFFT...
HA-HA-HA-HA!
NOW OPEN TO PAGE 119 AND WRITE...
HAHAHAHAHAHAHAHAHA
HAHAHAHAHAHAHAHAHA
?

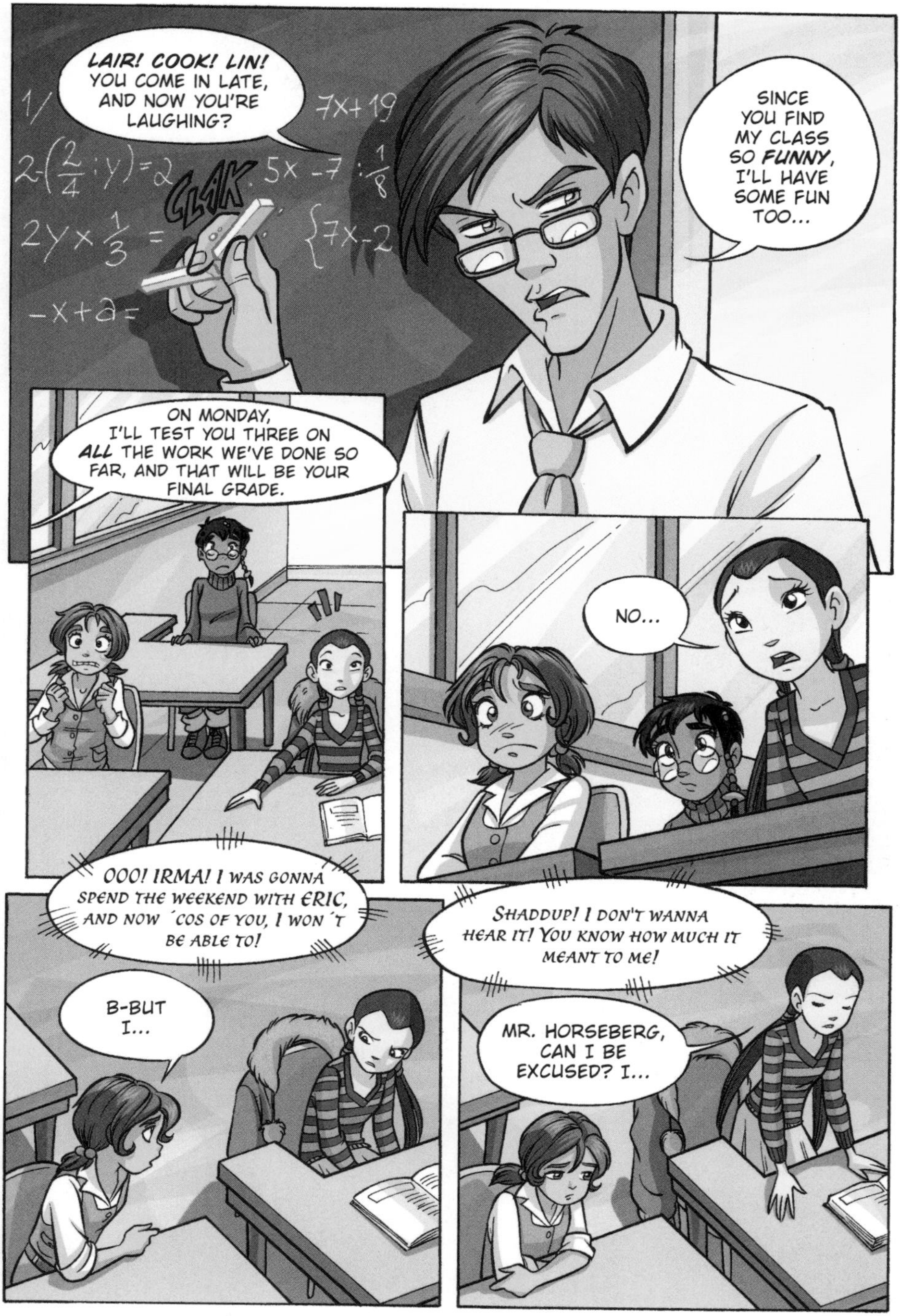
LAIR! COOK! LIN! YOU COME IN LATE, AND NOW YOU'RE LAUGHING?
CLAK
SINCE YOU FIND MY CLASS SO FUNNY, I'LL HAVE SOME FUN TOO...
ON MONDAY, I'LL TEST YOU THREE ON ALL THE WORK WE'VE DONE SO FAR, AND THAT WILL BE YOUR FINAL GRADE.
NO...
OOO! IRMA! I WAS GONNA SPEND THE WEEKEND WITH ERIC, AND NOW ´COS OF YOU, I WON´T BE ABLE TO!
SHADDUP! I DON'T WANNA HEAR IT! YOU KNOW HOW MUCH IT MEANT TO ME!
B-BUT I...
MR. HORSEBERG, CAN I BE EXCUSED? I...

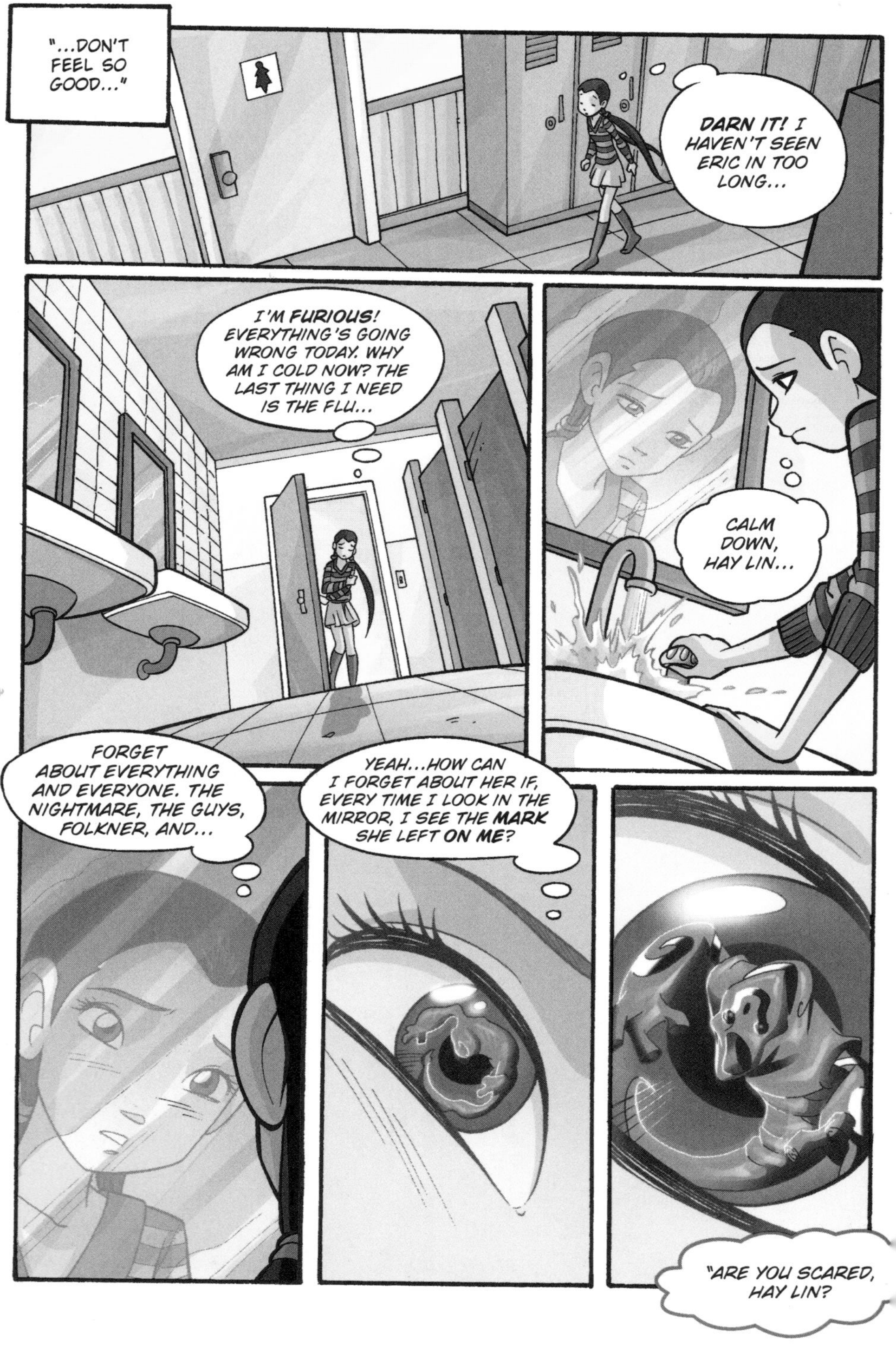

"...DON'T FEEL SO GOOD..."
DARN IT! I HAVEN'T SEEN ERIC IN TOO LONG...
I'M FURIOUS! EVERYTHING'S GOING WRONG TODAY. WHY AM I COLD NOW? THE LAST THING I NEED IS THE FLU...
CALM DOWN, HAY LIN...
FORGET ABOUT EVERYTHING AND EVERYONE. THE NIGHTMARE, THE GUYS, FOLKNER, AND...
YEAH...HOW CAN I FORGET ABOUT HER IF, EVERY TIME I LOOK IN THE MIRROR, I SEE THE MARK SHE LEFT ON ME?
"ARE YOU SCARED, HAY LIN?

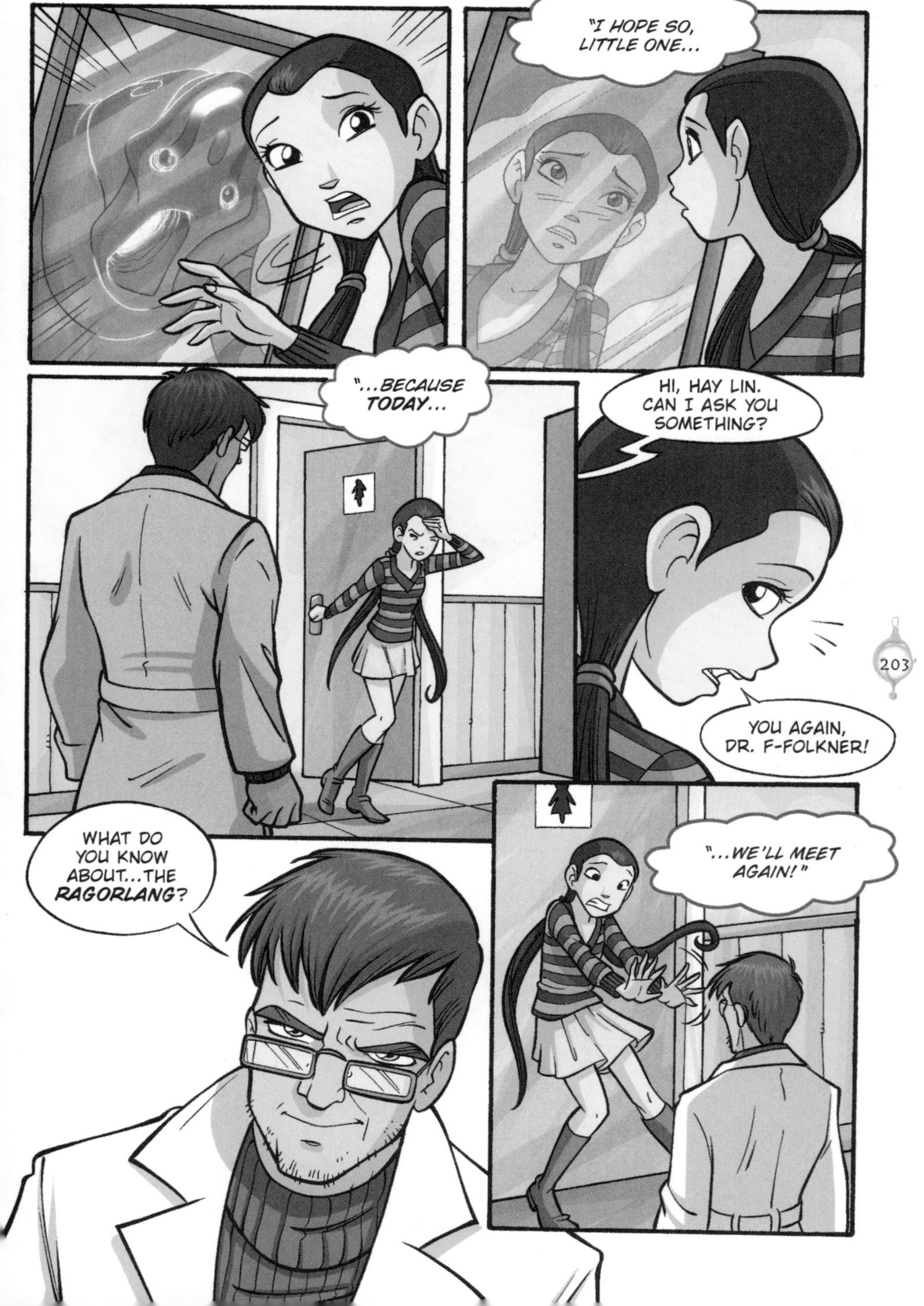
"I HOPE SO, LITTLE ONE...
"...BECAUSE TODAY...
HI, HAY LIN. CAN I ASK YOU SOMETHING?
YOU AGAIN, DR. F-FOLKNER!
WHAT DO YOU KNOW ABOUT...THE RAGORLANG?
"...WE'LL MEET AGAIN!"

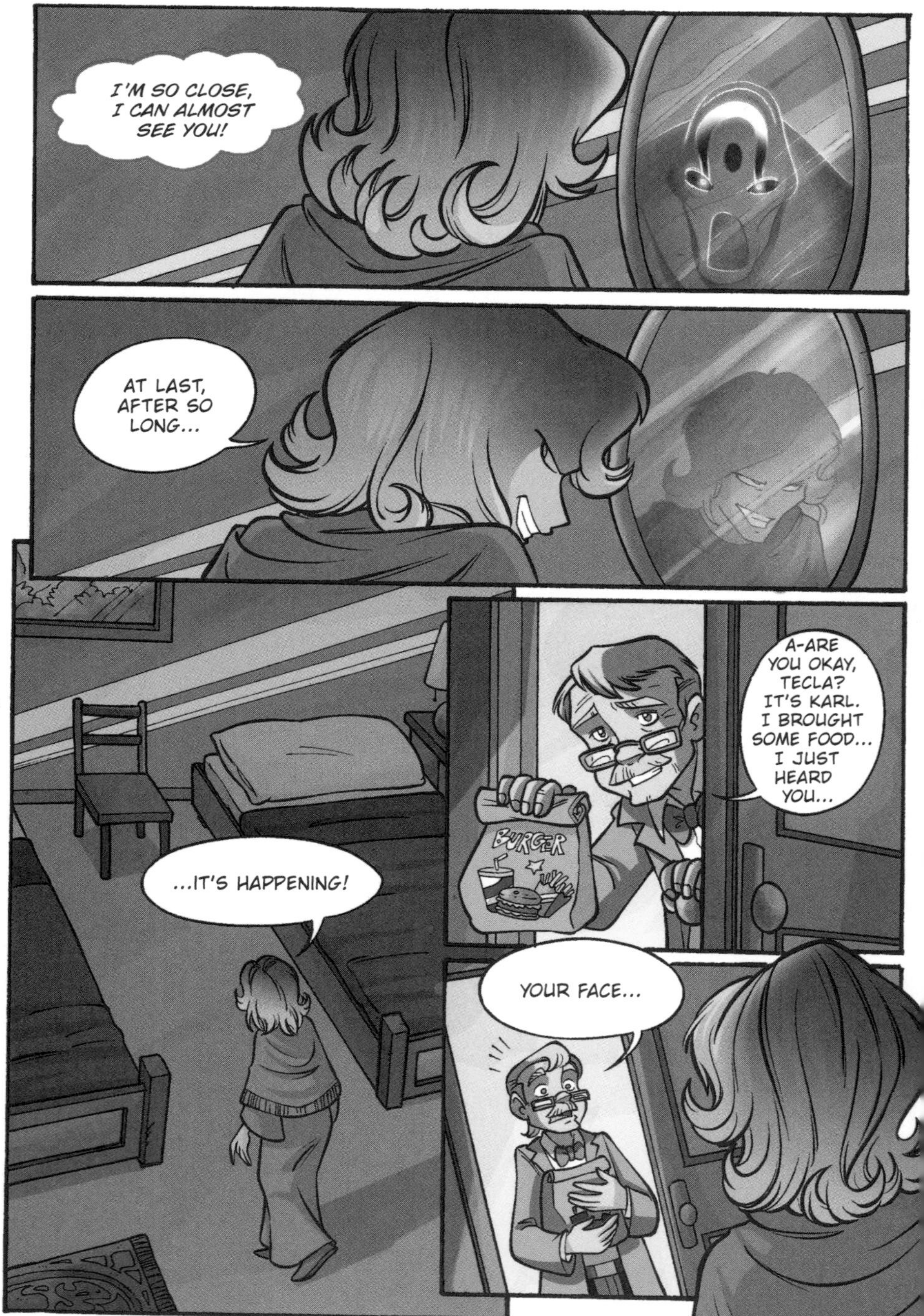
I'M SO CLOSE, I CAN ALMOST SEE YOU!
AT LAST, AFTER SO LONG...
...IT'S HAPPENING!
A-ARE YOU OKAY, TECLA? IT'S KARL. I BROUGHT SOME FOOD... I JUST HEARD YOU...
BURGER
YOUR FACE...

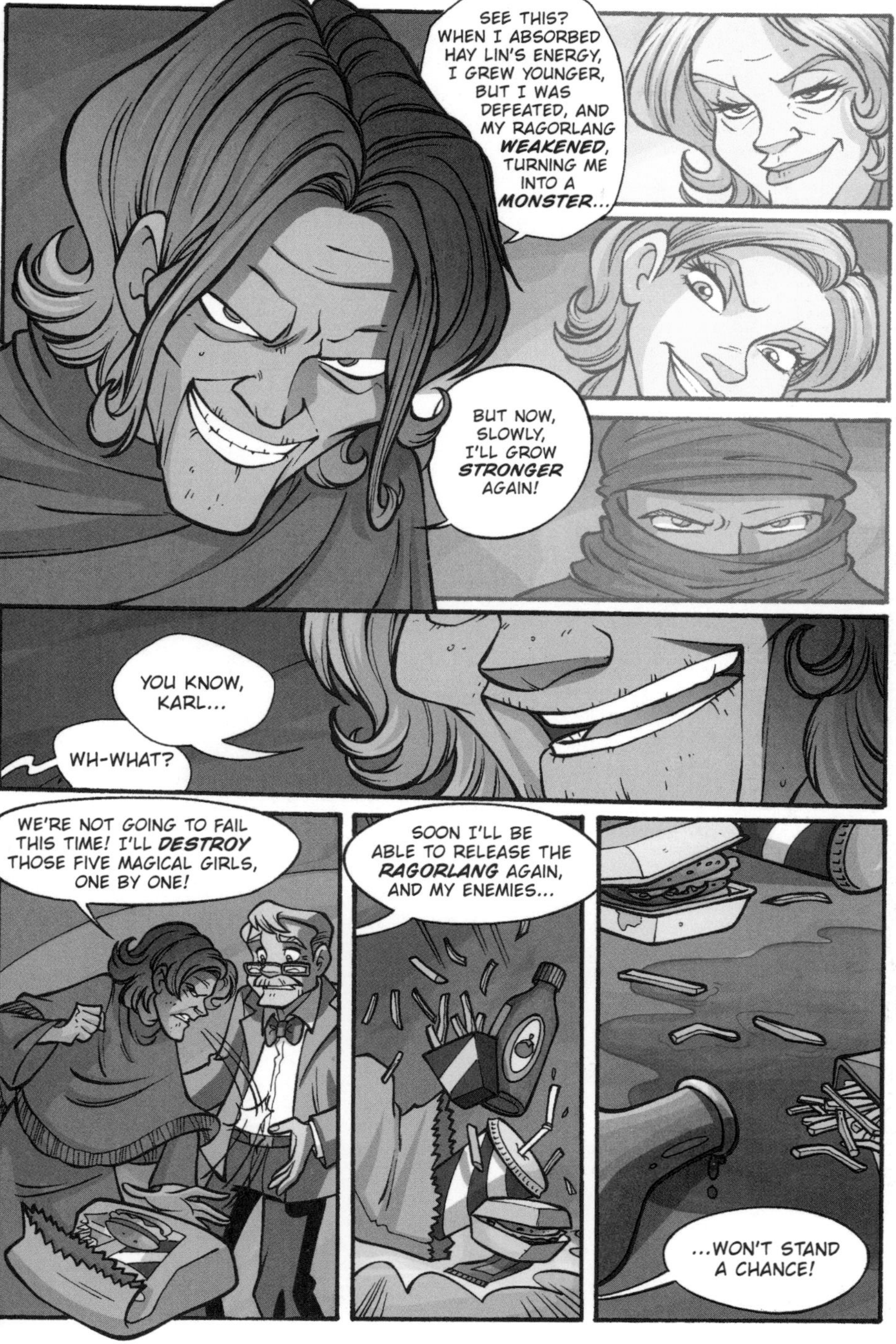
SEE THIS? WHEN I ABSORBED HAY LIN'S ENERGY, I GREW YOUNGER, BUT I WAS DEFEATED, AND MY RAGORLANG WEAKENED, TURNING ME INTO A MONSTER...
BUT NOW, SLOWLY, I'LL GROW STRONGER AGAIN!
YOU KNOW, KARL...
WH-WHAT?
WE'RE NOT GOING TO FAIL THIS TIME! I'LL DESTROY THOSE FIVE MAGICAL GIRLS, ONE BY ONE!
SOON I'LL BE ABLE TO RELEASE THE RAGORLANG AGAIN, AND MY ENEMIES...
...WON'T STAND A CHANCE!

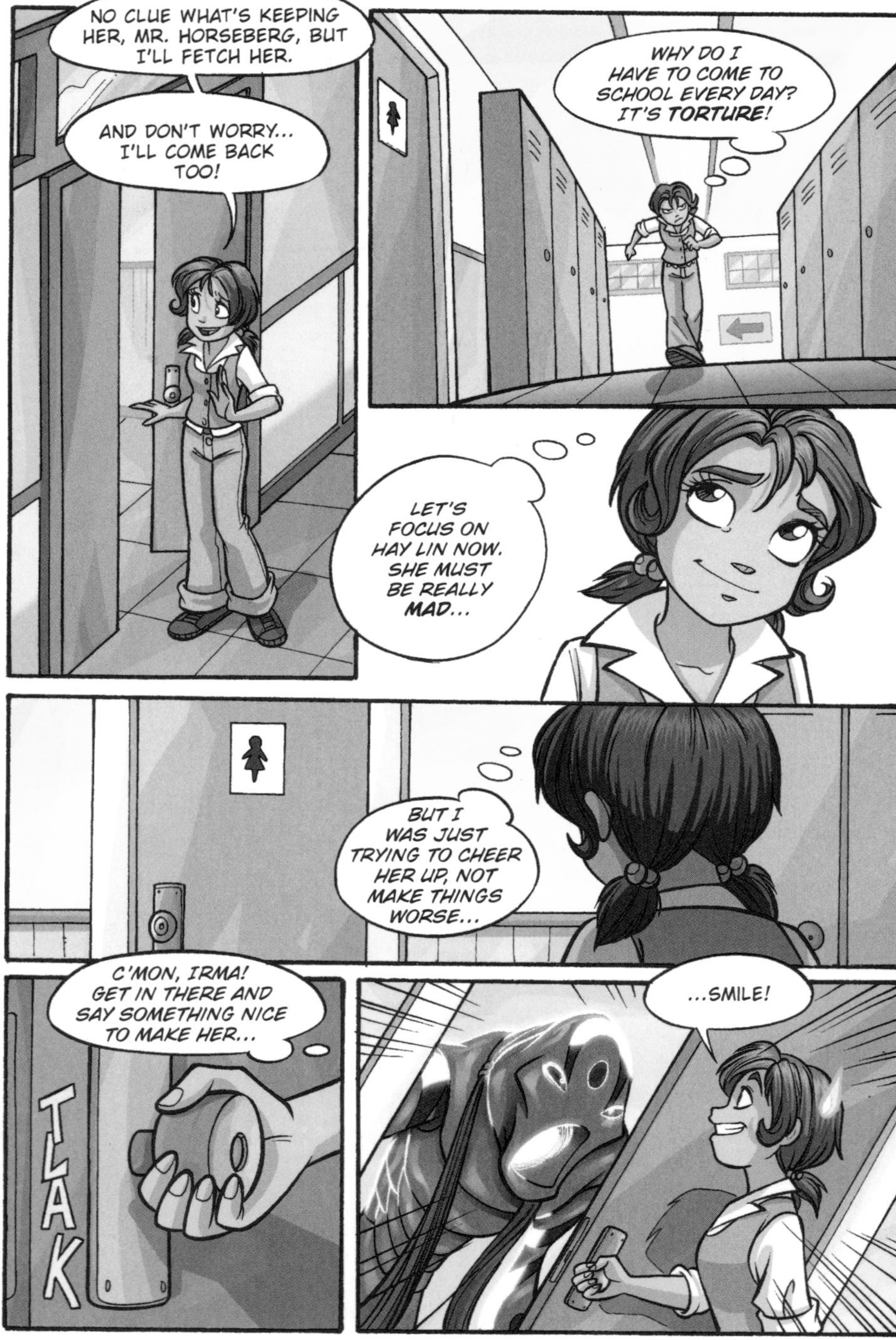
NO CLUE WHAT'S KEEPING HER, MR. HORSEBERG, BUT I'LL FETCH HER.
AND DON'T WORRY... I'LL COME BACK TOO!
WHY DO I HAVE TO COME TO SCHOOL EVERY DAY? IT'S TORTURE!
LET'S FOCUS ON HAY LIN NOW. SHE MUST BE REALLY MAD...
BUT I WAS JUST TRYING TO CHEER HER UP, NOT MAKE THINGS WORSE...
C'MON, IRMA! GET IN THERE AND SAY SOMETHING NICE TO MAKE HER...
TLAK
...SMILE!

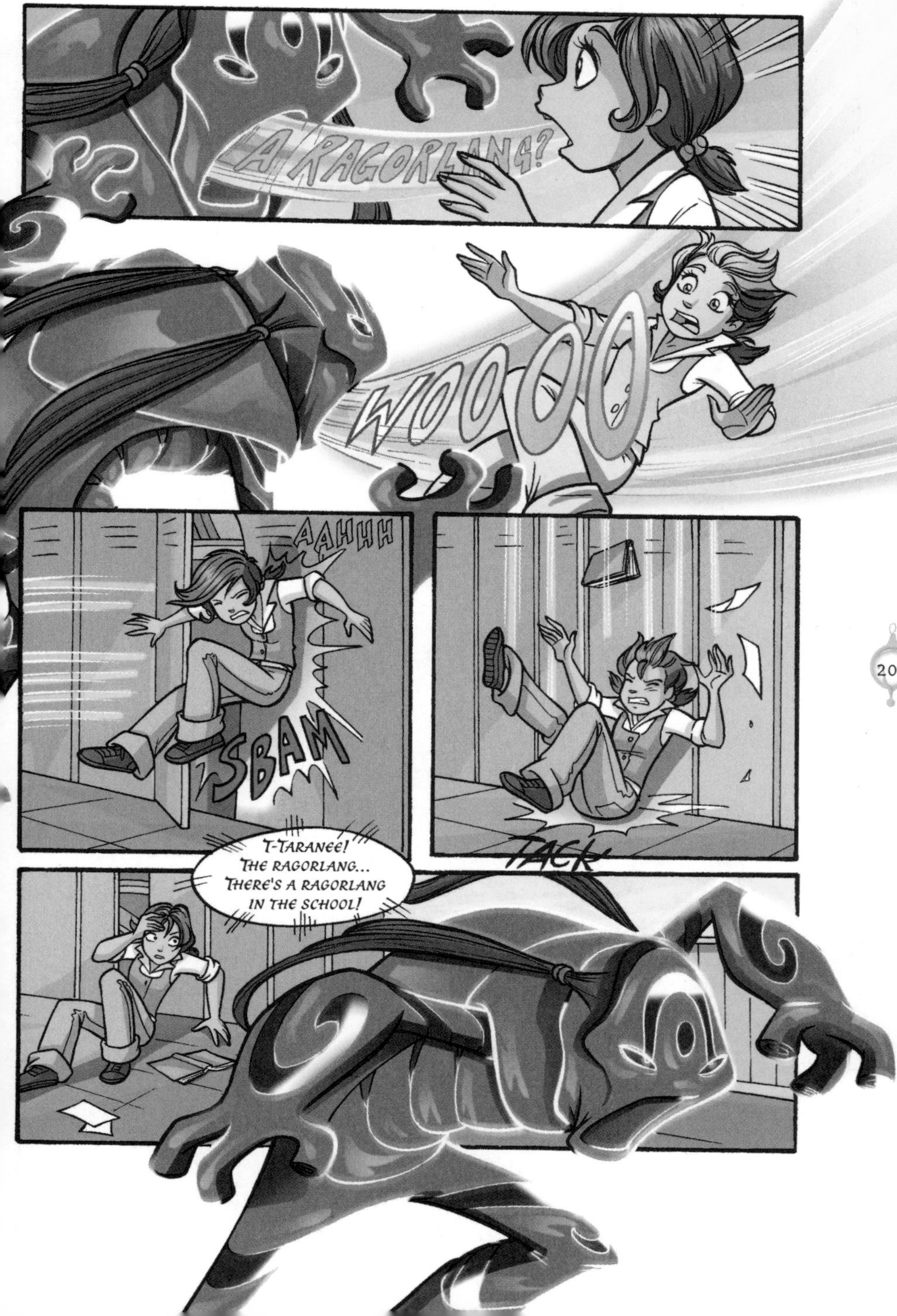

A RAGORLANG?
WOOOOO
AAHHH
SBAM
TACK
T-TARANEE! THE RAGORLANG... THERE'S A RAGORLANG IN THE SCHOOL!

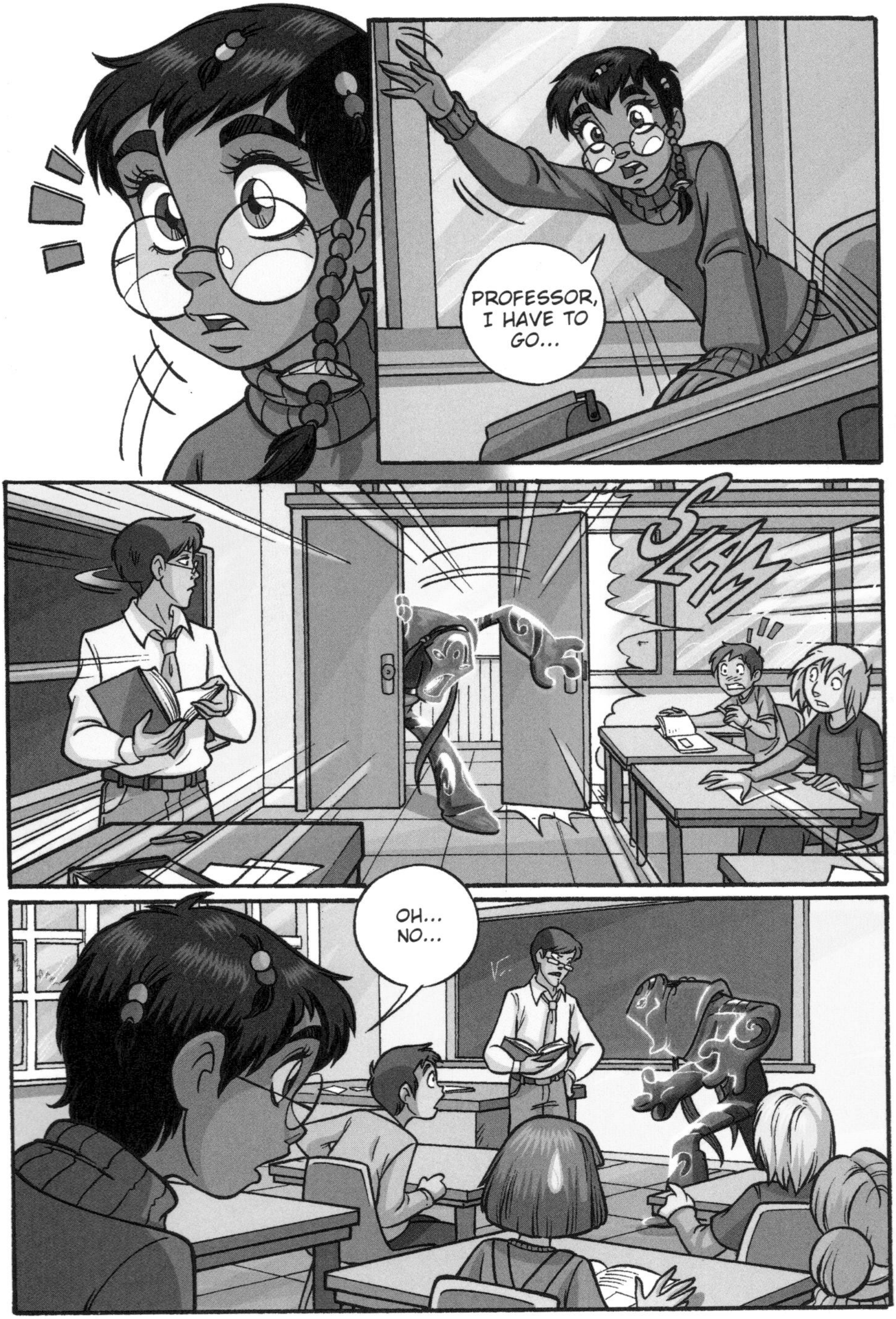
PROFESSOR, I HAVE TO GO...
SLAM
OH... NO...

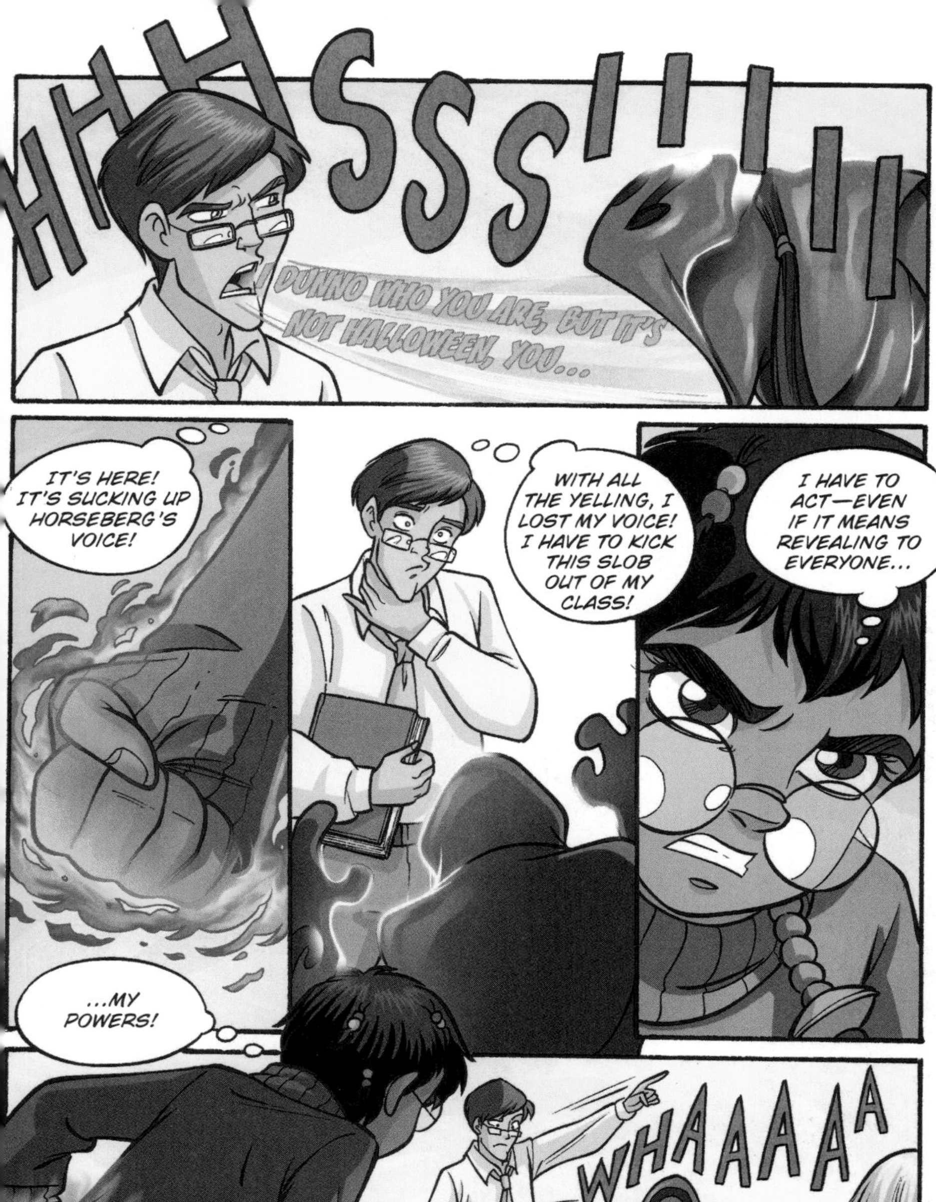
HHHSSSSIIIIII
I DUNNO WHO YOU ARE, BUT IT'S NOT HALLOWEEN, YOU...
IT'S HERE! IT'S SUCKING UP HORSEBERG'S VOICE!
WITH ALL THE YELLING, I LOST MY VOICE! I HAVE TO KICK THIS SLOB OUT OF MY CLASS!
I HAVE TO ACT—EVEN IF IT MEANS REVEALING TO EVERYONE...
...MY POWERS!
WHAAAAA

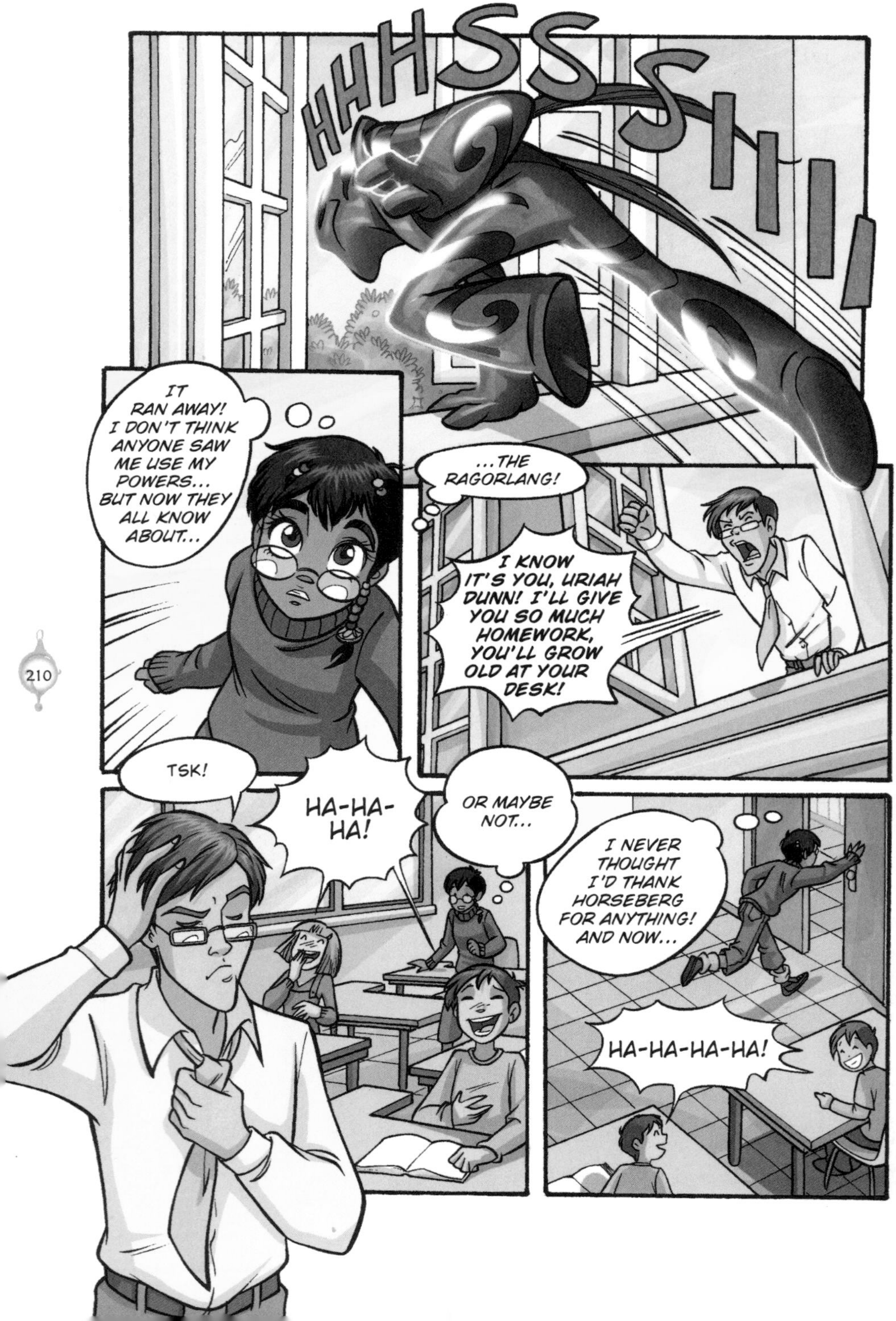
HHHSSSSHIIII
IT RAN AWAY! I DON'T THINK ANYONE SAW ME USE MY POWERS... BUT NOW THEY ALL KNOW ABOUT...
...THE RAGORLANG!
I KNOW IT'S YOU, URIAH DUNN! I'LL GIVE YOU SO MUCH HOMEWORK, YOU'LL GROW OLD AT YOUR DESK!
TSK!
HA-HA-HA!
OR MAYBE NOT...
I NEVER THOUGHT I'D THANK HORSEBERG FOR ANYTHING! AND NOW...
HA-HA-HA-HA!

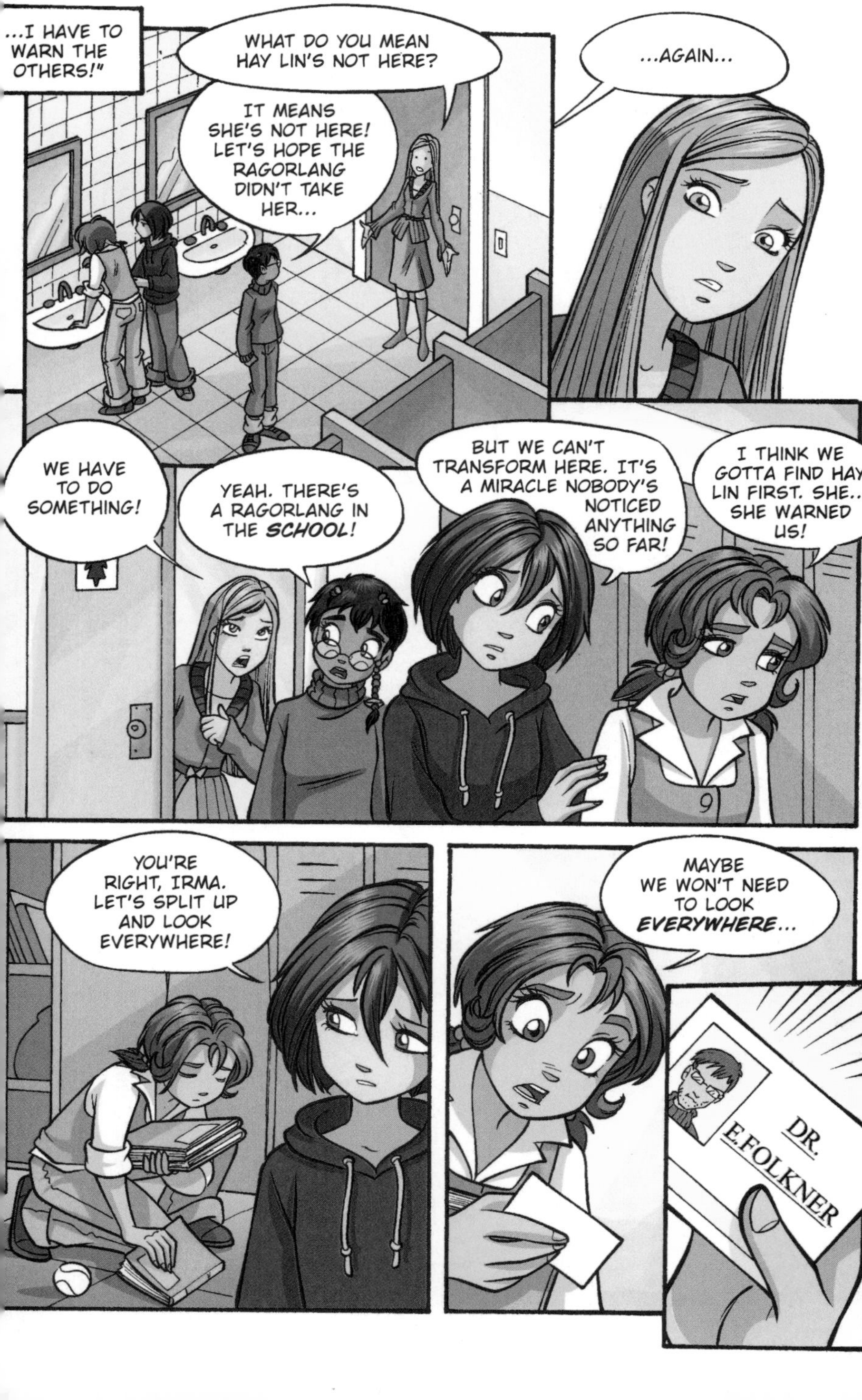

...I HAVE TO WARN THE OTHERS!"
WHAT DO YOU MEAN HAY LIN'S NOT HERE?
IT MEANS SHE'S NOT HERE! LET'S HOPE THE RAGORLANG DIDN'T TAKE HER...
...AGAIN...
WE HAVE TO DO SOMETHING!
YEAH. THERE'S A RAGORLANG IN THE *SCHOOL*!
BUT WE CAN'T TRANSFORM HERE. IT'S A MIRACLE NOBODY'S NOTICED ANYTHING SO FAR!
I THINK WE GOTTA FIND HAY LIN FIRST. SHE... SHE WARNED US!
YOU'RE RIGHT, IRMA. LET'S SPLIT UP AND LOOK EVERYWHERE!
MAYBE WE WON'T NEED TO LOOK *EVERYWHERE*...
DR. E.FOLKNER

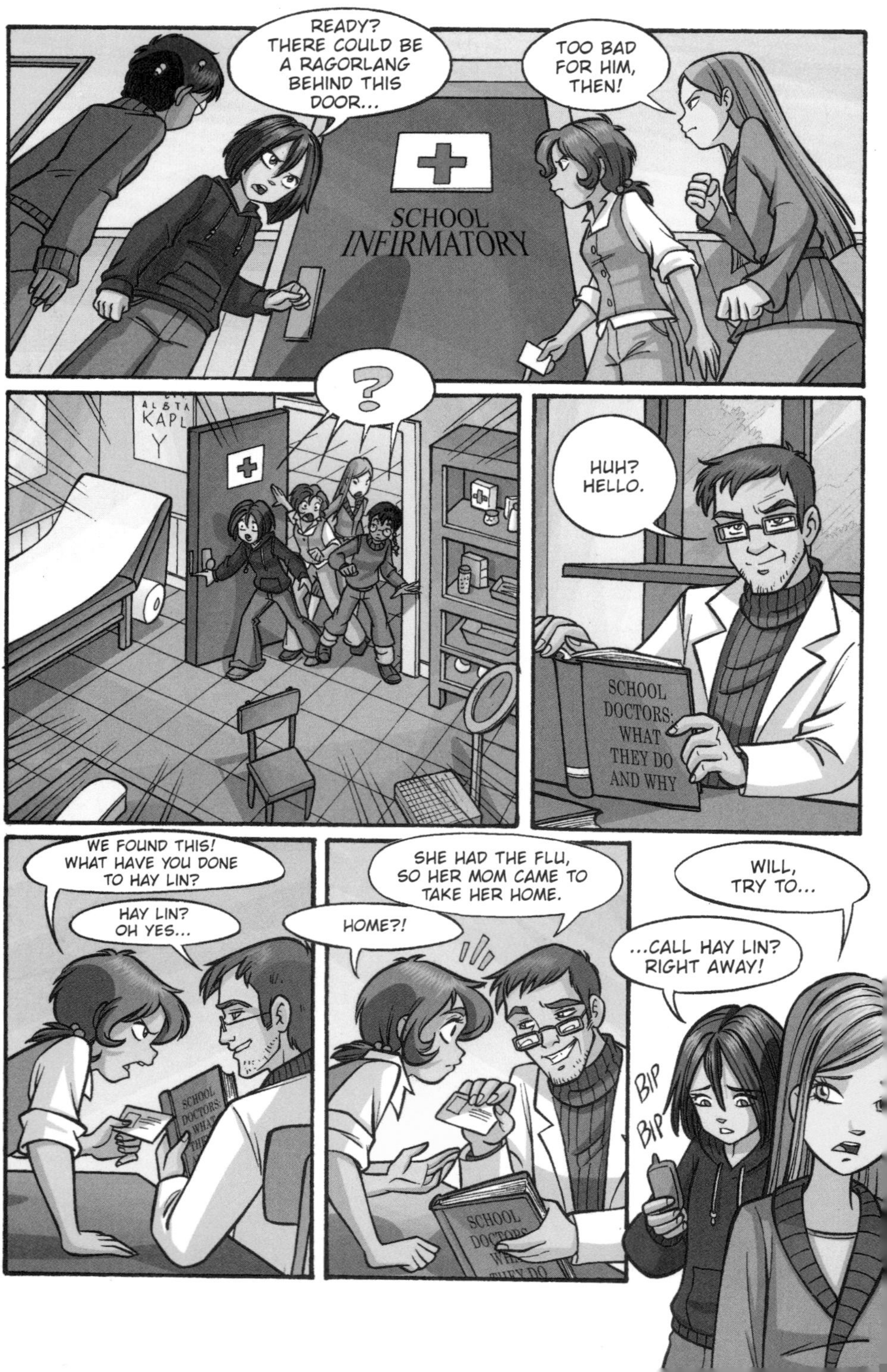
READY? THERE COULD BE A RAGORLANG BEHIND THIS DOOR...
TOO BAD FOR HIM, THEN!
SCHOOL INFIRMATORY
?
HUH? HELLO.
SCHOOL DOCTORS: WHAT THEY DO AND WHY
WE FOUND THIS! WHAT HAVE YOU DONE TO HAY LIN?
HAY LIN? OH YES...
SHE HAD THE FLU, SO HER MOM CAME TO TAKE HER HOME.
HOME?!
WILL, TRY TO...
...CALL HAY LIN? RIGHT AWAY!
BIP
BIP

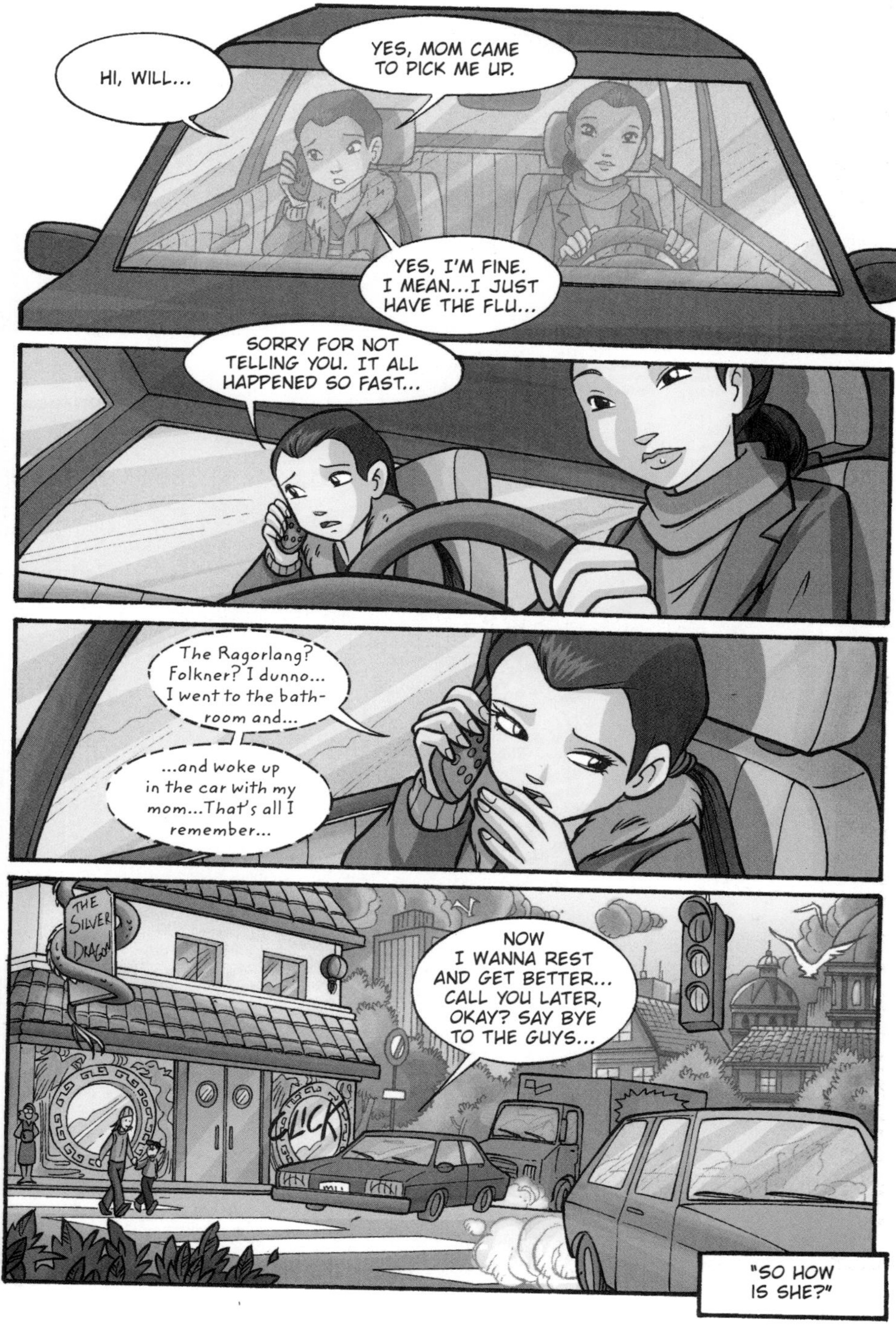
HI, WILL...
YES, MOM CAME TO PICK ME UP.
YES, I'M FINE. I MEAN...I JUST HAVE THE FLU...
SORRY FOR NOT TELLING YOU. IT ALL HAPPENED SO FAST...
The Ragorlang? Folkner? I dunno... I went to the bathroom and...
...and woke up in the car with my mom...That's all I remember...
THE SILVER DRAGON
NOW I WANNA REST AND GET BETTER... CALL YOU LATER, OKAY? SAY BYE TO THE GUYS...
CLICK
"SO HOW IS SHE?"

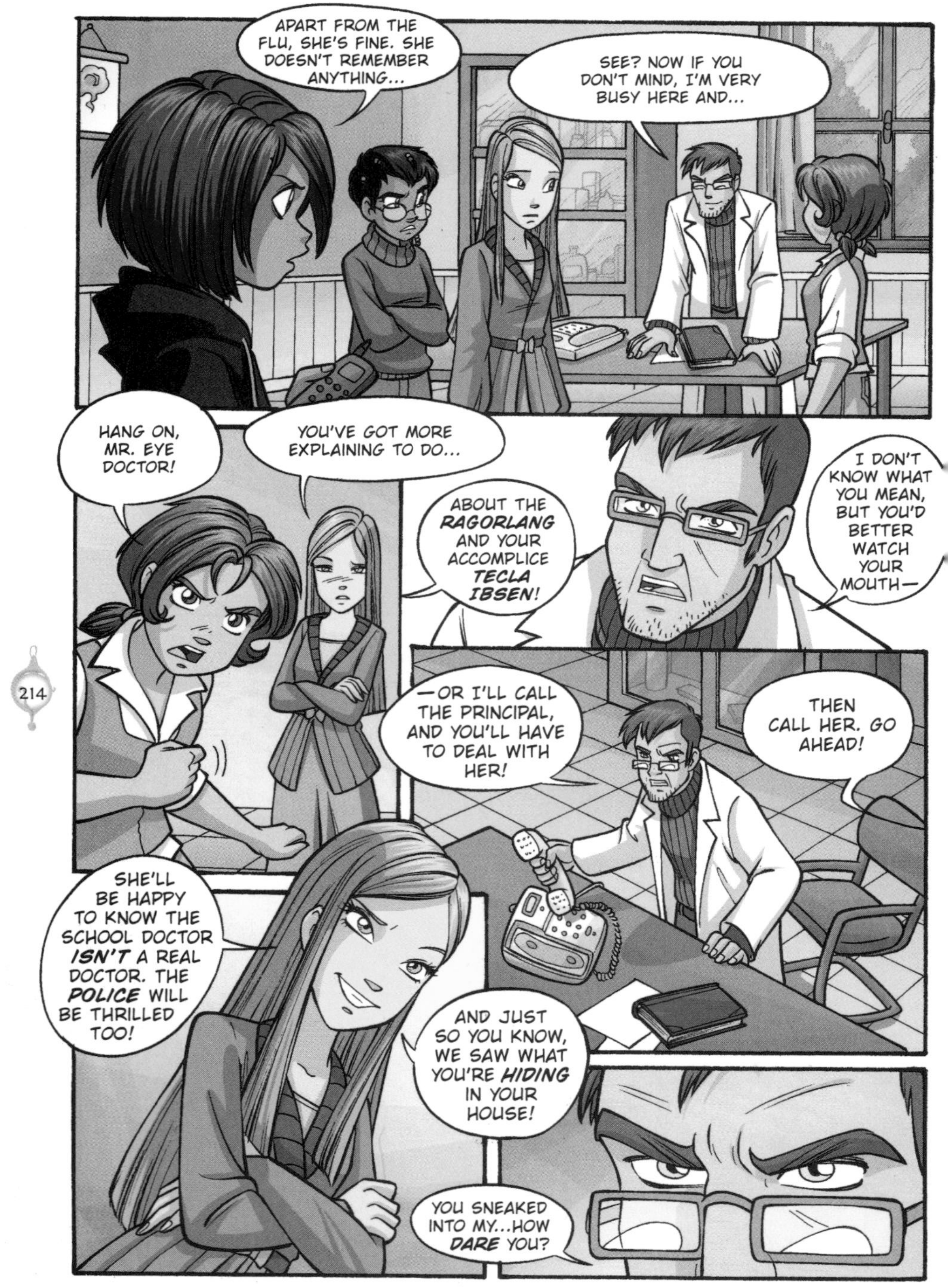

APART FROM THE FLU, SHE'S FINE. SHE DOESN'T REMEMBER ANYTHING...
SEE? NOW IF YOU DON'T MIND, I'M VERY BUSY HERE AND...
HANG ON, MR. EYE DOCTOR!
YOU'VE GOT MORE EXPLAINING TO DO...
ABOUT THE RAGORLANG AND YOUR ACCOMPLICE TECLA IBSEN!
I DON'T KNOW WHAT YOU MEAN, BUT YOU'D BETTER WATCH YOUR MOUTH—
—OR I'LL CALL THE PRINCIPAL, AND YOU'LL HAVE TO DEAL WITH HER!
THEN CALL HER. GO AHEAD!
SHE'LL BE HAPPY TO KNOW THE SCHOOL DOCTOR ISN'T A REAL DOCTOR. THE POLICE WILL BE THRILLED TOO!
AND JUST SO YOU KNOW, WE SAW WHAT YOU'RE HIDING IN YOUR HOUSE!
YOU SNEAKED INTO MY...HOW DARE YOU?

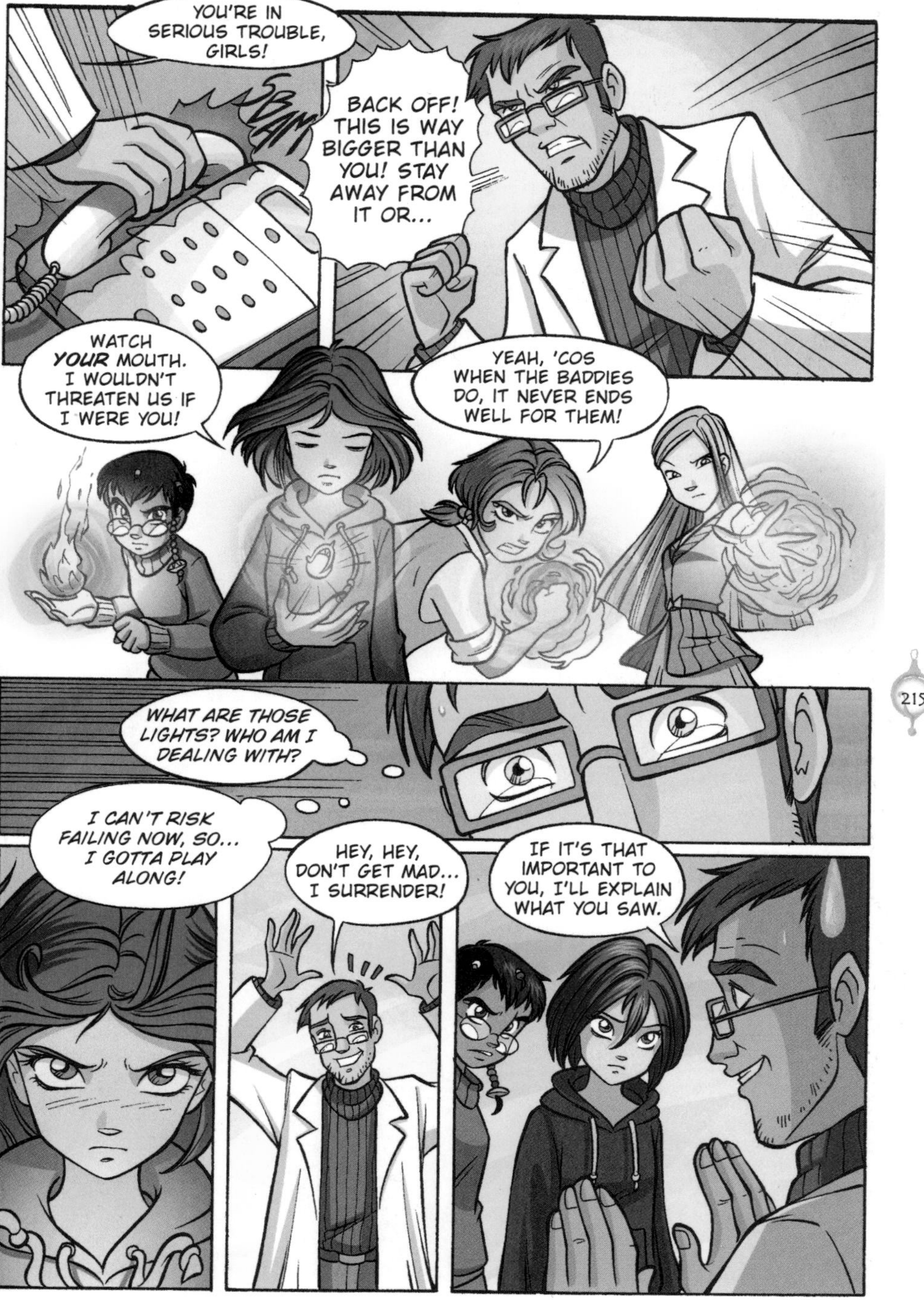
YOU'RE IN SERIOUS TROUBLE, GIRLS!
SBAM
BACK OFF! THIS IS WAY BIGGER THAN YOU! STAY AWAY FROM IT OR...
WATCH **YOUR** MOUTH. I WOULDN'T THREATEN US IF I WERE YOU!
YEAH, 'COS WHEN THE BADDIES DO, IT NEVER ENDS WELL FOR THEM!
WHAT ARE THOSE LIGHTS? WHO AM I DEALING WITH?
I CAN'T RISK FAILING NOW, SO... I GOTTA PLAY ALONG!
HEY, HEY, DON'T GET MAD... I SURRENDER!
IF IT'S THAT IMPORTANT TO YOU, I'LL EXPLAIN WHAT YOU SAW.

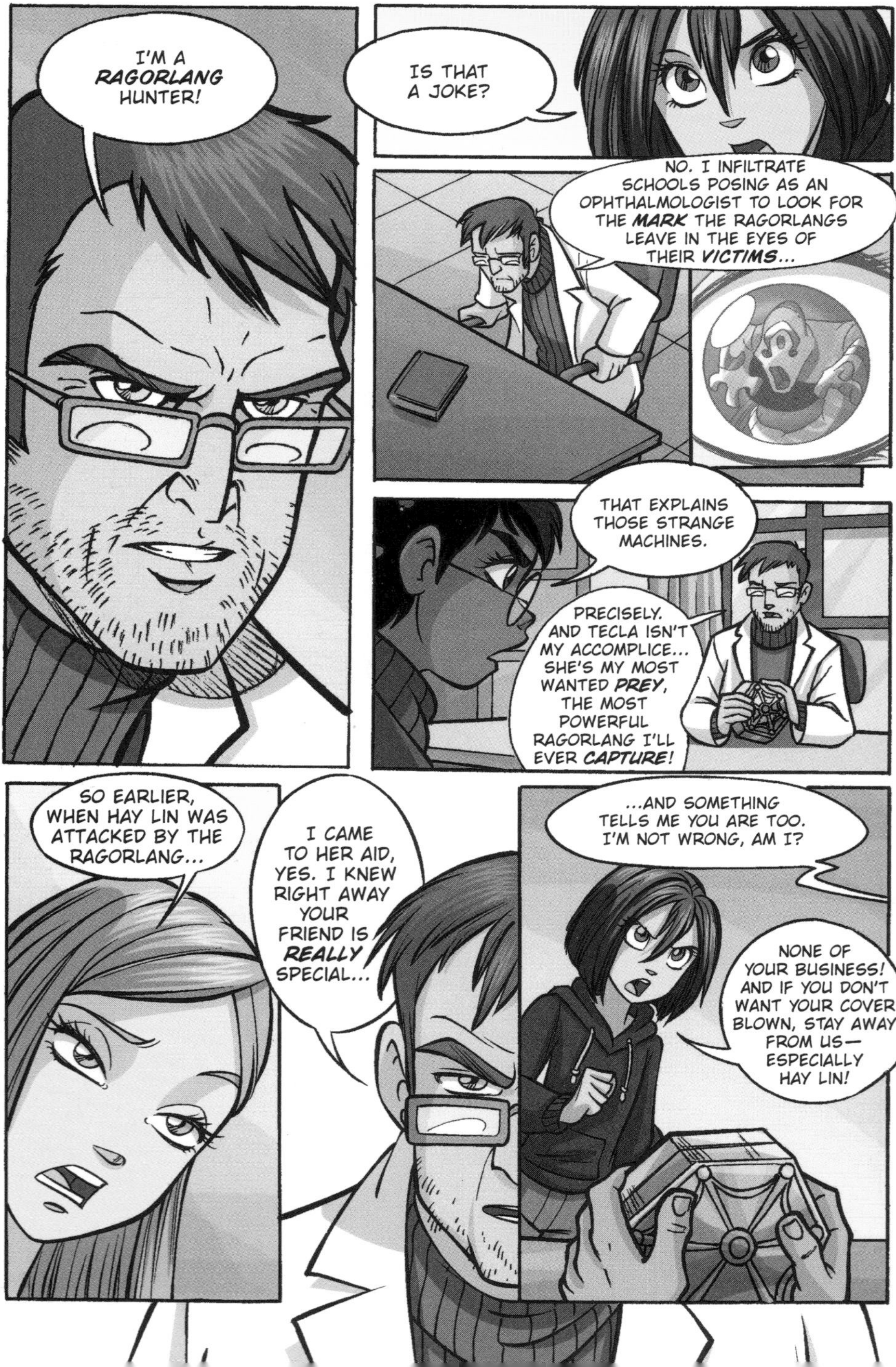
I'M A RAGORLANG HUNTER!
IS THAT A JOKE?
NO. I INFILTRATE SCHOOLS POSING AS AN OPHTHALMOLOGIST TO LOOK FOR THE MARK THE RAGORLANGS LEAVE IN THE EYES OF THEIR VICTIMS...
THAT EXPLAINS THOSE STRANGE MACHINES.
PRECISELY. AND TECLA ISN'T MY ACCOMPLICE... SHE'S MY MOST WANTED PREY, THE MOST POWERFUL RAGORLANG I'LL EVER CAPTURE!
SO EARLIER, WHEN HAY LIN WAS ATTACKED BY THE RAGORLANG...
I CAME TO HER AID, YES. I KNEW RIGHT AWAY YOUR FRIEND IS REALLY SPECIAL...
...AND SOMETHING TELLS ME YOU ARE TOO. I'M NOT WRONG, AM I?
NONE OF YOUR BUSINESS! AND IF YOU DON'T WANT YOUR COVER BLOWN, STAY AWAY FROM US— ESPECIALLY HAY LIN!

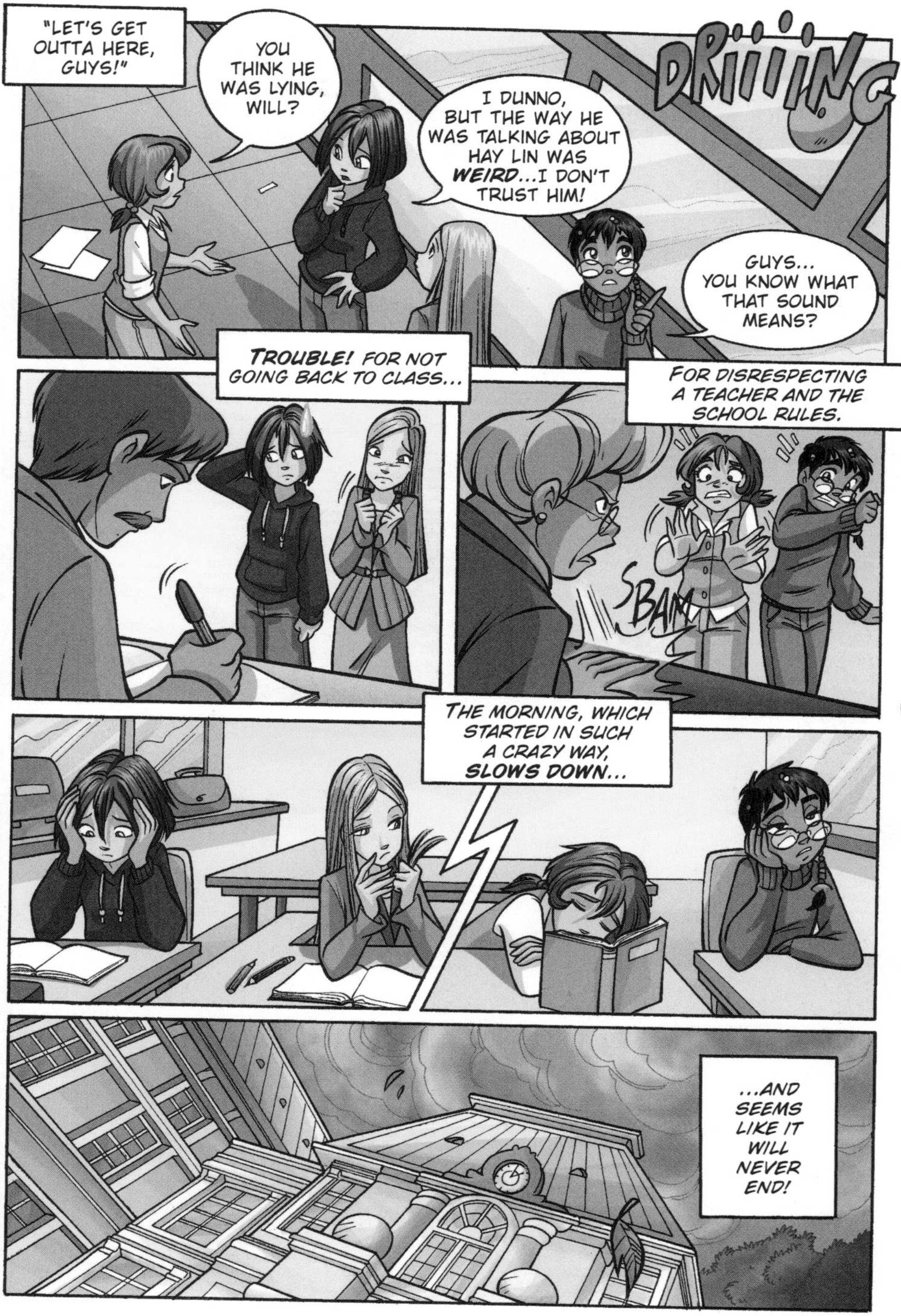
"LET'S GET OUTTA HERE, GUYS!"
YOU THINK HE WAS LYING, WILL?
I DUNNO, BUT THE WAY HE WAS TALKING ABOUT HAY LIN WAS WEIRD... I DON'T TRUST HIM!
DRIIIING
GUYS... YOU KNOW WHAT THAT SOUND MEANS?
TROUBLE! FOR NOT GOING BACK TO CLASS...
FOR DISRESPECTING A TEACHER AND THE SCHOOL RULES.
SBAM
THE MORNING, WHICH STARTED IN SUCH A CRAZY WAY, SLOWS DOWN...
...AND SEEMS LIKE IT WILL NEVER END!

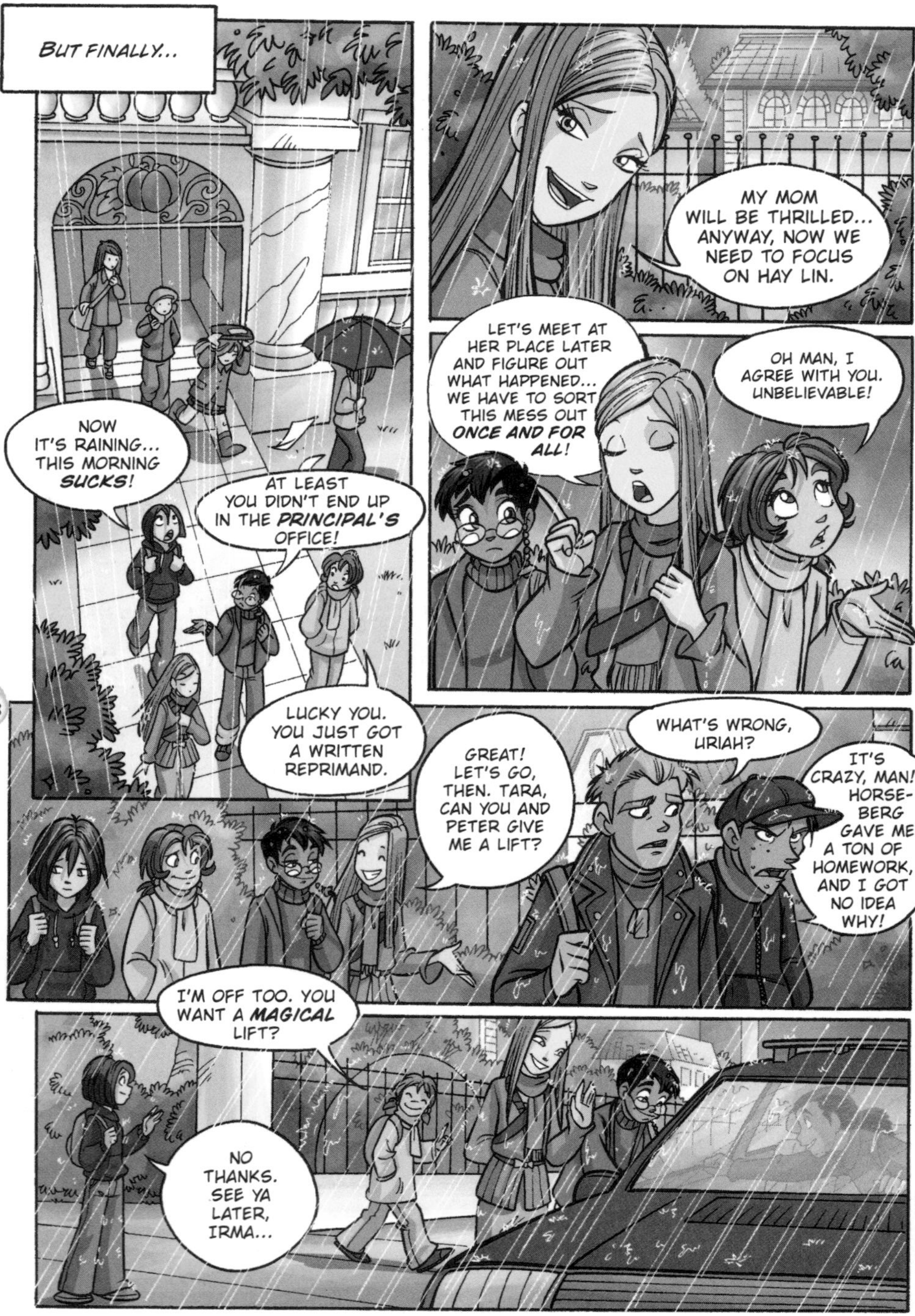
BUT FINALLY...
MY MOM WILL BE THRILLED... ANYWAY, NOW WE NEED TO FOCUS ON HAY LIN.
NOW IT'S RAINING... THIS MORNING SUCKS!
AT LEAST YOU DIDN'T END UP IN THE PRINCIPAL'S OFFICE!
LUCKY YOU. YOU JUST GOT A WRITTEN REPRIMAND.
LET'S MEET AT HER PLACE LATER AND FIGURE OUT WHAT HAPPENED... WE HAVE TO SORT THIS MESS OUT ONCE AND FOR ALL!
OH MAN, I AGREE WITH YOU. UNBELIEVABLE!
GREAT! LET'S GO, THEN. TARA, CAN YOU AND PETER GIVE ME A LIFT?
WHAT'S WRONG, URIAH?
IT'S CRAZY, MAN! HORSEBERG GAVE ME A TON OF HOMEWORK, AND I GOT NO IDEA WHY!
I'M OFF TOO. YOU WANT A MAGICAL LIFT?
NO THANKS. SEE YA LATER, IRMA...

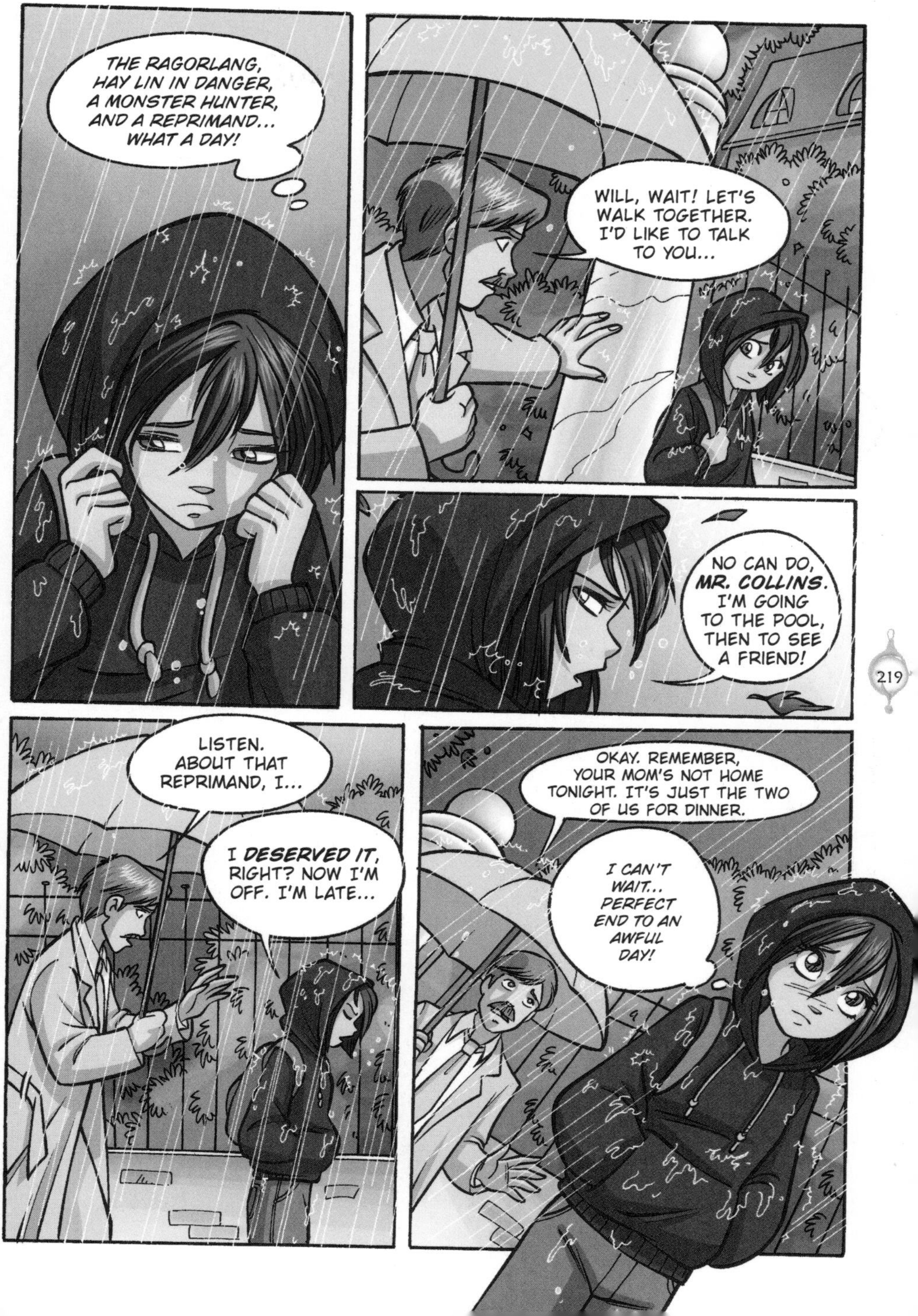
THE RAGORLANG, HAY LIN IN DANGER, A MONSTER HUNTER, AND A REPRIMAND... WHAT A DAY!
WILL, WAIT! LET'S WALK TOGETHER. I'D LIKE TO TALK TO YOU...
NO CAN DO, MR. COLLINS. I'M GOING TO THE POOL, THEN TO SEE A FRIEND!
LISTEN. ABOUT THAT REPRIMAND, I...
I DESERVED IT, RIGHT? NOW I'M OFF. I'M LATE...
OKAY. REMEMBER, YOUR MOM'S NOT HOME TONIGHT. IT'S JUST THE TWO OF US FOR DINNER.
I CAN'T WAIT... PERFECT END TO AN AWFUL DAY!

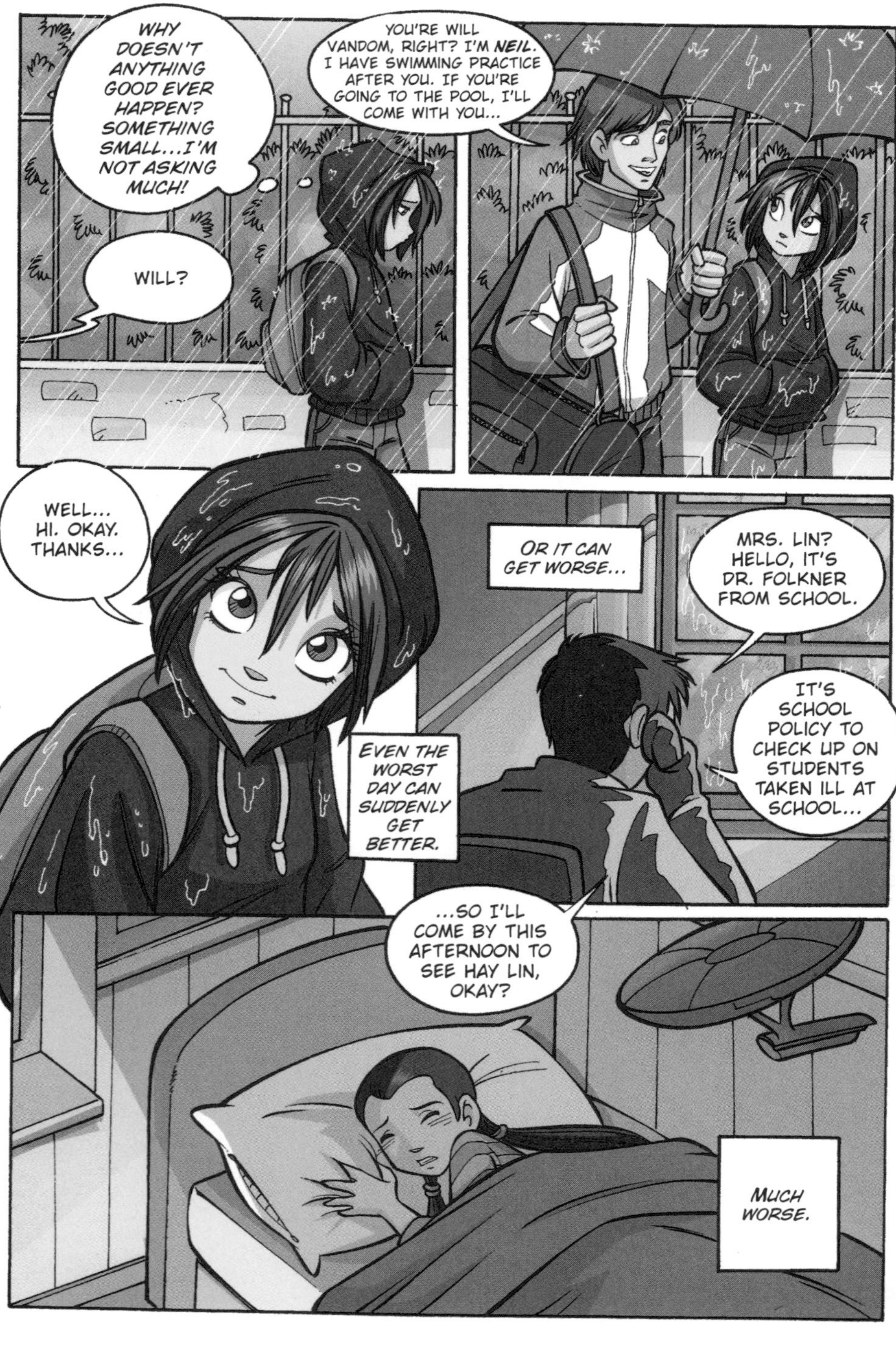
WHY DOESN'T ANYTHING GOOD EVER HAPPEN? SOMETHING SMALL...I'M NOT ASKING MUCH!
WILL?
YOU'RE WILL VANDOM, RIGHT? I'M NEIL. I HAVE SWIMMING PRACTICE AFTER YOU. IF YOU'RE GOING TO THE POOL, I'LL COME WITH YOU...
WELL... HI. OKAY. THANKS...
EVEN THE WORST DAY CAN SUDDENLY GET BETTER.
OR IT CAN GET WORSE...
MRS. LIN? HELLO, IT'S DR. FOLKNER FROM SCHOOL.
IT'S SCHOOL POLICY TO CHECK UP ON STUDENTS TAKEN ILL AT SCHOOL...
...SO I'LL COME BY THIS AFTERNOON TO SEE HAY LIN, OKAY?
MUCH WORSE.

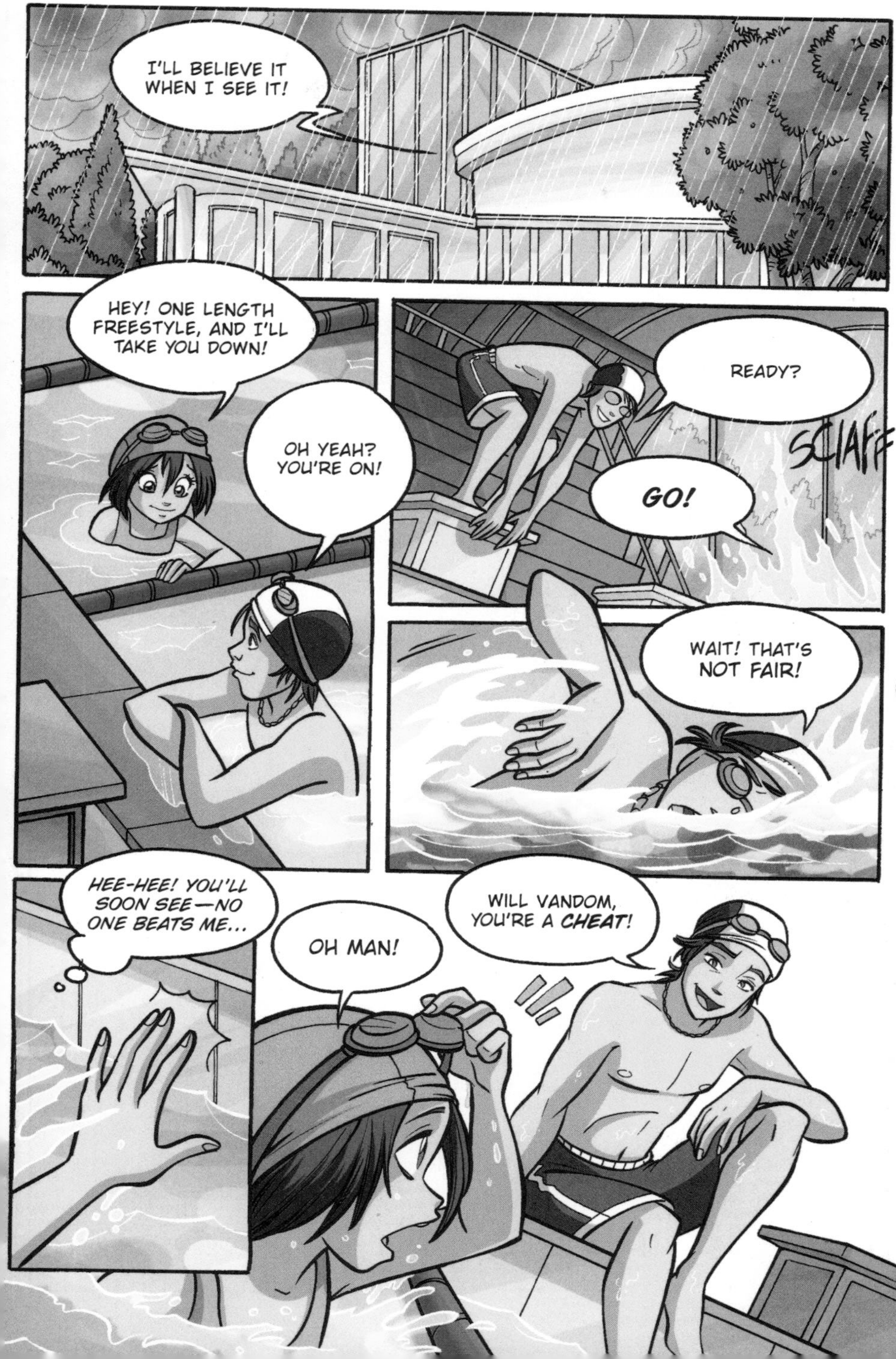
I'LL BELIEVE IT WHEN I SEE IT!
HEY! ONE LENGTH FREESTYLE, AND I'LL TAKE YOU DOWN!
OH YEAH? YOU'RE ON!
READY?
GO!
SCIAFF
WAIT! THAT'S NOT FAIR!
HEE-HEE! YOU'LL SOON SEE—NO ONE BEATS ME...
OH MAN!
WILL VANDOM, YOU'RE A *CHEAT*!

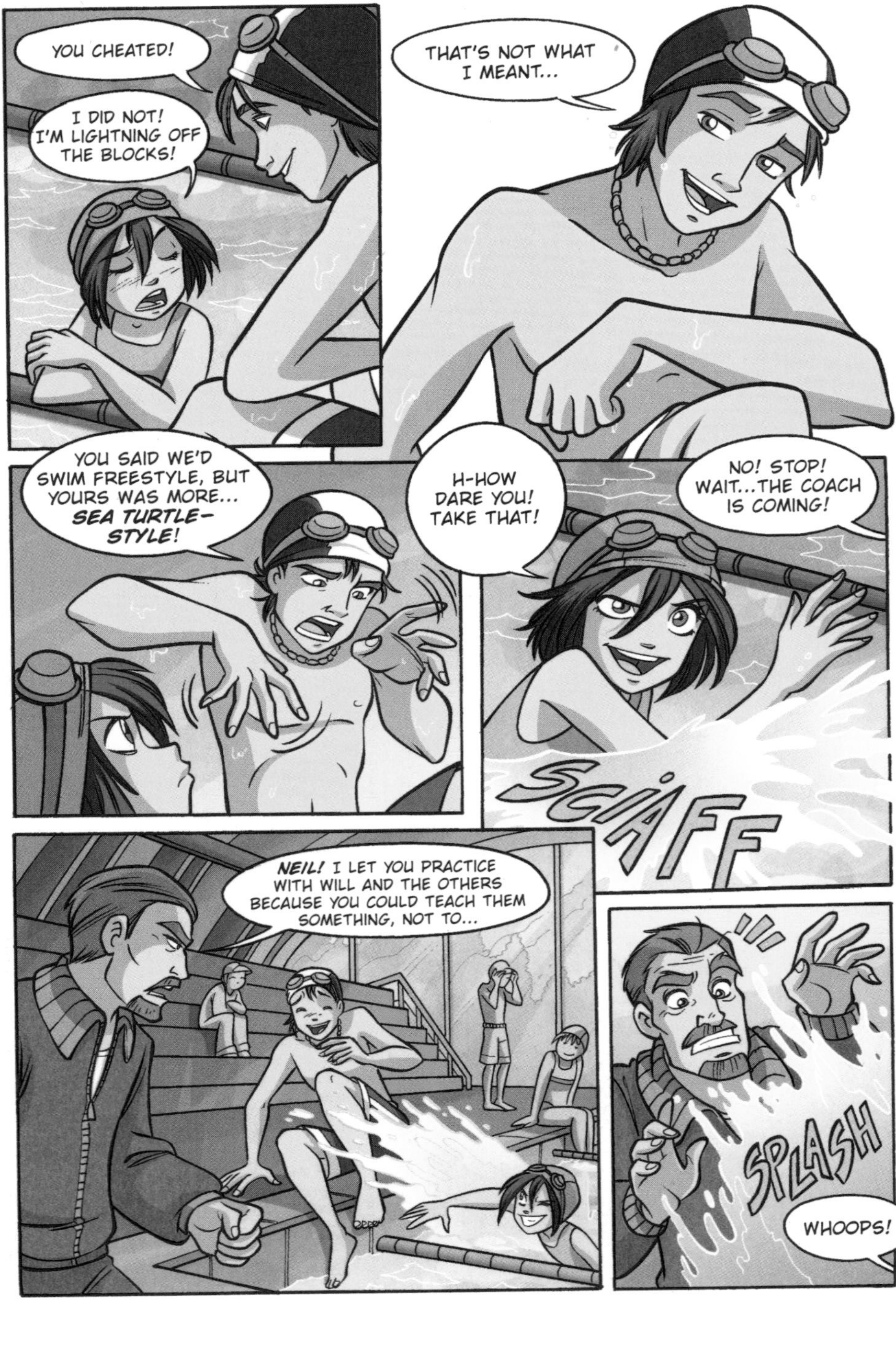
YOU CHEATED!
I DID NOT! I'M LIGHTNING OFF THE BLOCKS!
THAT'S NOT WHAT I MEANT...
YOU SAID WE'D SWIM FREESTYLE, BUT YOURS WAS MORE... *SEA TURTLE-STYLE*!
H-HOW DARE YOU! TAKE THAT!
NO! STOP! WAIT...THE COACH IS COMING!
SCIAFF
NEIL! I LET YOU PRACTICE WITH WILL AND THE OTHERS BECAUSE YOU COULD TEACH THEM SOMETHING, NOT TO...
SPLASH
WHOOPS!

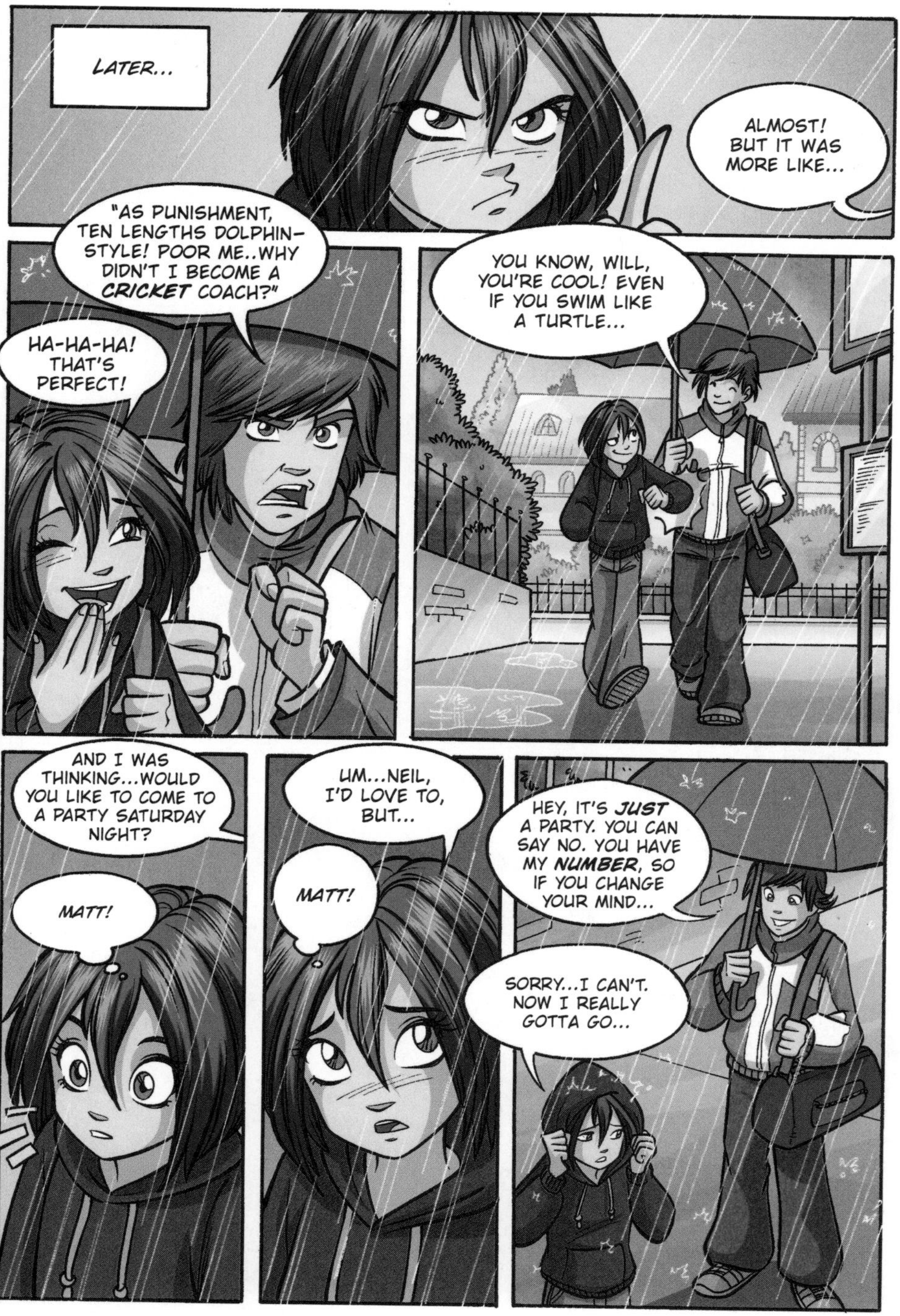
LATER...
ALMOST! BUT IT WAS MORE LIKE...
"AS PUNISHMENT, TEN LENGTHS DOLPHIN-STYLE! POOR ME..WHY DIDN'T I BECOME A CRICKET COACH?"
HA-HA-HA! THAT'S PERFECT!
YOU KNOW, WILL, YOU'RE COOL! EVEN IF YOU SWIM LIKE A TURTLE...
AND I WAS THINKING...WOULD YOU LIKE TO COME TO A PARTY SATURDAY NIGHT?
MATT!
UM...NEIL, I'D LOVE TO, BUT...
MATT!
HEY, IT'S JUST A PARTY. YOU CAN SAY NO. YOU HAVE MY NUMBER, SO IF YOU CHANGE YOUR MIND...
SORRY...I CAN'T. NOW I REALLY GOTTA GO...

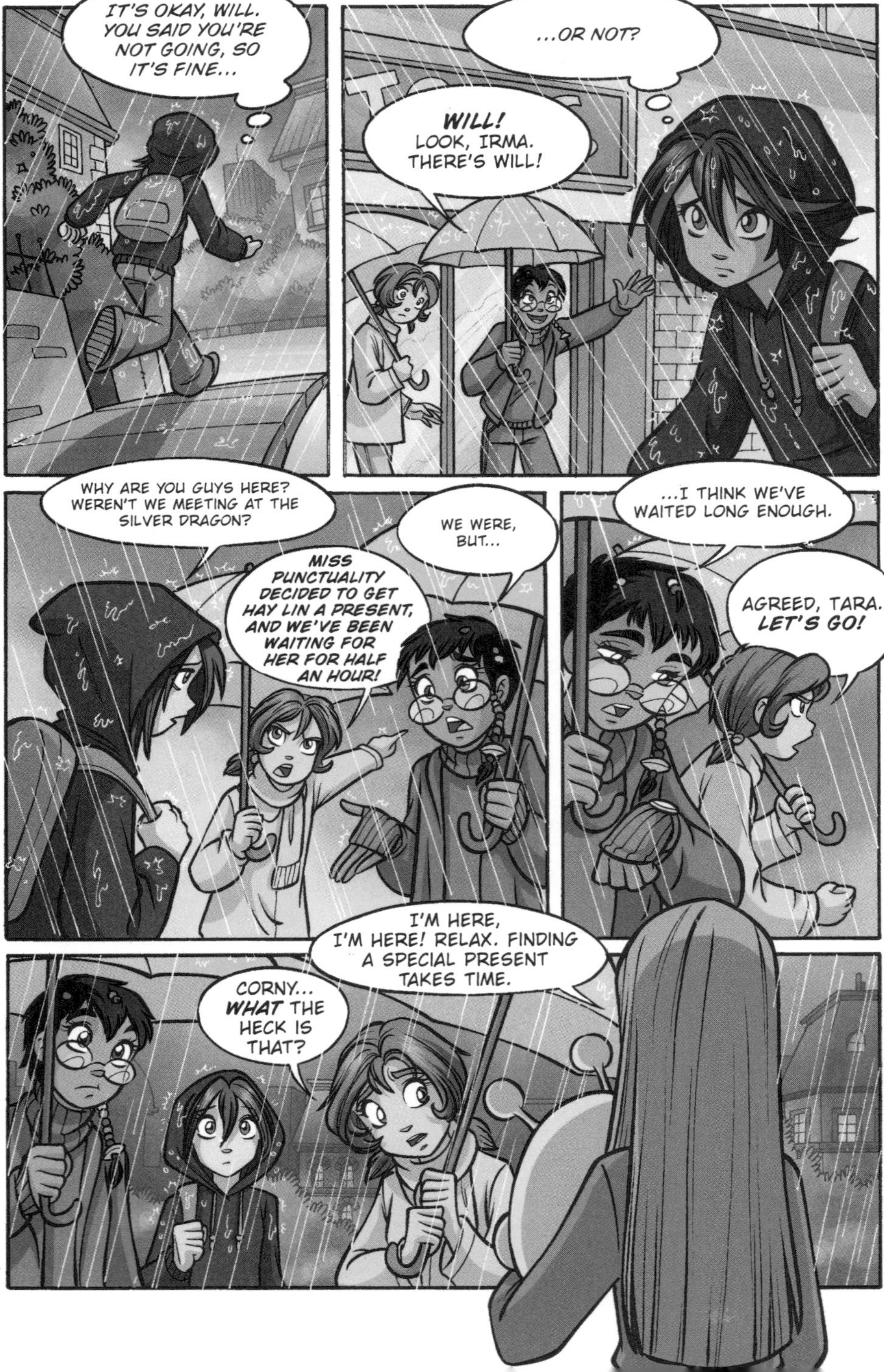
IT'S OKAY, WILL. YOU SAID YOU'RE NOT GOING, SO IT'S FINE...
...OR NOT?
WILL! LOOK, IRMA. THERE'S WILL!
WHY ARE YOU GUYS HERE? WEREN'T WE MEETING AT THE SILVER DRAGON?
WE WERE, BUT...
MISS PUNCTUALITY DECIDED TO GET HAY LIN A PRESENT, AND WE'VE BEEN WAITING FOR HER FOR HALF AN HOUR!
...I THINK WE'VE WAITED LONG ENOUGH.
AGREED, TARA. LET'S GO!
I'M HERE, I'M HERE! RELAX. FINDING A SPECIAL PRESENT TAKES TIME.
CORNY... WHAT THE HECK IS THAT?

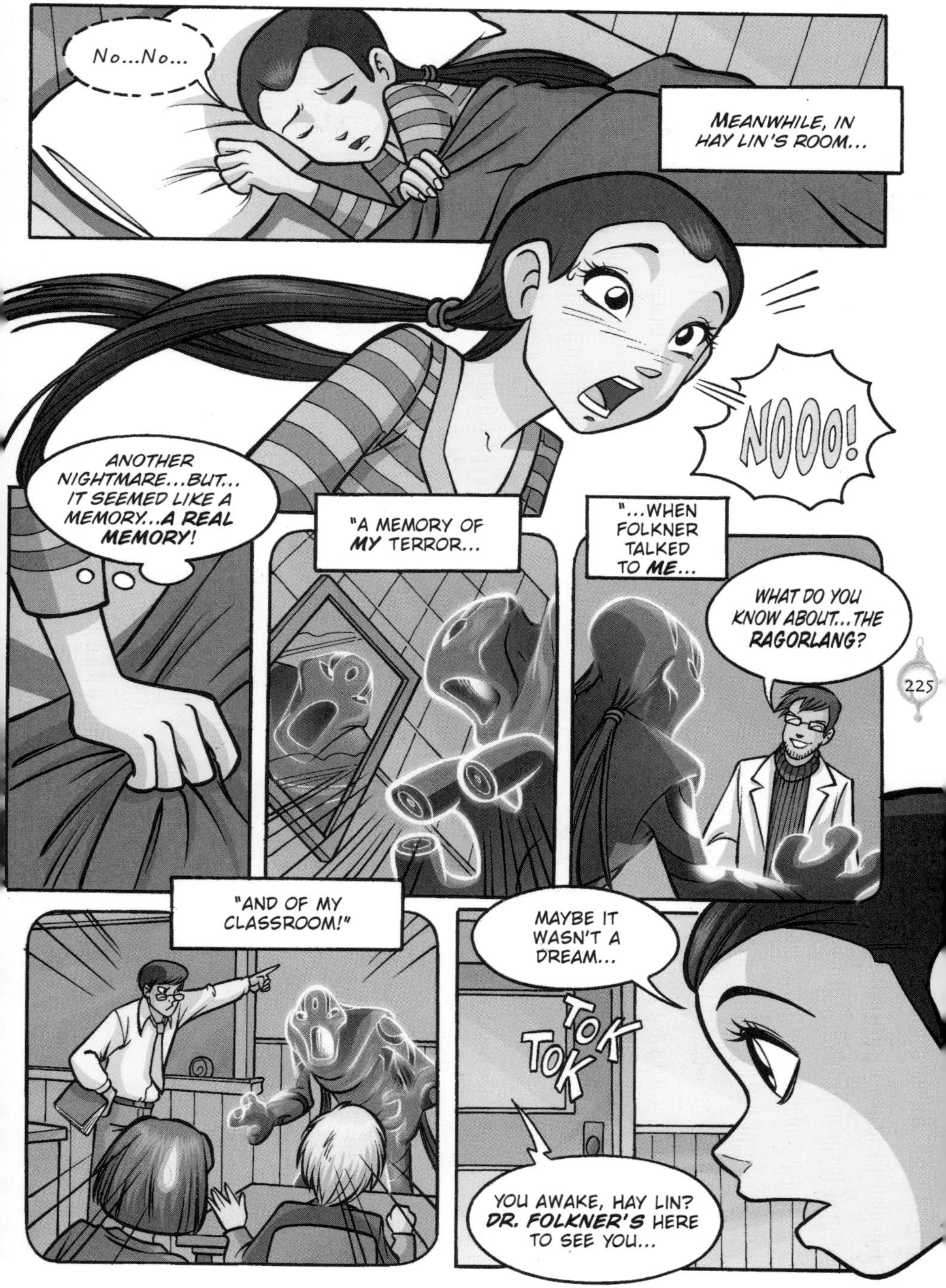
No...No...
MEANWHILE, IN HAY LIN'S ROOM...
NOOO!
ANOTHER NIGHTMARE...BUT... IT SEEMED LIKE A MEMORY...A REAL MEMORY!
"A MEMORY OF MY TERROR...
"...WHEN FOLKNER TALKED TO ME...
WHAT DO YOU KNOW ABOUT...THE RAGORLANG?
"AND OF MY CLASSROOM!"
MAYBE IT WASN'T A DREAM...
TOK TOK
YOU AWAKE, HAY LIN? DR. FOLKNER'S HERE TO SEE YOU...

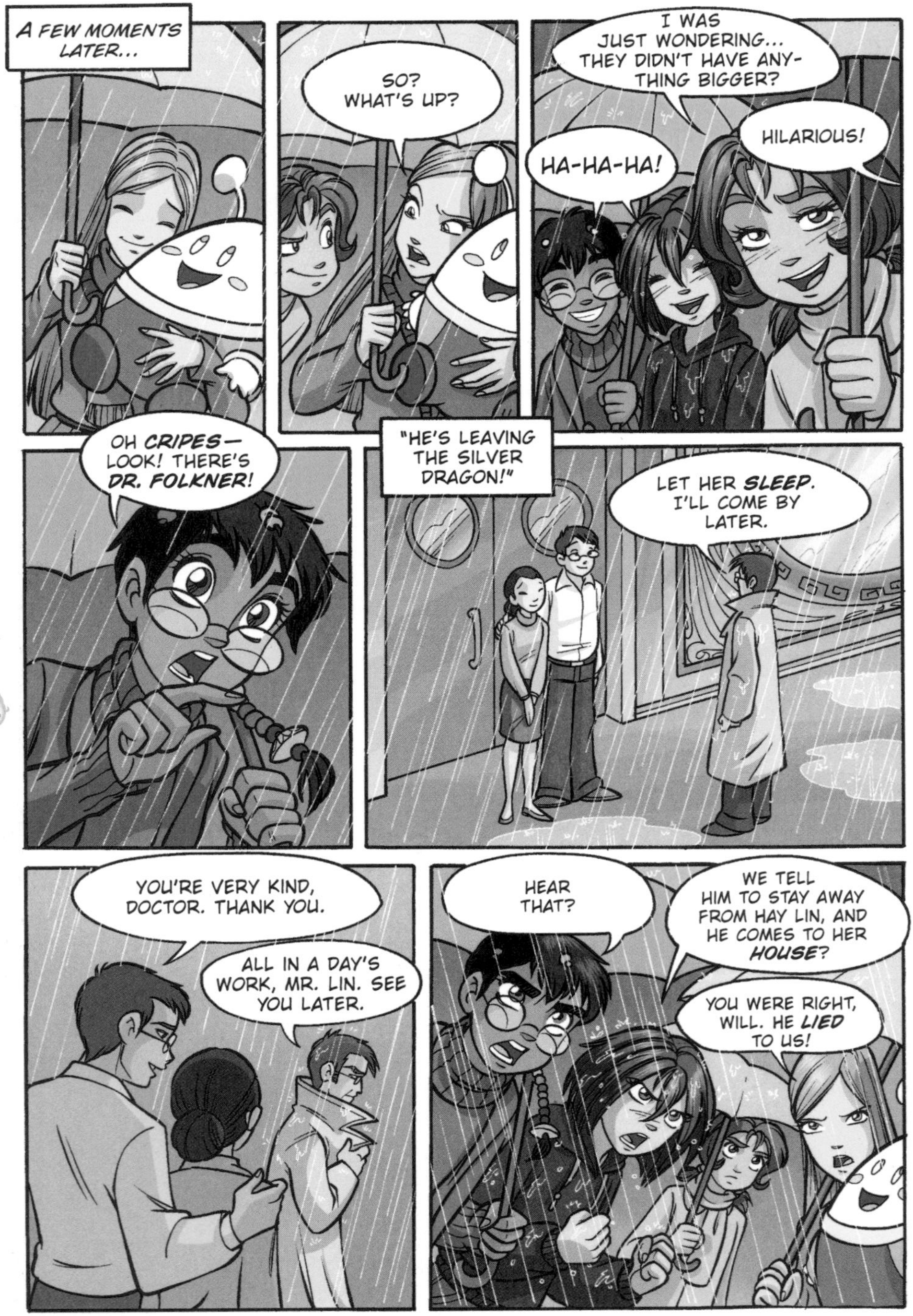
A FEW MOMENTS LATER...
SO? WHAT'S UP?
I WAS JUST WONDERING... THEY DIDN'T HAVE ANY-THING BIGGER?
HA-HA-HA!
HILARIOUS!
OH CRIPES— LOOK! THERE'S DR. FOLKNER!
"HE'S LEAVING THE SILVER DRAGON!"
LET HER SLEEP. I'LL COME BY LATER.
YOU'RE VERY KIND, DOCTOR. THANK YOU.
ALL IN A DAY'S WORK, MR. LIN. SEE YOU LATER.
HEAR THAT?
WE TELL HIM TO STAY AWAY FROM HAY LIN, AND HE COMES TO HER HOUSE?
YOU WERE RIGHT, WILL. HE LIED TO US!

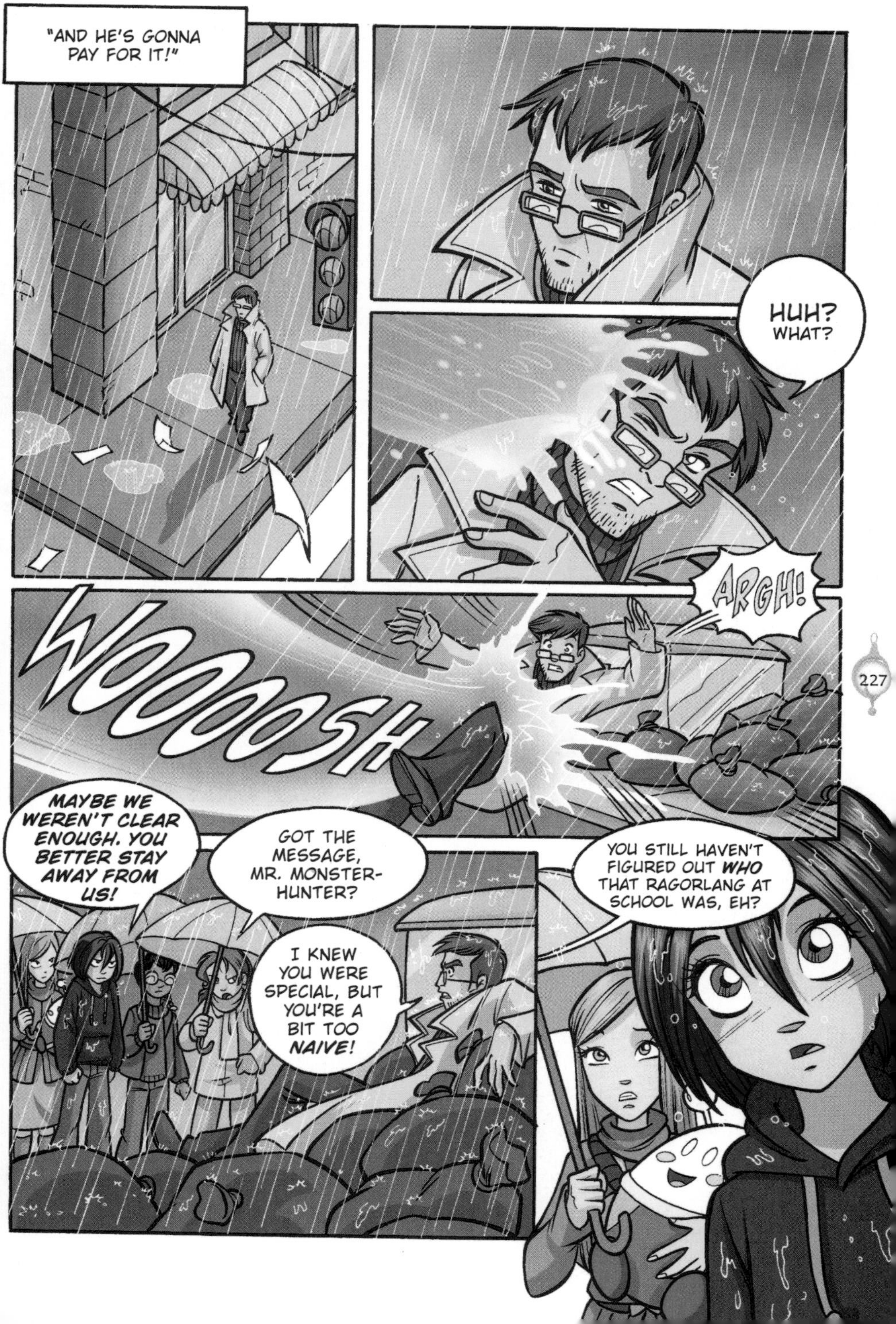
"AND HE'S GONNA PAY FOR IT!"
HUH? WHAT?
WOOOOSH
ARGH!
MAYBE WE WEREN'T CLEAR ENOUGH. YOU BETTER STAY AWAY FROM US!
GOT THE MESSAGE, MR. MONSTER-HUNTER?
I KNEW YOU WERE SPECIAL, BUT YOU'RE A BIT TOO NAIVE!
YOU STILL HAVEN'T FIGURED OUT WHO THAT RAGORLANG AT SCHOOL WAS, EH?

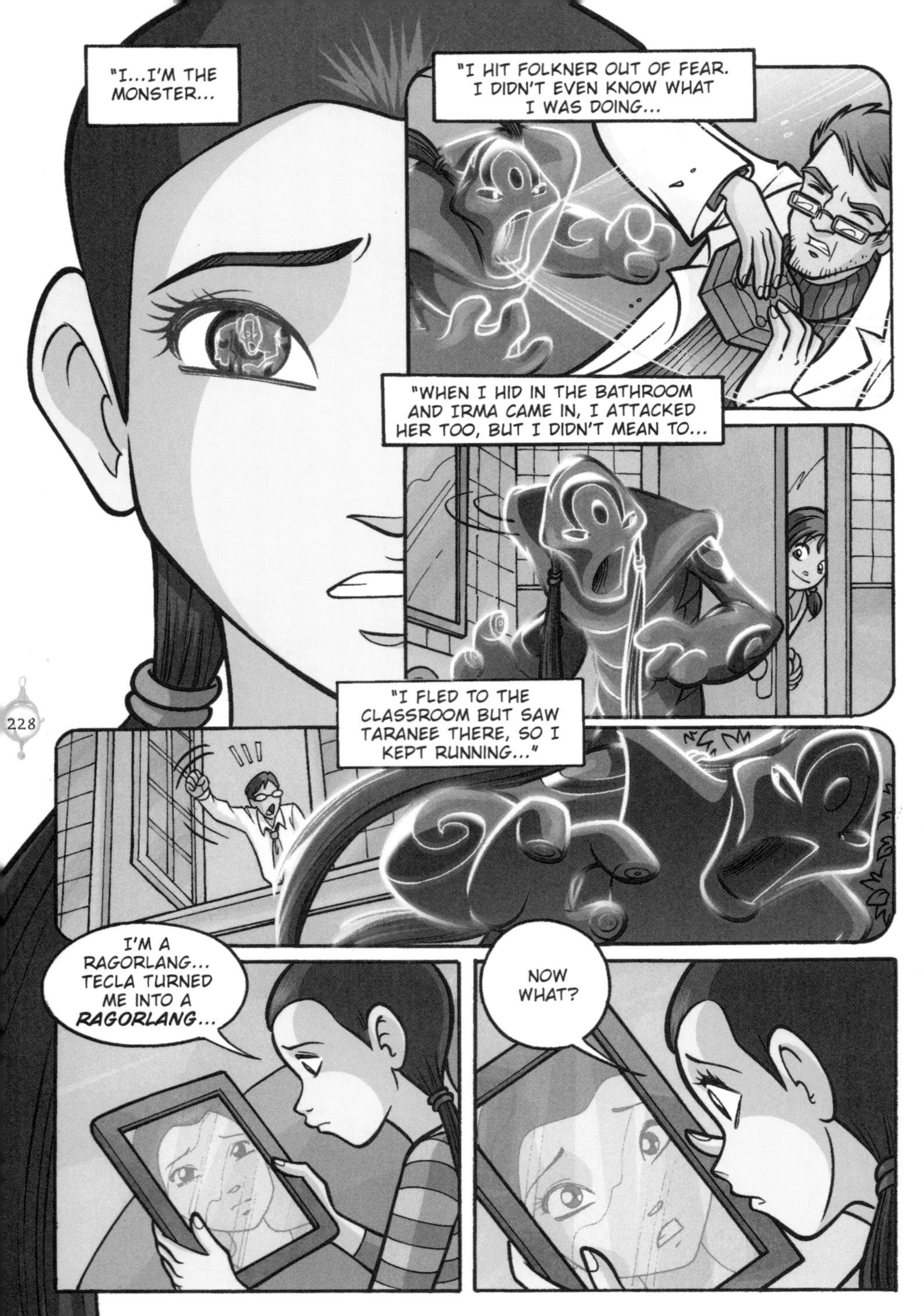
"I...I'M THE MONSTER...
"I HIT FOLKNER OUT OF FEAR. I DIDN'T EVEN KNOW WHAT I WAS DOING...
"WHEN I HID IN THE BATHROOM AND IRMA CAME IN, I ATTACKED HER TOO, BUT I DIDN'T MEAN TO...
"I FLED TO THE CLASSROOM BUT SAW TARANEE THERE, SO I KEPT RUNNING..."
!!!
I'M A RAGORLANG... TECLA TURNED ME INTO A *RAGORLANG*...
NOW WHAT?

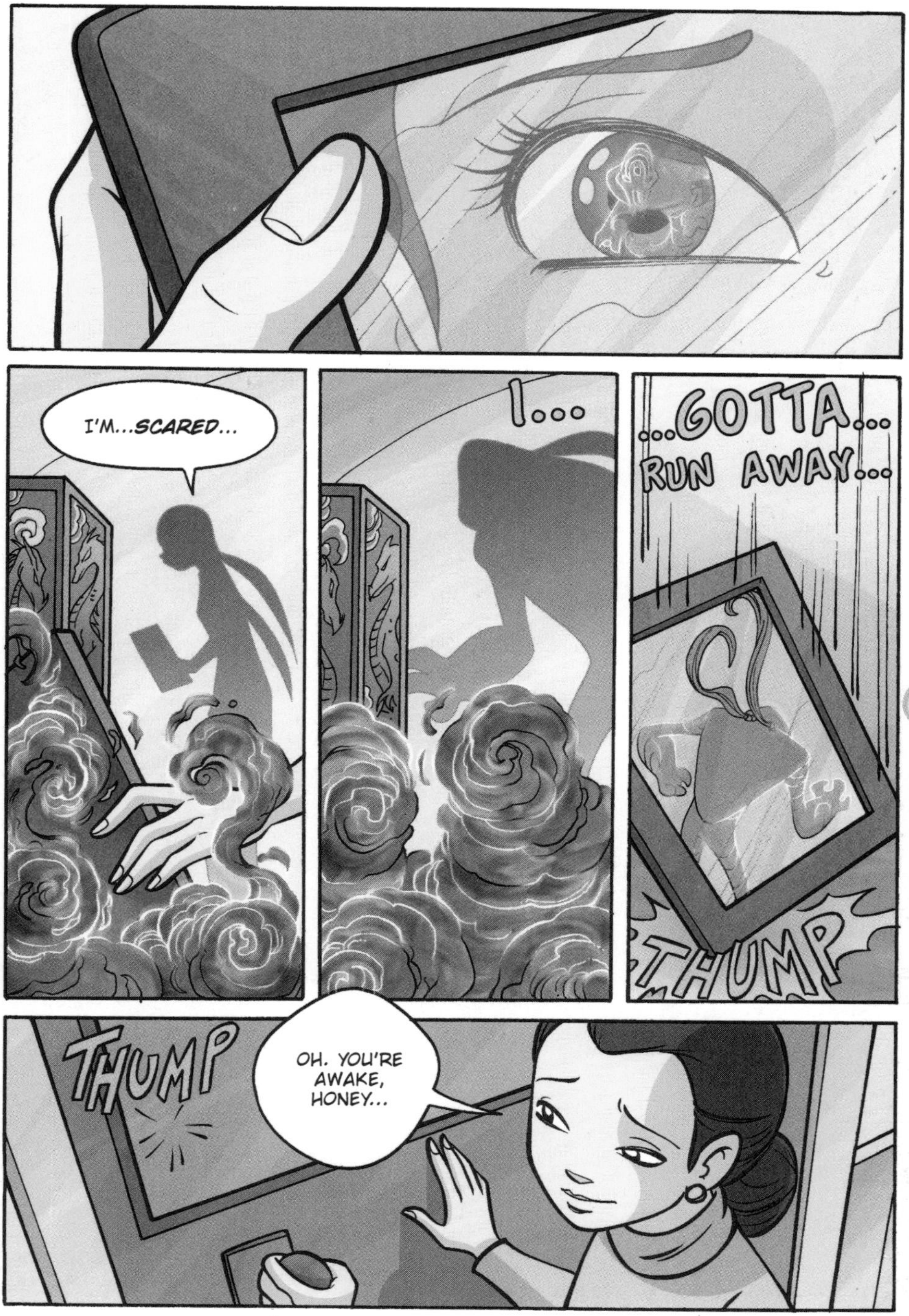

I'M...SCARED...
I...
...GOTTA...
...RUN AWAY...
THUMP
THUMP
OH. YOU'RE AWAKE, HONEY...

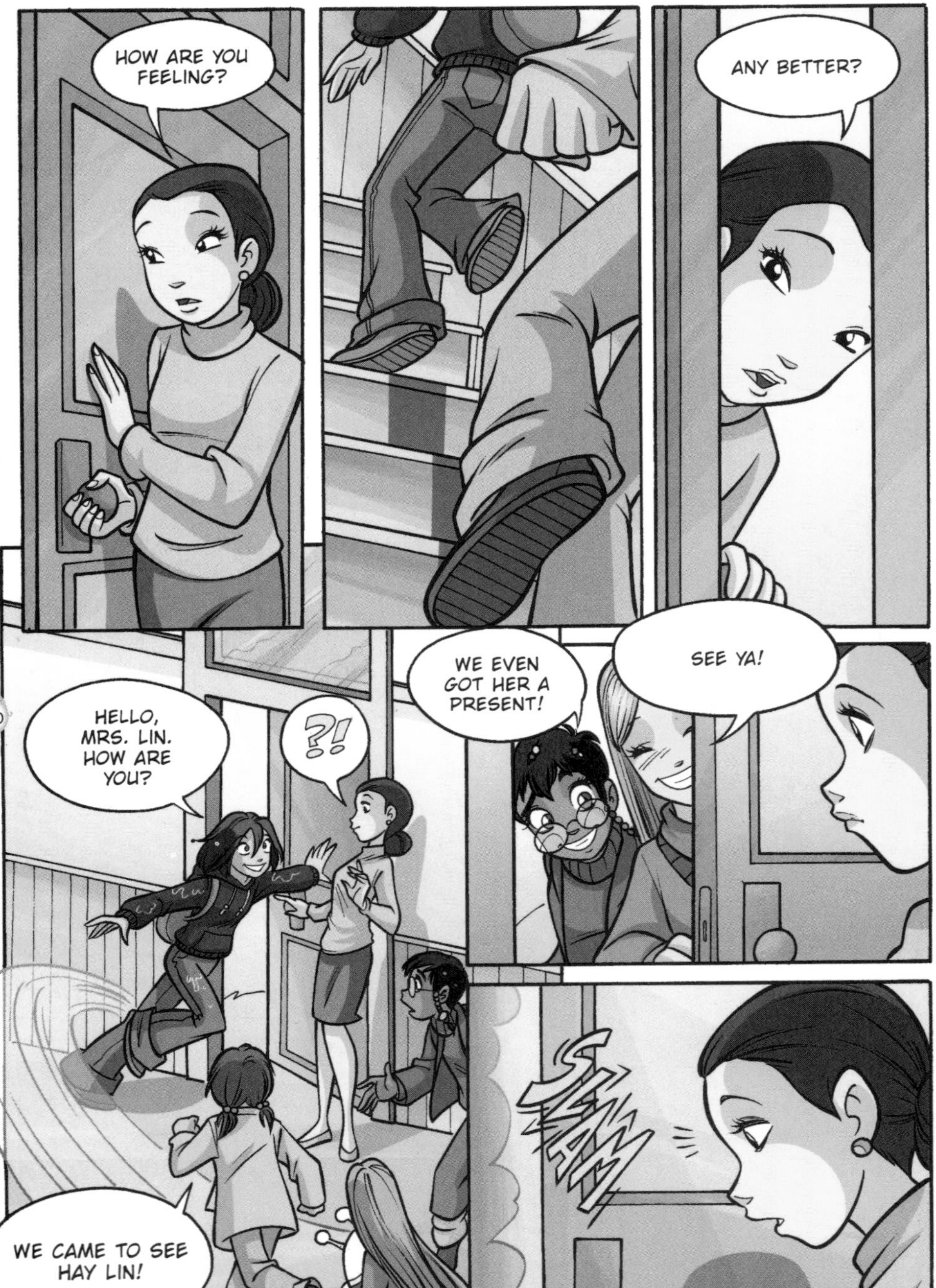
HOW ARE YOU FEELING?
ANY BETTER?
HELLO, MRS. LIN. HOW ARE YOU?
?!
WE EVEN GOT HER A PRESENT!
SEE YA!
WE CAME TO SEE HAY LIN!
SLAM

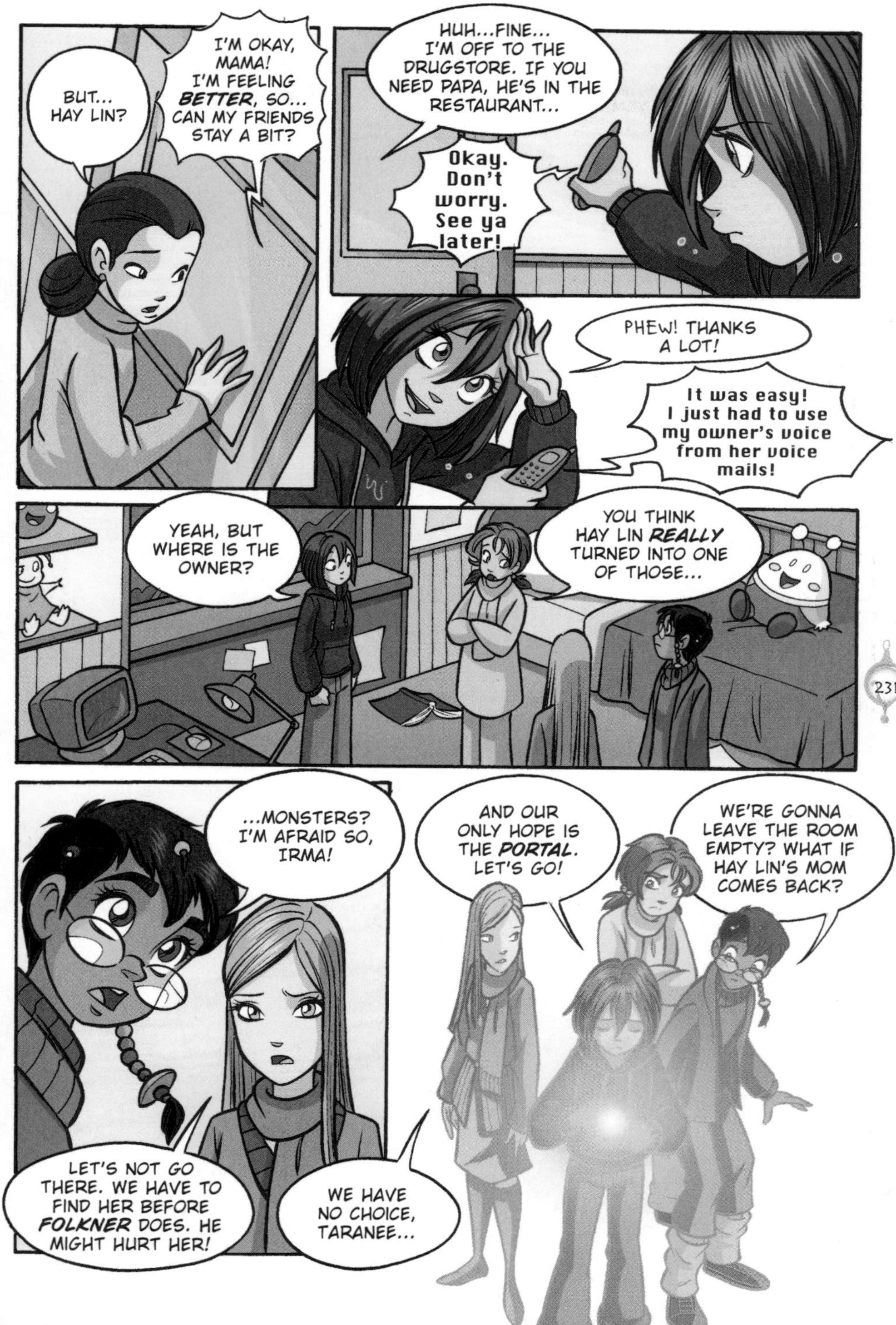

BUT... HAY LIN?
I'M OKAY, MAMA! I'M FEELING BETTER, SO... CAN MY FRIENDS STAY A BIT?
HUH...FINE... I'M OFF TO THE DRUGSTORE. IF YOU NEED PAPA, HE'S IN THE RESTAURANT...
Okay. Don't worry. See ya later!
PHEW! THANKS A LOT!
It was easy! I just had to use my owner's voice from her voice mails!
YEAH, BUT WHERE IS THE OWNER?
YOU THINK HAY LIN REALLY TURNED INTO ONE OF THOSE...
...MONSTERS? I'M AFRAID SO, IRMA!
LET'S NOT GO THERE. WE HAVE TO FIND HER BEFORE FOLKNER DOES. HE MIGHT HURT HER!
WE HAVE NO CHOICE, TARANEE...
AND OUR ONLY HOPE IS THE PORTAL. LET'S GO!
WE'RE GONNA LEAVE THE ROOM EMPTY? WHAT IF HAY LIN'S MOM COMES BACK?

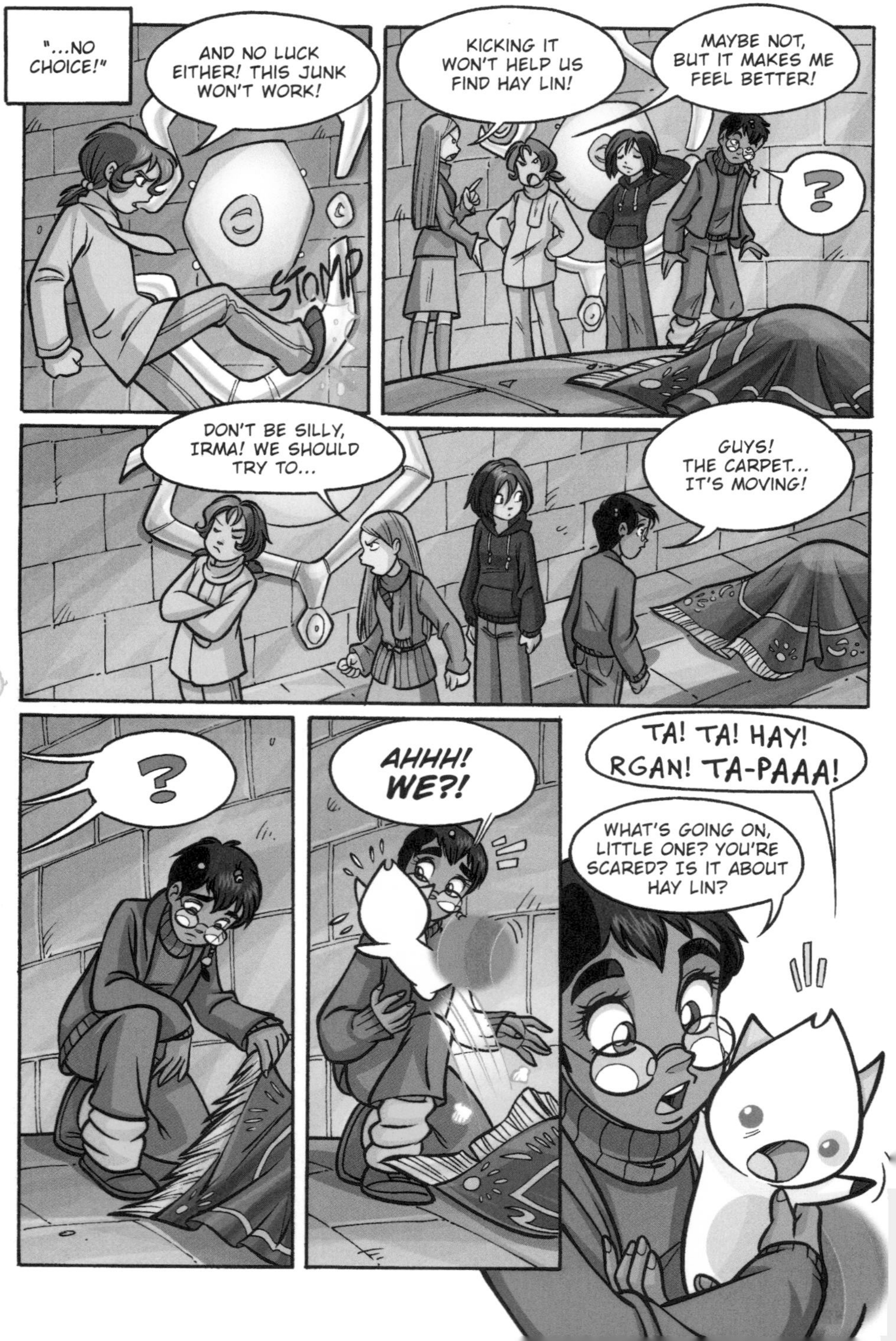
"...NO CHOICE!"
AND NO LUCK EITHER! THIS JUNK WON'T WORK!
STOMP
KICKING IT WON'T HELP US FIND HAY LIN!
MAYBE NOT, BUT IT MAKES ME FEEL BETTER!
?
DON'T BE SILLY, IRMA! WE SHOULD TRY TO...
GUYS! THE CARPET... IT'S MOVING!
?
AHHH! WE?!
TA! TA! HAY! RGAN! TA-PAAA!
WHAT'S GOING ON, LITTLE ONE? YOU'RE SCARED? IS IT ABOUT HAY LIN?

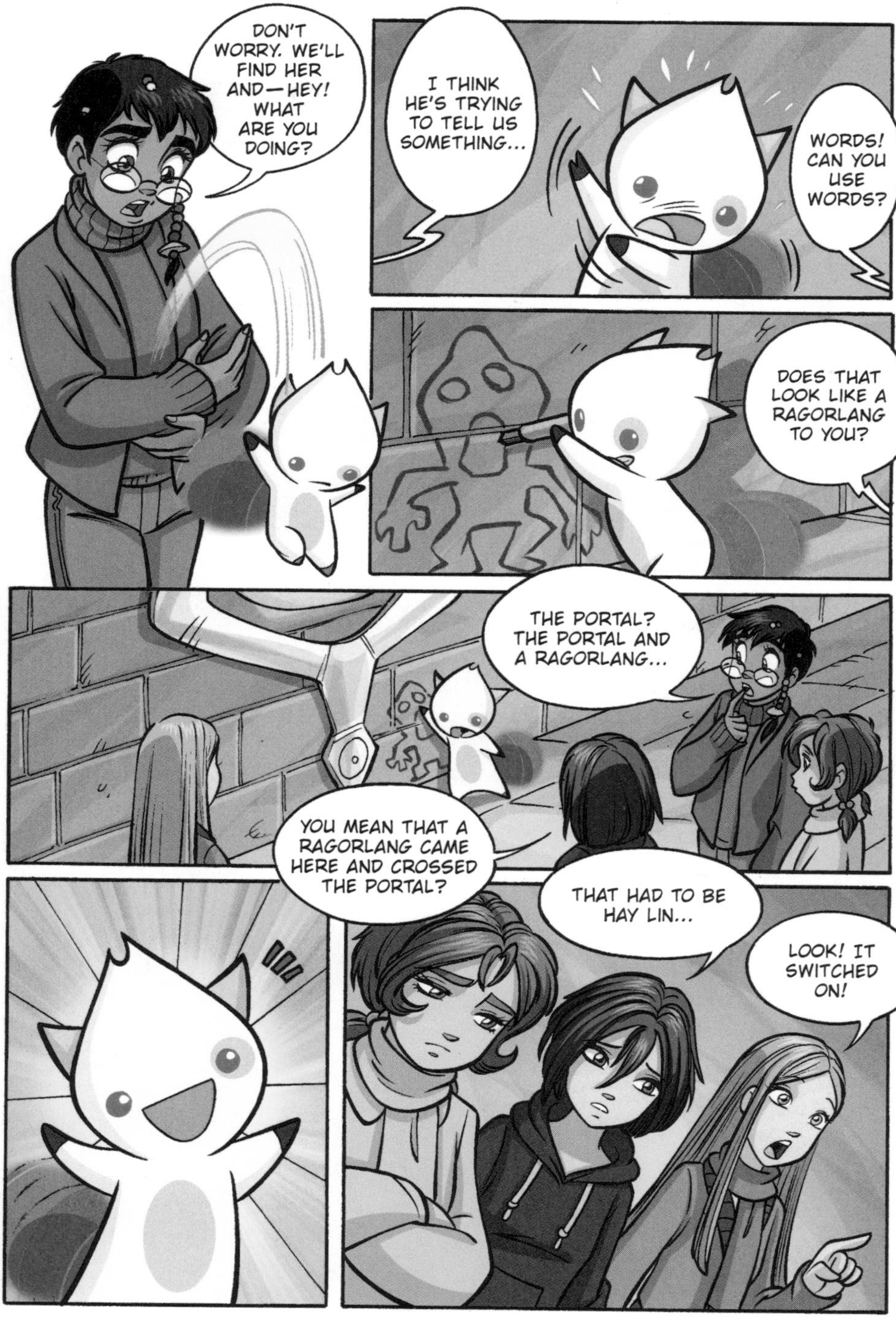
DON'T WORRY. WE'LL FIND HER AND—HEY! WHAT ARE YOU DOING?
I THINK HE'S TRYING TO TELL US SOMETHING...
WORDS! CAN YOU USE WORDS?
DOES THAT LOOK LIKE A RAGORLANG TO YOU?
THE PORTAL? THE PORTAL AND A RAGORLANG...
YOU MEAN THAT A RAGORLANG CAME HERE AND CROSSED THE PORTAL?
THAT HAD TO BE HAY LIN...
LOOK! IT SWITCHED ON!

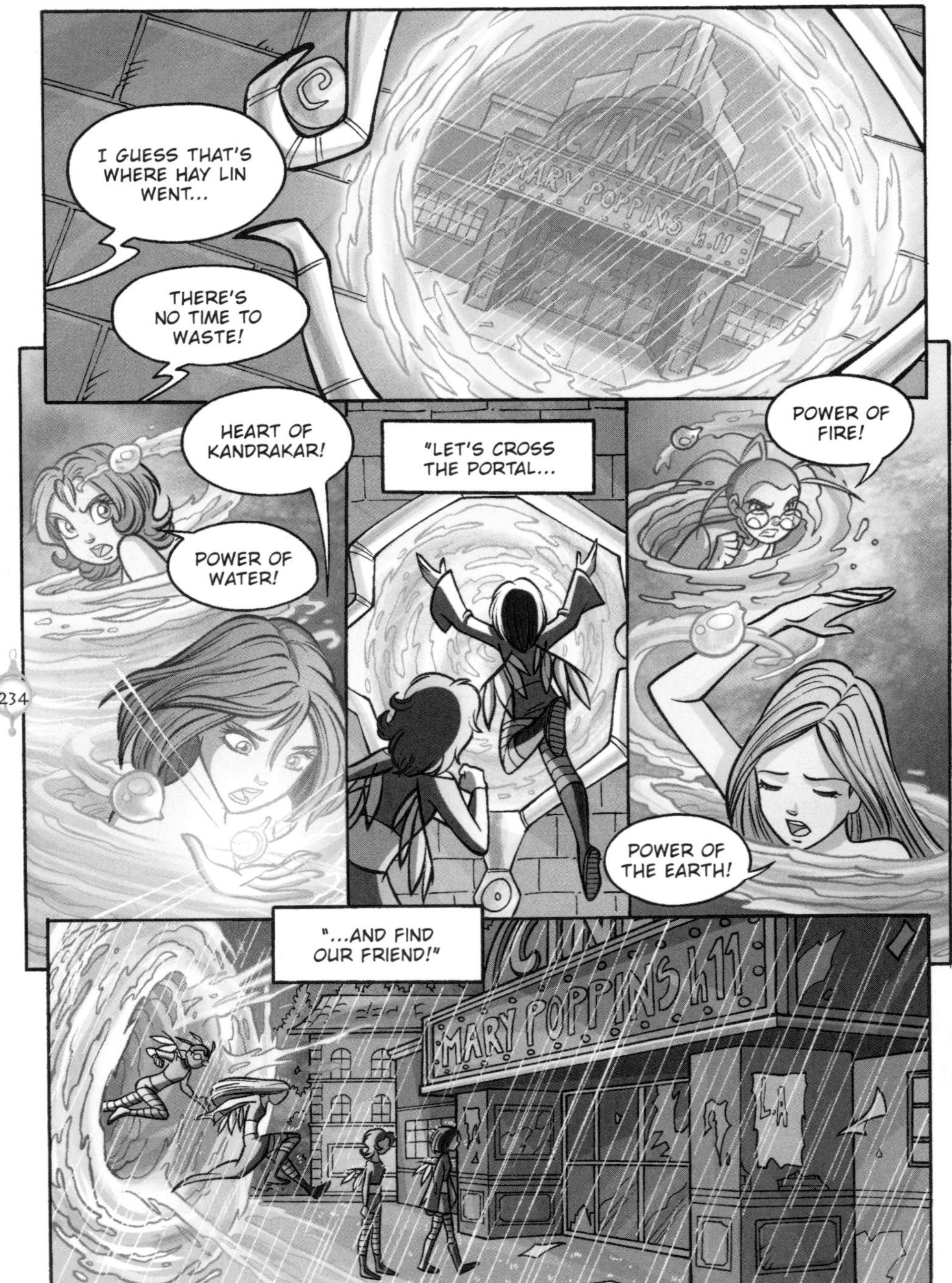
I GUESS THAT'S WHERE HAY LIN WENT...
THERE'S NO TIME TO WASTE!
CINEMA
MARY POPPINS h.11
HEART OF KANDRAKAR!
POWER OF WATER!
"LET'S CROSS THE PORTAL...
POWER OF FIRE!
POWER OF THE EARTH!
"...AND FIND OUR FRIEND!"
MARY POPPINS h11

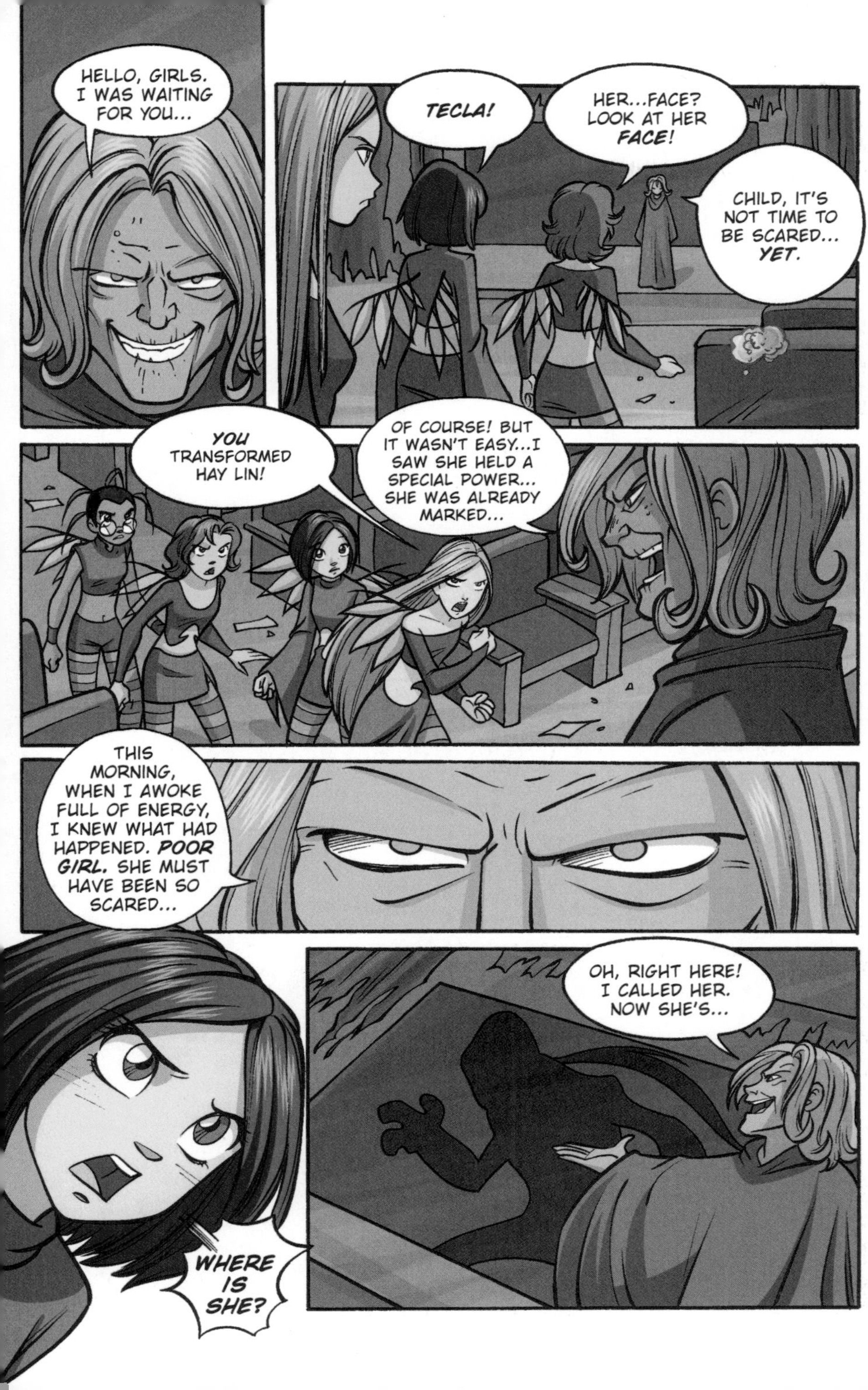
HELLO, GIRLS. I WAS WAITING FOR YOU...
TECLA!
HER...FACE? LOOK AT HER FACE!
CHILD, IT'S NOT TIME TO BE SCARED... YET.
YOU TRANSFORMED HAY LIN!
OF COURSE! BUT IT WASN'T EASY...I SAW SHE HELD A SPECIAL POWER... SHE WAS ALREADY MARKED...
THIS MORNING, WHEN I AWOKE FULL OF ENERGY, I KNEW WHAT HAD HAPPENED. POOR GIRL. SHE MUST HAVE BEEN SO SCARED...
WHERE IS SHE?
OH, RIGHT HERE! I CALLED HER. NOW SHE'S...

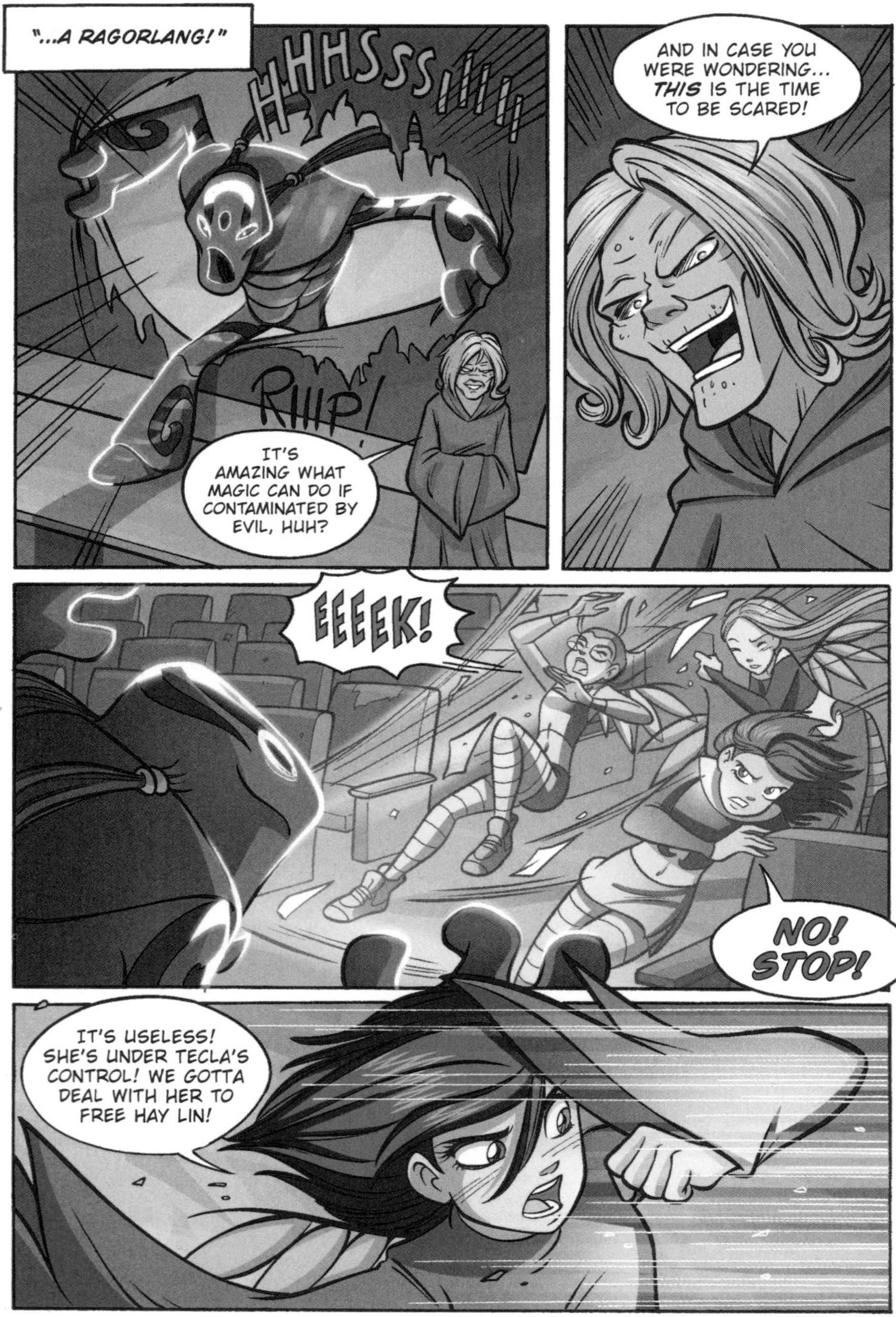

"...A RAGORLANG!"
HHHSSSIIIII
RIIIP!
IT'S AMAZING WHAT MAGIC CAN DO IF CONTAMINATED BY EVIL, HUH?
AND IN CASE YOU WERE WONDERING... *THIS* IS THE TIME TO BE SCARED!
EEEEK!
NO! STOP!
IT'S USELESS! SHE'S UNDER TECLA'S CONTROL! WE GOTTA DEAL WITH HER TO FREE HAY LIN!

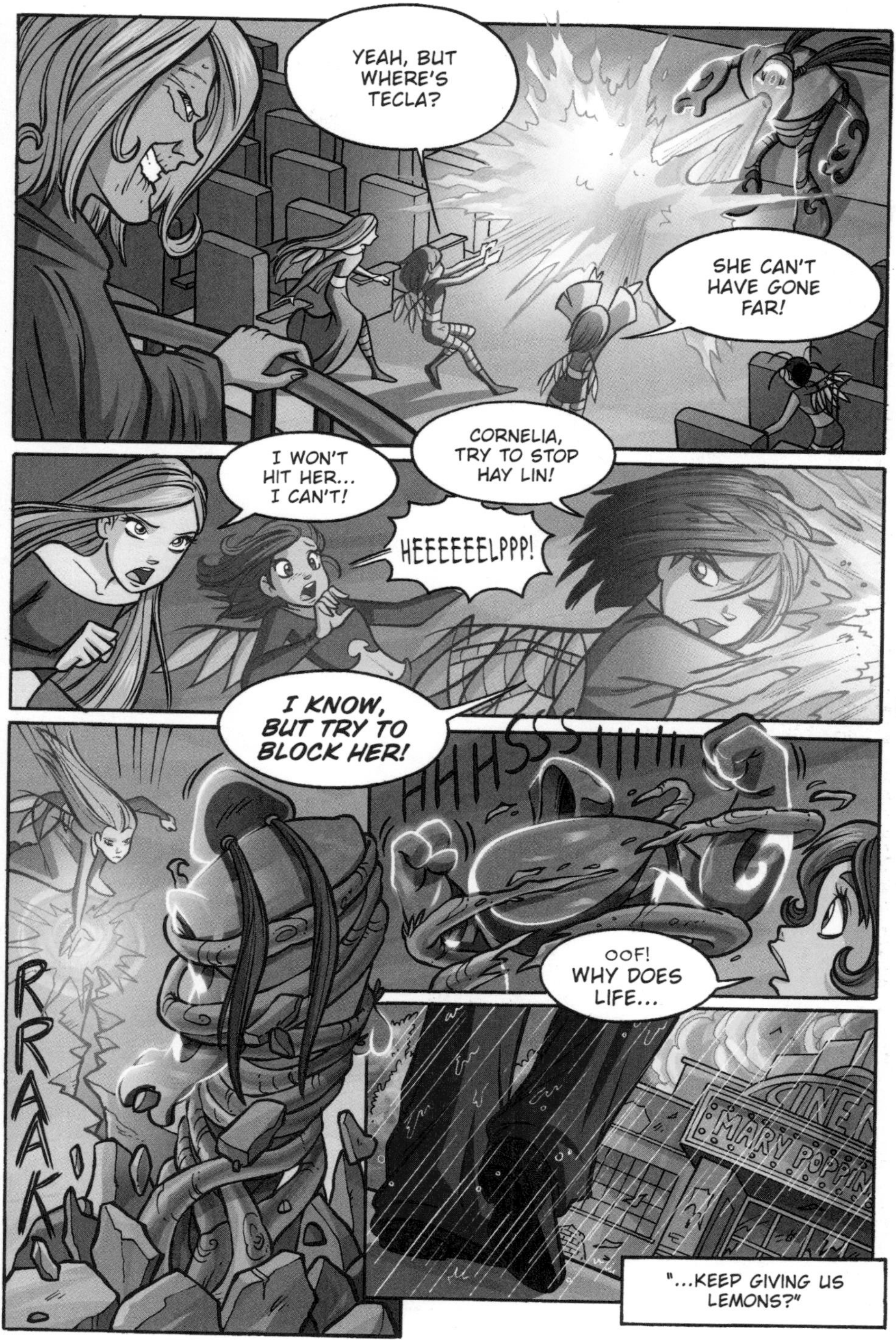
YEAH, BUT WHERE'S TECLA?
SHE CAN'T HAVE GONE FAR!
I WON'T HIT HER... I CAN'T!
CORNELIA, TRY TO STOP HAY LIN!
HEEEEEEELPPP!
I KNOW, BUT TRY TO BLOCK HER!
HHHSSSHHHH
RRAAK
OOF! WHY DOES LIFE...
CINEMA
MARY POPPINS
"...KEEP GIVING US LEMONS?"

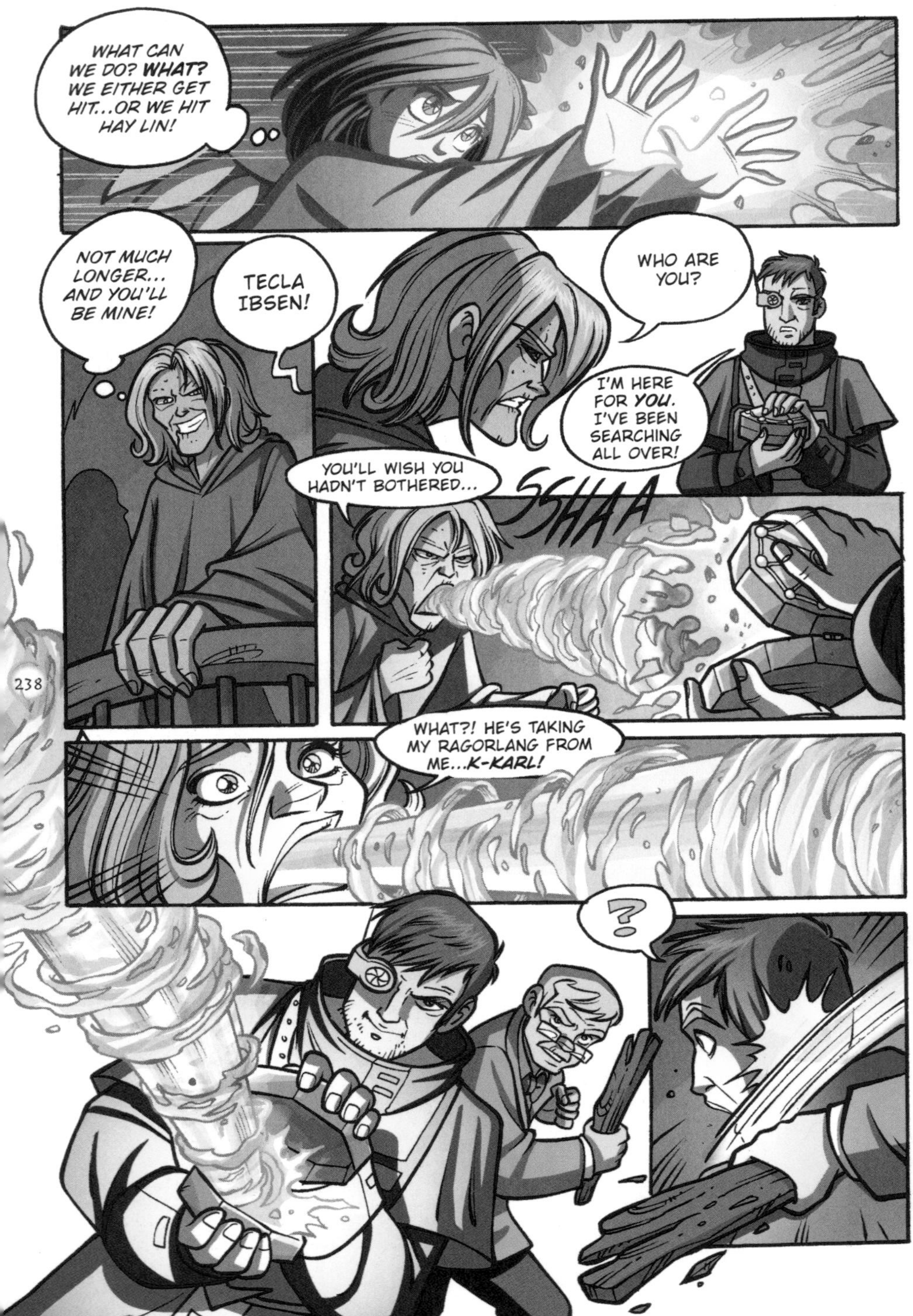
WHAT CAN WE DO? WHAT? WE EITHER GET HIT...OR WE HIT HAY LIN!
NOT MUCH LONGER... AND YOU'LL BE MINE!
TECLA IBSEN!
WHO ARE YOU?
I'M HERE FOR YOU. I'VE BEEN SEARCHING ALL OVER!
YOU'LL WISH YOU HADN'T BOTHERED...
SSHAA
WHAT?! HE'S TAKING MY RAGORLANG FROM ME...K-KARL!
?

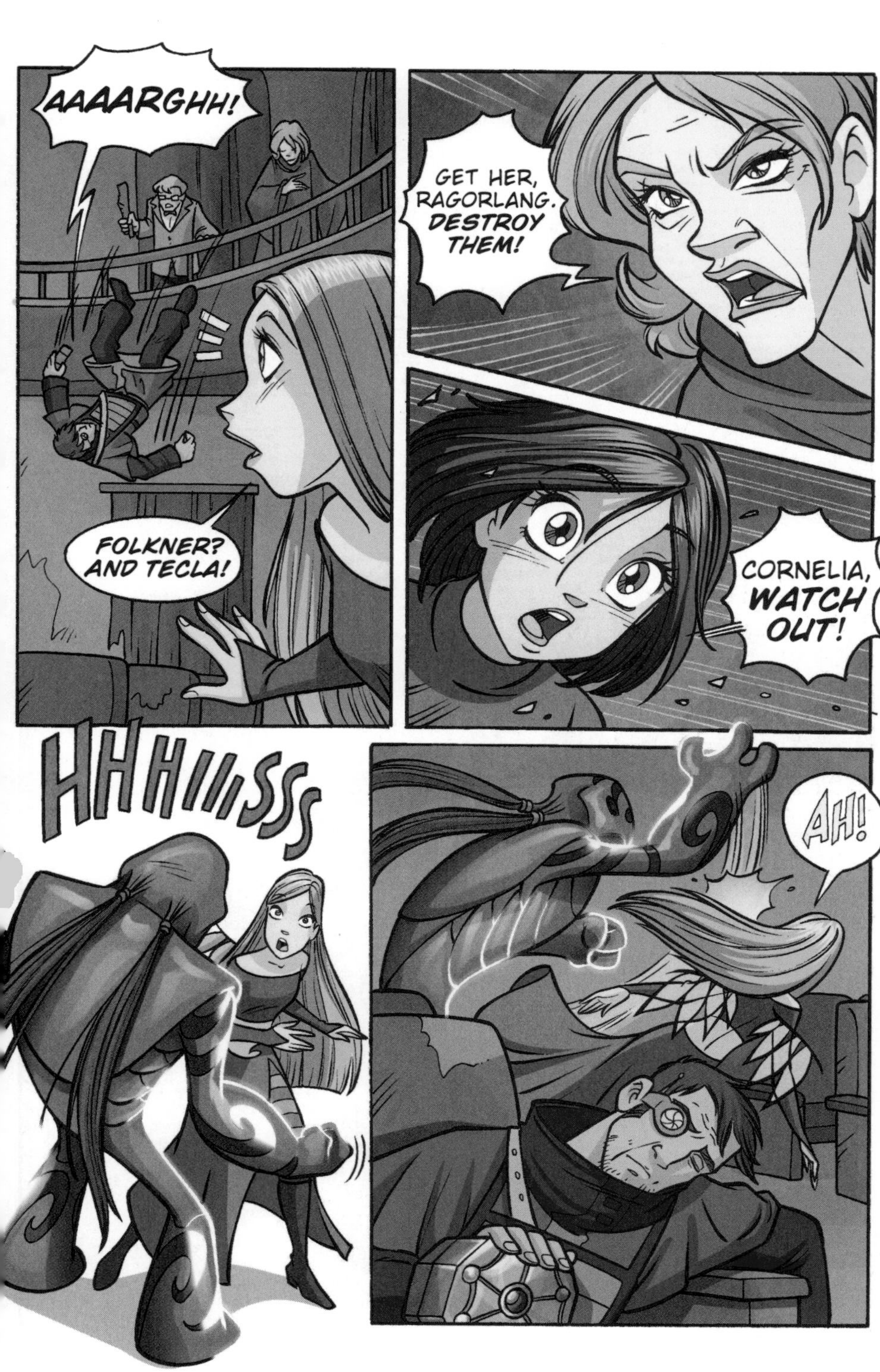
AAAARGHH!
FOLKNER? AND TECLA!
GET HER, RAGORLANG. DESTROY THEM!
CORNELIA, WATCH OUT!
HHHIIISSS
AH!

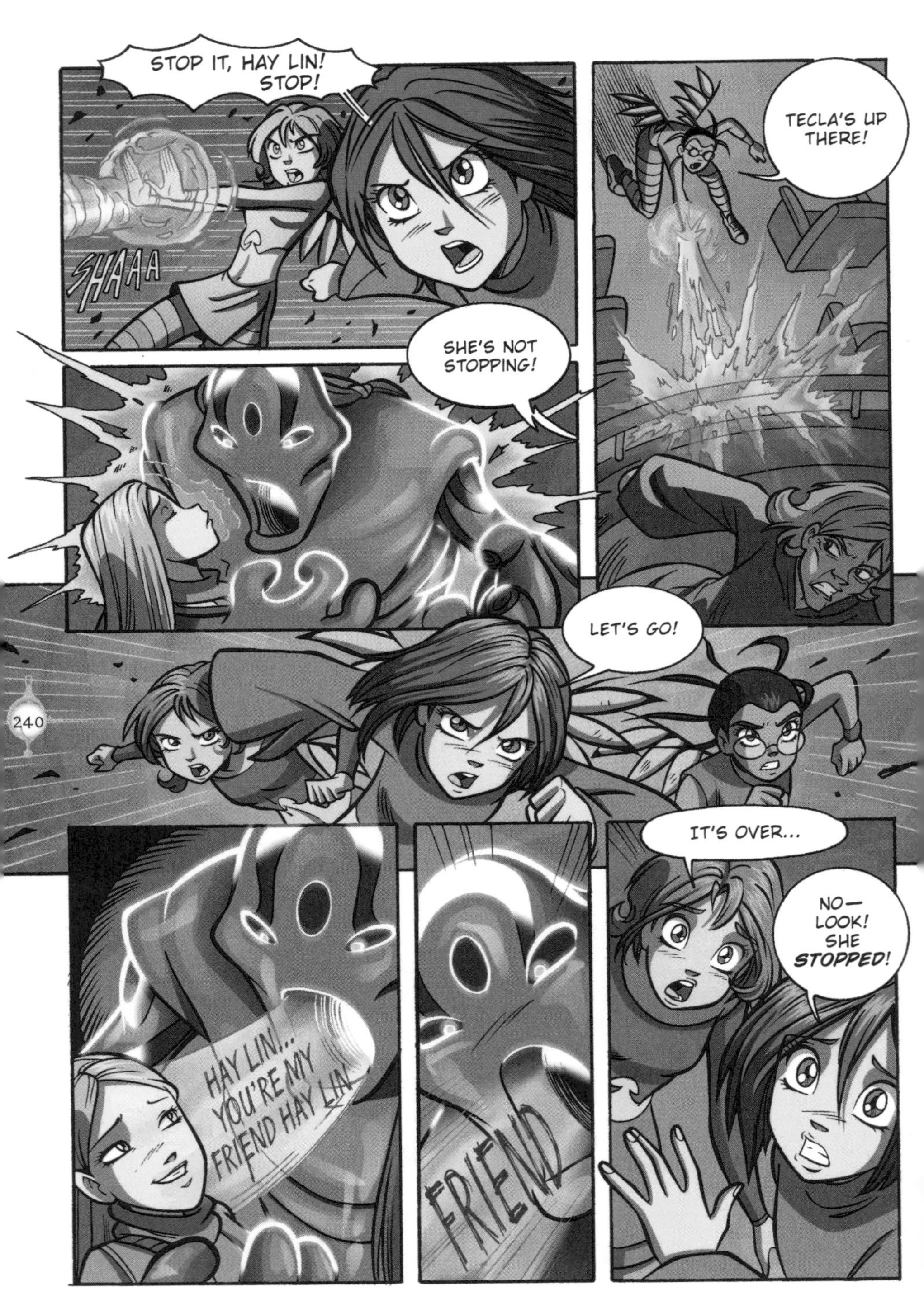
STOP IT, HAY LIN! STOP!
SHAAA
TECLA'S UP THERE!
SHE'S NOT STOPPING!
LET'S GO!
IT'S OVER...
NO— LOOK! SHE STOPPED!
HAY LIN... YOU'RE MY FRIEND HAY LIN
FRIEND

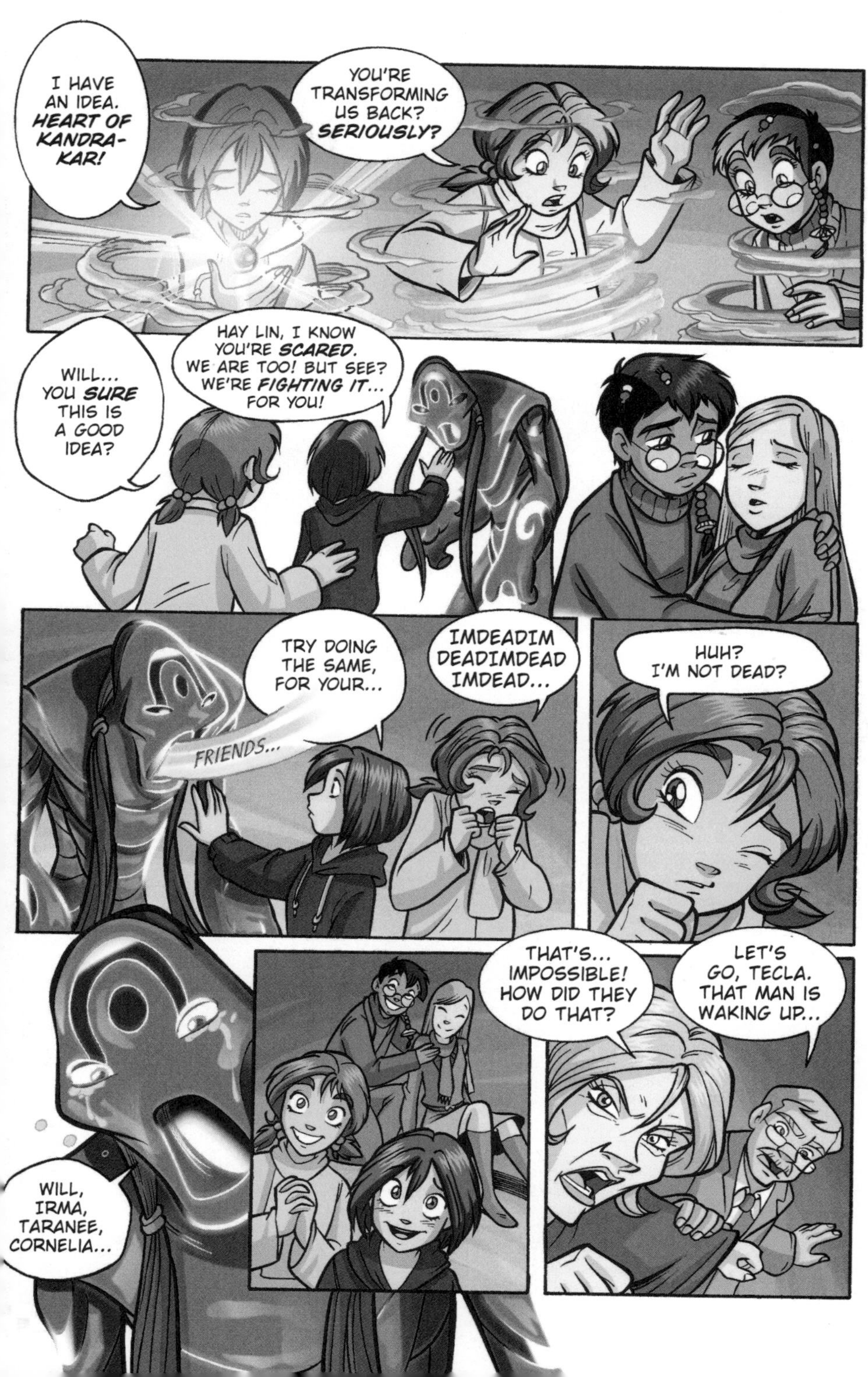
I HAVE AN IDEA. HEART OF KANDRA-KAR!
YOU'RE TRANSFORMING US BACK? SERIOUSLY?
WILL... YOU SURE THIS IS A GOOD IDEA?
HAY LIN, I KNOW YOU'RE SCARED. WE ARE TOO! BUT SEE? WE'RE FIGHTING IT... FOR YOU!
TRY DOING THE SAME, FOR YOUR...
FRIENDS...
IMDEADIM DEADIMDEAD IMDEAD...
HUH? I'M NOT DEAD?
WILL, IRMA, TARANEE, CORNELIA...
THAT'S... IMPOSSIBLE! HOW DID THEY DO THAT?
LET'S GO, TECLA. THAT MAN IS WAKING UP...

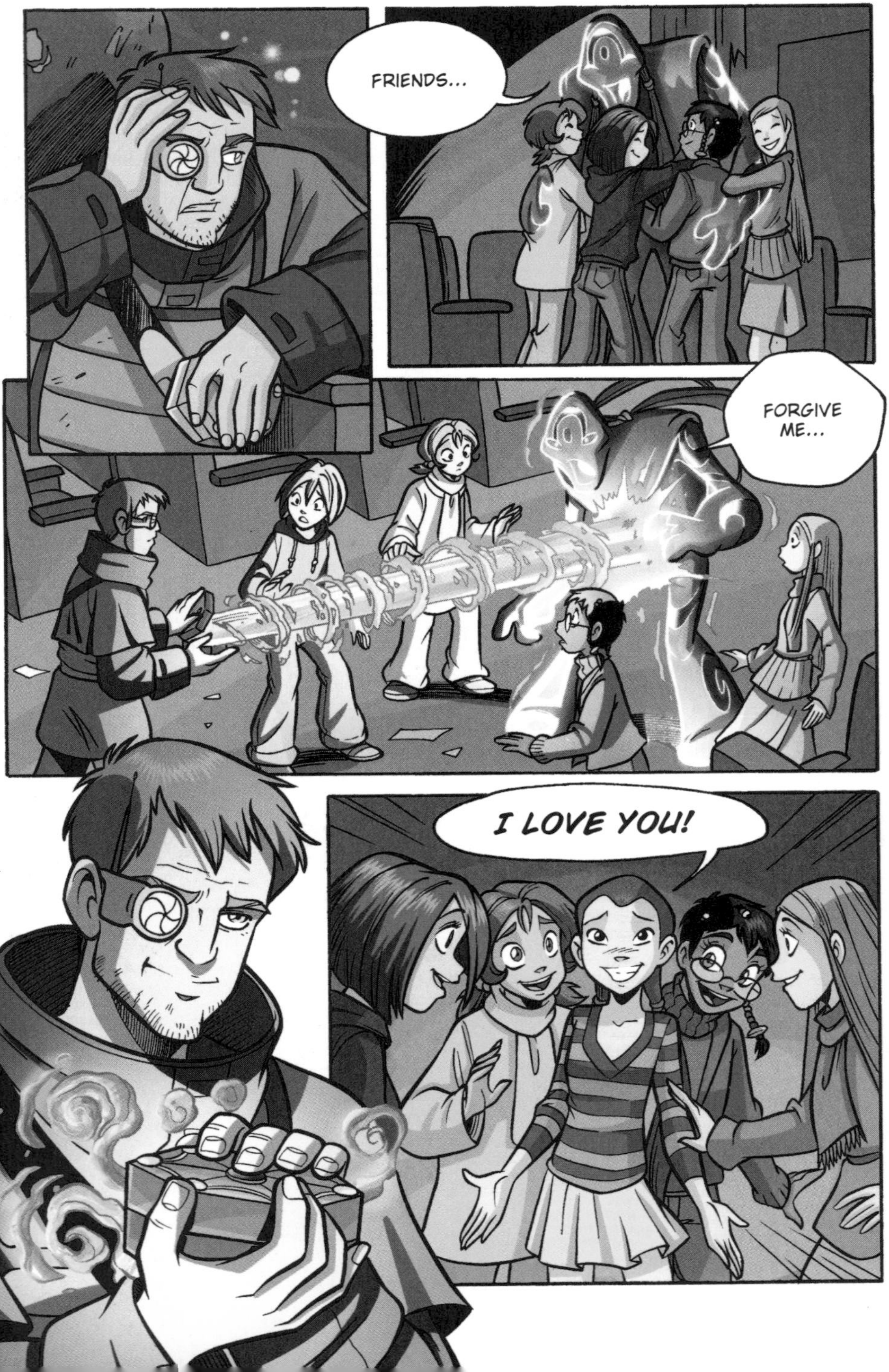
FRIENDS...
FORGIVE ME...
I LOVE YOU!

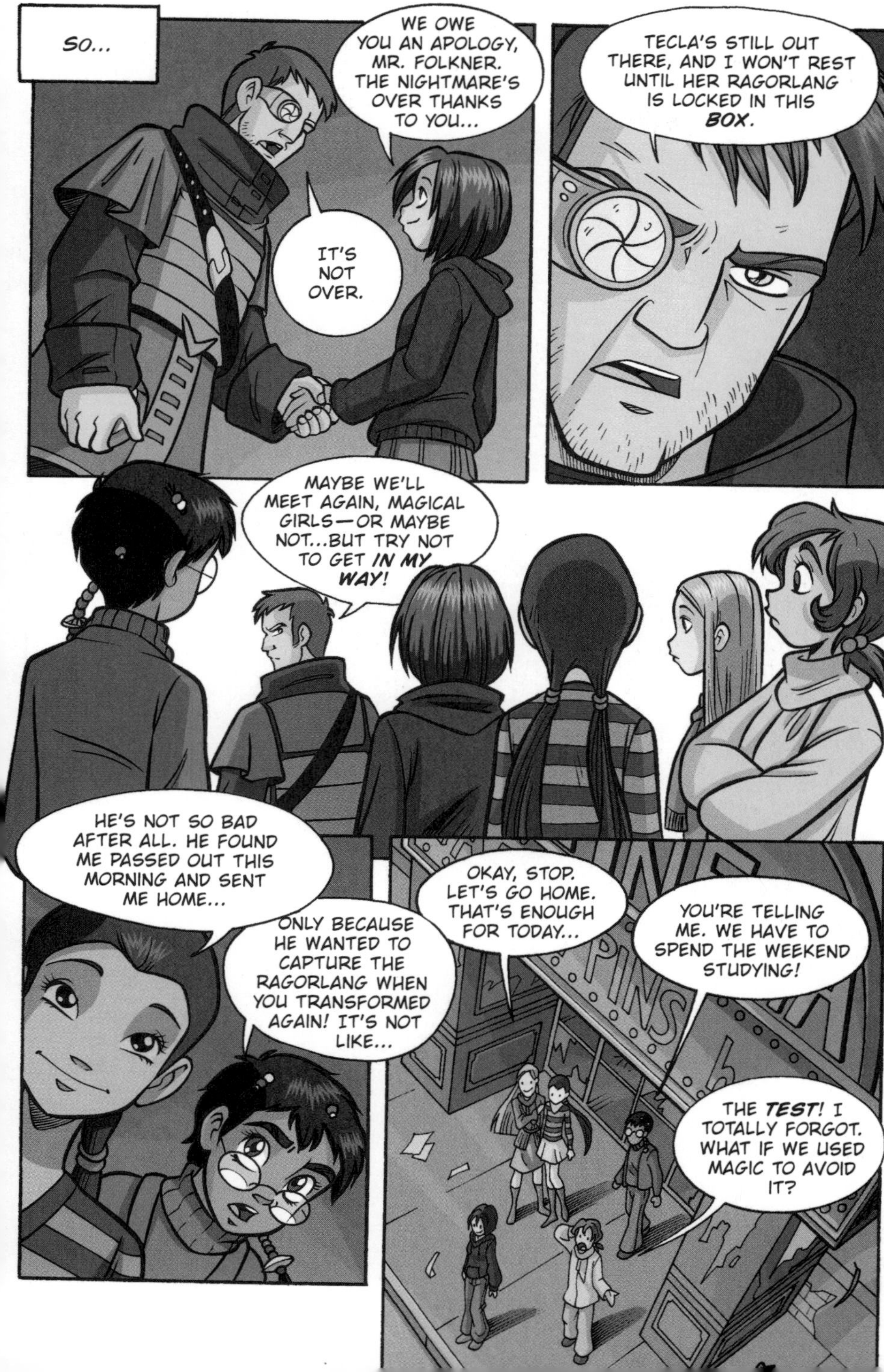
SO...
WE OWE YOU AN APOLOGY, MR. FOLKNER. THE NIGHTMARE'S OVER THANKS TO YOU...
IT'S NOT OVER.
TECLA'S STILL OUT THERE, AND I WON'T REST UNTIL HER RAGORLANG IS LOCKED IN THIS BOX.
MAYBE WE'LL MEET AGAIN, MAGICAL GIRLS—OR MAYBE NOT...BUT TRY NOT TO GET IN MY WAY!
HE'S NOT SO BAD AFTER ALL. HE FOUND ME PASSED OUT THIS MORNING AND SENT ME HOME...
ONLY BECAUSE HE WANTED TO CAPTURE THE RAGORLANG WHEN YOU TRANSFORMED AGAIN! IT'S NOT LIKE...
OKAY, STOP. LET'S GO HOME. THAT'S ENOUGH FOR TODAY...
YOU'RE TELLING ME. WE HAVE TO SPEND THE WEEKEND STUDYING!
THE TEST! I TOTALLY FORGOT. WHAT IF WE USED MAGIC TO AVOID IT?

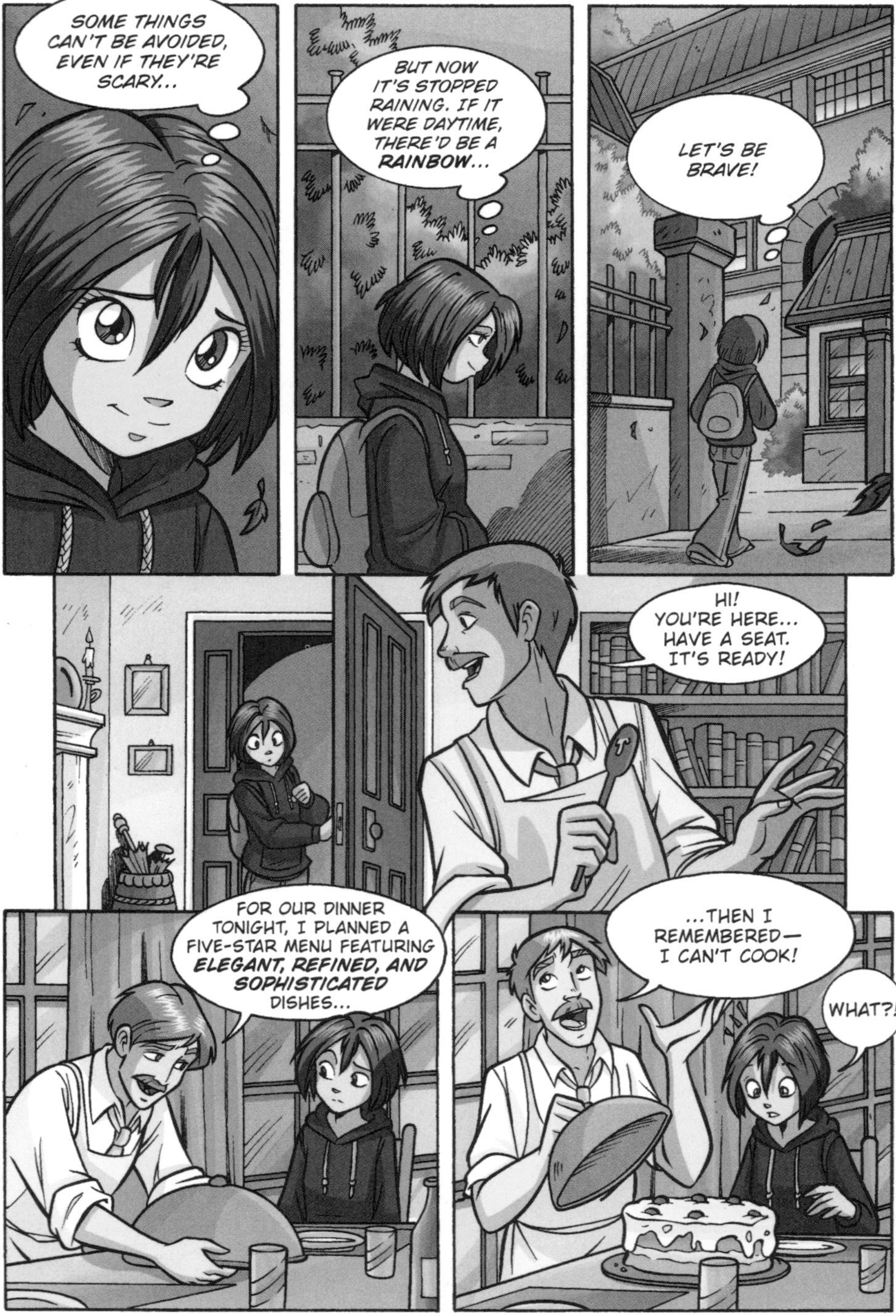
SOME THINGS CAN'T BE AVOIDED, EVEN IF THEY'RE SCARY...
BUT NOW IT'S STOPPED RAINING. IF IT WERE DAYTIME, THERE'D BE A RAINBOW...
LET'S BE BRAVE!
HI! YOU'RE HERE... HAVE A SEAT. IT'S READY!
FOR OUR DINNER TONIGHT, I PLANNED A FIVE-STAR MENU FEATURING ELEGANT, REFINED, AND SOPHISTICATED DISHES...
...THEN I REMEMBERED— I CAN'T COOK!
WHAT?!

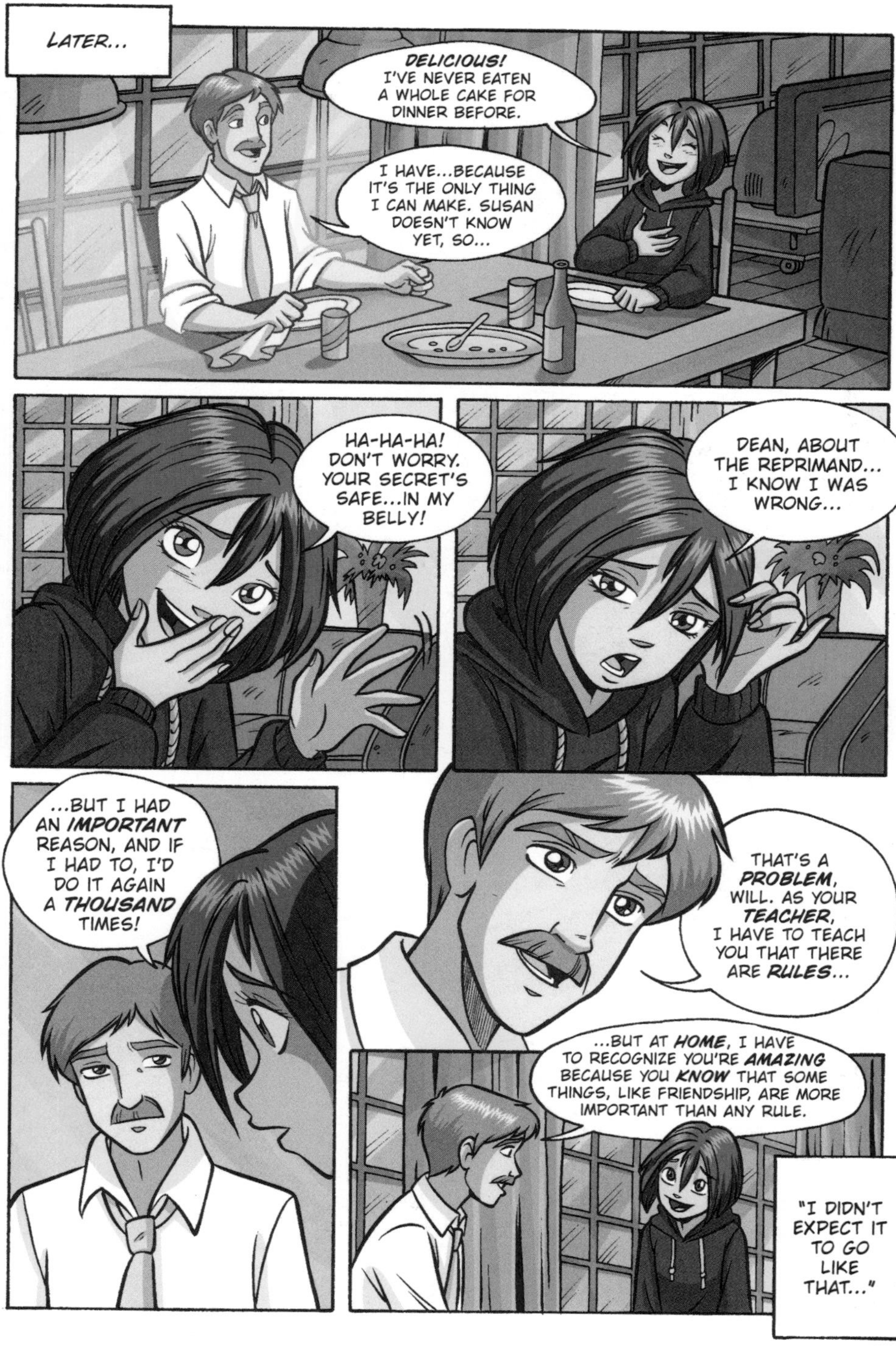
LATER...
DELICIOUS! I'VE NEVER EATEN A WHOLE CAKE FOR DINNER BEFORE.
I HAVE...BECAUSE IT'S THE ONLY THING I CAN MAKE. SUSAN DOESN'T KNOW YET, SO...
HA-HA-HA! DON'T WORRY. YOUR SECRET'S SAFE...IN MY BELLY!
DEAN, ABOUT THE REPRIMAND... I KNOW I WAS WRONG...
...BUT I HAD AN IMPORTANT REASON, AND IF I HAD TO, I'D DO IT AGAIN A THOUSAND TIMES!
THAT'S A PROBLEM, WILL. AS YOUR TEACHER, I HAVE TO TEACH YOU THAT THERE ARE RULES...
...BUT AT HOME, I HAVE TO RECOGNIZE YOU'RE AMAZING BECAUSE YOU KNOW THAT SOME THINGS, LIKE FRIENDSHIP, ARE MORE IMPORTANT THAN ANY RULE.
"I DIDN'T EXPECT IT TO GO LIKE THAT..."

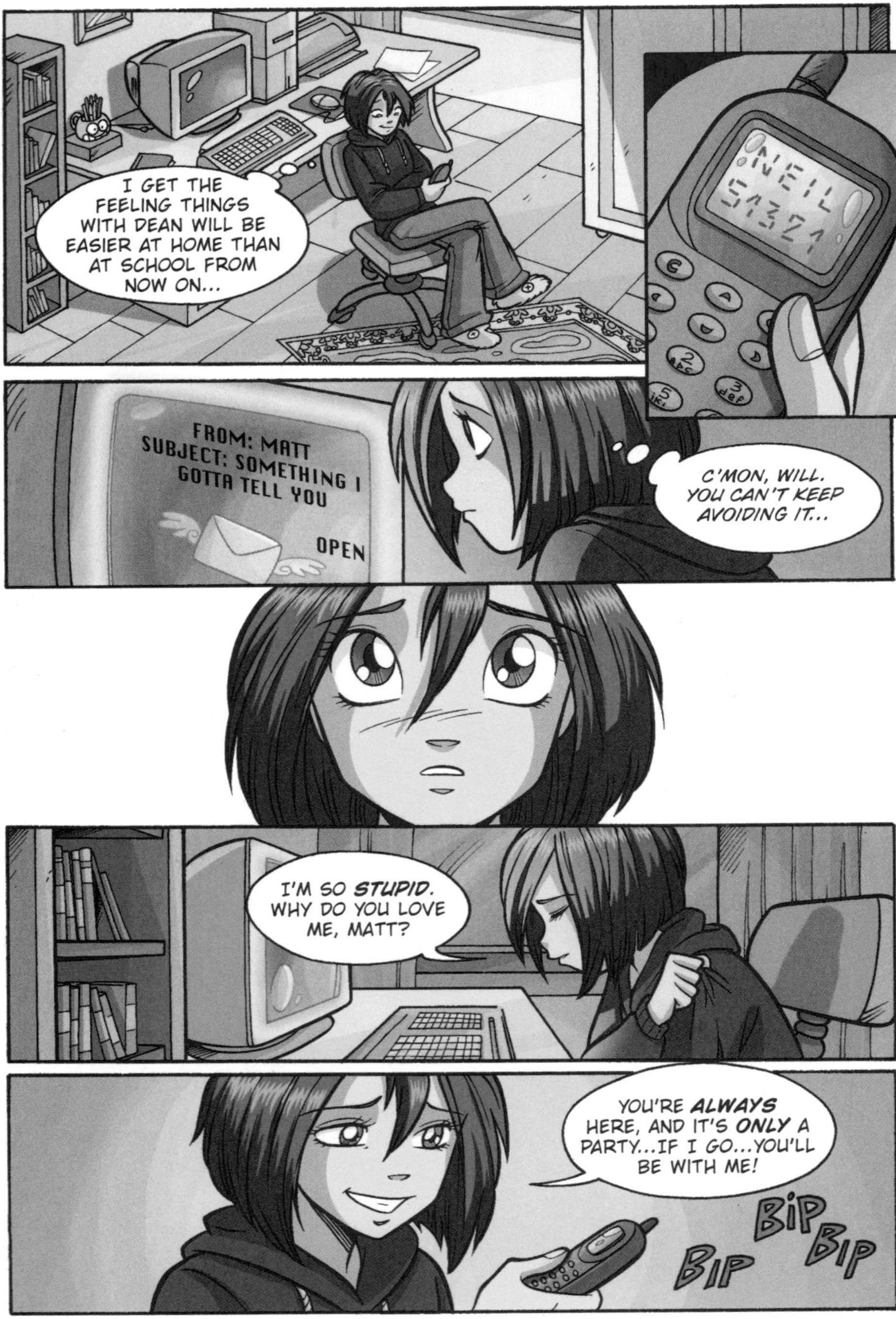
I GET THE FEELING THINGS WITH DEAN WILL BE EASIER AT HOME THAN AT SCHOOL FROM NOW ON...
NEIL
54321
FROM: MATT
SUBJECT: SOMETHING I GOTTA TELL YOU
OPEN
C'MON, WILL. YOU CAN'T KEEP AVOIDING IT...
I'M SO **STUPID**. WHY DO YOU LOVE ME, MATT?
YOU'RE **ALWAYS** HERE, AND IT'S **ONLY** A PARTY...IF I GO...YOU'LL BE WITH ME!
BIP BIP BIP

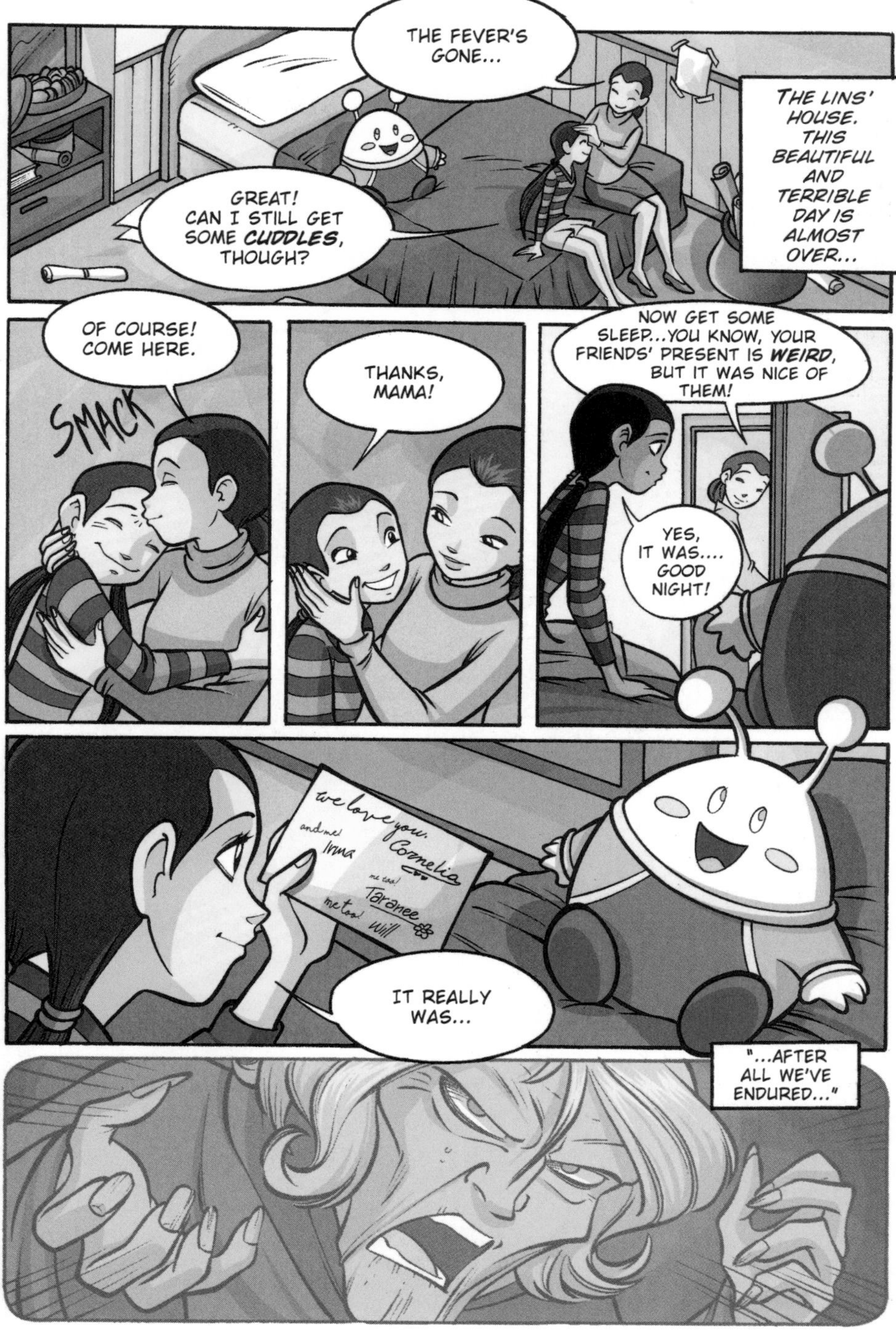
THE FEVER'S GONE...
THE LINS' HOUSE. THIS BEAUTIFUL AND TERRIBLE DAY IS ALMOST OVER...
GREAT! CAN I STILL GET SOME CUDDLES, THOUGH?
OF COURSE! COME HERE.
SMACK
THANKS, MAMA!
NOW GET SOME SLEEP...YOU KNOW, YOUR FRIENDS' PRESENT IS WEIRD, BUT IT WAS NICE OF THEM!
YES, IT WAS.... GOOD NIGHT!
we love you.
Cornelia
and me! Irma
me too! Taranee
me too! Will
IT REALLY WAS...
"...AFTER ALL WE'VE ENDURED..."

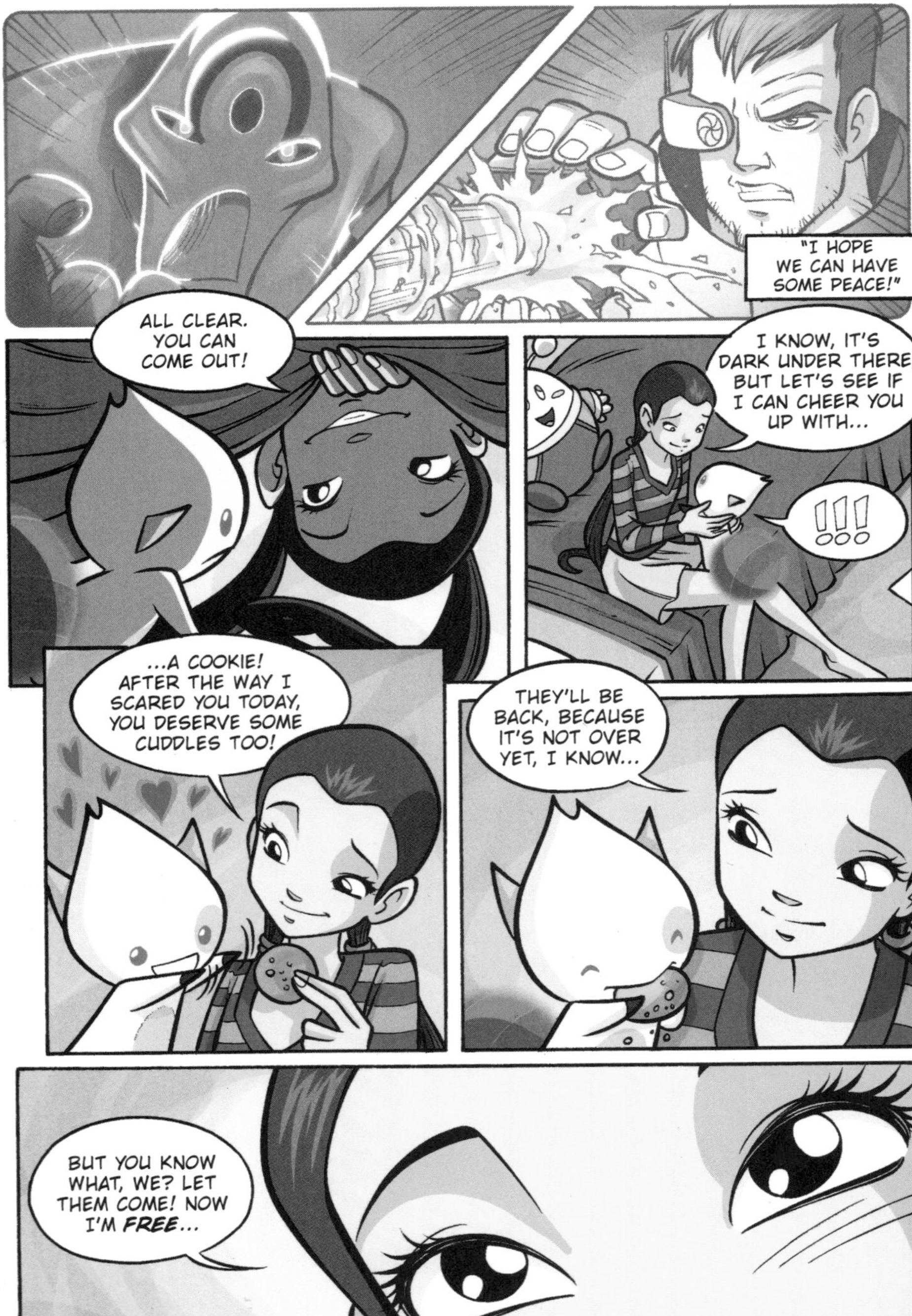
"I HOPE WE CAN HAVE SOME PEACE!"
ALL CLEAR. YOU CAN COME OUT!
I KNOW, IT'S DARK UNDER THERE, BUT LET'S SEE IF I CAN CHEER YOU UP WITH...
!!!
...A COOKIE! AFTER THE WAY I SCARED YOU TODAY, YOU DESERVE SOME CUDDLES TOO!
THEY'LL BE BACK, BECAUSE IT'S NOT OVER YET, I KNOW...
BUT YOU KNOW WHAT, WE? LET THEM COME! NOW I'M ***FREE***...

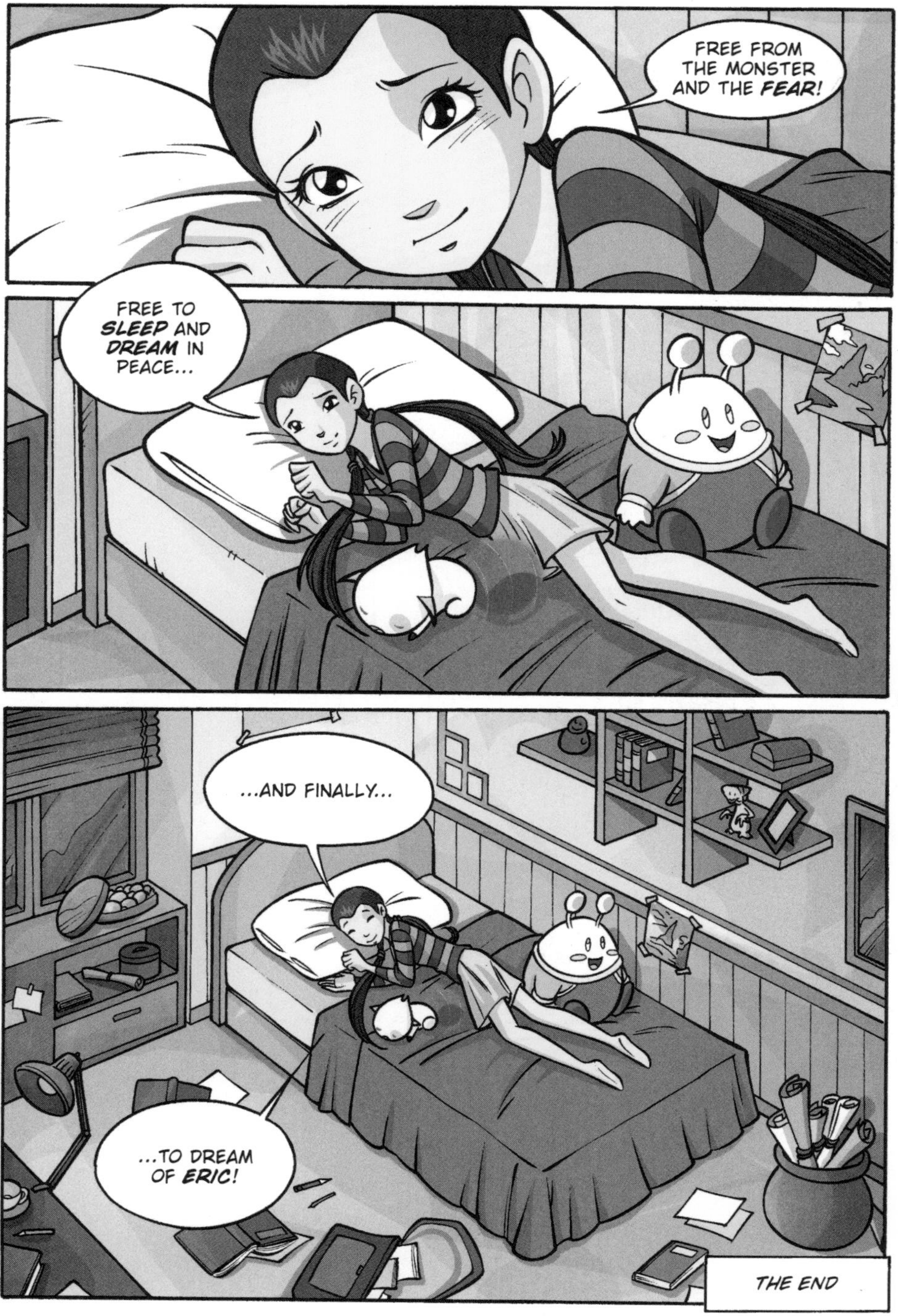
FREE FROM THE MONSTER AND THE ***FEAR!***
FREE TO ***SLEEP*** AND ***DREAM*** IN PEACE...
...AND FINALLY...
...TO DREAM OF ***ERIC!***
THE END

W.i.t.c.h.

Will Irma Taranee Cornelia Hay Lin

Read on in Volume 19!

Edward Folkner

The fearless Ragorlang hunter

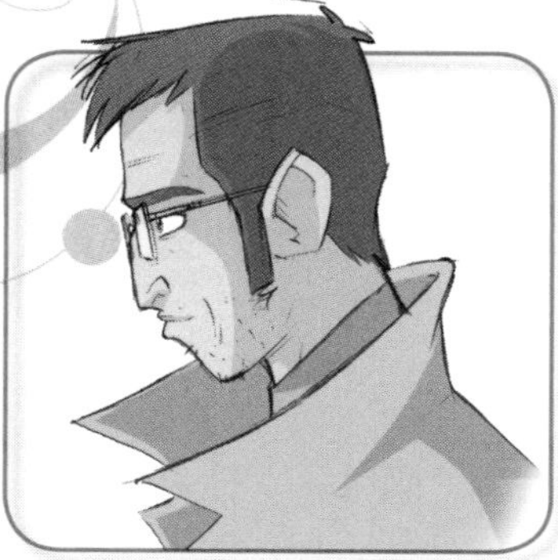

THE HUNTER

• Dr. Folkner, as he is known at Sheffield Institute where he's the school doctor, is a creepy character. Hay Lin sussed him out when she first visited him for an eye check. He's not to be trusted.

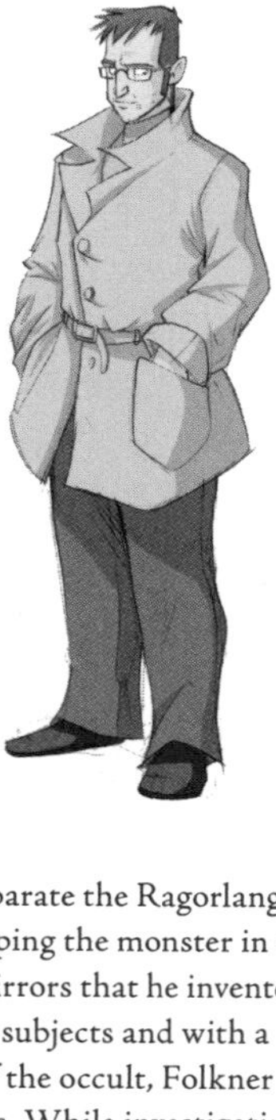

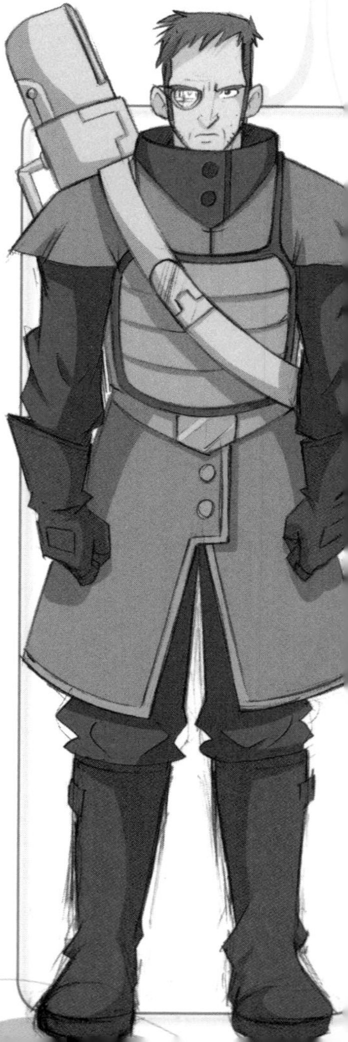

THE INVISIBLE MARK

• Folkner is hunting the most powerful Ragorlang—the one released by Tecla. Posing as the school doctor, he hopes to find students bearing the "mark" left by the Ragorlang—an almost invisible mark in the victim's eye which can only be detected by special instruments, similar to those used by ophthalmologists.

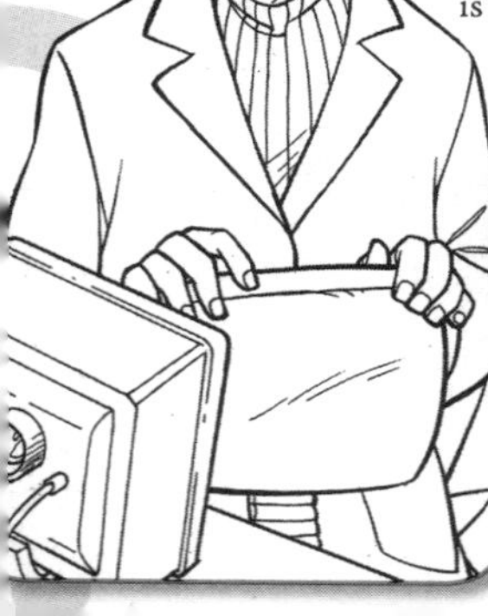

THE BLACK BOX

• Folkner wants to separate the Ragorlang from Tecla's body, trapping the monster in a black box lined with mirrors that he invented. As a specialist in many subjects and with a profound knowledge of the occult, Folkner is extremely dangerous. While investigating Tecla, he discovered W.I.T.C.H.'s secret!

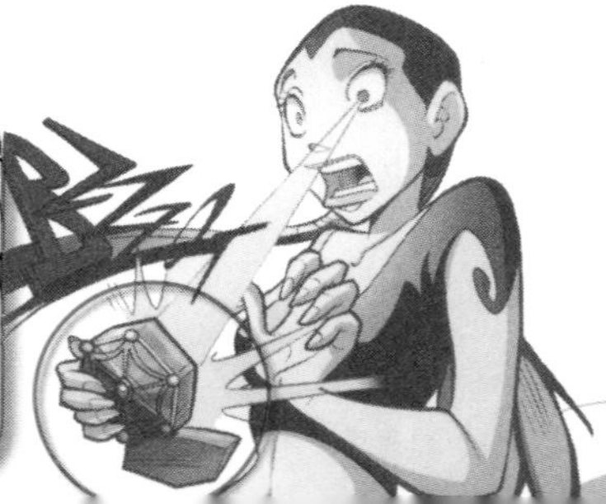

Everything about We!

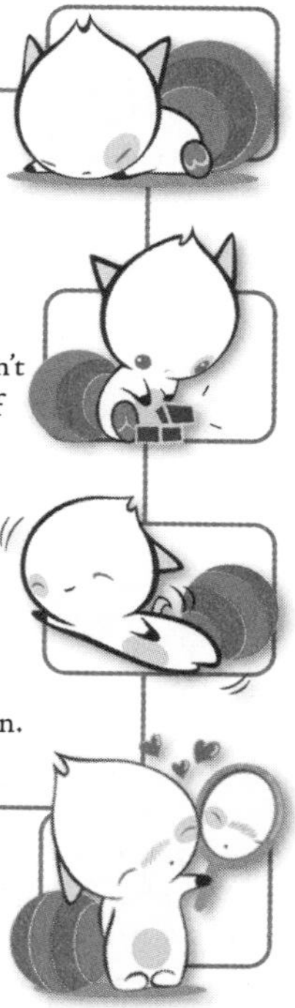

Who is he?

We is W.I.T.C.H.'s cute, curious, and mischievous mascot.

Where is he from?

He's from Basiliade and sneakily followed the Oracle to Kandrakar. Since he was very lively, it wasn't a good idea to have him live among the Wise Ones of the fortress, so the Oracle gave him to Orube, who's also from Basiliade. So We moved to Heatherfield, where he felt at home right away.

What is he like?

His fur is super soft, and his tail fluffs up whenever he's excited. His tail is also the only part of his body that can't turn invisible. If need be, the rest of him can. He can be sweet and funny but also cheeky.

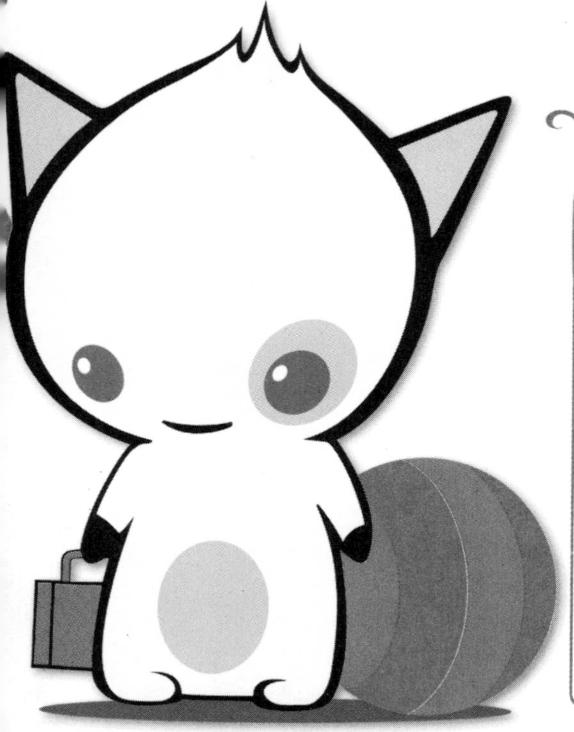

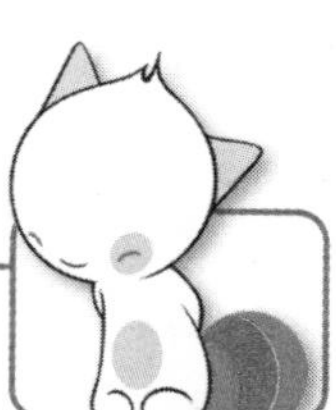

Fun facts:

1. The name We comes from the marks on his paws.

2. He loves cell phones. He talks in his own special language, adding the letter "W" to most words.

3. He always carries a tiny suitcase from which he can dig out anything.

4. He's not-so-secretly in love with Cornelia.

W.I.T.C.H.'s

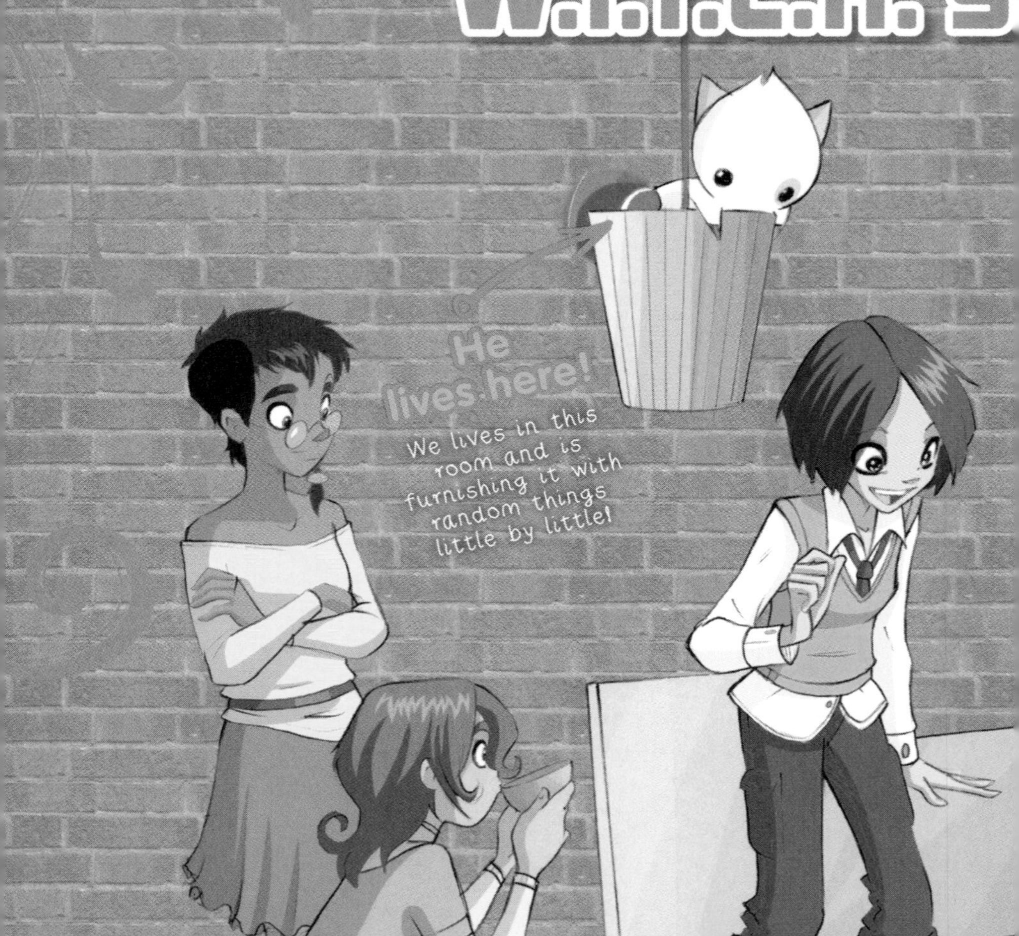

He lives here!
We lives in this room and is furnishing it with random things little by little!

WHQ and the portal

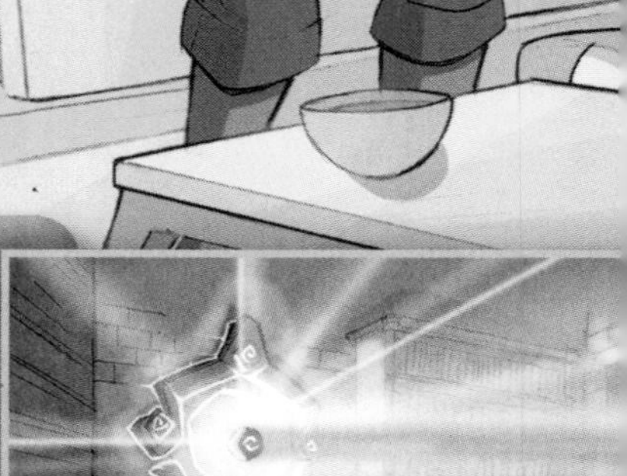

WHQ (short for W.I.T.C.H. Headquarters) is inside Ye Olde Bookshop in Heatherfield, currently closed for renovation. The portal on the wall was a gift to the Guardians from the Oracle. It's a magical pathway connecting Heatherfield and Kandrakar. The portal is also a kind of "eye" that can pick up W.I.T.C.H.'s thoughts and feelings.

Headquarters

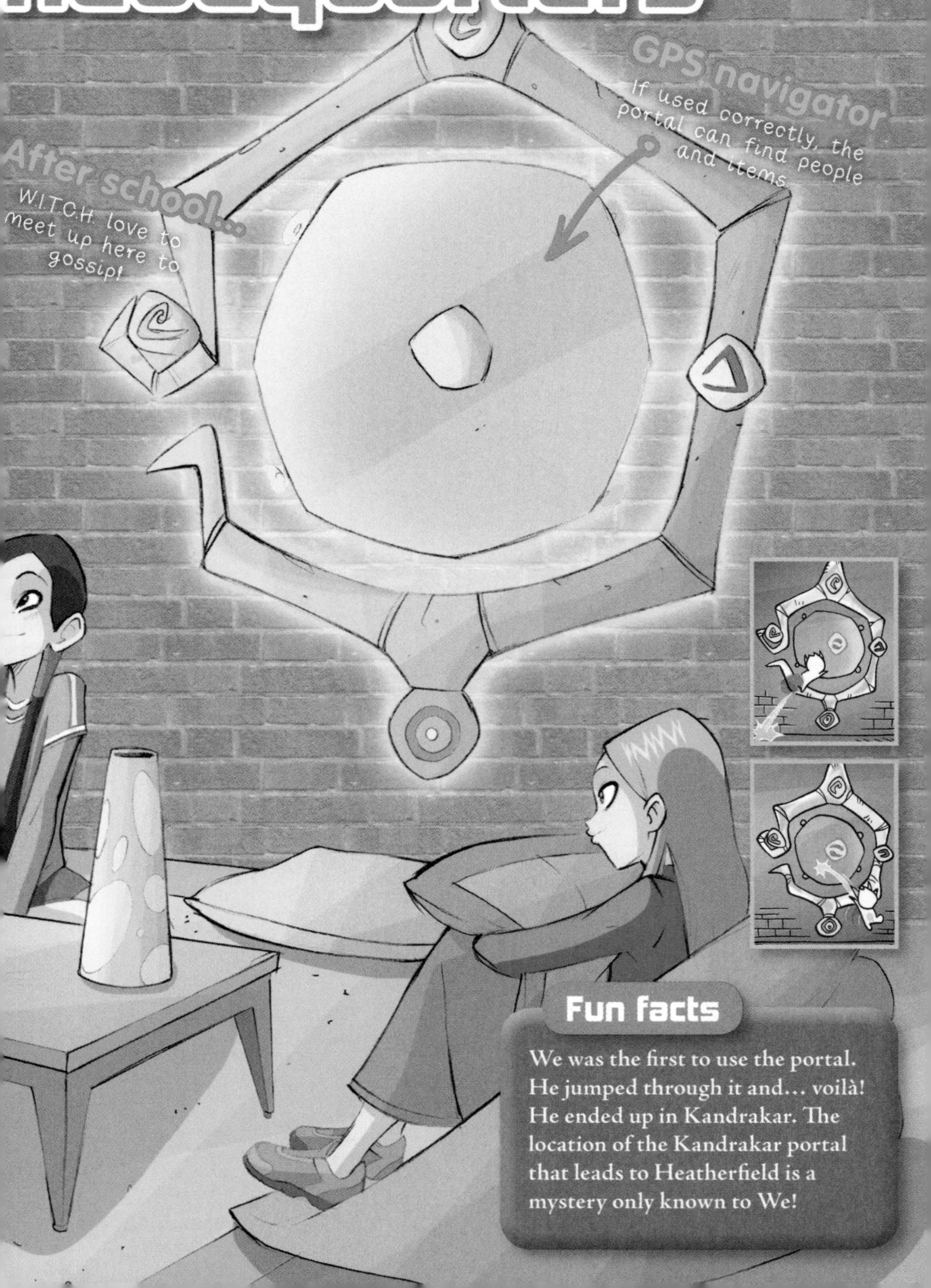
GPS navigator
If used correctly, the portal can find people and items.
After school...
W.I.T.C.H. love to meet up here to gossip!

Fun facts

We was the first to use the portal. He jumped through it and… voilà! He ended up in Kandrakar. The location of the Kandrakar portal that leads to Heatherfield is a mystery only known to We!

Part VI. Ragorlang • Volume 2

18

Series Created by Elisabetta Gnone
Comic Art Direction: Alessandro Barbucci, Barbara Canepa

W.I.T.C.H.: The Graphic Novel, Part VI: Ragorlang
© Disney Enterprises, Inc.

English translation © 2019 by Disney Enterprises, Inc.

JY
150 West 30th Street, 19th Floor
New York, NY 10001

Visit us at jyforkids.com
facebook.com/jyforkids
twitter.com/jyforkids
jyforkids.tumblr.com
instagram.com/jyforkids

First JY Edition: November 2019

JY is an imprint of Yen Press, LLC.
The JY name and logo are trademarks of Yen Press, LLC.

The publisher is not responsible for websites (or their content) that are not owned by the publisher.

Library of Congress Control Number: 2017950917

ISBNs:
978-1-9753-3224-2 (paperback)
978-1-9753-3225-9 (ebook)

10 9 8 7 6 5 4 3 2 1

LSC-C

Printed in the United States of America

Cover Art by Manuela Razzi
Colors by Andrea Cagol

Translation by Linda Ghio and
Stephanie Dagg at Editing Zone
Lettering by Katie Blakeslee

THE DARK SIDE

Concept and Script by Teresa Radice
Layout and Pencils by Alberto Zanon
Inks by Riccardo Sisti
Color and Light Direction by Francesco Legramandi
Title Page Art by Alberto Zanon with colors by Andrea Cagol

BEYOND BORDERS

Concept and Script by Bruno Enna
Layout by Daniela Vetro
Pencils by Federico Bertolucci
Inks by Marina Baggio
Color and Light Direction by Francesco Legramandi
Title Page Art by Giada Perissinotto
with colors by Andrea Cagol

RADIO SILENCE

Concept and Script by Teresa Radice
Layout and Pencils by Giada Perissinotto
Inks by Marina Baggio and Roberta Zanotta
Color and Light Direction by Francesco Legramandi
Title Page Art by Giada Perissinotto
with colors by Andrea Cagol

THE MARK OF FEAR

Concept and Script by Teresa Radice
Layout and Pencils by Giada Perissinotto
Inks by Marina Baggio and Roberta Zanotta
Color and Light Direction by Francesco Legramandi
Title Page Art by Giada Perissinotto
with colors by Andrea Cagol